MYSTERIES OF MOTION

BOOKS BY HORTENSE CALISHER

Novels
False Entry
Textures of Life
Journal from Ellipsia
The New Yorkers
Queenie
Standard Dreaming
Eagle Eye
On Keeping Women
Mysteries of Motion

Novellas and Short Stories
In the Absence of Angels
Tale for the Mirror
Extreme Magic
The Railway Police and the Last Trolley Ride
The Collected Stories of Hortense Calisher

Autobiography
Herself

HORTENSE CALISHER

MYSTERIES OF MOTION

DOUBLEDAY & COMPANY, INC.
GARDEN CITY, NEW YORK
1983

Library of Congress Cataloging in Publication Data

Calisher, Hortense
  Mysteries of motion.

  I. Title.
PS3553.A4M9   1983   813'.54
ISBN 0-385-18406-9

Library of Congress Card Number 82-45593
Printed in the United States of America
First Edition

Designed by Judith Neuman

1

GILPIN'S RIDE

READER, I'M GILPIN. This is our ride.

Strictly speaking there's no evening here in orbit but we keep to schedule. Lately, always at this hour, we feel a soft lensing-in gain on us—one more of the body's circadian rhythms for which there is no medicine. Our bodies seem to hope that some of you may now be watching us on satellite. The day salon, which has intermediate gravity, comes to seem to us more limbo than real. Passengers who were not in our cabin return to it. We six are in the non-gravity cabin closest to the tail.

You find us then exactly as we left you—how long ago? The positions for entering this life or leaving it resemble one another, just as with life anywhere. Once again each of us lies strapped to the Foget couch, which will allow maximum acceptance of G-force. We're ready. One of us has helped in the other five, taking his or her turn at being left to do this alone. Not recommended, but unavoidable. Each of us now lies suited up from visor bubble to box toe. A space suit is in effect a small spacecraft in the shape of a human being. Or so they insist. Inside, a life-support system pressurizes, humidifies and sucks wastes, to small limits. Smallness has great meaning here. The identity badges on our breast pockets, turned on in more active hours, are once again unlit. At the moment you catch us a lack of friction is all-important. Or perhaps a moment ago was. If we are not dead—we are forestalled.

I identify us:

On the first couch, left to right of your screens, is Mulenberg, longest of bone. At times he sings, but not now. Second comes Oliphant, a woman, and almost as long as he. Next should come the man Lievering, also known as Jacques Cohen, but his couch may be empty; this has happened before. He has the lightest foot in space—or spirit—of any of us. After me comes Wert, shortest of the men, who even when rigid has an air of looking behind him. The suit on the sixth couch keeps its gauntlets crossed where its belly must be; it is some months with child.

There's an extra person in our cabin, who should not have been here. Off center, in the shadow behind us, can you see a suit that hangs from the cabin wall, anchored only at its nape? Its arms float. We called him Mole. That suit can't look younger than the rest; I only imagine it.

I am the man in the fourth couch. A book is in front of me, clamped at eye level. Drop an object in non-gravity and it's lost to you. The book is the *Decameron* of Boccaccio. I have been reading aloud from it. One hundred tales to while away the time, as first told to each other by some nice young people in flight to the countryside from the Black Death. Boccaccio himself died well over six hundred years ago in 1375. Gentle Reader is what you and I would have been called then. In tribute to our noble birth, since we could read at all, and to our hopefully amiable temperament.

One hundred lives are believed to be aboard this vehicle. I offer you the private logbook of six, along with sketches of whoever else may wander in. Sometimes I may be Gilpin there; sometimes I can even bear to be "I." You understand that; this is a dilemma you and we share. It's in the spirit of the times, this twisting to avoid being a publicly machined shadow. The others here feel the same. Take us as we are, in the broken cinema of our souls.

In return we ask a favor. Be gentle no longer. Let your birth be what it may, but for whatever you hold dear give up the temperament. Listen to us with claws open as well as hearts. Cross steel in front of your own vitals, for whatever grace period this has given ours. Get up ever earlier in your mind to study the voyage we make.

Reader—ride with us. Not for our sake alone, not for yours, though soon you may be making your own decamerons into our blue. For the sake of that once gentle brown humus from which we all come.

Where the journey begins.

ON CANAVERAL

ON CAPE CANAVERAL, on Gantry Row, sea birds wheel above old space machines abandoned on that shoreline to rust in the sticky salt air, sometimes coming to perch on forked cornices and broken parallelograms no odder than those they might find on a forest floor. Vines creep over pitted metals once forged to absolute specification. On Gantry Row the birds and the jungle fernery are the space-age's sole archivists.

Here engineers from the great inland installations come to loot these old rocket shapes for a spare part or idea still usable, or to sit on the beached sawhorse of some module once smartly vertical and stare at that quiet line where sea meets sky—the obsolete old horizon which any child these days taken aloft on school trips to witness the first truths can tell you is merely the old shoulder curve of a planet he or she may someday leave. Or a couple of men who've already been in space as non-operating personnel, lodged by day shift in the roomier white gantry of the lab but maybe sleeping by "night" in those constraint bags in which a body hangs in non-gravity as on a butcher's hook, will be playing at toss with one of the small rubber balls which out in weightlessness help keep the muscle tone in the hands. They may play until the sun goes down, none of the spots of its eon-slow death here visible. Or they might simply jog the water's edge, shouting to each other at the lovely downpull of gravity in the legs—according to the aeromedics not the best deal for the veins of bodies evolved from the non-erect, but still what they were born to. This day a pair have brought a bottle, congratulating the whisky as they pour it for not flying out. Clearly they are veterans of the way matter behaves when it is not "at home."

Farther down the beach, a man seated on a triangular shooting stick and balancing a briefcase on one knee watches them with a freshman's envy. Weightless travel could be tolerated, and like jet travel soon would be by all but the few made markedly sick by it, but it took learning and could be curiously tiring. In plain language, it was still a strain for humans to be in an environment where they couldn't fall.

Nobody stayed on Gantry Row late enough to watch the moon come up. Or bothered to bring a man or a girl. The moon is business now. Like most heavenly bodies, it has suffered the decline in personality and charisma which comes, as in old love affairs, from accumulated familiarity and even the most special handling. Those beachcombers on furlough probably work on it, or on a materials-processing station "nearby." For the five nights Gilpin has stayed on here after dark, playing hooky from the fancy government motel up the road where all passengers for his flight are quartered, he and those busted old rocket shapes have had Diana LaLuna to themselves in all her phases, and it's been a quiet affair. The moon no longer has much of a sex. On Canaveral maybe even the dogs don't bay at it.

On the long-ago night of the Apollo moon shot, Gilpin had been a student on work holiday, gorging himself on boar during end-of-summer festival week in a small mountain town in Tuscany. That night, as all there agreed, "she" had lost her virginity—though a clutch of roisterers, dirty old men clapping their hands to their wine-soaked crotches, had kept shouting that the old man up there had lost his balls, until the matrons serving the tables in the straw tents set up all along the town's central *strada* had had them thrown out. After which the women, tightening their downy mustachios with a ripple that ran from one headshake to the next—"*Aie, la Luna poverina, aie!*" had handed all the rest of them in the tent a free extra plate of meat. Mouth full, gazing up through the starry, straw-rimmed tent hole as if he were watching a rape from a manger, Gilpin had quoted Sir Philip Sidney's address to the moon. Only the first line of it, which was all a sophomore could recall, but aloud, for hell, this was Italy: "With how sad steps, O Moon, thou climbst the skies!" Telling himself he was participating in the death of a portion of the world's poetry and was possibly the only person in the world to feel this. Next morning every columnist in the Italian newspapers had felt the same.

The following day he sat in a different stall with his real feelings. Here the wine drinkers were the younger men for whom babies were beginning to spill out—not onto the floors of their grandfathers' farms, sold now to foreigners, but into the new apartment villas on the edge of town, which the government had had built out of the local tufa stone. Tonight they were drinking grappa, which cost more than their own wine, but maybe because they knew him as the boy who since spring had lived on an absentee *inglesi*'s farm, trucking in the olives to the press like any of them, they wouldn't let him pay. He'd have to hang along until sundown when they'd all go off to the café where perhaps he could treat. The sky he saw through the straw hole was a bright, hard Tuscan blue, and empty. He had no quote for it. Now and then one of the men shook his clenched fist at it admiringly. Once a man let his thumb slide slowly through his other four fingers, two on a side, and everybody laughed. In the tent hole the sky dimmed to "mountain's breath," as the dusk was called here, then to a soft ripe-olive black.

Later, in the café that was the village's grange and heart, he and they trooped past the grannies and mothers who sat with the children at tables near the entrance, past the confectionery counter where girls clustered to talk with the two young daughters-of-the-house from whom he bought his ration of one mouth-filling inch of custard pastry with his after-work cappuccino every midmorning—all the way to the bar at the far end, served by the *padrone* himself. Among the gathered men he recognized the butcher, his cheeks as yellow as the tallow he worked with, who could be glimpsed every Friday through the bead curtain of the barbershop, confronting the mirror with a hair net on his head. The barber himself, that pink-cuticled Aesop, saluted him. Well apart from these townsmen there stood or leaned the town's portion of granite-wrinkled old men, in pants of stone also and boots cast by time, who every evening were maybe let out of the vaults of the Etruscan museum across the valley. There was one ancient who never got past the café entrance, standing inarticulate for whole evenings in front of the tinseled, glassed-in Motta chocolate display, staring in with dazed other-era eyes.

Gilpin had ducked through all of them, into the communal pisshole at the back. When he came out they were all on their feet, even the mothers guarding the pointy-lashed teen-gigglers whose baby-ready breasts poked at him from their blouses. The slim doe from the town's gas pump, who bent her valentine-shaped jeaned hips under his nose to feed the *inglesi*'s car when he brought it in but wouldn't let herself be spoken to, now smiled at him. Each and all had a glass in hand, holding these out to him. *Moona-shot—Moona-shot-Americani!*

That long, classically segmented room, lantern-shadowed yet lit with candy-paper frolic, smelling of after-work wine and ice cream, coffee and field stink and talcum powder, murmuring with three-generational tales whose nuances of wit and death he would never get to the bottom of, and underfoot with children treated like everybody's saints, had all summer seemed to him a bright parable of the world—and still does. He understood that they were making the ritual their rightfully developed sense of occasion demanded of them, and that they felt extralucky to have a real American on hand for it. A drink was thrust into his hand. And no, they still wouldn't let him pay. *A-pol-lo-o!* a man shouted from the back—*Viv'il machina A-pol-lo!* The old man transfixed in front of the glassy display mouthed it—A-pol-lo.

Dice Moona-chut! one brash kid in knee pants heckled him, but was hushed from behind. The old man stared in at the chocolate, as he had all summer. A mother detached herself plumply from a table to go behind the counter to remove the largest bar of chocolate, nodding to the owner, who nodded her credit or extended his own. She slipped the bar into the old man's stone hand and ankled self-consciously back to her corner. *A-pol-lo* the tables murmured, and crossed themselves. Together, Tom Gilpin and the old man wept.

All this time the *padrone* had said nothing. A large man a cut above all his customers except the banker and the pharmacist, he dispensed an air of refinement and benevolence combined, the first maybe from the pastry, the second from the wine. Whenever he chose to speak in his cleanly, Jesuit-schooled speech he was listened to. "We must hope—" he said. He hadn't crossed himself. Instead, he pointed to the rafters. "We must hope they do things decently, up there."

So, as a result of that night, here's Tom Gilpin out on Gantry Row waiting for the moon to come up. On his next-to-last-night on earth, for an indefinite time. As it is for the woman he is waiting for.

The two beach players are gone. The alternate pock of their ball still echoes. One of the men had thrown from a heavy crouch, the other with a baseball windup. Low tide has left their departing tracks indented, the oddly feminine footprints of men in Texas boots. The two sets of tracks narrow up the beach toward the weed line and converge there as if the two had lifted off, bounding up with cells suddenly light. A man newly returned from the world of non-gravity might well be excused for momentarily thinking so. A man about to go might do worse than take an image of those imprints with him.

His old Brownie camera, normally carried though seldom used (a person with a camera is noticed less, and that's his preference), will go to the one-room historical museum in the disused lighthouse of his island birthplace, a still functioning rarity of the sort the islanders prize. They generously feel that he is something of the same. His briefcase, made from a sharkskin his father once spent a whole winter's after-lobstering hours curing, must go through tomorrow's documentation procedures or else be left behind; he hasn't decided which. Where he comes from, the past has always had to earn its keep through use.

In the pocket of his T-shirt there's a pad and pencil picked up in the motel room. Shirt and trousers are of the loose kind he's worn for years; he'll miss their brownish maroon and round-the-world weight. The pad has a legend on it in Old English print: *Compliments of the L-5 Society of Tucson,* a group of space-habitant enthusiasts from years back. Their joy must now be high. The childish, peanut-shaped footprints he's now drawing lead straight into that legend. The white page itself looks like air to him. But even for an artist, which he's not, it isn't easy to project weight.

Thrusting the pad into the briefcase now stuck into the sand at his feet, Gilpin stares out at the once multitudinous sea.

Until that night at the *Porchetta* festival he'd had absolutely no interest in what was going on in the heavens, nor had any of his college crowd. He'd gone back and quietly tacked onto his art history major a raft of courses barely squeezed through, mainly intended to lead to astrophysics. The winter company of physicists could be wonderful, especially in Boston, where the cold nights gave an Early Cantabrigian cast to thought, and the good wives of those who still bothered to have them served up Early Revolutionary meals which cleansed the bowel accordingly. Yet one of the impurer sciences—aeromechanics, say— which soared as greedily as those others but maybe unfortunately got there, might have served him better by far. Meanwhile, he never did abandon his own much scruffier crowd.

The weekly opinion sheet he still owns, begun as a graduate-student journal, hand-set by two others and himself in the gilded but otherwise bare ballroom of a Housatonic River mansion inherited too soon by one of them, has at one time or another probed many antitheses without plumping for any. During the early years it kept wickedly changing its name to suit, under the impression that no respectable idea ever stayed the same. The end result was that their faithful subscribers, at first young like themselves, then aging along with them into the merely young-minded, could always trust it to be the same.

Now that Gilpin is notable, one of his partners of that long-ago ballroom has just written him, in what can be taken for congratulation if read hastily. "Don't you think, dear Tom, that like most radical journals we were only hoarding up our mutual angers for our friends? Have to hand it to you: yours have been more consistent than most." Effective, he really meant, but a power in the International Monetary Fund deserved to be answered truthfully. "No," Gilpin wrote back, "my milder fate is I've always been able to be too lively about what I believe. Which is what makes me a superficial person."

One just anger, unhumorously hung on to, better unified a life. In private, each shift had been painful, while he waited for a true commitment to appear. No one had been more surprised when it had, bringing along with it for the paper the underground name a popular success could now let itself be known by—*The Sheet.*

Life's been easy on him. His father and mother bought out his other partners so they could back him themselves, which hadn't mattered since he and they already knew how well they'd indoctrinated him. His mother, a moneyed Boston girl, had married herself to a Maine lobsterman during one of those ever-recurring periods in American history when such doctrines as Save the Sea, Screw War, Up the Rich, and Know Your Natural Body had all seemed to render one happy savage sense. Absolutists both, they'd reared him to believe that what you did daily, you did both within and to the cosmos.

In bad moods, he now sees his inherited categorizing of all people as a kind of cheaply moral packaging, of which his reforming madness may be the very slightly nobler side. Down at the bottom though, all the Gilpins were popularists, notoriously in love with that whole-flesh collective, mankind. "Who on rainy days," his self-taught father would say gloomily, "is only poor bloody *Pithecanthropuserectus* beating the children to stand up straight." But who, on moonlit nights when the catch was running—same old silver but new shoals—was surely the Fisherman, eyes intent.

The moon on Canaveral is now high enough for Gilpin to see that long before Italy his life's tone had been elected for him, by his having been brought up on almost the smallest of habitable islands: three quarters of a mile wide by one and a half long, highest headlands in the North Atlantic, and the farthest out to sea. Visitors compared it to the Grand Corniche, and as a boy he'd thought maybe this was so, if that place also had a thick central wood in which one could wander as in the Black Forest, and a crabbed lower coastline on which a visitor could either miss footing and not be found among the bayberry bushes until the following year, or else turn from walking out on the flats for clams to find the sea a solid rip tide between him and shore—which some dudes did every season, since no native would warn them. And if that Corniche place was also separated from the mainland by a moody packet boat called the *Winnie Mae*.

The island had once been a commonwealth, like those slightly larger sectors of the union, Virginia, Pennsylvania, Massachusetts and Kentucky. So when the boy thought of ideal government, a commonwealth was what he thought of first. However, a disproportionate amount of the island's scant land, and with it a controlling vote in all matters of principle, was held by one man said to be an heir of Thomas Edison, who appeared on island for such meetings only. It had been this man's habit to acquire more land when he could, preferably a plot with one of the island's scarce old houses on it, which he would then raze in the interests of the wilderness. Since he was also opposed to the islanders' having any of the ugly electric cables with which his ancestor had civilized civilization, this left them either to propane gas cylinders always overdue from the mainland, or Aladdin lamps whose tendency to flare up and blacken made for uneasy book study, or to the occasional illegal generator whose noise ruined both conscience and peace. So, when Gilpin thinks of what elective power can do, he thinks of this man.

There'd been little hardship, except for a lack of company if you didn't either drink or go to church. Garden season was two months, with no pasture for livestock, barring the few deer which the summer residents sentimentalized and the islanders shot at after Labor Day. There'd never been small fauna, and by agreement no rabbits which might overrun. In compensation, the wildflowers grew extra-foxy-faced and lone. Tourist summers were overpeopled and the comforts they brought effeminate—a time of foreign occupation with the sea still the only way out. Winter or summer, if you wanted whisky, which the islanders drank but didn't sell, or schooling, for which there'd been no teacher until Gilpin's tenth year, by which time three other mainland girls had married fishermen—you went across for it. When they needed a doctor, the Coast Guard flew one in by hydroplane, telephoned for at the only store. Conversely, one season when new wells were wanted, the tall well rigs had come across the watery plain, shuddering off the boats like totems come to tower over each backyard in turn, in order to divine its spring. Then the rigs had lifted themselves up with a shake of smart metal and had lumbered off again. At fifteen, he felt the humiliation.

One summer twilight that same year, just as he was taking the garbage downhill to dump it into the harbor, with the whole island spread beneath him in the glittering light and a buoy lowing like the island's one cow, a three-masted schooner—which, unknown to the island, a mainland agent had had restored and was running a cruise on—had sailed out of the Grand Banks of cloud to vanish and reappear behind one headland after another, her sails bellied pink with sunset—a paper ship with a dark hull borne on by all the ghosts of travel, above its mizzenmast a star. The blood drained to his feet and he felt gravity, that mother quicksand. Dreamstruck, he carried the garbage back up the hill. It wasn't the ship he'd wanted to be on—not those old ropes—but the star.

His boyhood has deeded him that transportational dream which moves nations and every so often ground-shifts the world. At those times the world is half spirit, though its goods might seem to be all that is marching, or its flags.

The dream in the bone is of migration. Scratch below the supposed goal and every man, every nation, is an islander like him: One day— a farther shore. It sounded like a religious antiphonal because it was one —the hymn that all the boyhoods and girlhoods sang: *One day—the mainland.* Once upon a time his own country had founded itself on a radical twist put to that refrain: One day, yes—*and for all.* What he's done—subversively, some say—is to have reminded them of it.

The moon looks stationary now, in a fleece of moving cloud. The heavens are being sucked clean by the vacuum attendant on the great wind drifts. This part of the shoreline is a bay really, with a bay's muted climacterics. The hurricane winds from the West Indies, among the highest in the Beaufort scale, are usually diverted, as they had been from Gilpin's small island. What he'd had there was talk of them, giants treading near his father's thumb while it traced a nor'easter in terms of Ferrel's law. Any moving object on the surface of the earth, Tom, is deflected by the earth's rotation, to the right in the northern hemisphere, to the left in the southern. On their dining table there was often a small cylindrical cheese with green flecks in it, called sapsago. The moon's made of green cheese, his mother said. "Have some."

Stomachs remember. In his, now, comes that veiny flash which had irradiated it on first reading Goddard—a short article, drawings and print elegantly faded, entitled "A Method of Reaching Extreme Altitudes." On his return from Italy it had been his conceit to read from early space history on rather than back, so that he might pass historically through any ordinary citizen's amaze—for in his innocence he supposed that all educated citizens, and to a degree even all those in the simple soda parlors of the world, were keeping up with it. He'd begun in the dark ages, with the legends of spaceships in the records of Tiajuanaco. Passing from Leonardo's notebooks to the eighteenth-century Turkish admiral Piri Reis's atlases from the Topkapi Palace, said to delineate topography only now observable from aerial photographs, he'd lingered on such nineteenth-century curiosa as Joseph Atterley's *A Voyage to the Moon.* Goddard, writing diffidently of how to prove a rocket could go as far as the moon, had been his first modern.

That terse prose, learned by heart as Gilpin had once learned tags from Emerson, came to seem of the same order, colorless as a Maine landscape and as full of astral light. A powerful special pleading rose from its few pages, elusive under its author's reserve. Gilpin was often to encounter during his long private education the scene and sound of a mind ahead of its time, but this was his first brush with it. Leafing through the volume in which Goddard's article had appeared, he found much the same number of pages devoted to the discovery of a new species of Piper bird from Panama. Goddard himself had at the time guardedly advocated rockets merely for meteorological and solar physics findings. *"The only reliable procedure would be to send the smallest mass of flash powder possible to the dark surface of the moon when in conjunction (i.e. the 'new moon') in such a way that it would be ignited on impact. The light would then be visible in a powerful telescope. On the moon, distant 220,000 mi., with a telescope of 1 ft. aperture ... we should need a mass of 2.67 lbs. to be just visible and 13.82 lbs. or less to be strikingly visible. Larger telescopes would reduce mass. (At sea-level ... we need 602 lbs. for every lb. that is to be sent to 'infinity.')"* In the library of the Massachusetts Institute of Technology, ostensibly silent, but like all libraries burring with brain sounds as the past ran in front of dozens of pairs of eyes, whispering its counsel and its devilment, the younger Gilpin's eyes had smarted, learning their true dimension. *Robert Hutchings Goddard,* he'd said slowly, aloud. Rows of faces fish-gawped or monkey-giggled behind the paw. A librarian had ejected him. For "pranks."

Two days later he'd been reading in bed, his buttocks warmed by a girl—in those days there had been time for girls. But it was Hermann Oberth, onetime doctoral student whose rejected thesis had become one of the bases of modern rocketry, who was really in bed with him. Even Oberth's equations seem to him clearer than other people's. "If the acceleration due to gravity were less—for instance only 12½ ft. per second as on Mars—a man could stand like a ballerina on his big toe." His fairly clean 1957 drawing of the elbow joint of a space suit hadn't been too far from what Gilpin will insert himself into tomorrow morning. Yet this same finicker Oberth, when he came to speak of psychological man, could suffer the most terrifying lapses of the critical sense, hazarding in a chapter on the future, and after he'd set forth entire

space-station projections in perfect, trustworthy and prophetic order:
"Further hope for more righteous times to come is encouraged by the
invention of the lie detector."

When young Gilpin the grad student came to that fool pronounce-
ment, he rolled onto the floor, kicking out his heels and inadvertently
hitting the girl in the eye. Apologizing, "I'm trying to stand on my
brain. Like on a big toe." To console her further, he'd clawed among
his scattered books and read the passage to her.

"They all have these last chapters. Just say utopia, and they all go
slavering. Without a shred of evidence like they'll spend pages ac-
cumulating, on, say, how a water-glycol system acts in space. Or with
none of the hardnose they'll give you on, say, what makes a gyroscope
go crazy just at the last." He quoted Oberth again: " 'The gyroscope is
a mysterious object for minds romantically inclined.' " Meanwhile patting her purpling eye. "You know, it's as if man is not an evidential
creature. Or not to them." She wasn't consoled and huffily requested
a cold compress. In bed again, he suddenly shot up on the pillow to cry,
"I've got it! It's sainthood they're after. Like in any new world—and you
can at least trust them to know it'll be that—sainthood has to be involved. Oh, not for them. For mankind. And that means you and me,
Madge." She'd crawled out the other side of the bed, and being already
in her cuddly fake-fur jacket for warmth, grabbed up her sandals and
left.

He hadn't detained her. He'd found his vocation. Or its practical
application. His intellectual friends knew of course that "outer space"
was getting nearer all the time. "Galaxy"—a puzzled Spenser specialist
had remarked, "you don't see words like that used *poetically* anymore." They knew too, of course, that the planet was very careworn.

But even if he could woo them to a space museum, to join the hoi
polloi who were there for the wide-lens movie and any fantasy they
could get, their eyes skewed and wandered. It had nothing to do with
them. They hadn't yet made the connection. All the while those silvery
vortices were drawing near.

Later it would be the hoi polloi, so mournfully willing to shift the line
between fantasy and what they know will be foisted on them, and still
so graceful with animal trust, who first listened to him. Plus the young,
who like Gilpin once had no track record to risk. Or of course, to wield.
Though once, early on, he would be listened to by a couple of stock
manipulators keen on the "commercial" possibilities of space mining.
Other hallucinations of theirs, not so soon to be corroborated, meanwhile sent them to jail.

He has a classmate (a novelist whose books concern themselves with the Colorado wilderness, and why not, of course?) who for years has spoken of the UN Committee on the Peaceful Uses of Outer Space (learned of from a UN Christmas card Gilpin had once sent him) as a Yuletide joke. Later, the space shuttle had passed him by like a rude bee not native to the West. More recently, hearing that permanent space habitats must apparently be confronted, since his friend Gilpin is going to one, he'd smiled the old science fiction smile, exactly as if offered a blind date with the robot girl who lived under the rainbow. "I still go in for the human quotient."

So do I, Gilpin thinks. Don't I? Under the moonlight, the waves of the Atlantic for as far as Gilpin can see repeat themselves like the border of a Greek vase, flat black ripples raising evenly their small hatchet heads. Grampus waves, his father had called them, for their resemblance to that blunt-headed cetacean. "And because they mean a blow." Fishermen, like other technicians, taught the particularity of things. His father would have done better than he with the finicky threadings and built-ins of a space suit. Though, since laughter was the only stimulant he ever indulged in, his having to pee into an inside catheter, meanwhile pedaling for exercise on a bicycle ergometer, might have been too much for him. "Your mother's the one for concepts, son." Meaning that her money had made her vague. "I have trouble with them."

So had Gilpin the grad student. But reading back after his girl Madge had gone, he began to tally why even ordinary citizens still relegated so much of what was happening in the world to science fiction. They themselves were fiction, to the scientists. You and me, Madge; this is our revenge. On the bed, she'd left some scrap notes he'd hoped might be for their class in thermodynamics where she was the better student, which had however turned out to be three separate ways of making piña colada. He'd saved them tenderly. They're in his archive yet. You and me, Madge, you and me. Those of us who in this migration, not being military enough, or technical enough, or even "healthy" enough, might someday have to go in steerage, or even be left behind.

For he had just that day come across a chilling passage of a different order. A "hypothetical letter" from a space colonist describing the voyage out, as imagined in the 1970s by a Princeton physicist named Gerard O'Neill, it dealt with those who were to be the new saints. "The three-week trial period is to sort out cases of severe space sickness and to find out whether you are among those who can adapt to commuting each day between normal gravity and zero. That's important because our homes are in gravity obtained by rotation, and many of us work in the construction industry, with no gravity at all. *Those who can adapt to rapid change qualify for higher-paying jobs."*

He'd sat in his wicker chair with the book-crammed side arms; then he'd gone into the kitchenette to make that piña colada. Not enough. Never enough for all the civilians who were going to be di-di-diddled, once again. Oh, Madge, where will you be, in your funny, cuddly coat? In which crowd? Who will catalogue us, people of the earth? Who will lobby for us?

So he'd resolved to. While finishing off all three batches of the colada. By family tradition he was heir to a long line of public defenders. The family mailbox, snowed in year-round with severely black-and-white begging envelopes and his parents' doughty return-mail checks, had been his chore. Because of this and perhaps the island postmistress's glare, he'd foreseen a certain style for himself. He would keep in touch with all the crowds he could, but by needling influence, not being it, his own modest role to be held to minimum in hope of retaining sense and compassion enough always to recall what the human quotient was. That presumption was to give him recurrent twinges. Last year, pushed by fame-guilt as well, he'd at last taken his own gravitational training. Only to empathize, never intending to make use of it. On that score he'd intended to be that darling of the syllogicians, the last man on earth. He'd never meant to go.

Tomorrow. To the first public habitat in space. Current winds at Canaveral launching site being roughly north at 10 miles per hr., waves 1 ft. every 10 seconds when he came out on the beach, but within the last hour increasing rapidly to perhaps wind NE at 14, waves 2 ft. every 4 sec.

Human gesture has been swarming toward him these last days, grow-ing like British pennies in the pocket when you are on the way to France. That summer of the schooner, a woman who'd been in school with his mother had visited them on island—by then a haggard unisex redhead in meager-hipped corduroys and crunchy sweaters planing her breast points, who smelled of alcohol and perfume, had gelid, perfect skin, eyes that picked off men, and a vague, unlipsticked mouth, inner-shaded to mutton, which couldn't eat without smear. Yesterday in the motel's coffeeshop he'd seen her double. Staring at him instead of his father, she'd wiped off the orange mustache of his mother's vegetable soup with the same backsweep of the hand.

His last week in Washington, going to the dime store, he marked how the girls there still wetted a finger and sleeked a brow. In a New York

men's room, old Captain Stanley's double groaned with pleasure as he
urinated from Gilpin's father's scow. Outside later, truckmen at a load-
ing entrance cocked their brogues like early balloonists. Here at the
motel, the cashier, desked like Gilpin's banker in front of a high window, continually polished the sun from both their bald heads. And last
night, waking from height dreams of a house he'd once owned high on
a cliff over the Mohawk River, where a contractor, come to estimate a
retainer fence, had once stepped back fatally far, Gilpin saw him again
in midair, hands spread in apology.

He's looking at the still grounded people here with the same embarrassment which during his travel-slumming young years used to crawl
in him at the sight of primitive peoples—even when they were still
speciously safe in their rain forests or on the hot Kalahari sands where
they carried pure water with them in their own buttocks. He knew too
much about their future. Now he's staring that way at his own kind.
Professors with fine teeth and solid families, who jogged the parks
displaying both, or vagrants with winter-rheumed noses and feet clot-
ted into their shoes past hope of ever shedding them—it's all the same.
He's standing on the borders of their innocence, which is gravitation.
That dower-right of their bodies was about to be corrupted in a way
which taking to the air within the stratosphere had never done. In a
plane, no matter at what speed, a human body still pulled its own
weight. The machine intervened for it, bargaining with Earth for motion. But now we desert into an element where the body can never be
quite natural again.

A sudden bulbul murmur from birds nested somewhere in this dark
machinery jungle makes him shift on his own perch, his worn black
leather-and-chrome shooting stick. From Allahabad to the Moscow subway, on ski lifts and in the outback, its cup and his bottom had developed such a comfortable triangular relationship that on his own three-
week test trip in to orbit a few months ago he'd sorely missed its
reassuring pressure, which wherever he and it go has meant "You and
I—and gravity—are meditating. Taking it all in." He'd even begun to
wonder whether that rounding of the face which, due to downward pull
on the facial features, so alters the physiognomy during orbital insertion
mightn't already be taking place, perhaps permanently, in his backside
—and during the intensive checkups on return had even asked them
to measure its radius.

He's certainly carried back to earth with him that squared-off position
which shoulders tend to assume during the first liftoff sensation of hanging upside down. The flight doctors can't understand why he should

have retained it. He could have told them. Fright. Three weeks in cosmic fright. True, he hadn't vomited like some. Nor had any serious arrhythmia as a result of the changes in total body water from induced electrolytic charge during weightlessness. And yes, he'd taken the wee pills for sleeplessness, plus those yellow gobbets designed to offset other "abnormal" responses to interruption of his body's preferences. Which medication had worked optimally, allowing him an eight-hour shift of perfect fright-sleep, and a functional fright-shift by day.

So he's come through with a perfect record except for one slip, due merely to a minor astigmatism interacting with faulty design—when he'd defecated into the Water Distillator instead of the Hydro John. Which had been taken note of as a viable criticism.

Even his question about his backside had to be taken seriously, for aeromedical research, they told him, had turned up some dandy commercial by-products from even odder observations. "No, his *er*, coccyx-to-buttocks periphery seems normal. Left cheek, that is. Let's measure the right." Behind him the murmuring of the doctors in the return room went on happily. "Decline in red cell mass, median on allowable scale. Muscular-cellular deterioration—hah!" They spun him round to the front on that one. "Slight change in vertebral alignment"—murmur, murmur—"no, no aberration in the right cheek either. But aha, look at that leg. And this one. Yep. Considerable decrease in the girth of each calf." Smiling at him when they saw his apprehension. "Everybody does it. Just as you've almost totally lost the antibacterial immunization given you before going. That red-cell loss *will* have to be taken care of. Weight loss, eight pounds, which is about average too—but pick up on it, fella, you don't have that much to spare. You may have to wear a neck brace for a couple weeks, and your Eustachian tubes may be blocked fuller than you're used to. It's all *absolutely* normal. Watch your balance of course—*lo—ook* at that guy over there trying to negotiate the staircase. For God's sake, don't jump off anything in a fit of absent-mindedness. You won't float."

One doctor had remarked on a change in the occlusion of his teeth. No surprise to Gilpin, after three weeks of trying to keep their chattering from notice in an environment where every human being, the minute unhelmeted, hungrily scrutinized every other: *You* all right, Jack? Then *I'm* all right.

"What you been doing?" this doctor says. "Grinding them?"

Gilpin sticks out his jaw at the pair of them. He feels heavy again, healthy heavy enough for anything. Gravity is laving his feet. The trend in these halls is to discredit it, whenever possible. Birth pains, for instance, are now blamed on G-pull. One of the docs is a woman. He thrusts out his lower lip at her. "Grit," he answers. "Sheer grit."

So he'd passed. Certified for the first civilian flight of the first passenger space shuttle, the *Citizen Courier*. Only a last-minute outcry had kept NASA from naming it the *Mayflower*. Space humor was analogous to sailors', and from the same tensions. The habitat they're going to, until then referred to as the L-5 after its position in space, has been rechristened Island U.S.—pronounced "Us." Still, he's going. He's already a guaranteed aristocrat. And barring certain enthralling considerations—like, would any children born on habitat be non-G inured, or would some of them do so badly in non-gravity that they'd have to be sent back here?—so will be all his heirs.

The waves are now becoming those individual ones the eye vainly keeps trying to hang on to. He hears a few more birds being unhappy, or alert. A sure sign of weather, and before morning. At the launching only the reporters might get wet, stationed in an open reviewing stand a mile and a half away. All the active button pushers will be in underground shelter, with the instruments. He and other passengers will board via a germproof corridor. Test flights like the one he'd taken weren't launched from the Cape but from other round-the-nation installations which had no such corridors, maybe on the theory that passengers who didn't disembark in space wouldn't contaminate it. Was it possible to taint space just by being there? He supposed they were doing their best and would only find out for sure later—possibly when large, catarrhal clouds surround later colonists with their own grandfathers' germs, or some little lice creature, of the hard-shelled sort that survives eons of non-atmosphere, arrives on habitats now projected to be in the dozens internationally, in perhaps thirty years. Human ecology didn't change; its "neighborhoods" always went downhill. Then its "best people" moved on.

They were saying the whole planet might eventually have to. Move on. The whole population even, piece by piece. Fleeing the scrap-heap Earth cities that still burned so beautifully at night, the countryside that still loped green and tree-frothed at the transportation window but had lost its cow-dung innocence to canals of fetus-deforming scum, and the air which was a nimbus of cancerous fire invisible, so that we were all fire-eaters now. While our children would grow old and diseased.

It seemed to him, no expert, that there was a curious ignoring here. Your child would grow old and diseased in any case, in what used to be called the fullness of time. If when you first saw the little greased eel when it was expelled, bright with red energy or washed candy-pink in

the calm arms of a nurse, you were also shown projections of the mum-
bling, warted bag of dropsy which age might make it, arriving to die
maybe in this same hospital or one like it—what then? You'd perhaps
blind your eyes with spread palms or shout, "I don't expect us to be
immortal!" Secretly thinking, "Though perhaps, by the time *he* grows
. . . Meanwhile, I'll do something for him, along the way."

In the fullness of time. That was what had been lost.

The solution had seemed to him simple and ark-like. He shifts the
briefcase stuck in the sand at his feet; the tide's nibbling in. The case
contains his master set of those issues of *The Sheet* which have had a
humble place in history, dating from a front-page opening blast seven
years ago—the day after NASA's plans for the present habitat had been
ratified, with a dainty absence of hoorah. They knew all the implications
far better than the laity. On the left-hand side of the page he'd used the
Bible: St. Paul's injunction that we must be members of one another,
and on the right the Statue of Liberty's injunction: "Give me your tired,
your poor," etc. Both under a wartime-size double head: EVERYBODY
MUST GO—WE HAVE THE RIGHT. Subhead: *To Go or To Stay*. It
looks very amateurish now.

He dislikes the Atlantic down here. A northern sea by rights, where
it goes warm it also goes glum and sly, with none of the Pacific's jade
openness. Still, on reentry from test flight they had all been whelmed
to see it, even in its great reversal. As mariners of the non-air, an
element which by now seems to him the very color of equations, and
in a descending rocket plane, the sudden sea below, that heaving
known, became a giant lily pad whose domestic dangers would have to
be relearned. In a queer way they had returned newly vulnerable,
having to be careful not to slip in the bathtub, like the old astronaut,
Glenn. But the sea mystery, once dominant in his life and the planet's,
could not be relearned. The mystery of the planet itself, was it burned
out? Or like St. Elmo's fire—the sailor's false beacon, that luminous
electric discharge into atmosphere from projecting or elevated objects
—merely gone on ahead?

That flight had been eight days and return—and only in orbit. This
one will be twenty-one days, and will touch down. The *Courier* itself
would be returning here, not with their crowd but with technicians
previously delivered to the habitat in batches, by smaller shuttle units,
analogous to the huge *Courier* somewhat as the older DC planes had
been to the wide-bodied jets. He's resisted knowing more of either
general operations or technical detail. If he's to go, then let him be a
passenger as the airplanes or the oceangoing steamships had known

them—thousands of us, committing ourselves to the air in a delicately preserved myopia, or to the sea.

During his training trip, the whispering headphones had prophesied continually. Island U.S., though as yet only a "commercial" installation, was located at one of the more suitable Lagrange points. There had followed a short vita of Lagrange himself and an explanation of his discoveries, of the sort Gilpin is learning to tune out. For his instinct to remain passenger-passive was proving right; if you listen too hard to the technology, your ear goes deaf to its implications.

Tonight there are no stars. He's tired of stars and no longer ashamed of it. In orbit there'd been a fixed rain of them, curving and recurving again, so that he'd seemed to himself imprisoned in a kind of star torture, trapped inside one of the exhibits at the old Hayden Planetarium. And in the window of his future quarters there was promised him a view of the firmament, traveling with him and the flat's perhaps every-two-minute revolutions. What was the atmospheric mix prescribed for habitat?—he's been told but has forgotten it.

On-Island, as the phrase had been on his small one, his dependency will increase a hundredfold. Sunsets and sunrises to be arranged. He thinks he can tolerate that. His own planet in its decline has already inured him to much. What he doubts he can take is to be dependent on an elect few for all the tastes of life. For, far as he could tell, these new worlds which their planners spoke of so blandly weren't to be worlds of grandeur, but merely virtuously free of both dirt and spontaneity and subscribing to their creators' ideals of comfyness.

His travels have taught him that middle-grade scientists tend to have petit-bourgeois tastes; it is the rich or the poor who are inventively grandiose. It's just possible he can take utopia. It's foregone that he won't be able to take utopians.

O Tom Gilpin, keep looking up. Layers of ozone blackened only by solar absence, grubby-warm ocean on a pre-storm night, as you need no satellite to tell you. A damaged moon shining on the rusted molybdenums and non-biodegradable plastics of migration-first-stage from a planet which has lost all its physical unknowns except the wherewithal of the first act of creation. Then why is it still all—choose your words carefully—what it *is*? Which seizes the throat and no adjective can describe—or only all of them in all languages. Which tears at our vitals as if these were made to be its abacus. The one mystery left to Earth is now leaving it—us. Then let it be us in toto. No other way are we dignifiable. No one part of us, no one person, is completely dignifiable alone.

A stentorian blast blows suddenly from inland—*Mmmmmm-ah-ah-ah—mmmmmmm*. Birds shoot up and past him on its trajectory, circling in wide agitations to get above the sound's crescendo, returning in downward swoops tuned to its decrease. This nine o'clock siren has taught even the night birds its musical phrase. A creature like him has to stand in its volume, letting the decibels drain down. Yet he'll remember Canaveral as a white, even silent place. So much of what it builds is reared behind muffled walls, components assembled in hangars whose vastness makes even the hammers go tick-tock. From these hangars, big enough to house pyramids, constructions are wheeled like huge geometric dreams, which afterward swim like colloidal shapes on the eyeball. Someday masters and apprentices both may be moved in entirety to Outer, where metals have no weight and the cold amalgams can be fused at low temperatures untenable on earth. By that time, in the improved skyworks of a later era, even average personnel should suffer no pangs of transferral. Or so he's told.

A chill shivers his bones, in spite of air so hot and close that the waves appear blunted. These days there's a subliminal thrill that comes of already being half able to look back at oneself from up ahead—at one's old former planet, that spent cannonball. Some here work under that condition constantly; they come out of their labs and projections dazed by the time thrill, the space thrill, frozen into weird concentrations from which they have to be won back. These are the ones who tonight, as on many nights, would be flown to other cities, to the brothels or opera houses of their choice. Those are the lighter cases, the more conventional ones. One brilliantly indispensable woman, whenever at the end of her brain tether, is flown to Finland, where she does time in a center for autistic children, being fed and serviced like one of them, beginning to babble and fling herself about the minute she enters. Though there are such centers here now, she'd refused them. "Finland's staying," she'd said. "Nobody's going yet, from there."

Contrarily, one man, a mathematician, goes only eight miles, to a health spa whose attendants have instructions to cocoon him in wet blanketings, rolls of bandage-thin ones from which every half hour they are to unwrap one only, with nursery endearments. Once this is done he emerges silent but warmed mentally, and goes home to his wife. There are those who have to be whipped, and neither claim nor evince sexual excitement—unless the return of the terrestrial time sense can be termed sensual. Epileptics, whose brain explosions dislocated them temporarily from internal time sense, were said to be able to work in these future-chill-prone environments without need of other release, their own intermittent attacks, if courted and unmedicated, taking care of it. Means to guard them while under attack were being pursued, for the possession of that other resistance, especially when present in high-caliber brainworkers, would give them top priority.

The wind's rapping at the loose flaplock of his briefcase, stuck there in the sand like a secretary displaying the boss's importance to the other board members here: Sky, Moon, Sea, Attendant Galaxies—and an expectantly wired world. He's spent a third of his life in all the slots of influence, from the walnut miles of government offices to the veiled, holy white of its "installations," at one moment gossiping away in anarchic little cafés, at another lolling in a press lord's yacht. Through the sexes too, he's gone, and out the other side—as can happen to a man really spermed only to an idea. In the shape of history, persons like him are maybe merely that—one motile cell, moving like any sperm, under one enormous general purpose and one very small autonomy. The papers in the briefcase contain his message. Everyone must go, if the world is going to leave the world.

He'd expected to be laughed at and had been—hugely. Receiving letters, however, from a couple of men at the Goddard Space Center, some half dozen from university centers, and a bid to testify before a Senate committee neither he nor the country had yet known to exist.

Nowadays, he sometimes sees his old second broadside—the one with a picture of the Ark, captioned *Two by Two—The Elite Is Everybody* —framed in a union hall or cartooned in some Christmas annual, and marvels at what a curious progression the advance of any idea is. He himself had been the quietest of rabble-rousers, intending only to start little avalanches of concern here and there, to tickle awake those whom the globe's anarchy still surprised.

So at last he has reached that middle mass which can assure an idea that everybody knows it exists. His has even been heard to tremble in that pale underground where anemia keeps the sights low—among the socialized poor. One constituency he has had with him utterly—the fierce young. In their company, he keeps to himself how transitory he knows their help must be—on their way, as they are, to all the other categories.

Now he is better known in Washington and the country at large than he ever wanted to be. Two years ago, via a behind-his-back campaign of a former employee retired to the life of sentiment, scotch, and long-distance telephone calls which old newspaper people so often fell into, he had been nominated for the Nobel. Rhoda, always excessive, had had public contacts unfortunately wide. More seriously, he'd been investigated as a lobbyist and cleared, again publicly. He had emerged from between those two prongs as from an Iron Maiden, purer in reputation than the innocent, and to some conservatives more dangerous than the humbly criminal.

From there he could watch with a certain arrogance. His hooted-at insistence that none must be disqualified, none favored—by then a great sticky orb of controversy and study—had rolled on without him. As long as the reformer is merely maligned he is safe. But once his words have been acted upon in his favor, what then? He has to be sure as a god then, that the arrow thrown was the rightful one. He has to be proud as a lord, of his own life. Gilpin is not. Should everybody go; should everybody even want to? Why should he bother, how dared he? What is—natural selection?

Then he'll see something to humble him, perhaps the gulping smile a very small child makes, as if it's sipping life. And he'll be out of that bramble, a man with his eyesight scratched in again. I love, I love, I love.

That too can be publicly dangerous. But that he will risk.

"You'll want to go yourself, of course, Mr. Gilpin." As if this man wouldn't know otherwise. In space matters, walnut offices are for those who still dealt in tycoonism; when you get to steel and enamel like this, and one beady model instrument neither a clock nor a Cellini, then you know you are in the white gantry of the Ship of State. "And Miss Oliphant. See by that article she wrote she's passed as a candidate also." This man has a face like an almond with the skin still on, the husk having been ground up to make his smooth-to-gravelly voice. "My wife and girls so admire her."

In the desk picture the wife is white, the daughters and their light-haired brother not so brown as their father, who is nowhere near so dark as Veronica Oliphant—who likes to wear white fur against her black, and has her own place in the public eye.

"Ah, you two'll make a fine couple for the ship. A useful one," Perdue says. Not saying in which way. Private lives were not to be private on the *Courier*. It must already be in the précis, each computerized, psychographed, and even collaborated upon by its subject. It would be known to Perdue that their relationship, Veronica's and his, has never been sexual. That Gilpin has no such relationships now would have been gone into, as far back as Madge. While candidate Oliphant's style in that respect may be part of what Perdue's girls admire her for.

"We're not precisely a couple. As you must know."

"Forgive me. Yes. We've had to study up beforehand," Perdue says with distaste.

"It's all in the public domain." Loudly insisted upon at last, by the public itself. "You don't forgive the process?"

"We abide by it. Dealing with the results as we can. Why do you ask, Gilpin? Balk, did you? When you had to go through the process yourself?"

"Only out of humiliation. I've so little to hide."

"I must say. How a man of your background could be so—"

"Foolish?"

"As to trust those data boys."

"It was either them or the military."

"Or us." Perdue actually smiles.

"No one class can be allowed to choose the inhabitants of a new world that rigidly. That's been my whole point. Besides, it never works." He'd kept his eye on the family picture. The son's hair is pale like the mother's but wooled like the father's. On a longer head, but with the same snub face. Wonder who that boy admires?

"What's your alternative?"

He sighed; he sighs a lot in these offices. "Choose by lot." Which of course they haven't done. "From a representational pool of humanity, constantly added to. Tied first to the birth rate here, and only then to their capacity for Outer." Actually he'd been improvising, as usual— adherence to principle being all he wants. In any policy to do with human beings, the means of execution were never ideal. His century has taught him it ought not to be. Let there always be a ragged, civilian, amateur eye.

"Mr. Gilpin, you may be very glad your ship's crew was not chosen by lot."

"Oh—with margins for operating personnel, of course." That's the loophole. They always see it.

"Everybody in a habitat in space ought to be operating personnel, for Christ's sake. Just as on any spacecraft."

"Until when? The millennium?"

Perdue's a graceful man. "Here's your promised list, Gilpin. Actually the data boys haven't done so badly. Every economic and social factor represented." He lifts a brow. Impossible, as they both know. "To an age curve." That's easier. "Over twenty-one. No children yet. But those belonging to present and future passengers on the qualified lists will be sent for later. And four of the younger women are pregnant. Two men in their eighties, three women. Low for the national percentile, but there it is. As has been so much discussed—death will inevitably be represented." In time. Agreed. "As for your lame, your halt, your sick—" Perdue blew out his breath. "That's impossible. We must *not* be burdened. But you do have—let's see—a blind person. Blind since birth, graduate degree, very nimble—useful member. Also, a paraplegic. Did remarkably in vestibular training. . . . Actually, in non-gravity no limbs can be rather good, you know. Or no use of them. Also, a few who wear hard-of-hearing devices. No sweat there. Plus one mildly retarded clerk, who's worked excellently in the postal system." He smiled again. Gilpin had refused to. "One mild emphysema, ditto one cardiovascular, et cetera, et cetera." He hesitates. "No known carcinomas. Sorry, but we simply couldn't. Because of the viral evidence, you really can't expect . . ." He broke out still another smile. "But a very nice pair of female trusties from St. Elizabeth's Hospital. Manics, both of them, on lithium dosage compatible with what we—" Might have to administer when aloft—to anybody? "Want to look it over, before you take it along?" He holds out the list. Take it away, he means, his wrist trembling with rage.

Trembling too, Gilpin bent over that first passenger list. A note appended to it reminded that each name had a case history not here attached, copies to be distributed to all when aboard. In addition, films on each person would be available for showing in the ship's common room, later to be filed in the Island's computer library, the file to be cumulative as the Island's population grew.

"So there you'll be," Perdue said. "One hundred and eight average citizens, supposedly. Only nobody who passes our training can be average—you ever figure that?"

"We never campaigned for average citizens. Only for representative ones." He's spent years explaining the difference.

"Well, you've got them. All the right wrong people."

"Wrong from NASA's point of view." Which by such a narrow margin he's kept from being his country's? Or hopes he has.

"From any point of view, they're a disaster. Why start out with the flawed—valuable people or not—when you can so easily find the healthy equivalent? The functioning one?"

"Maybe we value their viewpoint. Humanly." He loathes the language, but sees no way out of it. "And these people will function. Your crew saw to that."

"At a cost of ten months. Why did you do it, Gilpin? I understand you've spent years. Healthy people are just as human as the sick ones."

And the rich as human as the poor, and those in prison as much as those free, and the bad as much as the good. Or vice versa. He'd have had to admit thieves and charlatans and worse—all the human mix— if it had been up to him, but his own guilt is that he's always known how far he can practically go. "We want them both. Or rather, all." He makes himself grin for the thousandth time. "In heaven—as it was on earth." Except for the cemeteries—no room for those. All of them have signed a cremation release.

"It could be heaven in a way, you know." That rainbow stare could gimp a scientist's face as much as any evangelist's. "In a way, organic life itself will be an intrusion." This from a man who had started as a biologist. "Why not at least"—Perdue leans across his clean-swept desk —"I've a handicapped younger brother myself. Expect to miss him when I go. But—" He claps his knuckles together.

"You going with us?"

"On that first trip out? Uh-uh. I've opted for the second."

"You expect a hitch?" Gilpin gets the freeze traitors deserve. For they've had their hitches. "Don't see much of those displayed at God-dard."

"Any hitch won't be in the machinery."

But in us rabble, he means. Perdue has hazel-green eyes which start out of that skin like electric lights during day, oblong nails and perfect cuffs, but spare as he is, his uniform appears too small for him. A man of contradictions, who has no sense of them? Or a sense so fine that he daren't notice it.

Gilpin got up to go. "Well, I'm sure you'll make it, Admiral."

"I expect to—use my influence."

"A lot of people will. Have." He put the list in his briefcase. "We never figured on reforming humanity, you know. Only on including it."

"For better or worse? Like in a marriage?"

"It is a sort of contract," he says, surprised at the personal note. "Between the old Earth, and the new . . ." He would never get used to calling that thing "Earth."

"Sentimentalists. Just like God, you people. He never would take the last step." Perdue draws a finger across his throat. Above it, his brown face is more like Buddha's than Gilpin's will ever be like Christ's. "Rested on the seventh day, He did. When a look at any back alley in Washington would tell Him he should've—revised."

"Maybe the Islands'll do that. Ultimately. Produce their own natural selection."

"Natural— Huh." Perdue matches his knuckles, silently. "That takes time. Eons of it. We only have space."

At the base of the spine is where the future thrill comes, Gilpin thinks to himself. Just above the coccyx, like the budding of a diviner tail. "Perhaps we'll meet out there then. To continue this." Gilpin's glance crosses the desk picture. Perdue hadn't been in uniform then. "That your son?"

"Mmm. Eighteen now."

"Who does he admire?"

"You—" Perdue said.

"Gilpin! Gi-ilpin?" The cry comes from the beach behind him. "Is that you?"

Who else would it be, waiting for her company these five nights, secure in the knowledge that only on the last one would she come? He and she tend to meet that way, on the last night of professional involvements, or the beginnings of new ones. No friend of his life has ridden the years better, linked as they are by work topics and an unspoken tolerance of each other's private lives, neither conducted in directions which ever meet. Yet after all this time her voice retains its Barbadian reserve; she's an island person too. Until tonight, he's never thought of it.

As she clambers toward him across the scrub, the long silver boots she wears catch the light like pistons. Those yard-long legs, skinny as a Giacometti figure's, are her main African feature. Nefertiti's, the lazy newspapers like to call the suave shape of her head. To him she has the snub face of a neat French child, blacked. In his own childhood attic there are files of an early humor magazine which ran cartoons whose pickaninny voices ballooned in white captions from blank dark. But night doesn't make black faces harder to see; they make what light there is more apparent. Hers catches the moon's web like obsidian. Tonight the white shawl top which is her trademark is only a sweater. But even in the jeans she wears to the office, exotic for *this* particular aviary is how she seems anywhere.

"Tom. Tom."

"What's wrong?" Has she the look she had the night they met years ago, strangers on a ratty antique plane whose seats were granted only by favor? A waif—but even then at her own request. And ready soon enough to be a queen.

"Those palm trees, just outside the motel. The ones wired for music. There was a man standing underneath one of them just now. A—

passenger. But he's not on the list." She crosses her arms, gripping her shoulders, her eyes dilated.

He's never seen her like this. "A passenger? You're sure?"

She holds out a wrist. On it, the same mark as on his. The passengers are of divided sentiment on that mark.

"You've checked the list?"

"The motel's. At the desk." The words come numbly, slurred. But she doesn't drink. "I was in my room. Working on—something of my own. A part I can never get right. I thought maybe here." She shook her head. "So I went walking. God—that must be the biggest motel in the world; I saw almost no one."

Yet they are all quartered there, under security they themselves assent to. A valuable cargo, two years in the making.

"Then a door opened and closed, down an aisle. He came out of it."

"Some man you know?" His spirits sink. So many of them.

"I knew the shirt. Funny. Those sleeves always too short for him. Or shrunk." She'd never said "always" about any one of them before. "And the shape of the head. From the back. So I stopped at the desk. He's not on their list." She shivers. "Those palm trees outside, they're not for real. Did you know?"

"Yes." Vinyl, each must be, all twenty-foot-high spread, and down to each bristly calyx, which bears a torch.

She's staring past him at water, scrub, and sea, past even the celebrated shape of the module he's leaning on, discarded here so far back in the space program, to sink into the hoped-for anonymity of rust. "Your briefcase. Look at it."

Water is rocking it. Tide is coming in. While they watch, the undertow drains past the case, giving it the illusion of motion—a brief running-out to sea—then leaves it high and dry again.

"My past. I was going to let the sea take it." So much impedimenta. Like the apartment he'd finally disposed of, his lawyer protesting such a giveaway—though already some citizens were getting reluctant to buy. On leasehold, the agreement was. With "ground rights." For ninety years, unless the owner returned to Earth within a specified time. There would be more leases like that, more and more, coming on like that wave there, rising for its one moment of identity.

"Is the official list in it? Let me see."

The briefcase wets his knees as he opens it. But his clothes too are to be left. "You should've had a copy. Everybody did."

"I do have. I was saving it. To read on the—the plane." She flashes him a rueful smile. Her life has been predetermined by planes; she's one of the diamond successes faceted daily between those time-cutting wings.

He takes a small flashlight from the briefcase, holding it over the page for her. For years she'd worn her head shaved close; now it's grown out again into its old coiled pattern of tiny braids dividing the scalp, like plowed fields photographed from a satellite. The ears are the smallest adult ones he's ever seen, and perfect. He never kisses women anymore, nor men either, but those, bent over the list like a child's, he could have touched. Nineteen years since they'd met—she's now thirty-six. On the forefinger going down the list, the heavy carnelian ring which had been her father's, then her stepmother's, is gone. Given up. Though they never speak of her early history, he's had intimations of it, as well as of the shape of her present habits, though never the details. Soon, if he wants he may have those as well. Like everyone else.

The finger going down the list is slow. Over a hundred passenger names, each with its small vita attached, introductory to the dossier to come. Once aboard and out of orbit, the full dossiers, drawn from both human and computerized interviews with the life subject and all that life's contacts, will be available in various audiovisual formats, not neglecting plain print. So that at any unsuspected time your life might be unwinding in another human consciousness, or hers or his in yours, or you might consciously pursue a particular record on a basis less fragile than friendship or love. Optimally, everybody might, with everybody. Easier on an enclosed vehicle than on a planet-at-large, as Earth is now being referred to. Easiest of all where there will be just enough world, and time. On habitat.

"It will be the extraordinary documentary project of the age," one editorial had said enthusiastically. "All subjects have cooperated as entirely as if on the private psychoanalytic couch." Which also has been utilized. "A two-part dossier—on the one side its research routes in microfilm, on the other the unified document in readable type, multilingual and transferable to sign language or braille—is an awe-inspiring sight. Holding one in the palm is like holding a human consciousness.

Palm holding is certainly stretching it. Those things weigh four pounds. He'd been reminded at once of Hermann Oberth's lie detector. Openness is trust. Without further character delineation.

"I'd forgotten," he wrote to Colorado, "that only island amateurs like me could dream of modestly doling out the crumbs of justice; my century returns them to us on the double—as boxed cake."

He stares at Veronica Oliphant's forefinger, painfully tracking down

that list of names. Behind each of which now waits the four-pound box.
His little idea of equal opportunity in the new New World may have
boomeranged. Governments have to be founded on ideas—yet what
government can be trusted to execute them? "Who could have
dreamed we were all to become members of the members-of-one-
another gang so quickly? Hope St. Paul will be pleased."

The finger pauses.

"Find the name?" He averts his head, not to pry.

"No. Another man I knew once. Not too long ago."

He knows her sexual style. Or suspects it.

"Fancy *him* being along. Mulenberg." She seems amused.

The forefinger isn't. At last it stops. The hand drops to her side.

"Not there? The other one?"

"No. But I saw him."

One man, out of her many? He's sure of it.

The battered gold locket she always wore—she isn't wearing it. He
turns out the flashlight.

"Turn it back on," the voice beside him says.

When he does, she's holding out the locket. "It's what I was going to
throw away." The long arm goes up. She throws, not with a woman's
wristy toss, but like a basketball player. They watch a sparkle arc upward and silently down, too small for sound. They might have been
watching through a telescope the fall of a spacecraft eons away. He
thought of the gold oval, so recently on skin, twisting now in the salt
wrack, a whole portion of meaning. For a second, the power of the sea
is returned to him. Then he recalls where they are going, how far.

"Was there a face in it?" He'd always wondered.

"Not—so you could see."

"You saw *his* face, though? The man under the tree?"

"Maybe I only thought I did. That's what I'm afraid of. Because then
it would mean that I still—" She spat her disgust into the sand.

"You?" One of the unique reporters of the world, the world said. "You
saw. What you saw."

Her body planes are always interchanging the way a good dancer's
do, hoarding their own secret central motion under the body's leger-
demain. "His every feature is the same. The same. Only—it's a face that
doesn't startle you anymore."

He's known beauties, male and female both, who've aged that way.
Just gone ordinary.

Her face never moves much. That's what makes it such a lens catcher.
"He didn't know me. He didn't—even know me."

"That's impossible." No one could ever not know her, once seen. There are age marks. Yet, under forty still, it's as if she'd had irremediable spiritual surgery at seventeen and done nothing since—except not ripen.

"We were right underneath one of those torches."

Twenty-nine of them there are, one to each nonignitable totem-high palm, making a gigantic flaming avenue suitable to the scale in these parts, and to the intention. No expense has been spared so that this gateway to the cosmos, from which will go forth this first journey of the new aristocrats, might look as much as possible like a Chicago steakhouse. He could see her standing there, a movie girl no one could miss.

"He was checking his watch by the clock on the tower."

A huge digital one, well lighted, which gave calendar and weather information as well. So the man she'd seen wouldn't have been the blind passenger. Merely an anonymous one, who somehow carried the mark printed on each of them four days ago.

He isn't happy about that wrist mark. This one isn't a tattoo, but more like those purplish proofs of payment rubber-stamped on the back of one's hand at the ticket doors of conventions or benefit parties. Early on, NASA had proposed an invisibly permanent heraldry. "Some census mark will be necessary to distinguish between Earth and habitat residents, *as between any borders.*"

The whole fourth estate had reacted magnificently, especially television, whose voracious news maw, needing to be fed every hour on the hour, had found itself to be, like all "open" news, the unwitting ally of a sort of liberalism. "Invisible!" had come its roar. "Invisible?" So all passengers have these highly photogenic, two-year-durable, allegedly non-counterfeitable rosettes.

"So he had the mark," he says, and sees her shiver. But not for the mark, he thinks. For the man.

He feels the removal he always does, from all those still down there in the hot sexual morass, swinging by their genitalia to the ancient reproductive current however they mind-alter it, and therefore, in spite of all other marvels of brain, ever slightly blunted in their face-up to the rest of the cosmos. Yet who would think of this world traveler in terms of that old melée? Or with her narrow rib cage against a child's cheek.

"What were you doing, Tom, when I came along the beach?"

"Baying."

"At the moon?" She stretches her long neck at it.

"At everything."

She opens her mouth, a small orifice but more expansible than most. A curdling sound pours from it—more than a scream, not a shriek—long and idling. Not a bird flies up. Too late for it. Saluting the moon, she shrugs at him. "That my old friend you're leaning on?"

It's the old piece of hardware said to belong to the ill-fated Apollo which had blown up and burned on pad, immolating the three astronauts, Virgil Grissom and—who were the other two?—its fused horror now no more than an iron grimace on the air. She'd once written an article about it. Some said this wasn't the real relic; there was none. Who'd been the others of the trio? For the life of him he can't remember. In the space museums now, there isn't too much space devoted to failure.

"After your story came out, they came to get this. But they must have got the wrong one." And no wonder. Far as the eye can see, the ever-accumulating old shapes litter the shore.

She strips off her sweater, draping it there. "Bye. Bye-bye." Underneath, her bikini is wet; she swims and swims here, with that other restlessness which must keep her young. Athletes have the same—a constant need to make muscle patterns in space.

"Where's your white fur?"

"I was going to leave it. Finally I packed it. So—it's being documented."

Everything on the ship has its own document as to its chemical composition and reactivity in any spatial situation. There are to be no accidents this time, though the rocket plane will contain some paraphernalia left over from equipment specifications well back in space history, which if one thinks a minute are far funnier than that fur. Shark chasers, for instance, and pocketknives, and seawater desalting gear, all for use in the event of what was marked on each: JETTISON. Odd stuff, for those who could not possibly ever again land by themselves on that fleck, the sea. Had someone forgotten to eliminate old checklists? Someone always forgets something. Why does that warm him suddenly, instead of chill? Out there, where a bit of the wrong friction could send them all to blazes, there'll be no margin for endearing human clumsiness.

"I had a girl with a fur once." He smiles at the puppy thought of her, of the real girl. Except as Madge the symbol, he hasn't thought of her nor heard from her since the day she left.

"In the days when you had girls?—Or boys. According to the office."

"Ah, the office."

She stretches, preparing to swim, then hangs back.

"No, don't go in that. I don't like the look of it."

They both accept what the other knows. Sliding to the sand, she puts her head on her knees. Often they share these pleasantly collapsed silences. They free us, he's thinking—though not to the same things. In our separate ways we suffer from the same dualism. Or enjoy it. Neither of us cares to confuse mind with body. Or body with mind.

And he likes to guard people, from a distance. Though those high-jutting knees of hers, meeting the shoulders in one limber furl, seem not to need it. On the other hand, those silver boots always scuff.

His attention goes from her to the sky and its portents. That's dawn over there, not to break for hours yet, only a hectic itch in the sky, like an irritation in old skin. He'd found himself watching nature signs more too these last days in the motel, as if at the last moment these might still tether him.

Under his feet is the scruffy, barrier-island loam which privately he can never admit to the same company as the kneaded brown humus of his New England island, chastely containing itself as if for conscience' sake, behind the harsh salt rock. We're going to detach ourselves from the Earth pull, whatever else happens. We're really going to do it. The draw of the Earth, all the way down to its fiery, quaking bowels, will no longer be the strongest part of our ken. *Oh, only a slight detachment of the feet, lovey,* they'll say—they're saying. *You won't miss it that much, ducky, that heavy deadness in the soles of your feet, in your limbs. Think, now, of lifting a steel T-bar with your fingertips in the nice dustless factory*—where dust, they don't say, can be a bombardment. *Or of pedaling out into the late afternoon like a Nijinsky*—with a paramour chosen for the same metatarsal tolerances? *Oh there'll be gravity, dear,* false of course, and maybe not quite so forceful in the psychology; ethically we may even in the future wish to float rather than to weigh. But there'll be enough candy-gravitation to keep us all sane.

But the trek that starts with the feet always rises in time to the head. There had never been any of mankind's that didn't. We're going to float out of Earth's ken—and out of our bodies, as we now live and breathe. That's the real import beneath all the glory-talk.

"I've been a fool," he said to her. "No matter how many times they say they'll ferry us back, in our heads we're going for good, aren't we?" Forevermore. "No matter how long it takes."

"Never takes as long as they first think. After the first time. The shuttles didn't." Leaning back against the scabbed metal of the old module, she stretched her long arms in joy he could see well enough. "Yes of course, in the long run. Haven't you been saying it?"

"It's just getting to me. Look out there." The heavens are all fleece now, and stirring. The rising wind would be whipping her garments and hair if these hadn't been pared down in the style that even at seventeen had made her seem a world traveler, all silhouette bone. "Must be blowing fifteen, twenty knots. There's going to be a storm—and it won't matter in the least."

Smiling, she moves her head from side to side against the module. Except for its rust, she fits it, and into it or its newer versions, as well as any flesh could—a Jeanne d'Arc with the fire well behind her, ready to assumpt to heaven in her silver hip boots. "And you don't mind it in the least. Do you."

The wind's bristling at his T-shirt like an animal held back. A reverse wind—that means a vacuum deadness somewhere. This, though, is no hurricane blow—that hollow roar as if the longest freight car in the world were pounding along sixteen feet up in the air. He wets a finger to test the wind, sees it in front of his nose—and bursts out laughing at the sight. Freight cars!

"Tom." She pats not him but the shooting stick.

"Oh—I know. I don't expect Allahabads up there. *Out* there. Or Chicago either."

"You saw the drawings. The models."

"Whose greatest concern—if I get it right—is whether our habitat's to be wheel-shaped or cylindrical? Oh, I saw."

"You won't be looking at the outside shape. We'll be living inside."

"All the time. Yop—it's getting to me." There was an acid taste in his mouth. His father had always claimed one could taste lightning, in the yallery-greenery charged air before an electrical storm. This wasn't going to be merely one of those. Shrubs were flattening. The blunted waves could have come from a child's drawing.

"Poor Tom. You just belong to the old gravity generation."

"You old—hang-glider." He'd watched her at it more than once with his head back, teetering sickly. Though he'd often flown in the plane owned by the office, which she sometimes piloted.

"You *talk* free-fall, Tom. You've got the head for it. But not the feet."

"Nonsense. I just have a hypersensitive middle ear." But he knows he must seem like those thirty-year-olds who kid themselves they're doing all right at the teenagers' disco—and he's not thirty anymore. In the space museums the crowds of young people saunter without surprise, chewing computer gab like gum, swapping old mission names—Saturn, Vanguard—like batting averages, and forever emitting their weakly hiccuped *"you* know, y'know?" between the snappiest logistics. Coming up to him shyly, in a museum or on a street, to say, *You Tom?*

He's that, yes. Their hero. Whose muscles creak doing their dance. "So you really want to go more than anything. Down deep in your cells even, you buy the glory of it. You really want to go."

She hesitated, looking out to sea, "Not more than—anything. There's something else I—" She shrugs that off. "But yeah. Down deep. It's my kind of unknown, you see. You and I, we don't have the same unknowns. I almost don't have the same as the young ones. But somehow, I make it. I slip along in."

And he'll be tagging along because some joker wants to see the reformer swallow his own medicine? He can think about that on the way out.

"We met on a plane," he said. "Seems appropriate we should be ending up on one."

"Even if it isn't a plane but a two-stage rocket." She shakes her head at him fondly. "And not an end— Ah, Tom! Look at you."

His fear of heights is anticipatory, as much for others as for himself. Worst when those he loves lean over the high railing. He never gets sick at sea. But these days no credit's given for that.

Once in a while there's mother in her, though not especially for him, perhaps not for any man. She mothers dramatic old women, or sick ones, in lieu of the stepmother she adored. As once in a while there's still sex in him, though for no one in particular. He tends to let the impulse pass. As Rhoda, the office manager, has said with the bitterness of the unrequited: Being, like Jesus, too busy for it.

"Tom. After all that training—you're still plumb scared?" She can't help the smile; people can't. Lack of the physical prowess you have yourself is funny.

"Maybe I am. Right now I'm too busy for it. Look."

The shooting stick, plunged at an angle deep into the wet sand, is moving, almost imperceptibly. One has to know it well to catch the glint on its steel boss. It has known many soils and pavements. There's a technique to placing it well. Often it accompanied him to the office, where he had no regular desk. *Fidus Achates,* Rhoda had snarled at the stick when he retired her, *why doesn't he retire you?*

Now the stick appears to be walking, or inching. Not horizontally. No wind. A downward pressure he can feel on his own head. But he isn't moving. Or is he? He kneels. The circle of sand around the stick, flat as a Humpty Dumpty face, tells him nothing at first. Then he sees by a slight winkling that the sand surface is moving centripetally, as if the stick is being sucked from below, with scarcely a grain displaced. He lays his ear to the ground. Nothing. The birds are saying nothing. Then it's not a land wind. Or not that near.

"Maybe it wants us to kiss the ground," he says. In return for all the clay and river bottom which humans have walked on, and for all the *lutum*—the first mud—before. Plus all the pavements since. Kiss it, Tom, for all the places you've been, or won't get to now. He's never seen the crocodile loam of the Okefenokee, so near to here. He notes that the shooting stick is really in gyroscopic sway—or would be, if of the right shape. It's being pressed *in*. His ears feel the pressure now.

He stands up, peering east. In the new light he can see the horizon. Air from the sea crowds in toward them, thick and white, water-heavy. The sea is being brought to them. "Hey—"

The way animals—men and dogs—foresense a great act of weather is in a sudden confusion of terms, an eerie loss of measurement. On-island he used to see his dog circle and circle, nose down, eyes sleeked, as if she must run the great rat to cover. Far out there, high above the seam between sea and sky, the clouds open on a cauldron of lurid light, its edges boiling westward in furious gray. Storm? Or break of day? For a minute he can't tell; then the funnel rises like a bulging sinew connecting earth and heaven, streaming toward them, in no wind. Centered in the lost elements, the storm is walking the waters, neatly compacted as a tower and higher than Canaveral's hangars in the distance. There's a smell of sulfur, hugely rotting, electrical. Not bilge. This is fresh water, a column of it, riding the salt. Slowly. There's no wind. But they had better run. "Get going." He grabbed her. The last thing he saw was his stick, keeling gracefully, lost in a slur of waves.

"What is it, a tornado?" she said in his ear as, arm-linked at the waist, they ran on sand, laboring, hiking up their feet against the draw of the planet. Ah, it's your last pull at us, is it?

"Dunno. A tornado's twenty to forty—" he gasped back. Miles per hour, or knots? He was confused. Tornadoes were choosy. They could blast a street to lumber, zigzagging around houses left quiet as stars, suck dead a farm's whole herd and featherbed the farmer meadows away from his tractor seat, safe in a tree. People ran anyway, even into motels that had no basements, and shut the wooden doors.

They ran inland from the promontory, pounding dirt for a quarter mile, then pavement along the road coastward again, to where the motel sprawled, accommodating hundreds, every room with a beach view. White water, such views were called here. They neared the motel's breastworks, high, fretted panels of pierced stucco, fronded Hawaiian. The torches were shut off now but the palms were rustling with a steady marimba swish. Above the guard wall, lights were popping on along the indented cornices and swooping balconies which allowed each guest his outlook. The castle had been warned. He turned around, to the sea.

The funnel has advanced, is still advancing, grand as a pasha in its turbaned top. "Get inside," he snarls. "Aren't you?" she replies, and stays. There's no rain, no hail; he wishes there would be. "Not a twister, is it," she says. Now there's absolute calm, even from the papery false palms. This is the moment before the bad one. They could be sucked seaward in a subtle undertow of currents, when that thing hits—but he doubts it. This is that storm which walks the waters for mariners only. "I never saw one of these," he says. "But I've heard of them." No time for more. That mushroom at the top, hanging pendant from the storm cloud above, whirls downward, tapering. Wooing the water like a tongue.

Go on. Demonstrate. To see it miles away and clear makes him want to weep, though he knows it's no spectacle for him alone. One presence, anyone's, makes it the spectacle. Down the ages, that's been enough. "Here it comes—" he yells. "Fujiyama." Tumbling back in silent boulders, the sea flowers upward. Atmosphere spins to meet it, charging down. On impact, the horizon crinkles. Parachutes of water pouring upward bring a cool sluicing air to his flesh; then there are sea mountains, moving whalebacks of gray, between jeweled eruptions lambent at the core, which mean sun behind. And now the breakers come, tons of water swelling in sequences of glass, wallowing on the shore. At last in a sound one can hear.

Halloo-oo, it's over, fishermen say. And here we fine creatures still are.

"It was a waterspout," he says, still exultant. No, I don't have your unknowns, but you see the knowns I have. "Deadly. But they don't come on land. Let's go in."

She bends suddenly, bobbing her head between her legs, crock-kneed, the way dancers did. "Not yet," came muffled. Peering between her legs at the motel, she straightens slowly, keeping her eye on it, then hitches her behind at it and begins threading the clipped green maze which intercedes between them and the motel steps. The maze is one of modern landscape architecture's hostilities, dealt the paying customer. If you can't solve it, you step over a bush or walk the perimeter.

She takes it head on, now and then grinning at him. Collapsed on a garden chaise, he now and then waves back. She and he alternate their childhoods with each other. Or their silences. That's why people tend to couple the two of them. They rescue each other from the general coupling game.

Though the motel itself was only yards away, the path between maze and steps was intricate, another cheap manipulation, done at great cost. Inside there were more, in the public-complex style of grandeur—phony with real marble, for all this was government-owned. He frankly savors its quadruplicate comforts—four pillows for every bed, swimming pools lying like mirages every few yards across the false lawns, free snacks at the cocktail hour in the five bars. There's a sense of citizen swag flowing in every corner, and although brought up on the hard virtues of a Doré Bible, he's a citizen. On rainy afternoons on his island, after an hour or two with those steel engravings, he used to feel as if those Old Testament dramas—the Red Sea rolling back, Samson's thick neck under the temple columns, all the illustrations so thronged with people—were literally taking place in his own inflamed insides. Tonight, exhausted, he feels the same, hoping he isn't going to go on feeling Earth-responsible.

But maybe they'll ask us to breed selectively up there. It would be natural. He's had urges toward parenthood. Which any clear-eyed single person can tell you has nothing to do with sex. Perhaps in time the old master-race theory can seep in without ever being enunciated—what is this selection of machined, closed worlds, if not for that? While down here will be the ragged red-eyes, lupus in the dark, waiting on the property left behind? He thinks of the girl who wants Veronica's fur. Or those hedonists who flee to the hills to braid flowers and stories, whenever there comes a plague year.

Or the solitary, who writes his journal of it.

She's back.
"You solve the maze, or step over?"
She won't say.
He reaches out to press a button on a nearby tree. Nothing happens. Down at the swimming pools the trees burst into song at a touch. Or are left on, murmuring. These must be time-clocked. "Maybe I won't go." Would they allow it? "Maybe it's more honorable to stay."
She sticks out a long leg, cocking the boot. "Maybe. But not for you."
Of the two civilizations kept always in mind, one was the world where we actually lived among our own offals, with occasional opal sky-peeks

and sudden choirings of architecture. The other was that ideal place which the early church fathers of anywhere, East or West, had formed in our heads—a heavenplace of orthodox avenues cleansed hourly with youth serum, in a white nimbus of air. Meanwhile the middle-class utopias, white with plastic, whirring with Ali Baba effects, sprayed with fake ozone and greened with refreshants of chemical sweat, were what we were getting, and would get some version of in Outer. Yet the impulse is still lovable, like a child's dream of birthdays. He has to see it; she's right.

Just as he wants to see this morning, now warming up over the beach with fumbling touches of light as if searching for what to illuminate—a crab's shell with the creature gone, a stone to make glow like a palladium. And all sleepers, jaws agape.

Last night in the motel bedroom he began to yearn for the art he owned at home. Reproduced or real, it studs his consciousness. His apartment's monotonously long corridors had been chosen for it. Passing down these of a morning, each work chimed, to him, steppingstones into the daily cave. Selecting for that ditty bag of personal possessions each passenger was to be allowed, he had put in one art catalogue, its choice an elegy, and the worst wrench so far.

Up ahead, the motel's Spanish-stucco writhings and ice-cream peaks have dawn on them. Behind each window is some life version from that catalogue: Henry Moore's Shelter drawings as official artist for the second world war. Behind that window there, or that one maybe, the Pink and Green Sleepers with the monumental curved blanket—four inches by two and a half, the four-fingered hand, huge with slumber, the two heads under their curving shroud, and on the right—inch and a half by two, the great scratched pink shoulder. From now on, only human art would be set before him—real figures he will have to trace and compose, without guide. The idea awes him, yet sets him up foolishly, like a Sunday school warning.

He might as well begin with her, gawping up at the façade, arms akimbo on the minimal hips, at first sight fashion's very gargoyle, her aviatrix bones drawn with the whirlwind diagnosis with which artists like Reginald Marsh or de Kooning drew women—but with the subtler shadow of the girl he knew. A small head, Senegalese in origin. One man has maybe followed it here, perhaps two. And a friend. Yet in that ebony oval, which contains a brain of worth, he sometimes sees the black mummy face of the relic nun at Assisi, that hard licorice which priests of the moment had surely always anointed, perhaps with local wax. Beneath which it still has its own purpose, undefined.

"Solitude will be the sin, you know," she says. "They're already trying so desperately to get us to love one another."

"I know." The briefings have talked out all the group techniques of the waning century, from Rolfing to champagne, to fun with trigonometry and baroque music, to Albert Schweitzer and anti-perspirant. "Like St. Paul again. And with about the same results."

"You're getting very religious."

"Tendencies—tend to emerge. In any closed environment. As at a house party. Or a death camp. I see the next three weeks as somewhere between. So do they."

"What a bunch. Our—managers."

"Sure are." Texas professors, born in Russia some of them, but already with barbecue manners and Hollywood haircuts, both sexes of them. East coast think-tankers, fragile as prep-school geniuses, whose hound-dog heads one wanted to scratch between the ears for encouragement, until one saw the wild, monkish eyes. "My apartment co-op, the tenants never really believed they were their own landlord. *We're* our managers. And—though that bunch may not know it yet—they're us." Even Perdue. He's us too. And doesn't know it yet.

She hums mockingly, one of the tunes which had purled at them yesterday all through lunch. "Tom. You're taking all this so—" She touches his wrist. "I know you always do—who better than me? But this trip—can't you understand that for a lot of us, it's only *flying*. Don't overload it with—" She sighs.

"Significance. Sorry to be a bore, but I never talk like this with anyone else."

She smiles. He sees that he does. "Okay, then. Let's go eat."

They both burst out laughing. They've had their last meal. Until embarkation it'll be all liquids, rarefied but adequate.

"What's in those pep drops, Tom? I can feel the vitamins dance. Bee jelly and ox blood?"

"And powdered unicorn horn? Doubt it. Merck's best formula for aerospace."

"Anyway, I'm not hungry. Feel as if I never will be. You?"

"No. On a slight jag, though." He's just realized it. "The potassium crazies."

"And I don't pee much. You?"

"No."

Their voices die between them.

"Last words," he says. How strange it's all going to be, citizens. No account may ever give all of it.

Her eyes dart from side to side. Does she think of Peenemünde, the old site of the German military park, placed there because rocketeer Wernher von Braun's father had once gone duck hunting in a remote town, and the son had remembered—from which, doing her last article for *The Sheet,* she'd flown on here? Or of the Jet Propulsion Laboratory of the Guggenheim Aeronautical Laboratory of the California Institute of Technology—JP of GALCIT for short, where she'd been before? Or of what she's going to wear for the flight? Which is the same as for him. He checks his watch—his old Waltham from the island, which he's sending home. Past midnight. Once they get inside, they won't again be allowed out. Strange, that not more of us are wandering.

"May I offer you my arm?"

She takes it, in style.

"And my love." Just in case. It's wise to say.

"And mine. Remember."

"I shall."

They swing their joined arms and start up the path, between the double rows of palms. From these, a man emerges on their right, pacing head down, one arm behind him across the small of his back.

It's a European posture, Gilpin thinks in that first impression which takes precedence over all. Actors walk so, playing unworldly persons or famous ones, Stanislavsky method. Or it's in the striped suit, out of place for the tropics. Or that iron-gray, maestro hair.

The man steps to the center of the path, silently presenting himself. That is his posture.

His face. What must it have been, if it's ordinary now? Elongated by youth, would it have been an El Greco? Squared by middle age, it's no longer a face from those high winds, but one can see that it's been there—and hasn't yet settled for handsomeness. Perhaps the extraordinary has since gone into the whole man, who now bows as if they have merely met on the path, and goes on past. Yet he had intercepted them.

They watch him enter the motel. He walks determinedly, the one arm still folded behind his back.

She doesn't speak. My life's never been weighted like that, Gilpin thinks. By another person. I love by accretion, finding that no disgrace. But I've no background for joining in the dramas which fall upon those who've loved otherwise; I lack the proper conventions. I speak from the off-side. People don't seem to mind. "Thought maybe your locket had washed back in and he'd picked it up." Finding it empty? "Was there ever a picture in it?"

"Never. I wore it for the continuity of it. For what had been me. Or I thought I did."

"Is he the one?"

"Now I'm not sure."

"Neither was he." Then it must have been that man. "Lievering," he said. "Wolf Lievering."

"You remember?"

"Everything you tell me. Which isn't much."

"More than you do."

"There isn't more." He'd long ago made it all public. He knows that people find this hard to believe.

"We'll both soon know." She grimaces. "About everybody."

"Or perhaps he's crew. Operational."

"Wolf? Hah."

"What's his field?"

They're all booked under one, she to be the official photographer, he the historian, their particular cabin to be shared with, among others, an industrial consultant and the head administrator and wife; whether the wife has another function as well, he doesn't know.

We're booked as for any archaeological expedition, he thinks. Our quarry being the future.

"His field? Language. But it was in what he was, more than what he did."

"And what was that?"

"He—displaced people. From what they were. Everywhere he went."

He'd certainly done that to her.

"Ah—one of those." A charismatic. Evangelical or not, they're always trouble.

"Was Lievering himself a displaced person?"

"I never knew." She shivered her arms up, stretching. "Let's go in now."

Both turn the other way, toward the promontory they have just come from. Strewn with omens, it can no longer be seen.

He stretches an arm. "Which'll weigh more out there, d'ya suppose? The future—or the past? . . . Yes, let's go in."

As they do so, the palm trees on either side of them burst into a musical signature. Reveille.

Inside the motel for once and all until liftoff, every window that I, Gilpin, looked through became a haunting, by an Earth already half departed from. The motel was an excellent limbo. Downstairs, once past the porte-cochère, there were no windows. The grass-green sward of the rugs, interspersed with blood-red sofas and chairs in suites of three against walls of plastic stone and plywood forestry, projected a present world one would do well to find repellent. Either the authorities knew what they were doing to the psyches under their care, or hadn't a clue as to how cleverly they were managing—about par for government. I note how I have already begun to think of them as the authorities. I go into the bar.

There's no piña colada in front of me today. Much as it had done for me once, I hadn't cared to try its properties since. My glass holds whisky, Irish ordered but bourbon received, which could mean that on Canaveral even the bartenders no longer bother with terrestrial geography. The whisky in any case is forbidden—and that always helps. During these last hours we are on our honor not to have alcohol. Last hours help too, toward a rushing sense of what's to be done—for I never can believe in them.

As Gilpin, I do perform publicly rather well. But the *I* of me will not move except to an inner call which Gilpin has no power to provoke. Tapped once before, I recognize the sensation, never having expected it again. Not that the mission I've spent most of my span on is fulfilled. The missions that adopt me are not that sort. But once again, I'm on call.

In the movements we make toward one another's mystery, surely there is where life most is. Those ever-shadowy movements—who does not make them, and who is exempt from studying them? But on the *Courier* I would be closest to the nature of motion itself. This is why I and the others, and a great nation, are being drawn there, and why history is. For when people are in thrall to a certain physical motion, then life appears to them to be at its height. Meanwhile, swung like an undercarriage below any large vehicle is that other continuous movement—small, rotor, and fatal—between the people themselves.

I hear my own cadence—the part of me that comes from fisherfolk, who are in motion all their lives. We at home were always at once in the trough of the wave and on the anxious shore. We were always listening to the voyaging.

Time to go up. I felt great.

On the way, I stopped at the bookstall and inquired for any publications of the L-5 Society of Tucson.

"Sold out. Days ago."

How clerks love refusing. It salves them for being clerks. Shortly, I'd be where I would be refused nothing—of what there was to be had.

"Offer me something," I said.

He stared. Silently he reached into his stock and held out a heavy, lustrous art book, a copy of which I had once owned. Years back NASA had commissioned certain modern artists to paint the space effort, which from craft to environs they had done. I thumbed the preface, supplied by a curator of the National Gallery. "Artists should be key witnesses to history in the making. The truth seen by an artist is more meaningful than any other kind of record." Depending upon who picked what witnesses. First Edition—marked down to twenty-five dollars. It wasn't the visitant I'd have chosen from my lost library, but it was one. I held out a credit card I still had on me.

"You a passenger?"

"I am."

"Sorry. No credit cards."

I had a hundred dollars in scrip. We all had been issued the same amount, to cross the border with. The clerk's face lit up. He took the small orange and green slips and put them in a special drawer of the cash register. He was collecting them. He didn't bother to wrap the book.

So burdened, I climbed the stairs, the soles of my shoes sticking to the risers, partly from reluctance and partly from damp. Halfway up there was a botched crow's nest where carpenter and material must have come to the end of a contract, though a table and chair were provided, in case one wanted to watch the crowd below. I no longer did. They had been my collection. I took out my remaining scrip instead. Beautifully engraved peacock-feather style, with a leaf-crowned, plump-cheeked Hebe or hermaphrodite on either side, the stuff still had the look of IOU's. The slips measured about four and a half inches by two, much smaller than our civilian dollars. Each was marked MILITARY PAYMENT CERTIFICATE on its shorter ends. I hadn't noticed that before. The legend on the two long sides was harder to read. On top: FOR USE ONLY IN THE UNITED STATES MILITARY ESTABLISHMENTS—BY UNITED STATES, and on bottom: AUTHORIZED PERSONNEL IN ACCORDANCE WITH APPLICABLE RULES AND REGULATIONS. This lettering was very small, but in caps.

I knew where they'd got the whole idea. This was army of occupation currency.

I left the book on the table. Those were not my witnesses.

Upstairs the motel was all luminous white and gray-blue, as if they were already progressing us toward the germ-free corridor. They had given us each a two-room suite. We were to fraternize, like members of an expensive tour, on the eve. So far, in this wing, nobody had. So here we were in our usual ragged enclosure. Each mind enclosing itself, while making frantic land-ahoy signals to its proposed destination.

In the day of the wagon wheel, or the freighter coaling into a sunset, or the ocean liner with its cups of tea, or the trains probing the Rockies and carrying a honeymoon couple or a corpse, a life and its journey were synonymous. The two voyages were one. An air trip is a pocket out of life, an anti-life means to an end, with a tray and a toilet between. But in outer space, with the means so huge and the journey so far, what then? Time—what would it become? All that gear—would it become household, or at least a caravan? Put real people there, with real lives behind them, and could the old continuity come again?

Which would win out, the voyage or the life?

My bedroom has a vast window, from which I can see the dish antennae that dot the Cape, giving its outline an extra blur of puzzlement. There is a pair of binoculars on the windowsill. But I have no further urge to enumerate surfaces or distinguish them. My mind has taken on the mnemonic position. From that moon-flat perspective I can see how foolish my last remark to Veronica was. Which will weigh more, the future or the past? Nothing will weigh the same from now on, certainly not time. Down here a duration, out there would it be more of a distance? As the human faces around one flattened or curved with speed, how would one make contact with the minds behind them? Based in bodies constantly bombarded, would the minds sharpen or drift? Or cling to performance, as the best grip on the moment-at-hand?

This is exploration a priori. Of the first things. Into elements we are not adapted to. We are going backward, into anti-civilization. With everything of course mechanically provided for. Who can know what selves we will find?

Good-bye Amerigo, Eric the Red—who merely knew what they were looking for.

I passed an air-cooled hand over the pane, as if clearing a windshield that was clouding up. Good-bye my own, my native land, body, foot.

On the desk behind me a tape recorder was provided. I had been encouraged to use it. I pressed the button for tape. The slow hiss came on.

"I should have kissed the ground," Gilpin said.

MULENBERG'S INTERVAL

ON THE OTHER SIDE OF THE WALL a big man lies calmly face upward on the motel's fine mohair bedspread, fully dressed even to his shoes. This indicates what he is in the main: a hotel traveler, first by trade, but in recent years from need—psychological, for he is very rich—and by now, from personality. Two of his residences, unlived in for years, are finally up for sale. We report on them from the real estate firm's brochure—and on him.

Outstanding Private Retreat within Routt Nat'l Forest [which is in Colorado] some miles north of Steamboat Springs. Secluded in magnificent hidden mountain valley, 160-acre ranch in a setting of spruce, aspen, pines, lush grass and wildflowers crossed by trout-filled Reed Creek flowing through beaver ponds to lake. In this awe-inspiring forest setting comforts are twentieth-century. Beside picturesque pond, outstanding architect-built 10-room residence with huge glass areas, heated swimming pool, caretaker and guest houses, 2 original cabins and homestead, with professionally developed nurseries, plus stable and complement of maintenance buildings. Offered furnished and equipped at $1,750,000.

The price is intentionally low. He'd held onto the homestead for his great-grandfather's sake, the nurseries for his father's, until sure that his heirs were no longer any more interested than he in those fragile interviews one holds with the dead.

The second ad reads:

Chance of a Lifetime: 4920-cattle ranch in Oklahoma Panhandle. I-deal cow/calf operation for one man or family. Strong grasses, healthy climate. Cross-fenced into four pastures. Two good sets of working pens. Well watered with 10 windmills and 3 electric pumps. Good fall hunting with dove, quail, prairie chickens. The bonus on this ranch is a $500,000 Grecian mansion: fully carpeted, seven chandeliers, 4-car garage, central heating and cooling, large porch on three sides, enclosed atrium garden. Formerly used as retreat for corporate executives. Outbuildings for domestic and other help, offices or storage. This unique package ready to go at $2,000,000.

Ditto on the low price. Bought for him as a corporate necessity and in place of some holding-company stock, the house wasn't Grecian, the acres no longer a real panhandle. A prairie chicken might be good to eat but was a laugh to hunt. Quail there were not. He wouldn't shoot dove. Windmills anywhere were a pleasure, but Oklahoma was not Colorado. All of which he'd known at point of purchase. Far as he knows, they were right about the chandeliers. Sale money for both places would be disposed of for him in the usual style, by three balustraded banks. He is no longer corporate. But he expects to be back. He always does—come back.

He's lying on the bed because, though the day's been as medically arduous for him as for the rest, he can't expect his five o'clock whisky, nor is he any longer surrounded by the array of leather goods—portfolios, attaché and dressing cases, framed pictures and walleted cards —which normally keep him company in such rooms, and he has made all his telephone calls. There remain early bath and bed, and the visit of the aeronurse with medication. He plans to make no ceremony of any of these, neither whooping and soaking in the bath, nor masturbating in his last private bed-to-be—which he hasn't done since a boy—nor pulling the young nurse in with him, though in spite of sex being proscribed here on grounds of energy loss, she's made signs. He knows pretty well what will or won't be provided out there, industrially and domestically, since he's already been functioning as ordnance coordinator between Earth and habitat under a command order which transcends this flight, and reports direct to Perdue. On whisky supply, the answer—a tie between the brass and the doctors—is wait and see, and meanwhile send beer makings. These, dispatched on the last shuttle but one, all chemically documented and stowed along with other oddments the habitat can't yet fabricate or cannibalize meteors for, must even now be fermenting. The civil administrator-to-be, an excellent man heard of in the Middle East years ago, is his own nominee, which pleases him. It has pleased him, maybe childishly, to circumvent Perdue in several instances. Ordinarily Mulenberg doesn't much play industrial politics. If you'd had the goods early enough in your own career, you didn't need to. But it appears that many on the project consider it their civic duty to circumvent Perdue.

The view from the window? He's looked at it once and is done with it. It would never think of haunting him. That man Gilpin's moral flushes—what's known of them from his publications and appearances before congressional committees—seem to Mulenberg the man's personal style, a freedom not to be infringed upon. Along with most of the country, he thinks of the man's dramatics as astringently good for the nation to consider, if not to accept totally. To this he has a private addenda: Gilpin's face, narrow but benevolently engraved, is to him an eighteenth-century American joy. Rarer still, Gilpin's manners are the same as his character, yet another anachronism of which Lafayette and de Tocqueville, Mulenberg's early heroes, would have approved. Mulenberg's own trade, which a daughter had once put on a college application (under Father's Business) as "tycoon," has circled him among pretty many of the world's greats without ever making him feel himself infectiously one of them. But he has a shrewd sense of when someone obviously moves in a broader than normal scale. Gilpin is what Mulenberg thinks of as a world person, probably the only one on the ship. Having so judged him, as with the view he is done with him.

For Mulenberg this trip is transportation like any other, toward a goal. Born with an indifferent sense of direction even on a horse, he early made the pragmatic jump toward pure passenger. In the process of that he cares little where he sits or is; he expects to be delivered. He regards all science as in the business of General Delivery. He does commit the folly of still passively trusting it, which that same daughter has pointed out. As a passenger, he makes that choice. He regards this trip as a particularly long one in an advanced kind of plane, the rocket principle being merely an elaboration and the pretrip training a necessary sport, or stiffer-than-usual massage, of the kind often recommended for businessmen. The training has been hard on his outsize bone structure but has flattened his belly. Once on habitat, even temporarily, which is all he plans, he will follow the rules, however peculiar, as he would in any factory. It's all a means toward the goal.

If he were in an airport now he would go straight to one of those machines that write insurance policies and take out one for the largest sum permissible—always in favor of some far-fetched or far-flung recipient who may well have forgotten Mulenberg exists. It's a form of gambling and of faith—one of those private rites by which one tries to link oneself lyrically with other people, always safely absent. "One of your Swedish actions" his long-dead wife had called it, meaning those fits of mythic gloom which sometimes moved people of their ancestry.

Many of his unaware beneficiaries have been women. For the last three years always the same one. That cuckoo little act, repeated at every airport, has become his guarantee, keeping death away from him, and other men and other destiny away from her, while in life he has hunted her. The stupid miracle was that even given the trips to Saudi, away from Western planes and the magazines that went with them, he hadn't found her sooner. He could never for so long have kept himself from finding her—a fact now admitted—if all along she hadn't been so near.

On the night table is his evening dose of that yeasty yellow brew which will keep him hale until his first flight meal, meanwhile lessening the amount of excretory waste. As with all NASA-related inventions, from a personal feeding tube to that shuttle component which might yet revolutionize ordinary jet flight cost analysis, the company that worked it up has waived rights to the invention only, not to such product applications of it as might be marketable. Should the company disclose the invention itself, it forfeits that competitive position. On the surface, all very tidy-fair. Except, as Mulenberg knows, the real competition, such as it is, comes at the beginning, when investigational research is assigned—the same few favored companies like his being most often tapped. It's natural. You give the contract to the company with the most experience at getting the particular thing well and quickly done, which experience comes from—the habit of getting contracts. As the yellow stuff rolls past his closed palate, a fish glue trying to smell like almond, it amuses him that in outer space—he can't learn to say Outer —the discretionary facts of business, no matter how mixed with meteors, smell as usual.

Somewhere, on another floor perhaps, she must be downing the same potion. An exquisite stealth creeps over him. She's here, garnered into as safe a cage as ever a footloose woman has wandered into, wooed there by the delicate octopus arms of secret government. Although she'd been a first-class prospect, he hadn't dared wait to see whether she would qualify on her own before he committed himself to leaving. They wanted him; they must be sure to have her. Though of course he hadn't said so. His direct request had been for Gilpin, who it was thought had already pressured for her, or whose presence on the list was likely to affect hers. . . . All in all, Mulenberg has influenced the choice of five candidates: himself, William Wert and wife, Tom Gilpin —and Veronica Oliphant. He himself had plumped for training at a far station and arrived at the motel only yesterday, so has yet glimpsed none of them.

He can wait now. Bliss enough to know she's here and even to be in the same cabin, on terms chaste enough to appease any sultan.

Setting the emptied medicine glass on the night table, which is a beveled-off block of crystal-white quartz the designer must have deemed in tune with what was going on here, his hand shakes. The quartz is cold, and jagged to the hand. They've all been warned away from harboring too many lonely images of space, of what the layman thinks goes on there in monster ice geometry. Keep it joky close, the way the Apollo astronauts did, yesterday's indoctrinator had cautioned, that holy look on her face at every mention of the imperial three. Keep it human. He's doing that. He's seen the glassed-in museum display, with YE OLDE LUNAR SCRATCH PAD—mottoed in Old English type— taking top billing over even the biomedical harness, or the gloves with the wee lights in their fingertips for non-atmosphere's frauds, or the personal radiation dosimeter and the oxygen-supply energy masks. He's already peering ahead to the little packet that jogs along, chilly or hot, alongside every human adventure. There it goes, on earth as it shall be in heaven. The discretionary facts.

He slips down. That stuff was sedative. She too must be sliding down into the warmish pillows of the last-night-on-earth's womb-bed.

Surely their two dossiers must be tangling and melding there. Where even the feathers have weight.

THE EXPLOIT

THE SIX-FOOT GIRL loped toward the men standing under the New York Athletic Club's summer canopy, going east fast on long, bare grape-black legs. Passing them, she slowed, her arched sandals hitting first with the insinuating ball of the foot, then with a sharp click of the stilt heels. In the draining light, Mulenberg noted that the polished head and stalk neck rode their own caravan motion at the angle of a giraffe's. But it was Ventura who spoke, his pale, unhealthy-looking cigarillo drawing to a glow.

"Model?"

The girl's crushy white dress, thick but floating, shagged on behind her. "Never."

"Classy dress."

Mulenberg drew deep on breath; he didn't need to smoke. Across from them, directly west of the south end of Central Park and backed by a sky of cracked cloud, the Gulf & Western Building, where his office floors were, rode like a chandelier lit and paid for by shahs, some of whom he'd met personally. Coming in there twice a month on the easterly route, returning west again on a string of South American cities, and so home to the ranch and small wells which had begun it all, he'd made the world his triangle. And this city, this corner, its apex. Twice a month. Only fools demanded that a city be pasture—or even have pure air.

"Classiest street for it in the world," he said, elated she had looked at him.

"You should know." Ventura was sincere. In the steamroom, where men sat as if at pot, and talked like it, Ventura's sallow, forty-two-year-old body, canalled with black hair, gave him a sinewy edge on Mulenberg's giant, Scandinavian-pink forty-eight. Until Ventura opened his mouth. He was now from Garden City, Long Island, where he'd built his Spanish villa before his troubles, his tennis court in spite of them, and lived with his family. Such as it was.

Ventura had married too young, Mulenberg had first thought, rubbing elbows with him at the Oak Room bar—and now that he had the export-import business, with a thirty million gross that was always needing capital but took him high flying, he must be saddled with some pasta-fat mamma-tits at home. But no. A snapshot of a shapely enough woman, with tragedienne eyes. "She is mostly confined," Ventura said. "Oh no. Not to a string of kids." There was a picture of the one kid, a weakly little boy standing knock-kneed between the mother-in-law and the housekeeper, two wizened plug-uglies with outlaw mustaches. "To a sanatorium," Ventura'd said. "Psychological. I spend the average of a new Buick, every month. Working my way up to Cadillac." His pride in that had almost outrun his appropriate sadness—in which case Mulenberg would have crossed him off—but not quite. So they'd discovered that they belonged to the same club in more than one sense—and not only to the old A.C. behind them, now boozing and steaming itself, or jockeying for the night to come.

For they also have the same excusable habits, if not tastes.

Twice a month, they join up briefly before exerting these. Always they meet over a game of something, toss-ball or ping-pong, and have a drink or two afterward—never dinner. Neither of them likes to eat beforehand. Ventura likes to eat afterward, with the girl and her pimp. Mulenberg has never in his life dealt with anyone but the girl herself, and devoutly means never to, though Ventura has "a very quiet list"— more shadowy than shady, ranging from art-gallery swamis who could also supply the human frame, to stock runners who knew a ring of not-too-middle-aged receptionists, to Bronx warehousemen who had a pliant ring of "cousins." All of them small merchants in fact, with a fly eye for the fringe product, but still the kind of manners you could eat shrimp with. Ventura has a knack for finding such men through his business channels. Such anecdotes as he has come from those dinners, little accounts as pale as those cheroots of his, and full of that nameless middle-class yearning of, say, twenty years back, which Mulenberg recognizes; he had come from it.

Neither of them ever described an evening's sex afterward. "The exploit," Ventura called it. He sometimes went so far as to qualify it. "The exploit—was fine." Mulenberg never replied in kind, or mentioned what he had done afterward. He wouldn't mind eating with some girl who might spark him to enough concentric tenderness to ask her, but for a long time now, though the exploits often went beyond fine, he had dined alone.

Neither he nor Ventura ever set foot in a house. But unlike Ventura, he had to see the girl first. To tell the truth, he even hated beginning on the phone.

"Yes, I should know," he said ritually. "Ten years, my wife's cancer took." Rabbit-punching her first in the guts, then in the lungs and breasts, and finally—in the brain. He never showed pictures. He and she had had relations almost to the end. Anything he'd done while away from her had been for forgetfulness. Or, just once in a while to touch health. "And I tell you—not Paris." Where, out of provincial convention, he'd started his rounds away from her. And where it was all foozle and flame on top and scrawn below, and gardenia stink instead of washing. "Maybe Berlin was the best once. But before our time." Blue angels everywhere now, greasy-chopped little waitresses and countesses both. It was there he'd lost his taste for eating with them afterward. "Barcelona?" He pursed his lips out of consideration for Ventura's mixed Latin heritages. A gentle town. Where the girls wore handsome underlinen, but where the church horned in, even in the lowest quarters. Especially there. And upper-class connections had been beyond him. "Got more of a high out of that church. The crazy one you didn't like."

"The Sagrada Familia?" Ventura and his wife had traveled doggedly for her health. She'd never been irrational, he claimed, and wasn't now. Only depressed. "Crazy barbaric," he said now, meaningfully. They were both still watching the girl, paused for traffic at the far corner but easily sightable by her height and that dark back veeing deep into her foamy white. "You and your street Scheherazades." He was always warning Mulenberg against street pickups. "Someday, you'll overstep."

Someday Ventura would. Then this pally on-the-sidewalk twice-a-month confab of theirs, which was beginning to itch Mulenberg already, would be quits. "Bet you she turns the corner, down Sixth," he said.

"You're on." Ventura checked his watch. "Bet you breakfast, tomorrow morning."

If she did, it was at least fifty-fifty she was taking the high-class route she clearly rated, though even Sixth was a little too far west. But if she turned down it, walked a couple of blocks south and turned west again, she'd be almost across from Carnegie Hall—in whose aged flank a nightspot called Miss Lacey's, now replaced by a coffee shop, had for many months drawn a slow cortege of limos containing the escorting buckoes in their platform shoes, frilled shirts and ten-gallon hats—and girls like her. That place had been raided but its clientele still lingered, as he sometimes did, eyeing the satiny new doorway across the street, of what looked like only a disco so far. Where the tall, sooty couples going in— men outfitted in fawn suede from tip to toe, girls with the same daz-zlingly snub ebon eyes and paper-doll hips—might just possibly be merely social couples from that new world of black designers, black theatricals, to be seen in the glossies the air stewardesses were always handing him. He kept up with all his neighborhoods, making it a point to apply the same impersonal research to evening prospecting as to shale engineering. It never hurt to. That way, it never hurt.

"There." Mulenberg leaned forward, craning. "Turn *south*, little lamb. *There.*" He straightened up. "She's done it. What did I say."

Ventura laughed, chewing the now dead cigar. First time Mulenberg had ever seen him light one. "Little breakfast, then, on me. We can go brunch at the World Trade, maybe; don't have to stick to the A.C. Or take a long morning snooze"—he waggled his thick eyebrows—"and make it lunch."

There was something over-velvety about Ventura's clothes, though nothing Mulenberg could put a finger on. For all his own married years he himself had worn Hickey Freeman "executive" suits, which did well by too much waistline, except that the whole world knew this was why you wore them. Now, thinned by health clubs, he wore "international" jackets made of the angel-light leathers and silks that life had awarded him, kept the beard that grief had for a while grown on him, wore the now acceptable boots and string ties of his youth, and was comfortable for the first time since. Ventura had one of those bluish underbeards shaved sexily to the bone and there was a sheen to the guy's hair; under the midtown arc light he looked stagier than Mulenberg wanted to spend Sunday morning with. A man whom only height saved from wearing those elevator shoes.

"Bet you she comes all the way around the block again," Mulenberg said.

Ventura checked his watch again. "Got fifteen. Then, I've gotta." He always had an appointment, sharply kept. Often in the Oyster Bar, south side of the Plaza Hotel. "Give you anything she's a model. Or an actress, maybe. Going to meet her numbers runner, or her rock-jock, at that new African movie. Or even a college girl."

"Upper Lexington Avenue, you might be right. Or the Village— absolutely. But not this street," Mulenberg said happily. "I tell you what. Same stakes, but give me a handicap. Make it twelve. Twelve minutes. She took long steps."

Ventura nodded, slowly. "So she's it, huh." When he shrugged he did do it like a shorter man. "Wish you luck."

Mulenberg turned to watch the crowd milling along past the white-striped hotel marquees which were heated in the winter, the iron coach lamps shining down from another era on traffic signals, the car headlights and the muted glow of closed shop windows silky with tourist-deluxe ivories, or burning with flowers too precious to be sincerely sent to anybody. Central Park South at night was always a stage, moving with the same masks as on streets he knew in Rio or Caracas, or like on the Élysées or the Veneto—and these days even with the same authenticating touch of beggardom, in a deep niche or curbside. But this street at this hour had for him another pressure behind it, sweet over the gasoline cording his throat strong. It was partly the park, wrinkling behind all like one of those blurred Barbizon prints in hotel bedrooms —although his travel triangle included several such parks. From here he could see, high up in the Gulf tower, his own office floors, barred with light. Standing here with Ventura, mentally he could turn on the faucet of the bar sink in his own private lounge stories above, and see all his rainbow success flow from it—while down below here, he teased the whole funicular schedule of his life with a little healthy risk. This was the stage *he* was on. It was why he stayed at the A.C.

"Three minutes." Ventura looked worried this month, baggier under the eyes. "I wouldn't go with a college girl if you paid me. It's been offered. On my own tennis court."

"And you wouldn't go with a black one," Mulenberg said idly. He knew the answer. Not a question of color.

"None of your crazy barbarics. I want to be *reminded.*"

And you don't, Ventura meant. All he knew of Mulenberg's wife was the name inscribed on the watch Mulenberg took off, poolside, and that Mulenberg had met her in high school, going on to college with her, back when the money was potatoes—and from them, from both their parents' farmlands. But he was right.

"How is your court?"

"Wet, dry. Grassy, muddy. Even monsters. Woodchucks, moles. Two fifty a month, the lawn service. I do it myself. But the kid is learning." He has a tired, responsible smile. Mulenberg likes him again.

"And the business?" All Mulenberg knows is that its profits, dependent on many painstaking Asiatic hands in obscurely shifting places, are far too small for the gross.

"It goes." Ventura was staring up at the Gulf & Western. "Why you don't just sit up there—and phone. From a gold-plated mouthpiece. I'll supply you one. Made in Hong Kong."

"Why don't you? Phone. From the warehouse in Astoria."

"Because the place is loaded with family. I have brothers-in-law the way other people have warts." Ventura threw up his hands. But he was enjoying this. "Six minutes. Where you suppose she is, already on Fifth Avenue? Looking in the window, Bergdorf's? Or'd she cross to Tiffany's window, look wistful, and get picked up by some other john?"

"Tell you what," Mulenberg said. "I can't stand brunch. But I lose— what do you say to a tip on a modest killing in Saudi crude?"

"That what they're calling money these days?" Ventura said lightly.

"When it comes in tankers."

"Tell you the truth, haven't seen much of it any style lately." Ventura's eyes closed. "And what if you win?"

"Settle it later."

Ventura's eyes opened. "Made a bet like that myself a while back." He shook himself. "Then you think you're going to lose?"

"By a hair. But I feel her, loping along." He positively could. It was like an inner rhythm. Of the luck that came to him on this corner, behind which the A.C.'s back end gave off an odor of steak-fart and french fries into the pearly light pouring upward, natural but powerless against that oil rig of his on Columbus Circle, from the dirtier end of a park "built in the already outmoded style of Louis Philippe," as he'd read in an article on it while waiting for a plane in the executive lounge at Düsseldorf. Sending on a contribution to the park's restoration fund, afterward.

"This is one of the great romantic streets of the world."

Ventura ducked his head. "You better watch yourself."

He laughed. A shock of world-stained blond hair fell over his eyes. He wiped it back. "Not tonight. This is always my lucky night."

"Yeah, you told. About Rome."

"Did I?" In his mind these adventures were always private, but this corner must make him loose-tongued. It hadn't been a pretty exploit. He'd picked her up from a doorway on Trastevere where she was lounging deep in shadow. An old trick, but even when drawn to a lamp she was extraordinary, tiny and cream-skinned, an absolute Italian beauty with a chorine's legs, and costumed like a legionnaire, except for the round bellhop's hat. He didn't like costumes, ordinarily. In the cab she'd smelled fresh enough, of that same mink-oil hairwash all the office girls there were using. Until they were inside, she hadn't smiled.

"Then she opened her mouth, you said. And the whole Forum was in it."

Brown, rotting stumps. Little tombstone teeth. In gums of ancient red. He'd paid her off at once, as kindly as he could.

Ventura was putting the frayed cigarillo in a case. He caught Mulenberg's glance. "Expensive."

"Must be. Never before saw you light one."

"Come from India. My swami gets them for me. Want some? I can get them for people."

"India. Who the hell gets cigars from India? If you can call those cigars. Hate to tell you what they remind me of."

"What?" Ventura has a funny half smile on him.

"Of my sheepdog pup's—" He didn't like to say it. Of a thing a man put in his mouth.

Ventura looked down at the case, a flattish wide one containing maybe twenty of the skinny smokes. "Thank God they don't look like mine."

Mulenberg stared farsightedly at the corner where the girl could come on from either Fifth or Sixth, if she was coming. Out of the edge of his eye he saw Ventura was anxiously monitoring also. Wanted to win, no doubt about it.

Ventura turned suddenly. "I like them *normal*," he said with vicious emphasis. "Normal for *me*. Some nice-looking woman, not a girl. With brown eyes. And hips. In a pink slack suit." He grinned "My swami orders those too. On the half shell."

Mulenberg thought he knew now what there was about this man that gave one such an advantage over him. He had the over-limpid aura of a man who didn't know his own processes.

Turning away uncomfortably, Mulenberg saw her. There surely— that floating drapery, center crowd, half down the block. His heart pounded.

His elbow is touched. "Let me get a girl for you, Jack. The right way. Your taste even. I have an idea my swami's—pretty dark."

Ventura's first name is Clark. Mulenberg has never called him by it.

"There she is," Mulenberg said. "Look at her. Sailing down the block."

"Down a *street*. But you win." Ventura tried to grin. "It's twelve, on the nose."

They both have stopwatches.

"Thirteen," Mulenberg lies. "I told you. By a hair."

"You're—" Ventura grasps for his hand. "A good guy."

"My lucky number."

Ventura gives a slight shiver, as if to say "Not mine." Eyes half shut, he watches the girl as if she were cargo. "That material she's wearing. We stocked it."

"I'll put the order through Monday morning. In your name. Quarter shares in a tankerful. Of the best Arabian light."

"Monday." Ventura rubbed his eyes, sighed. "And today's Saturday. All day. Well—so be it. I withdraw brunch."

The girl neared them. "The best Arabian—" Ventura whispered slyly. "That a brand-name?"

Mulenberg, nodding, signaling him to blow. This was often the way it happened. He *found*—as huntsmen said of a fox discovered. And Ventura left, for his appointment.

"Arabian *light?*" Ventura was laughing. "Ah, I don't blame you. But watch yourself." He left, going off toward Fifth.

And Mulenberg, stepping forward from under the marquee, drew breath for what he'd come here to find. The perfect synthetic experience.

The girl took his arm, riskily. Close up, she was absolute black, too much so for the West Indian mix he'd thought her. Black marble, and taking the evening afterglow on small mouth, nose and shining cheekbones, the eyes big under wingy brows. The mouth parted, on pearl. No, ivory. Her ears were crimped as tight to her head as he'd ever seen, as if a doting mother had nibbled off excess.

Only the hair was bronzed, straight hair, not fuzzed but braided into many small weavings curved from center skull and rounded on the nape, giving the effect of a madonna's coif.

A beauty, though not being the expert on blacks that Ventura supposed him, he had no idea of her nationality. But she must be an amateur. She was doing it all wrong. Coming right up to him. Standing there. Eye to six-foot-three eye. She was his height exactly. Or a quarter inch more.

"Slip me the telephone number," he said dead-mouthed. "And walk on. Smile how-d'ya-do and good-bye. And walk on. Police." There was a campaign on. They were picking up anybody and everybody this part of town. Said the Club.

Smiling, she slipped her arm further in the crook of his. Dangling from her wrist, a fluffy pouch brushed his hip. But to Mulenberg's credit, when the cop came up he stood where he was. At that point he caught sight of the television camera grooving up to the three of them.

So had the cop. Caught in the simper with which ordinary people faced the tube, the cop righted himself. "ABC Playhouse?" he barked. The camera crewman—there was only the one, a short young man, black too—nodded. *"That* program, huh," the policeman said as a second cop came up, the other half of his detail. "Now don't all crowd in," the first one said loftily to the two or three persons already gathering. "This lucky man's going to win something. Aren't you?"

Mulenberg nodded slowly. At the girl. "If I'm smart."

The second policeman dismissed the crowd with a circular spin of his hand, as if winding them up. The two officers then walked on.

The girl flattened herself protectively against Mulenberg's shoulder —she was too tall to cuddle, or too proud—and urged him toward the Seventh Avenue corner. It was easy to do as he was being bidden, or forced. Their steps matched.

The crewman, toddling his camera, followed them.

One block south they went, to Fifty-eighth, where they crossed the avenue and continued west on the south side, and now indeed they were in front of the Playhouse and its almost eternal line of freebie ticketholders waiting to be let in to clap for tonight. Gawking self-importantly, about to inhale the same high ozone as some Hollywood star only fifty feet from them, they took no notice of Mulenberg and his —escort. As he'd suspected, he and she weren't destined for the Playhouse itself. But as they swept or loped past it—for he'd caught her ball-foot, heel-foot stride—the crewman detached himself and his camera, disappearing with it behind an iron fence well beyond the main entrance, which Mulenberg, idly passing, had often noted. So this was what that so secret-looking television-palace door was merely for.

This whole operation, or abduction, if that was what was intended, was so amateur. Except for the girl herself. He now had hopes of her. He could feel her funny purse knock-knocking against his thigh. He was meant to, of course. He thought maybe she already knew he was enjoying it.

It was Mulenberg's by now self-acknowledged fate to have a body— and a soul also, he was convinced—which only a well-managed copulation brought to full integrity. At such a moment, not only the limbs, mouth and hands accessory to the act moved symphonic with his genitals. In his head, imagery moved musically, toward accomplishment. Ideas fruitioned and took root. All of him swam in a piety of the whole and the solvable. And though it might be fate's ultra-seminal joke on him, everything conceived, including his children, had at first worked out.

Until his wife's death he'd never even realized this. For so many years his sexual life had been at home exclusively. When this had had to change it seemed to him that he simply left his deeper needs—including a liking for his wife which was more than love and not far from holy —in home's hands. During the intervals of her illness when he did seek out other sex, it was always in a foreign country, a foreign language, allowing him a minimum of self-observation. At the same time his business was blossoming, so that he was really learning more about other cities than about other women. Meanwhile, each time that he could return to her, the drama of her diminishing body held him fast. All his spiritual remission—which was how he vaguely saw his own process—was surely there, had been kept for him. For the last year and a half of her life, staying at her side, he went without sex—and continued so for months after she was gone. Somehow he couldn't get back to it. At last a friendly pal in Oklahoma—a banker more worldly-wise than most of their neighbors, and with a property adjoining Mulenberg's—one night came to the homestead where Mulenberg was malingering while all business and family success slid from him, and brought with him a compliant and quite appetizing woman. "Had to be," the banker had said later, and sharply. The woman, a widow, had been his sister-in-law, and he'd hoped for marriage for her. "You didn't drink."

Within a meteoric week of that night and the next, Mulenberg's spirits and fortunes had risen again, in an almost palpably breeding way. Yet the woman herself, aside from her decent manners, in no way resembled his wife—nor those other women either. Perhaps it was her very median-ness which had convinced. On Mulenberg's newly embarked-upon travels, doubly extended because of the necessary business repairs, he'd begun to test carefully, finding that to a degree beyond any the banker would ever dream of, there did seem to be a most solemnly direct line between his copulations and his successes or failures.

Though he had no special perversions, he did prefer that his girls, those goddesses out of the machine who performed his fate for him, be sensational rather than cozy—and, wary of personal connection, he never repeated them. Both habits seemed to him deductively natural. His subconscious clearly was afraid it might find out that its "process" could happen with anybody. The conscious Mulenberg had proved it. He would never again, of course, leave that process in the hands of one woman. After the Oklahoma widow, none of the women he chose was his contemporary, or came from anywhere near his own lifestyle—nor did any of his night attendants ever look anything like Trixie Bjornson, later Tess Mulenberg.

The girl leading him stopped him short, in front of a narrow brown-stone wedged between two warehouses. They were now on a block between Seventh Avenue and Broadway, across from an all-night ga-rage in the open rear of a big apartment house, a 1940s affair of bow-knotted bay windows and freckle-colored stone. The house they faced had a ground-floor store to the right of the entry, a discount toiletries, shuttered now. Three steps led down to the outer door; probably a buzzer system released a locked inner one. Three stories rose above; the first one up had boarded windows, probably an extension of the store. Two upper floors of flats, that would be, either floor-throughs or divided front and back. After college he and his friends, making their maiden flight East, had lived by the dozens in such houses, then cheap. Brownstones, recessed yet street-wise, anonymous by the thousands, servicing the young of his day, the archaically old, a host of failed sexual partners not yet known as "singles" and all the human degrees between adventure and atrophy, were for no other reason always memorable.

They went down the steps and through the outer door. Yes, there were the letterboxes: three, a bell-press below each. Would she buzz now to some accomplice above?

She took out a key hung round that long neck. He noticed the skin texture, not oily brown, not powdery slate—a satiny opaque. Two of the letterboxes had names he couldn't distinguish; the third was the store's. Two floor-throughs then, no duplex. A fine indolence idled in all his limbs. Adventure always took him like this. But though he had luck, he never depended on it.

"Give me the gun."

Turning without the slightest wince—yes, her eyes leveled with his —she handed him the purse which had been bobbing against him. He slung it on his left wrist and followed her up the stairs. One flight. Two. Not a stickup then, or a kidnap; maybe she carried the gun the way some women now carried police whistles or spray cans of Mace. Or maybe the two floors did constitute a house. Where the women shang-haied the customers? If this turned out to be some sort of setup, would he leave? He wasn't sure.

The second floor had only one door, with the customary peephole. Nobody peered from it. She opened up. He followed her cautiously, into a lighted flat, and stood there blinking. He was no longer a man whom the sight of a home rug or a remembrance of candles made nostalgic. Rooms satisfied him, or were ignored. But here was the flat in which he and his kind, two years out of school and not yet going back home, had lived with their new wives or girls, or alone. There was that same fireplace—more depersonalized, no matter what the incumbent put on its mantel, than the young Mulenberg, brought up on a ranch, had thought a fireplace could be. He'd had just such a black iron grate. Along with the day bed, in his time covered in one of those monosyllabic all-wear fabrics: "Duck? Rep? Sail?" which the clerks had used to emit like hiccups. Her couch was puffed leather, old and good. There were the books, quite a lot of them, and the single desk, with just such a reading lamp as he would have coveted. To his right, the windows that would give on the street were heavily draped; he'd made do with the landlord's shades. Beneath the windows was a second and ampler sofa he could never have afforded. Opposite him, a fold-back door would open on the "efficiency" kitchenette, spick-and-span or roachy. Or with dime-store ruffles edging the shelves, if there had been a girl. To his left, back of sliding doors prized if remaining, or vanished as here, would be the windowless inside bedroom; he glimpsed a coverlet. Beyond, separated by a screen, probably a third small space, dressing room or studio, or for the too-soon child. In the bathroom at the very end, the door would be hung with a robe and a mildewed towel, or a robe and a nightgown, with the douche bag meekly below.

But this place, though it might look much the same, even to the trivia of color, pottery and picture flung overall like a light scum attesting to the owner's modernity, must cost a packet now.

Besides, just beyond the kitchen there was a bar. Even with only four bottles on it, it wasn't due the owners of his day for another ten years. He walked over to it, easily but slowly, in case there was a catch to this somewhere. There was of course—he could feel that. But not whether it would be dangerous. Or rather, how.

She let him examine the bottles. A Chivas, a Jack Daniel's, a Russian vodka. She must have a good clientele. And a Campari, a drink you came down to, rather than chose. Were her clients all old? Though he wasn't, chill struck him. There had to be a connection, spotted by her, in him.

She was holding out a glass to him, not dime-store. He poured himself a Daniel's, sniffed it for knockout drops, reached into the cabinet below —yes, an ice bucket there but empty, brought it out with an inquiring stare, nodded over his shoulder at the kitchenette, and was rewarded with a nod.

No roaches in the kitchenette, no ruffles either. Opening a small undercounter refrigerator exactly like the one in his private office, he gazed at two splits of champagne, a paté under a glass bell, four large mushrooms also under glass, some French mustard and a round of dark bread. No chic white wine. But the soda was where it should be, lined up on the door shelf. Sitting on his haunches, he brought out two bottles and held them poised. He felt his age, and yes, his inexperience. That was what she made him feel, already. Untutored, in he didn't yet know what. Was she never going to speak? He wouldn't until she did.

He came toward her, the bourbon in the left hand, which almost certainly had a gun inside the purse knocking at its wrist, the two sodas in his other. The two bottles clinked. Was she deaf? She'd served herself a Campari and was drinking it all the way down, watching him. Corny drama-school trick. Even so, he appreciated the line of her throat. Could she be stupid, lusciously thick with it, a pig of the sort some men were happiest with? Not with that arch to her nose, the thin ironic mouth. That figure of hers meant nothing; he'd seen the same glory on an institutionalized moron. The flush whetted her high cheekbones, as if the Campari were coming up in them. He marveled that he could see it; her skin in its own way was changeable. Under that silver nail lacquer the nails would be as ham-pink as any honest serving-girl's. She wasn't one of them.

She put her glass on the table between them with a straight-arm sweep, waited for her draperies to be quiet again and said, "You're smart."

A pulse jumped inside him. So was she. So was her voice. Let his subconscious tell him why he felt so relieved.

He opened a soda and drank from the bottle, setting down the bourbon, the full soda and the empty, to leave his hands free. If she thought he was, he had better be. Smart. Weighing why this should count, he faced her and opened her purse. Yes, there was a gun in there. He slid it out. Dainty as her refrigerator but a lot older, though it had been kept fireable. Carefully he flicked it, and once again. Loaded. Tiniest safety he'd ever seen. He wondered where she got the cartridges for such a toy. It lay in his palm, scrolled like a watch. On the barrel an ivory square about the size of a sugar lump was etched with a curly black O.

"Yours?"

"My stepbrother's." Her accent had a lilt. West Indian? Dominican?

"What's your name?"

"Veronica." Not much left of the accent, whatever it was. Been around New York.

"Veronica," he nodded. He always asked it. First part of this—incident, that was routine. "Nice name." He always said it.

She moved past him to the table where he'd set the bottles and the glass, shifting them all to a tray. Right; they'd make a ring on what seemed good wood. But unnerving. Usually, in these small matters the customer was always right. "Sorry."

She turned to face him. "Veronica—Oliphant."

He blinked. It was the photograph on the table she wanted him to see. And the name—to hear? He came closer. In the picture this girl, younger, was centered between an older woman, handsome but nothing like her, and a young man much like the woman. Light-colored, both of them. Mulatto, East Indian or West, Mexican or South American highland—the two of them could be anything, almost. Not the girl. An intensity at his elbow made him go slow on the man. "That lady your mother?"

"Stepmother." She gestured toward a gaunt old rocker in a corner. "Died year and a half ago. She had a weak heart." She tapped the picture, looking up at him. "So does—Ollie. That's his excuse."

For what? Was he supposed to know?

"Your brother." He made it a statement.

Her elegantly small nostrils clenched. "Step."

He blinked. What was safe? "You two look younger there." It stood to reason, if she did.

She shrugged. "My first year in high school. I knew from nothing. And he didn't wear those turbans yet."

"Turbans," Mulenberg said. Rapidly he went over all the turbaned locales in his triangle. "Make one look older, don't they. Make him." Wasn't she going to tell him her brother's full name? How could he get her to? Then it struck him that Ollie could be short for their last one. Meanwhile he'd have sworn he had never met that young man anywhere. "So. Oliphant."

"We'd just come down," she said, staring at the picture.

"Down?"

"From Montreal. He never tell you?"

Who did she think he was? Somebody else. But who.

Mulenberg looked down at the gun in his hand. Very slowly he said, "He never—tells me much."

Those wingy brows tautened. "Doesn't sound like Ollie."

He moved the gun in small arcs. "So you're—Ollie's sister."

"Step. There's no blood between us."

And she didn't want there to be. He twiddled the gun. "That camera-man—he Ollie's pal?"

She laughed. Alto, even beautiful. But he didn't like it. "Mine," she said lightly. "He does work for the network, but not as a cameraman. We borrowed it."

"You work for the network?"

"I—have."

"Were we on camera?"

"No. Or, I dunno. Why should we be?"

"You tell me. You did the corralling."

When she grinned he could see that early picture in her. Until she knit those brows. "Blackmail, you mean? Nuh. Even Ollie wouldn't."

Enough. "Who owns this place?" Mulenberg said, hard.

She heard. Straightening to it. "We both do. She left the house to us jointly. Vivie. His mother. To keep us together." Again that shrug. "He lives upstairs."

"He up there now?"

"Of course not." She cast him a sidelong glance. "Isn't he—waiting for you?"

So she'd taken her stepbrother's gun? But a man could have another one. Again he went over the countries, the cities: Teheran, Bahrein, Afghanistan. Nothing in Libya, Algiers. Africa wasn't his beat.

"Why'd you bring me here, Veronica?"

He saw he'd reached her. Their own names always did.

"So you—wouldn't keep too many more of—" She trailed it off softly. "Those dinner dates."

Dinner dates. With whom? She couldn't mean him. A faint something stirred at the back of his brain. He couldn't quite get to it. Plunge blind, then. "You've seen me before?"

She nodded, quizzical.

"Where?"

She tossed her head at it. "Where do you think? In front of those steps you and your sidekick are always standing. Same place I picked you up from. Nuh." She snorted, snapping her fingers.

He thought no white fingers could do it like that. Like castanets. "Other nights, you saw me?"

An underburnish warmed her again. "Four times." Was it a sigh? "And once—I followed you."

That would be four months. "Since February?"

She gave him a teachery look. "March, April, May, June." This was June. "In May I—even followed you. Getting up my nerve. But then you—"

"Last month?"

She nodded. "May."

Last month. "But then I—but then I picked up that girl," he said. A tall blonde in a bright green dress and though it was a cool, bright day, wielding a parasol from which several other men already hung by the eyes. Picked him up right outside that shop which sold sexpot underwear. Walked Mulenberg three blocks before she would speak to him. They had dropped the competition by then. When they connected, she closed the parasol. Explaining later, "It makes me more statuesque." A girl from Florida, with a greedy swamp smile. Not a great find. "At the corner of the Hilton—better than the Americana corner, anyway."

She wouldn't grin. A whore would have.

He went up close enough to her so that he could feel his breath rebound. "What do you know? About Ollie and me?"

"That you've borrowed too much money. From his friends."

"Bor—" He hadn't borrowed money for years except for tax-deduction purposes. Whereupon his accountant would advise, and it then was done for him. "Who are—?" An uneasy crawling tickled the back of his neck. "I mean—which friends?"

"Which do you think?" Bending forward to the table on those long swoops of arm, she shook her head slowly. "Couldn't figure you. You're not at all what I expected. Nuh—I suppose everybody's dumb somewhere." One long hand pinched her other upper arm with a tug, as if she was righting a sleeve. She expelled her breath. "Get out of it with Ollie, Mr. Ventura. He's bad news."

His mouth closed with a snap. Ollie. Ali. Ventura's swami. All in a second he saw the moneybags under Ventura's eyes, the trap he must be in, and he, Mulenberg, might be in. Saw his own too-late-stammered-out identity—and himself on the floor, a mistaken-for corpse.

On his right the one window facing north glowed with the last light; the other was fully draped. Though the bedroom was unlit, a light was on in the bathroom beyond. Striding through the bedroom, he flung open the bathroom door. Nobody there. But he didn't feel foolish. Eyeing a closet door opposite the bathroom, he tried the key, all the while keeping his back to the wall. The closet was shallow and full of clothes. He left it open. Fire escape. He'd forgotten that. It was off the bathroom, outside a padlocked window paned with metal-reinforced glass. Nothing but a fireman's ax would get through it. Or a machine gun. He came out, closing the door behind him, the toy gun trained. On the front door. But when they came in she had locked it, triply. She was standing in front of the kitchenette door, watching all this. He sat down in the cushioned rocker. He didn't have a weak heart. Its pounding beat slowed. He still didn't feel foolish. "How do I—" He choked on it.

"How do you know I'm not in with them? You don't." Her head

arched, smacking the doorframe. She rubbed it angrily. So full of nature he had to believe her. And she'd let him have the gun.

He lowered it. "How did you know I was—who you said?" He didn't want to say Ventura's name.

"I didn't." She was still angry. "All along, I figured it was the other one. He looked the part. In every way." She made a sullen mouth at him. "Until that last time when I followed you. Ollie caught me at it. Thought I was following *him*. The way Ma used to."

"Following him? Where?"

"On his route, where else? From the A.C. block to the Plaza's front steps, and all the way around again. Ma found out long ago it was Ollie's drop. For anything. He won't use limos." She slapped the table. "Those Plaza steps, he never even goes up them. Just a gander at who ever's waiting, then pass on. To maybe a park bench. Same thing going past the A.C. Where he caught me. 'You should've worn a turban, sis,' he told me. 'Nobody ever catches on to me. What's one more turban?' And he's right. In that crowd to be really noticed, you'd have to be a—a two-headed—" she flung up her hands. "Pterodactyl."

He stared. "A what?"

Her lips twitched. They were fuller than he'd thought. "What I said." She pressed those long hands together. "First time I saw the two of you standing out front there, I was just passing. After all, I live here too." She came closer to Mulenberg. There was no scent to her. "Once Ollie found me out, you bet he liked it. Thinking maybe I'd join up with him after all." Her mouth tightened again; the voice had softened. A shoulder came forward, her eyes brooded. Coaxing something out of herself; what did she remind him of? Nothing. Or all women. "But then, all of a sudden he let me know he knew. Warned me off. Trouble, he said; didn't say for who. But I could tell; he'd mentioned you and them once. Ollie talks."

"Ollie's drop," he said. For girls? For anything, she'd said. He thought of Ventura's pasty cigars.

He got up out of the rocker. "How'd you find out for sure? Which of us was—which."

Wasn't she going to answer? Maybe, but in her own time. Outside, the dusk was turning on, in city glitter. She went to a lamp shaped like a stocky two-foot glass mushroom. At her touch it glowed orange, stem and all. For a minute her hands, laced on the glass, were charcoal with a penumbra of pink. Living with a woman like this you would have to get used to another style of fleshly being. "Ollie fingered you. I asked."

To put her off the track? But had she believed him?

"And you were—disappointed. In me."

She wasn't going to say. " 'That's him,' Ollie said. 'The one with the beard.' "

"You could have checked the Oyster Bar. One of those dinner dates." But she hadn't. Not if she still thought he was Ventura.

"Uh-*uh*. Ollie's not alone there. He's watched." She was toying now with a little pierced-brass pot, lifting the lid, replacing it. "And I would have been, later. I won't have that. I won't have any truck with that. Not in this house." She arched her neck in a way he was getting to know. "And I couldn't have brought you here."

They examined each other.

"And I'm not what you expected?" She'd watched him the way adolescents in his home town used to obsessionalize from afar some candidate whose orbit they never had enough nerve to break in on. The summer he'd worked in the depot, the stationmaster's young niece had brought the man lunch every day. Mulenberg could hear the slight creak of the basket now if he wanted to, smell the chicken salad, see his sneakers scuffing the cinder dust, feel his chest swell valentine-warm, and watch the girl float in from her galaxy, her eyelashes permanently lowered, as they had been for thirty years. He could stand here in his own star drift for another thirty; she would never raise her head.

But this girl had broken into the orbit, and decoyed.

"Or am I?" The one expected, all this time? She'd created him by watching, then drawn him into the actual. Whatever her reasons at first, he could feel their velvet now. There was no death in her.

He moved in close enough to see into the brass pot, which held a small green cone of the kind his mother and her friends, ladies of the western provinces, used to burn before dinner parties to keep down the cabbage smells. The way this girl's hands hoarded the pot—different, the way the one hand scooped a matchfolder into its palm, cat's-paw. The way she looked at him, from snub eyes. He felt that slow, cellular bloom of success start up all along his body hairs. His eyes unfocused, on the cone. She struck a match to it. Spiraling up into his arms with the smoke.

He tasted her with it. She tasted him. The stuff of her dress felt like coarse sugar. All their body planes fitted, except for her breasts—cones too, not sloped. Together they dawdled across the floor, a double snake, vertical. At the kitchenette she stopped them, bending to the ice door. Two champagne glasses were on the drainboard already; he'd missed those. The two splits opened between her knees with an inching caress; her eyes were uplifted to him, but inward. The refrigerator hung half open. And her mouth. "Sexy icebox," he said. He could scarcely speak.

The frail glasses seemed to fill themselves; the two bottles disappeared with a clink. She stood tall, one shoulder bare where he'd dragged at the dress. She's had a blueprint of how this is to go, he thought; she's had it right from the start.

He slipped the dress from her other shoulder. Now both were bare, symmetrical. He had his own blueprints. He touched the neck hollow, that U-shaped pulse center-collarbone, which sometimes winked like an infant's fontanelle. Certain places in a woman's body were more vulnerable than sexual. A Montparnasse street girl had once angrily clawed his mouth away from her nape. Saying, "I am whore. It is owed to respect that," in argot he'd later got the barman to translate. "What the hell did you do?" the barman said. He'd brought in emotion—or whatever that had been to her. Somewhere he'd slipped the traces of what was decently, routinely lecherous. Maybe this came from his long troth to one body. Toward any female body he had no class-consciousness.

This could get him into scrapes. As Ventura had warned.

The girl was waiting for him, ruefully. They never liked to have a man's meditation slip from them. But this girl was far more impenetrable than her skin; he had no clue to her.

"Pterodactyl—" he said slowly. "Are you a college girl?"

For a second, his mock horror fooled her. Then the two of them rocked with laughter.

They idled into the bedroom, hands joined. The bed was brass, its coverlet of some harmless, babyish cotton such as his daughters had had. He tossed the gun on it.

Her body was willowy and shaded, like the ink strokes made by an old-fashioned nib pen. In the end he put his mouth into her bush, then his hardening self, and almost his heart. Almost all the way, he felt her follow him. They dozed then, the semen stealing down their legs.

He woke guardedly, afraid she wasn't a whore. She was already awake. "How old are you, Veronica?"

"Twenty-seven." She grinned. "Going on thirty."

She didn't look it. But from the texture of her sexual responses he'd thought she might be somewhere along in there. "And what's your nationality?"

The chain of a locket she w   e lay tangled in his beard. The locket slipped to his chest. Above him, her eyes veiled. "Next question: And how did I get into this? Right?"

Under the beard, his face fell. If she wasn't a whore, how did she know?

"My own mother was from Senegal, emigrated to French Canada. My father was Jamaican, brought up in Barbados. He met her when he was on a mission to Montreal. He settled there. She died when I was four. That answer you?"

"Some." The accents. But what kind of mission?

"Ollie's mother, Vivie, was Bajan. His father was English. She never said who." Whenever she mentioned the woman she gestured to the room, the chair, as to a presence. "Daddy brought them up from there. Barbados. To Canada. She was our cook. I was fond of her. Later on, he married her. Then he died, too. While I was still in grammar school." She raised up on elbow. "There. That what you want to know?"

She knew it wasn't. And, like him, that there wouldn't be time for it. He touched the snailed hair. "Who does that for you, your—?" He'd almost said "mother," not thinking of the woman over there, the step-mother, but of the household women of his hometown boyhood, at their windows leaning over the Sunday school child. Probably his ideas on black life were as virtuously out-of-date.

"A salon. Called—Le Zebre."

Took him a minute. Le Zebre. A second-floor sign on Fifty-seventh. Catered to black women. Le Zeeber it was called, hereabouts. "Like a map," he said, touching her head. "Of waterways." Or jungle trails seen from a small plane.

"Takes half my take," she murmured, stretching. Even on elbow, they were the same height.

He kept his voice down, also. "How much is it? Your take."

"Six-seventy."

He wasn't staggered—quite. For her class of girl, then. And pimp. And gun. Which was now on the night table, her side. He'd put it there. If she was a pross, everything in the last couple of hours was out of line.

"An odd sum. Veronica."

Those eyes showed nothing. The mouth did. "After *taxes*. Per *week*."

In the middle of their scuffle he saw his watch. More than two hours. "Will Ollie come here?"

"Never. Not since—Vivie." She punched a pillow. "Oh, he lives up there. When he's home. Has his girls go there. Not for tricks. Vivie wouldn't have it. Just to hang around, powder their noses." The bed-sheets were pulled every which way; she straightened them. "Or you know. When it's for him." She raised her head, flushing. He was beginning to know the ways of that skin.

But—how much she knew of that life. When it was for *him*, she'd said. Even if she'd turned red for it.

"Bet no one ever called you Ronnie."

She sucked in her lips. "Not quite."

"What, then?"

No answer. Eye to eye.

"What *is* your job?"

"I'm—on a magazine."

"Oh? What kind?"

She hesitated.

"Fashion?"

"You could say that."

His daughters had taken such magazines. Some subscriptions had continued long after the two were out of the house.

"*Vogue? Harper's Bazaar?*"

"You're—very in the know."

She wasn't going to say. A model, then?—how many ways had Ventura been right? He'd have to breakfast with him after all. And talk turkey to him. Doubling his own promises to the man if necessary. To keep him away from his friends. In thanks. "I must have seen you in one of them," he said. "I think I did."

"They always think they did," she said.

When they were twined together again, he said, "Four times, you passed those steps on my account," and kissed a breast. "Once a month. For four months." She didn't answer. But when they were apart again, except for the long fingers plunging his hair, stroking him nose to beard and finally patting his crotch, she said, "You're safe here. Problem might be—to get you out."

He roused himself. "I'll take care of that." Again he touched the scalp between the minute braids, captured the long fingers—knobbled like a newborn calf's leg, he told himself, double-jointed the wrong way.

He knew very well what he was doing. Separating her into parts, so that she would have less personality for him.

"I thought you would," she said.

They regarded each other, stony-faced.

"Got a cigarillo?" he said. "One of—Ollie's?"

It was a cheap thing to do. He didn't smoke. She took so long to answer, serve him right if he'd axed things by it.

"I don't keep that stuff in the house. Any of it."

Both were breathing competitively fast; the second time around had exhausted them. Less mystery to it already, he told himself, and there'd be less and less, yet he was wrenched. He allowed himself to touch the old locket she wore, too battered for her, rumpled gold, with a pearl

washed to a bead. His hand was slapped back. Well, they all had their
—nape.

He left the bed, not looking back.

When he stood at her window again, showered and dressed because
she'd made him go first, he craned to see whether she could see the Gulf
& Western from here. Though at night its huge lighted shaft dominated
Columbus Circle, where Columbus himself seemed turned to stone on
his pedestal by the sight of his new world, here, only a quarter mile
away, it was blocked by the hodgepodge side streets in which the real
city hunched. During his first years as a "worldwide industrialist," when
mountains first shrank at his bidding and his handshake could lift important citizens toward him as if by their lapels, only his ceaseless circling
of the world had kept him democratically sane. All the while his money
power seemed to be educating his eye to be an emperor's, the airports,
revolving before him like one-and-the-same lecture hall, reminded him
that anybody with a flight bag was now equally an imperialist of space.
In the struggle between money and people, he could even see that the
side streets were always slowly winning, although the actual people
struggling in them might never for long be the same ones. Maybe this
was why these little city apartments still got to him, sunless little caves
of self-important shadow, shunted to violet, hoarding their contents
against the running footsteps of outer life. He'd better leave, for the
sultans and their sticky palaces. His next stop was Bahrein.

"What you looking at?" She was behind him.

"For my office building." He didn't turn. "Think I'll sleep there tonight."

"Which one?"

"The G & W."

"The—? Oh." Her nostrils indented. Small, well cut, they moved with
each of her expressions. Not all of which he had learned yet. "Can't see
that one from here."

He saw that she'd changed to a housecoat; this too was often routine.
Hers was neatly tailored and initialed. Her legs were too long for it.
"But it's there."

She shrugged. "Heard it for sure, the other night."

"When they bombed it? Cuban nationalists. They only got some windows. Pieces of the steps."

"Cool."

"Who? Them?" He wouldn't put it past her.

"You," she said. "But they weren't Cubans. They don't spread the red
that style."

"How would you know?"

She turned aside her head.

Against his will he came closer. "Do Ollie and his friends? Spread the red?"

"Them? Nuh. They'd sell nitro to a nipple-baby. But not for love."

"Love? You call that—that mass mayhem—love? What they do anywhere? Terrorists?"

"Know any?" She had a scent now, sharp as her voice.

In Venezuela, his first job. Maybe. In Iran once, never turning his head. "I'm not sure. I—prefer not to."

Her nostrils dilated again. "Practical man."

"Have you? Ever known any? Or maybe . . . victims?"

This was a new face on her. She knew that, quickly receding backward with it, skimming quick as an animal into the brown alcoves that a floor-through handily provided. That was why certain people lived in such warrens, often without knowing so. And often at great price. He heard the bathroom door go *plock*.

Know any now?—he should have asked. Would ᵗʰᵃt explain everything? Her brains and her looks, for instance—the way those people now did things. And why she hung on here would be understandable too, in a house that would have so many—outlets. Also her collection of near-nationalities; weren't nihilists, anarchists, terrorists, as often trying to get into the world of nations as not?

Above all it would explain what infused this room, a sense of some passion hoarded, which he'd first taken to be wholly sexual but was extra to it, free-floating in the room and around her person almost palpably, like the sense of purpose that clung to a lab technician's shoulder blades. Work—the way it molded, anywhere. Work was what he himself went around the world on, seeing the fanatic patterns it made in other people, as clear in the Ottoman Bow Grindlays Bank in Muscat, as it had been in the shack on the North Concho where his father had taken him, aged eighteen, for his first pair of handmade boots. Such work as he was imagining for her would explain the money and her easy way with it. The magazine would explain nearly everything—except him.

Unless, lured here because of what he was, he was the explanation. He'd long since stopped worrying how his life looked to other people. Bad enough to know so many of the secrets behind the headlines that the most honest of newspapers went limp in your hand. Or to be able to recognize, in the chilly intimacy of those haunts where the future was architected, people who knew much more. He hadn't been born poor enough to crave being as rich as he had turned out. He *had* been born free enough to see that power, once it continued past the possession of the mere decencies of life, always became incidental to something else its possessor's temperament wanted—in his case, to see the Earth exhaustively, below its crust and above. Wittingly, his life had become a construction toward that end.

"Your husband keeps forgetting who he *is*," a vice-president, flown out to the ranch to persuade Mulenberg to attend a promotionally useful royal wedding, had exploded to Mulenberg's wife. Often true, but not that once. The royal highness in question wasn't his friend; to have the power not to go was a luxury he did like. He'd just returned from a site, not Oak Ridge but related to it, where he'd seen projections, still controversial, which might change man's relationship to Earth entirely—and had been standing outside the bedroom door, his arms full of impatiens plants for his wife's window box, wondering how that humble, tough plant would take to non-gravity (the decencies of life were becoming so curiously mutant). He heard the visitor repeat himself, a characteristic of vice-presidents which came from there being so many of them. "Who he is, Tess. Why won't he remember it?"

From her bed, his wife said—bless her—"Because he never intended it."

Outside, the street was quieter now. This was the lull while people were at the movies, gone from the restaurants, not yet into the night clubs. He could go.

She came out of the bathroom turning on lights, turning off shadows, confident. Who was she?

"You okay?" he said.

"Cramps."

"Mental or physical?"

"Works both ways." She reached to pull the window drape across, then thought better of it, staring out. The initials on her housecoat were the right ones. "I was in Cuba once. Ten years ago."

"At seventeen? Doing what?"

"Cutting cane."

"Cutting—what the hell were you doing that for?"

"A girl like me?"

Nobody laughing, this time.

"Oh, not for Castro," she said. "Didn't know I liked beards yet. . . . And sure 'nough not for the hammer and sickle—never heard of them till we got there. Then they gave us each a cane knife, shorter but just as sharp, and explained the connection."

For a minute he had an extreme sense of what she was. Versatile. "What'd you go for then?"

She hadn't touched him since he'd left the bed; now she seemed about to. His flesh tensed, not knowing what it would do.

"For love."

He was silent.

"To get out of it." She was watching him almost tenderly, not like a colleague of the night. More like one of the club's exercise pros, monitoring his charges, whose history he knew without having to be told, from the rich fat on them. Watching them jog off the pounds of the night before.

"Hungry?" she said. Like them, without moving an inch.

He was starving. Girls sometimes offered. If the place was theirs. "No thanks. I couldn't eat a thing."

"I bet." She folded her arms. "Well then—I'm waiting."

So was he. For a sign of how he was to do this. "For what, Veronica?"

"To see how you make it. Out."

He picked up his jacket then, feeling for the wallet from which he'd removed credit cards, leaving only his Blue Cross card and the couple of hundreds, in tens and twenties, from which he would have settled beforehand, normally. There were girls who flapped a bold palm sideways for it, elbow on hip; there were a few who took it with a tea drinker's pinkie; most took the money matter-of-factly, slipping it quicker than the eye into some marsupial pouch. Then there were those who looked him over and upped the price; others took something off first, maybe a bra. He didn't choose all variants, but he knew them. His coat had an extra silk slot, pointed out to him by an unamused Edinburgh tailor, to keep extra bills in, in case he was rolled; he'd never been. The identification card said John Mulenberg, One Gulf & Western Plaza; if he were blown up or otherwise illegally damaged, would Blue Cross pay?

Hustling into the jacket, he side-glanced her bookshelves, tabbed in sections extending to the ceiling: Literature, Philosophy, Physics, no other science, nothing on his own long-gone subject, geology. A lot of poetry. No fashion magazines that he could see, a lot of small ones, mostly pamphlet size. No Marx. "You still go to school?"

"Uh-uh. Just leftovers." She was amused.

A few shelves down, he saw why. Way up high, two diplomas, hers, high school and college.

"Any books in that office of yours?" she said. "Or only ledgers?"

"A few of each." He was prowling now for the focus to all this.

Sometimes you found such a thing right on the person's own body, openly displayed in reactions they thought hidden. Or you had to dig for it, the way a man from the De Beers diamond trust had told him their miners were probed from anus to crown. You would get nothing as easily as that from this girl.

Sexually, he now felt happy and lumbering. The girl standing at the window, her housecoat fallen back to show lacy bra and pants of a tan that made her skin slate-blue, lounged there with a slackness she couldn't conceal. As his father used to say, working beside him in the family greenhouse, he had brought her off. Have to bring a woman off, Johnny; they feel things, too. By rights, all animals. Shouldn't wonder if the plants.

But this woman wasn't putting her history on the sexual line exclusively. Or not anymore. Must he give her money now—or not? Under those eyes roving after him he had an idea he'd be clouted for it either way. Depending on why he was here. Or as who.

Ventura. He'd altogether forgotten him. To be taken for that over-sueded man who nervously mowed his lawn by Garden City protocol and at poolside proudly slapped his hairy, veinous self—that was to laugh. Yet Ventura ought to be thanked. In the morning Mulenberg would advance the tanker money and up it a trifle, saying "For the boy," or some other sentiment. Ventura, by now inured to owing, would put up no argument. What a weakness, though—not to know when other people had payed out enough rope.

This girl would always know. Meeting her glance, he got that. Within the hull of whatever her obligations, mental or real—people always had both—she would manage herself. Somewhere beyond, though, she had her own romance she was keeping up.

A shiver went over him, but he kept on pacing, around the books again, past the old woman's chair. He could still feel his luck, luxuriant even, as always just afterward. But like any physically based confidence, always on the borderline of change. Sometimes he felt the one overbalance the other; he knew damn well which he felt now. There were places one had to leave with more style than one had entered with; she'd as much as said. Not much admiring him for being practical. He set hands on Vivie's rocker. Funny how he could see the stepmother, the son, clear as clear. "Can't decide about you, Veronica. For an amateur, you're pretty professional. For a professional, you'd be pretty ama—*Hey!* Watch it."

But she'd only flung out her chest, flung up her hands.

The rocker between them rocked.

She brought her hands down, long and two-colored. Maybe the only consensus to be made on her was that she was beautiful—and that there was no knife in them.

"You'll have such a very nice long couch over there to sleep on, nuh? And a cozy little office fridge, like ours here; Ollie copied one of those." The accent came out hard for what it had been all along—British West Indian. "In your little office suite. Maybe large enough for a party of ten studs and their girls—but they always like to call it the *little* one. It occupies that part of their lives." She squeezed her shoulders forward in that hoarding way she had. "Maybe this is my little apartment, huh? Maybe I play that game with myself." She shrugged. She tossed her head. " 'Come right to the office marked President,' *they* say. 'Forty-fifth floor. *I* am not the President, of course. But I have a key.' "

"I have a key," he said.

"But you don't aim to take women there," she said low. "You aim to go with them. I saw." Suddenly she pursed her double-curved figure into a simper, tiny-footed it up to him in exact imitation of a pross making like a chorine, tickled his lapel—and before he could move slid his wallet out and handed it to him, straight-arm.

Sick—a little—he opened it.

"Professional, nuh?"

"Yes."

"Put it away."

Waiting, she clasped her hands behind her neck. He saw how the waterways on her skull ran toward it. "When I was a kid, Ollie used to take me along with him, evenings. To deliver the goods. While Vivie was at work. She didn't know." Her speech was suddenly straight New York. "All they did when he and I got up there was sometimes to give me a Coke—just a black kid tagging along. Ollie only books white. But when I got home, I used to mime in the mirror everything I'd seen— like coming out of a movie. Vivie caught me at it, slapped me to the floor. So after that she took me with her."

"What'd she work at?"

"Cashier, in night clubs."

He stole a look at the diplomas.

She laughed. "Vivie framed those. I must be the only girl went through Hunter High doing her homework in a ladies' lounge."

"But you went back. To the Islands?" University of the West Indies, the college diploma said. A.B. English Literature.

"I got too—" Looking down at herself, she closed the housecoat. "Tall."

He reached over and pushed the coat open again, exposing a nipple, stroking it until it swelled forward through the silk like a muzzle. "So they sent you back. To be safe. But you still got to—Cuba."

She pushed down his hand. "Ollie's not mean. Not really mean. But he's foolish."

"He doesn't come in here, you said."

"No. But his friends come to this house."

"Puerto Rican, some of them?"

"You crazy? Bad boys from Brooklyn, they are. Warehouse Brooklyn." Her lashes were short but thick; they could veil. "Or don't you know."

"No Cubans?"

"You mean political? Ollie? When Vivie used to talk about when Stokely was in the islands, Ollie could never keep in mind who he was."

"Stokely?"

"Carmichael."

"Who was he?"

"You never heard of him?"

"I only have a B.S."

She laughed. He still didn't like the sound of it.

"He was a black radical. Of the sixties. Married to Miriam Makeba, once." She saw he didn't know who that was either. "A singer."

"Oh?"

She stared down at his hand, hers, interlocked at her waist. Only his hair made him the taller one. He felt her breath flow on his cheek. "You're so white."

Nobody move, he thought; this is where nobody moves. Not even the belly, retracting in. He had only to nuzzle in, in order to kiss her. Not appropriate. Simply stand here. Hold.

Under his glance, below the two of them, the desk. On it a couple of books—a thin clothbound one and what looked to be a dictionary, and the typewriter, in it a page inkily typed single-space, much crossed out. He was farsighted. Jaggedly irregular lines, with ink interpolations. Stanzas. He craned to read:

Miss Lacey's nightspot is gone from Carnegie Hall.
The *Times* printed her soul food on the women's page.
Come dinner-sinner time
The pimps brought her black girls at a crawl,
Revving up around the corner, turning on a dime.

The last word was blurred. *Turning on a—* Of course. *Dime.*

"Miss Lacey's!" he said.

She broke from him, backing up, grasping the corners of the desk behind her. "You knew it?"

"Never was inside." He put his hands in his pockets. "Were you?"

"Me? Did all my homework there."

"That some of it?"

"Some old stuff." She edged in front of it.

He was quicker. Holding her down, off, with his left arm, he grabbed up the sheet of paper with the other hand and held it at arm's length, reading out:

> "Half-ass time—" the tires whisper "—Oh, Miss Lacey,
> Gas cost something awful, girls blow your—"

He bent. "*You* have an awful habit. Of blotting the last word. *Mind* —that's it. 'Girls blow your *mind.*' " He angled his head down at her, squirming hard and slow there under his arm, not kicking. Slowly turning his torso, he dropped the paper, to secure her with both arms. "Yours are longer; mine are stronger." He held her off, opposite him. " 'Half-ass time'—I like that." He shook her gently toward him, toward his kiss—and let go like lightning. She'd bitten him.

On all fours, she smoothed the paper as if it were silk, got up jointedly, cradling it, and flashed it into the desk drawer, the thin book after it. Would she force in the dictionary, too? No.

"Good thing you didn't have the gun." There were tooth marks on his thumb. "So that's what you do, eh?"

She didn't raise her head.

"Didn't mean to be nosy. But I sing a little."

She stole a look at him. As if he were nuts. He supposed he didn't look like a singer.

"Tenor, in the college choir. Baritone now." A good voice, *a cappella* trained, but not above soft jazz. He thought of singing a phrase or two of the oratorio he still sang in the shower. *Fac mē-*ay, *cruc-é* ay, *cus-to-di-*eri . . . and then, high: *Mortē—*ay *Christi-*i, *prae-mu-ni-*iree. No, he couldn't make the *Morte* anymore. Maybe "Mountain Greenery?" *In* uh, *a* uh, *moun-*tain greenery, *where* uh, *God* uh, *paints* the— No, not her style—or his either; it was this room had reminded him. "So is that it?" he said. "In the little midtown hideaway? Your job?"

There was no piano, but probably they didn't do that anymore. Used a Moog synthesizer, for all he knew; no more thumping it out one finger, chopstick style. Maybe she simply sent in so many words per weekly retainer. Sweeping out to have her picture taken for an airlines magazine afterward?

Or—she was looking at him so blankly—was a job altogether too old-fashioned an idea? These days the young ate air and farted music, living meanwhile on borrowed mare's milk, quite successfully. Or only taking on a job to support a supremer habit. For this room didn't lie. He whistled under his breath. In his travels, whose evenings could sometimes veer remarkably from industry, though money made the connections, he'd recently bought one daughter a requested present in a painter's studio in the Marais in Paris, had dined with a playwright in Ireland who'd had cattle to sell, had had a concert on the viola da gamba tendered him and his "party" (a pliant girl brought along by his host) in the rooms of the celebrated Swiss player, and only last week had had a predinner drink in the Via Margutta flat of a plane mate who dubbed for the movies—and he knew that there was always something scrappy yet indivisible about the rooms of those who were in the business of art. "So that's what you're so—terrorist about," he said. "You write songs."

Was she going to drop on all fours again? "I what? What did you say?"

What had he? If a pair like them were to spend a year together, there might be whole lists of things that were inappropriate, except for bed. Maybe even in bed.

She had a good, slow smile, pulled from each side, like when a bow of ribbon was being made. He'd done that, for daughters. Her eyes went wet. "Guess that's what I do, yes, I write songs. Always the same one." She put her bare foot on a stool, leaning an elbow on the bent knee and chin on elbow, the robe's hemline stretched taut as a toga, her scrolled head forward like a fish with one ravishingly neat gill. In bed, too, any attitude she fell into had seemed new to his eye. He watched that ear of licked bronze. Suddenly she crossed her lips with a finger. "Shhh." Was she going to sing?

Then he heard a familiar mechanical sigh.

"Didn't know you had an elevator." An old one, rumbling in its cage.

"In the back. I don't use it."

"Who does?"

"Ollie. His girls."

They heard the elevator door slam closed. Uncertain steps came nearer, a woman's. Or a small man, he thought, one of those jockey types in narrow, high-heeled boots?

"One of Ollie's," she said.

The steps teetered off. A woman's, yes. "Drunk?"

"Not Ollie's. He caters well."

"Like what?"

"Young widows. Who want a guru. Housewives who want to swing. Staten Island. Queens."

"Nice girls." He made it sound as if he knew them. "Normal ones."

"Some of them don't know they're whores, if that's what you mean. Or not yet."

"No—barbarics," he said. To those long, votive feet, the eyes which when startled sprocketed in circles of white.

She still leaned on the stool, chin cupped in her hand. Light struck her eyeball from the side. Where his eyeball sank shrewdly under its ridge of bone, hers jutted. Into another world. But they could meet.

"He tells them I'm his tenant. So they won't have to know it's no Indian who's shoving them."

She was saying it crudely on purpose. To get his eyes off her. To get hers off him. Like new glue bonding.

"Sing something, why don't you?" she said. "Before you go."

"For my supper?"

"For the one you didn't have."

"Why not? What's in a song?"

Hard to start cold, but he did it. He made the *Morte* without cracking. "*Con-fo-ve-ri—*" he finished. "*Con-fo-ve-ri-ee—gra-a-tia.*" He'd never much known what the words meant. Perhaps she does, he thought, from her face. What kind of a song had she thought he'd sing her?

Outside in the hall, running footsteps. The door was beat upon. A woman's voice, yelling or sobbing incoherently.

He turned up his palms in excuse.

She got up and walked to the door, not tiptoeing. Peered through its peephole. Looking back at him over her shoulder.

"Who is it?" he mouthed.

"Never saw her before," she said aloud.

Again that hoarse babble.

"All right—" she called through the peephole. "Wait till I unlock the door." She motioned to him. "Go in the back room."

"Not my style," he said.

"When I tell you. In my house."

He stood fast. "I don't do well in them."

"You did well enough."

He went. Vanishing just as a woman, sobbing again as if on signal, fell through the door.

In the bathroom, the door ajar, at first he heard nothing.

"Yeh look at me," the woman then said. "Oh, God. Lookit. All down me. I run the whole three blocks from the Plaza like this, what is this town, nobody even stops me. . . . Upstairs, nobody's there. I figured I could change—there's always clothes there." She broke into tears again. "I din know where else."

"Here. Sit."

"God, look at it. A bran new outfit."

"Sit." There was a sound of water from the kitchenette, a clink of glass. A gulped thanks from the woman. He peered out. A screen jutted between here and the bedroom; he could see nothing. He drew back.

"I'm—a lady who visits Ollie," the woman said when quiet. "The landlord. I guess you know."

"How do you do," the girl said.

"He ain't come here, huh? Tonight?"

"He doesn't come in here."

"Yeh," the woman said. "This is a neat place. I was going wear a stole from home, last minute I dint, not with this outfit. A designer suit, this is. Ollie said." The sobs began again, a little forced.

"I understand he gets them wholesale," the girl said.

A pause.

"Maybe it'll clean," the girl said. "What is that stuff on it?"

Silence.

"The gutter," the woman said then. "They trun me out of the cab."

"Ollie?" Mulenberg could hear the note in the girl's voice. "A—cab?"

"Listen," the woman said. "You got to fix me up. If this dress was clean like an angel is between the legs, I couldn't go out in it now. Not this color. Listen to me."

"I'm listening," the girl said. "Tell me how Ollie came to be using a cab."

"He wasn't. Not him."

Silence.

"We was in the Erster Bar," the woman said then. "Him and me. You ever seen it? Hah. I work my sister's bar, Rego Park. Ollie did business my brother-in-law. Till I go out with him. I live with them. 'Go out with him, Concetta,' they say, 'you don't need to come back.' " She stopped short. "So now. I need to." Not crying now. Making that bad, gone sound, muscled from the gut, of the self gagging on itself. "So we was there. Us and a third party. This third party likes to eat after—understand what I mean?"

"A—third party?" the girl said.

"I never done that before, I swear. But Ollie says I don't do his friend that favor—next time, I pay *him*." She hissed that, Mulenberg thought. Or spat.

"And what do I know, the guy turns out such a nice guy. More better for me than Ollie. 'You believe in sympathy on sight?' he asks me. 'Not love,' he says. 'But sympathy. My wife's an invalid,' he says. 'And you're a war widow.' 'I'm not,' I said, 'he's doing time.' Ollie give me such a look. 'I wasn't supposed to say,' I said. And the john said, 'You won't lose by it.' Carlo, he said I should call him. He had another name now, but he was christened it."

Her chair creaked; she must be plump. From twenty-five to forty-odd, she could be. Young for any stage of it. Mulenberg's head ached and he felt the palpitation that overbreathing brought on him. In small rooms. Claustrophobic tachycardia, his doctor called it. "Other name for it's ambition, Mulenberg." But this time, heart pounding, he was breathing for somebody else. As he listened, the rosary of Ventura's very life was slipping through his own fingers, payed out in jerky film shots he could do nothing to stop.

They'd been eating peach Melba, the woman said, with a caress for it—"You know, raspberry sauce, with a real peach"—when two men walked in and sat down with them. Only the younger, blond one spoke. "Canary-yellow his hair was. Dyed. I never seen nobody so immaculate. Nails like pearls." Then this man had reached out and overturned the guy Carlo's cup. To Ollie he'd said, "Swami has to go to the gents', don't you, Swami?" And Ollie went. Then—"Mr. Ventura's cab is waiting." To the john.

"I said, 'Ventura—what a lovely—' " the woman said. And a knife had shown, between those nails. "A shiv. He had it under his cuff." So she and Carlo were led out at knifepoint—" 'Put the bill on my charge,' that blond kid says to the maiter-dee"—and into a cab. A big Checker. "There wasn't nobody in it." The blond and Carlo got in the back.

She'd been put in front with the other man, and cuffed to keep her eyes closed. "We drove like crazy then, round and round." But once she heard Carlo cry out. He was making a big killing on Monday, he said. " 'A money killing, I mean. I swear it on my boy.' " The blond one didn't answer; then she heard a—sound. The cab went on driving until at last they stopped. Then she was thrown out, on her hands and knees. Heard the cab pull off, and opened her eyes. They'd dumped her off half a block below where she and Ollie had entered the restaurant. "That alley the Plaza service trucks must deliver." Between two of the trucks.

He saw his one hand clutched tight around a towel rack, and beyond it the woman who must be standing up now—he'd heard the chair creak —in the muddied dress. Pink dress.

"Turn around," Veronica was saying. His own thought.

"I'm—scared to."

Silence. Veronica padding around her.

"Between my shoulder blades," the woman whispered. "Not wet anymore. Is it there? . . . It's there, isn't it."

He could see the dark red spot himself—not Peche Melba.

"No wonder you felt it," the girl said.

A scream from the woman, as if she herself had been knifed. "He fell against me. Oh, Jesus, Holy Mother—I'm going puke."

He had to pry his fingers from the towel rack.

In the kitchenette the woman vomited, the water ran.

When he blundered into the room she raised up, covering. In black bra and pants, and gartered stockings, her heavy rear stuck out ostrich-style over thin legs; she was about as he had thought she'd be—above it all a squeezed, once-madonna face. Fortyish. Her mouth gobbled at him, speechless. From now on—the mouth was convincing her—the sight of any man would terrify her.

He wasn't too sure of that, but he had to look away, and speak with his eyes, if he could, to Veronica. How else could it be said? Explain me.

The woman did it for him, croaking: "Who's he?"

"A singer," Veronica said.

"Get her into something of yours," he said. "I'll put her in a cab."

The word "cab" was unfortunate. "Home," he said to the woman. "I'm sending you home." His office voice; he felt ashamed of it here. But it worked.

"Nothing of mine'll fit her," Veronica said. The plain truth, but still withering. "Maybe—jeans."

"Not jeans," the woman said. "My sister—"

"Expects you to come home in something nice, hmmm?"

In tears again, the woman nodded into the bath towel being handed her. Amazed, he saw the girl wasn't being sarcastic; the woman was half-smiling at her. His presence had done that to them. To their sympathies. Or his voice had.

"Wait—" Veronica said. She was into the bedroom in a flash and out of it again, walking like a bridesmaid, gold folds glittering on her arm. "Here."

"Jesus," the woman said. "Sequins."

She'll say the Lord's name to that or to murder, Mulenberg thought.

Or to her own vomit. But it's only lack of taste. She's one of those who're too stupid to be venal. That's why she's here.

Veronica was already helping her into the garment, a long, draped one with a cape. They managed it, although the woman was hard put to walk. Sequins crunched. "There. It's not hard to get to Queens from here." Veronica handed her her bag. "But I wouldn't take the subway."

"Thanks, doll. Oh thank God, I never let go of my bag." The woman looked down at herself. "Oh gee. The bag don't go bad, hah? Oh gee. Listen. I'll mail this back to you, hah?" He could hear the reluctance in her voice.

"Keep it," the girl said. "I never wear it. It was a gift."

"From him?" the woman said.

Veronica stared at him.

"No," he said. "Not from me."

The woman looked down at the stained pink suit. "From Ollie?" She whispered it.

"From my brother?" the girl said, conversationally. But that was the way she said almost everything—as if what she was really saying was stowed away elsewhere. "Yes, Ollie gave it. But to our mother, not to me."

"Your—" The woman looked at him first. Then, a hand over her own mouth, at the girl. Then at him, again, as if to say Hear that. She made a throaty sound; would she puke again?

Mulenberg shook her. "On your way." The muddied thing on the floor had tangled between his feet. He reached for it. "Here. Take it along." Over her head he said to the girl, "The police might damn well be watching for it. Why should you have to get rid of it?"

"Who's this one?" the woman said, her eyes narrow. "He your brother too?"

Mulenberg was dumfounded. A minute ago pathetic, gulled by everybody including probably the sister-in-law, now she was nasty, fully street-wise; he could well see her behind the bar in Rego Park. Or buying Ollie. Or being bought. Everybody was at least two people— why not her? But what's done it?

She was edging away, even guarding herself, with the gilt gift dress. Fear was doing it. Not of him. Of the black girl.

Who saw. Walking toward her, very slightly smiling. As the woman backed up. To the door.

The woman gathered the gold folds around her. "I'll take it, don't worry, I'll take it." The handbag she'd thanked God for being left with was large, almost a satchel. She knelt and stuffed the pink suit in, averting her eyes.

If she can get back to Queens in time, Mulenberg thought, she'll be able to avert her eyes to anything. The bar in Rego Park would be open. It was only eleven o'clock. "You have cab money?"

She got to her feet defiantly. "My own. No money ever passed."

"Hurry then," Mulenberg said.

The two women turned on him as one.

He was the voice of reason here; why should they be glaring him down? But for the moment, they had puke and blood between them. And the two dresses.

"Listen—thanks, doll," the woman said. "And—listen, I'm sorry. For —you know."

Veronica seemed to.

"It's only—you know. Like I was knocked for a loop." She couldn't seem to take her eyes off the family picture on the coffee table. "Upstairs they all think you're only in his stable. Only that he don't want them to know." She spat toward the picture. "My sister was right. She trun him out the bar. 'He has the evil eye,' she said. 'Only on that kind of Indian, it don't show.'" She clutched her throat, the gilt cape, her satchel, her mouth dragging at the corners. "Oh God, oh God." The door slammed.

Together, not saying a word, they turned off all the lights and watched her from the window. Down below, the street lamps bloomed romantically. The restaurants were letting out. She got a cab almost at once.

"Ought you to get out of here too?" he said. The hand in his was unresponsive.

The police. What right did he have to say that to her? Or that she should run? Whether they came at all would depend on what had or hadn't happened to Ollie in the gents' room. He squeezed her hand tight, shook it between his clasped ones and let it go. The way people do at wakes, he thought: too late. Muttering an excuse, he made for the bathroom but sneaked instead into the bedroom, felt for the gun on the night table and pocketed it. She shouldn't be found with it. His wallet slid into his hands by magic. Or prophecy. Nothing in it except his money. Or his health. He bent to the tumbled bed, smoothing it. In the all-night New York glow which seeped anywhere he could see the soft, innocently hatched pattern of the quilt. He laid the Blue Cross card on it.

She was still at her window. He chose not to turn on a lamp; she hadn't. Taking her in his arms again was like holding a long swathe of the dark itself, turned into a body more body than most. An ear more than ear. Though his tongue had been in there earlier, he held his whisper decorously away from it now. "Veronica?"

Her eyes were the darkest part of her. Almost closed.

"I'm not Ventura." Guilt flooded him. "I'm Mulenberg."

Her eyes opened.

In his mind's eye he got out of there, out the door, down the stairs and into the street. He could feel the whiff of free air on him.

When she moved across the room and away from him, there was no emotion to it he could identify. Don't put on the lamp yet, he wanted to say. Gradually, he could see her now sitting at her desk, her back to him. Sitting on, she might not have heard him. It began to be comfortable there in the semi-gloom, restful. One's feelings put out in front of one, lambent fish. Dusk all night—it was part of the trove of this city. He would like to remark on this. And on how her flesh made less noise than his, in the dusk.

"When did you know?" he said. "That I wasn't. Him."

She turned on the desk lamp. A glare. Two-bulb strength.

"Stay where you are." She stood up, flattening herself against the desk, her palms inching protectively along the drawer where the typed page was, and the book. In the same way his mother had touched the secretaire where she'd kept her rings. "Stay, I said."

He hadn't stirred.

"The gun. Give it here now," she said, as to a child.

He laid it in her lap.

She stood up, holding it absently. She was adding him up, from head to heel. His shag of hair, which she'd tousled, saying, "Has those streaks women pay for. But this is natural." His jacket—scanning it now for what it must have cost. His cock.

Or she was separating him. Into disposable parts.

Meanwhile edging him toward the door.

"You knew it from the first," he cried out.

She drew herself up, mouth parted, neck arched, shoulders lofty, eyes veiled to a spot behind him. For a held moment she was taller than he was. "How do I know—" she said deep "—what I know?"

Then he was outside the door.

He took the elevator, letting the slow old cage shake him hydraulically. Downstairs he shut the inner door slowly; he wasn't going to run. His knees were still locked tense in the effort he'd made up there, not to crouch at bay. Or to spring.

In the entry, he listened upward. Nothing. The floor was that fine old marquetry tile, the mailboxes had polished-brass fronts. He wasn't going to scrutinize them. Over the transom, he saw the house number in reverse; he wouldn't need it. In spite of him, the weighted outer door slammed. Don't look up at the window. He looked, seeing curtains drawn, light faint behind them. Then he ran.

He reached the Athletic Club and still hadn't sweated.

Must be he jogs regular the three swimming coaches nodded to each other, lined up in his floating head like a row of bank examiners. *Now that Ventura, he never jogs.*

Mulenberg had never jogged in his life. When he spoke to the desk clerk, chill seemed to vapor from between his clicking teeth, but the man, wearing a light summer jacket, didn't budge. No, Ventura hadn't returned.

Whether or not it was Ventura sticking in his gorge, or his own helplessness, he must eat. No use going to the local police, who would only hold his hand, saying, "Wait."

"Where's the local police station?"

"Fifty-sixth," the clerk said. "Wallet?"

Mulenberg shook his head—"Car"—and walked out.

No fewer people were passing; the avenue was just as luminous as when he'd left it. If this were anywhere in Oman, he knew people who if necessary could get him to the Sultan. Or in Yemen, some official of Elkershi Shipping would get him to the Minister of Planning by afternoon grapevine and back, in time for tea in Hodeidah. Not that he would learn anything more than a hint of who, why and how—or, courteously as a blank wall bowing, that he was not to learn, ever. Even if the result was nix, he was part of the power structure, even of violence. That was the high-class route; that was trade.

Here in his home office, it was still possible to know or explore the vast network of manipulation behind ordinary blind trade—he wasn't fool enough to think otherwise—but democracy was slower about the violence, and seamier. Or it could even be corrupted by its own honesty; too often it left the organization of such matters to people outside the pale. To what proportion he didn't know, but if he went to the local police here, they mightn't either, which would be impossible in the Middle East.

But—to tell anyone must involve the girl. That was unthinkable; he'd been trying not to acknowledge this. Yet if he would go that far for her, why had he run?

Normally by now he'd be ravenous, like tonight not having eaten since noon. He'd formed the habit of dropping in after these excursions to Trader Vic's, where, no matter how late, he could sink into a straight chair opposite the plangent, circular shadow of one of the high-backed rattan ones, letting himself be served soft-footedly by waiters with the silent, nurturing expressions of amahs, and eating largely of the salty-sweet, piece-y Polynesian food, which he never at other times craved. Maybe the same need for saline replenishment was what sent Ventura to the Oyster Bar.

Shrugging off that, he plunged out of the A.C.'s marquee, strode east along Central Park South, hesitated at the Trader Vic totem, passed it, hitching his jacket, in whose left-hand pocket he now remembered he had a folded-up tie for the restaurants which didn't credit Western strings, and walked up the Plaza's main steps, intending to cross through to the south side. Though what could he do on entering the place—inquire for Mr. Ali, check the gents' room? But his knees were being undependable, an extreme sign that his large body had to be stoked. The thought of oysters sickened him.

Inside the hotel he walked on to the central heart of the place, the landing which descended to its main entrance, and stood there as he had on many such nights. On these lone dark sorties the place had become his real companion; in other cities he had similar ones, which commercial travelers like him (for he knew himself to be that, no matter the scale of it) cherished and compared. Life had by-passed certain of these Grand Hotels, the Plaza-Athénées, the Ritzes, for luxe; they could no longer be emotionalized. Broader-based old nineteenth-century joints like this one were the best. These days their dramas were increasing again. The Arabs were seeing to that. Such hotels were now their western palaces. A Sultan of Oman had exiled his father to the Dorchester, where Mulenberg had run across him. A former Prime Minister of Yemen, whom Mulenberg had known years ago, had been murdered outside his London hotel.

Here, his real allegiance was to the Oak Bar where his father, that disciple of open spaces and potting sheds, had nevertheless first taken him, saying, "When this ranch first started, John, even Andrew Carnegie was from the sticks." And where, about a year ago, he and Ventura had met.

That's where he should go. Where he'd find the man miraculously resurrected from the grim dreams of his friend Mulenberg, munching peanuts and chatting tennis to the barman. Alight with the gaiety of his recent exploit, but dropping no word of it—except to his friend. Freed for the moment from certain money worries, but not mentioning that to a soul. Fresh in from charming that Concetta woman into such sincerity that he himself had been won by her. As he forever expected, hoped to be. Sending her by go-between beforehand the expensive pink suit. Fretting over the style of Mulenberg's adventures. Craving for himself only whatever normality life still might give.

His friend, Ventura. To whom he still owed a cargo of Arabian light.

But who was not in the Oak Bar. The barman, a new one, checking his receipts in an empty house, gave Mulenberg a "That's it, buddy" stare. Though it wasn't closing time yet, maybe he was tired of humanity and had decided to risk it. The place felt like London after hours— or Saudi Arabia. Like all the enragingly dry ones. No, it felt worse than that—later than any of the late-night cities he knew so well. He felt caught between the pincers of all the places known in one way or another. With no name in his wallet. Even though two beds legally his, at his office, his club, were within blocks of here, and a ticket for Bahrein was in his morning file.

"Oyster Bar still open?" His voice felt rusty.

"Couldn't say."

He turned down a corridor, traversed it twice, turned wrong, and was almost lost. Hotels of this vintage tended to confuse, with a plushy mix of grillework and a constant dirty renaissance of doing-over—but he always got lost anyway in large buildings. His staff teased him, thinking this was because he came from the wide-open West, when it was actually in part why he had left, with his father's sad compliance and a headshake from his gimlet-eyed mother, who was a quarter Indian and rode their land and all the outer hills like a map maker. As a boy he'd had almost no sense of topography, having to acquire the local one over and over. These days, he was relieved to let the airlines do all his geography for him, traveling in the company of many first-class passengers of all nations who, whether or not they knew it (often a woman confessed it) were exactly like him.

Maybe there was no inner entrance to the Oyster Bar.

The central entrance to the Plaza itself coming round again, he walked out onto the wide Fifth Avenue steps. It was late enough for the horse carriages to be gone. No, there went a last one disembarking its tourist couple or pair of lovers against the park's slotted murk. A mild heat lightning vibrated the whole square, so well known that memory had postcarded all its views into one: from the General Motors Building's faky plaza across to that old à la Vieille Russie corner store, which through the years must have sold and resold all the Czarist loot there ever was, all the way down to the Bunny Club. Which served you girls

in can-can stockings, who in turn served you hamburgers with a body
bend as prescribed as the protein in the burgers—and in fact couldn't
be seen from here. In between, the flower-bedded horse and rider in
the center of it all flashed off and on like a souvenir from another era
entirely. In front of him the steps were crammed; must be a street
performer. They played anywhere; the police had become benevolent
patrons of art. But here came a police car, sidling the roadway at the
bottom of the steps.

Leaning forward, Mulenberg jostled a man, who only kneaded him
in closer, as if to be one flesh here was what was wanted. Others did the
same. "Sorry—" he said, but no one heeded. He was working his way
right and halfway down when a woman asked, "What is it?" A young
man answered, "They found somebody"—and Mulenberg stopped.

He put his head in his hands and raised it again. At peak hours, the
hotel's islanded driveway streamed with limousines, private cars, and
cabs depositing or picking up. After theater a few select cars were
parked, hired limousines waiting for their clients but not averse to
being bribed for a quick in-between run; he'd often done it. The police
car wheeled next to a gleaming one of these, whose chauffeur standing
alongside saluted. One vehicle was parked ahead of his. A big cab, lights
out.

A Checker? He couldn't tell from here.

"Watch it, honey pops." A pair of leather-boys he'd jostled opened
their teeth at him.

"That a Checker, down there?"

The two exploded at each other, in mime. "Can't have that one,
honey. It's took."

Whee-ah, whee-ah. An ambulance was having trouble getting
through down there. The cops toughed the crowd back. A searchlight
went on.

It was a Checker. They brought the two thieves to the highest hill,
was that the way the Bible said it? And left them there. Outside the
hotels was the way they were doing it now. Parked.

The body came out of the car slowly onto its stretcher, passed along
to the men in white who covered it. The crowd strained forward anyway, Mulenberg with them. Not long back, an elderly colonel, dying of
natural causes in a public place and with all his papers on him, had been
hauled off for burial in potter's field, while his family hunted him; their
outrage had caused a *Times* editorial. Had Ventura his credit cards on
him, anything?

In his own thinned wallet a roll of bills lodged, anonymous. Tomorrow, en route to Bahrein, the wallet would be fat with identity again.

A soft shrill passed through the crowd. Two plainclothesmen, one of them hatted, had partially uncovered the body. A forehead. A black crest of hair.

Not enough to identify your own brother from.

The two men, staring down, had an exchange.

Gamble on it.

"Officer! Officers! I think I know that man."

The way twenty or so heads around him shrank back, then closed in —he recognized a movement herders knew.

The two men cased him, exchanging glances; had this fellow said something obscene? "Ste-p up."

He tried to.

"Let him through, d'ya hear."

He'd walked through such hostile aisles before—more tailored ones, but the eyes quite as ready to make him pay for it.

They uncovered the face. A blue-chinned man turning to putty under the cheekbones, thick, naked yellow at the nose, but not long dead. Not long enough. They must have left him alone to it.

Mulenberg knelt. Ventura's long-lashed eyes glared askance, the eyes of a horse about to spook. Like all the dead, he knew something. He was the victim of it. Of what all would know. Those left behind rushed to close the eyes for that reason. More than for respect.

Except for the police. "Know him?"

The victim, as the police reports would say. Maybe this had been the origin of his own contempt. The other guy in the deal. He shook himself, as he often did after a big one.

"I know him," Mulenberg said, leaning over Ventura with the heavy bated heartbeat of the better businessman.

So he got to the station house after all, going with the willingness of the respectable. When he gave his deposition there was a moment, when asked his name, when he trembled. But not because he had no identification. This was easily explained—and could be corroborated. He'd merely been for a walk.

A solicitous young rookie was sent back to the club with him anyway. Invited upstairs, he accepted, cannily scanning the signed portraits of shahs, sultans and sheiks which Mulenberg set out in every hotel room, on the certainty that now and then an original would turn up. Once the officer had properly refused a scotch on grounds of duty, other virtue spread from him. Mulenberg could have refused to come along, he instructed. Strictly speaking, it was no crime to know a corpse. "First thing they taught us at John Jay College of Criminal Justice. No honest citizen ever knows his civic rights." He then accepted a cup of powdered coffee. But they'd had to gamble on it, you see. "You could have been some kook who was connected."

Mulenberg sank into a chair, the scotch, a hotel staple he rarely drank, warming through him. He jerked his head awake, clicking up his jaw. "I knew my rights."

"You did, eh?"

"But honest methods are often slow."

"How about that. How *about* that. You're damn right."

They almost shook hands on it.

"Sorry about your friend."

They'd told him nothing, he realized. "Who found him?"

"The doorman. He noticed the cab."

"There long?"

A shrug.

"Did he die there?"

"They'll tell us. Chances are the cab was stolen. We don't know he was robbed. He carry much?"

Mulenberg looked up. They'd already asked him that. "I just don't know."

"He wasn't rolled. Now—a pross'll do that. Or two of them. Maybe no time for it."

"A—? Oh." Mulenberg cocked his head innocently, shook it doubtfully. The scotch seemed to run to the tip of his ear, reddening it.

"Too bad," the officer said. A wedding ring shone on his stout finger. "That could leave it random. Junkies. Punks."

Mulenberg stood up. "Will you people notify his family? Or shall—?"

"Being done."

"Because I leave for Bahrein tomorrow evening."

A good citizen always babbles openly to the police.

"Have to do our jobs." On his way out, the officer stopped again in front of the photographs. "Know all these guys, huh? What're they like?"

Mulenberg laughed. It felt good to. "Not like us."

The officer gazed at the picture of Mulenberg's wife and daughters. "Your friend. Would you say his habits were more or less like yours, sir?"

"Guys, you mean?"

"Yes, sir?"

"He liked it normal," Mulenberg said.

Those were the hardest, he was informed again. Citizens just out for a walk.

On leaving, the young man had clearly already forgotten Mulenberg's name. "Well then, we'll do what we can, Mister, er—"

Mulenberg was having that same image—of wafting the other man over the doorstep by his lapels—which he often had ending a successful conference. "It's an odd one." What he always said, but suddenly he was shaking again. By an exertion that left him limp he didn't voice what some demon was pressing on his tongue: Ventura. "Mulenberg."

When he shut the door, he looked at his sheiks. Though they were of diverse nations, the West rightfully thought of them as one. Collectively they often reminded him of those pottery horsemen of some Chinese dynasty long before Ming, who sat welded to horse and lance, and through these to ground and sky. Though he'd never seen any of these live men on horseback, when dealing with them he sensed brotherhood in their buttocks, even through their business suits. They still traveled together. Though their women now carried Vuitton bandboxes and they themselves put slim attaché cases of black ostrich on his desk, or stood in the airports centered in mahogany hills of Italian leather, they were only changed on the surface from the days when they'd villaged forth behind perimeters of waxy or dirty linen pouches containing honey and dates. They all had the same luggage, carrying their oasis with them everywhere. They left the lowly spiritual labor of building the world up from scratch every morning, the tramp stews of going it alone, to nations built up of separatists like Ventura and himself. They had their feet on more diurnal rhythms. To them, an individualist was simply a man who had to travel without kin.

He felt hungry now—not ravenous, but ready. It was never any good to think of the world too much in terms of nations. Between any two poles there existed that modest vale-in-between where people could talk. Though he'd never been a Christian by more than birth, when singing his Latin he could still feel a vague churching. Even though Ventura's failure—for to be murdered was to fail—wasn't his, surely his own success could be partly Ventura's and without charity; he still had a tanker that belonged to the man.

Trouble could come—and demons too—from finding the vale of such human connections too modest. For he knew why he traveled. People said they traveled for adventure, or learning, and often thought so. More often they were like him—if they had enough money for it. As long as they skipped on, they kept themselves from the event chains that made up ordinary life. This time, too, would he run?

Downstairs, he met several club members he knew. Too bad; they'd remember him. When involved with crime, or with happiness, keep yourself unmemorable.

Outside, New York's most faithful star, that low one—was it Venus? —shivered like an asterisk which wasn't sure what it was replacing.

I will not have revelation, he said to his wife—and stopped short. He'd loved his wife best for being able to talk to her, even after the sexual furor had waned. Ventura had at least talked to his Concettas; maybe the live wife in the madhouse, lately refusing to see him on his Sunday visits, had kept that connection warm. For ten years he, Mulenberg, had triangulated the world to keep from himself what many men did—that the people they liked best in the world to talk to were women. His wife's long dying had been his excuse for doing to himself what he had tried to do to the girl, Veronica. He'd kept himself from personality— his own—by separating it into parts. He and Ventura belonged to a nation whose men talked best and closest to their women, but hid it from themselves. He, Mulenberg, was still talking to the dead.

"Father!"—his kinder, hippie daughter had groaned, hauling him backward at his wife's funeral. Since that day the other daughter had never written. The burial dress had torn to the breastbone. In her coffin, his wife, a five-month skeleton, had been plumped by the undertakers into a kind of sharp-nosed girl he couldn't get to. Clasped by paws of music, she had escaped.

Since then, her zombie, floating through the cities, had been made to keep appointment with him, in perfect, synthetic ritual. She never looked like herself. He never spoke.

The big wooden totem at the Trader Vic's entrance loomed again in front of him. This time he went in.

One of the dimmest restaurants in New York, and usually empty when he arrived—he'd never been too late for it; maybe it never closed. Since it was always the same, he could have the impression that its braziers burnt only for him; that was its specialty. He was welcomed and seated. The lotus-shaped chairs, printing verandas on the pink dim, were meant to inspire him with fake Polynesian feelings, but the place would accept real ones, if held quietly. The same elegant male amah served him. A tall Chinese with a long, grandee head and gold patina profile, he could have sat for an ambassador. Or stood, for waiters did not sit. When he bent to his male customers, speaking with curled, lacquer lips, in the dimness their white faces, raised to that head, were bowls of milk, curdled with beard. Mulenberg knew his lofty impatience with the need for pussyfooting race relationships sometimes didn't jibe with the facts. His somber assumption of equality or worse unnerved his junior executives. Nor could its recipients always believe in it.

The waiter, at least, brought him his usual drink with a smile, and a table telephone. He always phoned a daughter from here, once a month —not the hippie one, who had no phone in her hutch in the California foothills, but now and then sent him a glittery three-dimensional post-card addressed in roundish script, but the one who didn't speak to him. He phoned person-to-person—so that she could know it was he, and so that he could hear her voice. To the operator, at least, she always sounded in health.

"Bring me a phone book."

He was sitting as usual opposite one of the high-backed chairs. By every color curve, the woman he'd met tonight belonged in it, a queen to the bone. It wasn't her skin that would complicate things between them, or his cheese-curd face. But she'd done her homework in the women's lounge at Miss Lacey's. Her mission, whatever it was, would have come from it.

He wasn't surprised that her name was in the book; that would be her style—a woman who had picked him up, had walked that route for him. My kind of style, he thought. His daughters had no style as yet except reactively, and maybe never would. His wife had been a lovely amulet stored in his armpit—always under a man's wing. In life no doubt better than his bereft memory of her, in death she could only be the fringe product of his shoddier sense of romance. His mother on horseback, rating him for his trail losses with the Indian red high in her cheek, had had maybe a touch of this girl. But he wanted neither of them now for more than the reminiscent love he bore them. He could say this and be understood—by that girl.

What else could he say of such a girl—other than that she'd picked him up? And that she knew what her own mission was. For which she would walk any route.

That he wanted her to walk his, from now on?—how could he say it to her? Anything thought of brought that laugh of hers whipping into his ear. *Come to the office of the president. I have the key.*

Yet they shared something more than the flesh. That brutal some-thing which had bedded them. He could see her going around the world with him because of it, he trying all the while to find out what it was. Or to avoid knowing.

The phone rang and rang; she might be debating whether to answer it at all. Or had already gone out again herself, to wherever such a girl would go? Not to a lover, lockets or not, not now. Nor could he feel around her any sense of other kin. When he could figure out where, then he would have her. He would not tolerate her being lost. Or rather, that he could be left behind. Where could she go that a man like him couldn't follow?

Find her quick, then, and tell her. Pay her, or beat her, to remember it. That the dead all say the same thing: You better watch out.

But when she came on with the same sharp "Yes?" that he himself answered a phone with, relief choked him, so that he answered from the nerve of himself.

"Will you—eat with me?" Mulenberg said.

She sat over the poem she might never finish, only enlarge or refine, maybe letting it hulk on her desk, on all the desks, until in the end it went down with her life. Meantime, it served in secret as her real calendar, neglected for weeks for the ordinary one. To tick it over always brought her back to herself. Its three stanzas belonged to three periods of her life. When she was in her teens in New York or Barbados, and first had feelings she could phrase. When she returned here from the West Indies with a university-educated psyche which by then she could no longer sever from the dreams or facts of cunt. And the ever-budding third stanza which contained her life now.

Under all three she could hear that missing stanza of her time in Cuba and its aftermath, which her pen could not write.

The poem, typed single-space, with all its hand-written annotations forming like coral, occupied one long page, and was untitled. Lievering always told his classes that the title of the piece was the most unimportant thing about it. "Ladies and gentlemen—" his brilliantly echoing, brittle Anglo-German voice said, "—can one title a life?"

His white, seraph's face hung over all his pronouncements like a pained medal struck in memory of the era he carried with him without ever speaking of it, as a child thrice removed—Berlin to England to the West Indies—of the Holocaust. Details were unknown, but there was a sense of villages destroyed behind him. Even though he was un-branded and had gone to an English grammar school, his parents' history, if not his own, elf-locked his face. Everyone wished to cherish his remarks, but outside his presence could no longer remember them. That presence, facially beautiful—as well as spiritual, ruined and in-tense—couldn't be borne for long. That was his history.

She had been the one who'd borne it long enough to remember those remarks. At seventeen. Thirty-five, he'd been then. Now, wherever he was, he was about the age of the man who had just left. The men she chose kept pace with him.

Otherwise, he was now a man in a locket never opened, and in a stanza as yet unwritten. Once she had tried to incorporate that year, from an autumn to an autumn, during which she had been first Lievering's student, then his protégée, finally his lover, and through all of it his companion victim. Instead, Lievering's voice, too nasally distinguished by its own pain, had incorporated itself into her life. For in a way, some would say, wasn't she still answering him back? Except that no one had more than an inkling of her true life scheme, either of her poem or of her actions outside of her rather public job. And no one, certainly not Lievering himself, had known precisely what his voice had been asking for.

"Is this—yours?" he'd said in his soft, compelling out-of-class manner, not looking up at the student who, only in her second week at the university, knew she was already being called the "New York transfer," for having asked to be exempt from a freshman English course she apparently thought beneath her.

"Yes, it's mine, whatever it is," she'd replied, recognizing the folder of work submitted to substantiate her request, from which he was holding up a page. Her last defiance. For then he'd raised his head. Lievering had no idea of the effect his face had on people. Or his manner either. If they were at first stunned, then thralled and at last too irritated or wrenched by their pity for him to further bear his company, he always ascribed their jitteriness to their reactions to his "thought." But he could never merely beguile just enough for people to tolerate him, much less want him about in the ordinary way. It was like meeting an archangel momentarily, one just fresh in from tortures lucid behind him.

Ten minutes later you could scarcely bear to have tea with him. Or with his intensity, which he was so unconscious of or familiar with that the effect was of some ravening bird always at his elbow, visible to all but him.

His face, uniquely his if ever a man's was, had at that moment raised its suppliant eyes at her. Her flesh felt the shock.

Outside his office, two boys and a girl passed and grinned in at her knowingly. She'd expected yokels down here, and there were some, but many of her classmates, long-legged exquisites dressed by the island's crop of clever designers, or by their mothers' expertise, had been members of the new native middle class, children of merchants or, like herself, of the new black diplomats. Movie-tutored, sent to Montreal or

Toronto for singing lessons and expecting to explore other resources of the Empire later, they were a knowing lot, with a softer, tropical version of British manners. Lievering's classes, where his strange spirituality could enliven, and where the disease of hesitation from which he suffered was lessened by his knowledge of his subject, were always packed.

They had been a confident lot also. While the inhabitants of the greatest cities were often barred by private owners from direct access to their own city's beaches and waters, by law no Bajan native could be kept by the richest estate from strolling the morning or evening shoreline. So, when she and Lievering had apparently become a pair, gossip, though strong, had been surprisingly free of racial sentiment alone. Or they knew Lievering. So they went on past without rescuing her, which they might have done, watched her and Lievering's association grow, in class and out—and left her to discover him.

"Read this out," he'd said, at the torturous pace she'd mistaken for a stately one. As if he thought a poem was important—anyone's. But she was to learn that so might he pause before any of the details of life. A crumb on the floor, a bit of sauce on a spoon, a telephone call, a pencil raised, would all halt him equally. The trivia one must pass through in order to exist burred and gouged at him as if he had to react to each with an outsize sensitivity. Whatever had happened to him—or to his parents—had made it impossible for Lievering to summon the slightest indifference.

Already dazzled, bemused, she'd looked down at the stanza she had written. Hunter had been a smart, hip school, poetically oriented the way her whole generation had been, via the sluices of rock music, the jazz prose of popular journalists, and the sing-alongs of radical politics. Except for the page Lievering now handed back to her, the folder on his desk contained essays and stories only; she hadn't really chosen poetry yet. "Miss Lacey's" had already chosen her. Those years as Vivie's inherited stepchild and Ollie's evening sister, and as a quiet high school girl among whores, had focused her. As Lievering would later even congratulate her for, Miss Lacey's had been the "concentration camp" experience of her life.

She'd never written of it before, and no one else had seen the one stanza. She read it out, in its first version:

Miss Lacey's is gone from Carnegie Hall.
Times published her soul food on the Women's Page;
Pimps' limousines brought her black girls at a crawl,

Revving up again around the corner, turning on a dime.
"Half-ass time," the tires whisper, "—oh Miss Lacey,
Gas cost something awful, girls blow your mind."
Across in the building built like a Florentine bank,
An old white lady sits, eating Bath Olivers
From the gourmet store; Taste like beaten biscuit
If you squeeze your eyes and come from Georgia—
And who doesn't like watching whores?

But Miss Lacey's is gone now, from Carnegie Hall.

She read well.

A long pause. "Yes—" Lievering said then, "—it's yours." She felt as if he'd given it to her.

As in a way he had. Raising her head, she gazed absently around the apartment the man who wasn't Ventura had just left—into which she herself these days came perhaps once or twice a month. Mulenberg, he'd said. She'd remember it; she remembered all of them, always asking, if they didn't give their names, always knowing when they gave them falsely. No matter; she treasured them. These were their names to her. The import with which they always told or concealed the one name that held them together always surprised. She herself would have enjoyed being named to the hundredfold, one for each hour, each dress and each outer garment she chose to cover it, each country her lucky job submitted her to, and each stopping place. And each man on whom she perpetrated adventure. To which man she always told her real name. A name was a word. Words were her honor; those she would never falsify. Why should she? Through them, she'd learned to move with the current, poetic or not—and that it was useless to falsify. Hopeless.

Stretching her long arms high above her head, she exploded a great *waw* of breath. She was full of hope.

She bent to her page again, seeing in the gap between first and second stanza what hadn't been written there.

That week following, Lievering had invited her and another student, an upper-class Bajan boy who'd once lived in Philadelphia, to come out to dinner with him and a pair of visiting professors from the States. Part of the learning process, he'd said: the university would pay. Lievering was poor—but he was also said to have the habit of it. Which she and Vivie did not. She and the boy knew they'd been hand-picked, and not only because they were bright students; the boy because he was a cripple, she because she was—she hadn't yet known what. In class Lievering was firm. Each poet, he said, has one ikon the student must search for. Raising his arms crosswise, he added more haltingly, "Each person." The crippled boy nodded, rapt. Maybe Lievering had already searched out his for him. She already felt she was to be given hers.

That evening, Lievering and the boy picked her up at home. Vivie had approved of Lievering's suit, worn daily in class and bought a lifetime ago in London, but ignored the boy, as she'd ignored all people of color since returning to the Islands. The boy owned the car which brought them; Lievering had never owned one. It was hard to imagine his tautness at any wheel. But though he exclaimed at the luck, he wouldn't have elected the boy for that reason. Later she would understand better the workings of his innocence, which wasn't childish but desert-dry, absolute. Fatality had picked him clean. Since then he'd lived in the great, nervy spaces between good and evil. To him, anything blown at him by either was gratuitous. No wonder hesitation was his disease.

So, for instance, a friend and a friend, pressing their wits together, had blown him into the university, which like others, as soon as the discomfort he occasioned outweighed his gifts, would blow him out again. For although he was neither mad nor sick, he had a fault of memory which kept him remorselessly and inconveniently in the present. Where a normal personality's sense of the past gave it footholds to live forward from, articulating these as it went, Lievering's past, of which he couldn't or wouldn't speak, co-existed with him, only partially latching him on to a present he wished to live by entirely. Slowly as he spoke, ate, taught, he was lucky to do it at all. His silent central pain took the form of ever-heightening discriminations. He could just barely choose—his speech, his bread. In harness with other people's easy onwardness, this could grow worse. That night they had a demonstration of it.

"Where we going?" The elder professor had been white, a psychologist with a desk body and gold-scrolled glasses, and genial in a hard way. The younger one, whom he'd introduced as Terence, hadn't seemed like a professor at all. Robin, the cripple, who was yellower than most people of color here and not as pretty, was already irritated with him. "We could eat here at the hotel," Terence said. "It's *very* super." He was a smooth copper color, with features so little raised in his round head that he looked to her like a melted penny.

"We're on tour to study race relations," his elder said. "Why not go where race *is?* I mean—both, of course." His laughter did nothing to age him.

Lievering smiled.

Terence whistled. "Anybody ever tell you you look like Raphael's David? That one in front of that gallery in Florence?"

"Michelangelo's," his elder said.

His friend had mugged up at him. "We were *both* there."

Robin had jerked his bad foot.

"Buonarroti?" Lievering said slowly. Informing always eased him. "Yes?"

They waited again.

"Well, then—what do you say?" The elder professor had written a well-known book and was a leader of men. "Where we eating?"

"There is a restaurant." Lievering had doffed his schooltime tie for an open collar with long lapels, neatly darned. Always interested in white bodies, she'd noted his well-modeled throat.

"Bridgetown? Outside it, huh. West?" In the end, Robin, interpreting Lievering's vague gestures, limped the way to the car, seating Lievering in front with him to direct. Or deflect.

They drove for hours. At first, when eating places were passed by as too neoned-up or not the one, they assented, but soon they began to understand that nothing being good enough for them, nothing was what they might get. "Any, but *any* old tippy-oh joint," Terence said fretfully from the back seat, where she sat between him and his friend. But Lievering was hunting the perfect place for them—one he'd heard about but had never had the money to dine at himself—and urged here, backtracked there, through woods, half-lit hills, and down the crashing coastline, they had found it. She heard Lievering give the relieved sigh of decision resting. Though the place was a burnt wreck. They all stared at the charred heaps smelling of sweet-potato ash, the spars sticking up like a ship in starlight. And the sign.

"Take us back to the Sandy Lane," the professor said.

On the way back, he and his friend had a low-voiced exchange, half French, half English. *"Incroyable,"* Terence said. "But he *is* marvelous." The professor answered in English. "Not for you, doll." Adding in French, "So is the girl. Marvelous." Terence replying with a French snigger; "And not for *you.*" Adding, even with a frank glance at her, "What's she along for?" "Dunno," the other had answered. "Dunno if *she* does. Where *are* we?"

She'd breathed to herself, softly. It was like being a child, and not being one. "Does *he* know?" Terence said. "*What* is he?" Not one of us, the other had replied. "But yes, beautiful. If you can call it that. *Spirituel.* And after a moment, "Now I remember. He's supposed to have been in one of the death camps. You see that mark on his chest? Though I never saw the mark on a chest before." "Where *have* you seen it, *cheri?*" the brown one said. And then, "Oh Lordy-lordy, where *are* we?"

"At the Sandy Lane," Robin had shrieked from over the front seat. "And she understands French." One could never tell what Lievering had or hadn't heard, but he was already out of the car.

"Good," the old one said nimbly. "I invite you all." His glasses beamed at her. She rather admired him.

"No, no," Lievering said. "It is my responsibility." In the starlight his head, furled in its collar, hung in its own cloud. He went on in, up the steps.

Terence groaned, clapping his hand to his forehead. From behind his fingers he peered at her.

She leaned across him to the other one, who returned her glance more openly. There were no race relations yet, as far as she could see, between any of them, but you never knew. Should she speak English to him now, or French? English. French on her part now wouldn't be polite.

"It's a mole," she said low. And crossed her legs hard, over the sudden liquid pang between them. That was it then. Why she was here.

Terence uncovered. "*What* is?"

The older one nodded at her. He'd known why she was there before she had. In the years since, she'd often wished she knew his name, to tell him what had become of her, if she was ever to tell anyone. He knew his business, that one. "The mark," he said.

Lievering was back. It was after hours, he told them. The hotel restaurant was closed. The town was. There was a tremulous dignity about him. He'd done his best. The expected fatality had come upon him, resting him. Perhaps he lived for it? For he had the panting air of a dog after a chase, quarry or no. A weal of satisfaction came out on his face like a crack in sculpture, mortalizing. "There is nowhere else. Unless, Robin—" had a suggestion? He didn't finish. It was now in their hands.

It was always in somebody's. Whoever, rent by his broken grace, would do something. That night it was her turn. She was filled with joy at the workings of things.

"Vivie'll feed us. My stepmother. She's great with ham and eggs." And with little else, since leaving off being a cook, but they needn't know this. "And she always waits up."

"As late as this?" the professor said gently.

"She still keeps theater hours. From where she worked."

"Miss Lacey's?" Lievering nodded at her.

Robin swung on his heel jealously.

Ordinarily, Lievering's reference to the poem would have been a betrayal. She'd been grateful. She too had a past, for which so far the island's bland lightheartedness had done nothing.

"Miss *Lacey's*," Terence said. "Lord God." He hitched a hip. "And did you work there too?"

He resented her being taller, and his sweetums being nice to her. Ollie'd had a few sidekicks like that who'd called her "the giraffe." She spat lightly at him, a ghostly *p-r-r-t.* "And there'll be plenty of race relations," she'd assured the other one. "Some months here, Vivie just can't stand the blacks."

At her desk now she chewed her pen, silently laughing. Outside in this side street it was now the deepest trough of night, just as it had been there—and equally set for a scene she cherished and couldn't get rid of. Loving her own seventeen-ness for the first time it had strutted in command of anything. For the feel between her legs of those hot, plushy labia with their contracting Venus valve, moving toward the presence of Lievering, while by instinct she turned her back on him. In those days, too, her head was as open as a begging bowl; anyone with a mind to could drop a coin of idea in. She had some of those yet. But most of all the scene held Vivie on all cameras—*paisan* scourge, beloved half-mother and link about to break—handsome by then in the andante style of middle age about to fall. To die.

Their small cottage, white enough on the outside, had been shadowy as a hut within; the rent from the New York house tenants had had to pay for all their keep plus her own tuition, plus the lawyer for Ollie's latest scrape. She'd pointed the other four to its privy, meanwhile calling in to Vivie, then had led them in and seated them on the one room's scattered cretonne pallets, doing all of this with a child's offhand certainty that everyone else lived as it did, though she knew well enough that Robin's parents lived in a large house high on a hill. Vivie, for her heart's sake resting high on a frowzy pillow, in her lap their collection of tattered magazines from New York, wore a headkerchief which misrepresented her entirely; under it was hair oiled Spanish style and amber ear drops from Veronica's father. The cardiac blue in her lips shone electric on her pear-tinted face. When she smiled, she never showed gum. When she was stormed up, as then, her cheeks paled like knuckles, reminding all that she could outwait anyone. As she had outwaited Veronica's mother, loftily confessing it. "I did your daddy best. I'll do you—as good as him." Seeing their entourage, she settled the large Canadian coin-silver brooch in the grandee calico ruffles she'd worn over crushed kid-leather boots long before the era had caught up with her, and lifted her chin.

The professor introduced himself with a polite little speech, somehow including Terence without naming him. Vivie nodded, joining the two of them with a glance before turning to Robin, who still had not sat— not because of his brace, but for the awkwardness of being in such a poor house. His parents, returned now from their Philadelphia teaching jobs, the father to Parliament, the mother to society, had snubbed Vivie at the freshman reception but had greeted Veronica for her father's sake. Vivie nodded to him, elaborately. "Rest your leg."

Vivie could be cruel, the girl thought now, in the way of all people who knew the schemata of the world, who had swum out beyond the breakwaters of sentiment. Like Shakespeare, like all good dramatists, if she'd written plays she would have lopped off heads.

Lievering had come up behind her to kiss Vivie's hand, but she'd already seen him, in Vivie's face. She herself had lost his name and couldn't say who he was, already focusing on an image of him separate from the man before her and reduced minute enough to swim her bloodstream without the man himself ever having touched her— a merman of the blood, inside his own icy capsule, in a forty-year-old graveyard suit made before he was born. Lievering kissed the hand, in slow motion. Then the six of them—Robin, the pink professor, the angelically fair and dark-haired Lievering, copper Terence, her black self and Vivie already blued with death—sat looking at each other, in all their colors of skin. It would be the last time she thought of it that way—skin.

"Who *hurt* you?" Vivie was saying to Lievering. "I'll cook you a meal."

Whatever Vivie's circumstances, she kept the makings of one special meal always with her as insurance that sooner or later somebody worthy of it would crop up. Only Ollie, when he flew down for one of his hideouts, could make her break into her hoard, since he always replaced it. Two weeks before, he'd done so from the gourmet store on Fifty-seventh Street, the same one that had appeared in the Miss Lacey poem. The packages always caused Veronica a certain eerie misery, hoarded too. Having only one street to be homesick for must be shameful to those who had whole villages at their backs, home towns doubly luminous because they'd never been out of them. Yet it was the street which had pushed her to poetry.

Just so, when she'd first been entered in a Stateside school as a transfer from Canada and from Bridgetown, the weight of other languages at her back, other worlds, had made her a solitary. Though the teachers tried to make kindly class-use of her foreignness, they couldn't really treasure it. Nowadays the good schools were packed with children who from choice could have ranges of cities, different families, behind them, and these children were no longer tentative. The world now belonged to their kind. Rich suburban kids holidayed in the same Puerto Rico the city poor had emigrated from. A few of the forward-looking rich now even sent their young to her former school for the ethnic polish money could not buy. The world now belonged to the smartly drifting children of successive worlds. If you came from what had once been sought after as an "integrated" background, you had to catch up.

Meanwhile, Vivie had served them up Ollie's apology for the amount of his bail money—tinned grouse and asparagus, augmented with a sauce made of the eggs she and Veronica would have had for supper if alone, a pudding of the local breadfruit with which the subdued Terence comforted himself largely, and a mess of dried fruit soaked in rum. It was a talented meal, no doubt about it, and nobody else could have done it even with that provender; the girl was pleased to see Vivie resurrect herself. Lievering ate in the non-grabby way of Europeans, the fork confiding close to the knife, but his aura of poverty left him for a space, and when Vivie brought out the goose-quill toothpicks she used to pinch from the cashier's desk, he exclaimed. The quill lolled between his lips. Because he was strange was no reason to think him unsophisticated; he might even be the victim of his facial architecture. By that time Robin had excused himself to take his father's car home. Terence, who was wishing loudly for his own record player, brought out a brandy flask. There was a sense of family the girl would often see later between people temporarily brought together from the ends of the earth. The professor was regarding her thoughtfully.

"You going to write a book about us?" If he was, she meant to read it.

"Not yet. And not about us." He smiled back at her.

"I only meant—I'd want to read it."

"Always reading." Vivie leaned back against the pillows she carried everywhere to warm her, even here. The kerchief had come off.

"His partner at home really writes them. We just collect info." The oil Terence had eaten glistened on his forehead.

"Why are you so tetchy-mean?" Veronica said to him.

"Why aren't you?" Terence retorted.

She didn't get it. She saw Vivie was frowning at him.

Lievering stood up to go. Coaxed to faculty events or student pow-wows, he always left early, from the outer edge of them.

"How—shall we get back?" the professor said. His one awkward remark.

Lievering had forgotten they had no car. It was plain that walking was his transport. Asked, he confirmed this.

"Everywhere?" The professor was interested.

"Everywhere," Lievering said, with the polite little laugh that folks said behind his back was still so German of him. Would he kill a person who said that to him? She imagined herself saying it and pulling the toothpick, slowly, from his full lower lip.

Vivie went to the phone and cajoled them a late cab. They took Lievering with them, though he'd hung back.

"Do the dishes tomorrow," Vivie said when they'd gone. "I enjoyed that." She was already letting her hair down on her shoulders. In their side-by-side cots it was like a dormitory; each had a night table at least, and separate clothes pegs. On the center table where the girl did her studying, there was still the pleasant essence of guests. She lay weakly, face into the pillow, in one of the starched nightshirts Vivie still ironed for her.

"I don't like you to tiny your braids so close," Vivie said. "Not down here." Vivie's hair was long and flat, from the part of her that was white Dominican. Up to that time they'd done their hair themselves, or Vivie did hers. This time another girl at school and she had done it for each other, copying a style in *Ebony,* but not because it was African. Vivie had no patience anyway with the new negritude which automatically vaunted its own characteristics no matter what. Not all black was beautiful, she said, any more than all white was. The whites understood this, and laughed behind their hands. Conversely the soft, Englishy Bajans infuriated her as too supine, too regular. Sure, they were in Government House—but when the wife of the manager of Barclay's Bank had her Sunday afternoon cocktail, did she invite? All of their race relations were still with *each other,* Vivie had said.

But I'm past all that, the seventeen-year-old Veronica thought, way past it. I don't want to get into it. I just think my hair suits my head. "It's cooler that way," she'd said. "And I'm too skinny to wear one of those heavy Afro heads. Anyway—you looked marvelous." And you cooked marvelous, but how to say it so it won't recall to you our former seven courses, and Father sitting down to them? How to say it so it won't reproach? For our hundreds of omelets since. "That professor, I promised he'd see some race relations." Fights, he meant—though he'd deny it. "Dinner so good, he didn't get any." She rolled over on her back.

Vivie stopped brushing, holding high the oxblood coral brooch she pinned up her back hair with. She pursed her lips to herself in the mirror between the beds. Lipstick didn't hide the heart trouble in them. "Didn't he though." The brush clattered down. She came to the side of the other bed.

"What you looking at, Vivie?" It was an old game. Vivie'd used to poke for ear dirt, knee scabs. Now there weren't any.

"At your being too skinny."

The girl sat up. "What did you say to Mr. Lievering? I saw you. What did you whisper to him?"

"Didn't whisper."

"What then?"

The coral still nestled in Vivie's hand. She smoothed the girl's starched chest on the heart side, as if trying to erase the small breast behind the cloth, then pinned the brooch there, gave it a fillip, and folded her hands together. "I said—'You better love her, yes? Yes, you better love her,' I said."

By the time it was spring and Easter holiday, he still hadn't. All the school year their separate partisans had watched what nobody called a romance. For the students, it might be their own destiny they were watching; for the faculty it might be their children's. To those families who made the color line a matter of keeping peace with the British residents, or more often with themselves, Lievering and "the New York transfer" were a threat—with their high-class openness on what could well have been managed behind closed doors, colonially. Especially when their daughters brought home the news that the girl wouldn't marry him. As Bruce Le Sueur said—that smart, Empire-educated banana-colored professor with fine mustachios who taught Spanish, published ballads in Bejan dialect and was her and Vivie's one confidant —"It's now a question of the Old World and the New World seducing each other. The battlegrounds being poetry and the apocalypse." Meanwhile, those economics and history professors who'd brought Lievering to the college through an all but defunct group left over from one devoted to helping the Hitlerized, and who knew his tiny salary, were waiting, as Bruce said, "for that classless devil—money—to enter in."

There hadn't been time for that. Even if her upbringing after her father had died hadn't made her money-energetic and unlikely ever to look to a man for it, by Easter she'd been emotionally exhausted, as in some trial marriage whereby she'd acquired nothing but knew everything. Though she had told Lievering she was no virgin but the veteran of one protracted high school affair and one party, and although he'd had his liaisons and a short-term marriage once, to an English girl, her own body lay between them, as he said, like a too newly cast sword.

His body, thanks to that other greater concern, memory of the worst, had long periods of half-forgetful abstinence, which gave his infinite discriminations free rein. He didn't want marriage, but for her sake he wouldn't touch her without it. He didn't want children, not his children, but if they two married, they must. For her sake. "How do you know you can have them?" she said cruelly. "I don't doubt *you* can," was his response. Her reply—by then enlightened by milder incidents like that first evening's—"So I'll have to do it for both of us?" But in class, and on their long afternoon walks on the oceanside, or the shorter nighttime strolls which never ended up at his boardinghouse, he was master. That was what she had no hope of explaining to Vivie, that the poetry ran between them like an ever-nourishing stream. Until, thanks to Vivie really, she was able to judge even that.

Easter had frilled the native parts of the island with Anglicanism. Even the orchids looked sedate. Conformism—or rather, what Bruce called "our light air of seriousness"—was briefly in control. "Mostly of party and dinner manners only," Bruce noted, and really in reaction to the tourist beach orgies just past, plus the last spate of royal visits and dinners on gold service, for some of which Vivie, reawakened to her own gifts by the gossip on them since that night, now catered.

"We don't want them to know we don't fast Lent," Bruce said. "We still have the old colonial habit. Still think moral superiority helps." He'd pointed from their porch to four children tottering in the wake of their mothers like invalids, their swimmer's bodies crammed into spiky collars and hard, shiny shoes. How strange, she'd thought, meanwhile sipping one of the rum juleps Bruce came for, that the passion of Jesus should bring this. The solemn week before, it had also brought to the university a band of American boys and girls, mostly from the richer and more personal colleges, who after some preparatory sunbathing here, were off to help Castro with his crop of sugarcane.

"Cuba's not even on their way," she'd said disapprovingly. "Anywhere." Actually she was intrigued. Many of the young American visitors were from in and around New York, and a whiff of that style, unenclosed or always prepared to be, had come back to her.

Bruce had laughed. "She's the most moral of us all, eh, Vivie?"

Lievering, rocking in Vivie's proffered favorite chair, nodded. Like a relieved suitor, the girl thought. "But those Americans. They have a fine spirit."

"Listen, they don't even know whether there is a crop!" she'd exploded. At him. For though he was no Marxist, he in a sense had lived his whole life in a kind of negative politics. The smell of any commitment made him lift his nose. He was obliged to, of course, by that history of his. But what it really came down to was that any well-fed American youth, on a holiday spree for the politics they took up the way their parents did jogging, could freeze Lievering in his tracks with the word "anti-fascist," neither of them seeing that it was the last half of the word he was really reacting to.

Those nights when she stared into the mirror she looked to herself skinnier than ever, and without bloom. To see as much as she did about these three people, that they couldn't see themselves—even about Bruce, who never brought his simple fat wife and dull kids here or much anywhere, and constantly engaged himself for flash lecture tours away from them—would it make her preternaturally old?

"And she's practical too, eh, Vivie? Like you." Bruce knew how to get round Vivie. So that the drinks could keep on coming?

Vivie had looked better those days. Since the word had got around, their larder bulged with food of her own providing. She catered for the British carpet king who had defected from all his creditors at home and ate mournfully from his gold plate because he couldn't go back to them, for the absentee British lordling who'd built his powerful American wife a villa with a shell-shaped bed, facing seaward, that she was never in—and for two gentlemen who sang *Iolanthe* to each other at dusk while feeding each other sugar cubes.

Vivie had charged the tiny carpet king the most, for his sins, until she saw how his own great Danes bullied him.

"Whyn't you all three go? See about that crop." She sat tall, sipping the rum that was better than any lipstick. Her boots and calico were the same as always, only fresh and new; the lord's American wife, on one of her flash visits here, which resembled Bruce's trips in reverse, had copied them.

"Easter present," Vivie had added. "I'll pay fare."

"Uh-*uh*," Bruce had said at once. "I promised me old woman. We partying the kids." Away from the college and his Spanish classes, from his Bajan wife and his ballads, or even the choir where he soloed Schubert lieder, his voice took on a new, syrupy porch-lolling Veronica hadn't yet identified. "Nuh, I know that Castro, nuh. What a man. A big man." Bruce had met him once. The American group had an invite to do so. "He'll like Veronica." Bruce appeared to be watching the sea line, though they were deep in hedge. "And she'll like him."

So, two days later, the college, where Bruce was a powerful mover, had offered Lievering his expenses plus a little extra in return for going to Cuba as faculty adviser to a small "observation group" of its own students, who would accompany the Americans. The West Indian students were not to work in the fields, as a sop to opposing faculty who, fearing involvement, had fought the whole idea bitterly. That, and one conservative's comment, "It is not necessary to observe every kind of politics," had decided Lievering. He had refused the extra sum.

The trip had few student takers anyway, or parents who would allow them to. Robin's had flown him out of the country fast for a suddenly trumped-up Easter in Philadelphia and the promise of his own car. So she and Lievering had arrived at the airport, separately though mentally together, along with two raffish couples who played *vingt-et-un* in the university lounge with English Rothmans dangling from their lips, also a Haitian girl, distant cousin of its dead dictator Papa Doc, who still heard his voice mystically and thought in Cuba she might be a kind of royalty; and two rather delightful Bridgetown thugs who were surely after marijuana and general opportunity and were later found not to be college-registered; and the good Americans.

So it would come about that, pressed by these motley forces, she would discover the blaze of open fields, cut her mouth on cane whose sweetness in memory could make her jaws ache, and would find her present profession—all the way thinking little of any of it. For during those same ten days, she and Lievering, after six days of silence between them, followed by four days of what?—dialogue, mutual feast and rape? —and after being sung toward their rest by a host of radical angels, plus one little psychoanalytical plumpie who'd pushed back her own braid to whisper in Veronica's ear, "You be the giver, he the taker; it's more hot that way," had been married. Or had assumed or pretended they'd been married, by a role-playing divinity student later revealed to have been "not quite ordained." After which ceremonies, in what was still the most theologically satisfying hour of her life, she had given Lievering his icon—and had left for New York.

In a whirlwind of self-righteousness, and hoping to spend all her remaining money on a first-class ticket. Wanting to step out into that armored city with an outward show to match the brimming verge of all her felt power of limb and mind. Out of the first vortex, and still under twenty. But not at all understanding that if "this neo-neo-world of our time," as Bruce called it, had responded to her as if she had been made for it, that was because she had been. Nor that, in the Mosaic-lawed realm which underlay all eras, what you did to another life as formally as she had—was formally done to you.

The phone rang now. It often did on her nights in this city, at just about this time, when she was at her desk still reading between the lines, before the poem resumed. She was under no obligation to answer. It would be Rhoda Esher, still keeping lone vigil in the bar to which all the staff went for a couple of drinks once the weekly magazine newspaper—or newspaper magazine—they edited had been put to bed. Or Rhoda would be lordly drunk at home and reminding all hands, up through the senior correspondents of whom Veronica was now the oldest, and not excluding the publisher if she could catch him at home, that she, Rhoda, at the advanced age of forty-five was still executive editor—which meant chief midwife in charge of the passage of ideas into computer print-out or cartoon or telecommunication, for what Rhoda herself called "one of the thought publications of the decade."

The trouble was, on these calls Rhoda was reminding herself that it was not her decade. Tom Gilpin, the publisher, must now be in his late thirties or more, but by means of his careful brownish mummery of non-clothes, non-living quarters and even non-consorts, plus a sober ability to think backward while ethically moving forward, he kept this hard to observe. The public, saying admiringly that Gilpin was even adventurous enough not to mind that his creation had gone big-time, couldn't know, as all Tom's own staffers did, his intention that one day, "like all organs of opinion without action," it must self-destruct. "We'll grow up, Rhoda," was all he'd say to her if her call got to him. Adding genially, "And so will you. Calm down."

But Rhoda had been trained in old-style media where news was thought, and thought was only a barely printable news which would have to be processed. The lack of routine blood-and-thunder in their own pages disturbed her profoundly, in somewhat the same way that the idea of a routine act of love made the younger staffers conversationally uneasy. In either case, she had a tin ear for their subtler violences. "When she begins to call us existentialist—we'll have to can her," Tom joked. "She's incurably in step."

Veronica herself took all her assignments straight from Gilpin—an art in itself. Let the phone ring.

No—Ollie. If he were still alive, he'd phone. She picked it up.

Rhoda, when primed, spoke in squelches, with the sound of a carrot being fed to a horse. No doubt her big breasts, always to be seen in the comfortable gap of her blouses, were as usual pressed forward like an offering, but this meant nothing; they were merely what got between her and newsprint. Somewhere inside them, within that anonymous evening bulk which could be so bulldog smart the next morning, was the curly-top redhead who'd come up from Arizona to make her fortune. Whatever Rhoda's vortices had been, she now wore her hair in a flattened mat on top of her head. "Know I'm pissed. But did I hear it on the telly or dream it—that the Pope died?"

To her and her kind, the girl thought, the globe was still like an old eyeball which on the instant went red and veinous with every dire fact. "Tell Tom, why don't you." Rhoda thought Veronica was softer than the others only because she listened. When it was really because of Vivie that she couldn't stop respecting middle age.

"He won't"—squelch—"put it in the issue."

"The issue's fine, Rhoda." Full of non-purpose, the way he likes it. Shaken loose. So that anarchy may bloom?

"Thanks to you. Still have some sense in you."

Did she? According to Rhoda? Then there must still be some of what Rhoda called "sense," to be rooted out.

"Says you're going to Montreal for him."

Gilpin? He wouldn't have said it like that. He knows I go for myself first of all. And approves.

"Even so, bet you won't put in a thing about the people leaving Quebec. Or how U.S. border banks are closing their accounts to any more of their cash. Will you?"

No, not at all likely. The story she'd asked to go up there for had only a beginning, in a group of grade-school children watched one chill, vivid morning from a café terrace in the Old Town's square, she being the only outside customer. There'd been the usual number of Scotch-Irish-looking kids, some dark-eyed pinks who might have been French, and a couple of blacks from somewhere in the old French Africa, with faces chiseled like her own. To these had been added, obviously new to the class—and like primeval Canada no longer smiling—two broad Eskimo boys, or Aleuts, who every time they linked hands were persuaded to unlink them. By a teacher with a small-coin mouth. There'd been less than a dozen children altogether. In the old square, early in the term. That was all she had. She must be careful not to make too much of the ethnic distribution, as some would. "Yes, it sounds like one of yours," Tom had said. It was; she already knew that. One of the pieces that kept her and the poem going, and made people recognize her picture. This was all she knew about it as yet, except that the piece would rise and take flight as she herself never could, and at a certain same angle she would feel in her guts. "The language of nihilism—" a commentator had said of them, "and full of hope." Tom had reported that, his scarab eyes veiled. "Jesus," she'd answered, "that could get me canned."

"All the other mags have had stories on the Quebec thing." Envious pain of that sort turned Rhoda sober.

"Maybe Tom'll run a picture, Rhoda." Vague, menacing and costing the earth to arrange properly. "Of the curbstone of a bank."

"Oh, you're all, all—"

Alike? No, not really. Except that none of us can help seeing these days that what's "significant" to people is no longer the key to them. What means nothing to people, to us—is what must be looked for. Flags of nothingness, which may one day ring the world.

"Rhoda—"

"Oh, all right, all right. Say it. What you want to say."

What an order. But it came to her.

"All Popes die."

Rhoda herself hung up. Better that way. Among the staffers, whose real united front—youth—Rhoda never mentioned, there was an implicit agreement to keep propping her up. In case Tom should after all decide to have his non-way.

She turned back to her desk.

It had been a silvery island afternoon when she'd left for Cuba. Vivie, so prophetically right, had tried to equip her like a bride, but she would take only a change of dungarees and underpants, a shirt and a bikini for sun work, a poncho in case of mountain cold and one of the wide-necked cottony blouses, approvably peasant-revolution, which the American girls wore for everything. At the last minute Vivie had tucked in a gift-wrapped package she hadn't opened but had let stay. Looking down at her straw case the night before, its contents seemed to her like a vocabulary, suitably stripped down for voyaging. Expanding easily into the airy silences in which she would swim nude, sleep raw. All of it underwritten by the sandals she stood up in.

Only last year she'd still been jealous of the clothes she saw on the island's international residents—thin voiles and lineny wools which hung from their lamb-pink or artificially tanned limbs like paper sculpture, gilt sandals which scrolled the toes and ran up the ankles as if hardened from the money they walked on. Vivie couldn't make those clothes no matter what skills or New York supplies she had; they were heritage. The hacked leather and metal-blazoned denims the American boys and girls were wearing were merely emblems, half army regulation and half spectator, and like the banners carried into football stadiums, never sported by the team itself. The Americans hadn't really divested themselves of anything. In among them under the lush green breeze of the airport, which like all airports seemed to have no past and one narrow future, Lievering, in the dim European suit which was never precisely cool enough or warm enough but would probably do him at either pole if necessary, should have looked ill fitted out for this group and its purpose—too baroque.

He hadn't. His face had been open to the world. He'd been born his own emblem. She looked down now at her own hands spread angularly on the desk. So had she. That was why she had wanted him. For a time.

When they arrived, there had been a crop. "Arranged for—" the camp cynic, a boy from Brandeis, said, "like everything. Those canes look old." Maybe so; they never found out, or even whether sugar crops went in seasons; the rest of the group either ignored such things or took it as a sign that miracles came naturally to the elect. Who were to meet the island's dictator at a still undated event listed on their schedule as "Agenda, with Music."

They were to have seventeen days there, most in the mess hall gloated, before their intricately chartered flights flew them to ports from which they could reenter home. Some were plodding on to colder socialist countries, chillier in temperament as well, which would allow a witnessing visit but had refused any offers of work. Castro's generous acceptance of their work gesture had won their hearts, and the velvet climate he provided went to the head. After peppery-sweet suppers from which pig or whatever it was had been removed on gentle notice from the vegetarians, the lanes were full of hand-holding couples murmuring decorously to each other, "This is a Latin country," until the gloaming was over and they could dive behind a hedge.

On the fourth day she and Lievering, gazing helplessly at each other across the sea of talk at mealtime, joined the strollers, walking like the other couples but not touching. "It's like the evening promenade in little Italian towns, the *passeggiata*," he said—but here talk, which at the university had been their niche away from others, belonged ceaselessly to the crowd. They were thought to be a couple; wise glances came their way from other pairs, but when night fell they separated, each to one of the cots which to the property-shock of some had been discovered to be catch-as-catch-can, yours only for the night.

Conversely one's assigned place in a sector of a work gang was for the duration unchangeable except by committee, yet the following day Lievering had crossed a cut field—she could see him coming, bare to the waist and in a regulation khaki sun visor too small for him—and joined her line, inserting himself sometimes ahead of her, sometimes behind. Either way, she wielded her knife silently, taking her dippers of water, her scratches and her reliefs as they came. It's courtship in dumb show, she told herself. Or like that push game men play hand against hand, the bodies not quite lunging. Something must give.

On the sixth day, working so close upon her that she feared she would cut herself, he said suddenly, "Fall out of line." The singing in the fields was constant; he'd had to repeat. When she'd done so, he led them to the main hall. A few dropouts were asleep there, hang-jawed, saved for beauty by an upflung arm, a curved cheek. There was a smell of fruit and chocolate—a five-pound box of French candies, filled with citron, which somebody had opened that morning, as well as whiffs of chewing gum and toothpaste and feet, and vegetable fart.

"It's a children's crusade," Lievering said. "Not a pimple here. Or wrinkle." Was he telling her that she too was a child? He was smoking a cigarette, which did scare her. He hadn't smoked since he was seven, he'd told her, when they did it for hunger with rolled cornhusks, which was all she knew of his childhood. She stared at her dust-burned feet; they were farther from her than normally. His hands were shaking. This place was called "the camp"—did it remind him? "Get your bag," he said.

He walked her down a dirt road—she knew the distance because he told her so: "Two miles." There were cars to be borrowed but he hadn't thought of it. She carried her own light suitcase. Now and then they passed a small, loaf-sized cottage. Things were neater here than the group had expected, though the gardens could be tangled, bearing grossly whether tended or not. It was past lunch and into siesta. As they walked, the strange all-day hubba-hubba from the fields—military anthem, reggae, a tape of Piaf singing *À l'autre côte de la rue,* and one insistent, lemony harmonica—gradually died. The sky was a flat blue. She felt they were walking on it.

Yes, he said one more thing. "Put on your hat." She was carrying it on her wrist, a wide, black-straw brim of Vivie's from which she'd once cut out the crown. In the fields she sometimes put one of the provided khaki caps on top of it to further protect her exposed head, but not now. As they walked, the big black disk balanced her. Since childhood she'd been one for costume, and was always secretly conscious of her own silhouette. At going on for eighteen, she thought of this as insincere. Under the hat brim, sweat formed a diadem from which pearls slowly fell. Her wickedly long stride kept her slightly ahead of him.

They stopped at a cottage which had been whitewashed and had a flowering vine. A short-legged middle-aged Cuban woman came out to them, nodded, and slunk back in. Lievering put down his faded Aer Lingus flight bag. She held on to her satchel. They stood chest-to-chest, hers slightly above. "There's such a lot of utopia here," he said. It could have been the fields left behind he was saying it to. Or else the white-wash and the vine, and the coffee smell from inside. A cooling second wind came to her, from her own sweat. There were two orange flowers on the vine just under their noses. He saw them but didn't pick them, for which she was glad.

Inside, all was brown and white except for the fruit the woman served them, along with bread and pancakes. Wood and white wall, bare table, the dishes baked brown as the woman's hands. And a stair. The coffee came from a tin of the same American brand the camp was using. Outside back, near a privy and a washplace, two sun-dried towels hung neatly on a string. It had all been prearranged.

"So it's as you wish," he said, laying her on the bed, and she heard the faint, Germanic flavor. His eyes beside her, even as remembered these years later, were of an innocence to be relied upon. Or stamped on. Though he and she had at last gripped each other in the hedges, they hadn't yet kissed. Now her lips drew back in a snarl of need, and they did not. His bronzing torso, slightly small for his head, was familiar to her; the white hips and thighs, protected by his shorts, were a sur-prise. After one glance at the luxurious implant of his sex, she hid her eyes from it. His face was strained; she couldn't tell what he thought of her, stretched out on the coarse bed with her bony feet slopping over, but the foreplay of his hand was reverent. He was slow, but not as delaying, she thought strangely in that same moment, as "when in life." They seemed to her to be swinging in a jungle cradle of their own flesh. She forgot her own silhouette.

They spent three nights and two days in that place, deep in sex and bitter, fortifying quarrel. No wonder she'd come to think of day and night as one. As if sunk down a well, they were, with only the other's ladder to climb up on, or fall back from. The woman served them nameless greens and sweet farinas whose cooking smells were still with her, and once a birdling they ate with bare hands. On the wooden sideboard there were knives and spoons only, cups of baked clay, nothing of glass. Four thonged chairs, the one set of sheets, and the two towels, which didn't grow grimier. Plus that coverlet, how could she have forgotten it?—an heirloom or dowry piece surely, wild with the only color in the house. They were always afraid they'd stain it with sex; that fear had been their only expressed emotion. Unless they were all the time expressing one she still had no name for, as for the vegetables. The sex wasn't various; she was too young to invent, and what he was she still didn't know, but he came to her by ritual and she had no sense of want. In her young one-track way, which could envision no experience except its own, she was storing it all up, in case it never came again.

On the second noon, while they were eating, they saw the woman hanging out the sheets and, abashed, didn't go back up the stairs, though the woman's smile remained the same. Because the woman was another woman, she who at home roamed the nearby barrios and poked her head into every language, never addressed her, and had half convinced herself the woman was mute.

"Let's go for a civilized walk," Lievering said when he saw that audience of sheets, and though the road was dead in sun they had walked far from the house, found a ditch pool and bathed, watching each other in their first easeful silence. Nature lapped them in velvet-struck calm; their eyes stretched now to horizons; again they were abashed. In quiet, they walked back. The woman was gone, into the village or to wherever she lived, from which she came and went every afternoon leaving them one of her peculiar suppers; she was not the owner of the house. They mounted the stairs, so that they could quarrel again.

She had been right, to store it all up.

She couldn't smile even yet at that upstairs classroom, the bed lit like a boxing ring by two bodies' natural light. There had been no single contention between them. The match itself was that, conducted in the bright, floating anger generated by two opposing poles of life. Which had to meet. On the bed, her younger self crouched on all fours, its lean rib cage pushed forward—he said once, "like those figurines on old automobiles. On the radiator caps. I don't suppose you've ever seen one." She hadn't. She'd looked over her shoulder at her own buttocks raised high, humbled yet enraged that she should be compared. He sat at the head of the bed, hunched sculpturally to himself, clasping his knees, a man in one of Blake's circular drawings, with the same rayed, effulgent eyes. Held fast by student resentment, she hadn't told him so; he had brought her to Blake. "There are no men in Blake," he'd have said. "Only angels and unearthly denizens"—and he would have been right. She always knew what he would have said, even now. In the end who could stand it? He always rang true.

For good or ill, he'd taught her the sound of it.

"Are all—couples—as angry as we are?" she'd asked.

"We're angry because I'm weary. Both of us. And because you are yet not."

Weary of life, he'd meant, though she hadn't asked. Weary was still not the word she would use for him; she knew no right one. For the way he hung impaled on the brute past, with that awkwardness which made people avoid him.

"You don't have the—aplomb to die," she'd said.

He'd broken out of his hunched circle then, to cover her mouth with his hands. So that she couldn't answer him. "Where, my God, do you get the words?"

From the air, from the English. From Vivie speaking in her own father's voice, or now and then from a nursery memory of him, keen as a slap. From subway posters, travel brochures, a hoard of books picked up at the whites' thrift shop in Bridgetown, New York Public Library exhibits of medieval and other manuscripts—and from Bruce, sitting on the porch. Though she sometimes got them wrong, she was going to be better at the words than Lievering was. She let them *all* in.

"I made you break the circle," she'd said. "Didn't I." And didn't explain, didn't have to. "That's what words are *for*." Down flat on her belly then, with her face in her paws. In wonder. And that's what I'm here for. She was half off the bed, her arches scraping the floor in that long length of leg she always carried below her. Like a second body, he once said.

"Maybe they have you on the planes now," he'd said. "Those ornaments." There was always a moment when they slid into sex. One or the other would weaken. She held still for it. "Maybe on the bombs, even," he said. A spark from his fingernail pricked her hip. "I can feel the lines of speed on your side."

The next day, the last in that place, Lievering went for a walk by himself; she'd refused. When he was safely gone, she went to his flight bag. He'd left the suit, oxford shoes and raincoat in which he'd traveled back at the main hall, not worried, as he said with a wry face, that anyone would take them, though there had been thefts. In the bag she found the ancient black one-piece bathing suit he sometimes wore in the fields. He was at the moment wearing the white shorts he sometimes put over it. One extra pair of underpants. No pajamas, no socks. Those he'd worn on the plane must be with his shoes. The shirt he'd worn hung on the door of the bedroom's one cabinet; he'd put it on for dinner the night before. The cabinet's door swung emptily open; emulating him she'd hung nothing there either, keeping what she had in her satchel, removing and replacing her few needs when the other was out of sight.

She had an idea he did that even when he was alone. The shirt swinging above her as she knelt had been rewashed; he was more scrupulous than she and was probably now taking a swim. She hadn't had it in mind to do this when she stayed behind, only not wanting the walk or the swim; her muscles were stretched to an all-over ache from an invigoration whose details still crammed her head, and she enjoyed the musk of its sweat. Feeling in the bag, it struck her that what she was doing was a domestic necessity; she was investigating her possible future household. He'd asked her to marry him, and she'd half agreed.

She drew out a crumpled drawstring pouch made of tough, sueded calf of the same yellow-brown as the shoes foreigners to New York sometimes wore. In it was the comb she'd seen him use, and a bunged-up locket. The pearl had half its skin gone but the case had a rubbed glow. Nothing inside it. She put the locket and comb back in the pouch and put the pouch back in the bag. Underneath, between it and the bag, almost like a false bottom, she felt a book, and drew it out. Only the dusty green cover of a book whose narrow spine never could have held much. No print there or on the cover, which had once been a fine one. Inside, the spine had been stitched with white book string, to which a few bits of thickish paper still adhered, parts of pages once. Closing it, she found she'd been holding the book cover upside down; its title was on the other side, boxed in by a gold line: *The Elephant Sonnets.* Underneath, neatly smaller: Wolf Lievering.

She knew his first name of course. Since neither he nor anybody ever used it, she'd early on looked it up in the university catalogue, where all the faculty vitae also listed publication, if there was any. His had listed merely his British grammar school and university, a sparse number of teaching jobs, not all of these in colleges, and some British Council lectures around the Indies, of a sort of which Bruce had said, "Anybody down to a button can always do those." Bruce's own books were often on his tongue and on other people's; that was the way, down there if anyone published, whether or not it ever got out to the great world. She was sure neither Bruce nor the university had ever heard of this book.

She sat back on her heels. When she did that, her knees stuck in front of her like a grasshopper's, Vivie teased, and she'd always laughed back. She didn't care about it any more than she cared she was black. "Hump it, you don't," Vivie said. "You just know you're beautiful." Maybe so. Let them all think that took care of it. Rather than that she cared so much about something else, it neutered the skin right out.

"You won't marry a black man now," Lievering had said yesterday —"I'm sorry." She knew this hadn't been said from vanity but from the built-in prophecy of his teacher trade, which saw the young come and go. "Won't I?" she'd said then, standing tall and honestly wondering. He had groaned, squeezing vertical forehead creases which did nothing to age him, and asked her again to marry him. "People like me, we go on and on—but you'll want to stop somewhere. Women do."

"Or start," she'd said. Even when she'd still been full of him.

When she put the book back in the bag, the seam between the bag's zipper and old fabric slightly tore.

She stood up, hearing Lievering return. "Dinner's ready," he called up the stairs, and she shuddered. It had been the first thing he'd ever said to her that sounded too ordinary. "Put on your shirt for it," she'd called back. A sense of what she meant to do rose in her, more in her blood than in her head. He'd come up the stairs, his thick hair slicked back in wet runnels, and had done as she said, buttoning himself up with his slender blue-white hands on which the shadows fell so well. There had been the glory about him of a fine instrument on which tragedy played; people must be excused for adding to it. But that insight came late. At that moment, she simply waited for him to finish, then took his arm with a new intimacy. "I smell," she said joyously—and told him she would marry him.

That night they retreated each to a side of the bed in a kind of truce, in which he drowsed. She couldn't feel single that way, and found she wanted to. On a mat downstairs, she stretched out and slept soundlessly, creeping back before he awoke. Vivie had once said that except for after pregnancy, when all women's bodies repaired themselves in sleep, most unions were divided into those where it was the woman who slept later, or it was the man. If it was the woman who got up earlier, then that was the time when all the marital poisons festered in her. "Even me with your daddy. Maybe we have such a time the night before, I want to kiss his feet. Maybe I'm up early to set his birthday cake. But when I see him sleeping up to heaven with his face so smug, I just want to press the pillow on him." Asked what she supposed the men thought if the woman was the lazybones, she'd cackled, "Nothing, the thick creatures. They just go on out."

When he woke that morning, she was staring down at him, with his coffee in her hand.

When he'd drunk it, he ruffled through his hair, which had dried in straight-up patches, said "Comb" to himself, and went to the flight bag. It struck her that he said that every morning. It struck her that he was speaking faster than usual these last days—maybe only to her, as stutterers were said to do with children or members of the family. If this didn't make her feel closer to him, it must be because she'd been watching him for so long. When he opened the flight bag, the zipper tore all the way down its length.

He smiled. He didn't often. "Got this bag in the attic of the boardinghouse. Somebody'd carried stones in it."

"Or—elephants?"

She'd thought he would change color or even rant at her; kneeling there naked he'd merely retracted backward at the bent nape, the stomach, as if a force at his shoulder had tapped him, saying "Detained." He dropped the bag. "You looked. Inside."

"That's the way I am." She straightened herself.

He stood up to her, nodding slowly. She meant he ought to know that about her beforehand. He saw that. Oh, there was never any lack of understanding between them. "You needn't have troubled. To say."

"*Who* tore the pages out?" She'd waited all night to ask. Still hoping it wasn't him.

"I was in hospital. After the book came out. I did. Under the influence of a drug." He shrugged nakedly. "They thought it best."

She fought off an impulse to draw a shawl around those shoulders. They didn't have a shawl between them, anyway. In a way both of them had wanted to be minimal, to live it. He giving away his tiny salary to people on the boardinghouse street who needed it more than he did. She always wanting to move on. Both of them needing the drama of it.

"Who'd printed it?" she said sadly.

"A fly-by-night printer in Cornwall. Friend of a girl in the hospital. He did it for free. Hipped on type, he was. Not on the material." He brushed his palms together in that ridding motion. It would have been the last copy he'd had. No need to ask.

"A wonderful idea. The poems must have been." By now she thought she knew enough of his mind to apprehend in part what they might have been. She could hear the elephant, plodding down the fragile sonnet structure, thudding through that foliage. The behemoth, breaking down the words that held it up.

"I wasn't as young as you are." He snarled it. "When I wrote them."

"Why'd you keep the cover?"

"To remind me. Not to try again."

Her breath had indrawn itself in a *s-f-f-f-f* of horror. "A word is a *wing*. You taught us that yourself." In those classes where he'd taught them to handle other men and women's poetry the way children were taught to respect knives.

But it was as she'd suspected. He didn't believe that anymore. How could one—unless one believed in it also for oneself?

He was watching her, sadly. "Good teachers get—such strict listeners." He twisted her face toward him, her head still bent sick, shook her until her jaw clicked. "Listen, Veronica." No more *Ronchen* then, grunted from the deeps of sexual energy, whispered lightly at its end. She saw where that long held-back energy—eruptive, ritual—must have come from. Brooding, she scarcely heard at first what she would hear forever. "We make nets of language. But the blood always comes through."

She went all shivering then, so that he had to sit her down on the bed, which sank beneath them, those knees of hers sticking up akimbo, so that she could almost glimpse between them their pink root. Perversely remembering when she had tried to stanch her first menses with spider web. Having heard that it worked on wounds.

"What is it? Are you ill?" He was chafing her temples, her wrists.

Her mouth wouldn't work, but only because it was so full of him, the entire gist of him, though she hadn't the scope yet to say. How she had all his reasons now. With such a fall from belief as his, who wouldn't be beset by infinite discriminations? Given that head of his at birth, dragging it down to such a minimum, who wouldn't own that pained beauty-medal of a face? He didn't despise as he thought he did, not enough for action. He merely despaired. He was in despair over the language he had been committed to by temperament—since for him, no language could compete with his early events.

She hadn't been as wrenched for him then, though, as she was now, meanwhile crossing her fingers in holy spell against such a fall happening to her. He'd had language sufficient to the day, to his days. What he hadn't dared was to push the language to meet the life, which meant pushing on the life—to meet and pass those early events.

She'd taken his face in her hands then, kissing him for those as she hadn't before; it wasn't necessary to know them in detail before believing. How heavily it weighed, to know a person so; would she ever want to again? Even the knowing might infect.

But she had a discrimination of her own, to keep her strong. To be hoarded, never told, except in its own fashion. No, Lievering. We net the language *for* the blood to come through. I will. She began to shiver again.

"I made too much love to you," he said anxiously. "You're frailer than you look. No? What then?"

She stared unfocused at the patch of white his shorts had shaped between the navel and thigh. You're so white, yes. How we ever going to *get* to you? But who would ever believe that wasn't the real contest between them?

He was persisting. "Tell me what, then? Is it that I mention blood?"

Poor wolf, she said under her breath. Poor wolf of the camp fringes, do these still shine so brilliant through your child-dusk? Let her fix his face in recollection, alive—and asleep. A man to remember, only. With him—because of the camp, or because of what he'd made of it—one could never know for sure which was character in him and which experience. Nor could he.

She shook her head. "It's the morning sickness," she said.

When she saw what he made of that, she began to laugh raucously.

"So now you do what *I* wish," he said. Meaning, marry him.

They'd had no further talk, having to dress hurriedly. The tall, makeshift scarecrow of a boy who was the group's only missionary had enthusiastically arrived. At night he recruited the love lanes; once she'd joked to Lievering that he could be their minister. "Jimmy Odgers here," he said to each couple approached. He called that up to them now, the two of them framed there in the crude window hole. "She made up her mind yet? I took me a chance." Her head and Lievering's, stuck there like Punch and Judy, had looked down on him. Hers wouldn't turn to look at Lievering's. So that's where he'd walked to. So that's the way *he* is, she thought. But he doesn't say.

Downstairs, lethargy took charge of her. No more talk. "They married to avoid talk," a Bajan neighbor woman had once said to Vivie of a local pair. Mr. Jimmy Odgers chattered on, but that wasn't talk.

When they were in his truck, the woman who'd seen to their wants came from behind the house and stood by its vine. When the truck started up she yelled something at them, fluent if not melodious. "What's she saying?" Lievering had said, through the engine racket. "I paid her." As the car wheeled around, the woman, standing stolidly, yelled it again, shaking the vine. A scab on her lip made her look as if she had two mouths.

"Good-bye—" Lievering called out. "If that's what she's saying."

Receding from them, the woman brushed her palms in riddance. Veronica, stashed in the open truck between the two men, leaned across Lievering and out the side, aping her. "Whore," she said, leaning back. "That's what she said. Didn't she, Jimmy?" She glanced at Wolf Lievering beside her. "Don't know what she called *him*."

Red-faced, their driver hadn't answered. Born a Mormon, as he'd already told them, later serving with a Catholic mission in Africa and now a part-time faculty member of a Methodist seminary in Tennessee, his ear tips were always red anyway, as if constantly tweaked by God in three forms. Bumping along the road back to the mess hall, she'd learned where the wedding would be. What she'd thrown up as a tease Lievering had tentatively acted upon, speaking privately to the missionary who had then, he now confessed, "Blowed it up to a nice big ball. People here need somepin like that."

She saw from Lievering's profile that he was appalled. Or maybe was pressing back what she was reassuring herself of—that Mr. Jimmy Odgers was still a minister in embryo. To be fair this was a fact that Jimmy himself had repressed. Still there'd been a specious uncertainty in that truck, rising from all three of them. When they had a flat tire Lievering didn't help.

By the time they reached the mess hall she'd decided to go through with it. If she was pregnant it was merely with a growing sense of herself and of the rhythm she meant to follow. She entered the hall, whose dirt floor and grub odor and general laissez-faire gave it the air of some zeppelin-sized, Eden-destined paper bag which had burst its sides, scattering garden-fresh youth, three-day-old opinions, and all this could lead to. Portals, visionary but apprehended, rose up ahead, mistily waiting for her and the others, sooner or later. She knew only that those categories one was expected to live by must have a thousand names ever freshly reincarnating—and that she would not comply.

Lievering and she, they learned, were to be married out on the fields, and as arranged by Odgers and delighted mass sentiment, on the very patch she and Lievering had worked. The marriage was to take place in the presence of everybody, which here was felt to be presence indeed. When, left alone, she searched her straw bag and this time tore open Vivie's star-papered going-away gift, her eyes smarted. Back home there was a woman on an island near theirs who made huge-sleeved blouses pieced of tiny, fluttering, leaf-sized parts, each attached at one point only. Brides queued up to buy them. Vivie had offered her two, each folded like a parachute, the one red-black, the other tawny and blue—vine and sky. She chose that one.

From the crowd of watching girls dressed in a range of work outfits dramatizing what they were here as, one girl, in khaki and clogs but capless and with a crinkled waterfall of hair, tore open packets for her to blot the road dust from her face. Getting into the spirit, another in bandanna and thongs from which swollen toes protruded brought her a bucket for her feet. She wiped her sandals herself. She always had spare jeans; no one else's ever fitted her. She let someone squirt perfume. Except in those cuddles of self-savoring which kids had, or for Lievering and the metaphor, she didn't really want to smell. It was then that the plumpie girl had sneaked up and hot-whispered her advice— to be a giver. Three glee-club-trained sisters then opened their mouths wide as fledglings and serenaded her in one angelic voice. Through all this she wondered what the men might be doing to Lievering. When she was ready she was offered a wreath crown, but refused.

When she saw him approaching her over the sharp stubble in the center of a ragtag wedding procession like her own, tenderness locked her throat. At that distance, away from his intensity and from her so recent enfoldment by it, she saw again how the beautiful head was too large for him, the rest of him a degree too small. He wore the shirt he had washed, open at the throat, and his town pants. The wreath they must have offered him was around the preacher Odgers's neck. No one could make Lievering do what he didn't want to—at least not in the small things. What he did want, that was another matter. He'd succumbed to this ritual somewhat as she had, because it coincided with rites of his own. But she would never have to pray to remember him with dignity. As he came to a halt beside her there was a tinge of irony on the near corner of his mouth. She could admit that there must be a number of categories he had escaped.

After this wedding there'd be one more. She closed her eyes for it. Odgers, maybe from unease, married them—or made his pantomime —hurriedly. "Now, do you take—" he said suddenly, from a mixture of verse and admonition, saw that bride and groom, each sunk in reverie or willfulness, might never respond, and with a mutter went on without. "By the authority vested in *you*—" Odgers said, "I pronounce you man and wife." Lievering had no ring but gave her the locket. She gave him nothing, as brides were allowed to do. And as in her heart prepared. For a minute there seemed to rise an awful brass admixture of song sadly falling off, and squawked instrument. Then much too many

cheers. Someone snapping pictures, hands high. Oh Vivie, you won't
want those.

Then she saw that the whole field had turned from her and Lievering
toward a small cortege circling the fields—a soldier on motorcycle,
followed by a soldier-driven jeep with a sole occupant, a bearded man
in the same khaki cap as those the camp issued, backed up by a very
small, monotonously tootling band. It was the Agenda, with Music.

A wave of people melted past the two of them and toward it, like
movie extras driven by a blow-horn. She was in luck. She reached out
and gave the stunned Jimmy Odgers a push. "Time to pray. Why not
to him? Castro. Looks like a good guy. Go on. Git." He seemed guiltily
glad to, not waiting to be thanked. "Why—" she quavered, watching
him spring in a wide circle, dipping elbow on the turns before he took
off straight, "he's high on something. Don't believe he is a preacher.
Want to bet he's not even ordained?" Then she was alone, with Lievering.

"Good-bye," she said. "I don't ever want to stop," she'd said. "Not like
you imagine it. But we both got our wish."

Then she ran, hobbling and slithering her way across a field that was
like a patchwork of good intentions, though in one corner a stand of
cane was still uncut. Four of the students, one morning rising earlier
than the rest to join their disgruntlement over "conditions," had been
found chanting "Stand-out, Sta-and-out," against "bosses" who they
couldn't quite be persuaded were themselves, or their representatives.
It had been a curious political fact that the four had been among the
most physically conservative in the camp as well as among the richest
—as one of the loose-smiling Bridgetown thugs had said, "People not
used to wearing each other's socks." Credit-card radicals, who'd wished
to keep the revolution as tidy as themselves, and as conventionally rich.

"Save me from organized protest meeting, rump or any other kind,"
Tom Gilpin would one day say. "If you can protest only by shooting off
your mouth *en masse* or standing on some sort of regulation, you're no
use to us. We want people who are their own protest, in every cell.
People who're surreal naturally—and I don't mean freaks. Powerful
mutants, who will never want to be the main drag. But who in spite of
themselves may end up being it." That's what Tom's ambition had been
then, though ambition was a dirty word with him. It had been appropriate that back there, hacking her way across a field and away from her
own false wedding, she'd been about to meet him for the first time. The
man who, as he sometimes told her, was the asexual influence in her life.
Who comported himself as if he meant to be that in everybody's.

When she reached the dirt road which led to the mess hall, she bent forward to a wind though there was none, stretching into a long, chopping stride; these legs of hers could run. They breezed her right into the middle of the hall before she could rein up at the sight of the two boys she thought of as thugs—punks wasn't quite the word either—going through a row of people's bags.

"Just lookin'—" the tall one named Marcy had said lazily in the American rock-singer talk they both affected. "Like the ladies in mah brother's shop." On the island his brother ran a smart boutique. "We didn't take nothin'," the fatter one, the sidekick, said. The first one clicked his teeth. "Tuh—should have done. For the symmetry." If they had, where would they put it, wearing those scroungy T-shirts and sharp, pocketless jeans? "You looking for dope?" she'd said. The side-kick had giggled, teetering. He opened his mouth wide and took out a bridge made of four or five teeth. "Got it in Amsterdam." In places it was crudely hollow. "Leaks a little," he said happily. "Look over here," Marcy said, pointing to her bag. "Miss anything?"

Against her will, she searched. "No. Yes." Vivie's other blouse. "Look down the line, missy." She didn't want to. The blouse, tucked well under, was in the third bag down, belonging to the plump girl so interested in her wedding night. "Imagine—" the other boy said, popping in his bridge. "Pinching your going-away outfit." Marcy was rescattering all the duffel bags, backpacks and suitcases in canny disorder. Spies, were they? And for whom?

At Miss Lacey's the pimps, stool-lolling in their wild livery and five-pound shoes, had talked a code as complicated as lying, though their brains were caramel—which clearly these boys' brains were not. If the two weren't pimps, which she was sure of, nor yet quite students, which she would bet on, nor merely thieves, then what profession did they belong to which gave them a tinge of all three? And whom did they work for?

"Let her have the blouse," she'd said. "Let her have him. If she can wear them. It wasn't really a wedding, was it?" She glared at them hard, convinced they would know.

"I sure suspicion not." The expression of Marcy's face was quite brotherly. Not like Ali. Like an elder brother for real.

"If it wasn't, why'd you go through with it?" The giggler had a pie-face which said nothing. Maybe other parts of him than his bridge were hollow too.

She scowled hard over his question. Why had she? Outside, strains of music were approaching—that band. And probably all the followers,

streaming after it across the fields like in some movie the extras themselves were making, on location the world, and scarier than any Hollywood. "It was on the Agenda, I guess."

They burst out laughing. Years later, bumping into them in Amsterdam, she would spend an evening with them in a café on the Singel
Canal, learning that they still spoke of her, and that two things only
counted with them: money and wit. Who they worked for was no
mystery—themselves. After that, anybody. Even Castro.

"Looky here—" she said on her wedding day, "will you help me get
to New York?"

"Go from Barbados," Marcy said.

"Vivie'd never let me. I'd have to finish out the term."

Plainly they knew of Vivie.

"Can't get to the U.S. straight from here," Marcy'd said severely,
lifting his long, cropped skull and cleft upper lip. Long gray peanut of
a boy, with smart-curved principles not good enough for his brain.

"I'll go anywhere. On the way."

"Like us." The fat one giggled.

"I've got money." She fanned out her travelers' checks and hard
dollars. Vivie'd given her the year's tuition and allowance all at once,
to put her on a par with the rich girls whose parents were money-
training them. *Not that you're not money-trained, lova-bunny. But to
have confidence.*

She'd had it—her own brand of it. She had it yet—what would others
call it? Nothing, if they didn't have it themselves. That deep fund of the
will to live, will to express, into which, when trembling, she could dip
as into a purse.

"Whee, lookit what she got," the sidekick said. "Look at all that
lovely paper."

"Lovely," Marcy said. Absently he waved the money aside. "What say
we check with his nibs? About a plane." She was made to put the money
away; on the Singel they'd laughed at how little it had been. Her ticket
back to the island was acceptable; the sidekick pocketed it. "Take your
bag with you," Marcy said. "Okay, you want to leave her the blouse?"

"I'd like to leave something here." Sky filled the mess hall's high
window. The troupe's scattered goods, from rush baskets to chromed
record players, glinted with a second-sight doubleness. Memory had
already painted this.

"Ain't you?" the sidekick had said. "Ain't you already done that?"

They led her outside the mess hall, across the beat-down grass where cars and trucks were parked hit-or-miss, and out to a break in the road, where they planted her.

"Stand just here," Marcy'd said. "Just as you are. Don't move."

Here the road branched. One way led to the village two miles away, where if you were bored with end-of-the-world talk, as some of the flightier Americans labeled the afternoon seminars, you could wander in and out of the sandy bare post office, once a chapel, where only a native could mail a letter anyway—that is if the postmistress was in attendance, instead of only her hound bitch. Or you could go into the café, as Veronica and Lievering had done, and have iceless syrup soda in which floated some slippery berry said to come from palm. The other branch of the road led to the cottage from which she had come.

Far down the road to the village she could see the trailing crowd, now almost orderly. What they were following was hidden, but must be the jeep. For some reason she felt herself to be watching a battle. Perhaps it was the way the two roads deployed, clean as map tracings under the fiery sun. Behind her, all the random vehicles seemed aimed at the post office and café, at the garbage cans, at her. Scraps of half-known battle words filled her head: advance guard, sentinel. Was that what she was? The sun beat down. The music was only distant noise now; then with a last *whang* of brass it stopped.

She'd forgotten her hat. Maybe the woman had found it by now, and adopted it. Or maybe it still lay on the nail where she herself had hung it, watching the departures of people as only objects can. Let it. She hated the thing. She began to cry for it, in hate. There was a handkerchief in her bag but she wouldn't bend for it. Stand there, they'd said. She bent her head to one of the big sleeves which puffed out on either side of her. The crossroads made a breeze here, lifting each point of cloth on them. The motion of her own dress always seemed to her part of nature's motion. As much as any of those insects called the Articulata, who were all segments, she too was bodywalk and brainwalk joined together, centered in a circle of its own traversing. She began to laugh.

Luckily. The staff car, the jeep, emerging from behind its ambush, the crowd, was bearing toward her, creeping so slowly it seemed not to move, only to be steady on the air like a mirage, in its own plane of light. The khaki figure in front, khaki-capped, held binoculars, trained on her.

Twenty yards or so from her, the jeep stopped. She held steady, estimating the yards—about the same distance she'd once measured from Vivie's island house door to their landlord's, after which their own garden could legally begin. The binoculars came on, didn't lower. She could feel the gaze behind them, not only the one known from movies of the face, or pictures, but brown and intimate, boring into her. The jeep wobbled—bad terrain, your nibs—but the hand and the gaze held firm. So did her sleeves, not billowing. The jeep came to a stop.

For a minute, she'd thought he was going to motion her into it. Instead he said something over his shoulder, from behind the binoculars. The two thugs, who were in the jeep in back, scrambled down. Then, lowering the binoculars, he doffed his cap to her, and she saw that he, too, was laughing. The brown glance was as she had felt it would be. There was a military name maybe for its mixture of geniality, chill and range. He said something. The jeep wheeled at his signal, ground the dirt and took off.

The two boys ambled toward her, looking the same as before; they might have just dropped off a bus. They'd stayed that casual the whole time, all the way to the plane.

"What did he say?" She wasn't going to leave this to guesswork.

The sidekick answered for them. "He said, 'With those sleeves, *she* should fly.'" He doubled up on the grass, then got up and scampered; his bridgework must be leaking again—he was high.

"It was him, wasn't it?" she said. Nimbly, so that she could withdraw the joke if need be. "Castro."

"Naw, he has a stand-in," the sidekick said, blowing on a grass blade he'd plucked. "They switch shifts at the barbershop."

"Come on, both of you," Marcy said. Then he did make them run, but only for fun, when they went back to steal Jimmy Odgers's truck. Locked, but the sidekick had a ploy for it.

They drove leisurely after that. "Fifteen miles," Marcy said. "No hurry. They'll telephone ahead."

"Telephone?" she said. "How?" None for miles. The crowd had grumbled. One scared kid had left. Needed his wiring.

Marcy, who was driving, tapped her chin with his free hand. "Walkie-talkie."

This time she was too proud to ask to whom.

The airfield was ragged with plants, like small airports one still saw on Long Island in those days. Out here it contained itself in its own hard gray air. "This isn't Havana," Marcy said to her. "Plane's an oldie. You game?"

Three smallish planes were on the runway, each of a different shape. They're planes in a dream, she thought. I won't have any trouble. "Where's it going?"

"Honduras. You can make New York from there."

She smiled. In dreams they didn't tell you.

Getting on the plane, while Marcy was in with the pilot making sure, the sidekick slipped her a packet she got rid of her first trip to the lav; it was hash. "Guy sitting next to you's going to New York," Marcy said, returning. She hadn't had to pay. "Compliments of the management." Neither had the rest of the scanty passenger list. It was a government plane. "So, toodle on, Sister 'Ronica." Acid-yellow irises, set in his lanky skeleton, gave him a dandy's look, or as if a painter had arranged him. "Keep up on all points." He hopped off.

The plane had been ancient, with velvet couch seats that seated three and braided blinds that pulled down. Her only seatmate, who was Tom Gilpin, caught her noting them. "From the old Tempelhof-Moscow run, the pilot says. New engines. He swears." She had no idea how far back that dated the plane, or under what circumstances, but was flattered her seatmate took for granted she did. She would later find that the world's hip travelers had a common fund of round-the-globe informa- tion, extending even to certain "in" acquaintances—journalists, photog- raphers and other media people for whom travel remained as much ego as business—and especially so among Americans, who even yet seemed not to "have" their travel as nonchalantly as other nations. Living and working among them, she would acquire some of that ferment. Mean- while seeing how this same sophistication, adopted in one's greenhorn years, could emerge in the successful of her trade, often still technically young, as a royally deadened innocence that kept them from those very "sources"—strange roots and sailors' warnings—which best fed their profession.

That day, knowing none of this, she'd accepted Tom's courtesy to the young for what it was, not suspecting in him deeper agonies of kindness. He'd seemed to blend untroubledly with the era of the plane—if he'd had a homburg, as perhaps one of those gentleman philosophers of Karl Marx's London, dapper with intellect, whose photos were in Lievering's office at the college. Or like one of D. H. Lawrence's Laborite-socialite co-weekenders in an English country cottage—on Lievering's other wall—if he'd had a cap. Later she would know that he always blended. He never wore the homburg. Or the cap.

When the middied stewardess came by, he'd said quietly, "Note, she has real cartridges in that silly belt, poor girl." And in a minute Veronica and he were talking, laughing. She told him about the group she'd just left. "They don't want a revolution," he said. "That kind just wants to be intimate with one. The way some romantics want to be, with crime.

They're political—prurients." He wasn't surprised she knew the word, only charmed when he heard from where—a Sunday-school tract "against lewd and prurient practices," hung behind the bar at Miss Lacey's. He was the kind told you true things; you had to be reciprocal. She told him a good many, omitting Lievering. She'd go back to finish at the university later, she said. But for a while, she'd work; she didn't yet know at what.

"I was an escapee once, from Harvard." She was awed. "From there? I don't see why." He'd chortled. "You're right. I've always said it that way. But it is pretentious."

At the time, he'd had a reddish mustache and beard later shaved— he'd been in the Middle East and acquired a skin infection. He'd been to China early on, also. And yes, this was a government plane. To Honduras, where she could pick up a plane to New York. He hadn't asked how she had boarded; maybe he'd seen. "You a friend of Castro?" she'd asked. "I met him," Tom had answered. "He's easy to meet. No, I just came to observe." He did that everywhere—"to complete my Harvard education," he said, grinning. "Maybe my mind's so open there's nothing left in it but a draft. Shaw said that, I've heard. Probably bamboozling his audience into thinking it a bad thing." He was like some of the British residents in Barbados, she thought, rich enough to eat cities like candy—and wasn't startled to hear that before going to New York, where he lived, he was stopping off at Palm Beach. "To settle my mother's estate while she's still alive," he'd said, smiling. "She wants to live in France."

What was his regular work? "Settling my father's." He sobered. "Not quite the same. He left me an island—in a way. He was a fisherman." But soon he was going to "gainfully employ" some "boys and girls" to refurbish a newspaper-magazine. "Leftist?" she'd said cannily. He took a pineapple juice from the tray the stewardess was holding out to them. "Left of what?" He pointed to the stewardess' belt. "Her?" No, he'd said. "Can't hack anything political anymore." He voluntarily etymologized "hack" for her. "Afraid some of my vocabulary congealed at the prep-school level. Because I never went to one."

Ailpen, she thought he'd said his name was. His voice walked on New England stilts, finickily distant but polite. Telling her, as she sat there with her newly married thighs hugged tight so that their sated wet wouldn't stain the socialist velvet she was being flown free of charge on, that the Age of Politics—"Capitalize that"—was over. "Outmoded. Gone. Political theory of any kind. Just packing the belly with diamonds real or fake. Can't feed, can't cure. Only kill us, throe by throe.

No, just give me a news sheet to publish for a while. I don't want a cause."

She sensed he was talking to her the way one might to a person one would never see again. "What'll you put in it, then?" she said, dazzled. The stewardess was offering them lunch. He waved it aside for both of them, producing delicious sandwiches with some native relish in them, fruit he said was a variety of loquat, and finally a flask, all from the sloping pockets of what she saw now was the softest approximation of an ordinary business suit, mulberry brown, fine-woven to appear coarse, made sloppy with special care. The flask held iced wine. She slid into luxury easily; Vivie'd always said she would. Though hanging onto his words as if to a shelf. Not everybody fed you them. "Now to your question." He accepted coffee for both of them, smacking his lips over the deep bean flavor, looking at her grampa-thoughtful over his cup. His eyes were red-brown, fox-hazed like the rest of him—like maybe even his tongue. "We have the power," he'd said. "Ideas will come."

Later on she would know, as all the office did, that he talked like that —professionally—only to new recruits or other amateurs, being himself, as he said, the extreme of those. "Part of the open mind, to be that." With the experts of anything he kept a polite distance. "They're all old." But that too was a pose. Or a ploy.

Originally, his money might have embarrassed him. There were times when he hopped athletically from one non-pose to another. But underneath, like an iceberg—whose chill his own could resemble—he had seemed to her to grow ever solider. Inside him, somewhere in that flickering underwater bulk drilled with light, there was concealed—she was sure of it—a cause.

"A good question, yours," he'd said. "But I can see you don't think mine a good answer."

"It scares me."

"As it should." A forefinger smelling of orange rind tipped up her chin. "Run scared," he said. "We all do. But *run*."

She froze. But only because the last man to touch her had been Lievering.

The stewardess came over to her, apprehensive.

"It's all right," he said to her, "I'm non-molesting. This is an interview. Cold."

The attendant, a ripe girl, tall for these parts, with strained eyes, shook her head at them worriedly.

"Really not," the reddish man said rapidly. "I like women. But they fit the anatomy so exclusively. While the males now, they want to own your mind—homosexually. And the world's." Ostensibly he was talking to the stewardess, picking up and reflecting over each bottle on her tray; of course he was talking through her at Veronica. He set down a juice bottle, shaking his head. "Mind you, I'm not cold. Just thoughtful."

His intelligence was reddish, too, the girl had said to herself. Open in manner as a moss rose, but flushed with its own secret pigment. Generous to the blush-point, but furtive on all its inner action, even the best. She had views on what pigment did to thought. (Since then altered some, but maybe not too wrong on Gilpin. He was still fond of the word "cold.") He'd turned his modest, cool glance back to her. "Perhaps I'm nearest to a—paedophile."

In those days, words she didn't know could make her angry. But also, the trapped stewardess had been near tears. "We no 'ave." She wailed it like an aria. "We no 'a-ave it. Coke." Then had fled up the aisle.

"Listen—" Veronica had said to him. "I don't care what you are. You know any Cuban Spanish? Whatever that girl speaks? Go up there, then. Apologize to her. Say something nice." He'd gone and done that presumably; she'd seen him talking up there at the head of the aisle; had heard the stewardess's Carmen-laugh. So he could speak—something. But when he returned, Veronica was sitting across the aisle instead of next to him.

"Want to know what I said to her?"

She shrugged.

"I said—" His eyes drooped inward. "Maybe I said—I'd kiss her, if she weren't wearing those cartridges."

She'd been sure from his expression that he hadn't. In after years, once they'd been reunited, he'd continued the joke: "Want to know what I really said to that stewardess?" he'd say, leaning over her desk at the office (never at his home parties, where he was always formal and oddly circumspect). Then he'd manage something outrageous, or interesting.

On the plane she merely nodded, returning to her scrutiny of the woman on her right, a beautiful mixed-Asian, lithe in a Western black silk shift, on whose bared copper arms and neck yards of eely gold lifted like gills with each rise of the plane.

"You're right—I'm rude," he'd said, settling behind his newspaper, a British one.

The Eurasian was talking to the man on her other side, with whom she was traveling, but from time to time she and Veronica had covert female communication by glance, the woman eyeing Veronica's blouse, the girl wide-eyed at the woman's feet, whose rubied claw-toenails curved over her sandals, long as guitar picks, ending her body in two pronged, erotic paws. She would walk arching each foot, the hip following, Veronica thought—her own body power aroused—and according to the earth-matter beneath her would shuffle, scrape, or click. And saunter best down a staircase. She was no feminist's riddle; she was any woman's. For years after, striding a city pavement or lugging a flight bag, Veronica would remember her.

Furtively she had opened Lievering's locket. It was empty. As it should be.

From behind the newspaper, Tom's card had been dropped in her lap. "Interview successful. Want a job?" He ducked inside the newspaper before she could answer. In the moment that the plane had begun its descent on Honduras she saw by the card that his last name was Gilpin (assumed, she'd somehow thought, until the telephone book showed her many Gilpins), and she saw one brownish pupil mischievously regarding her through an eyehole poked in the air edition of the *Manchester Guardian*, above a column headlined: *Paedophile Society Civil Servant Loses Case*. Child-lover, the word must mean; the civil servant being revealed in the column as president of a society which advocated sex with children, for which reason attempts were being made to oust him from his job at the Post Office, though by due process of law. "Den of sin, the P.O.'s—" Tom said, lowering the newspaper. "Always a cover for the sinister. Pals who bury the mater alive on Sunday, sharpshooters who pick off lovers' trysts." The picture of the civil servant was nothing like Tom nor the news story either. Still, it would be three years on, and she almost a year out of college, before, picking up the odd, intransigent weekly which was becoming her favorite, she saw the name of its publisher, and got in touch.

At that time he lived with a woman called by the single name Purvis, a neutered beauty more like a pet swan than a companion, who had silvered hair and wore blackish lipstick, glided now and then into his parties and, like many "art" photographers, lived silently in a welter of recorded music while printing into reasonable life what the rest of the world saw humbly with the disjointed eye.

Meanwhile Tom, whose paper foretold the death of coherent personality and a coming world of freebooting and free-associating instincts, lived a life organized to the last soap bubble, receiving both at home and office the crisply moral service once accorded nineteenth-century overseers. As for children, she'd never seen him with a young child, but had once heard him call them "the ultimate amateurs," and there was a column in *The Sheet* which was run by them. Otherwise—as he often asked the staff sardonically—wasn't he living the lives they all were? Modernist men and women, eager to swap communication for meaning, shadow for substance; purposefully aberrent and uncohered, preferring to live in the small mental huts provided for by nothingness, on the grounds that these were always enlarging.

Mightn't he himself be that powerful mutant he had once described? One of those personalities who could be found waving prophetically from the quicksand of any era?

In the longish apartment in which he and Purvis lived, a dun progression of rooms budding one from another in the old-fashioned West Side of New York way, there seemed to be no one room devoted solely to either person or any function. If he and she did sleep together, they could have done so in any room of the house. Clothes and other possessions, though always neatly accessible, were kept anywhere, in cupboards scattered throughout like dower chests standing ready to remind these two absent-minded chatelains of the normal duties of dress and ownership. Music was piped. Regular meals were eaten out or brought in and the two secretaries who saw to all this on double shift had an office in a smaller flat on another floor, as did the photographer her darkroom. Tom, so far as could be seen, had no personal office either here or at the newspaper. None of this seemed to have been done from any of the "decorator" impulses which made other people formally display their life stances.

So it was managed that Tom could commute between office and home in the thinking cell of himself with a minimum of personal friction and in the mulberry medium-weight non-clothes he continued to have made in replica—and that, so sustained, he could go everywhere and did, seeing by turns all the movies, print exhibitions and any other form of human endeavor, making all the city-influential committees and the national ones, knowing all "the" people, plus many who were not, and as she knew, reading well into all the books.

When traveling, he disappeared fruitfully under an even finer-grained version of this life plan, which saw to it that although he traveled much and unorthodoxly, the publicity never got to him. Publicly, he was known for—and in the usual way, heckled or given kudos for—*The Sheet.* Years were to go by, with Tom as their tartly frivolous, lazily dependable sponsor of ideas so popularly anti-popular as to be nearly invisible, before she saw how signally his mode of life left all the avenues of influence open to him while he earned no reputation for it.

Parties he gave sporadically, also in the name of *The Sheet*. "Parties are non-negotiable," he'd said. "Benign blockages. In the canals of human friendship." Yet, from any vantage she knew of he was a fast friend, even to Rhoda, to whom he often let drop those very remarks —because she wouldn't understand them?—which Veronica early began to save for her own image of him. "Learning to live undersea of politics—" he'd said when Rhoda grabbed him to protest the paper's lack of interest in the heads of nations, "—is not too far from learning how to conduct oneself without the pull of gravity." And when Rhoda took him to task for their lack of coverage on Russian bomb capacity: "Talk about the end of the world has such a bad effct on people these days, don't you think? Makes them so nervy about their bank accounts."

Which made Rhoda ask the others whether he meant people wouldn't buy the paper, or he'd run out of income for it? For as fast as it made up expenses, he doubled them. His maternal grandfather's money had in fact been based on paper mills. "Paper to paper, in three generations," he'd say, grinning, and some wag had had it lettered over a door. The younger staff did agree that he wasn't mystic in any of their modern ways, and only tepidly self-investigative. "Yoga?" he'd said in answer to a devotee. "That's for self-violinists. Along the muscle path. There're others." During her own tenure (now one of the longest, for those hired as promising in one direction usually left him in order to fulfill that promise in another), among the groups he'd sponsored with more encouragement than money had been a Puerto Rican boys' soccer team and a Yorkville girls' folk-dance group, each of whose members casually called on him and were chatted to without barrier, but to whose events he never went. "Children are curative," he'd said of the paper's column, "for about as much as we can bear." One office verdict on his sex life was: "Polymorphous? Possibly. But not perverse enough to practice it." He had a bad word or a comic one for most every human institution, yet never an incendiary one. Where in all this, then, was the "cause"?

When she'd come for the job, going to his office in between her modeling assignments and finding him listening to the life story of an émigré Czech carpenter who was hanging some shelves, his first words to her were, "That tall. I'd no idea. Your pictures don't show it." At Honduras he'd left the plane ahead of her, not from rudeness but to leave her to herself, and had never seen her standing up. Yet obscure as her work as a model still was, he'd followed it.

"How are you with the camera yourself?" he said, meanwhile watching the carpenter delicately insert a thin sliding shelf. She'd felt as if she already worked there and had merely come in to confer. "My head's my camera," she said. The carpenter was now feeling the dowel of a drawer, taking out a file. "You don't mind the emotions of that?" Tom said, faintly smiling, still eyeing the carpenter, who was working on with the jauntiness of an expert under watch. When she opened her mouth to answer somehow, Tom put a finger to his lips. All this time she'd felt as if she was being calibrated. They'd stayed on until the man, with a final caress to the small finials which ended each shelf, touched his cap and left. "He works slowly and wonderfully," Tom said. "No contractor will hire him." Later, both office and Tom's house had broken out in aisles of the misty woodwork, until a staffer had grumbled, "I'll be here tomorrow in a powdered wig and black beauty patch," after which the man disappeared, and they were all guilty for it. "Go on, Tom's just set him up privately," Rhoda accused. "A palliative," Tom said. "It's one of the burdens of my mental life—that I have the means for them."

Standing waiting back there, she'd burst out, "Well? Am I hired?" He'd grinned. Though beard and mustaches were gone, and had never been more than brown, that foxy tinge was still on him, aged a little to auburn. "You've been working here all this time. In my head."

She'd answered that camera question correctly then. She was often to do that, not knowing why. She'd known from the first that she wasn't one of his palliatives—though to be certain, she was to work independently hard enough to become *The Sheet*'s star—and that the job was no prelude to her sleeping with him. Over the years of her employment, as their cool intimacy developed, she felt that whatever he'd been once, he was almost asexual now, and working toward that as ultimate. Perhaps for the same hidden reason that he'd recently absolved himself from the politics which would have been so natural to his temperament, and was now toying with non-gravity—for by pulling some Washington strings, he'd spent time in one of those whirligigs with which they tested astronauts.

"Like getting a blood test," he'd shrugged. "Just wanted to know." And hadn't told the results.

At his parties, where she was sure he was learning too, storing up something as simple as one-two-three if she could fathom it, she'd studied his art collection, hunting for the missing work of the woman who lived there. Whose story was revealed easily enough one Christmas when Purvis vanished to the mental hospital he'd taken her from as the penniless daughter of a deceased friend. "She wants to be a man," he said, with one of his fuzzy blushes for his own generosity, not for the woman. "I'd've, hmm, paid for it, but they don't think she's—well enough. So by choice she's gone back. Her own works are all in the darkroom; there'll be a show of them. Which might help. Very violent stuff—she'll only show them when she's inside; isn't that interesting?" He'd patted the cheek of the youngest researcher, who wore her lover's diamond around her neck and his baby beneath her belt. "The world wants to change, too, but it's not yet well enough."

Had it struck any of the others at the Christmas party that by now they knew of dozens of tales happening in and around him, of which the keynote was always the same? "I'm nobody's confidant, just a repository," he warned. "And not always a silent one." For interchange was the modern way, he said, and people liked to bank on it. Of her own life he knew as much as necessary—which was the way she thought of it, and which had included Lievering.

She might tell him about Mulenberg, the man who had just left here, if she so chose, though because of Ollie she might not. Or, to dig deeper, because she was fighting against thinking of that man by name. But Tom knew her sexual sentiments, and would have guessed the style of her sexual life, though she never gave details. "Women too should be able to forage in that style," she'd said. "You're one of the ones who can," he'd replied. "Your professional life gives you the opportunity, the range—just like the men. And your looks. But they have tacit social approval. It's one sort of male style—recognized." And then more keenly: "For a woman to be the aggressor, selector of strangers—and without witnesses to confirm her choice of style—that would take a special inner cohesion. Wouldn't it? Almost another warmth—to replace the warmth?"

She'd all but confessed about the poem, saved only by an instinct that confession would disperse it, probably forever. As long as she had the poem, she could tell him, or the world, everything else. "You're my confirming witness," she'd said.

The second stanza of the poem was the poorest; maybe the period when she wrote it wasn't yet digestible, begun as it had been in the exciting limbo of her first jobs in New York. All those jobs had been in the back of something—a dry-cleaning store, a showroom on Seventh Avenue, and finally the Mercantile Library where she was dustily happy handling this merchandise, and was sometimes awarded unbelievably

odd but touching throw-outs, dead but smudged with eternal life—
histories of the ewer and milch cow, patterns for the bustle, and a
prospectus for an early computer: *Improved Mechanisms for Performing Multiplication by the Process of Repeated Additions—acc. G. Leib-
niz*—which she brought home to the "superintendent's room" in the
basement of Vivie's house.

She was the superintendent, on a promise to Vivie that she would go
up to Ollie's at least for baths. And so keep an eye on him. This she did
only when she couldn't stomach the public bath. The first time she'd
gone up, four of his girls, seizing upon her like a hostage—"You got no
tub down there, miss?"—had dunked and powdered her; no gang-bang,
but not knowing who she was they thought she'd sneaked her passkey
on the sly. Then they'd repentantly squirted perfume on her. So she had
learned their ethnography, noting how their slippage from better mi-
lieus was already or almost a fact, in their too suddenly loosed charity,
in the squealing rite they'd made of her and the foolish revenge they
took in it, in their delight in any unfounded event intruding on their
flesh-dull afternoon.

She was mostly dirty in those days, and drunk on solitude. Working
in the backrooms of whites, living below pavement behind a railed
window where a cosmopolis walked by at ankle level, she was saved
from hermitdom but freed from talk. At times she broke into poetry the
way other people broke into sweat. She didn't think of herself as a poet.
Like a menses, the attack came only at times, sometimes in those days
after her real menses, as in later days it would sometimes come after
a man. During that long-ago time, poor and solitary as she was, it didn't
seem to her that she was forgetting her dream of converging on the city
in all her powers; she thought she was accomplishing this. It had been
the vortex, and she had loved being there.

Then came a second limbo—with Vivie sick again, and she herself
returning to the university down there, to do her three more years'
degree stint in two, all the while with the remembered brass fire of the
city at her back. Lievering was gone from the island; he'd never come
back, nor had the university ever heard from him. Bruce, who'd since
been to Cuba, reported no news of him there. He could have left for
anywhere, with one of the American groups. It was what he would have
done, finding sudden truth in one or another of their allegiances, and
on their instance, or through his own fertile passivity, someone to drive
him handily across a sea—though possibly, when they got to the boardinghouse where he would live, or the school where he was newly to

teach, it would be found to have been burnt to ash. She couldn't further imagine him, except as a man with a borrowed Aer Lingus bag, hung against the sky of his own traveling.

Down there she'd picked and picked at the new stanza brought with her, just as when a kid she'd used to suck the chicken carcass until Vivie wrested it from her. But the stanza stayed as it was. Memory couldn't add more meat.

Down the hill the pianos still gape in Steinway's;
A salesman stands festooned. It's always noon there,
The walls are garlands where nothing sells.
The past works hard on Heimweh street
In halls that once we scribble at old scores.
Yonder, behind that window empty as a cracked harp, was a hall
  called the Aeolian;
In front of the new church store full of blond epigrams
Is a brass hydrant the bums love.
As the gods arrive, the pianos are leaving.
At teatime the traffic chatters Kafka
To a loud sunset. Hung on it is the quiet earring
Of the battering ram knocking down the old hotel.
In after-lecture fever
Japanese faces pompon midnight, as we walk home
(You have the landscape you're leaving
You have the living you get, all in all)
Miss Lacey is gone again, from Carnegie Hall.

Then she'd graduated, Vivie sitting blue-lipped in the auditorium in a nest of her adoring clients, all of whom, invited over Bruce's protesting whistle, and to Vivie's answering, "What you care, man? You sit *on* the platform," had sent cash presents also, as Vivie had known they would. The little British bounder looked forlorn without his big dogs. The two gentlemen, holding hands, had exclaimed in high voices at the beauty of the Bejan girl graduates. The lord's American wife, wearing a hat perhaps intended to camouflage her Stateside liberal opinions, came up and spoke in low tones to the diplomaed Veronica of her proud duties to come as "the emissary of your race." "Yes, ma'am," she said to the lady—"like you are, down here." And pressing a little song she'd written for the two men into the hand of one of them, and bending to kiss the green-jumpsuited little Englishman—"For the dogs"—she'd then flown home on the bounty of all of them. To get the job she shouldn't have doubted Gilpin would have kept for her. Then she'd flown back and brought the dying Vivie home.

"I'm always dying," Vivie had bounced at a too commiserating island neighbor, but up here in New York she couldn't believe she was settling down to it. "Someday, take me with you on that job of yours," she'd say. "What we races do to each other don't get melted down to scratch by a good job—but how it helps." Veronica herself began to realize the gradations of what it had meant to this high-nosed, charged woman to cook or not to cook. One of Vivie's forebears had been a white Bermuda landholder whose daughter by a native had in turn "housekept" for a white Jamaican hotel owner. "No Spanish in me. Your half-tone person always likes to claim some, your father used to say." She talked more now of the father.

Veronica recalled him as a giant of a man, with a calm maintained at high speed. A parliamentarian since the age of twenty-six, he'd been in the habit of saying that he'd always meant to take time out for race prejudice, but something else always came up. "I have got absolutely no prejudice against myself," he used to tease. "That's where people of color get it worst." But when he was crossed unfairly, or saw unfairness exerted against others of the race, the whites of his eyes turned oxblood. "You ever know," Vivie said, "the year you were born, your mother and father, he was in Rome for the FAO, they lived in a palace?" The ground floor of it, a UN rental. The girl had been shown pictures of the palely frescoed rooms, scantily furnished with huge pre-Victor Emmanuel sofas whose cracked-gilt curves exploded at the lens. "Your people always lived well."

After an attack, high on her crumpled pillows like a deposed queen, earrings awry, Vivie talked faster the more narrowly she'd escaped death; the megalomania was coming out in her, for "my girl." Like a last tenderness for me, her girl thought, kneeling at the side of the bed, fist clenched over the pill bottle. A tender oozing formed in her, for all the put-upon, living in courage, dying in protest, with all their passion for a wider expanse spread out exaltedly before them. The heart in Vivie's breast was breaking into floral offering. "Your father said I wasn't ever to hold you back from your own terrors, just because I didn't have them." Eyes closed, Vivie snorted. The heart beat visibly. Her girl laid her other hand on it.

They'd come back also to an Ollie changed to Ali by the turban whose expertise he demonstrated for them. Standing in front of Vivie's triple-paneled dressmaker's mirror with his arms stretched wide holding taut the two ends of snowy cloth, if he wasn't quite an Indian, nor an angel nor a devil, he did seem of a genus almost his own. When the turban's fat peak was complete he stuck a glass topaz at the crest, ramming in the stickpin so jauntily that it drew blood from his scalp; all his actions were flawed alike. Full-face, his upper lip was a cupid's bow nearly touching his nose. Glossy words came often from it, never outright lies. In contrast, when he was in a scrape his silences were thick with little peripheral fears from which Vivie would have to puzzle out what the main chance had been, and what had gone wrong with it.

Grinding her chair roughly back, she strode to the kitchenette, opened the fridge on the food party waiting there—what had possessed her, to buy two of this, two of that?; she wasn't hungry for any of it—slammed the door, and poured herself a club soda. To the left of the tiny counter, in the wall just above, a black mouthpiece protruded, the intercom between this flat and Ali's just above. Quick as that man had been, he hadn't noticed it. If she let her mind loose on him, she could imagine him and his life in more detail than he would believe, fleshing him out from others of his kind he might be superior to, yet still resembled. But don't dwell on him. By letting him be the first to come here, hadn't she already changed this place—since Vivie's death kept solely for the desk's contents and all allied broodings—into just that "little suite" she'd downgraded to him?

Meanwhile, knowing damn well that the idea of such a place, nested in the heart of the city and for her adventures alone, had excited her ever since Ali used to take her to those other more "executive" suites. With her orange lamps and the misty gray curtains shopped for like any bride, she'd made the place a hope chest for illicit weddings with the unknown, a den which only a certain diffidence and leanness of taste had kept short of the sordid. Was there any difference between her and him because this place was primped with books? Or because, unlike Ali, she didn't use it for livelihood?

Hers was a woman's fantasy. On the same level as any roving male's, but not stopping there—and poignant against her own will. For, in the fantasies of most women, these fests were never communal, jolly and shared, but private; their little magic carpets were still designed for only one guest.

Her own harsh laugh startled her. He hadn't liked that laugh—the man. Vivie too had always been at her to change it consciously, the way you'd change a name that didn't go with your beauty. But the laugh came from her cells, satirical. She put her mouth to the intercom and blew.

If her stepbrother, who always proudly referred to himself as "a 4 A.M. person," did prowl beyond the hours of even his raunchy crowd, this was partly because his milkweed energies collected late. According to Vivie, when he was a boy she couldn't get him up in the morning either for school or fun, and one exasperated afternoon had brought in all the neighborhood boys to see him drowsing in his tousled bed, hugging the pillow like a girl. The ruse had only put him farther outside the pale of ordinary boys. To Vivie's rage, he'd liked it there.

Perhaps there were even certain body rhythms, after-evening cycles, which helped make you a pimp. Ali the grown man complained to his mother that he wasn't "Garuda evil"—referring to the Thai devil doll he kept to scare the girls upstairs—but merely "fancy-chancy" in his tastes, meaning that his spirit oozed most comfortably into corners where moral standards were relaxed. His ever-pubescent good looks put the seal on that, as Veronica herself knew good looks could, verging with you to emphasize any path you took. Ali's skin color, though, which could pass for a number of indeterminate races, allowed him more experiment with truth. Long before she'd realized it, her stepbrother had served as her spore collector down among some of the world's dirty businesses she'd been spared but ought to know about. For this she was grateful to him. He'd saved her from being an aristocrat—the fake one that Vivie otherwise would have made of her.

As for Ali's rites with women, luckily his sadisms must be as relaxed as the rest of him, at their worst little social cruelties. Beyond that, there were many males not pimps who liked to have a woman only once. She understood this, or had. She'd brought men "home" in many parts of the world—hotels, apartments borrowed or rented for her travels, only never here. "Slap death a little, after I'm gone," Vivie had said. Her pupils had glazed, never her brain. "Young ones have to." Make this place yours, she meant; she'd known how much it wasn't yet. So— seized by that man's eyes, so ready to own the city as he stood on those steps, by that lion hair of his so maverick to the "business" rest of him, and most of all by the mane of travel floating behind him so clear—she'd told herself she was courting him as the first candidate, to make the home-place hers.

Ali wasn't answering. Barred from here, he probably never now listened for the intercom. After his mother's death, unable to come to Vivie either for the advice he asked for after the deed like a chaser after whisky, but never took, or for the bail money, which he did, he'd started coming to Veronica, until she'd at last shut him out. The house had been left to them jointly—by that same Vivie who'd sworn "on your father's head, and mine" to keep her girl from "Ollie's muck." After years of waiting for him to change, she'd finally conceded there was nothing to wait for. "When I'm gone, let him go." Yet in the end she had bound them together, in one of those counter-actions with which people both denied the whole tenor of their lives and admitted it.

Like me, she thought. Like mine. The unknown is harder for a woman to acquire. When will I learn that mock weddings are not the way to it?

She bent her head to the next stanza, of which, though it wasn't done yet, though nothing in the manuscript was final, she was beginning to be proud.

> Upstairs, as the man and I bedlock, the alley panes blaze.
> Is that three zombies combing their hair,
> Or three hairy pots on the windowsill
> Of those boys who give harlequin cookouts?
> (Two pairs of opera glasses lying there, and a riding crop)
> And no wonder, with the MONY time-tower opening its dark
>   redoubt
> On a climbing string of light it douses again, dickering
> Like a stepmother letting you in, closing you out.
> Alto night birds scream in the late coffee shop
> "Look boy, you gave me a nigger cigar!"
> What's that mean? Why's there always a 2 A.M. pistol shot
> But never a 6 A.M. corpse?
> Toward morning the harbor's talking,
> Grave hulls at sea, yawing broad thoughts.
> The avenue rings with heels, like an apse,
> Society shadows the streets, the nation begins living,
> The day ferry jams the pier, the fur stores kneel in prayer.
> This street never wears out.
> Nothing too big for it, nothing too small.
> But how will Lacey come again, to Carnegie Hall?

With this addition the poem became a poem—she was almost sure of it. And the next stanza—would there be one? From day to day she was never sure. What would happen there? Each stanza so far was an era. One could never see at the time the eras of one's life. To say "Lacey,"

not to call her "Miss"—that was a change. She was concerning herself
with that when the downstairs buzzer was pressed.

Who? . . . *My name is Mulenberg . . . Oh no, you don't. The night's
over. I've shut you out.*

Then she heard the elevator, sighing upward. To get to it, if no one
upstairs answered your buzz, you had to have a key.

Ollie, then. She was glad—that she was glad.

Sly, loose, mean—though never to her—and sweet (for until her teens
he'd been the most beguiling companion), yes, he lived in the mulch
between good and bad, and had taught her it was there. Yet he had an
odd loyalty to what he was, a need to be consistent with it. Reject him
from your life, as she and Vivie, clasped in desperation, had once tried
to do, and you carried him like a stone in your consciousness, as if you'd
resisted a natural force—which perhaps you had. The elevator passed
her floor, sighing. Why'd he rung the buzzer then? Here it came, the
old confusion, hot and binding, the shifty yoke Ollie always brought
along with him. Behind her, the intercom sibilated. "Sister?"

He's safe. He's home. But don't answer. Don't get into it. Better to
carry the stone.

"Y-yes, Ollie?"

"*Shhh-h-h.* I must come down. And speak to you."

She clasped her hands tight. "Okay."

"Lis-sen. Doose the lights."

How Irish the Bejan accent sometimes sounded. It could pass for
Anglo-Indian, leftover Hindustani or what-have-you; the old Empire on
his tongue served him well. Whenever he had to light out, he fled to
corners of that empire, small islands or outposts, never to the continents. In her own travels she'd encountered other people who too were
bits and drifts of the Empire, as she was in part herself. Empires didn't
stop all at once, but turned human and fragmentary.

Ten minutes went by. Fifteen. Twenty. One of the things Ollie always
did was to make you wait. Learn to wait.

He was there, scratching at the peephole. The minute she opened up
and let him into the room he grabbed her wrist and led her quickly into
the walk-in closet in the bedroom. He was always at ease in the dark;
was that why his friends kept him on?

"There—" he whispered. "You can turn on the light now."

She fumbled unwillingly for the string. Disaster from his second-rate
crimes never touched his Roman-silk suits. Would blood have fallen on
Ollie? Did she want to see that, or not?

He'd changed to his flight uniform, so who could tell? The vanilla suit and turban were gone. Sharp jeans and two sweaters now, the string one and the cardigan, and the Fendi shoulder bag. An admiring twinge pricked her. He dressed for travel better than anybody. Except her.

"You forgot to change shoes." Tawny suede, high-heeled and buckled.

He hadn't been able to bring himself to. Or to divest himself of his rings. Garish ten-carat love knot or true green-gold scarab, fake solitaire and dim carnelian Greek seal from the first century, he'd kept them all.

Why was he looking at her that way? Pityingly.

"You'll have to get out of here," he said hoarsely. "By tonight."

When he saw she couldn't answer, he smoothed her cheek. "They'll be coming to wreck this place."

Vivie and she had lived under the shadow of many such "theys." "So you got out of the washroom."

His neck arched like a cat's. "She came here, the c——?" He always curbed his tongue to her. She was Sister. "Where'd she go?"

"Back to her Queens bar. In Mamma's gold dress."

"Mamma's— The one I gave her? What the hell you—?"

"She had to change too."

He put his hand to his mouth.

"You help kill him?"

He shook his head. "But they know I know who." From behind the hand, sludgily. Above the hand his eyes, brown and humid, were from a father Vivie'd never identified. Veronica's own father hadn't much wanted to give him their name, confiding wryly, People'll think he's mine.

"I'll have to make a clean break," he said. "This time."

This time. He'd never said that before. The times were always separate, always a surprise to him.

"Where'll you go?"

"Better you don't know." He always said that, heroically. Then came the letters for money, loud and plain, in between hints of return. Money to come back, money to stay—all the same money, Vivie said, and said. By the time he did come back it was all over, for one more time.

The weak bulb shone down on him.

So many things they knew of together, no matter what. For a moment she dreamed there, discounting what he'd said about the place. One of his little fears, which were relieved the minute he'd confessed them. "You hungry?" she said absently. What Vivie always said to either of them—the only way she showed her feelings. Before you go, let me pack you a lunch.

"I ate," he said, listless. "After they left. The restaurant. Safest place."

She recoiled. Garments hung behind her pressed against her, clustering. "You—ate?"

"He took them for four hundred thousand," he said. "I introduced him. I never thought he couldn't pay." His head swiveled away, then back. "I didn't have my gun, you know. By the way—where is my gun?" He fisted her lightly above the breast, half grinning winsomely. Vivie had always been stealing his gun, for his own protection. His sister was becoming the surrogate in spite of herself. He knew.

"I'll have to turn on the bedroom light."

"Okay, dolly. I'll stay here."

In the bedroom, taking the gun from the corner where she'd blindly stashed it again, she was arrested by the calling card lying on the bed. Smiling, she picked it up. So that's how he spells his name, without an *h*. And yes, there it was—the address: One Gulf & Western. She gave it a peculiar smile. She knew well enough that you couldn't see it from here.

How clean the card looks, how businesslike, almost chill. Just the name and the address, not even the company. A million miles away, and who knows how many dollars, from lives full of—clean breaks. She left it on the bed. Dousing the light.

Ollie was looking up at all her old files, stacked on shelves built around pipes which led upstairs to his kitchen. Not a good place for them, as she knew. "Here—" she said behind him.

He whirled around. "Jesus . . . Oh . . . I'm all jumps. . . . Thanks." The gun went in a sweater pocket at a crazy angle. At once he was nonchalant. "Now, promise me. Two hours, no more, you be out of here, okay?"

"Why should I?"

"It has to do with me, girl. I told you. They can't conceive of loyalty." The word purled. "Sure as Christmas, they'll come."

"For you. Not for me."

He stamped his foot. "Jolly damn." An island oath. Vivie's.

"It's your mouth they want to shut."

"Mouth?" He shuddered. "They are not so discriminating." Drawing her into the closet, he bunched her hands in his. "Honey—" It was almost an embrace. "For the house. They'll go for the house." He was sweating. "I have it on good authority. We have till 5 A.M."

It was the "we" half-convinced her, and that he was shivering. The clothes she and he were pressed against smelled hot of her own scent, lost between their two bodies, which were front to front as if to copulate, though he and she had always been sibling dead to each other. She saw that his face at last had no girlish pout anymore. Ten years from now, at fifty-odd, he would be what? She had no doubt he would be alive, somewhere. But this was the way she would see him, the two of them, closeted. She saw the buckle of his shoe.

He's all provocation. Yes, why not? They'll bomb the house.

He watched her glance out at the room, at her bookshelves and up at the files. She saw herself blown out of here into that freedom from possessions which so few could achieve on their own.

"Look, sis. You want the house, you can have it. There's enough insurance, you want to repair later. The land is yours, from now on. I shan't ever claim, I swear. But you must go now."

Moving her head carefully not to knock the bulb, she broke away from him and flicked on every light in the house. Shrinking back from the glare, his face worked like a bladder. She saw the Garuda he would be.

"Never, then?" she said. "Ever? No money from me to you? No letters for it. For bail, for anything? Not from jail, not from anywhere. Understand? I'm not to be Vivie to you? Ever?" She wasn't fool enough to ask his promise. Only enough to promise herself what maybe Vivie after all foresaw. That the stone itself, by its own doing, might relieve her of it.

"A—real clean break?" His big lip actually quivered. When she said nothing he whistled. "I'll—miss that rocker."

"You want to wait with me here instead?" she said, dry. "Bull it through, together?"

He did blanch at that. So it was true then. They would come.

"Do as I say." The dead voice he must beat his girls with. He never damaged the goods. "Veronica." Of a sudden he quirked at her winningly. "Please?"

Fascinated, she nodded. The alternative love and cruelty that members of his profession had to supply must make them supple as wands.

He heaved a sigh. "Five o'clock then, better make it. Five-thirty at the latest. And—" he hesitated. "And—don't go upstairs."

On his way out, he went right past the rocker. Not that he wouldn't miss it. Just that he had many sentiments.

From the door he leaned back in. "You're always going off on your own anyway, aren't you?" he said lightly.

"Fix that gun in your pocket," she said. "Liable to shoot yourself in the heart."

She didn't watch him from the window as Vivie would have done. He always got away, into rabbit holes near or far. His problem was staying away—from the crooked ruts he loved, for which he would violate any parole, even self-imposed. As those boys were sure to know. Never a sincere criminal, never able to convince them of it, he was most in danger from the bad company he admired, over whose superstitions he yet had a certain sway.

I'm getting tired of this window, she thought. I'd have had to leave it soon anyway. I'm tired of what it puts on me. Not that she ever expected to escape from what life had put on her, any more than Ollie could. But she was tired of this version of it. If she forgot her race more than most—or more than she should, some said—it was because in her work she saw how people were divided socially by primitive inner gaps as deep or even deeper than any the world put on them in the form of money or bloodlines, or skin.

There was the gap between the sick and the well. There was the gulf between those who had their dead already behind them, and those who didn't yet. The gap she was thinking of, and it was a social one, lay between those who had or hadn't clung to their own people. The final rabble, avoided even by one another, were those whose close family members, once strayed, were not merely lost but no longer counted upon. For there were tragedies of loss and shame the world over, but in the right sort of tribe even such lost persons were held consciously in the fold, ticked off by story or memory—accounted for. The worst blot was not to know where a family member was.

Ollie had made Vivie and her feel that way. Even though he was always coming back, they could seldom say where he was, even if they knew. One day, by some underworld twist they might never hear of, he was doomed not to pop up again. That was the real reason Vivie had held off from those Bejan island clans always proudly mapping their tributaries present and absent. It might be why, in her own travels, Europe centerstream didn't please her, and why she had fled the wedged villages of France. And hadn't been made comfortable by skin alone, in some parts of Africa.

Take up your bag now, baby. Kept always at the ready, packed with those cosmetic and medical needs which increased each year like one's weight, plus those charmingly interchangeable clothes which chemists now pressed upon one like an ideology—she half despised it. She glanced swiftly about her, her heart missing a beat, and ran to the desk. Always at the last minute before leaving here, she almost forgot. As if she wanted to leave it here, the one lover to be permanent. Stuff it in the bag now, the original manuscript. A copy, kept updated, was in the bank. The key to the bank went into her purse, its duplicate being with

Tom, who'd said when she gave it, "Mentally, I'm your nearest relative." She took the original with her everywhere.

Not that she fully believed her stepbrother—but Ollie was never trustworthy enough to be disbelieved on all points. She'd go to her office, where she often spent the hours from midnight on, until time to take a morning plane. There was a whole such afterlife in high office buildings all over the world—as if those huge unwalled fortresses could no longer be left to the ministrations of night cleaners, as if the world no longer could be.

Often she saw hired limousines arriving or drawing away with clients for whom the dawn hour might be either late or early. Tom had urged her to use a chauffeured car at such hours, but she never had; at times she had to be poorer than some, humbler than some, in order to be her old self, still embarking. Last two times up to Montreal, she'd taken the train along the Hudson, watching for the small, yellowed island—was it before Poughkeepsie or after?—on which lay Bannerman's durably ruined castle, whose roofless crenellations and broken spaces were what her overannotated poem might come to be. This time there were plane tickets in her purse. Then would come those children chirruping in the square, and in other city parts she would search out. Work was the best travel.

Good-bye, desk. As she turned away, the rocker's viciously short prong caught her ankle; it had been kicking them all for years. "No— you can't come back!" Vivie yelled from it into the phone, to Ollie in New Orleans, down there on his third lam in a year, fifteen years ago, the time he'd secretly invited his young sister to go along. "No, I've rented it to somebody," Vivie'd said, duller. "The whole house." This time, she's really trying to get rid of him, the younger Veronica had thought, from behind. "Vivie. Listen. He only asked me along for company. I could've always come back." Vivie had reached out—and slapped. Later, the tenant complained that their "son from South America" had had the nerve to let himself in and out of the place, with his key. Ollie, taxed with this on one of his hideaway calls, had yelled back, "You think I want to—that ratty old house? You think I like to go in there?" Why had he then, his sister had asked when they all three were together again. "What did you do here? When you sneaked in." He'd wrinkled his nose. No turban as yet. A broad leather hat, butternut soft, that she'd envied. "I dunno. Those velours drapes, ever sniff them?" he'd said, pointing. "I came and sniffed."

Half across the room she could smell them now, heavy with the niches and coral glints of childhood. In the reaches which had lapped around

Vivie, around their three. She walked over to them now, to draw them closed. Saw her own hand gripped on the tassel, where it always lingered. "What a fool I am," she said aloud, and ran to get her own passkey. "What a—fool." And ran out the door and up the stairs.

Loud colors get so shabby, when executed in paint. White floors get so dirty. Moorish arches hang by their matchstick portals, made in a Brooklyn woodyard. Rattan tables get picky here, soggy there. The looped bedcover droops from the sofa bed like a fallen breast. The girls have cleared out, leaving a pink cloy of face powder and champagne. Not the cleaning woman's day. Ollie, who could always rise to an occasion once a plan had altogether failed, had thought of everything.

She found what she was looking for in the kitchenette, wired to the oven clock. She'd never seen a time bomb before. Nor likely had Ollie. The thing hung from the oven door like a sick black bat. It looked like all of Ollie's contraptions, as if it just might work. If she turned back the clock, though? She crept forward, not daring to. She gave the clock a bitter smile. It was set for seven o'clock. There was also a smell of gasoline.

Was he trying to pull a fast one on those louts—to make them think some ally had already taken care of him? She'd never seen any of this new crowd more than in a brush on the stairs, but knew from Ollie's boasts what they were like—like all his crowds, routinely too smart for him. Or was he doing it for the insurance—odd of him to know how much? For which, as total owner, she'd be such a plausible front. To be applied to, later.

She bowed her head, in Vivie's old attitude. Repetitive grief was gulled grief. Her head whipped back. Call the bomb squad—why not? Up near the curved ceiling there was now a weight lift and a leg exerciser hanging from hooks on which the shelves for her father's books used to be. So long dead, he and her own mother, so honorably. Did such deaths still fund hope? Was it possible that Ollie had been funded by Vivie's? For she did half-feel that admiring tug of the heart-brain when a life reverses itself in front of your eyes, as possibly a better one than thought.

She drew away, carefully stepping backward, shutting the outer door infinitesimally slow behind her, as if it led to a house of cards. Not because of the bomb only. Ollie's good instincts were not like other people's. Even his reforms could have a ramshackle guile. Yet it was possible, the way even a swami's dreams of self-magic can be. Possible that he too, her brother Ollie-Ali, was at last tired of this house's version of his life.

Leave his gamble to simmer there, then. At the worst she would be an accessory after the fact—for both of them.

Minutes later she was ready to go, dressed in a floating but serviceable gray, whipping a gray scarf around her head and neck, even enjoying the self-drama of rising from these dead steppingstones out into the cloudy walkabout, with her spirit handy to her flesh and vice versa—when the phone rang.

A preliminary? One of Ollie's crowd, checking it out? Taking care of it ourselves, boys. Won't answer it.

Or her brother. Reneging again. Vivie was never able either. Not to answer.

"Yes?"

A choking. Or a groan. From a wounded throat.

It's the one they thought they killed, flashed through her. Ventura. Calling from somewhere, for Ollie. Or Ollie, himself? They got to him. The phone cord twined from her, blood-clotted.

"Will you—eat with me?" the man said.

The phone slid from her. She bent to pick it up, the house sliding neatly after and from under her, without ever a bomb. The drop came when you looked up and saw where other people still normally were. Up there, up. In that dialogue where I was only two hours ago. What can I answer him?

Her name was coming to her like a pulse, breathed in her hand. She brought it to her ear.

"Veronica. You all right?"

I'm all right, in my own way. But if I open up to you, I'll whimper.

"Please, I know you're there."

She swallowed. "Tell me your name? Again?"

That was a strange sound he made.

"Mulenberg. John Mulenberg."

She saw him clearly, everything he was. If he were standing here in his full strength the floor would humanely provide itself under her again. And she would delude herself that she could get to him for more than a night.

"Say something," he said. "Anything."

After a minute, he said, "I'll wait."

How smart he is. Don't cry over it. Her eyes stung.

Ask him then. The question that welled up in her wherever she was in the world, from a distance she was only beginning to define.

"How do I get to you? How we ever—going to get to you?"

People like me. To people like you.

Would he think it the basic cry between man and woman, or black and fair? Or rich or poor? If she herself knew who was asking, who was replying—would that be the answer?

She could have sworn she heard him smiling, before he said from confident lip, *"We—get to you."*

That was the answer. That she knows only the question. That he has only his reply.

"Yes—I have your card," she said. "Your calling card." The phone was an extension on its own wall switch. Gently, she pulled out its plug.

Now she was ready. Her overnight bag could still be swung over a shoulder, though in addition to her month's supply of interchangeables, it now held the boots and woollies she'd need if she went north. She'd always wanted to visit Calgary and the Rockies above it, ever since riding up in a Montreal elevator with a young woman carrying a thick hide suitcase out of another era, with a sticker from there—a rawboned white girl tall as herself, with ankles like hocks, long feet shod in new white kid, red hands and a face brilliant with quiet—a young moose who'd parted the foothill forest in order to check in at the Ritz.

She herself kept certain places like that stored always in the back of her mind. To go to, as now. In emergency.

Montreal itself might just now be as hot as New York. The manuscript was in the central pocket of the bag over her left shoulder, the typewriter case in her right hand, carried under her mottled cape of all purpose. She knew she looked internationally handsome, seductively capable, a spender though probably not rich. Trained by Vivie to love clothes both for vanity's sake and for their artistry, in her long mirror she saw a woman who had learned on her own to value them for their guises, which could both influence her thought and externalize it, all the while hiding her good mind. Men used clothing in much more muted and less conscious ways, which at times she envied. A man's dress, much closer to uniform, gave him the same solidity of intent and maneuverability which his lack of protracted reproductive process did. Their vanities, like their energies, could be applied straight to the main chance. When she wanted a man, it was in part for this. She didn't see herself as ever wanting a particular man's child. The poem was her child, born to her in the washroom at Miss Lacey's, at the time when it became plain to her that her body interposed between her and all revolution, because men noted it.

And now, ready to wheel and go, she suddenly let go of everything, typewriter banging to the floor, the cape puddling after it. The shoulder bag unyoked itself and slid. Kneeling at the open refrigerator door, she might have been searching its contents like a scholar, or adoring them. She saw nothing, blindly. Squatting on her haunches, she wolfed abstractedly at random, paté, mushrooms, bread, the door hanging wide. Now and again she rested her head on her long thighs, inching her head to the knees. Her shoulders heaved, but only in digestion. When she'd finished the solid food, she closed the door in reflex, her face still a blank. Opened it again. Only mustard left, soda, champagne. Shutting it again noiselessly she stood up. Head bent, eyes inward, she reassembled herself, leaving without a backward look.

Outside, she walked rapidly in flat rubber-soled sandals. On the road, she never wore high heels. The city at this hour, with its stars waning, its buildings coming forward out of night into the stone of themselves, its milk-and-porridge needs beginning mildly to clink, was her precinct. In her cub reporter days she'd often left town at weird times or worked an excited, self-imposed midnight-to-dawn shift because she loved the office then, a catacombs for one person, neatened by cleaning women and lunar light. On a view.

Inside the office and her own cubicle, flinging her gear on the tweed couch, she sat down at her desk to watch it. How kind big buildings could be when deserted, how permissive. This architectural kindness was rarely spoken of. Structures of many sorts had it, as if from an instinct beyond their builders. Seated here she felt nurtured by an amah's arm from behind, urging on her the orange-blue over a bridge, the wet fishgleam on a junkyard's immortals. She had mappings here, all pointing outward. When she sat here in the early hours, she was always about to set out.

She'd walked the few blocks here piloting steady on that. Each time, crossing the broad convergence of streets in front of the Gulf & Western, mounting the small apron of steps and past the guard's trusty joke —"Only two of us holding up the world this morning!"—she was walking toward this.

Wherever "John Mulenberg, One Gulf & Western Plaza" had his office here, his view wouldn't be quite hers. Perhaps his was at the very top—not counting the restaurant. This seemed likely. They might still pass each other unaware for years—or meet soon, one dusk or morning. She ruled no one out of her life, not even Lievering. But that was the range of possibility she liked best.

Over Jersey two helicopters were homing for the city port like mechanical bees. She had a license to fly dating from a period just after graduation when she'd been acquiring every physically useful talent she could, from snorkeling to marine navigation, since these too were ways of conquering the world. Or in order to demonstrate—to the gods, perhaps—her lost faith in language alone? Never. Or not yet. If that ever happened, didn't she know what she'd have to do? Hunt him up —Lievering. To apologize—"Now there are two of us."

What did she mean by language? Faith, hope and principle? Or only that the act of enunciating was the mediatrix to all grace? All she knew for sure was that once she'd found it, the act of announcing had been her way out of the wilderness of early being. So that when in days before she'd have sobbed or raged, now instead a rod rose in her, ramming those valves shut. Cry on the page, the rod said.

Years went by before she knew that this, too, was worship—and, like all worship, could be dangerous. In any act of words there's praise, she thought. And I don't yet fully know what I praise.

That man Mulenberg had thought her a terrorist. She smiled to herself, meanwhile overlooking the angled warps of the same view he at best might have eight or so more stories of. A singer, he'd sensed the timbre her life sounded, when like a bell it was struck: that she was organized around something. True to the times, he'd assigned this to the political—and hadn't been altogether wrong. There were people who were linked to the political world merely by what they themselves were circumstantially. Many an émigré thought himself a revolutionary for that reason alone. And it appeared that all revolutionaries thought of themselves as émigrés emotionally, when really both might be merely among those who were displaced in life by having had a world view thrust upon them. Like greatness, she thought. So that though they talked of themselves as part of the "new world," they didn't yet know what that world was.

Over beyond Columbus Circle, in that welter of lower rooftops whose tarred surfaces were catching the first sun gleams, her own house lay, a molecule helping inch life along. Or actually far smaller, in the atomic scale. From a period spent at an institute in La Jolla, writing up a pair of physicists who felt themselves to be turning into biologists (quite as naïvely, it turned out, as pilots might dream of being trapeze artists), she'd learned certain rudiments from the one who'd fallen in love with her—and although she tended to mistrust secondhand knowledge picked up sexually, she did know that in the realms of matter, a molecule was now very large. Would her house, however infinitesimal, soon be made to puff up higher than its neighbors, sending up a heap of tumbling clothes and small criminalities? She couldn't stay to see. But I'm glad I ate that stuff in the fridge. Got the jump on whoever. Maybe even Ollie's crowd, ignorant of Ollie's effort and, like many of the gangs, now reportedly masking their ordinary crimes and vendettas by aping the style of the political ones, would indeed come for the house.

Ollie had wanted the rocker. She'd have settled for the bed—Vivie's old couch bed, bought in the Maritimes on her marriage holiday with Hervé Oliphant. Vivie, during her last weeks in it, had worn a white cap belonging to her own grandmother. By every atavism she could pry from the past, she'd meant to control her own death. On the appointed day, not revealed to Veronica beforehand—"But I keep hinting to God, baby, and I think He's clinching it"—she would, as she said, "take up my bed and walk."

The sofa bed here was comfortable on a daily basis but it was essentially an office sofa and never really slept on, unless the secretary to all the staff writers, a lean man, pork-white with former priesthood, used it for bouts with the pickup boys Rhoda alleged but no one ever saw him with. "Truth is," Tom had said, "I've stocked the office with idealists, lapsed or practicing. And in exact ratio to their kin outside, no one of them agrees with any other."

Which am I?—she'd thought, but wouldn't ask. "Neither," Tom said, as if she had. "Or both." So was he, then. That was their link.

She took up her bag again, slinging it on the worn harness made for her by a leather shop, once she'd caught on that there were parts of the civilized earth—Orly in August, Grand Central Station forever—where she must be her own baggageman, and left the building, signing out for the guard, who this time said, "Early bird leaving early, huh?"—a man whose sedentary profession obliged him to have the last say.

Outside, she could have waited for a cab to pass, but chose instead to cross the Circle and walk along the southern rim of the park. There was always a line of cabs waiting in front of the Athletic Club. Sometimes they took you on, often they wouldn't, citing their "regulars." Once, late for a plane, she'd doubted the existence of such a customer at such an off hour and received the driver's haughty reply, "He prefers to remain anonymous." It was a need for independence that took the drivers suddenly. They all had it; those who could afford to indulged it. She understood it well.

The park, running along beside her, smelled of its city-peculiar summer—those low green melodies which were never quite snuffed. Approaching the cabs, she saw from across Fifty-ninth Street that they were all Checkers, empty, or maybe the drivers asleep. Some people were afraid to take cabs at these hours, but to her cabbies had always been the city's nurses, its twenty-four-hours-a-day attendants through whose changing licenses one could clock the city's migrants—the world's. Since the Vietnam war, a lot of Thais. Ever since the Papa Doc era, a lot of Haitians. Recently some Turks, whose significance she didn't yet know. And now and then one of the earlier progenitors in his privately owned medallion cab, a Brooklyn Jew or Queens Italian family man who'd put his sons through college by means of this equipage bearing you, waxy as a mausoleum and tartly clean. People brought their own murders with them, most of the time.

She peered in the window of the last cab on the line. Empty. In the next one, the driver was asleep. Now that the street was deserted she could see what an ugly strip of false Paris this sector of it was, gaining breadth only far toward Fifth. Here no late lovers stood entwined. Above the A.C.'s marquee, its oblong windows, so nineteen-twentyish narrow for the view they commanded, squinted like the small eyes one sometimes saw in the handsomest Irishmen, some of whom had founded the place. Was that man now sleeping in a room up there, or had he phoned her from his suite in the building she'd just left? Where would the two of them have eaten? Now that he was safely by-passed, she could allow a certain interest. All things could be of interest to those who were resolved that people were not permanent.

Should she tap on the glass? The cab driver was slumped over his wheel, poor man, which kept on turning maybe even in his rest. But it was his profession to drive her to hers. Battista, Juan, his license said. Maybe from that Puerto Rican barrio, two blocks from her own block, whose whole motto was a shrug. Sure, why not wake him to a good airport fare. She was about to rap when the blast came. Like nothing she had ever heard before. Sucking the air in. At once she remembered the beauty-supply store, stocked with inflammables, at the bottom of her house.

He opened an eye. Saw her over the half-rolled-down window. Eye to eye. "That wasn't no backfire," he said, as if to a regular. He got slowly out of the cab. "Wonder where." Looking up, they saw nothing. The great buildings, plane on plane, hid all perspective. Vibration lapped their ankles. Two more cabbies joined them, staring up. "Listen—" her cabbie said. They heard it, a slow brown web they couldn't see, settling. Rubbling the smacked light.

"Terrorists," he said. "Wonder where."

The silence yawed her sideways. "Maybe—Fifty-fifth Street."

He caught her elbow. "My wife's afraid to go to the bank, the department store. Where you going?"

"Kennedy."

"Right. Let's get outa here."

They were at the Queensboro Bridge before they heard sirens. Once out on the structure, she leaned out to stare back. The river wrinkled under the impossibly looped guy wires and spidery fenestrations which the years had flung over it. Faded red-brick warehouses with postscripts from the soaps and comforts and inventions of a century ago were riding cozily alongside the cab, to blot out, on the far shore, the high-pointed spires and glass forests of now.

"See anything?" the driver asked. "Them bomb clouds, they last forever."

She shook her head. He was a good driver; he didn't look behind. Her life surface was pocked with encounters like this, the small businessmen of the traveler's experience, often more memorable in a penny-hard way than the persons one shared ideas with, or loins. "Vignette people—" Tom, to whom she'd confessed this, had said. "Everybody's more comfortable with those. Nobody really wants the big story."

She hunted for the driver's face, furtive with kindness in his back mirror. "I saw a bed. On a cloud."

His eyes found hers for a minute, shifted.

Studying the cab, she saw that it was an owned one. Pictures of the children, a bobbing luck animal in the rear window, a Sacred Heart up front, where it counted most. The back seat and floor had been scrubbed with that disinfectant which smelled like violet gargle. He'd made his traveling nest. Even revolutionaries would, or anarchists, only moving their gun gardens and ticking toys from time to time, by error or trial. But moving on was essential.

People who inhabit revolution—who are they, what are their types; do these eternally recirculate? Not all of them from a beggar's opera. *Some people who inhabit revolution*—that may be all. Like the title of a print picked up in a bookstall off the Thames. Or always obtainable on the Rue de l'Art. Some people inhabited revolution who didn't know they were there. Who felt they were part of a new world, yes, but hadn't yet imagined it.

Suddenly the driver laughed out loud. "The Klondike Mattress Factory sign. That's what you seen, hah. From 1928. We have all kinds products here, this bridge. Used to have even the Victor Victrola dog."

They rolled down into the ordinary streets, short-cutting through the one she always looked for, where two tiny villas fought a war of large roses. He didn't remark on it. Their encounter was already over, their little personal spurt. Like an orgasm forced out of life, between two strangers. Like a house. Like a bomb. She could still hear the rubble.

I see a bed rising. On a cloud. Vivie's dying on it in great gouts of bedcloth, rising up to shriek, "I don't know—what I know"—then falling back, a spent sheet, a gone breath, cold wax in a frilled cap. She'd knelt beside the bed, receiving the shriek in her arms, stuttering out, "I'll know it for you." As it passed through her. Gone.

She crouched in the cab, her pack still on her back. When Vivie had risen like that, it had been the last paroxysm of what she did know, gazing back at the tender expanse of all of which it was no longer her time to speak. This was what all the dying must feel: Make haste and speak; make everything speak, count—she, Veronica, would feel it too. All the sentient living felt it: their solid, eminently sure and even practical death jogging beside them, who are still full of supernatural life.

Up to a point, the old ones did your dying for you. She was no longer that young. Or houses did it for you, falling down, fading out. Now she must do it for herself. I don't yet know what I know, or all I know. The energy of it poured through her. Her fingers trembled with knowledge. I am the *terrorista*. I am the revolution. I am the new life.

Her own dying had begun. She hid a grimace of satisfaction. At the lifetime it could take.

THE CORRIDOR

As Jacques Cohen, who was once Wolf Lievering, is being inserted into the longish, flat tram which will transport their group from the motel to the pre-liftoff corridor, the aide, who has helped each heavily suited-up body to load in, bends over him to deliver the usual briefing. The rule is that no passenger, once suited up, is left too long uninformed or isolated. Identity, propinquity and a constant camaraderie of fact is always urged upon them. "This group," he's now reminded, "is not necessarily the group which will be in your cabin. This group may be more or less random."

More or less. An accident of the sequence of motel rooms from which the tram has rolled them, stopping in turn at each door? The room sequence can't have been left to accident, since nothing has been. The aide isn't lying, or even attempting to prevaricate—a word Lievering's father had favored, sermonizing on its derivation from the Latin verb *varicare*, to straddle. Since his father's birth, in the first quarter of a century now drawing to its close, the nature of lying had merely once again changed. He himself wouldn't at all have minded being called Lievering again, a name he'd neglected rather than defected from.

"Your own special medication is around your neck, Jacques." The aide, reading from a list, has never seen him before but all of them affect intimacy. Especially now that no one can literally see the passenger. "Each pill is separately ejectable. The pouch records how many taken, and at what interval."

Lievering coughs. "And bears the prescription on its little tum." He is still rather proud of yesterday's attack outside the motel, if it was one, the first in so many years and mild, but proof that the hospital, sponsoring him as valuable because of it, hadn't recommended him for nothing.

In fact his mood is still warmly elated. This country prefers the elated, and rewards them for it.

The aide pauses, but without comment. They are trained to be intimate toward, not with. "You'll be in the corridor approximately forty minutes. You must ambulate only twice, on signal." Though the suits are modified, it would be unwise to drag that load about. "The corridor is windowed. One window to each of you. No plane-time Coke or chips, or last book purchases." The aide's voice is grimy with joke. "But the window's yours." Have a look, a long, long look—the voice doesn't say. But before it moves on to the next, Lievering's shoulder, or the place where his shoulder would be, is given a last cozy pat. "There'll be music," the voice said.

He is already enjoying the uniform. Actors were said to take confidence from costume. As a kid he'd had a clown suit once, and a band uniform and shako, which he'd enjoyed, though never performing in them. Saying to his disappointed mother, No, I'm not in them for that. He didn't intend to stare through that corridor window, though, while some prophylactic ray removed the germs from him. He had no further need to look. The past is his real alias. He is unloading it.

One becomes exultant through being a rejectant, though philosophy tended to deny this. He'd been born one of the Rejectimenta—a popular word in that household of German pomp and Jewish martyrdom combined; therefore his creed—or naked impulse—is a rejectant's; it is natural to him. This is what they want here, don't they: natural selection? But he would have come anyway. He's the one who can admit that they are well rid of a planet hung in the heavens like the withered-prune testes of an ancient Jehovah, still spawning horrors that change only in versatility. Good will is its farce, recitable every Christmas in twenty-four languages, by popes and presidents kept swaddled away from the ordinary living which went on in any of them. As the world wanted. While outside its basilicas, the faithful poor kneel in the slime behind the faithful rich, Jews are burned in one style and Asians in another, and all over the earth the miserable child becomes the woman and the man.

When he thinks like this, rhetoric fills his mouth like spit. He can forgive the actual soil of the earth its quakes and other Incan calamities; what he can never forgive are its countries of the mind, their terrible and persistent inequity. In which the occasional joys and goods are always lost, just as each personal body in its time is lost to disease. Gratuitous evil? There was none. We were all on evil's salary. Gratuitous good is his scourge. For he can see that these occasions exist: balms that are offered, children who are not whipped—and groaning out of some blackish studio behind the Loire or the Thames or the Neva, or curling at the base root of some buddha tree, the true blood whisper which says, "I am Thee." Under all the filth, those little white worms of good? He can't wait for them to be butterflies, or whatever the optimists think they will be.

The one day he'd gone back to Berlin, a birthplace never seen since, the windows of the shops had been assaulted by drifts of may-flies, their wings folded back like dead Giselles, gauzy and sweet. A hand could lift hundreds, in one ball of carnival fluff. *Schmutz*, the shopkeepers said, brooming and hosing—and they had been right. On the sidewalks, the West Berliners allowed glassed-in display stalls, unattended, in each some bit of merchandise with a placard directing the passersby where to go for it—and why not? Why shouldn't the pavement, too, have its profit, say these pragmatists, pup-pup-pup from their sputtering, consonant-plopping mouths—and they were right. Inside one stall, against whose panes were piles of the bug-gauze, there had been a single gold sandal, wonderfully embroidered. The sun had struck sandal and bugs to iridescence at the same time. *Fabelhaft*, a couple stopping to admire had said—and they were right.

From there he'd taken a bus to Checkpoint Charlie to see the atrocity photos, then the subway train which passed directly over the Wall so that you could see its sentries and the barbs sticking out of its concrete, and after that had spent the rest of the day in whichever East Berlin museums were open, all of them being closed alternately, as announced from day to day, so that one could never be sure of one's choice. He'd managed to see both the Pergamon Porch, an ochre Greek frieze of figures, the largest he'd ever seen torn from its home sun, and the Ishtar Gate, a great green-blue and gray tiling with seneschal lions, the longest ever scooped from its native sand—surely the two best museum rapes he had ever participated in. After that and a fruitless search for a meal, all the restaurants in the open museums being closed, he walked down Unter den Linden, wide and free now of armies, and lightly goose-stepping, brought himself to the door of the university library where Marx himself had worked—whose brass-dragon knocker he too had touched. And he had been right. Going back over the border he stood next to a young couple, East Germans, bidding farewell to their West German mother who clutched a small bouquet of dreadful cotton flowers and seeped rheumily at the eyes. Entering the Demokratik Republik, one had to be yelled in by number and passport; leaving was by gate and silence, but equally secure. On return to West Berlin, he'd eaten soup at the Copenhagen, from a menu choice of thirty—on the good side surely. In the cab to the airport the driver proclaimed that Berlin's city services, including the refuse-disposal stacks which made a kind of skyline on the city's interrupted leaden cloud, were the best in the world. And he had been right.

They were all of them right; each had his or her small mite of it, on an earth irreparably wrong. So Lievering nursed no illusions about doing his best as a matter of principle during his own term on it, or even his worst, which would have been merely romantic, could he have brought himself to it.

Instead, that protestant saliva of his constantly filled his mouth. Where had it oozed from, stuttering him? From his schooling in England, which had had so much of it? Or from before? His parents, two young Germans fat as *Blutwurst*, hadn't been cooked by the Third Reich's ovens but had merely escaped, along with their year-old boy, plus both sets of grandparents, who in the course of time had merely died. On arrival his father had almost immediately qualified as a librarian in Bloomsbury, where he got words wholesale, of which supply the boy could never get enough. Even his mother's cranky-looking amber and garnet jewelry had survived.

They had been a small family from the first, graspingly close. All that was left of Berlin for them to mourn for were a few friends, along with certain brands of cocoa and *Rindfleisch*, which lacks London had soon repaired, even to the *Kleine Konditorei* where they could eat éclairs on Saturdays. Not being very Jewish—not for centuries, his mother said— they had left no God behind. His father had joined the Fabians, or what was left of them, their refugee services being far the best. Via their thriftshop Wolf had been clothed by Harrods up through grammar school. A German kitchen could be steamingly excellent anywhere; his mother's glazed carrots could have been served *sous cloche* at the Savoy. So, everything they had had been secondhand but of the best quality—including their tragedy.

Who could be apostate to that—to an inoffensive run of luck? Instead, he had been assimilated to it (a word the real Jews used disdainfully), except for that mouthful of words he could never speak. Words of all sorts cluttered his mouth, piled there like the world's error, but he couldn't speak them. His mother blamed his trouble on his looks; of course she was in love with him. "Too much of an introduction, your face."

His father found the way out for him, as well as how to make his son profitable. Wolf's mouth? Other men's words, if put there indivisibly, would spout from it. They had memorizing sessions in which Der Vater became better than the therapist, having far more words than anyone, until an apoplexy fatally cured him of them. His son, writing down the inherited words by the thousands, was borne on to university anyway on a scholarship, and got a first. His mother, driving the two of them home after watching him get it, and still gazing fondly, committed their sole family accident, from which Wolf's face, like the family jewelry, had survived intact. It was not to be his fortune. She had characterized it correctly; it overexpressed him. Meanwhile, behind it, his own words once again jammed.

In hospital, delayed there by recurrent attacks of petit mal ascribed to the concussion, he began again to dispossess the words, this time by writing them, in stanzas flowing evenly, a process of which the neurologists approved. Meanwhile, news came from a last correspondent cousin. In San Diego, at the zoo, this cousin's four-year-old son, left loose-handed by a gossipy mother, had been drawn between the bars and trampled on by a suddenly rogue elephant. Maybe this boy, too, had had a face too much for him. Day after day Lievering would try to draw both elephant and boy back again through those bars, rogue and child made whole again by the words from his pen. "Beautiful . . ." the girl printer from occupational therapy said as she worked at the font setting his lines, and looked at him.

The sonnets—by compulsion exactly as many as Shakespeare's—were finished and the printed book of them done by a Cornish printer who visited the girl, and the girl herself departed, back to her winter job. Older than he, she'd already had a book of her own design printed by a London publisher, and a winter lover who worked in the same firm. The copy of Lievering's poems sent to this man (one of an edition of twelve and the only copy sent out other than the one to the author's father's former library) came back with this man's critique scrawled over the colophon: "These poems have no tact."

It was true, as Wolf saw at once, a comment worth more than the design it had smudged. Agony without genius was gaucherie. Between elephants and boys, between himself and the world—and whose tragedies?—his poems had foundered in that all-embarrassing slough where, for real seriousness, he should have shut up. By the end of the day he'd had his own revisionary attack, of grand mal this time. Just before he fell, he saw the book squarely and himself holding it, the way a runner who hasn't placed dangles his track shoes, walking back. The words were nice, like a collection of gems all of the same size. The poem was the perfect product of his training. He was secondhand all through.

On that score, he found himself more interesting to an American doctor on the staff than to the English ones, whose society engendered the problem quite regularly. "Happens often," one of these said harshly. "You are what you are. You had better get used to it." The American, who was a Jew also, smiled, overhearing this, and beckoned the patient into his office, closing the door.

"*We* never do," he said. "And I'm not so sure they." Fact was, their caste system actually helped them handle it. "Meanwhile, fella, you're just as much a victim of the death camps as if you had the mark on your wrist, only you're second generation."

In a low voice, the patient had whispered back, *third.*

He was ultimately told that the stifling bourgeois Berlin household which his parents had replicated behind their Bloomsbury shutters could have been their own repression of inner damage done. "But they had you, on whom to focus forward."

And I don't—do that, the patient said, low.

"Ah, come now. We're very much interested in the problems of art, back home." The doctor collected paintings, satisfying his passion at the flea markets in Hampstead and Camden Town, though last week he'd seen a find at the Leicester Galleries—described with ardor—but the salary paid him here was low. "We lead a more random life over there in the States, you know. Art is a way to cohere."

Other people's art, the patient said, stronger, though he still stuttered, or did what he did—more like an occlusion of the lips.

"People who have all the sensitivities of art, the intelligence—but no talent for it," the doctor said sleepily, his chestnut eyes half closed. He had a fine hooknose, thin and avid, a beard as curly as one of the prophets and two advanced medical degrees over his desk, all at the age of thirty-eight. "They're one of the negative problems of art, that's all. How do they find their audience? Or become audience. In order to live. For that's your problem, isn't it?" The patient gasped—at having an all-over sore flicked like that. Though it was a help, to be recognized. He broke down.

"I'll tell you what some do," the doctor said, when that was over. His eyes again were half closed. "You find yourself another audience, quite cynically. One where your sensitivities can work out, never forget that. Often such people make remarkable progress. More stable than some artists." The patient kept his eyes on the doctor's powerful stub-tipped fingers, the fore and middle ones stained bright yellow from the butt always burning there. "And in time," the doctor said, "you'll find little places *you* can bear to be audience." His beard vibrated with energy.

Or false prophecy, the patient thought. "Or you can stay as you are, Wolf." They had never yet told him what that was. "You can keep your pathological honesty about the state of things. Schizoids have the same. No, you're not schizoid." The doctor took a puff, which he did rarely. "But it will make you just as unacceptable."

I'd prefer that, the patient said.

Nobody said anything for a spell. The butt smoldered down. "So you got rid of all those lovely books Angela's boyfriend printed," the doctor said then. "How?"

I burned them, the patient said. *Like Hitler.* He watched the butt. Matches weren't issued to patients in this wing; the doctor would know where he'd got them. The butt was flipped away.

"In that case, my wife has the copy you gave her, Wolf—remember? If you want, we'll bring it to your plane."

That will be honorable, the patient thought, but didn't say. But not so important now as doctor thinks. For patient was over and done with that now, and had already made plans to teach, as well as to emigrate. Otherwise, except for a mended head and the medicine provided in case of another attack, which they somehow doubted would occur, he was just as he'd been when he entered—the world still black and swelling in his heart, brinking at his lips. He will just have to find another way—to the tragedy.

"We're all secondhand," the doctor said, pleading. Just then the dustbin caught fire. The two of them beat the fire out. Over the drenched basket, patient and doctor faced each other. Clearly the doctor already hated the sight of him. "You . . . are . . . very acceptable," the patient said.

To the plane, the doctor's wife, a small, dissatisfied, pretty bundle with a very sharp eye, did bring the last copy of the slim green, too elegant book. Patient had brought the picture from the Leicester Gallery, purchased with his mother's insurance. From now on, if he didn't save as his parents had done, the authentic might come nearer, though not in that picture—as he could tell from the wife, who worked at the Courtauld and had done classes at the Slade.

"Oh, Larry—to make *him* buy it," she'd said crossly, turning away toward the patient. He *had* been made to. She knew what she was about. "It's music Larry knows; did you know? All too well—the prodigy. But we don't have a piano now. . . . Here's your volume, Wolf."

Before the plane left she snapped his picture, fixing on him her glittery currant eyes. She'd never expected to be a painter, he thought; she lives free of such things. Yet, older than the doctor, she was bored with him, as she had confided, adding that to have that happen with ever younger men might be her fate. The doctor, after a flurried *You shouldn't have* was offside with the picture; he was one of those whom possessions helped.

"You reach your cousin?" she said in a whisper, though there was no need.

"Yes." Lievering was en route to San Diego, where he would live at first with the cousin—whose wife had been put away—and work at the lecture job the British Council had found for him. She scribbled off a note and slid it into the book. From the gangplank he saw that the picture taking had been an excuse; she was storing up his face. Though he would have liked to return the compliment, he couldn't; he'd never been able to store up faces. Once aloft, he'd opened the book, oddly thin in his hand—and yes, she had done it for him; she'd torn out the pages. Instead, there was a note. "Larry's sicker than either of us, but stable. You knew you were being bad for him; that's why you bought the picture, wasn't it? I think the way you speak is in tune with what we all know—why cure it? He says that though you may be a shining light of something or other, people can't take it. And that all we've done is to move you on. I'll be leaving too, one of these days. Send me your address."

He hadn't, but she'd got it somewhere. For as many months as Shakespeare wrote sonnets—which extended through his jobs in Mexico City, Bogotá, Costa Rica, Valparaiso and Jamaica, only ending just before he got to Barbados, he continued to receive her forwarded envelopes, each containing one of his own sonnets on a single page. Each he destroyed, but not before reading it again. She never wrote her own address, though by the postmark she was still in England. When the envelopes stopped, he was sorry. Somewhere, in her own way, she, too, was the stutterer.

Why should this tram ride to the corridor remind him of that long-ago plane ride which had got him out of Cuba? Because he is cargo, once again.

"We're taking you to Paris with us," the American kids had said, leaning flush-faced over him, their ready-made icon. He's lying on one of their sleeping bags, in the old mess hall to which they'd carried him from the field. Lucky he hadn't fallen on the sharp cane stubs, they said.

"You fell so light," a boy says, bending from skyscraper height a baby face nested in fluff beard, "you chew peyote?"

He can smell the boy's sneakers. On the path, he fell, they say. When his fake bride ran from him. As yet he has no sense of what they refer to. He tests his tongue—not bitten. So far as he can feel in his still levitated state, he has no bruises. Never any thrashing about, none of the harsh side effects. He falls silently, dance-relaxed, returning charged, as if from flight. He's a secondhand epileptic, too.

"No, he fell like he was smote," a girl says, huge-thighed over him. There's a snicker from behind her. He can smell the girl's crotch. Sitting up, he feels surrounded by kindly, foolishly nodding sunflowers. They have a charter flight out of here; they'll arrange everything. Two of the richer kids will pay for him at the other end, if need be.

"No sweat," the same boy says, encouraging. They mistake the stony face he has after an attack—and to all accounts, before—for refusal. "We'll demand you."

He sees they've already chartered him for themselves; he's now their cause. He's so often been somebody's. Still, it's staunch of them. His first words try to warn them. "I've already—flown," he said.

In the plane he dreamed muzzily, tended dotingly by that girl. The others chaff her now and then. Barbados sinks back, a gem-fruited paradise tainted by England, like William Blake's. He will not even cable it good-bye.

In his room in the hotel back of Saint-Sulpice where they all landed, he came to his full senses just as the girl, chap-lipped with love, babbled toward him in her great stolen sleeves, otherwise naked white from the waist down. He'd never beaten a woman before. The girl adored it, but didn't get her just deserts afterward. Holed up in the *salle de bain* down the hall, he checked his wallet's small contents, his returning self—that solitary pensionnaire—and his British-schoolboy knowledge of the warrens of Paris. He could always make himself lost to people anywhere, imitating that hunted need to run which he should have had.

This underground ceiling, traveling with his trolley gaze, is broached with slender pipes that remind him of the old *pneumatique* tubings in the Paris department store his mother had taken him to on their first trip there. Fat brass cartridges had zizzed overhead in constant tic-tac-toe, one finally zinging down into the cage beside their clerk, with a magnetic goosing she acknowledged by a plump sidelong hand—the very soul of French commerce. Shortly after his arrival in Paris from Cuba, the French language was to furnish him a livelihood, as a translator of whatever of their own books might require an Oxbridge tone. Still later their medicine, breezier than Britain's, would dismiss his disease: "You don't have a disease, M. Cohen, but a philosophy."

He had taken the new name in order not to have his real one on any book. The name had belonged to the little cousin crushed by the elephant. This way he could at least keep a connection with what his own life had not yet imposed on him. At the local *boîte* off the Place des Vosges where he brought his work of an evening, he knew he was regarded as one of those boulevard intelligences who ate little but a roll now and then plus ambiance, all on credit—the sort whose luck now and then cashed in. His ability to live so minimally was at first admired by the others there, who assumed him merely adroit at hiding what he must be hooked on—if not art or perverse sex, or film, then at least the ordinariness which was clearly denied him—each of the other patrons interpreting him in terms of his or her own cravings. He was too clean to be one of those secret layabouts who merely preferred filth—and besides, they saw him every evening. Once his neighborhood circumstances were known, it was proposed that in spite of his provocative looks he was one of those scared, sexless creatures who prefered to live in boardinghouses rather than either full-bloodedly in the family, or in one of the torturesomely calisthenic love relationships now become fashionable. When it was finally plain to them that he could live even as he did, yet not diminish the dignity of what he was, they were infuriated. What insult, to do without what they could not dispense with —how dared he lack interest in the good things of life?

Ultimately the bar, like most, accepted him pridefully as one of their mysteries, a testament to what a century exhausting itself in explaining things had almost forgotten—that there were wells of personality which couldn't be bottomed out. One of which, after many removals, had settled off the Place des Vosges.

Lievering was sensitive to the progression of all this. His relationship with himself was that of a man who kept a domestic animal which must someday rear and sink its teeth in him—or might not, fooling nobody but him. He took patiently all the explanations of himself now and then offered by itinerant girls, psychologists, experts on the refugee syndrome, and the other authorities which any good bar was heir to. The regulars had turned their back on him.

Once in a while he did venture into the bookshops and cafés of the more crowded arrondissements, but there his face was still too much his fortune; one day a sneaked flash-shot of it had turned up outside a famous tourist brothel, inside which the male candidates sat illuminated like the girls in Amsterdam—though only at the groin. His publisher informed him of this, with that interested French tolerance no church could keep them from. "We thought you were celibate." He was. After this he kept to his district, where his landlord was his reference. He never went near the universities, knowing enough by now to mistrust his power over the young.

Actually he had a room with a fine, scholar-attuned brother and sister whose quarters were as minute as his own. At dusk or some portion of the day, it was merely manners, or the compassion of the like-crowded, to leave them to themselves. At the three home dinners per week for which Lievering had contracted, M. Aaron, a second-generation mathematician whose father in his own *bachot* days had known Einstein, fed Lievering wine "to make the words come." Lean as some medieval apothecary too enlightened to take his own potions, M. Aaron wore his white hair navy-cut, over an eye flawed from the time of his compulsory military service as a youth, and scrawled his nighttime equations on the sheets. Their kitchen was draped with these, waiting their turn to be transcribed. One which had never been deciphered waited grimly, a faded battle flag of the intelligence. Mlle. Elise, the elder sister, has all these years washed Wolf's handkerchiefs. "Nephew," M. Aaron called him. "Everybody's nephew, all your life. I know your trouble."

But how can he? Monsieur's own mother had been taken away during the occupation, even though her own whole ancestry had been Huguenot. Two of her uncles had paid their dues at Passchendaele. Ever since the Age of Enlightenment somebody from that family had paid his or her dues to history. Even the mild old sister's blood runs more comfortably because of it. "Our tame cougar," M. Aaron says, watching old Elise pass Wolf the honey jar yearningly. "Who thinks he is only a cat." Wolf's real name is known to them; they like to pun on it. But he'll have to leave them soon; their knowing comforts are pressing him. All Paris is ameliorating him; having colleagues is its way of life. He leans forward, refusing the honey, trembling. "Hatred is hard to keep."

Shortly after, Lievering, against his anti-crowd habit, went to see the Beaubourg. He'd never been able to resist heights—not the alpine ones but the human eminences. But break a habit and it entangled you even worse. High on those glass chutes he'd bumped into a classmate named Dysart, later briefly a colleague in the West Indies, and now a poet traveling the world's universities, though far more successfully than Lievering had. The black fur on Dysart's protruding upper lip no doubt still waggled low Scots at all the girls en route. Indeed, he was hoping to welsh on next year's job in order to follow one of them who had a little money of her own. "Just the man, Lievie. You be my substitute." He wouldn't take a no. "Not a British Council job this time. I'll go guarantor. My God, mon, at university you got a first, as I remember. Dear God, mon, they're only Americans."

And how was Wolf living? Dysart was horrified. Translations—slim pickings at best, and weren't the French all now wanting the American style? Lievering saw his suit being inspected for signs of starvation, and all but confirming it. True, his publisher kept him only on sufferance; these days the office sighs that greeted him were large. Though the Aarons, who must be paying much more for honey and washing powder than when he first came to them, had never increased his rent. Dysart, staring at him over the bock they'd stopped for, wasn't yet aware of his own irritation. They always thought Lievering never saw it. Lievering had paid for the beer. The time had come once again to relieve them all of the burden he is to them.

So, once more, he'll go where he's pushed. Leaving is the only tact he knows.

"Oh yes, you'll remember us," old Elise Aaron says, her eyes as bitterly red as her hands. "Like the cat."

"You can sit up, suh—Jacques," the aide says. "No need to lie back." The tram, which must hold at least eight suited-up forms, each one in its high-backed niche unable to see the one ahead or behind, has stopped. This underground runway, leading from the motel to the degerming corridor itself, which in turn gives directly onto the launching pad, had been built by a contractor already under indictment for its deficiencies—a risk which exhilarates Lievering. More may be ahead. He sits up in his clown suit with its big, reassuring box toe, eyeing a ceiling slightly chipped. M. Aaron is still following him, a pneumatique just for him. His cataracted eye looks even wiser than his good one. "I know only one way to live," he'd said in adieu. "Collect people, Wolf. Not hope."

Arriving at the college in Richmond, Virginia, to which Dysart had sent him, he finds that the drawlers there, calling him Doctuh because of his Ph.D., remind him of a voice tickling out of a past scarcely thought of since—of Odgers, the false preacher who had performed a marriage on him. These gentle Virginians whom Lievering coaches at night— women mostly, pursuing what is here called "continuing education," under the assumption that life itself hadn't done that—soon teach him the difference between their state and Tennessee, and try to take him in socially. The richer ones are romantically certain that their Palladian houses will foster in him a renewed dreaming of England—which happens, though not in the kind of dream he could have told. In practice though, Richmond, like Paris, is too cheery for him. Yet Paris's cultivated satanisms and haughty intellectualizings of fashionable religious pain had been no anodyne. The haunted picture frames of those martyrs he and his family should have been part of still attend him—empty now even of the shadowy glass.

Is it because of them that the actual people who have passed through his life have less than the usual force in his memory? Though those who have can be summoned if need be in scenes quite accurate, even his parents have fallen into this void. He must possess less of the wavelike returns that characterize the brain life of others. Though he's no blank, memory is not where he partially lives—except in the case of those martyred ones whom he lives with eternally. "Because of them you have no minor guilts," the doctor for whom he'd bought the picture had written, incidental to thanking him for it. "Your memory's non-Freudian. It bears no ordinary grudge. People won't love you for it. We can neither stay away from the sight of it nor watch you for too long. You can't conceal. That we're all of us in the same grim present. Stammering on. Heard from my wife?"

Lievering has never answered. Bills are the sole mail he replies to, twitching on the dot to the few he receives. Letters offering tentative life intimacy, or those follow-ups on how he's getting on, from people themselves mired in the art of getting through—how can one answer them? They are like dreams.

One person who had never so applied was Veronica Oliphant. She'd been all his present for a time. When other women offer themselves for that, which still happens, he remembers her. Not because she left, but because he had been the guilty one, in trying to make her part of his present for always. Once in a Paris bookshop he'd been confronted by a poster of her. *Writer for the Damaged Age,* its flyer said. So that's what she had become. He'd stood there in the sadness of all follow-ups. So she had joined that journalism-by-the-decade which could make any running sore of mankind into a local case of the megrims. An age was never either damaged or pure, but a temporal flash which blinded its inhabitants, some of whom would hear its magnificat, others only its black Mass, the greater body of them never seeing the flash at all. An age was always everything. No style could contain it. He had merely made his choice of one. Veronica had had reason to be afraid he'd make her doubt words. She had seen him plain. That was what had enraged her most—that he might regard that kind of seeing as the immemorial function of women. Some of the best men and women acquired those more manageable angers early, in place of the impossibly durable, purer angers of dedicated life. But when he left the bookshop, he'd again forgotten her. Now and then his organ autonomously recalls her bed.

He's in his fifties now—a time when a man begins to notice that his heroes have remained forever young. Lievering has no such real faces to go by. But even a hair shirt wears into positions of rest. Once more the monastery of himself is being broken into. These Southerners he's among know how to tolerate worth without competing with it, tranquilly leaving it to its eccentricities. When his teaching begins to be bruited about and the college transfers him to day classes, his ladies give him as good-bye present an antique roll-down map of the Virginia Commonwealth. In their talky, secret way they must have discovered how life anywhere is only a setting to him. "As it is so much for you women here," he exclaims, thanking them. "Though for you it will not change." He's said the wrong thing again, as he can see by their flushed faces. In spite of this, they invite him home. People are startled by what a man like him can live on emotionally. They don't want to know about it, but against their own inner warnings they keep inviting him home.

Along the farms on the James River which a few of these women have inherited or married into, their teenage sons are now hunting the land with Geiger counters for their own Civil War artifacts. "Hunting your martyrs?" Lievering asks.

The boys take to him. Sometimes on weekends he goes out with them on their queer walks, which are neither exercise nor dreaming but somewhere in between, and may end up with some rusty proof that people other than themselves have lived. Tow-haired and snub, or brunette and oval-faced, these boys have the polite remoteness of their fathers, set forth in soft, murky voices still almost feminine—though their own mothers, chatting peahen high, are another version of female entirely. A code of manners sifted down from French dandies in Baltimore, British adventurers, black slave nurses and butlers, and maybe an infusion of North Carolina mountaineer, sits like armor on these boy knights who have no horse for it, though they sometimes speak of shaggy farm mounts, or the occasional birthday colt.

The chain between each boy and his father is clear. In their grandfathers' time, they tell him and believe, the riverbed had still been frog-pure. Under their grubby campfire hands the ground between the pushed-aside twigs is desperately old. Urgent dying still leaks from it. The scrub trees here nuzzle these boys like family furniture. Down on their knees in the leaves, they smile over their shoulders at him. War, that old status quo, is as usual again crumbling their horizon. Boys from this territory respond quicker than most.

One day it strikes him that they're using him as a kind of Geiger counter for themselves, for powers they think he has. They know their scraps of flintlock or cannonball better than he ever can, excitedly ignoring him when one is found. Though they sometimes sling words as neatly as tackle, they aren't bookish. But now and then, when a boy says a thing or asks it, all of them will wait for the answer. "Roun' heah" —one of them says now, holding up what he's just identified as a musket strap, a piece of ossified leather at which all are staring—"roun' heah, where it so comfortable, it ever *hard* on you?" The face of youth straining for knowledge must be more weird than any in purgatory. Its destiny is more sure. "—Doctuh?" the boy said.

Sometimes he almost can't bear it—their destiny. But surely by now his company won't add to it. Soon, though, they might not be able to bear him. Before that happens—at least he judges it so—they take him along with them to the Goddard Space Museum—and there, poking about in a file of the latest aeromedical news, he stumbles upon a series of brain-wave studies done by the space program, which indicate a possible niche for him in it. When he does qualify, he tells no one the basis for it. As he prepares to leave Richmond, the boys drop by his office singly or in pairs to tell him how "super-pleased" they are. In the documented personal pack already incubating for him on the shuttle, he's taking a few of their exhumed knickknacks to the new world for them. If they had after all begun to tire of him, or of his halting answers, they hadn't yet been aware of it. He's escaping just in time.

"We should all be such epileptics," the team at St. Elizabeth's Hospital had agreed, examining him for the project. "If that's what you are." They doubt it, as other doctors have—two major attacks, only the one in the psychiatrist's office in the British hospital corroborated as serious, though not positively identifiable. The second—the Cuban one—almost twenty years ago. "More like trauma reaction, both times." He's told them the circumstances of each. "Too exaggerated for trauma only, don't you think?" one doctor argues. Has patient had no other instances? "In bed—" Lievering tells them, sometimes a stoniness he recognizes comes over him. When he's at the nadir of aloneness, though this he doesn't add. In this state he sees distant light ahead, and finally breaks through to it. "In dreams." Laughter. "Wet?"

Lievering looks patiently from one to the other of these mouths flipping his life from lip to lip. Swollen young medicos, grown fat and fork-tongued in the consulting room and the lazing air of the District of Columbia, what do they know of the need for tragedy? But he can see their medical greed.

"Why d'ya want to go?" one asks.

He's already told them how after an attack or a threat of one his speech difficulty vanishes, returning only as an accompanying sense of electromagnetic confidence, charging all his muscles with good will, gradually wanes. He never uses his pauses consciously, but they guide him well. Always toward the truth. "When . . . I am . . . in attack," he answers now, "it is like . . . what non-gravity . . . must be. I am sure of it. And . . . I have never been . . . as happy . . . as I am then." He's spoken the truth. Why should they look so stunned? And judgmental. He could have added, It takes the place of the poems. But holds his peace.

"After all, do we want anybody out there in attack?" the same doctor who'd not thought his seizures negligible says thoughtfully. "We only need the temperament." A tiny, bitten-off man with a navvy's biceps bulging on the short arms sticking out of his surplice and the hands of a plump child, this doctor's shiny brown eyes remind him of the organ-grinder who'd come once a week to their London street, though Lievering's mother had never once tossed him money—whose eyes had been exactly like the monkey who had turned the man's music box. Or the monkey's eyes had been like the man's. "We'll let this man train," this doctor said.

When Lievering returned from space training, this doctor was there to talk to him. Dr. Carlucci—the head. In the interval, Carlucci had taken the trouble to hunt up a couple of the translations by which Jacques Cohen had once made his living. "Had to look up too many words," he grunted—the standard complaint. Again his eyes reminded Lievering of the monkey's. "But your training record aboard—my God. Suppose you've heard?"

"No." But he couldn't help knowing how he'd soared and modulated to that state of being as if he'd been born to it, often helping out others like a good bath attendant or lifeguard. Never spilling a drop of food. Moving with the angle of vertigo, not against it. Never faulting space.

"They say—" People hesitated with Lievering. It was catching. "They do say here, Mr. Cohen—you sometimes blurt painful things. Uncomfortable to others, that is." The doctor scratched the report on his desk with a minute nail. He wasn't a dwarf but only barely not. The Apennines still produced foreshortened men like him. Dwarfs were sometimes used to get into the tight corners of aeronautical assemblages under construction. Maybe they used a Carlucci to pry into the inaccessible corners of a person. "Jesus—people are still going to be themselves in space. What in heaven do those bozos expect?"

Lievering smiled. "Heaven."

Carlucci sat back. "Any trouble with women, out there? Or men? No? You mustn't-a smiled much. You've got quite a—physiognomy." He poked Lievering's chest. "Big word."

"I don't mind it anymore," Lievering said. Meaning all of it, including the jokes. As for his face, he knew it was now mostly like anybody's. It could look better or worse.

"And was space like that to you? Like you said? Heaven?"

These men were such idealists, with such pale, well-bred ideas of how to reconstruct the mind. Like Dr. Larry, who had prided himself on having reconstituted his own. They never dared see that other world, of mind spitted on a pain-stick like a brochetted live bird, its sinewy nostrils filled with blood, its twisted neck a fowl's at the moment of death, its eyes glazed with *the* knowledge. They think you can wipe that away.

"Not heaven—no. But for me . . . as I said." Being in non-gravity does resemble, more protractedly and mildly, what he feels at the beginning of attack. Except that he's fully conscious.

"You want to go back out there then? Start a new life?"

"Start it?" What an absurdity. "A life . . . can only . . . be continued. Or . . . my life." He hesitates—long. "But if you said—finish it . . ."

"You ever suicidal?"

They seldom asked so abruptly. Though death was now mentionable in the States. Formerly it had been a social sin, better concealed. Now, at his college and others, they took classes in it. As if by studying it they could beat it. "Not—so I don't notice it," Lievering said. Careful to smile.

Carlucci burst out laughing. "You sure know how to talk to us."

"Not I. The century . . . knows now . . . how to talk to itself. Too late."

He never sees why what he says should be uncomfortable. Only catching on when they physically begin to move away from him.

"Never been in non-gravity myself," Carlucci said. "How's it feel?"

"I only know . . . how I feel."

"Yes?"

The psychiatric "Ye-es?" He recognizes it. I feel marvelously afraid —dared he say that, if he wanted to go? It's like an exercise that sweats me into a relationship with people. But the clearer he said things, the farther people retreated. And they were right.

As usual, truth came out of him. "It makes me feel firsthand."

Carlucci had lowered those eyes. But he raised them again. "They said you were a real Nijinsky out there. What do you say to that?"

Lievering leaned forward. Don't frown so, his mother said adoringly at his side, in the window of their London house. Keep the mouth smooth, she would say, in creamy German. His lips now felt numb. "You have monkey's eyes," he said. "Too . . . full of good."

Yet Carlucci okayed him anyway.

"People are always . . . taking chances on me," Lievering-Cohen said.

And your luck runs against them, or you do—is that what this monkey-man would say, with a last grind of his box? When Carlucci leaned forward, his pouty little arms curved to the table like a pair of tongs. "I like—freaks."

The trolley's moving briskly now. Lying in the notched seat, feet supported, Lievering feels a carriage-child's passivity creep over him; he'd been wheeled until he was four. Ahead of him a helmet projects above the seat back; the person wearing it is very tall. He himself is already getting used again to the peculiar majesty of being suited up, which makes all one's gestures minimal yet enlarged, within the limits of an environment which will make most gestures nothing. One may scream murder in such a suit, or mourn the world like Samson Agonistes —and be taken merely to be wanting air. Soon his limbs won't weigh at all. He's waiting for that, craving it like a drug which wouldn't end consciousness but give it a rest from being itself. Like his attacks.

"No germ-free corridor on the training trip, was there?" the person in front suddenly calls back. "Wonder what it's like." A baritone voice, very American. "Seen the pictures, of course."

What's it want then? Something.

"There'll be"—since Lievering can't lean forward, he projects his voice—"windows." As in a coffin, a needless expense. A modern coffin though, designed to keep him very much alive. Delight floods his muscles.

"Ri-ight." The voice has relaxed. "Er—Mulenberg here."

After a minute Lievering answers. "How do you do . . ." Not because of his two names. He's simply never learned to do the quick name swap over here. That conception, too, will soon be a farce. Let them have their windows, their labels, while they can.

"Not too far to go naow, you two, Jacques. Jawn. Yo' group's the layst in the tail." The aide, trotting alongside with his final tender namings, disappears backward to a trail of other names: Tawm, Bee-yal and others too faint to catch, floated up in his soft—is it Floridian? He

reappears like a marathon runner, his slug-white unarmored face oozing alongside their visored ones. Been years since Lievering has seen
gardens with those huge slugs in them; they, too, are England. His
imagination's already rising, leaving behind it a planet of ever paler
faces, slug-dotting a wasted Earth.

CANAVERAL

The tram emerges, megaphoned from the tunnel onto a wide clipped
field, richly cared for. Cricket could be played here, or any of those
antique games men play with quoits or bats. The sky is cruder here
though, a heavy moist white.

The large voice breaks forth again, amplified for the benefit of the
millions invisibly here.

CANAVERAL

How good of such a place to be so musically named.

Now he sees that the tram he's on is actually the last segment in a long
chain of them extending die-straight across the green all the way to the
huge hangar itself—a structure said to be higher than any of the pyramids, and certainly glassier, its walls constantly exchanging polyhedral
light. One of the many mirages here which have to be taken for real.

The tram stops short. Figures clad like his own begin to dismount
jerkily, like the old movie continuity for which he used to haunt picture
houses from the Tottenham Court Road to Ealing, as soon as he was old
enough. Railroad cars, circa 1914, with French soldiers descending
pell-mell from all doors, in leg wrappings thin as lingerie. Or would it
be 1939, and the Hitler troops entering the Sudetenland? At which very
time his father, watching the foreign press sluice past his leather corner
in the library at Bonn, had taken warning. He'd been proudest of the
fact that his profession, "Words alone!" had saved his family. "When
there began to be all those early articles in the American press about
what fine, smart chaps the poilus were—then one knew there would be
a second world war." He'd however hated the Pathé newsreels first
exported from there, and all the other reeled-back history his son became addicted to. All that filming only made it harder to believe in life.

Lievering's tram car is longer than it seemed underground. So is the
one ahead and the one ahead of that, in diminishing perspective up to
that door in the hangar which must be the entrance to the corridor.
Figure after figure is getting down from the cars, slow as robots—or
civilians—in the outmoded heavier-model space suits demanded by
Congress, which NASA had vainly insisted they wouldn't need.

How could I think there were only ten of us, in a last tram? That steward hypnotized us with his fake warmth. They intended it. All the figures have dismounted now. So has he himself. There are dozens of us. But ours was the last cart. Suited-up figures surround him, tentative, even chatting, not sure what's up yet. Not too organized. That's good though—isn't it? That aide's merely wan from working inside, down in those basements where he can't get the local tan—nothing sinister. We're in the open air now. If Lievering moves slightly left to see around the side of that enormous hangar, he'll see the vehicle itself. Instead, he looks behind him, at the carts. Yes, that's what they are; why didn't I see that before? Carts. But we've not been packed into them. We've been allowed to get down from them. In the open air.

He'd rather stare to his right, a mile and a half across the nibbled green flats to where the reviewing stands are, low, white and rambling, with an indolent air of gentleman sport. They remind him of the sheds on a Virginia polo field the boys once took him to. Or the judge's stand on the country-club grounds where the dog show was, where a dachshund, placing its paddle feet as if it were as tall as any dog, had won best-of-show over a doberman. A dog show was by nature a setting, a Sunday afternoon movie still. Yet shift to the handlers and the pens and another professional reality took over: the animals themselves. No animals here, of course. Even the vegetation's been quieted. Lievering shifts himself slightly left.

He can never quite believe in any airborne vehicle. So small when not in motion—even the largest of those with intentions of flight. So able—even the smallest of them—to carry destiny for the likes of us. He's long known what the shape of this one will be—not one of those penis-style rocket probes. A double vehicle-on-vehicle with a third disposable belly, each parting from the other on signal. The hangar above is higher than the UN Building piled twice. That thing, its progeny, aims farther than the idea of nations. Yet when the thing lofts, in stages that he, deep in its middle belly, will jolt to but not see, when its groaning metal and plastic is finally data-processed out upon a magical evening which is now pinkly descending without the aid of any artificial intelligence whatsoever—

THE CITIZEN COURIER

—will look like nothing so much as a fly copulating with a fly.

Up ahead, the citizens are lining up docilely enough in front of the hangar's back door—or is it the front one? Lievering can't get over how informal it all looks, how casual they're being allowed to be. Yet could they flee? Soaring as the hangar is, its door is barely man-high. All man-scale grandiosity, from cathedral ceilings to floor lamps big as cannon, has stopped at the motel. From now on there'll be no more earth-style architecture, good or bad. He already knows that from the training trip. No more grand porte-cochères or arching buttresses, designed to elevate man's sense of himself, but always to human scale. The kingship is now in the amount of distance subdued. Aboard, all equipment focused on his body needs will be on as small a scale as humanly possible. Though he minds this less than some, over a time it can be subtly demeaning. He wonders whether others have noticed this. Perhaps. At the door, two florist's baskets, of the same height as the door and filled with red flowers, flank it gracefully.

As the passenger line keeps forming and filing in, the aides monitor it, one to every four or five passengers. A hand flicks his visor. His aide, his own *personal* aide, is smirking. "Jacques. Visor up!" He's the only one around him who's kept it closed. The air on his face is fresh. Yesterday's storm has helped. "The last storm," they said at morning prayer at the motel, "that you folks'll have to see."

At the door proper there is no step. Each space suit, short or tall, lifts its heavy feet apologetically. Each passenger's elbow joint is carefully assisted. They're being loaded in now, not let out. He sees that clearly. The carts were only interim.

In exchange, he'll have what he always wanted. The setting will be real.

As he nears the corridor door, the flowers redden peculiarly. They're not flower-flesh but nylon, or vinyl. That makes no difference now. All the settings of his life have been unreal to him, secondhand because he was—and only he upheld them. A setting, to be real to its inhabitants no matter how strange it is, needs only enough of them to sustain it mutually. He has colleagues now.

He turns from the passengers ahead of him to look behind him at the crowd of lay advisers clustering in for a last stare at him and his kind, brushing their hands together in send-off relief—and pride. Across the flats, in the sporting pavilion, the reporters stand ready to caw and cheer to a popeyed world. All the watching world is in the same state of lagothalmia: the state of being hare-eyed, unable to close the eyes. Against these marvels.

His elbow is cradled. He sees the nonexistent step.

"Look at all those lovely roses," the aide said.

He passes through an airlock, the first of the many to be. Inside, he's not surprised to find that the "corridor" resembles that official waiting room through which one passed or did not pass into East Germany. Though no passport numbers are issuing in amplified hullabaloo from the row of bank-teller booths along the left wall—*sieben hundert-neun-und-dreissig, sieben hundert-ein-und-vierzig*—and there is no tic of unease from the room at what may have happened to seven hundred and forty, the spasm of waiting in all these figures is similar. The chairs are semireclining, and properly notched for the suited-up. Nobody is ambulating—the training lingo for stretching the legs. He sits.

Those promised windows have television sets in them. How wise. The coastline, hallucinated with giant cake-plates and tongs like a kitchen for ogres, is already in the past, not to be seen again except as part of the rough crumple of a distant earth-ball. He'd expected some soft, degerming hiss here; there's not even a disinfectant smell. All done with rays? So is all of life, the briefers said. Avoid sinister thoughts.

There are only twenty people here. Four rows of five. He will never see all the passengers at once. The delicate balance of the craft will not tolerate all that much breath or flesh together at one time. Or all that personality? Gantries would number four. "Gantry" seems to be the word for common rooms of varying function. He intends to look up the etymology. Library hours are to be rotated. Maybe, as on the training trip, mixers will be arranged. He anticipates being a good sailor again, freer than most. For the sinister thoughts which seem to him natural.

PLEASE   WALK   ABOUT   NOW

He smiles. The sign talks like him. But here unspelling everybody around him to chatter, to inspect the breast-pocket name of his or her neighbor and to stroll, slowly extending the appendages. Gravity is still normal here, though everybody's already unsure of it. There is laughter. "Home room!" somebody calls out. He doesn't understand the phrase. A woman falls in step with him—an astronomer who briefed them at the motel. Luckily he remembers her, as he does all teachers. By her manner, she is one of those women who remember his face. It seems they are patrolling in a circle, as was done at recess in old-fashioned schools here, where you changed teacher and room for each subject, arriving end-of-day at your "home" one.

"Or like they do in the entr'acte, the Vienna State Opera," Lievering calls out to the circle. He's joining in. Above their frieze of figures, the neon sign glows like a votive lamp. In outer space every object will be seen as intensely intimate, in a perfection of nearsightedness. "Round and round they go. Glass cases in the center of the grand salon. They never look at them."

Lievering stands stock-still. He sees he has drawn ahead of the others. He'd spoken slurred. Was his upper lip deadening slightly, in the familiar sensation? With his canvased hand, he can't feel for sure.

Suddenly a tall sentry is at his side. Is there already something noticeable about him, his movements? Safer not to look up. By the uniform, it's not an aide. Another passenger. He keeps his head bent. Straining to instruct his body—to what?

"Or like the *passeggiata*, nuh?" the interrupter says, "in small Italian towns?"

Who would not recognize that lilting, roughish voice? He doesn't need to check its name. Looking up against his will, he has to lift his chin. She was always taller than he. There it is—that snub black pearl, her face. But exactly as was. They promised real people here. Not dream visitants.

Who have real names on their breast pockets. *V. Oliphant.*

So she's followed him here. Where people flee a man, there are women who will follow him because of that.

"So . . . *Ronchen* . . . we were . . . married after all."

"Nuh."

That Bejan grunt which can mean anything. How he remembers it. She pokes a finger at his own breast. "Jacques Cohen? Who's he?"

Dream people poke you like that.

"A child in those sonnets. Who was crushed by an elephant."

"Ah. Him." Her glove goes to where her neck hollow would be, just below his eyes. "I threw him away. Just yesterday."

That laugh of hers, sharp and akimbo as her knees, comes from her bone structure. Hooting at her passion to be more than beautiful. People who want to be artists beyond their means for it—one ought not to be tender with them. He would have told her in the end, that her poem wasn't much. Life must have done it for him. "I . . . saw a poster of you once. In a Paris bookshop. On the Rue de l'Art."

"I saw a shot of you. On a doorway off Pigalle."

"Mistaken identity," he said. "Was yours?"

Nuh. Isn't she going to say that this time? In any of its variants? He remembers how sex could stretch that monosyllable of hers, when she was stricken on those heights. "You look just the same," he says, stern for both of them. Though he at least has grizzled. "What . . . hasn't happened to you?"

She isn't going to answer. Yes she is, in a whisper. "Why are you here?"

When he spreads his formalized sleeves they seem to him to be addressing a multitude. Or making ready to deal with an instrument panel too big for him. "To find that out."

"The town innocent. Here to tell us the truths. All of them."

He sees that she is real.

"You do address me . . . like a wife. A Xantippe." Pronouncing his father's term for household shrew the German way—Ksantippeh—he smiles.

What a glow of anger women can keep for life!

All that has faded for him. What he sees are her haunches, narrow as a borzoi's, high over her supple back in the Cuban sunlight, the small udders of her breasts almost touching the bed's pagan-streaked coverlet. In whatever anagram her body used to place itself her legs were the most of her, her chin more often student-deferential, against her neck or cupped in her hands. While the belly, flat as a primitive spoon, disappeared into its own shadow, over the pink slit that his mouth or his hands or his sex were always grasping for.

"I know the anger was there," he says humbly. "Like a navel between us. But it's gone."

Not mine. Is that what she's said under her breath?

A figure tall as hers looms up to Lievering. "Ah, partner, saw you debark behind me. Glad to get off that thing. Don't like tunnels." It half extends a hand, then remembers its glove, laughing in its hearty baritone. "On my way to those television screens. They're taking messages. From the dear departed—that's us. To those left behind. What a shivaree, eh. Two-way though. We'll still be able to see them."

The tall man pulls up short, puzzled by Lievering's impassive face. "Excuse. Could have sworn you were the guy riding in the seat behind me." He bends, peering. "Cohen, is it? Howdadoo. All get to know each other in time, eh?"

"He moves on, is all. Nuh, Lievering?"

The big man exclaims, turning. Slowed by his equipment, he raises his arms to the speaker, dropping them at the sight of her, his massive fair-skinned face on a level with hers. His creased eyes, blue under flat Baltic lids, hooknose and Roman-modeled lips are in their own way as symmetrical as hers. Everything about him is huge, except his whisper.

"Veronica." His glove goes up, smoothing his own cheek. "Gave up my beard back there; we all had to." He knocks back his helmet to show thick gray-streaked blond hair. "Mulenberg here." His shoulders twitch off a yoke. "Ah God." He hides his face in the glove, smoothing. Whatever painful is going on in him, he doesn't want the suit to hold it back. Straining at electronic latchings that took an hour to gear, his head comes all the way forward of its plastic bubble, on neck muscles that must have an ogre's strength—how does he manage it? On joy, whimpering with relief. "Ah God." He takes a step forward, slowed as they all are. Maybe it's the urine-pouch, slung along one thigh, which makes him smile. He's recovered himself. "Still got your gun, Veronica?"

Two passengers largo between her and Mulenberg, turning in unison. They are ambulating. "Oh—" the bright-eyed astronomer says, still paused wallflower-near. "Didn't I have you two at the briefing?" They blink politely and pass on in slow motion, to some music which has already begun in them. It's very like a ballroom here, Lievering thinks. Both the amenities and the small, ignoring cruelties preserve themselves wherever people are—even here. For underneath all of it is the waiting room.

"Did the police ever come?" From that muffled voice Mulenberg might be on his knees, only the space suit saving him.

She isn't going to speak to him.

Strange clarities rise in Lievering, flowing from the base of his spine. People are becoming nearer and dearer. He sees their motives, in aura above their heads. Her anger glows like a spotlight drawn by that able draftsman, fear. Of such a nearness happening to her? With any man? Yet this man and she had been naked together when they last met. The man has that falling sickness in the limbs which comes of it.

"I followed you—" the big man says. "I took out insurance at every port."

Such scenes have no place here. Those two can't feel that yet. Out there—it will all be in the present. His own limbs are already lighter. All the falling sicknesses of love which straddle everyone over the abyss of human obligation—while the bellies wobble in the thick spermal rhythms and the women spew out in water and caul the soft skull of some new candidate—all are to be lifted off, in the purer current to come. That thin-aired sea of exploration where everyone will float impersonally. Can't those two feel the hangar's growing iciness? Gravitation is departing, lifting off the human onus. In our asbestos-colored new skin, we ambulate. Soon to rebound from one another if we accidentally collide. Yet because of that, plainer to one another than in the sweaty bumble we're leaving. Colleagues! He must speak to them.

"Domestic scenes—" Lievering says. Because his lips are numb he sounds satirical. Can't be helped. "Have no place here. You'll see."

Veronica raises an arm. Will she hit him? She did that once. In the hut, one morning. When he woke. A blow to the face.

She drops the mitted hand, on which, as on his and the other man's, are tiny flashbulbs, minute but powerful. "I'll save it for the sharks." Her croaky, gawky laugh—why should it change? Salt on her own wounds. He'd cherished her for those, a young girl's wounds. He can yet, for wounds still to come. To all of them.

He's standing on illuminations that drift below his feet, arched now like Nijinsky's, whose foot bones were said to have had a special, space-conquering conformation. She and he are together again on the one perch which united them, from which she must have thought she could scramble—into the Paris bookshops.

"*Ronchen!*" How strong his voice is, unimpeded. "Did you ever finish the poem?"

PLEASE   STAND   BY   FOR   INTER-
                              VIEW

Amplifiers don't interrupt; they impose. Unlike those at airports, this one can be understood. They are each to take their turn at the television interviewing stand.

"Have to say good-bye to my daughters," the big man says. He grimaces. "Daughter." He makes no move to go. "So, you write poetry, Veronica. Not songs. And who's he?"

They all have two faces. First Mulenberg's suavely canny, corporate face—and now this one. Even the lady astronomer, eager beneath her sharp, teachery visage—a pince-nez face modernized with big, college-girl glasses. Lievering can see better, now that the air in his nostrils is slowing with his heartbeat. Mica sprinkles the air here, linking vortices when he blinks. The underlying face is always innocent.

"Songs. No, I write songs." The face Veronica turns, first to Mulenberg then to him—black-glass eyes and cheekbone dazzle—refracts only. Have they upped the candlepower here? Or has she her visor down? "The pretty little gun, Mulenberg? My brother took it. It's not been heard from. The house went, later that night. A bomb. Just like at Gulf & Western. Only our insurance company didn't pay for it." She's spinning like a ballerina now, showing first that face which had peeped soft behind the explosions of orchids in a Barbadian garden they went to once, then this visored bulb of glass. "The poem, Wolf? Sure, I finished it. I always do."

The face stops revolving; he can't see at which half of it. But the voice is directly in front of him, nude, sprawled. The coverlet they used floats in front of him, bright as chicken's blood and blue shell, then levitates away. That's the way I am, her hand says, caught in his old Aer Lingus

bag. Her breasts shudder gleefully to one another; we smell—of ourselves. "But this time I left it stuck in the mirror, at the motel."

She turns to the big man. "Who's he, Mulenberg? He's—a man who
doesn't follow anyone."

Cruelty of such quality is bracing; and means that Lievering is right.
Its ugly armature, present in each beginning innocent, grows to be the
hidden sculpture interlacing the world. Look at those two, Mulenberg
and Veronica, walking away—look how the man is trailing her. She only
had to whisper to him. I'll eat with you now, she said.

"On the motel mirror," Lievering murmurs. "Like a calling card."

The astronomer is still watching those two. "Maybe it couldn't be
documented."

He laughs. It purls from his mouth like from anyone's.

PLEASE   AMBULATE

"What a conversation we're having," the astronomer says, keeping
pace.

He looks at her more closely. She's the passer-by, and knows it. At
university he used to feel sorry for this kind—always at the edge, with
nobody bothering. Until he saw that those who could persist at it developed the hardest integument.

She's still searching out that pair. "He misses his beard, he can grow
it again out there. My first uniformed job, I was project manager of the
first satellite to study X rays in galactic and extra-galactic space—and
know what I missed? My ear hoops. Still do. My analyst says it's very
human of me. But then he says that about everything I do—almost." She
touches her spectacles.

He must be staring at them. Inside his mitts his fingers splay out as
if light radiates from them. Energy is coursing through him.

"I wear contacts usually," she says, flushing. "They corrupt the telescope some. You allow for it. But no light plastic's allowed in here." She
gazes up. "On account of the proofing."

"Gas, you mean? Or rays. I should have thought of it. We should have
asked, yes? But people don't, anymore; there's too much gear."

"Oh, nothing like that. Just antibiotic spray, I imagine."

"Mustn't let the stars corrupt your judgment," Lievering says loudly.
"We ought to be scrutinizing everything."

A space suit cocks at them to show a bare, sunny hawk-face and passes
on.

"Who was that?"

"Gilpin," she says. "That's him."

"Who's he?"

"You can't not know. How could you get here? Without knowing."

"By way of a disease they're not sure I have." His head is filling with its golden confidence. This is the brief period when he knows it. Shortly he may not.

"That what you're leaving behind? Half the people here are leaving something."

"I always leave."

She nods eagerly, in the manner of people with analysts. An aide, passing through the rows head bent to his basket, hands them each a vial of the familiar yellow stuff. She hands hers back. The aide takes a second look at her. "Sorry."

"Observe," Lievering says, "looks like mucus, but tastes like papaya. That tells us something." He's lost his stammer entirely; his voice is that warm authority which once taught, serene on other explorers' heights. "Reality's so patchy these days. Patchy newspapers, television." He nods toward those windows. "Patchy pain, even with all the analgesics. Weather, too. History. Patchy war." Hurry, before his mouth fills with his tongue. "Only a few basics to trust. Like dying. Or starving. Or being tortured. Or giving birth, I suppose—if the woman sticks with it."

He bows toward the astronomer's well-masked belly. In a city on the brink of war, his mother, with no hope of hospital or drugs, had had to stick with it. Which left her with a disproportionate respect for women's bellies, much urged on his father and him at mealtime, when theirs could merely feed. Only money could make her more emotional. "On that vehicle we'll be able to believe everything. Because we'll have to, eh? We'll pool our knowledge, too. And call it faith—eh?" He tosses his emptied cup into the wire cage intended for it. "Last time we'll throw anything. Huzza!" His voice is loud even to his own ears, a nasal evangelist occupying his mouth, his smile stretching to cover the vast replica of himself which is swelling from its own outline. Hurry hurry. Believe.

A young male aide touches his shoulder pad. "Interview, Mr. Cohen."

"Right." He's never used that expression in his life. Far off in the beautiful double helix of consciousness this fact records itself. "But call me Wolf. We're all ordinary martyrs." Ah, but he's being grand; he can only hope that a few ancestors are watching. "And this lady here?"

"No, I stay," she says to Lievering. Her teeth dazzle him. All light-reflecting objects now have penumbra to him. "I'm ground staff."

"Commander Townsend. Assistant on the project to Admiral Perdue," the aide says gravely. "In charge of substitute personnel."

Squinting, Lievering sees that though otherwise suited up like the rest of them, she has insignia buttons on her female-softened epaulet, and she is wearing plain black leather brogues.

Suddenly she thrusts up an arm. As if they hadn't been talking. The arm comes out smartly, angled at the elbow but with the mitt facing inward instead of out—as necessitated by certain straps. At normal gravity, the official space salute became a caricature, a paramilitary *Heil!* Once off earth it took on an uneasy beauty, interposing between him and the floating universe. Thine own hand, solid before thine eyes. Antiposed to another from the same regiment. While both souls float.

"Perdue—? *Perdu, perdito. Verliert.* Lost. . . . Excuse me. I was translator." His own words, backed up in their cells like worker bees, are about to swarm on him. Emerging again from his father's lists, brought home to rehearse him with (nothing like new words for unlocking the larynx, *mein Sohn*) from books he has translated, or from the dictionary itself, they come zooming in, on the eve of attack. They may be that high noise which other epileptics hear. Bringing on the real altitude.

"Mr. Cohen—Wolf. Is anything wrong?" This aide has a British twang to him. They come from all over.

"I am—somewhat elevated. I do not usually fall. I get to non-gravity, it cures it. We better go. *Auf Wiedersehen,* Commander." When there is penumbra around a face he can often see its past youth. She'd had a merrier, turned-up nose once, now eye-contradicted. The eyes are narrowed in salute. But she is a wallflower still. Brushing her insignia, his mitt rests for a second on her jacket, where the breast would be. "Stars on your shoulder. But you still need the earrings."

The aide takes Lievering's elbow, his own face stiff. When they get well away, a goaty snuffle spurts from him. "You always that frank?"

"I'm a man who has brain explosions. I can't afford delusions, too. Even other people's."

"Science boffin, she was. Very good, actually."

"I see." He can't bother to, really. The apperception he's entering is too bright for detail.

"Shall we press on?" the aide says.

"You are British?" Lievering speaks idly. Heavy. The world is too heavy.

"Emigrated."

"Ah. Britons of character don't, much. Not to here."

"I say. You all right?"

The sound of Britain, or used to be. In the face of all insult. *Are you all right?*

"No offense. I'm one of them. You may go now."

"My orders are to see you all the way into your jolly little niche."

"I will have company."

The screen he's placed in front of is still blank, though he sees others are not. All down the line suited-up figures like his own are waiting or talking. There are no booths, no boundaries. Why should he feel alone as one does in a hospital—isolated with the true destiny of all, while others outside are still partying? An émigré into death, lacking the healthy character to stay on. For death is the treason each of us is doomed to commit. Was that from Pascal? Or another from that weed-swamp of ideas Wolf Cohen-Lievering is afraid to attribute to himself?

But he is not alone.

On his left, in front of another screen, is the big man, Mulenberg. Mulenberg is in a dream of himself. People always are, but this corridor, lifting off one veil of dross, allows that to be seen. Lievering's head, moving on his neck like an idol's, feels uncomfortably large. He shoves his helmet farther back. When his head bursts, it will have room to.

A man now appears on Mulenberg's screen. "Your daughter's in the studio, sir."

"My daughter from Mendocino, yes. Tessa. Good girl."

"Your daughters."

"Guilford? You called Guilford?" Mulenberg chokes out a phone number. "Guilford, Connecticut. You have her on the line?"

"She's here in the studio, Mr. Mulenberg."

"My—other daughter? I have—two."

"Both of them are here."

A pause. "Maidie. Maidie." Mulenberg, peering so close to the screen that Lievering can't see it, lays his head on it.

On the screen to Lievering's right a different interlocutor appears. A personality known even to Lievering, who's never had a television set, he's both conscious and unctuous, full of his own humility and fame. The man in front of that screen is Gilpin. Now and then one sees such profiles, in engravings of whose period one is always unsure.

A delegation fills the screen in front of Gilpin. "Your home island is here, Mr. Gilpin."

"Nettie! How's the P.O.?" Gilpin's saying. "Rector. Cap'n. Jennie and Rose. You Wiswells. Grown so I wouldn't know you. Lee Willipaw. Lee —you keeping the folks in gas, propane and natural both?" This is a joke. Apple cheeks, male and female, quiver over Sunday-best. How clear they are. They seem to have no penumbra at all. "Clarence"—

Gilpin says—"Clarence Mock, what you doing off-island? You win the Old Boys' Race, that old tub of yours?"

"Ayuh."

"Mr. Mock is eighty-nine," the interviewer says. "Mr. Mock—what do you think of this voyage of Mr. Gilpin's?"

"Twasn't his idea."

Behind Lievering, laughter vibrates. Other passengers, waiting their turn, have gathered in close. He can smell the unique must of space-cloth, of the flesh behind the cloth. *Before your attacks, Cohen, any delusions of smell?*

"Happens every year—" Clarence Mock says. "Somebody invents the wheel."

"Tell 'em, Cap'n. We don't think ahead—we pioneer." Gilpin's boyish voice goes nasal—an orator's.

"Sure thing," the old man says. "Puttin' you some of my Old Boys' stew in the deep-freeze. For when you get back."

More laughter.

"Make it myself," the old man says proudly, to the interviewer. "Save up the tongues and cheeks for a whole year."

"Tongues and cheeks?" the interviewer says. "Lordy. Of what?"

"Cap-n," Gilpin says, "you shouldn't have come, maybe. Any of you. Not on my account. For the people here to make wrong use of you. You belong on-island."

"Don't you worry, boy. You puttin' us all on the map."

On Lievering's blank screen an interviewer now fades in, and toward him—to his enlarging vision perhaps the same one. One screen, one vis-à-vis, one journey. Through the airlock, all in lockstep. If he's in attack now, between him and the people pressing behind him there'll be no room to fall. To be crowded is also to be of the crowd. This is what comes of not hating enough. They are holding him up.

"Some young people here to see you, Mr. Cohen. What's that you've got there, boys?"

A Geiger counter? Sweat's breaking out on him now in radiant pores but he can't explode yet, he has to know.

It's a musket. Leaked part by part from that dried-blood earth of theirs, where nothing else grows so hardily. Over hours of tramping they've dreamed for years of putting a whole one together. Perhaps the fathers have helped. Or the great-grandfathers, sending up from the gun-pits of the eyes and the musket-slits of the pelvic bones a last black mucilage.

"They wanted you to know, Mr. Cohen. Will you speak to them?"

Their scrubbed faces shine in the pitted, mauve odeon light. Baby hawks, they have no auras yet. They are themselves. If the martyrs are always ordinary people, with ordinary lives, at what age does it manifest?

"I— We—"

His mouth's too full of stammer again.

Next to him on his left, Mulenberg is bellowing, his housed arms gripping the screen as if to tear it loose. "I promise. I promise you both. I won't be just a passenger." Lumbering aside to give place to the next figure, he lurches toward Lievering to give his shoulder a grotesque pat of partnership. His face is beatific and wet.

At the beginning of an attack, Lievering's brain always fixes on one of his father's old word lists, always the same one. Before and after, he can never remember which. It will come of itself. Fall now, Lievering, and be done with it.

On his other side, on Gilpin's screen, the old captain's finishing up his recipe. "Cod's tongues, yes. Taste like oysters if you make it right. And with the cheeks."

"They throw the rest of the fish back, no matter how big," Gilpin's saying. "Captain Mock will tell you why."

"Because the sea is our dominion," the old man says, gleeful. "What's that your dad used to call us, Tom? And because we don't like cod."

"Mr. Cohen?"

At what age is a life ordinary? When there are no guns? No border numbers? No waiting carts? In the moment before his head bursts, Cohen-Lievering searches for what his own number is among the hundred here. *Sieben hundert neun-und-dreissig, sieben hundert ein-und-vierzig*—or that lost one in between. He sees his own life-on-earth clearly—like everyone's a numbering, heavy and secret to itself though to others lightly passing. Until the score comes in, the personal number from outer space.

He stretches a gloved hand toward the boys. "We came here in carts. Near and dear. Remember that. Thanks for bringing the gun."

He can now smell the brain in his own cranium. Oh lens that only slightly corrupts the stars—now let me fall. But the suit, with its minute nailings, holds him strong. He tears off his left mitt, holding up to them the thin naked fingers with the clearly stamped purple blotch just below the thumb. "But I like having it. The wrist mark."

Now can he fall? Now that he knows?

Next to him, Gilpin, hearing what Lievering said, recoils. *"Pithecan-thropus erectus,* Dad called us, Cap'n," he says, and spreads his arms to the fading screen, embracing all shadows on it and behind it. "Remember me to the sea."

As he turns away a figure approaches him, lifting its squared feet in the same slow motion as his own. Amazing, how human characteristic can seep through even a space suit. Or youth can. Mooching space as if it owns it. Ignoring those who are not immortal. Ain't everybody seamless flesh? Not a country boy, this one. No musket. But what's a boy of that age doing on this side of the screen at all?

Passing the commander, who has already spotted him, the boy grimaces a silent, chimp *Boo!* at her, and winks at the officer at her side. The chimpface sits puckishly on his own. The wink is too old for him. The commander's face is racked with surprise. The other officer, holding her back, returns the wink.

I know this boy, Gilpin thinks. Seen him somewhere—that almost white, woolly hair. Or I've known his like always.

The kid comes on with majestic gawk, his helmet knocked back like a cyclist's. He stops in front of Gilpin. His eyes are like all of theirs—glowing toward the existential raids to come. His mouth is sweet with awe.

"You Tom?"

LIFTOFF

THE HARDEST THING to fake had been the wrist mark.

Mo-o-le-son! Mo-oleson Perdue-ue!

As the boy is lifted off and up, and hung by his heels, the flesh on even such firm cheeks as his enlarging downward while the blood drains from his fingertips, the Space Angel, a grotty character from a comic book often foisted on him and his sisters when they were kids because of their father's profession, keeps calling his name with the silvery insistence of a receptionist.

Swung by his neatly boxed feet in the alternating light-and-dark of a cabin which lags forever behind him, he zooms upward to the last point of toleration—and rides on from there, a clot of body from which its own mass is dripping, like in the Francis Bacon painting his mother is so proud of, in the dining room in Washington. He's a haunch of gravity-dripping meat in space—where he's never before been. That cheap little Angel is even a help to him. —Son-nee! Sonny Perdue!

He hasn't been called that since he was a home-boy of fourteen arriving at the prep school which promptly dubbed him Mole, and after four mutually guarded years had last June formally extruded him. "Into thy hands dare we pass the torch—?" the headmaster muttered, ceding him his diploma.

"Torch for what, sir?" He'd known the proper answer: To light up the world. But why let on? They might think they had taught him it.

By now the world—which isn't quite synonymous with his father, though both senior and junior Perdues have it tough not to think so—may already know where Mole Perdue is. Snot drips from his stowaway nose.

The name on his breast pocket says FRED KIM. In that grisly corridor he'd seen nicknames, tribal aliases for some of the blacks, and even flashy acronyms. The project encourages the personal touch—but keeps an encoded master list. *The important thing is to be easily identifiable in space.* But the name on his pocket is different. It isn't him. His roommate Freddie Kim, two years older because of travels as a State Department brat and other early sorrows, was the one who had taken the training. Yet down below on the sidelines afterward, between studying the mockups in the museums and working out on the non-gravity training gear which a young Perdue could cadge access to, they thought they'd done pretty well with Mole. "When you get out there, though, the motto is learn, learn—" Freddie'd said worriedly. Yearn, he'd said, actually. He was tall for any part of his mixed ancestry, making his and Mole's measurements fairly swappable, and though their racial mixes were nothing like, these made for a sort of resemblance even the school had recognized. Temperament was a horse of another color. "Now lemembah, Mo'. In space no moh joke. This one's big enough."

Mole tries to laugh. The angle between upside-down diaphragm and esophagus must be wrong for it. His temples are splitting—if they don't watch out up there on the flight deck, that *point of toleration* of theirs is going to get beyond him. There's no second wind out there, Freddie says in his stopped-up ear. No second thoughts either. You have to be with it all the time.

How long will this vehicle continue to rise? He tries to recall the manual—those infantile arrows crossing the white page he's now on. At two seconds: *The vessel will have cleared the launching pad.* At six seconds: *Fuel rockets burn out and drop.* Into the Atlantic Ocean—or was it the Indian? No, that's where they dump.—Six minutes: *Main engines shut down. Smaller orbital engines take over.* He sees them, two doll-baby turbo-maneuverers at the edge of space, nidgy nudge. Oops. Over. Into orbit. Your weight will drop to zero. 00000000.

It hasn't, yet. His outline still fills his couch. His straps still bind. Sequence, though, has been lost—gone with a seven-million-pound thrust. Time is in his own limbs now. He has no other vehicle. He is rising alone. *The air will remain at sea level throughout. Do not hyperventilate.*

Out there, the mind grows very thin, Freddie said. Too fond of abstraction. Keep to the concrete. Okay then. His heart's pounding like ... a power mower. The grass on his family's place in Kentucky—where the first known Perdue had been a groom, to put it gracefully—is blue.

As in a Van Gogh. Whose madness seems to him worn out. Once it had been so coveted that it had been put in children's bedrooms. His Utrillo, at the other end of matters and in the front hall, stank of the false peace made out of one persistent village street. Every century makes its own madness and then makes peace with it, his father says. Making his own. Of course they're all busy now totting up their century. Keep away from fathers this century said, early on. Well, he's doing that. He begins to laugh. He chokes.

"Don't swarrow—" Freddie said, watching him work out on the space simulator. "Roll your tongue." Loll it, he meant. How can you, from upside-down-sideways? He's going to choke to death. In the holds of old schooners, old storybooks, cargoes shift, bilges drown. Breakers smash over the poop deck and onto the unused lifeboat. And stowaways die. No matter how rich in privilege. Die in dark green pools of second thoughts.

He's not died. He's merely going to be sick. All over his nice new suit. *Speed may induce peristalsis* the book says, with a complete failure of style. Means your guts veer ahead of you and have to be convulsively repossessed, about every three secs. *Count*—the briefers said at the jolly motel; when in danger of losing your bearings, *count*. Okay, Mole. Count motels. Can't be too many like that one. Better still, imagine yourself with a girl. Last summer's French one. Who made love at high decibel but would never *thou* him. Alleging that her aunt, who wouldn't approve, was in the next room. Which the aunt turned out to be, concrete enough to make tea for them.

Soyez le bienvenu, M. Mole.

For surely his body ship is leveling. The cabin, which he seemed to have left so far behind, is catching up with him, enclosing him again with its warm accordion. Slowly the horizontal reenters his veins, like bliss. Like the warm brim of milk held out to delirium. You're no longer a reversed clot of consciousness, rushing the dark. Loll your tongue now, Moleson Perdue, Jr. Breathe.

He's forgotten the information panel. Up there in the sight of all. What he wants is that lighted part in the middle. Two words on it; he sees that much. ON COURSE. But the meaning won't register. *Temporary dyslexia due to deoxygenation. In some individuals.* He's grateful for that last. As an individual. A chimp must feel like this, confronted with the alphabet. Is he aphasic, too? "Abbadabba—" he croaks. "All Gaul is divided." No, he can understand what he says, and hear himself faintly. His ears are open, hearing the hiss of the pressurization system. Soon his brain will reopen too, and read. He doesn't have to wait for it. He knows where he is. He looks down at himself. He is floating against the straps.

Superfly, the vehicle, is still keeling, but less and less. Soon he'll be sitting at almost the same angle as in his scull on the Chesapeake. Turtle haven't been in the bay since his waiter great-grandfather served soup made of them in the dining car from Philadelphia to Wilmington, at thirty-five cents a plate. Oysters are coming back to it. Keep things concrete. A sob-bubble escapes him. The window on his left is such a stately Magna Carta of the skies he can't look at it. A giant hand, placed at the small of his back like a generation of physical education instructors, is pushing his shoulders square. Not courage, just the effect of non-G.—the muscles in his back reacting to weightlessness. Feels like that long, gondola glide when you're coming down from sex; Fred was right. Except that you never land, kid. You'll grow used to it.

Oh land, Superfly—on land! Reel the film backward, so that he can walk out of this theater, rubbing his eyes. But that window's stubborn. Traced with God's own holograph. Give it the stare anyhow—a young man who's met Gilpin. He wants to smile, but his face has disconnected. *Do not disorient. You are in float.* The kinesthetic connect between body and will is different. He has the illusion now that the vehicle is static. This mean they're out of orbit and on their real way? He knows they'd've had to get free of circling Earth in order to beam their way to the living-station. But then, what about space being curved? A curve so vast it seems straight—still, no one's ever mentioned it. He does know for sure that when they lifted off the acceleration doubled his weight, and that now he must have almost none. And that's about it.

At least he no longer has the illusion he is the vehicle.

Truth is, he can't seem to retain that sort of fact verbally. Okay, he'd rather experience them, and maybe in time they will stick. "The facts fly from me—" he'd loftily told the exasperated Freddie. "Must mean I'm a real citizen of space." Nothing doing, Fred said, that day he got back from training. "You just refuse any flight fact. Any scientific fact, almost. Like it came from idiots." Then they burst out laughing, enormous gasps which flattened them to the ground, where they lay erupting chuckles until the museum guard came over to them. *Gad ap the floor.* "My friend has an exhibit here," Mole said proudly. "A space environment. He won a contest on it." Which was so, but didn't prevent them from having these bouts of laughter wherever they went. When together, their blood ran pure amusement. At what the world was, which in spite of all delighted them, and at what it would be if they could just get it out of the hands of their parents in time. "The fact

is—" Mole observed when they were out of there, "that you pronounced the *r* in "flight" perfectly. Just like an *l.*" And they burst out
again.

There was no hard reason for Freddie's accent, which wasn't always
stable, though never assumed. His parents, both born in the U.S., spoke
English perfectly, as had he until taken back to Seoul at the age of eight
by his feminist-dramatist mother—who then abandoned him to her
mother, the repatriated widow of a Korean émigré to New York who'd
made a fortune in vegetables. At the age of eleven he'd been bought
back by his own father, by then an illustrious architect passing through
on a tour of acclaim from his semiancestral Tokyo. "Acquired at gleat
cost," Freddie'd said, twinkling, "to go lound the woh-hld with him. My
accent's a somatic defence, my father says. That means—from the body
cells." He smiles. "My father's a little, bowing man who moves huge
buildings about like pebbles, to keep people from noticing." "What
difference does that make?" Mole said. "*Your* father's good." Since
Fred's mother—who Fred said had an ego as snaky as her neck—certainly wasn't, but Mole's mother was okay, he and Mole were more or
less even on the parental scale. They'd never needed to discuss what
they meant by "good."

Look at the window now, Mole. It's only space. You've heard talk of
it since you were born. Never questioning what was meant by it. Nor
had the talkers, in their hip circle no longer even saying "outer," once
that had been taken over by the amateurs. Space was what they wanted
certain things from. Not bothering to enumerate. When he'd wanted
something from it, he'd gone straight to them.

He spent his infancy at the knees of top NASA personnel, including
even a couple of the aging first astronauts, and knows how they love
jokes—indeed have to have them, if they're wise. Tom Gilpin's name
is anathema to all that crowd; that's how Mole first became interested
in him. To a boy reared in the clockwork suburbs of Alexandria, Virginia, and the capital's white miles of near-monument, Gilpin's island
youth, of which everyone Mole's age knows the details, is real beyond
hope—a father who was a fisherman! His own father he regards as one
of the smart ones, yeah, but fatally clobbered by having thrown in his
lot with the government, when he could have stayed an honest solo
scientist.

Mole understands well enough how his father's mixed blood might
have contributed to his ambitions, even if Mole's mother—who is an
eighty-eighth cousin of Freud and constantly improving upon the connection—hadn't already explained this to him, her verdict on Mole

himself being that he has no color feelings at all. She thinks that everyone, of whatever color or colors, should have the feelings which go with
these—for guidance in life. He does have one such feeling, out of kindness concealed from her, which tells him she can say this only because
she's white. As well as being committed to explaining his life to him
before he gets to it, which he's neutralized by shunting her off onto his
sisters, who needed that sort of thing until they married, which both
now are, to young NASA men. Physically he's a gangling version of his
mother, who has the crimped-gold hair and fair skin of some Viennese
Jews, though the long shape of his handsomely wooled skull and the way
his snub profile is indented there are, like his father's, faintly African.

He knows his father idolizes him. He has done his best not to make
conscious or unconscious use of it. Yet he knows he's here because of
it, as much as to follow Gilpin, his own idol. If the two idolatries inter-
connect, which his mother has now and then pointed out, then he
thinks he's made rather a neat response to all that—which, when his
father learns of his presence here and burns up the wires to talk to him,
it'll be Mole's turn to explain.

If there's time, which he sincerely hopes there will be. Because the
real reason he's here is, he has an inkling something might happen to
this ship. Or to put it another way—if something unforeseen or accidental does occur, his father and other NASA conservatives, while never
conniving at such an event, mightn't be averse to seeing such a project,
with such a passenger list, make an example of itself. Expensive, but
they're used to that. How many times has he heard them hold up their
flagship answer to expense: For the sake of future times.

So, Tom, I felt I had to come. So I did what you wrote you were doing,
in *The Sheet. Went down the white and walnut offices.* So did I, all
except Dad's, which you described so well. In all the other ones, though,
I did what I'd so often watched him do. Kept it simple and spoke the
truth—only not necessarily all of it. "Dad can't know about it," I said,
"because of that man, Gilpin." The smart ones just nodded, screwing
up their eyes. The dumb ones said, potato-in-the-mouth, what I'd only
had to hint to the others: favoritism would be alleged. All the way,
Gilpin, your name was almost enough. Plus maybe a little credit for me,
Mole, as a regular guy who wanted to join up early. From these men
he'd grown up with. "So you want to go. So, the admiral— Uh-huh.
What's your friend's name?" A tough bunch, his father's boys. When he
got out of there, respect welled up in him, for his father, too.

What he's afraid of is that he may want to be a hero more than a good
boy should.

The view from where he emerged that day had been part of his childhood and had grown with it. He'd always left these offices from the back. He was in the office yard, one of the atriums which often serviced government architecture there, sparing the Parthenon fronts. Pipes coiled from some basement hernia and went in again, thickly wrapped. Hydrants rose to brass caps on which he had often sat. Where foundation granite met gray earth, iron oxide fringed it like brown fern. Cellar door housings had wooden lids that flapped back as if for dogs. There was the mournfulness of retreated functions, to which nobody paid mind. The undisturbed air had a prism lightness. On the open fourth side, an aerial view of whatever the observer was tall enough for. In the foreground, for years, only an early print of a rectangular park of trees, dotted separate and from there the size of burrs, beyond these, green dales shrubbing an observatory dome soft and rosy as a mushroom, in rain or shine. Now, greater Washington was his, in a glorious, marble-reflecting sky, where even he its son could not always tell cloud from monument.

Come to think of it, none of the men propositioned had laughed.

"I'm laughing—" Mole says low, then stronger. "I'm laughing." He's sitting up now like a baby righted by its nurse. The sun at the window is a huge porthole of glare. I'm a barnacle getting a free ride on the universe. Glee shakes him. Freddie, by now in Osaka getting ready to build two houses—one "for quietude," near the National Park and in the style of the old catabolist school whose disciple he is, but also one house "for protective emulation," out on the highway and in the style of the sewer-pipe architects—can no longer share the joke. Fred has settled for the ground, Mole for the air. They'd always known they would separate, but not in what style. From now on we have our own jokes is all, Fred said, saying good-bye to him at the airport and handing him the book on the catabolists which is in Mole's documented luggage. Wonder what style is that motel you're going to? Let me know. Then for once the laughs hadn't burst out.

It's because of architecture that he's here. Because Kim's father—Eminent Kim, as Fred fondly calls him—had smelled a rat. A rocket buff from way back, at first he'd been all for Fred's going on the *Courier*. "Our firm did some of the industrial design for the living station," Fred said. He would never say "habitat." "We ought to keep a Kim foot in the door. My father went to see your father about it." Both boys know how Washington business is done. "But, Mole . . ." Fred's always very sober when he speaks of the firm, but this is more. "Yes, Fred?" He doesn't like to think of the two fathers together. "I'm to go for training,

Mo'. Why not? It's a plus. But whether I go on the *Courier*'s maiden voyage afterward—is watch and wait." Why? Something wrong with Mole's father's baby? Oh no—Eminent Kim says Commander Perdue's team has done a fine job there. "Admiral," Mole says, "he got for it. So what's wrong?" The project itself. Somewhere it's a bummer. What Fred's father had said more precisely was: "There's bad architecture there somewhere. Not on the drawing board maybe. But in the head. Or the heart." From a Kim, bad architecture was the worst that could be said. "I'll find out," Mole said. "Go to one of Mother's teas, if I have to."

In the worst of the hot weather Mole's mother handed out paper fans with the drinks. She said it made the gossip more informative. "Ah, Mole dear." For two months he's had his own place, on the proceeds of a summer job. The crowd has changed; it always does. But the tiny, packed house makes for classic parties. Amazed, she watches him take a drink, a fan. "Want me to help serve, Ma?" As a knobby-knees he often had, though she'd never prettied him up. Sadly smiling, she shakes the gold head people think she dyes. She and his father still make love and have no other lovers, no matter what is said. But she likes to watch others finding them. "Ah, Mole, if I'd known you were coming—there's not a soul here your age."

There isn't, but over there was the Eminent Kim. Neither he nor the gray-blond civilian talking to him is fanning. If you are a five-foot Oriental among all these gung-ho ramrods, perhaps you don't. But the other man, an Anglo type with a British suit and finish to him, but an American, who must be in State, maybe a Secretary, for few foreigners come here—what's he doing with that string of beads crawling through his hand? The Kim has nice manners. "This is the son of the house, Bill. And my son's friend. Mole, do you know Mr. William Wert?"

"Worry beads," Wert says, seeing Mole's look.

"Get them in that headshop, here in Georgetown?" Which sold all the casual machinery of meditation. When Mole was thirteen he'd bought a Turkish water pipe there.

"Inherited them." Under his linen jacket, Wert's wearing one of those transparent embroidered shirts from the Philippines. But the type he is, he could wear a monocle, too, and get away with it. "Cool me off better than a fan."

"Beautiful." Kim hands back the smoky purple beads. "See you're wearing a barong. Wish I had the nerve. I'm the only man here in my native dress. A dark suit." Kim smiles instead of laughs. But that's where

Fred gets his mirth from. "So, Bill. You liked the designs for the living station."

"Very much." Wert has a used face, but not a guarded one. "Don't see how you did it for the price."

"Cost." Mr. Kim's face clouds over. "The next highest bidder—too low to be safe. We know his ways. Wouldn't like to see it. Not for this. Fraid they were going along with it. . . . Mr. Wert's to be the civil administrator on the living station, Mole. He's going on the *Courier.*"

"But it was a plus for Kimco anyway, wasn't it, sir? Even at cost?" He's relieved when Fred's father, tossing back his Buddha head with an amused gape, admits it. He so wants him not to be a hypocrite. He doesn't see his own father anywhere.

"I like your hospital wing particularly," Wert's saying. "Hope we won't have to use it much."

"How many times have you been out there?"

"Once. It's no ordinary shuttle trip, you know. I do okay. Dull when you get there, though. With just a skeleton crew. Like a big empty stage set waiting for people. They're right to send that many. *If* they are."

"I heard eighty only, Bill. For your empire. I heard—sixty."

"Still a tussle going on," Wert said.

"They asked us to do the sick bay for the *Courier* as well. But we bowed out. Couldn't stick putting the body lockers damn under it. Some of my Korean ancestors buried their dead under the bed they expired in—but still. Hear they finally used an old Raymond Loewy design, modified. Very nice tambour. Though small."

"Body lockers, sir?" Mole said.

"I assume they don't bury—in that sea."

"Wouldn't be too sure what they do—hear about those satellites that keep disappearing?" Wert said. "No sign of them. Luckily none of that's my beat. For the living station, each passenger signs a cremation release."

"Not for the training." Mole shot a quick look at Kim. Freddie had left for that the day before.

Kim ignores it. "How'd you get the job, Bill?"

"Fellow named Mulenberg proposed me. Met him in Saudi, few years back. I had a—connection there then. With Ordoobadi International, their branch there. After I met you in Seoul. He's the project's civilian for ordnance. He said they didn't need a scientific chap for administrator, or want one—their military would take care of that."

"We have to assume they will." Kim's eyelids are as good as fans. "Mr. Wert helped me get Fred out of Seoul that time, Mole."

Wert twiddled each smoky bead as if it was a year. "Well, maybe this'll be the ultimate country, Ultima Thule. Actually, I'd turned down the job. Funny thing—Gilpin sold me on it. And certain—family matters."

"You know Tom Gilpin, sir?" Mole said.

"No, wrote him, though, after he spoke once. To a huge crowd in Boston, mostly your age."

"Fred, too—" the Kim said. "Is of the faith. So, Bill, you too think well of him?"

"Salt of the earth. Like his constituency." Wert bowed to Mole. "But like all reformers, sometimes inaccurate. The way he talks of the—habitat—you'd think that a living station was already a piece of Tivoli. When it's only—Paramus, New Jersey? Steubenville, Ohio? Haven't been back home long enough to know whether Gilpin'll be the salt of space—hmm. But his principles are as solid as—whatever's solid." Wert's manner was so knowledgeably tired you kept wanting to inquire of what. "He reminds me of Cobbett, or Jean Jaurès. You feel you could put his face on a stamp."

"Close yours, Mole," Fred's father says. "Or use that fan. Here comes your dad."

His father, embracing him in his complex way, which is never cold physically, scolds him for not coming home oftener, scrutinizes the full drink Mole still held in his hand—"Regular party rounder, eh?" and sends him off toward an army bigwig who'd unaccountably brought his pretty daughter; Mole knows why. Since he and Linda left school he hasn't dated her.

The general is evidently here for some info. Mole watches him operate. Of medium height, he works both up and down, sticking his short muzzle first at a succession of important wives, including his hostess. Getting nothing from Mole's mother because his father "never tells her business." Mole grins at his mother, who knows as much of it as anybody here.

When his mother leaves him to the general and four of the general's kind, plus a couple of under-secretaries and a covey from the UN—all anti-NASA either for good-and-fearful reason or good power ones—the paper fans really ploy. Mouths that are hidden can leak. No "that man Gilpin" talk is bothered with. The oddity of the passenger list is passed over as negligible, except for one snide reference to the choice of Wert. "It all figures," they keep saying. Something else is at stake. Linda's father leaves early, looking as if he may have caught a rat. Leaving her behind.

Mole, dragging Linda by the pinkie, says good-bye to Kim, who's now alone.

"Your mother's been so good to Fred, Mole. So good. I like watching her." Kim's snake-wife, Fred said, had cured his earlier geisha tastes; they now have a middle-aged Chinese housekeeper with cold flab cheeks and gold teeth.

Kim's really watching the admiral. Wert is being talked to. "Is Wert State Department, sir?" His father doesn't think much of Wert; Mole can tell.

"Not—quite. Or not any more. He has a past. Maybe an inch too honorable. For modern tastes." Wert, now edging toward the front door, caught their eyes on him, nodded ruefully, and edged his way out. "But he has his compensations. Evenings at seven, he goes home to them."

"Kim's keen," Linda said, leaving with Mole. She'd waved off her father the general, who isn't much but all she has. In revenge she makes use of him in his own style. "Where's Fred? In training? In *Courier* training? Gee." She looks frightened. "Gee."

Two days later, he had everything he or anybody could find out, short of espionage. If the dissident children of Washington were ever recognized by a foreign power as the prime source of info that they covertly were—the headmaster had once warned at Parents' Day—it could mean the collapse of government. "Space is *heavy*, isn't it," Linda sighed. "Gee, I love your place."

Two weeks later, biking off to the Smithsonian to meet Fred, who was having his picture taken there as a member of the training group which had come down from space Saturday and been released from post-training checkup yesterday, Mole *feels* heavy. What kind of torch is being passed to him, Linda and Fred?

"Oh—you know the Army," Linda'd said, picking fluff from his new electric blanket out of her long hair. They hadn't had to use the electric part. You know my father, she'd meant. Just as her pal Adrienne is Air Force and he, Mole, is NASA. Only the navy kids at school banded together, a breed apart, to take their fathers' side on things; when the sea no longer counts except to dunk spacecraft in, that's what you have to do. But everyone at school knew the echelons. By family, Adrienne was Mole's day-in, day-out rival for control of space, though in a pinch the Army—and Linda's pa the general—if here hand-in-glove with Adrienne's pa—was top-cousin, Army and Air being entrusted with that biggest hush-hush ambition: the big *W*. In Germany der big *K*, in

France la big *G. Krieg. Guerre.* Mole doesn't know the Chinese or Russki or other names for it.

After that came what Tom Gilpin called the big ruck and muddle, "the best of whom always write their names lower case." The civilians. Had Mole's father, the honorary admiral, forgotten that he was once one of them? No, it's cuckoo reverse. He can't.

"They don't want civilians on the platform," Linda said, lying on her elbow, as Mole was. She put the ball of red fluff she'd collected in Mole's navel. "I don't know why." This last was a fib, but they all had certain loyalties. Platform was what the general called the living-station. His father called it the NASA station, or now and then, depending on context, the L-5. "Why should he call it that?"

She leaned back admiring. "You have a deep belly button— Oh, I dunno. Maybe they want to mail things from it. Or load . . . 's what platforms are for, aren't they? What's your father built it for?"

For glory. But that was understood.

"To be able to build more of them," he said. "Because we're already ahead." She was broody, the way he'd found her when he'd picked her up at home the night before. When the general was between women his aides had to come play poker with him, with deuces and shop-talk wild and Linda serving them beer after beer.

"I don't ever want to get ahead, do you, Mole?" She was a neat math student—and by remembering the details of her childhood's banging around the world had won the geography-and-civics prize—but was otherwise simple. Any depth she had came from the broodiness. "Why do they hate civilians? Why does the admiral?"

He sat up, staring at his belly button. "Because they mess things up. You think they're counting on them to?"

She lay back, tracing a forefinger down his nose. "Oh, not my father. Not him. He's counting on yours. Any chestnuts to be pulled out of the fire, he says—he's counting on him."

"Very *old* chestnut, that idea," Mole said.

She said: "You have such a sense of style." He tickled her ear. They rolled over, sweating. "Look—" she said afterward, "it's still there. Your red belly button."

Then she'd reached over to the arm of his drawing board, where he'd set a jar of colored pens and pencils, in his first taste of domestic joy. With another girl. Carefully choosing, she bent to his belly, tracing a circle of dark blue around his navel. He knew it for an orbit at once. Next she drew an outer concentric one, in purple. For the largest, the yellow crayon she picked wouldn't show. She drew over it in orange instead, blurring the outline to make it a jagged one, with a flourish of her forefinger. Finally she dotted a black pen line from its arrowed end at the navel, down across the three orbits on his belly and into his pubic hair. "Where's that?"

She patted the curls. "Canaveral. Where the computer blocks are."

He'd had to laugh, even while concentrating on what she was telling him. "Now draw the *Courier*."

Fussing at already having used the black, she chose a thicker felt pen for it, first lightly flipping its point through a pubic curl. Her coquetry wasn't crude in itself; all girls used the material at hand. She'd got it from being slapped on the buttock for listening, as she trundled back and forth to the fridge for the beer. It was no odder than having an aunt.

She'd put the small black *Courier*-fly where he'd thought she might —not on the goal line to the L-5, the dark blue, but in the links between the jagged orange orbit and the undefined purple indelible. Where he'd been afraid she would. Then she slammed the pen and pencils back in the jar. "Game fini." He knew she wouldn't tell him more.

"Right over my appendix," he'd said, quickly clowning. "Will I have to have it out?"

But when they kissed good-bye at his door she clung a little, puzzling up at him. "We're civilians. Aren't we?"

The minute she was gone he'd rushed to the Goddard. Homework you did on your own was the kind that stuck. Days after, biking to meet Fred, it was still so much in his head that he plowed right into another rider parked at the bike rack. "Sorry," Mole had apologized, "—wrong orbit." He'd had to limp up to Fred, who began smiling at the sight of him and couldn't seem to stop; was Fred a little high? "Dangerous, down *here*," Mole said. They loaded his bike onto Fred's graduation present, a bug-car painted iridescent lime, and drove off to say farewell to Fred's exhibit at the Goddard, now in its last days. Mole didn't say he'd been there in the interim.

Fred had enjoyed himself, he said—though only intellectually. "That universe. Wow." But the going had been tough; he'd just barely qualified. He really shouldn't have. "But you know, Mole—they let me through like a breeze." Stopped at a light, they looked at each other greenishly, until the car behind tooted. Fred was driving. "Now tell me about your research," Fred said.

When they parked, Mole still hadn't spoken. "Ooh, the Goddard's an airy site," Fred said, walking up the inclined approach. "But I know airier." Suddenly he'd jackknifed into a running stance and galloped a big circle, halting again at Mole's side. Some tourists stopped to stare, but when he kissed the ground they half applauded. He wiped the gravel from his lips.

"What kind of grass you on?" Mole said.

Where Mole is now, locked and floating, Fred's answer comes back to him. "Grass?" Fred said.

Inside the museum, Fred no longer looked high but inward, like a person who had some body condition he was monitoring. He kept hunching his shoulders in, squaring them out. Dead center in the lobby was the mammoth walk-in model of the *Courier,* bristling black and silver but empty, and only one kid leaning over the railing to read about it. " 'Actual rocket size thirty-six stories high.' Something!" the kid said.

Mole nodded. "The important thing is to be identifiable in space."

Fred didn't laugh. Fred, who was never rude, moved on, not choosing to notice that Mole's limp was real. But in an empty room halfway to their destination he stopped. "Your ankle?"

"You should see my belly." He still hadn't washed off the crayons. Why should he be whispering? "Fred—there's no backup system for that thing. None at all. What's that mean?"

His friend moved on again, Mole dithering after him. "Oh, I know in a way, Fred—if that thing starts falling in the drink, say. Like the oldest Skylab, only sooner. Or say it misses its rendezvous with the platform. Habitat. Docking the ship, say they miss, yes. But the alternatives, what do they mean? Like—what about burn-up?" He knew he was only playing the idiot so that it would be like old times. Having seen at once that it never again would be.

Fred's experience had changed him. He was grave. Was he grounded for good? "There's no backup for burn-up, Mole." The dickey phrase didn't make him smile. Or say smart-ass: You just burn, Mo'. In a jagged orange line.

But yes, there were other ways to miss orbit, he said. He detailed them.

"I don't believe it," Mole said, this time for real. "I just don't. Overshoot. Yes of course I know what it is." It was an orbit like any other, only drawn in purple indelible. "You mean you can just be kept circling? For how long?" He stopped Fred by the elbow: "How long, Fred? *Fred.* For forever?"

It was an off-day for the Goddard and the room they reached was also empty, except for the guard. The glass case with Fred's exhibit, a model for a civic center in a lunar colony at the site of the St. George crater, was still there. *A multilevel structure for two hundred inhabitants,* the card said. *With features to influence minds to new sensitivities toward the environment, during the colonists' leisure time away from normal routine. Access to the lunar surface being possible through airlocks.*

"I wouldn't do it like that now," Fred said softly. He continued to stare into the glass cage. "Forever? Well, that would depend. On the supply of what they call—'consumables.' " They waited for each other to laugh.

"Now that you've explained it," Mole said carefully, "I go for the backup."

Fred swept a finger across the glass case and inspected it. "So does the Eminent Kim. Computers alone can't always manage, he says. He thrust his thumbs in his armpits and "did" his father. "Much cost, yes, Fred. In proportion to time. A backup has to be on the ready. To build this one, maybe two years. But they could have. The *Courier* itself took ten. This pushy admiral, who gets his billions for NASA and does what he wants with them—why didn't he push for one? So, Fred, I fear this mission is too special for us. No, we don't go. Not this time."

Mole, too, stared into the glass case, leaning against it. You were not supposed to. Behind him the guard approached.

"Pity—" the Freddie image in the glass said to the Mole one. "Gilpin's still going." The name rang through the glass between the two images. They had discovered each other through him.

"Pity—" Mole said. It was one thing to doubt your father like any green boy, another to grow up to it. And still another, to realize in the same instant that you had inherited some of his tendencies—say a talent for plot. "Pity, Fred. That I can't go instead of you." "Pity." He almost screamed it.

It was then that the guard had to speak to them—men almost, shame on them—screaming "Instead of me," "Instead of you," to each other, wrestling in laughter—or was it laughter?—on the museum floor.

He can now read the ON COURSE perfectly well. Maybe he'd dozed, or dreamed not being able to. Nothing else is dream. He's here. The part of the panel he's to check for ongoing instruction now lights up in smaller letters: Water Intake. He's practiced anything to do with food or drink. He presses the armrest. A nozzle inches up. Wrapping his mouth around it, he doesn't need to suck. The water rises in tendrils, filling him. He doesn't stop. The nozzle has done it for him; it's timed. Here each encounter with an element has to be. The elements are fierce and sacred here. He breathes deep. What marvel. To be in a place where this is so.

They've put him in the cabin nearest the flight deck, with all his second thoughts. When he came aboard, the crew who'd settled him in seemed to be having some; maybe they'd figured he wouldn't show. Two had shown up at the motel to check on his nerves; he'd bought them Jack Daniels at the bar, joshing on his own with the bartender, for his being under-age. The two who in the corridor had picked him out of a clutch of other Class A passengers—that elite whose existence Gilpin had predicted—and had seated him, had then drilled him on what they called "the courtesies of the house." If ever in deep trouble, for instance, there were flanges he and others could activate with their breath. He didn't ask what trouble. "Not until we've cleared the launching tower," one said, grinning. "And never come near the flight deck," his buddy said. "We shoot." "Comprehendo," Mole said. His father's word—popped. Such a glister on them all of a sudden. He felt too young to interpret it. "We'll remember you to him," they said. "If the time comes."

The ship's commander or captain and co-pilot had remained invisible, though they must have been informed he's here. Though all these men who've been picked for the *Courier* seem to travel in pairs and to think in the same style, there's some other unity about them, nothing to do with their insignia or even their profession. Pilots and navigators, they're the active crew who in shifts must run this ship—and after a while it comes to him what else they are—the ones so far known to him.

Charlie Dove, Arthur Shefflin, Ervin something, and two or three others who are merely faces—they're men of a sort rarely glimpsed in that combined top sector of Air Force and NASA operations known as The Joint, which is his father's baby, though they sometimes figure in his father's irritable home-comments. These are the ones who never appear at the Perdue house, in that inner circle which swapped its laser-powered calculations across his mother's punchwork tablecloth, or lifted glasses white or umber with cosmic change. These are the staff who've made it to seniorship by every dogged effort and road of circumstance from honest to dirty, except—top competence. Or have it, but narrowly, without that extra flare of—comprehendo. Government was full of them, his father said. Life must be. His parents have a house-name for them: Grade A Dummyville. In a pinch they could be Comprehendo's burden, or could outnumber him. Or he could make use of them, with their flaws in mind. His father has staffed the *Courier* with them.

"Graduation's such a paranoid time," his mother had sighed, on that day very full of her noble ancestor. "You think everybody's at you to settle your values. When really, nobody's bothering except yourself." She took snapshots of him, her careful substitute for indecent kissing and mothering. "I was the same." The phrase which at once spoils all parental advice.

"But we listen to them. How we listen to them," Fred said, on the second-class train ambling through the Japanese dusk toward Fukuoka, and toward the summer jobs his father had got for them. "My head is all echo. Of course, I never let on." They were passing through frail paper villages, the houses like lanterns in the woods strung along the train windows. "Eminent Perdue never lets on about his values, he only acts on them," Mole said. "Then you deduce. What's that smell?" Hair pomade. The whole car reeked of it. "Have some." Freddie handed him a tin of it. "Put on a local value. Then you won't notice it." But they were already laughing more genteelly. The snares had begun.

Maybe nobody ever really plotted. There were merely marshes of obligation, campaign promises to one's friends and family, election gains and losses against one's competitors—who, short of the national defense, were the only enemy—and suitable expropriations of performance and inertia from time to time. While the wind debates over the stage-lit domes as intended, his father and Dummysville greet every morning, the Chinese property man distributes the sunsets and removes them, a Gilpin rises on the national scene on a cockleshell wave and a modern general crosses the Delaware to forestall him—and the oysters come back to the Chesapeake.

And out on his porch watching the skies for weather, some oyster dredger remarks to his wife: "See they've floated that *Courier* on billions of scrip. Rocketed it to the far atriums. So's that Perdue kid could stowaway on it. So's he can see that life is only Washington as seen from a hill. And so's he can deduce his father." The wife, maybe already pregnant with what may someday be another Gilpin, does not reply.

Maybe nobody's plotted except Mole. He knows what that means. An excellent schooling in Shakespeare, Aeschylus and all the other great comic books, has taught him it. Plus the headmaster's required course in Greek and common doom. The plotter is always alone with his crime. In a nimbus of further crime-need. He has Mr. Chape's own word for it. The class hadn't yet found out what Chape considered his own personal crime to be, but they knew the feeling. Mole Perdue, who so early on had deduced his father, has no choice but to go on with it, even from half a million miles away.

What Perdue, his father, loves about his wife is that she never messes up from too much of the same talent that keeps them socially above the ruck. Perdue knows too many high civil servants and "militicos"—a word his son has coined for him—to whose dinner parties people go already drearily certain that all the conventions of such parties will be observed. The real powers—that is, the admitted and known ones—rarely appear at such houses beyond the once-a-year obligatory showing. They come regularly to Elsa's because she has their own tone and self-confidence—more verve and racier conversation—yet her evenings or summer garden-do's never lose control. Those paper fans of hers are known all over Washington, and once or twice have made the newspapers beyond, after which she'd pulled in a little, without a word from him. Even their menus receded for a while, below their usual Viennese excellence. It isn't his job to be known.

Not nationally, and not even late in career, like such "character admirals"—his son's phrase again—as say, Rickover was. The Navy, being the sentimental part of the military, is different. Even the Army is, since an army, even one using weapons so rarefied as to be almost things of the spirit, has to be visible. Yet Perdue can't keep a free press from asking questions on the military or political aspects of such a mammoth effort as the space one. What he can do, and has, is to keep that side of it constantly forgettable. Just because of such a press, and such a public, rapacious for daily news and weekly features but over the long run indolent, it can be done amazingly well. Unlike the socialist world, his government doesn't have to issue calendared White Papers, or Five Year Plans.

His best contribution has been never to have one open season for congressional appropriation. Lots of small ones, rather, in which NASA can raise its "progress uncertain" or "timetable delayed" skinny palm, yet rarely make the front page. While even the tremendous commerciality of aeroresearch is not the biggest bell struck—nor even the profusion of watch parts and other micro-hardware you could manufacture cheaper in space. For every time NASA asks for more, it does so in a comforting sea of flash aeromedical news. Give an American a better heart monitor for hospitals and henceforth you have a hold on the heart itself.

Admiral Perdue's own father had been the first black Hollywood director to make it big, though even by Gramp's time the family had been cocoa-color to wash-pink. "The American public wants to be aesthetic," he always said. "Just you keep telling them they are—in wanting what you want to give them. You'll reap from it. But that's not the *hull* story." He always came down folksy on a word or two; only time you could see the Hollywood in him. "We still let in dissidents, remember? After any war. During some other people's. What people here want—an*ces*trally if you please"—he always said that for the gallery— "is to be let in. To anything. From art to politics. Even to killing—you ask it the right way. Everybody *want* to be let in, remember that. Everybody except those few at the top who already are. You don't really have to do it, o' course. Just give the look of it. I don't make art movies, except by mistake."

So—the civilians' shuttle plane, *Courier*, and its goal, the so-called habitat for civilians. Still a space station really, enlarged suburbanly. A mobile home, trying to look like a real house.

Who could anticipate that a Gilpin would train such high-class philosophy on it? Who could anticipate a Gilpin? Perdue, his father, shivers, stepping up the walk to his house over the little red hands of the Japanese maples, which always fell prematurely. The garden is the only place where to his taste Elsa goes wrong. Mole, in one of his unfathomable switches, likes the stiff flower rows, too many of them red. "Like jelly jars. A jelly garden. Goes with the house." Whose "expression," however, Mole dislikes, adding that too many of the Georgetown fronts have it. "Like a Pekinese the husband walks. Sour Ming."

Warmth chortled in Perdue. Son-warmth. Nothing shows in his face. The best of sons have to flout what their fathers do. He'd done the same. A father has to take his chances with it. Fred and Mole lolling with their knees sky-high the way boys do, saying, "We don't want to be just drop-ins, you know. Into college." Still he, Perdue, has done what he can to make old Kim keep young Fred at home. Off the *Courier*, that is, without making a point of it. Offering Fred a post even, to make further space environments. The best good deeds have to go unnoticed, when not of the sort to be told to sons. These days, when Perdue passes old Kim on the tow path where men like them jog, Perdue with his bodyguard discreetly jogging behind, old Kim's nod is maybe a mite cool. Perdue can tell. Men of their mixed bloods have an advantage. Their faces, not being of the dominant race, are not as interpretable. Except to each other. Must gall Kim that Mole has elected to go to Japan again, on last-summer contacts Fred had blithely shared with him. When it was Kim's boy had won the prize.

Perdue's next-door neighbor, a famous hostess, always has too many cars in front of her house and his. But he won't complain, because sometimes the parties are Elsa's, though not tonight. Two cars are from the working press. The press milks a lot out of this street. He has his eye on one of the other houses for his elder daughter; the younger one may in time take over his. Mole won't marry for years. He has his eye on those geishas, he said. Perdue smiles, though it doesn't show.

Tonight he and Elsa have a date for a drink alone; she knows the pressures on him. Staying on to check Canaveral round the clock—four nights now, five?—he's late for it. The last of the old black maids who wait at the corners for the Washington buses has gone home. Good, she won't look daggers at him for living here. Or murmur, "Uppity." Standing on the step, he looks forward to Elsa opening the door for him, wife-warmth flooding his heart. She knows a lot about the human heart, related as she is to the man who wrote the book on it. And yet believes so staunchly in the worth of his.

He shivers again, waiting. Early prizes can be saddening, later. Whom the gods love, et cetera. Gods are useful; multiple or single, they take the dirt off one's hands. He really believes in them. Let the Gilpins be the atheists. And there's no reason to be sorry about young Fred yet. It's all on the knees of the gods.

The door opens. The entry hall is so small, so low-ceilinged, the heads of the newsmen gathered behind Elsa bob at him as if on pikestaffs.— Oh, Lee—Her home-name for him—Lee—the *Courier.*—Yes, Elsa?— The *Courier*'s, all right, Lee.—Yes I know. Just left the office—. The press can't already be here for anything wrong there. Besides, he's wearing an intercom.—Gentlemen?—He knows them all so well. Saw them at the launching. Will go on seeing them.—*Lee*—. What's wrong with her? She never interrupts like this. Knows when to sink back, when to shine. Always at his side.

—Admiral?—the senior of them all says. Always ranks you, tenderly. For the blow that's coming. But from where?—Admiral, we're reliably informed that a passenger on the *Courier* under the name Fred Kim is really your son. Can you give us a line on it?—Her mouth is what's wrong with Elsa. There ought to be a fan in front of it. For she truly knows his heart.

Nothing will show on his face.

And that's the way it'll be. Sketch him often enough and it comes out paint. I'm not as sure of her; she'll never let on what she really thinks of him. But that's him. Except for too much of the NASA bit. That's

Gilpin. Funny, how it crept in. But in every other way, that's him all right. I'm always so shitty good at it. At putting myself in his place.

Mole looked down at himself. Wonder will I tell Gilpin? ... Know I'm going to. Funny, how when I went up to Gilpin in that grisly corridor, how he seemed to recognize me. Though that's only the man's way; they all say. If I tell him I'm here, won't I have to tell him why? He'll worm it out of me ... Know I want him to.

Freddie won't talk—if the press get to him in Osaka. But he's there. And I'm—wherever here will be. Somebody'll leak it. Maybe the somebody will be me. And that's the way it'll be. For the honorable admiral.

The sharp ache in his chest isn't a physical one. That's unfair. Everything ought to be physical here.

He ought to be hearing from others in the cabin. Not a rustle above the flight's steady wash. Soon the aides must come with food—or did muscle drill come before? He's almost hungry enough to raid the emergency supply under the seat. Would an alarm ring out? He's tempted to—just to hear something. No, can't afford yet to get caught with his hand in the cookie jar, or in any unspecified act. Maybe no one here can. Maybe robot-hands, not in the manual, would unfold out and discipline them. Or maybe no one's here, except him. Which would he prefer? He won't answer. He prefers to be a child at his window, waiting to be called to meal. When all children are good. Soon the mother-voice will chime.

He dares a look at the window. A tremendous corps de ballet of stars leaps at him and over his head. Shift focus and those stars are stationary, Mole passing. Fixed points, maybe, of a far somebody's toleration, they gaze toward him out of the uncountable woods. Creaturing toward him, who can fly. If he had his golden branch with him, his magical brass-bone, he'd play clarinet for them. He's trilling, the long note unfurling from his mouth. Softly, p'roo. Who'd think that one could whistle, in non-gravity? In his dream or doze, his cabinmates answer him.

A man's descending hand, naked out of its mitt, nicks past his shoulder but can't rest there. To his sleep-myopic eyes it's huge and sculpturally near, a marble hand from a Rodin, from a monument. The hand of God, broken from the largest statue in the universe, is at his shoulder. But on the underside of its wrist, on the soft inner part over the tendons, is a human mark.

"Haven't played the clarinet in years," Mole mumbled. He woke. "Who's whistling?"

"You started it." Gilpin, grasping a wall bracket, is dangling over him.

Mole's ear can distinguish two or three ordinary chuffers, an off-key Wish-I-were-in-Dixie and one fancy birdman trill. Everybody in the cabin must be at it. Testing space with the tongue. Tasting Outer. God, above him, has a one-day beard.

The space suit hangs on Gilpin shabby-perfect, the way his clothes used to when he was lecturing, easy togas for that well-known head. Which is staring down intently at Mole's breast pocket. The free hand, marble no longer, floats at his side. The unsupported feet tread air. Sweat starts from the stubbled cheeks—floating is hard work. The free hand lowers to touch Mole's ungloved hand, turning it palm up. Freddie had done the purple wrist mark on it with a tattoo needle. He's an able draftsman, but the marks on the two wrists held up for Mole's inspection are not quite the same. A bead of sweat, loosed from the nodding head above him breaks into a cloud of minute globules, dispersing out.

"Sonny Perdue?" God says.

Lying on his rack, Mole gazes up, the joints of his limbs lifting and lowering as if he himself is the air's articulation. Thought is breaking out on him, like sweat too, crusting his upper lip with what tomorrow may be beard. The whistling has died, silenced by the truer music of affairs.

"Saw your picture once, in your father's office."

Mole, staring up, acquires his first definition of God. God is whoever is ambulating, half-created by the horizontal's awe for the vertical.

"Does your father know?"

Mole smiles down, studying his own body's rise and fall. Suddenly, with a swift glance at the panel, which says nothing new, he thumbs the right spot on the couch arm, his straps fly up and he with them, grabbing the hand rail in the cabin wall just in time. He's panting, but where everybody wants to be, from Peter Pan on. Walking on air. From his cabin mates below, a faint cheer. "Know what?"

"That you're here."

Swung by their hands, he and Gilpin ride chest to bumping chest. Must he answer him? Can't have two idols; you must choose. Letting one destroy the other. According to all the comic books.

"*I* know." It feels to him as if he's chosen himself. Perhaps it's meant to. This is what Freddie couldn't tell him. I'm the real liftoff. As Tom here is. As all the whistlers are, in all the goodly vessels. We're the orbit in the greater dark, and we'll be the docking, or the overshoot. All of us—the passengers of ourselves. Even to any dummies on the flight deck.

Is he now in possession of all the flight facts?

Quick, the panel's glowing angrily. RETURN TO COUCH.

"Tom—ask you something?"

But Tom's head is bent. One wavering hand has slipped its rung. The other's about to, loosing him to be dashed upward, or from side to side. How it would actually be—Mole can't recall. But his muscles already move, as on any old playing field. One of his fists uncramps itself, snagging Gilpin by the belt. Straining Gilpin toward him, lifting him like a sack of nothing, a human bubble, he hooks him to the wall. Turning carefully, leaning into it, he does the same for himself. No time for the couch.

So they swing again, side by side.

"Thanks." Gilpin's greenish around the mouth. "You wanted—to ask me?"

Mole shakes his head—oops! The tendons he overworked there a moment ago stretch oddly light, but not without effort. There's weight in space, but it's not—weight. Let the question hang there. "Never mind."

"Sorry." Gilpin's grimace is new. Three years ago when Mole first heard him speak he had a roundish crowd-blending countenance hard to remember. Now his hawk-lids droop, scarab-patched. One would know him anywhere.

So this is Tom Gilpin. Not old, nowhere near aged, but one can see how his aging is going to be, with no return possible. So this is Mole's father as well. Those who have to tot up their century. Men of power have such killing smiles when they're weakly like this—but would one die for them?

Gilpin caught sight of the panel. He sighs, looking downward. "Is that couch a hundred miles away? Or only ten?"

They've linked onto the highest grips on the wall. Mole half wants to let go, to try how it would be to bob in helpless ricochet. How niggly careful you have to be here. "You just go down hand over hand. Hand *under* hand. And leg. See those notches? They're on the transverse. Makes it easier. Just be careful—not to rise." He grins helpfully. Down below, the others in the cabin, all second crew, are now sitting upright like good pupils.

"You didn't understand, Sonny. I'll make it. Just that I'm scared." Gilpin's eyes bore into his. "Still want to ask me something? Or not?"

They swing.

It comes to Mole how precious such a question would be. One of the durable ones likely to go unanswered, even by headmaster Chape.

Unasked, it could sustain him through the airlocks ahead. Only clasp it.
Is space an opening out? Or a closing in?

"Sorry about this, Sonny. I'm of the gravity generation."

"Name's Mole."

"Sorry, Mole."

Pass *me* the torch, Mole said to himself. To all of them.

2

THE COUNTRY BEHIND HIM

1.

"So, you found your new wife over here," Bill Wert said across their table. All the Garrick's other patrons were still at the bar. Club London didn't usually dine at six-thirty, nor Wert either.

Opposite him, the heavily mustached young Iranian, last seen eighteen years ago as a boy of ten, stared at him unnervingly.

"I m-mean of course, in N-new York." Wert sat back, annoyed. To all steadfast career officers in the Department, any place outside the U.S., even one's own club in London, remained "over there" even when one *was* there. Normally Wert concealed it better.

Young Bakhtiary kept silent. "New wife," said to any modern upper-class Iranian, was tactless as well; monogamy was what was recent to them. To say it to Manoucher, whose father, in defiance of both fashion and palace ukase had taken a second wife at seventy and was now, at over ninety, taking a third (which must be why the son, for five years at the UN without a break, was passing through London on his way home), meant that Wert had jumped nuances and was speaking as family, to which his unique friendship with the elder Bakhtiary entitled him.

Under that luxuriant mustache, which these days must make him appear old-fashioned even among his own countrymen, the boy eating now looked stolid and alertly stupid, the way all young men of his kind used to. In the thirty minutes since he and Wert had met, he'd seldom spoken without deliberation, as if the two long balloons of black hair on his upper lip gave him that privilege. Their tapered ends, if slightly elongated and tied behind his narrow Aryan head, could serve him as a mask, should he ever need one. All the young men had looked like that, in the provincial Azerbaijan of the younger Bill's first tour. While there, a tender sprig barely out of Georgia, he'd never met a Bakhtiary socially, or a Pahlevi—the patronymic of the former Shah—either. This young man's mother, the august first wife, had been a Pahlevi. With a long palace arm.

"In New York?" Manouch, tall even at ten, must have got this from her side. He wore a Savile Row suit and Hardyman made-to-order shirt —which he wouldn't have acquired in the present oil-money "Arab" sack of London, but by inherited habit. He put a manicured and wedding-ringed hand on the cloth. A squirt of mock orange, maybe Floris, came from him pleasantly. "No," he said slowly. "I would not have find a wife there."

Wert grimaced, not concealing it. He'd never again seen Bakhtiary the father, or any of the family since that time in Venice, eighteen years ago, when the old man's whole female clan had been accidental witnesses to Wert's tragedy—the death of his wife Jenny in the courtyard below the Bakhtiarys' hotel suite's window—and the old man had for a spell adopted him. But the letters from Teheran still came regularly, written in the elegant Harrovian script and grammar of maybe 1905— along with slang roguishly Americanized for his correspondent. *Bill, I'm getting hitched again,* last week's letter had said. *Do you know the Egyptian symbol for life—the ankh?* Bakhtiary had drawn it. *That's what a woman is. And the same shape.* Adding, as often recently, *You're forty-six, Bill, fourteen years younger than me when I first married. Precocious, you were to us in Venice, married at only twenty-eight.* The old man remembered everything—even that the day was a Wednesday, when Jenny Wert's motorcycle had toppled on the cobbles below the Hotel Danieli's balcony—and often described it. Never until now saying, or implying as so many friends did, "Bill, why don't you marry again? It's time."

"You mean you wouldn't want to find a wife there?" Wert said irritably. Frankness had kept his rank low in the service, though the home crowd had learned that foreigners tended to trust him because of it.

"In New York?" the son repeated, then logjammed again, in the remembered provincial style. Had he been brought up in the provinces? Was he a smart Bakhtiary, exported to the UN, or only a rich one whose way in had been bought for him? Could this son ever grow up to the thunderously willful style of his father? Who'd fallen from governmental grace a hundred times, and always on his feet—a dapper man, clean-shaven even then, who talked fast English and moved slow, clearly accomplishing mountains of the intrigues they called work, and twinkling all the while over "our little corruptions"—teasing all Anglo-Saxons within range.

Manoucher was staring at him again. Wert saw him as he would have been in Meshed or Tabriz early on, walking along pinky-linked with another boy, not ogling the girls, but falling into quenched, agonized pashes confided only to each other, or even for each other, marriage being so long delayed that it was said these belated husbands often preferred sodomizing their wives. What could one say of him now except that at twenty-eight, Wert's own age that time in Venice, but surely married early for an Iranian male, he was not precocious? He was the son. Some kind of duty plainly exuded from him.

"In New York," Manoucher said unexpectedly, "girls are only to be met . . . or is it . . . meet?" He laughed. Not a horse-laugh. A careful rumble. In a handsome voice. Displaying himself, as the young blades who'd come to Bill's offices in Meshed or Tabriz had used to do, half in the prime hope of being cronies with the young American.

" 'Met' will do."

"I go to school in Germany. My mother insist. She went there." He shrugged. And suddenly, he recited:

> Uber allen Gipfeln ist Ruh
> In allem Wipfeln spürest du
> Kaum einen Hauch.
> Die Vögelein schweigen im Walde.
> Warte nur, balde
> Ruhest du auch.

Manoucher's eyes were now full of tears, probably because he'd done it so beautifully. Like the would-be cronies. Who had wept, reciting lines from the poet Firdousi, which Wert could barely understand, then had pressed his hand, grabbed up a last tea cake, and left. "Goethe. The most beautiful short poem outside of Greek, my father say. . . . Over all hilltops . . . *ist* hush. In *allem* treetops, not even a . . . the birds sleep, the little birds . . . wait thou soon." He shook his head. "*Ist* about death, yes? Though it says not the word. Even my father say—not translatable."

"I agree. I know a little German." Wert smiled for the old man, who wrote poetry the way they all did, but in French. "When I was in Iran, the Bank Melli in Teheran had a resident poet. There's a Bank Melli in the General Motors Plaza in New York. Whenever I pass it, I always want to go in and ask, 'Your staff poet—may I speak to him?' "

Manoucher whipped out a hand, pointing it at Wert so like a gun that the head of the Garrick's dining room, a slim, finicky woman dressed like the governess in "The Turn of the Screw" but much more ladylike of course, turned her pleated bosom toward them. A diner or two, lately trickled in, turned also. "You are the same!" this Bakhtiary boomed at him. Pleasure stretched his mustache. *Ewig* the same. As you were then."

"B-but how do you know?" Bill said. "You were ten years old, maybe. And I caught sight of you only once." You having been sent out and away from the women when I was brought to them.

"And the speeching. Exactly the same." The young man sat back happily, his tie askew. He was one of those from whom Western dress, even when worn from birth, parted creakily in installments from neck to belly, pushed by fluid bones meant for the saddle or the squat. "B-bakhtiary, you called us, my father say. And he always call you—Buh-beel."

So he had, mocking Wert's accent. Come in, Buhbeel, and talk, he'd say, summoning Wert every day for a month after Jenny's funeral. Wert's office, briefing him on the old boy's power and riches at home, had thought it wise for him to obey; even though the Middle East wasn't yet Wert's line, they'd said, any bright day in a department of state it might be; he already knew Farsi. In their kindness—he now suspected —they'd also thought it good for him.

So it had been.

"How is your father?"

He knew at once, from the plumed drop of the boy's face.

"When did you last see him?" Wert said grimly, quite aware that this shouldn't have been said—and had nothing to do with nuance. This had to do with the son himself. A beloved only son. The second wife had had only daughters, five of them. Yet although these days the world's air spaces were fairly perfumed with "Arabs" traveling deluxe, with all their children and servants as was their custom, this son of one of the wealthiest—of a man who flew to Switzerland on a whim for a watch or a mountain walk, each being valued equally—hadn't seen his father for five years, Wert couldn't hazard why, except that it must be connected with the fact that the father himself, for all his travel, would never come to the States. Had young Manoucher been banished for offenses unimaginable—although what could offend such a philosophical father? What son could fall from the graces of a man whose mildly just letters reminded Wert of Lord Chesterfield's?

"He is preparing to die."

"Die?"

The female maître d' sent Mr. Wert, such a quiet gentleman usually, a reproachful hint; under her eye, the waiter brought cheese. On second glance, with that fall of chainy gold among her blousings, she looked Viennese, and less governess-y—more like a patient of Freud's. One of those same complicated bourgeoises with nipped waists, but who instead of having her pulings immortalized had gone and found her proper job. She looked nothing like an *ankh*. A pang knifed him, for the old man, and already a gentle, flowery hurt for the old man's letters, sheafed like a wreath of fathers and uncles—Wert lacked male family—in their special box. He'd been planning a second box. He blamed the boy.

"Oh, Mr. Wert—not for a year."

Soothing him, no less, this phlegmatic poem-quoter, product of too much wisdom at home. "Something—besides age then." Bakhtiary had long promised to live past one hundred. And believably.

"Cancer of the mouth."

No wonder Freud had come to mind. For the last year, Bakhtiary had been reporting on reading Freud for the first time, gently mocking most of the way, once or twice furious over trifles—and suddenly the subject had been dropped.

"*Ankh.*" Wert croaked it. "Know what that is?"

Manoucher smiled. "Anyone who know my father, know that . . . He didn't tell you about her? This wife? He is so excited." He shook his head, tenderly, the mustachios floating. "She is sixteen. Like my own mother was. Like the second wife, too. From Ardebil, this one." He pursed his lips. "But from a good family. A very proper choice." Yet some cloud now came over Manouch; he hung his face in acknowledgment. Recalling to Wert the oddly open charms of that household whose ward he had been for a month.

The women of course had been only a background mist, except for the servingwoman, a body merely, which served tea like a walking veil, holding itself in bas-relief, producing from its cloth depths an entire silver tea set balanced on one snaked-out palm—hot pot included. Nine youths, all cousins, had lounged in and out, half of them living at the hotel, the others daily visiting. All of them had had personalities as supple as water; one could see their thoughts. The older men, of whom there were three contemporaries of the old man, were desiccated, powerful and opaque. Two middle-aged ones were lesser versions of the same. This young man, clouding over so openly, was still certainly nearest the youths. "And she is *not* a *Universität* graduate," Manoucher said, the cloud clearing. "My father is so excited."

"The wedding will go on?" Wert heard his voice crack; let it. Some prejudices deserved to be shown.

Young Bakhtiary leaned back, straightening. "And why not. She already chews the *nun*—the bread—for him. He so tires of custard. Lamb he can no longer take, though she tries. From her mouth to his. She is a good girl. It is unusual, yes, for her to be already in the house." The *maîtresse* just then passing, Manoucher's eye flicked once over her fortyish but tiny shape, as his father's would have. "Of course, he is not yet—" He hesitated, but only for the word. *"Entstellen?"*

"Disfigured." Wert shuddered, hating the German, wishing somehow that Manoucher's second language—no, third—had been French, which was his own second-best. Ordinarily the Iranians of his day hadn't been linguists, as his colleagues on the Teheran desk had early informed him. Not a matter of talent. Too unbending, they'd said. Too proud.

"No," Manouch said. "The clinic assure us. Too deep."

"He's in hospital?"

"After the wedding. She will go with him."

"To chew," Wert said, to the depths.

"To Isfahan," Manouch said stiffly. Had his English improved, suddenly or not?

"Roses of Isfahan," Wert grunted. He had an ancient record of that name, sung by Maggie Teyte. He'd never been back to Iran; though he'd have been welcomed. He'd preferred the letters. Knowing too well what a tour back there might do to them.

"Indeed magnificent. And a good hospital."

"As good as Shiraz?"

"As good, sir." The eyes lowered. Did that mean that his father had given this second hospital to the nation as well? From certain profits received?

"And the girl, will she—?" An idle question. A Western one.

He shrugged. No, Wert thought—not pond water, that look of his. "She has never been to Isfahan. Or anywhere. She is very excited. And she may have a child. It is still possible."

"Artificially?" It would be a most modern hospital.

"Not at all."

Wert was being scrutinized to the pore, like some precious quarto under a lens.

As he reddened, Manoucher said softly, "Mr. Wert. My father want me to tell you that. And more. Much more. But in particular 'Tell him about the child,' he say. 'That it is possible.' "

"You spoke to him?"

"We speak daily."

So the son wasn't after all exiled. Or else peculiarly so. And now he was going back. In the middle of revolution. For a wedding.

"And—m-more?" Wert said, softly cooperating—as he had by God, in his replies to the letters all these years. Discussing anything under the sun, and whatever the old man called the tune on. Sometimes going so near the edge in matters of nations, or national philosophies, that once or twice Wert had felt compelled to show portions of the correspondence—by habit he kept carbons of his own letters—to his closest friend in the department.

I don't see any conflict, Nosworthy had said, chin tucked in at Wert rather too keenly. Unless anything from antiquities to the Roman satirists—to the preferred methods of *coitus interruptus,* was important to the national defense. . . . As he supposed they were, of course. Still, Nosy, as he was called, had leaned fascinated over the letter on the aforesaid methods: Of course, I see you've given advices from time to time. . . . As I see he's given you, here. Hah! No more than friendly. He'd slapped the letter admiringly.

"And more? What more?" Wert found himself speaking in the old Danieli rhythm in which, during successive afternoons of talk, he'd floundered further into Farsi. Like walking half a mile out off the Lido, it had been—into a sea which never had the decency to cover your head.

"He wants you to know," the son said, answering also in Farsi. "He wanted you to know especially. 'Tell him I will smell like roses till the end,' he said. 'She will see to it. Be sure to tell him that. . . . And I suppose you will have to tell him about the food. Manouch,' he said, 'tell him that the saliva of a young girl is sweet as sugar; he still won't like it; they think that unclean. Though they keep their own unclean body hair. So tell him this. Persuade him,' he says. 'That in the evening in hospital, in the last dusk, she will still do for my body what it can no longer do to her.' " Manoucher blushed. But perhaps at the *maîtresse,* whose skirt, flouncing near, like her glance on both of them, had brushed Manoucher's elbow.

"Why couldn't he tell me those things himself?" Wert said in English. "Write me, I mean. We never spared words. And I'd just had a letter."

"Oh he meant to. *Vielleicht* he meant to, Mr. Wert." Manouch gave him the gliding look they always did when they wanted you to know they were lying for courtesy's sake. Nosy would have called the look insincere. When it was just the opposite.

The boy's eyes were that extraordinary Kurdish blue. Some mountain infiltration, way back when? Though one wouldn't lightly imply Kurdship to a Bakhtiary-Pahlevi, except in family teasing. He began to remember the protocol, every item of which, the old man had said, had a desert reason. "Like our obsession with roses and fountains," he'd said, in his stiltedly perfect-spoken English. Slang he only wrote. "You Anglo-Saxons have the same, Beel. Climatic habits, I mean. Once, in the long vac, while I am at Harrow, I am invited to a school friend's family in the Cotswolds. After that, no one has to tell me why English parliamentarians have that sheep-snuffle. Or why their wives neigh like mares. . . . You must have the same cause and effect in America; what would they call it there—*print-out?*"

Bakhtiary was always subscribing to dictionaries of slang and obscure academic publications, as well as to dozens of the little magazines, cultist bulletins and pulp rags he called "Yo-yo." *"Because after a time, it doesn't bounce."* He loved all the new American euphemisms, the new graphs, as the fresh green evasions of a civilization reluctant to examine itself—"Dangerous, not to, yes, but it happens to you people every time." Why didn't he come to the States and see for himself?— Wert had often written, but this was never responded to. Just as for some years now—ever since the tenth anniversary of their meeting, on which date Bakhtiary had sent him a spray of the same small green sherbet-colored orchids he'd sent to the undertaker's parlor in Venice —he had no longer mentioned Bill's wife.

"Ought to get rid of that German stuff," Wert said. "Can't do you that much good at the UN." Or not with us.

"Father says the same."

"What's your post there?"

"Oh, quite insignificant. I am what you call—underfoot. To learn."

Which might mean either that the clan hadn't been able to buy him in—or that he was being groomed for the top.

"*Vielleicht*—what is the English for that, Mr. Wert?"

" 'Perhaps.' "

"Pairhops. No. Purr . . . haps. R-right." The son was making a steeple of his fingers as children did, with the thumbs serving as portcullis, or door. Opening these slowly, he looked in, spellbound. "Purr-haps it was your last letter from my father, Mr. Beel?" He closed the thumb-doors, crushing the steeple to fists. "It was my last phone call." He brushed his eyes. On the single-breasted jacket that bound him so perfectly, a button popped.

"Why didn't he ever come over here?" Wert burst out angrily. "He went everywhere else."

"He never tell you?"

"No."

"That it was because of me?"

"No. But I suspected it."

"Something bad, you thought."

Wert couldn't answer. His eyes stung. So for Bakhtiary Senior, no more of that tumbling exchange-bazaar of ideas—stopped now at the pen, stopped at the throat. Yet stipulating roses all the way, in the senses left to him. Wert remembered planning, years back, how he would take Bakhtiary south, to Athens, Georgia; they'd have understood him there.

"Nothing bad, Beel. I assure." The boy's eyes shone their improbable color. Devotion, in a blue mosque. "I will ask when I see him. If I can tell you. If I can speak for him."

Wert put his face between his hands, smoothing it, blew his nose. "Sorry. I get these irrational angers, these days. All my emotions seem to turn into them."

"And you are only forty-six."

"He did tell you everything." Wert put out his hand, was able to smile. *Can* I help?"

"But you have help already. *Wirklich.* Only because of my mission to you—am I allowed home."

"Mission? Thought you were just passing through."

"I see at once you will be too angry. When you walk in."

So this vague, rancid choler he couldn't shake must be plain to all— in his gait, his gesture, probably even the flushings of his skin. Like those men clowned by drink, whose veined noses marked them. "What is it? Your—mission."

In his mind he was already telling Nosworthy. One of those little corruptions, would it be? They had no sense of the level of these to Western eyes, since standards were simply not the same. As the old man had smilingly pointed out to Wert early, moral standards on both sides were impossibly high—but in reverse.

Would Wert be asked to use his "influence" precisely in some area where he couldn't imaginably either have it or exert it? Like getting a failed candidate for Oxford by hook or crook past the examiners, and in? Or persuading the Victoria & Albert to part with a piece of the national treasure—at a fine price of course—to some avid tycoon in Teheran? Where the university itself would have done the Bakhtiarys any favor, and maybe the museum, too. It wouldn't be anything military; that drama had long since been transferred to the corporations, in the open style learned from the West. No, it would be some amusingly human exchange, which, for the Bakhtiarys not to perform for the cousin or uncle who craved it would be a breach of the highest family faith. Or it could be a favor for friends—in which case the fealty required soared altogether out of sight. Wert wouldn't be asked anything directly connected with his job. Nothing small, that is.

"I have two missions," Manoucher said. "One—to get a sweater set, size forty-eight, for my mother, at Harrods." He snapped his fingers, grinning. "Accomplished."

"Yes, the pound may be down momentarily, now and then. But thanks to cashmere, never quite out. What's the other?"

Young Bakhtiary pressed his hands to his vest, looking up. It was an English vest—and ceiling—but Wert fancied that behind the vest's wearer he could see the sky in Meshed and smell the sulfur tinge of those winter afternoons when some celestial vegetable seemed to be comfortably burning, while a luminous-eyed young crony, backing himself up against the wall of Wert's study, recited stanzas nominally addressed to the Five Gates or the Tortoise River, but just barely grazing these loci of history with personal allusion, and choked up halfway through with fervor and embarrassment. Waiting for persuasion by all hands to help him through; which was ritual. After which everybody glowed with tea, and went out into the dusk convinced of human glory, and his own part in it.

It had been a marvelous way to spend an afternoon. Only the grudging would see it as one more of those late-marrying young males' substitutes for sex.

These days Wert himself couldn't persuade a flea of anything; he was tired of any of that, dejuiced of all early generosities, or ardors, and resigned to his own sex substitutes of the moment—a late-melting pub-love now and then, or more recently, a brisk smartener with a woman barrister who'd had her wrenchings also. By now he knew that a life spent in "tours"—the departmental phrase—had a way of putting the most colorful present into the past, almost as one experienced it.

Meanwhile, a single man whose general job classification—Cultural Attaché—might often mean exactly the opposite, could take compensation in a tinsely string of telephone numbers circling the globe, and often brightly renewable, especially on leaves home—since by now his sophistication on other countries was endless, and his own people, tired of innocence, were well ready for it.

But how tired he must be, to sink with such gratitude into these cushiony Middle-Eastern pauses, where there were stanzas of time between thoughts. As in the days after Jenny's death.

"Mr. Beel?"

He sat at attention. Importances often strung themselves along a man's life in the same recurring style, often with the same people.

"My father ask you tell me the history of that day. Of your meeting," he said, as if coached.

"The day at the Danieli."

"Please?"

"Name of the hotel."

"Par*don*. We were in maybe twenty hotels that year."

"Um . . . Excuse me—I do this for *you*?"

Manoucher thought, gravely. They had postures for it. "Us."

"My word." Wert always swore in the manner of the country he was in, a habit he disliked but couldn't shake. Blame it on a tenderness toward the foibles of far places and peoples, which gripped him the minute he stepped over their borders, making the host people his always excusable darlings and him their surefooted interpreter. When young this had made him briefly valuable at his job; now there was danger of its tabbying him; in his line, the men who went to the top were not the sensitives. Already this talent for observation may have cost him his nativity. For when he went home on leave (where if confronted as now he should be saying "Bro-*ther*" or "Kee-*rist*") that other stance persisted. He was always faintly explaining Americans over his shoulder to a savage interlocutor who could only be himself and who gave them no quarter—tenderness to the foreigner not being involved.

"Let me see—" He meant to exhaust all his own pauses. Meanwhile running over the possibilities. Could the dying Bakhtiary, reading late into the night, next to a bowl of roses as was his wont, have become convinced of a heaven of confessive therapy for all? Nonsense. They never even pushed Islam, except politically. To them, all the other garden-of-Allah Islam doctrine was already consonant with the existent world. Or else the rest of the world wasn't worth the conversion. Or not to Bakhtiarys.

No, it would be something practical, within the terms of what friends do for one another; the old man always insisted that Wert had done a lot. Could it be that after all these years they still thought that Wert had some actionable claim—against the city of Venice and its non-pavings?

Or the Lambretta cycle company, for making what it did? A couple of the older men in the Bakhtiary household in Venice had had an even odder expectation—that the State Department would surely compensate Wert for the loss of his wife, either by finding him another or furnishing him the wherewithal for a richer one. These two had even argued which alternative would be the fairer, while the head of the household, who knew that Wert by now understood almost everything in that language, watched him.

Old Bakhtiary had had one of those countenances made powerful by skin-disease surmounted; the pocked skin had stretched all-of-a-piece over the heavy features, a fine hide, worsting time even in the ceremonial picture sent Wert two years ago, when the old man had had a medal for state services unannounced. In the dim Italian voltage, the beard under the shaven cheeks shone dark green. Whether or not from his lack of skin mobility, Bakhtiary had only one facial expression—a dignified alertness to advantage, so steadily held to that one never had any clue as to his immediate acts. But as to his approving any long-gone claims—again nonsense. All the man's actions were immediate—though performed with an air of ageless calm.

The waiter was asking whether Wert and Manoucher wanted coffee in the lounge. Beyond, the *maîtresse* watched him and Manoucher with a care not all duty; yes, she was Wert's type, competently neat and with a businesslike sensuality, probably clever enough beyond her station to be companionable, maybe arrested by class difference but not crushed by it. Not at all likely to be one of the poignant ones Wert couldn't take.

"Tea," Manoucher said. "I'll have tea."

"A sweet? The trifle is good here." Wert was recalling those Venetian pastry wallows in which the male and female halves of the Iranian household had most nearly converged. The men, arriving one by one or in pairs, had indulged themselves patriarchically, as if they were doing this for the home, as perhaps they were. Clustering at the samovar, lacy tidbits in hand, they looked the more virile for it. The same physical heightening occurred when they leaned intensely over flowers, sometimes over a single bloom, or swarmed almost scholastically to examine a fresh bunch of freesias or iris. Extending into what in other countries might be the woman's sphere, and often in the most delicate attitude, their blunt masculinity seemed only to increase, even to its own scent, in a way that assailed Wert, abashed him and could never have been explained at home.

Giggles would come meanwhile from the women, eating too, behind a screen which the hotel had supplied. A sense of their family life exuded through its wooden lattices—of deferential girls, black-eyed swans barely out of the nursery, waiting to enter some other harem of family women whether they were to be the one wife or not; the older women were the go-betweens. In Bakhtiary's house in Teheran the women's quarters had still been separate; even in the relaxed hotel version Wert had seen how the day consumed itself for both sides in dozens of rumorous back-and-forth domestic transactions, beneath which the sexual, a blank to outsiders, must be explicit to all. Courtship, even for those of his young cronies in Tabriz and Meshed who'd been at university, and for the girls, just beginning to attend, whom Wert had glimpsed there, unveiled by then but black-dressed, off by themselves and still giggling—had been a matter of channels running separate. The groom of an arranged but delayed marriage occupied the engagement period in elaborate romanticizing to his devoted male friend. The girl would be always with women, presumably taking in whatever mid-wifery and suggestive passion she could over pistachio-sprinkled maca-roons—being urged to more whipped cream and filliped toward a man all in one. When girl and man finally met and coupled in the hot, honey cake dark supplied them, did they speak?

Manoucher, hesitating, was feeling his girth. He, too, saw the *maî-tresse,* and lowered his eyes. "No thank you, no dessert. Three months, and I am already getting the marriage-fat."

"Your father won't approve of that."

"I have to send pictures, every month."

Wert laughed. Everybody in Teheran knew the story of Manoucher's mother and father. Old Bakhtiary, having left his country as a young man "to see the world," had lingered mainly in Paris and other chic corners of France, until he was sixty and assumably well seasoned, when as he himself said, he had returned home "To found a family." In the year after the heir was born, when both parents had grown connubially fat, he proposed to his wife that they take a thinning cure at one of the spas known to him during his long golden youth. She, strong-willed as he, had to his surprise refused either to leave home for foreign uncer-tainties which might unseat her, or to grow thin—which both he and she apparently equated with modernity and the West. He had forced her to Switzerland anyway. It was rumored that she had then done the unheard-of—refused marital relations. The old uncles of the traveling household, however, blamed her later infertility—for which Bakhtiary had dispossessed her, on her weight. In any case she'd had no more children. The second wife, the old men had said contemptuously, was thin enough—from having only girls.

It couldn't matter much with the third wife—not for long.

"Your father has the best of both worlds. Actually he doesn't give a damn about ours; he's always mocking it." How much laughter there had always been around him. In his company, the younger Wert had felt pugnaciously in command of life and its golden days—with a good swathe of both still in prospect. Even now, whenever one of the letters came Wert saved an evening, dining alone over it in the black-and-silver Kensington flat he'd subleased from a transferred colleague who'd had a fancy wife. "Decoration by Heals," the lease agreement said. "Not to be tampered with." A while back Wert, moved to satisfy the old man's charmingly voracious interest in the lives of others—or in Wert's life—had sent him a picture of the sitting room's coffin-slim couches and starved, sculptural drapes. The following Christmas he'd been sent an enormous domed-brass brazier, centered in a multicolored circular comforter thick as eiderdown, under which an entire peasant family could lie old-style, feet pointed toward the coals. Since when it lay vivaciously on his black-cat floor and conveniently took the eye of any woman he brought home.

"Not you, Mr. Beel; he never mock you." Again the scrutiny, so strong it raised the nap on him.

In the lounge, Manoucher parted his mustachios over the tea. Just so tea had been drunk in Meshed, the young cronies in their badly cut blazers, bending in obeisance to the ark of friendship as if an invisible *imam* had given the signal, their intense eyes brimming over the cup at Wert, the host, at each other, in adoration of the situation of kinship, focused on the samovar whose cobalt flame they could carry anywhere. Sons-of-generals working as Embassy clerks, shy teachers who'd never before rubbed elbows with those except through this foreign host of theirs, and that one young poet to whom all deferred—Wert could never have explained to them how frail friendship was in America. In the red-velvet night clubs of Teheran at the time they could have seen the U.S. version of it in the executives and technicians of the Point Four program boozing over the caviar—a backslapping, sometime thing. Wert had later brought his samovar out with him along the roundabout route he had traveled home, scooping up the last sights of a country in which, still a tyro, he'd thought he might have left behind a life.

Rocking with him in the plane over the Elburz range, cradled on a bus seat along the Caspian and flying again over the desert-bordering bazaar cities in one of whose crucibles it maybe had been made, this bronze, crenellated pot with charcoal crumbs still in its belly, such an elaboration for boiling water merely, and indeed falsely stamped with the Russian imperial crest as so many were, seemed to him a concept he was bringing out with him, although when finally disposing of Jenny's effects he'd sent the thing itself to Jenny's parents in Illinois. By that time, Bakhtiary's letters had begun, and he'd had no further need of it.

His coffee cup clicked against his teeth. I know what I am to this boy-man of theirs, this possible tiger engrossed in training himself up from cubship. I'm a bequest. Or I'm going to be. It's been decreed. I'm to be young Manoucher's old friend.

"What can I tell you?" he said, leaning forward. "Our story? It wasn't much." In Manouch's hard blue gaze and just perceptible headshake he saw that it was. Or it flowered there, as he himself spoke. "We met in Manila, Jenny and I, my second tour. My first, as you know, had been in Iran—Tabriz, Meshed. In Manila, she was working for the Filipino professor who was our Fulbright Commission liaison." An idealistic girl from Antioch, she had hobnobbed with the young Filipino intellectuals who published *The Literary Apprentice,* teaching them Martha Graham rhythmics on the side and tangling too ardently with their anti-American politics.

"She was helping picket the American Embassy when I met her. A sailor of ours who'd killed a Filipino national had been sent home for trial, instead of being tried there."

The Roe case—in the light of the Marcos regime, what ancient history it was. It had been a period when all Southeastern Asia was hung with the lanterns of exchange scholarship, as if it was nothing but a ruddy international tea garden—and Vietnam had been only one more place.

"Maybe she married me just in time." Dressed in one of their Maria Clara blouses, a high-shouldered embroidered trifle which he'd ultimately sent home, too. "We were married at the Embassy." With a wedding lunch at the Overseas Press Club where, as Jenny had written her mother, they'd had custard-apple ice cream, and a group of dancers had done a dance of stepping over bamboo poles, called the *tini-kling.* "Venice, where I was sent shortly, was really our honeymoon." Living at the Danieli with other departmental couples in an expense-paid suite whose governmental arrangements dated from World War II, they had been part of an almost communal life which might well have seemed normal to that other Iranian household in the hotel.

"Yes, my father tell," Manouch said tenderly. "Four months. And such a pretty girl . . . he see her. On her motorcycle . . . I did not see her. But all our women talked of it."

"Middling pretty," Wert said. "One of our—girls. Nothing out of the ord—" Though sometimes in bed, in that silly-soft gilt gondola, as he leaned over that thin profile of hers, which was like a slash of indelible ink on the afternoon-shadowed sheets, the breasts like two small inverted cups, and the patch of pubic hair he and she had called her "mouse," he'd actually felt his heart stop, wondering if love-embolism could kill. "She shouldn't have been on a motorcycle at all in that city; I don't know how they sanctioned it, really. But she worked for the consulate, a kind of courier." And in those days the whole world was deferring to our American machine-style—even those wily thousand-year sailors the Venetians, with their brigand doe-eyes. "She was so proud of knowing all the streets she could use it on—a whole backyard network. Sometimes she had to part with it, though, and use a *vaporetto*."

One noon he and she had run into each other on one of those, and putting a finger to her lips she'd flirted with him until he picked her up, to the siropy outrage of two well-dressed sixtyish signoras behind, who kept *Cara!*-ing each other like machine guns. *Cara, can you tell which of the Americans are whores? I never.* Answer: *Psst, Cara. Maybe they all wear yellow, like the putanas in Russia.* When all four were getting off, Jenny, who was wearing yellow, turned to them, saying in Italian, "He's my husband, we're going home for siesta." Everybody laughed like crazy, and they all ended up for a drink at where the signoras had been heading—Harry's Bar. Where it was their habit to sit for hours in the smart leather hats one of them had made, clicking their bracelets, gradually removing an arsenal of cigarette holders, lipstick cases and other frippery from their handbags, and being persuaded by table acquaintances to take orders on all of them. *Cara* Marcella, *cara* Tonia; he remembered them yet—and how, when Jenny'd said to him, I parked the Vespa on the Zattere, they'd rolled their eyes at each other. *Chic!*

Nobody ever stole the motorcycle, no matter where she left it. Probably the whole of Venice knew whose it was, she'd said, giggling. "Such privilege, ain't it orful," she'd sighed. "And four months ago I was a radical." Seriously discussing their progress, they'd both concluded they hadn't yet compromised on any principles. But they'd meant to keep a sharp lookout.

"She'd only exchanged the trusty old Vespa for the Lambretta that day." Wert's thumb pressed his teeth: "She hadn't wanted to." But a requisition had been put through, in the lavish embassy style. And the order had come through. My darling old Vespa, she'd sulked—couldn't we keep it somewhere? "If she'd been riding the old one, maybe— But it was junked."

"No it wasn't." Manoucher sat up. "The hotel head porter salvage it. My father buy it from him. For me. It go all over Europe with us, for years. Our gardener in Teheran has it now." He pushed the tea away; China tea meant nothing to them. "You see, you were so romantic, to us. Both of you. So young. Together—in a marriage. So dashing. And no children. . . . To the women especially, she was. And so odd. Riding that *machina* like a horse. Astride." He was reddening. "And in those thin clothes." The flush deepened. "I was still with the women. When they heard that—sound—they all rush to the windows. I was not allowed to look. Never. But I already hear it wasn't the same machine. I used to sneak out to where she kept the old one. The porter let me."

The old Vespa. And Wert had kept nothing. Not even the samovar.

So romantic they were—and so practical. The porter must have been bribed; Wert remembered him. A bow for the Americans, but for the Iranians almost a salaam; he'd probably been on their retainer the whole time. Which hadn't prevented him from being the first to run out from his little office and pick up Jenny, or the doll bleeding from the nose that she'd become. Such thin, gauzy stuffs she wore that steaming summer, that day a green-and-red dress, picked up for a song at those stalls near the synagogue in the ghetto, which fell from her waist in points like a handkerchief. No helmet; in Italy then nobody did. She'd loved the way Italian men on foot sometimes paced her, running alongside her back wheel crying *Bella, bella* until with a wave she outdistanced them.

"Yes, the women saw it," Wert said. "And ran to your father. When I came in from the office for lunch, not fifteen minutes later, he met me at the door. He didn't want to let me talk to the women—but not because of your customs—not at all. He led me in there, when I asked."

He'd never forgotten the sight of that group of women, their veils rimmed beneath their eyes, clinging to each other in bas-relief, or as if in these quarters which they never left singly, some daily applied nougat paste kept them even from moving their limbs separately. One of them, on command from Bakhtiary, had been persuaded to drop her veil for Wert, giving her account. "The cobblestones spat her up," she said, to her husband, not dreaming Wert knew Farsi. "High in the air, with her *place* showing." Their word for Jenny's "mouse." "If she'd worn *chador* like us," the woman said, meaning the shawled wraps, without which in spite of the heat there, these women never left their rooms, "maybe the head would have been spared." Then like one of the Fates she'd raised a draped arm and shut her face from Wert's sight.

Once outside again, the old man—if one could call him that as the spry septuagenarian in a silk suit he was then—had apologized. "Fateh sours, from only having girls." When they went back to Wert's room and saw the Italian doctor in pince-nez and black ribbon, leaning over the pillow and the fall of hair on it, as in one of those Victorian lithographs —"A Medical Call"—old Bakhtiary had dropped on one knee slightly in front of Wert but still linking hands, so that Wert, forced down with him in that Christian posture, stayed for a minute there hand in hand, staring at the backs of Bakhtiary's shoes. Then his hand was released, so that he could go nearer. There Jenny was—or wasn't. In the silly gondola bed.

"Does your father still have shoes made to his own last in Jermyn Street, and then wear down the backs of them like carpet slippers?" he said smiling, and stopped short. Manoucher was again staring at him in that bug-eyed, Coptic way which made one realize that all the frescoes, from Persepolis to Greece to the Pyrenees, stated a simply observed physical resemblance.

"What—what . . . ?" Wert said, and stopped short. How much of this conversation had been said aloud. How much only thought? And for how long had he been speaking in Farsi?

"Ye-es." Across the dinky cocktail table Manoucher took Wert's hand and held it. Wert let it stay. The ill-lit lounge was occupied only by one other couple and a foursome, all of them British and busy at it, and the club was after all—thespian. And he did feel; what did he feel?

As if he was reporting on glory, a small tincture of it. And that Manoucher knew.

"She was so terribly nice, you see," he said in English. "Jenny. So—nice. And so terribly—" Close. The pacts they had had, the jokes—all so interwoven.

Jenny hadn't fenced him in by dying; she'd left him irresponsibly freer than he'd meant or hoped to be. She and he had meant to keep such a sharp lookout.

"Do you have a picture, Beel?"

"No. I kept nothing. Except something your father gave me, afterwards."

"She is a dark-haired, my father say. With a good white skin. And features not *dick*." His tongue made an effort. "T-thick. And she sometime play 'Für Elise' on the hotel piano."

"Mendelssohn's 'Spring Song.'"

"He say she does not have the blond nose American. Like this."
Manoucher pronged his own narrow nose into a pug. Wert burst out
laughing. This time the English people did look up, and away.

"More like this," Manoucher said, making a two-fingered aquiline
line on the air.

"Not quite. A slight wave to it. Like this." Wert guided him. "There."
He sat back. He felt nearer that bed than he'd ever dared go since.
"Actually, she wasn't that other kind of American, but one generation
only. Her folks came from Bulgaria but were Armenian; her maiden
name was Arkanian."

"So." The eyes glowed.

"Now's there anything else your connoisseur father would like me to
tell you?" Like: height five foot six, waist small, weight I dunno, have
a try at one-twenty, shoe size seven—large. And a head with a great
cave-in from which a cockade of brain protruded. Bakhtiary, who measured all women, hadn't seen her at her best.

"There is. But I *weiss* not how to say it." Manoucher threw up his
hands. "Promise you will not be angry," he said in Farsi. "Please believe
me. My father requests for reasons most *serious.*" The Farsi word was
actually nearer "real" as Wert remembered. Or real-to-life.

"Yes? What?"

Manoucher leaned toward him, a forefinger raised like a priest's.
" 'Be sure to ask him,' he said on the phone. 'I forgot to. I trust you to,
Manoucher. I can trust you to the end of the world. Haven't I done so?' "
Manoucher took time to smile at himself holily but Wert still couldn't
help liking him. Loving him was nearer the truth. "Go on, then."

"What was the color of her pubic hair?"

When Wert didn't answer, young Bakhtiary stood up.

Wert stood also. "This wedding of his—must have addled him."

"I could wish it even. Because of the pain he has. But no."

Tears rise so readily to their large, already moist eyes, Wert thought,
but is that bad?

They went out to the entrance and got their coats.

The doorman handed the red-faced, almost blubbery Bakhtiary his
coat, but helped Wert, whom he knew. Or because Wert was senior.
Outside, the London evening glittered like channel water, always a
puzzle to him how the nights here shone so, with so little light; must
be the wet. Through the portico they could hear this most obsequious
doorman in town, out on the steps now, letting in a latecomer. "Gu-
u-ude evunning, sah—" like a wipe-down from a masseur. But if you
asked to hire him or his wife to masticate food for an old man, they'd

have you up at the assizes. What was enlightenment, that it could patronize a young man for the tear in his eye?

"I get it," Wert said hurriedly. "I'm his bequest to you, isn't that it?" He raised a hand to the boy's shoulder, higher than his own. "I'll do my best to act like one."

The eyes above his veiled. When they were about to take refuge in oratory, they often lowered their eyes like this. To let you know. "It is my father's nature. To make gifts."

All of their natures. The cronies had come arms laden to the train on which Wert left Meshed, though he'd been there scarcely a year. "Come back," they said knowingly, more to this year out of their lives than to him, for they must have known he wouldn't. Raining on him pictures they had taken six months to paint, silver ashtrays marked with their own names, they had wailed it: Come back.

He should have sent flowers to Manoucher's hotel even though the wife wasn't with him; perhaps he still should. The sexual allocation of flowers meant nothing to them; there was a ritual. Not in tribute to people; he saw that now. To that sacred, irrecoverable time which had been between them.

"Have you a picture of your wife?" He should have asked at once.

He was proffered it. He took the thick cardboard to the light. Odd how in the Middle East they still managed these nineteenth-century photographs, with that same cold purity of line which used to come from plates which took hours of soaking to develop—and a long time to pose for. In Tabriz he'd seen ancient German tripod cameras. Though perhaps in this case it was in the purity of the sitter. On a polished white glare the head of a handsome girl perched in cameo. If that huge space between the eyes wasn't touched up—no, they hadn't minimized the thick brows—she must be beautiful, even with a mouth so severe. The glare wasn't entirely from the paper.

"Soraya."

"Soraya." Like the Shah's former queen. Whom it hadn't been polite to mention. "And like all your own father's brides—is she, too, sixteen?"

"She is twenty-four." Manoucher looked him straight in the eye.

"Ah, Jenny's age," Wert said too quickly. But very late, for them. Or used to be. In fact the respective ages of both were all wrong. Or more like us.

"Will she be joining you over there for your father's wedding?"

"She stays in your country. To make the house."

A German-style one, by the stern lift of that face? The Iranians had always admired German expertise.

"We are married only three months."

"Still time then," Wert said, knowing these jokes were in order. "To make him a grandchild." Oh he was trying. This time he knew he was speaking Farsi.

Manoucher put the picture away in an inside breastpocket. He had clouded over again. "She is—*Universität* graduate."

"Ah . . . so you met there." Wert had done this evening all wrong; he was years out of date on modern Iran. He should have asked Manoucher to meet him in the bar; maybe, in spite of the Koran, they knocked back their scotch like anybody—maybe the two of them should go for a nightcap even now.

"No. I never meet her there."

"Ah. You were engaged to her before." Before he was sent away. But would even that explain the age of the girl?

"No, I never meet her. She say she think she see me once, somewhere from far away. Before I leave Iran. But until she see me the wedding day, she is not sure." Manoucher put on his overcoat. Preening? Yes, a little. "It was I."

"Do you mean—?" Of course it was meant. A young man five years away in the raw city they all wanted to conquer. But where girls were merely met. A boy who was important enough to exile, or whose family was. For nothing bad, he'd said. If you were all that and a learner too at the Western arena where for all their public scorn they carefully sent both their richest money-splashing aristocrats and their finest talk-dragons, no, you wouldn't take just any wife. Amazing how they could act from conventions thousands of years old and still appear inventive. Confidence did it, roiling in this boy's veins as bright as blood.

The "boy" was fastening his overcoat, regally. The doorman rushed to adjust its collar, receiving his tip by a sleight-of-hand so fast Wert only knew of it from the man's face.

Manoucher nodded, standing tall. "I write my father, yes? And he send her to me."

Just then the *maîtresse* appeared. In the umber light of the old entrance she came toward them on neat feet, all the time seeming to move deferentially backward. Her gold watch swung from her blouse on its rose-velvet bow-knot, pinned to her collar, not to her breast, as a woman not in service might. She would always know her place. Yet the gold chains, which he now saw ended in a bunch of functional keys at her waist, stirred in reverse, faintly sexual. In her hand, held out to Wert, was Manoucher's button, the one he had popped.

Wert took it and passed it on. Bakhtiary kissed her hand.

"Mrs.—Vrouman." Wert wasn't after all surprised he remembered her name. These things had a way of storing themselves up for him. "My —godson."

Surely no member had ever introduced her before. She took it prettily. Perhaps she'd never before brought any of them a button either. "Vrouman—" Wert repeated. Though the "Mrs." might well be complimentary, in the same way that the British dubbed their cooks. "I had fancied you yourself were Viennese—" They exchanged looks. He had fancied. She noted it.

"No sir, I'm Dutch."

She left, thanking them with excess, Wert thought, even for what he now recalled the English would call her—a manageress. Until he glimpsed, in the kissed hand trailing behind her, a clutch of bills. He laughed. "So you noticed her, too." Manoucher joined in.

Out on the steps, "Gu-gude night, gentlemen," rolled down them like suet. "Shall you have a cab?"

"There are no cabs anymore and you know it," Wert blurted. Ashamed of himself at once, he passed the doorman a coin. "Where you staying, Manouch—the Savoy? My car's down the alley. I'll drive you there."

"The Dorchester." His eyes glinted.

Of course. Islam had bought it.

And miraculously, here was a cab. What's it doing, creeping up to them from where it had been waiting? Marvelously gleaming cab—the cabbie had a cloth still in his hand. " 'Ere you are, guvnor." Allah had dispatched him—having been applied to beforehand. The cab, on weekly hire for one night, belonged to Manouch.

Wert pressed his hand. "I'll be in New York shortly. Shall I speak to your wife?"

"I will not yet be home. But call on her," Manouch said in Farsi. *"Please."*

"Of course," Wert said, in English.

"My mother is with her."

"I always wanted to meet that lady."

"She knows all about you. Also, there is the other wife." Manoucher's teeth, suddenly shown, are magnificent. "My father's, Mr. Beel. . . . But Soraya does not like it."

"Ah well, two mothers-in-law." But shouldn't an Iranian girl—a girl who would still submit to being married as this one had—be used to such leftover polygamous households?

"My mother and the other wife, they tell everyone in Teheran they come to New York to wait for our child. Except my father. They do not tell him."

"Why not?"

"There isn't yet a child," he said, gloomy.

"Manouch. Only three months."

"And if Soraya—if there should not be, I could not tell him," he said distractedly. Suddenly he is a wild man, pulling at his tie, raking his hair.

"Manoucher. Why not?" Hadn't she been a virgin? Wert dared not say it. "Manouch, control yourself." It was what one crony back there had said to another, after the story of love unrequited, love hopeless, and more usually, love untold. He patted him.

Manoucher straightened his tie and hitched at the overcoat. It was polo-cloth color and cashmere, or maybe even vicuña, and the longest, thickest and no doubt lightest ever seen. No Briton had tailored it, no New York one either. A French expatriate from Algiers maybe, sodden with hashish. "Even it should happen—I do not tell him until his own wedding time is over, yes?" Manoucher said, in the sugary tones with which they said We are speaking the truth, you will understand, but not *the* truth. "That is his time; he should not be—worry-ed." Only this last word being in the English in which Wert had continued to answer him.

The thought of that ninety-year-old, spry in mind as he was, on his wedding-deathbed, being incantated over, tossed ribbons and chocolate, going through it, however it would be done, only to have the door closed at last on both his exertions and his suffering—it shouldn't bear thinking of. Why instead should Wert feel that he himself, for all his panoramas, hadn't yet had a life? "I suppose."

"We have our reasons, Mr. Wert. Always. Like you do."

Young Bakhtiary's voice is cold now, adult, remote. Not a godson's. What it says is: We know all the nuances. And now—would you like to cut things off?

"I assume you know your father's reasons then. Why for instance he would want to ask me that most extraordinary . . . personal—"

Bakhtiary bowed his head, almost all the way to his vicuña breast.

"But you can't say. You're not allowed to."

A headshake, violently *yes.*

"Enough. *Enough.*" The boy might break his neck. Even the cabbie was staring.

The doorman, of a higher caste, has turned his back. "Weddings—" Wert said. "I had only one of them."

The boy raises his head. How he does alternate his ages! "When we marry, we also *give* gifts."

"Do you." He was thinking of Jenny's "mouse," tangled wet with both their fluids, and so long now in its body's grave. If there was a grave. When he'd wanted to have his family ring, which Jenny always wore, buried with her, old Bakhtiary had whispered: "No, take it with you," and when Bill persisted, had removed the ring himself, while the Venetian undertaker emitted a shocked Catholic sigh. "Son"—Bakhtiary had said in English—"grave-snatchers, don't you see? What do you bet this man has a connection? In fact—" he'd said, switching loudly to Italian, "in Venice you can scarcely bury at all. Perhaps you want to send her and the ring home." Wert could have done that through the Department, and with flags, too, but instead left her in Venice, ringless. Later, sending the ring via Bakhtiary's kind offer to take care of such details for him—to the cousin in Georgia, who, awakened one morning by a solemn Iranian on her doorstep, had never got over it. Bakhtiary had had the ring delivered by hand.

"Well, whatever *he* wants of me, he shall have," Wert said. "Tell him —that it was black. The mouse was black."

For a moment Manoucher didn't get it; then his head cocked, smiling sadly. "Thank you. And bless you." They embraced, kissing cheeks. After a moment, Wert leaned on the cab door. "Shall I bring over your mother her sweater set?" he said in English.

Manoucher grinned. "Already done."

And probably by hand. "I'm loathe to let you go," Wert said, the old Farsi formalities liquid in his throat. "You can see, my dear friend, that I don't want to." He stood aside for Manouch to get in the cab. "Give your father my eternal love." In Farsi it was easier. "Tell him I keep his letters always. And the copy he gave me of the *Gulshan-i-Raz*."

"He gave you—that?" When Manouch was caught off guard, the mask made by the mustache faded. One saw the man behind it.

"I shall send it to your first son."

The boy sat back without speaking. Damn stupid of you, Wert. He stuck his head in the cab. "Manouch. The child will come. And in time, maybe, to have your father see the—what will it be?—the one hundred and seventieth of his line?"

"The seventy-sixth. He exaggerates." Was the kid smiling? No, but the man was.

"Right. Still, you're the seventy-fifth. To an American, that's—what's your New York address by the way?"

A card was slipped to him, bearing more numbers on it than he'd ever seen on one address. "Where's *that?*"

"Queens Boulevard."

They burst out laughing again. That used to happen—instant double laughter with the father. Who'd once said, Perhaps we two should be in oratorio.

"Thank you," Manoucher said. "For the mission. You cannot *weiss* how much."

Wert closed the cab door.

The cabbie gave a last slap to its gleaming fender. "Lovely soi-ght, isn't it? 'Aven't the time for a cleanup on the usual." He swung himself in. "Except I get one of these blokes. . . . The Dorchester, mi-ind you. Soaking in oil these days. Roight? Tally-o!"

Inside the cab, whose window was open, Manoucher, dark and erect, said no word.

Wert drove home roiled with emotion. Landscapes of it were passing one another in his breast, which must have been empty-ready for them. Meshed, Manila, Venice, and Athens, Georgia—as seen through Jenny's eyes. Teheran—though he'd never seen Bakhtiary there, or ever again since Venice. And Queens Boulevard, which he hadn't yet seen. In his youth, some such interweaving was what he'd come to the Department for. Yet he could no longer see himself making any new moves for the future among these scenes, even though he had no thought of leaving them. Other people might be kindling to new passions, or like the old man—to further news from life. But these days Wert waited for others to set things going; his own letters to Bakhtiary had said as much. Very liberating it had been, never to get a moral reply, and few direct ones. By the time they got around to answering each other's thoughts, these had faded gratefully past the contemporary. Any application to living could no longer be made.

He meant to take out the box of letters and begin rereading backward, down to the first, under which reposed the red morocco box Bakhtiary had given him after the funeral—opened then and never since. It contained a small white, plaster death-mask of Jenny. "One can get anything made in Venice," the old man said. "Better than a gravestone. One day you can break it. But not now."

Driving home, he began to be irked by the way the Bakhtiarys, father and son, were involving him. Not with their own private lives, which in spite of all the elegant public poetry, they kept hothouse dim. But if you were a serious friend, they would keep looping your own life around your neck, hanging it on you to confront you with it, as with the box, whose purpose had been: "Mourn now."

Wert parked the car again just off Kensington High, walked into the square where his flat was and entered the pub almost directly opposite,

glad that he was in England where, having had so much of the real
poetic thing, they'd developed antidotes for it. Neither a limbo nor a
place to let go altogether, the Hartsdale was a spot where, though he
was known, he might sit and consider his friends without having to
acquire more of them. It wasn't yet ten o'clock; he and Manoucher had
dined early. He sat over a shandy, considering much, then went to the
telephone, dialed the Garrick, and when it came on asked for Mrs.
Vrouman.

A female voice, presumably the kitchen's, answered: "She's gone for
the evening." No trick at all to get the voice to give him her home
phone; should that tell him something? At the home number, a much
superior female voice asked him to hold on, called out, "Helene Vrouman, Mrs. Vrouman," came back to ask, "You're not her mother's nursing home?—ah, good," and without fuss dealt him another number
where he could reach her. He was further convinced of the woman's
prospectively tidy cool; he admired the Dutch. It always pleased him
to find women of whatever class who pursued their solitary way with
sure, businesslike steps—almost as if, had he been the one to die early,
Jenny would have become one of them. Cleaving through life neither
remarried nor a mere widow-pensioner, and with a certain quiet personal radicalism—though by now emotional only, not political. The
third telephone number had a familiarity he couldn't place. He dialed
it. "Dorchester, good evening," the phone said.

Crossing the road to his flat, he thought of the quiet dramaturgy of
machines. They ought to be members of the Garrick, all breeds of them.
Somewhere on the telephone boards a few tumblers had clicked, and
here he was with more knowledge than he ought to have—small change
as such details were these days. Mrs. Vrouman—a woman who did
instead of didn't, which he'd sensed already—might fade back now into
the collage Wert had made of her, only forgetting the roll of bills, folded
perhaps around a calling card. But Manoucher—who wouldn't stay a
boy any longer, and whose missions either in Iran or in New York might
therefore not be a boy's—troubled him. He was glad of his own flat
coming up—in spite of its black-and-whiteness so comfortably chaired
and bedded that he could always sleep off any ambition there. And so
acceptably not his.

In the front areaway he passed the sturdy, smutted hedge which
never grew. Then came a flight of the spruce stairs he much preferred
to a lift. Inside, in the sitting room's grate, there would be a fire laid
pridefully high by the char whose away-all-day gentleman treasure he
was; each night he lit it, a happy arsonist. On a lean marble table in the

side hall he would find mail and packages brought in by the porter, who was old enough to love a lord and to settle for an American. A bottle of Bulmer's cider was always ready beside his turned-down bed. No messages in his box. How did irritation enter in? Through what cracks?

What he first thought he saw was a white furred arm reaching out from the grate and up past the mantel; then he saw the flowers on it, crusting thickly. He turned on a lamp. A potted plant the size of a small tree stood in front of the fireplace, one long dazzling branch arching toward the ceiling, then dipping gently to trail its blossom fingers almost in his brazier. Between that and his landlord's plinth-like marble tables there'd obviously been no place to set the plant down except on the hearth. Was there a card? No, but on the table lay a ticket which said just that—No Card—from a shop just where he thought it would be—in back of Park Lane, near the Dorchester. If he knew anything about Iranians, the pot would be special too. He knelt. It was. Thick putty-colored ware, calligraphed with early indigo, manganese purple and eye-blue, the kind of pot one saw only in museums or mosques. Or should. Sometimes there was a rare flush of pink on them. He touched it, half smiling. A lesson in how to send an unbribable deputy-ambassador—a legal pot.

He drew the curtains and turned on every light in the sitting room, rather as he did when he brought a woman here. To assure her of what was here and what uncozily wasn't—and for later, to be able to turn the lights out. The plant was as tall as a girl might be; its buds and flowerets were unknown to him. By now he was accustomed only to a certain artificial language of flowers, anyway. He was aware, for instance, of those beaky bird-of-paradise blooms which in Southern California grew outside any dusty insurance office but in New York lorded it over the tables of flash restaurants—and that his mother's favorite, the true American Beauty rose, seemed no longer to exist. His cousin liked freesias, which were available around her birthday. From an earlier time, there were garden sweetpeas, and those gardenias one had sent girls.

This great spray of brown bark and flushed white must come from a fruit tree, or what once had been one, tamed now to a shrub. Not apple, and not so pink as the cherry blossoms in Washington. He had an idea it wasn't from any of the places where London got its hothouse supply either—the Scilly Isles, Kent. Algiers, maybe? Gibraltar? Crouching on his heels, he leaned forward. Wound around the plant stem was a coil of what he could identify—those same tiny tree-orchids of spotty tiger and freckle-green which Nosworthy's wife grew on the place they'd

meant to retire to, before the blacks' unrest. "Who'd have thought it of
Jamaica?" Nosy had said, last time Wert went for a visit. "I tell you who
should have. Us." Nothing had rousted Nosy's gloom, certainly not
when Gail had said, "But Nosy dear, how could we have known? We
never had a tour *remotely* near."

He went to get his bottle of Bulmer's from his bedside and sat down
again in front of this plant, or tree, with that strange wreath at its base.
It was perfectly possible Bakhtiary had arranged for this flamboyant
bouquet, maybe even to be made to some exotic specific from the
Gulshan, which translated meant Rosebed of Mysteries. He saw Bakhtiary laughing up his sleeve—if his throat, in which the cells themselves
must be spreading like fantasy, still allowed that. Hell. Who else could
have sent that pot?

An hour later, finished with all the cider in the fridge and starting on
brandy, Wert was still sitting there. He seemed to himself to have lived
always between two parallel tracks which, as far as he could see into
future snows, were still separate. On the one hand, human nature was
the same the wide seas over. Yet on the other hand, everywhere on
those seas, and clinging to the gravels and fjords as well, there were
clumps of people cohesively different. This was why the world didn't
work out, and he had a job.

The big spray of fleshy blooms quivered now and then in a chill
current which came from an unshuttable register; the British never
really wanted to understand central heating, but like his old hotel in
Manila, where the showers had been present but unconnected—they
now provided it. Because of this inconveniently precious pot on his
hearth, he couldn't have the fire he preferred. It had taken over his
sitting room, a warning. Its givers meant it so; he knew them. Never
press a moral; give a gift that seeds the mind. Give no advice but poetry.
And never confer a favor without first asking one, so that the one given
may be acceptable. What favor were they going to ask—or confer—on
him?

Weddings—the evening had been full of them, all airborne on the
breath of Bakhtiary's mortality, under that jaunty boast of his, "I shall
smell roses all the way," which one had only to cut shorter to see the
meaning of: I shall smell. As your Jenny had, by nightfall. As one day
—you. This branch dipping its gentle tip into his gift brazier—was it a
rose? Named for a woman, as roses often were, or for queens? There
must be a whole generation of girls named for that deposed queen
whose picture used to be in every palace and hut. Like Manoucher's
Soraya, on whom he must call. Those tenacious tree-orchids, he had

seen their like long before. That tenth anniversary bouquet sent him by
Bakhtiary had been made of them—little Jenny-blooms with their
green-pink tattery petals in handkerchief points. All of this was being
done with their dreadful literalness. What was he being led through this
evening, like a man wearing a blindfold it was time to drop?

Women—the whole evening had been made to murmur suggestively
of them.

He was being urged to marry of course. But in all this sickly-sweet
barrage there would be some steely hook of the practical. He was as
sure of this as that he was now staring at an eighteenth-century pot
identical with one long ago admired in Bakhtiary's quarters at the
Danieli. Its replica—in an artbook of their national museum's treasures,
which had been propped up behind it—was as Bakhtiary had said quizzically, "out on loan." What the hook would be he couldn't prefigure,
any more than he could dispose of this particular pot by sending it home
to his cousin. He had the letters, which might help. Last week's was on
his mantel. "One must learn from the physical," Bakhtiary had written.
"Everything in the universe is anticipated there."

Anticipate he must. Or wait to be embroiled? What saddened him
now was that he had a year of grace to find out what he was targeted
for—about the same time as Manoucher had, to produce a son. With the
help of that wife. Even makers-and-shakers like the old man had to wait
for grandsons; who knew but that with the help of the little girl from
Ardebil he was hanging on for just that? Or to see Manoucher safely into
harbor somewhere. Both, more likely. And in the rhythm of their ways,
Wert too would have to wait with them. Because he was to be a legacy:
"To my beloved son, Manoucher, for use in the profession he has nobly
chosen: One tame diplomat, carefully cultivated."

Wert laughed. The flowers stirred. If that thing had been a woman
instead, its nearest rosy tip could have picked his breastpocket, or put
a token there. He felt ashamed, a recent habit. To its giver he was that
powerful entity which their like could spend a lifetime treading the
waters of feeling with—a friend. In turn, they were friends beyond any
shape of friendship Wert was likely to find at home. Certainly not with
Nosworthy, whose only real allegiance, after the Department, was to his
wife. As Bakhtiary had once commented, this was often the case with
the Americans. "We are still very Elizabethan in my country, Bill," he
wrote, "in more ways than one. Have you noticed?" No, he'd have to
read up on the Elizabethans, Wert wrote back, privately marveling at
how his own slapdash education was being returned to him—from their
side. Sometimes he did have the scholarship, and then his own brain was

picked exhilaratingly. What had this senior friend, compared to whose lineage even this pot's was new, ever really asked of William Graham Wert of Athens, Georgia, scion of only four known generations glossed by one part-time brigadier general? Only a correspondence.

Better put the brandy away, or he might weep into his cup—a picnic mug marked St. Ives, left over from a weekend with the she-barrister. When young, he and Jenny had wanted to learn from existence what things were proper to weep for. Only with Bakhtiary had he continued that pursuit.

The mug shot from him, but being of thick ware rolled oafishly on its side, where it did have a look of its round donor when she had her legs in the air. He'd had a pleasant enough time between them. Don't asperse that shingle she can hang out, either—her name scripted in black-on-cream, high on a fine law-court door. Given the temper of the times at home, he might well soon have need of the kind of advice she could supply from behind a desk, with her legs strictly together. "Everybody's now sunk in dollar-shame, for which somebody *else* must suffer," Nosy had reported. What if that bloody intractable, wise, sweet, and wily ninety-year-old should leave money—and pride would call for a whack of it—to him, Wert? He was going to be given something inconvenient. He could feel that for sure.

On matters of state, Bakhtiary always addressed him formally. "You understand us so well, Mr. Wert," he had written once. "I hope your employers appreciate it."

Nosy had paused over that letter, too. "Very complimentary. And what did you answer the old guy?"

Wert had written back, taking the trouble to underline, My *country* appreciates it.

Nosy'd slapped him on the back for that one. "Tough isn't it, to be friends with any other national? There was a Frenchman once. I'm not Catholic, but I was to be godfather to his first child. His wife kicked up a rumpus clear to the Vatican. Where her uncle was a cardinal. . . . And I was just coming *in*, you know. Wouldn't do."

"Just after World War Two was it?" Wert had asked. A lot of men like Nosy had come into the Department then, the last romancers of war.

"Right. And before Gail." Nosworthy had picked up again Bakh's little disquisition on coitus. "Right you are, Billy me boy. Keep 'em on sex. That keeps everything straight."

That damn plant hiding his hearth made him angry. He knelt in front of it. The pot, a vase really, had been affixed to a modern base made of their overbrilliant silver. They thought nothing of cramming the centuries together however hideously. Born knee-deep in the beginnings of world art, they could well afford to leave mere taste to the parvenu West.

He put his arms around the great chill vase, and by alternately tugging and creeping backward managed to inch it safely over and off the raised fender. Waxy buds pressed him, warm and resilient; not a one dropped. He was being resisted. Over a shoulder he saw that the plant's highest arch had gracefully entangled one of his landlord's rapier lamps. He got up to free it, his arms carefully circling. His hair was raked; a waft of bloom entered his ear. Once, in his teens, he'd marched in a hometown parade wearing a holstered flag which had continually streamed back over its bearer in a tussle the whole laughing town had been watching; this felt the same. He went down on his heels again, pulling. There. Done. The tree, for it was surely that, now half-barred a door, but one could brush past. By its scent, which seemed to come from both their exertions, yes, it must be a rose.

Perhaps he ought to give it a drink. In his bedroom he found the carafe on the night table freshly filled, although his good char, swerved off routine by the arrival had forgot to turn down the bed. Selfishly, he stood in the doorway and drank the water himself, watching the addition to his household. Maybe best to let it die, while he was in New York, with the char off duty. Calling on the daughter-in-law must be gone through, but was obligation enough.

That was the least a conscientious bequest could do. Being one—and he meant to be decent—was chancy enough. While taking all care not to be annexed. At home, friendship died when its generation did, but with them, maybe because they had so many more generations to look back on, its obligation rested ever heavier on the young. In Meshed, one of the consular clerks, an older man with a family, had been nearly bankrupted from supporting a widow with family, no relation, because of an obligation inherited from his own father. What Wert had to guard against might be Manoucher's supporting him—with favors impossible to accept. With a persuasion as mild and patient as their water buffalos used to be. If ever a man was marked by son-ship, that was Manoucher.

He began laughing again. The tree didn't seem to mind. That pot must have heard a lot of laughter during eighteen years with old Bakh, and after God knows what palace mayhem it must have survived. Smoking-hot intrigues in which somebody got the knife, rope tricks in which prisoners were hoisted to oblivion. Nowadays of course, the perpetrators were westernized—which to them meant merely: Your nation had better manage its misdeeds more openly; the world is looking at you.

In the Danieli, he used to visit their suite daily, with the sun streaming in gaudily on the fine Tabriz rugs they had laid over the hotel carpet, and the women walking past him barefoot to oil the rugs naturally—though outdoors they affected French shoes which peeped back and forth from each enveloping *chador* as if there was a second and extra-retiring woman within.

Fifty years ago or less, he might have had to have his balls cut off before he was allowed inside the door—or would have had his tongue cut out afterward. Once, there'd even been voluntary eunuchs; their power in public affairs had been so deviously great. In the old days, maybe they'd have sent him one. To brush his clothes, brew him syrup-of-figs when he was bilious, keep his diaries and any loose state papers suspiciously free of lint—and perform certain services for him when he couldn't sleep. As eunuchs had done for the women, it was said—for when wives accumulated, a wise husband kept them content. All the habits of the world probably persisted somewhere; there were no "ancient" ones. Pity Jenny couldn't know.

He got up, and tiptoed—God knows why—into the dressing room, where he refilled the carafe and returned with it.

Very gently he tested the water in the pitcher with a forefinger. Museums were humidified. The pot felt ice-cold. Delicately as a curator attending a papyrus, lightly humming under his breath and yet restraining an impulse to pour in instead the rest of the brandy, which was one-hundred-proof Metaxas and sure plant-murder—he watered the tree.

Whistling, he lit the char's pretty coal-castle with his usual pleasure, then sat suddenly back on his haunches. He'd been messed with that's what. Interfered with in his private music, shut away for years. He sounded the yearning whistle again. Orioles flew out of a nest in Georgia. His young wife to-that-date had never seen one. She'd had two musical calls with which she'd summoned Wert, birds, the family, the world. This one, which he'd just whistled, the motif from *Das Rheingold*, had belonged to her relationship with a previous man, and she'd worked ineffectually to get rid of it. The second, not a whistle at all, she was very proud of, as the most exotic of her collection of street cries—the cry of the man who'd been selling hundred-year-old eggs the night she first came to Wert's hotel in Manila. *Balooo-ch. Ba-loooch.*

A gray voice, it had been, smearing through the four o'clock morning grayness, selling what Wert still thought of as a gray egg. Though he'd never seen one, he knew of its rumored properties. "An aphrodisiac," he'd cuddled Jenny closer to say, she as pink as a bonbon against sheets which in those days, his poor ones, were gray as well. At daylight, two hours from then, she would squeal at the sight of the headless shower in his bathroom, but that was still to come. The cry outside was weird and yet consoling, a seller even at this hour, hawking known medicine for our ills. "For old men," Wert said to her, over her. Not for young men, growing in a woman's hand like a root, even at four in the morning. Yet the seller had persisted outside their window; maybe he'd seen Jenny come in. Calling the properties of his wares proudly as a proverb, the man kept on, while they'd climbed to orgasm and fell moistly. *Balooo-ch. Ba-a-looch.*

Wert called it aloud, inclining his ear. Yes, he still did it better than she had, which had annoyed her. Such anthropology was to have been her specialty; it was to have been the way a diplomat's wife who refused to be that only could stay with her husband and still be honorable.

She'd had a sibling's rivalry with him even then—not for what he could do, but over the general spoils of life. In time would this have grown on her like those calloused spurs on the heels of women who wore shoes too short for them? In ten years time, eighteen, which would bring them up to now, with her hair still clipped as boy-short as then, when it had looked like Paris, but on the more massive headline of a middle-aged woman where it might now look like Illinois, and with his own hair maybe falling below the ears in what in London had been a "Chesterfield" but back across the water had become closer to movie-style-at-the-country-club—yes, he could see the two of them. Especially if they'd had no children, as agreed. She by now ever louder in company over what she did, he by now the gentleman-husband-diplomat all in one, ever quieter over his own accomplishment, now that rivalry had faded, along with any further fears of love-embolism. Yet, maybe in her company a man who might have felt better about that accomplishment than he did standing here, after the years without her.

He could see it all quite coolly now. A man who, whatever, might one day soon have need of that hundred-year egg.

The fire was burning handsomely. The rose tree, if that's what it was, didn't yet seem to mind. Soon though it would surely need a tropical humidity, and more than the attentions of even a very good char. In all dispassion he must get rid of it. Getting properly rid of the pot itself would be harder.

Of course he was being messed with out of friendship, too. In the black and white of his rented house the Bakhtiarys, father and son, grew toward him, the old one and the young, forming three-dimensional and real from that long bas-relief behind them, the great backwall of polite nuance to which they had been kept.

When both sides knew it was shadow play, each had an obligation— not to move toward the real. That pair was going to. Why couldn't he guess how? When he already knew what his answer would be. It would be the one he'd been trained to give whenever the East-West balance was upset that way; it was given every other day, internationally. He would be the first to call them uncivilized. And to feel ashamed after-ward? Of them *and* himself?

"How there are friends!" Jenny had exclaimed over tea and cakes the afternoon of the morning he'd met her. "How there are friends in every place." That morning, he'd been sent out onto the Embassy's steps to deal with the daily picket line on the Roe case—or rather, with the Americans on it. "Send young Wert to talk to them," the deputy ambas-sador of that post had said to Wert's superior; "He should know how to talk to them; he's just out from home. What else are these young sprouts they're sending us good for?"

Only six months along on his first tour, Wert already had been silently instructed on what would and must happen to him. Ideals were never mentioned, or why the young sprouts like him kept coming on, once upon a time only from the "better" universities and families, now from almost anywhere in the States, in tune with the democratic—ideal. Each of Wert's older colleagues had at some point of intelligence or temperament recognized what his own first struggle had had to be: to remain, throughout all the motley years of foreign seductions, what they knew themselves to be when at home. In their native land? So it was in the songbooks maybe, when they were there. But to us out here, the young Wert coming out to be tested told himself, it was Home— where no "natives" were.

Out on the Embassy porch there was something squalid in the sun-shine that wetted him almost as soon as he stood there. He'd worn the lightest-weave American shirt made, a tropical suit, and a narrow tie. He was already having a tailor make him a suit of the local silk, which was permissible, and cheap, but he would not descend, ever, to the barong, however elegantly embroidered—a shirt so cool and transpar-ent that it showed the under-arm tufts and chest hairs of all men to be virtually the same. In every post he would learn that there were certain native garments which accepted the climate beyond where a man like him could follow. Southerner though he was, the heat seemed fetid to him because of the conditions beneath, which he'd by now blundered into like any ordinary observer—squatter-towns not yards from these clean steps, where naked babies crawled like red-eyed larvae; there was a city of squatters inside the cathedral itself. Soon the archbishop would pay them to remove themselves, for which bounty they had come. When they left, others would replace them.

"We have to be at the end of the rope to bring our families here," a man inside there had said to him. The cathedral, which was at the center of Manila's earthquake temblors and had more than once been destroyed, had recently experienced a new crack, extending into the sacristy, the chancel and under the statues around which this man's family and others had grouped a front line of sturdy wooden creates which said *whisky whisky whisky* in black letters, and might have come from the Embassy itself. Behind these they lived, on dun tickings spotted with the yellow salve of living. The priests sometimes came to spray for the lice that got into the pews. The man's wife had scurried to hide a pot warming on a Sterno can. "It's a holy place, yes—but—" The man's shrug was clearer than his English, learned as a boy here in the "American" war. Only the intellectuals here called it the Japanese one. Or those who were hangers-on at the Embassy. "And the marble is cool," the man said.

It was midday of what was said every month to be the worst month, and Wert's trousers clung like wet rags to his ankles. "Ayra—deeshun, ayra deeshun!" the man said, shaking a spread hand up, up to the vaults above, with a smile that included all cracks. A priest walking the nave stopped to watch Wert slip the man a coin. Nosworthy, at Wert's side, watched, too. "What's it mean?" Wert said when they were out of there. "Ayra deeshun. A sort of *Jehovah wills it* in Spanish?" Nosworthy, who was sometimes called Uncle in the Department because he was Uncle Sam-of-the-striped-top-hat in every dependable fiber, had blatted like a goat. His eyes looked tired, though; newcomers were sent to him to be told what to think, and it weighed on him. "Air conditioning."

On the picket line in front of the steps that afternoon, Wert saw Fernando Diaz, the tall, handsome graduate student who edited the university newspaper which had started the outcry, and Rony Cristobal, a talented writer soon to be barred from an exchange fellowship for being there. Just the night before, Wert had had drinks with the two of them, and sitting between them, a tiny incendiary girl with pearly, projecting skull-teeth, who had seemed to belong to both of them, but only politically. They relied on her for the anti-American remarks. After each one of these she closed her lips or tried to, then let them recede gumward, turning to each of her companions like a pleased dog.

"Why do you bother with us?" Wert had said. "We're out of here, officially. Soon we'll be phased out altogether." Fernando, who was as well read as anybody like him at home but wrote lavender verses which seemed to have little to do with either his mind or his sex (they all wrote, whether they were radicals, poets or medical students like the girl), said: "You people have been in the Philippines fifty years; you're in our blood and we hate you for it." Rony, a hard drinker, said moodily: "I speak English better than Tagalog. Better than Spanish. Tell me—do I write in it? No, don't tell me. I'll write in it—and I'll get nowhere. I won't deserve to, maybe . . . So I'll write in Tagalog, which is supposed to be *my* language. And I'll get nowhere."

At least we're not responsible for your Spanish, Wert had thought, but hadn't said; how could he? Yes, get out with the young ones; we have to know how they think, Nosworthy had said to him. The girl leaned forward, about to snap at him. Above her pearly muzzle the nose was a tiny sepal of flesh, pulled. "You people are in the world's blood." And miraculously, her lips had closed.

So, out on the sunny steps he had come, that afternoon. Or had been sent. His being there meant nothing—a ritual. Just the daily courtesy to the picket line. The ambassador before the current one had been a cultivated man who believed in talk, real talk. Nosy's version of the uses of talk was that it served but needn't mean anything. Wert on the steps still believed with that other ambassador. "Understand their courtesies; use these. They'll weep at the sight. Just so you don't," Nosworthy had said. "And it lets them let off steam." Still, out there hatless and exposed on the steps, Wert felt himself to be an emissary—and likely never to get over that feeling. "Always remember," the briefer in Washington had said, checking Wert's orders: "Wherever you are, you're us."

And wherever we are, are we the world? He hadn't believed it, even then. It was after five, and the streets of the central town were filling everywhere with ant-crowds arrived from all the crevices, not all of them young but predominantly so; by seven o'clock the streets would be milling, all traffic jammed. They crisscrossed the streets and stalled the cars—a hegira trotting neat and purposeful, knowledge-bound. It was the hour when the universities let out, or their evening sessions began.

Hundreds of universities, most of them private, Nosy had said. "And those size-two girls with flowers in their hair, don't let them fool you— nurses, doctors, dentists, biologists and all the rest. And the men—two professional degrees, three—even if you're going into daddy's bank . . . more especially of course, if you're not . . . Look down there."

They'd been in a hotel that night, the highest night spot in town, with the bay below. As many times as Wert looked at Manila Bay, whether it smiled with breakfast sweetness at the false front of tourists lodged along its shore, or sullened with black, peppery rains which vanished forward like motes into steam, he always saw it squawking with the triangulated flames of war, or jigging white and black with newsprint, or in the mysterious abyss of silence that came after gunshot or before. He never knew which war he was looking at, Admiral Dewey's little take-over, or that later spectacular whose winners were now leaving. "Look," Nosworthy said. "Dewey Boulevard's hard enough to cross at best. The whole Orient's jammed with students. But don't you worry. Over here they're good little boys now; they've learned their lesson. It's all for—" Rubbing his right thumb on forefinger and middle one, he made the immortal money-sign. "It's no moral rearmament."

So he, Wert, had come out on the steps, but not as to battle. Only to give the picket line the message they'd been given yesterday and would expect tomorrow. That the ambassador had taken cognizance. And would convey *their* message. To the proper authorities. The plaza was really very crowded; it was hard to say which students were on the line and which only on their scholastic way, in a city which appeared built on the square but where one turning could confuse even an old resident. In colder cities the poor couldn't rubble up a hovel right next to a Riviera-style hotel, as they had near Manila's main one.

Or, like last week, appear one morning in the rear slop yard of an Embassy which hadn't bothered to plant anything there—fourteen people matted together in sleep, or in the copulations which produced the round-headed babies lying everywhere among them—all with the diseases or hidden starvations that linked them bone to bone. That first morning, seen from the Embassy's back windows, as the sun glinted on an exposed cheek or bodice or the white sole of a child's foot, a chicken-chatter of wakefulness ran through the pile of them. "A heap of *people*, I've never seen one," a staff girl said, and fainted; then the mound down there gurgled and opened, maggoty face after face, saw the Embassy people staring from the office above and folded again, inching over each other but still moving—a mass of night soil for which there was no pipe. They had stayed on for days; a democratic ambassador could take no cognizance.

A few of the office girls, led by the one who'd fainted, began leaving the people-in-the-back their own lunchtime sandwiches of bologna or peanut butter bought at the PX market, where they were allowed to buy supplies along with the military. The courtyard people ate what they understood to be food, but left the rest. Their own leavings, of scavenged parings and rice thrown out by restaurants, grew ever larger; their garbage-hungers required refuse by the bale.

Then the rats came; maybe a baby was taken. One evening, in the dusk of the rainy season, their shusha-shusha rose more excitedly to the typewriters clattering up above. In a fog hung with neon, they were humping themselves together again, consolidating around some province they had lost. Again the whole office went to the windows to watch. Slaglike, they moved on, and out. Next morning, an Embassy aide was sent to order plantings; it was known that these people never disturbed gardens. Just to be sure, the aide, a smart cookie with a will to do for ambassadors what they couldn't on their own, chose a cactus furred with a delicate web which entered the skin like nettles—and the Embassy's slop yard was at last sown.

"Greetings, Mr. Wert." Rony came forward one *toro* step.

The girl between him and Fernando nickered in Spanish, spit flecking from her.

"Yeah, we know——" a young voice said, in sandy American. "You'll convey it to the proper authorities. And we're not that." The voice detached itself to one side; it came from a slim-headed American girl with one of those cowlick haircuts. Pretty enough. The collegiate ethic she took to be international shone from her. All the way from home. "*Are* we, Mr. William Wert." She raised an arm, and made an impish salute. With a hand, foolish girl, which held a roundish object negligently. He had time to see her gold wrist-bangle gleam, and to hear that she couldn't quite pronounce her r's.

Then the Embassy's armed soldier wilting at the doorway shouted, "She's got a grenade!"—raised his rifle and all but fired it.

Maybe the heat made the recruit slow. Certainly he was a green one. Wert knocked the gun up in time. Perhaps her saying William had helped.

He went down the steps to her. Shaken, she turned up her palm to him. "It's only an *atis*," she said in her stubbly home-burr, "that's all it was," and covered her mouth as if she saw the state of the world for the first time. "I know," Wert had said tenderly. Raising his head, he saw that the picket line was taking this as personally as he was. Grinning, blushing even, they were already making the proper poems. Taking the roundish object from the girl, he went back up the steps to the soldier. "Go inside," he said between his teeth. "But slowly. Like you're going to lunch. Get your ass out of here; I don't care what your duty-hours are." He turned the *atis* in his hand. "You trigger-happy fool, this is a custard-apple." The guard went off whining how was he to know—? The stuff these spicks ate, he'd said. True, the thing did look exactly like a grenade. If the shot had been fired, would Wert have had to blame this damned country? It was their fruit.

But when he took a good look at her, he began to shake, and his eyes cleared. That night, after pancakes and tea, a walk clear across town, a jitney ride to the Chinese section and a dinner there, he took her to the cathedral. In its depths the squatters were already bedded down. A tiny radio squealed red-eyed. A priest came forward out of the shadows. "They spray for lice," Wert whispered to her, but the priest wasn't doing that. Walking past Wert and the girl with quiet, tranced eyes, he went to the squatters' corner, made the sign of the cross over them and himself and hung a lamp for them.

"How there are friends—" Jenny whispered, "everywhere."

When she thanked Wert for saving her life he let her know how she'd saved his. So that he could still go on with his job in some dignity—a trigger-happy fool stopped short of the shameful, just in time.

He raised his head at that. The echoes in flats like these were thin but still serviceable. The story he'd elected to tell himself was a true love story. The lovers had saved each other in the end. She—to be spared for Venice. He—to be spared for this. *Balooch. Ba-a-looch.*

He was being brought nearer and nearer his wife by those two Iranians, but why? Were they repeating to him, as if there was some vampire-chance of resurrecting Jenny even yet—"They never really bury in Venice"? Or reminding him— Buried, maybe only in quicksand. But long ago.

He got up and put his arms around the tree that had been planted in his house. Holding its blossom-scent and prickle, cradling deep in boughy arms that bent for him, was like holding a woman whose name he didn't yet know. But there was no use turning out the lights.

11.

ON A FREEZING SUNDAY in New York some weeks later, he left the hotel in the East Thirties which for years had maintained an abiding home for him in the form of a hamper of two suits of different weights, two pairs of shoes, a raincoat, a dinner jacket and a small monthly storage bill inscribed, "Your pied-à-terre in New York"—and set out for Queens in his rented car. The car had the heady vinyl smell which nowadays came with so much that was brand-new; its seat belt yawped at him like a jailor until he locked himself in. He was home. On the seat beside him, wrapped by Fortnum's with the nanny care that sent biscuits unbroken round the world, was an unwieldy package containing an assortment of their finest, centered around one modest gift to be made at the true and highest Meshed level of eternal friendship—his own great-grand-uncle the brigadier general's silver collapsible traveling cup. All of this packed together in one very large pot of interesting design. "Can't afford to insure that, I'm afraid, sir," the tail-coated clerk said, admiring it. "That's all right," Wert said. "Neither can I."

He'd ended up buying a seat for the package in the plane to Washington, where it rode belted in like a passenger and spoken to coyly by the stewardess, after she'd finally agreed to allow it there. "Your wife's not on the plane, sir?" He'd shaken his head, staring moodily at his package. "For the wedding of our very best friend. Friends." He patted it. "Sorry your wife's ill, sir." The stewardess was sympathetically older than average; the airlines were permitting that. "The baby," Wert said. When she passed by again, she reached down and straightened his companion's seat belt. "Austrian wine cooler," he said. "Break like crazy. Can't think why they wanted it; they've been living together for years."

Though he'd never had need of the fantasy life, he'd rather enjoyed being cast into the expected social frame. He had a lot of random experience and information going to waste. No trouble for instance, to find a home for that plant; he'd taken it at once to a dead colleague's widowed mother, who still lived near Blenheim Park, in the glass-roofed atrium her husband had built for them out of complete disregard for the climate and an equal regard for an ancestor who had been the King's astronomer. She had converted the house to a conservatory, planted its ground to tree nurseries and now lived in a hut at the bottom of her topiary garden. Where, when she and he stood there by moon-light—in the midst of a grass-and-pebble chessboard on which the thirty-two tree-chessmen whose queen skirts and turreted hats she herself had clipped loomed like adversaries about to move—she'd sighed, "To think that I once collected Belleek!"

From her dead son, who'd sighed over that, too, Wert knew what that was. What did most people do with the odd knowledge and peculiar people they collected throughout life? They passed these on to their children, who often couldn't care less but in time couldn't help being immersed in the fabric, too. "What's Belleek?" one said importantly to one's girls—"Why, according to an old friend, it's an Irish china of creamy texture but nasty puffy shape—exactly like the Irish tempera-ment." Or to the boys on occasion, slowly and mysteriously, "Why that's a job for the King's astronomer."

For of course one gave them one's fantasy, as well. He could recall his own father doing this, though in the South of those days the whites more often relegated this duty to the blacks. Until Wert was ten, the cooks and gardeners of the town, the servants and the service people, had been his juvenile literature, a communal resource shared by all white children of his rank. And the blacks of those days, with more held-in fantasies than even their own children could support, had been glad of the chance.

So if now in his middle age he began to feel like some weighed-down collector whose bric-a-brac was turning to junk—was it only middle age? Or a profession where he remained a cultural tailor who never sent in the Sunday suit, a *diplomate* of the world's health, who must never prescribe? *Not* to reach even the brightest conclusion—that was his job. But privately, he had accumulated some.

Would he and Jenny have had children after all? Did he want them now? Other people's children were like other people's art to him; he had never wanted to possess. It was his belief that in the abstract, men never wanted children, and women rarely. When convention didn't force it, a dissolution of other needs or a generalized yearning did, or that great progenitor, accident—until they saw the child. Then of course, they wanted to do it again, for the drama it added to the most meager lives. Viewed even dispassionately, to put into the world something absolutely new, yet dragging in its train all the old mysteries, was a marvelous act. He could only hope he wasn't going to do something silly with women, or even with boys, though he had no taste for them. Doing either because of his sudden rosy passion—to transmit.

"*Is* it a rose?" he'd said to the widow, after she and a helper had lifted its clay pot out of the larger one, so that she could see its drainage—which had been as should be. The lorry he'd borrowed from the Hartsdale pub had a brewer's name on it. Wert wore a sharp cap to match, and felt the winds of Oxfordshire tanning his cheeks. "*You* look lively," she commented. "No. Not a rose or a daisy either, you clot. Nearer some form of mountain laurel, I fancy. I shall have to look in the book. If it's there." It wasn't. "Can't be a rose," he said, coloring, remembering his grasp of it. "No thorns."

Well, perhaps after all some hybrid; was his friend a grower?

"Used to be one," Wert said, digging in a toe. "Once owned some of the largest opium fields in Iran. Made his millions from them. But at eighty he got rid of them. And has given a great deal of money for a hospital."

"Ah so," she said without a blink. "Well, it's not a poppy. By the way, the hut won't take that other pot. The fancy one."

"That's all right. I only have it on loan."

She stopped to detach the withered wreath which still clung to the plant's trunk. "Why, these were tree-orchids—how prettily they've dried! I shall save them for my granddaughter, who's thirteen. At that age they press them, you know. Only us old parties dig." She got up heavily, dangling the circlet from a wrist whose withered state it matched. "These came with? *How* extraordinary. So an old party sent you all this, eh? Pity." She gazed up at him with the sibyl bluntness of all good gardeners. "Well, I'll board your plant treasure for you."

"No, it's yours."

She gave that English snuffle-click old Bakhtiary must have heard in the Cotswolds eighty years ago, and bent over the plant again. "Ah, you Arab beauty, I'll take you in." She fondled the thick stem. "Our village inn won't, you know. Take in Arabs. Nor my sister's hotel in Bournemouth, either. They do crowd one you know, abominably." She crooned over the plant, greedily. "But I'll take *you*. However did you get here?"

"I imagine she came by hand," Wert said—and drove the whole way back to London in astonishment. Uneasily, he rang Cicely, the barrister. They had a fine evening—though not on the rug.

In Washington two days later, he was having lunch at the Monocle with Nosworthy, in town on the same business—a departmental conference on the serious drop in quality of the new recruits. "We're getting only the squares," Nosy said. "White *or* black. Oh, the ones with good accents and maybe a little money behind them—we always got some. And the smart-aleck ones who want to be gentlemen. That's all right in a foreign service. As long as there's also a steady enough stream of men at the top with—not only brains, but *you* know. A fervor to—you know."

"Sure," Wert said. "Could you possibly mean—men like us?"

"Ah, come on." Nosy glanced from one tight little table to another. The place was a congressional haunt rather than one of theirs, which was why Wert had chosen it. "It's not the Viet war that pisses off the young anymore, by the way. That generation's gone."

"Where?" Wert said.

"Come on. Into the nation, that's where. And doing very well. . . . I went up to Harvard the other day. Two staff men we'd very much like to have. Collaborated on a position paper for us once. Smart as hell, one of them. The other not bad. Not your academic jerks, either. Smooth. Know what that smart-ass had the nerve to say to me? 'Mister, when I want to have a hand in my country's diplomacy, I'll join a multinational corporation—where I can have some real clout.' . . . And his sidekick agreed with him."

"Nosy—" Wert said, "you and Gail having more trouble in Jamaica?"

The answer was yes. They wouldn't be able to hold onto the house they'd put all their hearts into, unless they wanted to retire to a state of siege, political and vandal. His wife was desperate. "She says she's too old to rethink the world."

"But that's what old age is, isn't it? When you can't?"

Nosy was holding a cigar to his ear, rolling it between thumb and forefinger to hear any stale crackle. He still got them from Cuba. "You thinking much, these days?"

Wert took the offered cigar and lit it. "Multinationals? Bigger deeds, bigger words. When you and I came in, corruption used to be quainter though. More personal."

"Gimme back that cigar."

Wert was touched by the American shyness that could still hit a nail on the head with a joke.

"It appears I'm about to be tempted, Uncle. Not sure with what. Want to bet on it?"

As he told his story, beginning with the Garrick and including a good part of that evening's reflections—leaving out only the tree's effect on him, and maybe not quite—a pale, incredulous smile grew on Nosy's face, but he would say nothing, only shaking his head until Wert had finished.

"I'm fascinated with Manoucher," he said then. He made Wert repeat all the young man's utterances he could remember. "I might turn up in Iran; you never know." As to Manoucher's inviting the Garrick's manageress to the Dorchester, he'd guessed it almost before Wert said, "It's even possible he asked her there only for the company. They like female company, you know. Men of the harem nations. For itself." Nosworthy had once been in Turkey for a long while, and Morocco, too, though never Iran. "They like to be centered in it, that is; they're not like us. We get a mortal lot of it—but that's different."

All Nosworthy's conversational reactions were governed by what he could or couldn't tell either his wife or the nation—which by now might be identical. Though he was very good about the old man, very polite about the wedding. "They're not satyriasts; never think that. The dynasts mean so much to them." At times he could be a very smart man. "So you're going to Queens the very day of the wedding; who suggested that?"

"The Bakhtiary women invited me for it. The wives." When he'd called Manoucher's home, three women had answered, apparently on three different extensions. A fourth phone, over which he'd heard younger giggles, was picked up afterward. "They're going to hold a celebration throughout the day—I'm asked to early lunch. After the ceremony, which they're going to see by hookup, they hope to talk to Iran." Hesitated. "To the son I expect, Manoucher. And the—family. And maybe the girl." He didn't know the protocol. Or if there was one. Or whether they still honored it. "It's all been arranged."

"They must have rented satellite time." Even Nosy was awed.

Wert's conversation with the three women had been a kind of chorale, with each voice first identifying herself. "This is Soraya." The young daughter-in-law, it must have been—Manoucher's wife. "This is Fateh." The old man's second wife. And "This is Madame." Meaning clearly *the wife*. "Only Fateh spoke in Farsi as well as English. Giggling all the way. She sounds a silly type." The fourth extension's giggles,

Fateh's young daughters, had quickly stopped. On command of Madame.

"What does Madame speak?"

"Swiss French; she lives in Vevey. A couple of times in English, though." Stiltedly, but it might be only manner. Even the instrument, which vibrated when she spoke, seemed to know this was Madame.

"And the daughter-in-law? Manoucher's new wife?"

"English, good as you or me." In a dovelike, scarcely accented voice which Wert, brooding on its tone, could still hear. Resolute. Or some other old-fashioned word, or biblical one.

Nosy was delighted with Wert's plans for the pot. But when Wert pressed him for an opinion on what the Bakhtiarys might be up to, he would give none. "Well, you'll find out in a year, won't you? Their plans for you, I mean. I agree they have some. As for why Manoucher's in exile—" Nosy shrugged. "Maybe he'll tell you that then, too. Maybe it's even—something we ought to keep our eye on." He rubbed his hands together. "All I know is—I wouldn't mind having that young man in the Department."

On the nature of what gift might be in store for Wert, Nosy refused to speculate, only shaking his head and saying, "I doubt if you'll have to retire"—still with that faint smile. Insisting on paying the check, though, as if—Wert himself said—it was some kind of anniversary. Usually they each paid their own deductibles.

"It *is* an anniversary," his friend said. Outside the Monocle, they'd gazed at the wide expanse between it and the building beyond, and the rising breastworks of the rest of Washington. "Since Manila," Nosy said. Turning, he clapped Wert on the shoulder affectionately. Wert did the same, though he was usually undemonstrative with his own kind. Funny, when the European double kiss or male hug of warmer countries gave him no trouble, abroad.

"Well, let me know," Nosworthy said, when the departmental car drew up for him. "Gail and I'll be on tenterhooks."

Wert wouldn't see them for a year; they were going to Sri Lanka. Wert's hand was shaken hard in parting, and his face was stared into, keenly. "I always loved Jenny," Nosy said.

On the shuttle back to New York, Wert puzzled over that. Nosy had written him from Manila at Jenny's death. By the time they met again, three years had gone by, leaving Jenny both too near and too far to be easily spoken of, even if Wert's new arrangements—a woman here, a woman there—hadn't been plain. Now, after all this time, there was something . . . valedictory in what Nosy had said, yet he'd done it almost gaily. When did people say a thing like that to you? There was a tone in it which Wert recognized but couldn't seize.

In New York, the hotel manager welcomed him sadly. A new management and a renovation was in the works; after this year they could no longer harbor Wert's hamper. In exchange, Wert would have television in the room when he stayed there, instead of in the clubby old lounge to which the hotel, quiet as a library upstairs, had always relegated it, and though his new room would be half the size of this one, he would have a modern closet with sliding doors, instead of that clumsy old armoire. "Gentlemen are going out," Mr. Wemyss said. At eighty, and with a matching wife who still regretted their death notices couldn't be in the defunct *Herald Tribune*—"the *Times* is simply not the same!"—he was certainly one of them.

"Gentlemen are always on the way out," Wert said irritably. One felt the world was going to rack and ruin when one was of an age to feel it, irrespective of whether or not it was true. But he'd never before been classed as on that side of time's colonnades.

Luckily, the woman whom he always called first when here still lived in the brilliantly chintzed Park Avenue apartment a divorce had granted her, along with her three grown daughters. During a round of plays and dinners, Wert made her talk of her girls; he wasn't sure why. She was delighted to. Always tactful with his bachelor lack of interest, she never had. The three were all willful and all pretty. "Like me, once." Little by little her anecdotes slipped farther out, across table and into their bed. "Oh, with kids, either you eat them alive or are eaten," she'd say, staring at her napoleon as if it was a small coffin. Each night now, after love, she resumed her *histoire*.

She was a dear, kind woman; her house offered comfort artistically disciplined, and in sex her backbone arched with joyful intensity anyway he asked it to, her breasts pillowing him afterward. He tried to think of her, heroic among her warped nymphs, as all the lovelier for her distress. Blond hair streaming on her satin sheets, she looked it. "Oh, I'm so grateful I can talk to you about it, with most men you have to walk such a chalk line." Though the girls were all away on a school trip, the three now advanced on him, steady on over their acnes and abortions. He'd intended to ask their mother to stow his hamper in one of her many opulent closets, but after that night decided not to. Inside him, the vote had gone against her. It wasn't in this way he wanted to become part of the dynasts.

Besides, on these cold nights which were rocketing up the new year, all New York was a blue mosque. For sure, one would never meet a mullah there. The winds honking him across plazas had no underside from Russia; at their center he would never hear, like a tuning fork, the desert's stealth. But down on the Lower East Side, where he went alone one night to the theater, a vendor roasted something on a cart from which came that same Middle Eastern smell which had pinched the Tabriz evening with charcoal—here sweet potatoes, a good try, but not the great hairy beets smoking red and orange, under an Elburz sunset which had hung in the west like a fine rug.

In Tabriz, the men shuffling along under that burnished light in baggy pants, suit jackets and bent fedoras had looked to him like tailors from this neighborhood. Before him in a bakery window, soft powdered cakes oozed the same poisonous yellow in front of which he used to see the Tabrizi schoolboys hungering in pairs, their fifth fingers linked. He would never bump into a donkey here if he hunkered till doomsday at the crossroads of memory. But in a dairy restaurant he sat for an hour watching a couple of old men with a week's growth of beard, as they drank tea from a glass and played a game with counters, while their feet worked happily in and out of shoes worn down at the back. Borrowing the waiter's pad and pencil stub, he wrote the note he owed Bakhtiary, thanking him for the tree, admiring his son, congratulating him on marriage, and wishing him well.

Outside again, he dropped into a stationery store to buy an envelope and stamp. The stage-blue had intensified. The upper bodies of people walking were circled in auras fumed with their breaths. Across the street a gutted building reared, each floor of the façade more open. At its top the stone frame pointed toward him its triangular pulpit—but it wasn't a mosque. A letter box stood below. This city was its own city now, and the ruins were different. Staring up, he mailed the letter, to which he'd added a post-script. "Dear friend—don't send me too much."

That note must by now have reached Iran. To lie unnoticed maybe for weeks among the congratulations which in spite of all would be coming to Bakhtiary—and to the girl from Ardebil. Strange to think of today as her wedding day also. Would Bakhtiary be sitting apart, on his side of the house, complying with old-fashioned custom for the bride's sake, since for her sake little enough could be done? While in another part, intoned over by female relatives who saw all their history in her, she sat in separate ceremony, in all her lacy, provincial pomp?

The only wedding Wert had ever seen there had been a peasant affair not far from that girl's city, near the Caspian. Pious as the girl's promises might be, it was more likely she was some wealthy man's daughter, of the sort he'd glimpsed at their Embassy receptions in Paris—a rich Iranian milkmaid, modernized to the septum of her nose. In which case the male guests would be wearing cutaways, the youngest of the emancipated women might be bared and frizzled in the style the Department wives termed "Call me Babe," and after the ceremony, couples would jounce up and down together in their peculiar fox-trots, which seemed to be not so much revived from the nineteen-twenties, as saved ever since. Yet none of this meant that the girl's promises wouldn't be kept.

Teheran was eight and a half hours ahead of New York. The ceremony was to be at nine-thirty in the evening. So here he was, driving off to Queens for a one o'clock lunch—and already chilly and touchy, after early breakfast at the United Nations with a member of the American delegation, unknown to Wert, who'd rung him up late and hectically the night before.

"Woodrow Smiley-Brown—" this tall, bleached man said when they met, "and yes, I was christened for the late, very late President, father's friend. As father told me daily, 'They'll have to know their history, boy, to place *you*.' . . ." This over, he appeared less exhausted, keenly examining everyone who passed, and oddly excited by the UN restaurant— if one considered that he must see it every day of the week.

Pumping Wert, he was annoyed at him for knowing only as much as the next man on "the British temp-er-a-ment." He was one of those who visualized all national temperament as rather like the wooden plank on which the waiter was offering him smoked salmon—as a thin slab of some indigenous substance on which a nation's doings were daily deposited. But the term was useful; when it came up you knew either that the conversation would get nowhere, or that all human talk was in vain.

"No, I won't have more salmon, thanks," Wert said, "I'm going to a wedding in Teheran at one o'clock."

The man was duly startled; Wert had meant him to be. Over here he made use of the most shamefully childish tactics, probably because he no longer felt sure of what men were like here, or women either. In his travel-twisted way, he knew too much. He'd grown away from those home standards which, if kept rigidly, whatever they were, made a person certain of himself for life.

"Your companion going with you?" Wert's package, brought up from the parking lot, sat on a chair at the table's third side. "If so, you're both going to be late."

Smiley had been brought up to a certain coyness, Wert decided. As the father had. He explained, lightly sketching Bakhtiary and his entourage.

"Thought they'd discouraged multiple wives. That they don't do that anymore."

"They do and they don't." He wasn't going to explain Bakhtiary to this man. "Never multiple, though. Islam allows four, I believe."

"So you're going to lunch with three old ladies, to listen to their husband, the old guy—get married again. By international hookup."

"Two wives. Third one's the young daughter-in-law. And neither wife's really old. Let's see—" He'd been intending to do this arithmetic, out of a sense that there were already mysteries enough—and that he ought to prepare. "Madame the first wife was married when she was sixteen and he sixtyish; which would make her now about forty-six." He's amazed; Bakh always referred to her as "my traveling dowager." "So was the second wife, Fateh. When he was about seventy-two. Eighteen years ago; that would make her—my word. Only thirty-four. The new bride's the same age they were."

"Got a daughter at Brearley who's sixteen," Smiley said gloomily. "You ever feel that these older countries have the right attitude toward —got any daughters, Wert?"

"No. Though I have friends who do."

"Umph . . . This daughter-in-law—what age is she?"

"In a way, she's the oldest. She's already twenty-four. Of course, she went to the University of Teheran. But only just married—that's still very late—for their girls. Or used to be."

"It's us," Smiley said, still gloomy. "You may depend upon it; it's us."

"You know Iran?"

"No, I was a social scientist. Specializing in Africa. In the days when that was a small field. Or a big empty one. Southern Ghana—four years there. Then northern Nigeria, two more. Village structure—I wrote a book on it." He leaned forward. "What's your ambition, Bill?"

Wert hadn't been asked that question so bluntly since high school. In reality it was always being asked. In America, unless you had an ambition that showed, people didn't know how to ticket you. Even naked ambition, properly bared, made them feel safer. You might even go farther because of it.

"On my college placement bureau's form, I put—'to see the world.' They switched it. To 'Foreign Service.'"

"Heh." Chin on his big folded hands, Smiley was still swinging his glance keenly left-right.

"Later, for the Foreign Service application, *I* switched it, 'To see the changing of nations,' I put—I was twenty-three. They thought it quite elegant." The truth often was, even when misinterpreted. "Best little statement of the departmental cop-out we ever saw," Nosy had said. "Got you to Manila the moment we saw your resumé. We can use a young officer with your kind of talent for talk-talk." Leaving the young Wert with the first of the romantic sorenesses which were to replace each yesterday's heart.

"Well, you're seeing it." Smiley swept out a hand.

"Mmmm." Even at breakfast the UN smelled of polyglot sweets and sours, ethnic stipulations and aversions. The smell of any of those trading places where the map changes ran off the tables like water and populations blew before the wind—how this excited him even yet! "They thought I meant—change*over*," Wert said.

"Aren't you going to ask *me?*"

"You? . . . Oh yes. What's your ambition—Woodrow?"

"To have a village. An African village. Named after me." Smiley screwed up his eyes. "One of the chiefs had already adopted me." He said a series of African syllables, grinning. "That's me. I could still do it. Even these days. If I went back."

"Can't you?"

"I'm trying. That's why I'm here."

"Why'd you leave Africa in the first place?"

"Came back home to marry the girl I left behind me. Biggest wedding there since old Woodrow himself. She was the daughter of a dean." Two women from Sierra Leone passed by in their richly striped and segmented dress. Woodrow stared after them morosely. "Got hooked to stay on, at the college. And never got back to my village. Or had one named for me here." He grinned again. "The college already being named."

"Say"—Wert smiled at himself—already so American again. "Say, your father wasn't by chance *the* Brown. The anthro man. My best friend from home studied with him. One great man who was really great—he said."

Smiley's nod plainly had been nodded many times before. "Changed my name. Added on my mother's. Because of the overtones."

Overtones indeed. "I even saw him once." The old professor, pointed out to Wert by his worshipful friend had had that worldwide look to him even when shuffling unkempt down a university corridor, through colleagues tweeded up and suburbanized. They hadn't been able to do that either to his looks or to his tongue, which now and then made the papers with near-indecent pronouncements on American life. As a father, the old anthropologist might well have been one of those who should have had only daughters—at least in America.

"So when the bid came for here, I took it," Smiley-Brown said. "Got divorced over it. She said if I ever got back to Africa, I'd want to stay, and keep her and the kids with me, even marry them to blacks." He snorted toughly. "You married?"

"My wife died."

"Ah." Smiley-Brown gazed past him and out the window. "Sunday. Know why I like to come here on Sundays? Because here there aren't any. They've buried them, under their own Fridays—that's the Muslim one, isn't it?—and Sabbaths, and general hut ceremonies. The way they're going to bury us. Can you imagine any of our women here? In their church hats?"

"My wife never wore a hat."

"Ah. Both my wife and my mother did." Woodrow drummed his fist on the table. "My—stepmother does, too." He shuddered, opening his mouth wide.

"Ah," Wert said.

"My father remarried, you see, quite recently. So did my wife."

"Oh?" The traumas of the recently divorced or divorcing were always so stale and unvirginal. Must be why bachelors listened to a lot of them.

"What sort d'ya think those two would marry, Bill?"

"Mmm . . . m." The old guy, Smiley's father? Probably, by now—some woman who would clean him up. And Smiley's wife, breathing all this propaganda under that hat? Very possibly—a black.

Smiley-Brown was staring through him, and out the other side. "They married each other."

"Eee," Wert said.

"Our daughters are with them. They've bought a brownstone here, and are sending the girls to Brearley. After all his talk."

"And your sons?"

"Haven't any."

"Hah." Having exhausted his monosyllables, Wert looked at his watch.

Woodrow placed a hand across it. "Scads of time, really. Your boulevard's just down the road. . . . So you see what I mean, don't you? About the older countries."

Wert stood up. "Sorry. No, I don't see." What I see is the frighteningly personal drift of all men, behind their most seignorial jobs. I see the old ambassador at Manila, who hadn't believed in talk-talk, but not from international conclusions—only because the sexual tremors which engaged him from wrist to liver to brain weren't up to it anymore. Or that gambling French cultural attaché to whom all culture was a coin, including his own. Or even my own British opposite in London, who does act more impersonally than any of us, not as he thinks because his passion-for-no passion is so well ingrained—but because the passions of the belly, when sated five times a day, are more ignorable than the rest.

Three Senegalese Moslems passed in a waft of white. Wert sat down again. "It's true, they more often travel together. Arabs. But that's all I'll vouch for."

"They're calling themselves the *new* nations, now." Brown screwed his eyes to slits. "And why not—they've got real life behind their backs, re-al struc-tured *life* . . . while we-uns . . . Arrh, never mind us. Look there. And there. And there." One brilliant group after another, leopard-sashed or pinwheel-haired or in Arab white, went under his pointing thumb. Europeans and others from the West, or dressed like the West, also thronged the hall, but Smiley-Brown wasn't seeing them. Harder to, of course, but whether this was because they were more faded in color or more complex in spirit, only time could say. Certainly another quasi-European Westerner couldn't.

The room was full of people tangentially closer to Wert and each other than most, each conscious that this ribbon of humanity they were in was an era. The scene had that tremendous, noisy vigor which the centrally busy passing scene always did. He'd never met such publicly displayed human surety as was flaunted here—in a hall no longer in its heart devoted to the curatorship of the living world but crowding in for the ceremonious process of its dying. For the coming pyrotechnical death-talk, each country wanted the best seats in the house. There were no shy people here.

The hugely turbaned pair of Sierra Leone women passed their table again, ripely as chords in music. Behind them, traipsing on and off one game leg, went an old Hollander, Wetter Malm Schroon-Malmsey, whose names had eighty years ago been amassed to hide the Javanese grandmother he was now forever mentioning. On the committees which dealt with those political prisoners whose betterment had been his lifework, he had the most pacific of tongues, careful never to speak aloud the controversial word "freedom." While he talked, one could see again the stolid Dutch galleons which had steadily plied history while others fought. When worsted in an argument, he dipped his old bones and blanched-vegetable face like a third-rate actor, one hand on his heart, the other flung high in minuet. He believed in his own cause, yet like most here his very strengths came from a cynical flow exactly opposite. The most enduring international politicians had the same temperament as women of fashion; they were not profound thinkers but experts at seizing the infallible costumes of the moment, blithely aware that they already had fifty other exploded eras in their closets. Sincerity was not involved. Or the earthly paradise either—unless it happened to be à la mode.

"I rather wish I could be like the people here," Wert said. "They know for sure the passing scene is—just that."

"Ah, man—you want a village."

"Balls." Both their ambitions, so picayune. "But if I come across a tribe, a noble savage tribe where it's in the structure for the fathers to marry the sons' wives—I'm sure there must be one—I'll let you know."

"Thanks, there's a kind bastard." Smiley was bright red. "But now that you're offering—take me along with you, this afternoon."

Wert recoiled. "Why?"

"Maybe because I know the way. Queens Boulevard may be near, but it's not easy."

"I'll find it."

"Maybe because I haven't seen a wedding lately. Not one catered by Western Electric International."

"Sorry."

"Maybe because I'd like to meet those three ladies." With each try, Smiley-Brown leaned farther across the table, almost kneeling on his chair.

"It's a Moslem household. Can't take a man they don't know."

"*You* haven't met them."

Wert threw up his hands.

Smiley-Brown sat back with the calm which came from being beyond embarrassment. "Maybe because I want to hear that old guy give the responses, then."

Wert swallowed; red crept up him also. Anybody who bothered to look could see the two of them for what they were, two angry dogs from the West. "He won't be giving them." A wave swept over him. Two homesick dogs from the West. He could almost see Bakhtiary standing at his elbow in the stage fog which traditionally surrounded such visitants when they came to warn—or to give advice.

"Don't the men speak at their weddings?"

"In the only one I saw, bride and groom had separate rituals. But for all I know, this one could be taking place at the Teheran Hilton. With our ambassador acting as best man." He looked over his shoulder. "No, I don't really believe that . . . How would they do it in your village?"

"They—" Smiley-Brown shrugged emptily at his own fingers, elbows on the table among the dishes. "Nemmind." Chin in hand, his look swept round again. "Suppose you think I'm a monomaniac," he said hopefully.

"No." I think you're a fairly normal man, of the sort often born to excessive fathers.

"What, then?"

"I think—maybe you had to persuade yourself—that you were one. Or were persuaded." By the daughter of a dean. "And now it's gone. Your village is." Others having taken advantage of it.

Smiley-Brown had his head between his hands now. The waiter, hovering for so long, had left, perhaps thinking bitterly that people who could afford to conduct all their emotions in restaurants, did so at his expense. Or else that all the emotions of such people were table-size. Wert laid down a large tip.

Smiley-Brown sat up at once. "Sorry. I only see the kids every other weekend. This is the other week. They always ask me about the village. And never listen to the answer. If it has gone *kaput* for me, you're the only one noticed it." He laid a tip beside Wert's, patting the package which sat between them. "Help you out to the car with that thing? No? Don't blame you. I might jump in. . . . Well. Think I'll take this desperate character to a movie."

"Wait." Hoisting the package, Wert put it down again, back into the social framework where so much he had accumulated was going to waste. "Your girl goes to Brearley, you said? The—troubled one?" Though he hadn't quite said.

"See you know the lingo. Don't tell me you do have—"

"No."

"Didn't think."

Wert picked up a napkin and brushed at a spot on the package. "Why not?"

"Something two-dimensional about men your age who don't have offspring—troubled or not. Hadn't you noticed?" Smiley-Brown, having broken down in front of him was getting back at him for it. Whereas in Meshed, or Tabriz, they'd have linked pinkies over his outburst, and wept mutually.

"Hmmm." Wert looked down at himself. "Well, I've still got a vest." He pulled a pen from it. "Listen. Do me a favor. Call up a friend of mine whose girls go there, too. Spend the afternoon." Was this dirty of him, or samaritan? Dirty at first, but then the other. "You won't be sorry. Warm house." Soft beds. "Just don't say I sent you, mind. At least not at first. Today you're just a wounded parent wanting to talk to another one." Over here his suits never had any accumulation of paper. He tore off a flap from the package, wrote a name, number and address on the reverse side, and handed it over. "Her troubled daughter's name is Nancy, same as hers."

Smiley took the paper and read. Half smiling, he tapped his teeth with it.

"Don't get the lady wrong. She's a friend."

"But I'm not supposed to mention it, hah?"

"Not right away."

"Not until your own afternoon errands are complete, eh. I see."

"No you don't. Never mind. If you do choose to go, you'll find it—" How could he say it? It's where the two of you can weep mutually. "You won't have to—walk a chalk line there."

He let Smiley help him to the car after all.

"Oh I'll go," Smiley said, lingering at the car door, tensing his long unmuffled neck in the raw air. The sky had a leaden secrecy; it was about to snow. He shivered like a bird. "I'm curious."

No, you are desperate, Wert said to himself, stowing the package in the passenger's seat. Arms still around it, he stopped short. But how do I know?

Smiley was studying the reverse side of the paper with the telephone number on it. "Fortnum's. That the place where the grocery clerks— clarks—dress like—deputy ambassadors?" He let his eyes flick over Wert's second suit, the ten-year-old one, which he was wearing in defer- ence to the coming afternoon, and back to the piece of brown paper the wind was fluttering. "Biscuits, it says here. That great heavy thing holds biscuits? Poor - Soraya. And what was it—Fatima? You must be making a play for big Madame."

"They sent me a pot from Iran that's damn near a national treasure," Wert said sharply. "The old man did. I'm returning it."

"Did he now. Whatever for?"

"Wish I knew. And he'll only send me something else. For better or worse. As a valedictory bequest. I wish I knew what." Wert's neck felt cold; the dress muffler he wore was too thin. "The ladies know, I fancy. Over there, they usually know everything."

"And never say a word?" Smiley sighed.

"Never used to." Wert paused, hand on the car door. "Funny. I can almost feel—what it's going to be. But not quite. Some bloody complication I'd be very wise to—forestall. It's on the tip of my tongue, but I can't name it. It's even in my own day-to-day actions somewhere. Something quite simple maybe, that other people might even be able to see." He thought of Nosy. "Are able. Knowing me."

"Ma-an. Maybe *you* better go to a movie."

They shook hands lengthily, grinning at each other.

"Maybe your Nancy and I'll talk you over," Smiley said. "If we see anything, let you know."

Both laughed, and kept standing there.

"Going to snow," Wert said, staring up.

"Yeah." Smiley probed the gray sky carefully. "Going to snow."

Watching him go, Wert thought he looked jauntier. Starting up the car, he slapped its dashboard as if it were the rump of a horse. Nancy would be answering the telephone within say—half an hour. At least he'd done a destiny job as neatly as a machine.

Going around the block to change directions, he found Smiley on the corner, just hailing a cab. The traffic light held them fast. "Have fun in *your* village," Smiley said.

III.

SNOW COMING DOWN gray and fine; it meant business. Each car traveled the eclipsed morning in its own shroud. In his three-sided bay window he piloted a satellite lost on Queens Boulevard, in light spectrally broader than any in London. Through the swirl, high-rise apartment buildings lofted up into the mists, dull palaces all with the same portico, occasionally a delicatessen or drugstore alongside. They had no addresses out front; they were ashamed of having only these six-digit numerals. No doorman knew the number of the adjacent hive. Only one could tell him in which direction on his side the numerals went higher; across the avenue was an unknown continent. He had by now inquired of four, each a sorrier grenadier as one got closer, all with blank eyes and coffin-chins. Each portico gaped forward, an old alligator's upper jaw, its quartzy hide and gilt sawteeth chipped. Each man stood in the throat, the snow fogging all to an old movie frame. This was a foreigner's bad dream of America, but a cheaper surreal than it ought to be; what were the Bakhtiarys doing out here? Once, Middle-Eastern United Nations functionaries had crowded into nearby Queens before they found its Third Avenue equivalent, or the even newer galleries and black basalts of mid-Manhattan. But that would have been years ago, about the same time as when he and Iranians like these had first met. They were dragging each other back, maybe. "Afraid I'm lost," Wert said over the drugstore phone. "Sorry."

"Ah, of course. Where are you?" A high male voice, squeaky, elegant. A papal nuncio, met once in that Rome hotel where all the priests went, had had a voice like that. Since those traveled in pairs, he half expected two men to enter the drugstore.

Only one hatless elder came toward him, a fan of salt-and-pepper curls high above his head, the handsome face unknown to him, but not its nose curl, these black-silk brows, the cheeklines drawn with a stroke of the pen downward, the nostrils that moved. In it he saw all of them again.

"Fereydoun. Cousin. Come in my car, Mr. Wert." A 450 SL Mercedes, glowworm in the dim. He led the way, in that sloppy gait of theirs. Wert, transferring the package, couldn't see the backs of his shoes. Inside the car, the snow seemed scarcely to have wetted that morning coat and striped pants. It was all coming back to Wert, the way they took the current atmosphere deeply into themselves—flowers, heat, oases, rain—but not like Westerners, into the boredom of conversation. "I was not in Venice when you were there, Mr. Wert." He meant Wert to know he knew what had happened there. "I am with Madame. Always." He pushed that forward, for a reason. I am not with Bakh. But the voice was what astonished. One flute-step beyond mere homosexuality, or age, where among Wert's travels did it belong? Baloooch? No, not that. Rather, that remote flute which people played in mountain regions, anywhere. "But I have met your cousin. Your family house in Athens, Georgia—beautiful."

"You brought the ring home. My wife's ring."

Fereydoun's nod started the car.

Yes, they were dragging Wert back.

He won't dig in his heels, he wants to be. Already. "You're Madame's cousin?"

"Oh yes. But I am also Bakhtiar." He doesn't add the *y* or *i* that some do; there are variations. It's after all a tribe, a locale, as well as a name. And a force in their history.

"But Madame wasn't with you. In Georgia." Wert's cousin would have said. She'd gone on for pages as it was.

"No. Someone else take my place with her." The French had a name for such flutes—the *mirliton*. The car drew up a circular driveway and under a portico. They'd merely crossed the boulevard, to the high-rise opposite.

"She doesn't travel alone." Fereydoun turned off the ignition. He sighed. "But Bakh"—he paused—"he wanted to know what your house is like." His mouth went roguish, as if it talked out of school. As if it often did.

"That far back? I can't—" Believe it. But he could.

They got out of the car, Wert trundling the package. He's the family equerry, I suppose, his cousin had written, in her spritely imp-lady style.

He waddled rather, but was wonderful with the muffin stand, and compliments to suit. I shouldn't mind having one of him for my very own. And he knew the ring for what it was.

Their grandmother's sherry-wine ruby. She'd been enraged at the idea of its going into a grave.

Fereydoun's gait wasn't due to shoes, his sleeker than Wert's own, which the hotel's hamper hadn't improved. But I won't gossip about Bakh with him; I don't know quite why. At that moment Fereydoun turned—just inside the maw of the entrance, where again a uniformed man stood in diminishing perspective—and made a low bow of welcome, his hips drawing him back—Coppelia, a sorcerer's bow, a wheedling. Wert had seen old Prince Chumpot shuffle on his knees to and from the then young king of Thailand, but that was protocol. This came from the man himself, deeper than style. Fereydoun wasn't fat exactly, but pear-shaped, as the striped trousers made plain. Like that castrato tone of voice?

Among the Bagirmi, in north-central Africa, such men were said to still exist; a retired colleague had so described their voices. Above Fereydoun's wing collar and bow tie the neck lapped in a girdle-of-Venus fold. A chill hit Wert's stomach. No, his cousin wouldn't mind. Ladies from his heath, of her era, could still strangle a chicken because it tasted better after, or shoot a stoat. Or make fretful moan when the best chorister at Christ Episcopal lost his voice, due to virility. Once informed of what a Fereydoun might be, she'd never condescend to think of it further, and continue to enjoy her muffins. Like Madame? Because this would have been the bargain under which she could leave? Had been allowed to leave—Bakh?

They were now on the twelfth floor, in front of one of a long corridor of doors. Fereydoun had rung. "I have key. But ladies want to be warned." A laugh like a squeaked grass-blade. In the mountains of France they used onionskin for those flutes.

"I'm not dressed for a wedding."

Fereydoun sighed, tremolo. "The other side of the water—won't see." He's Bakh's era, if not quite his age. A fine-grained eighty-odd Those glandular eyelids, not born to that face? It could have happened, within the boyhood history of those two. Their country's history was full of sporadic reversions to its ancient practices. Hermias the tyrant of Atarnea—and patron of Aristotle—was one; they're not always tabby cats. Narses, the general under Justinian. Smart, and faithful beyond other—men.

Wert's hands were chilled. He rubbed them. Just that I've never knowingly seen one. His own genitals felt cold. Fool—it wasn't catching.

Fereydoun was scrutinizing him, his suit. Footsteps padded to the door.

"I'm—a bequest," Wert said. "Aren't I."

Fereydoun put up a plump hand. Not a hermaphrodite face, but of a special antiquity. The eyes mild with retrospect. Altered to it? The mouth went roguish again, tittered, and bit itself. "So—am I."

As the door opened and was held for them by a woman in *chador*, Fereydoun bent and transferred the flower in his own buttonhole to Wert's.

They followed the *chador*, a stolid gray servant-shape, unchanged. Ahead, down one of those lemon-pale hallways which promised one of the typical "living spaces" these modern buildings provided, all floor-lacquer and cream-colored slats and lozenge design, he heard a fountain of female giggling. Smoke drifted, underlined with perfume; was there ever any smell more enticing?—promising frivolity and a light session of human politics, nothing to do with government. At the head of the hall he stopped, in a waft of wheat-smell. But not wheat. *"Polo?"* he whispered. Not accurate, but the way he remembered their saying it. Their long-grain rice, cooking somewhere. Fereydoun's teeth glistened. Wert felt his own backbone melting. Oh my God, I'm going to be happy, he thought, dismayed. From the next room he could already sense that clan energy of people to whom roses were important, but who in their time had also lopped heads, grown opium, with a girlish smile for this when challenged, and two kings back had had a ruler who munched kebab while poets were hanged—and whose last Shah had once publicly bowed the knee to one. At Wert's side, Fereydoun chittered nervously. Wert remembered the other name for a *mirliton*. Eunuch-flute.

The serving-maid was beckoning. Amazing, how they'd used to do this from within that garment—and to see it still done, here in Queens —with the man next to him watching. Wert was made to put his present in a small room off the hall. As he set the box down in relieved good riddance, the name for what it had represented returned to him. *Pish-kesh*—the prefavor or sweetening. Or bribe. By which you are warned.

Ahead, the chattering has stopped. His own Farsi's already rushing back to him, clamoring a word for every object he sees, and all the old phrases he'd always been glib and good at orally, able to float in the give-and-take from street to embassy, though nearly unable to write or transcribe. Today, why appear to know any of it? Little advantage enough.

"*Alors*—" Fereydoun says, as if from now on they must expect any language—and they're in.

The first thing he sees is Bakh. The long walls of this triple-sized room are hung with rugs: the two end walls are huge movie screens, one blank. On the other, slide-projected larger than in life, Bakh's sitting in his garden, a girl at his side, facing the real-life family photograph below. Fifty to a hundred people must be in the room, lined up there, below the screen. Above them, Bakhtiary is in a black suit, on which Wert can sense the baking sun, a hand on each pommel of his high-backed chair.

"Bakh—" Wert says. It's much the same face, except for the sunglasses, which are on a table to Bakhtiary's right. He had wanted the people here to be looking at him. They'll be able to search his face for hours on end; he has the advantage of being a photograph. Any secrets are jewels inside him, safe. All the girl's jewels are on the outside—hung between her eyes from a headband, in her ears, at her bare wrists and throat. She's in Western dress, one of those wisps for summer, but grasps a shawl awkwardly round her shoulders. The small nose has the downward-curving septum, just right for a ring, but it too is bare. Her eyes are cast down though, on Bakh.

"She is first time out of *chador*," Fereydoun says, falsetto. Perhaps he can't whisper. "Ah. Madame."

They must have lined themselves up under the screen just before Wert entered. In the center is a long row of women of all ages, brilliantly dressed. In front of these are the children, party-dressed also. Behind the women, garbed in their black-white as if for a graduation day, as if they haven't moved since he last saw their country, stand the men. All bow formally. When Madame moves, the lines break up. In spite of the men's Swiss watches and Italian silk suits and the women's spicy French aura, it flashes on him what this group is. Perhaps it's the two young women with babies on their hips. Or that screen, high above them like a colored sail. They are immigrants.

Madame comes forward, robin-breasted in her purple sweater set, on the pouty legs which for Wert link all European women from Finisterre to Leningrad, except for the Swedes. Wert knows when a hand is extended royally. The hand he kisses is boneless in that peculiar way. Incurved, almost vestigial, it must never have done more than fold a napkin or slip on a ring; it may never have buttoned for itself or forced on a boot. Its exercise? Perhaps holding a sheaf of playing cards. He avoids the big pearl on it as he would a royal mouth.

An hour later, still seated at Madame's side, after as many innuendos as there are nuts in the dishes scattered everywhere, he's exhausted but has learned a good deal, though not yet what's in store for him. All this is surely intended. At first he'd wanted to drink only Coca-Cola out of sentiment for what used to be, but has been persuaded, though by swift gesture only, that they may not be as they were—so is now drinking scotch. Some of them may be. Wherever possible they convict themselves of nothing. Does the *jube,* the water ditch, still run through Teheran, even on the main drag, Pahlevi? He hasn't been able to get anyone to say. Perhaps they no longer want to say the former Shah's name. Madame, as he was surely told long ago, is family-connected. Or perhaps because they have moved on.

He knows now why they're in Queens. The place belongs ostensibly to Fereydoun, who was once years ago at the UN. Each time apartments adjacent or on floors above or below have been vacated, he's acquired them; he now has two floors, and after brief difficulty with the fire laws —a sweep of Madame's pearled hand—has built a staircase to suit. Though he is single—had her eyelids leveled for a moment?—he was brought up in a palace, used to space. He's of an in-between generation; though younger than Bakh, his father was a general with Reza Shah. The former Shah's father can be mentioned by name; he is history. Fereydoun is her cousin, all here being at the very least cousins, of near or far degree. He's actually the son of her mother's oldest half-brother, and as a young man wheeled Madame in her carriage. "Because of our mothers being so young, much is different with us," she says, again with a leveling. Wert can't detect whether or not she ever looks up at the screen; he's still waiting for her to mention Bakh. But a queen bee, if ever he's seen one.

What's exhausting him is his effort to see these people more than visually. Some diplomats never get past seeing foreigners as scenery; it's a hazard of the trade. He's never had that trouble, even with the Japanese, once even achieving intimacy with one, though in France. Oh he knows the odds of all of it, the self-delusionary traps. Yet these people keep peacocking themselves in his mind, as if it's in their very character. They have shallownesses he can't plumb.

Madame, fat as predicted but solidly so, as if every ounce counts for something, is hugely perfumed with a velvety scent meant perhaps to hide her competence. She's one of those short women whose groomings take their attraction from the concentrated area over which these must be displayed. The face is small-nosed but powerful; the thick black hair, cut and winged in points on the cheeks, has been ruddied with henna in the way of older women; he had been given to understand that this was the matronly thing to do. Madame's voice is ambery in French; her English grates as if she's swallowed a string of bronze beads; both accents are serenely heavy. If she squirrels meaning in her cheeks, one can always lean forward; he recognizes the habit queens learn from their husbands, or from a court. She hadn't learned it from Bakh.

Fateh, the second wife, hovering always near, is a thin fashion-plate, expertly auburned all over. An extremely routine sophistication, twirling from rings to dark glasses, to scarves to hair, makes her look older than she must be, no doubt intended, as the mother of all those girls. The rings, seven of them, are more astounding than anyone else's, but what's most extraordinary about her—realized when she came forward to meet him, bowed with her hands clasped over her face, and greeted him in Farsi—was that they had already met. It can't be, but of course is. After Jenny's accident. This is the same woman who, veiled like one of the Fates, had dropped her veil at Bakh's command. "With her *place* showing," she'd said of Jenny's fall. And now here she is, with her long silky legs showing, a little skinny and ankle-y, as if not yet used to it. Dressed in that color he's heard the chic Departmental women bill to each other like birds, *beige beige beige,* she looks like many women he's seen liberated from purdah or *chador* or even the nun's habit—absolutely correct at all times, for anything but home. Two of the girls she's had from the old man are in the background, mutedly the gigglers he'd heard over the phone, though not the Swiss school-girls he'd expected but highly painted young dazzlers.

A few of the older men remind him of those he met at the Danieli; one or two may even be the same. Young or old, the men have lost a certain naïveté; not even the patriarchs would now expect the Department to compensate him for the death of one wife by supplying him another. The world has grown smaller for them, too—and along with their loss had itself lost something. What aggregate innocences he's seen lost in his time—tribal to national, East to West, and now, ever heavier, his own West to East. *The noble savage doth not long maintain*—his father used to say, of the blacks who went north.

At closer range, the men here haven't changed in their surety—which comes out in dash in the younger ones, and in the elders in a mutual tribal satisfaction. Sexual authority, Bakh said once, feeds business too. "Our women make us all feel first-born. So a man can stay poor, with dignity." The women have had to make the most changes, or the most open ones—and suffer the most confusion? In the main it was the men who forced them to change. They seem to be bearing up. They speak better English than the men. If anything, they want to be Western. The men merely want the West.

"You still have your house?" Fateh giggles suddenly. For the past hour she'd been interviewing him, extracting just where he works, where he lives and especially whether he can expect to be posted again to Washington—all this with a spoiled-child's forward air which the other women falsely deplore. "Fateh!" they cluck, and smile. She reminds him of some Southern girls, half honey-giggle, half silly-sass, with an idiot gift for the socially useful impudence. But is this Fateh's character? Or her duty?

"House?" He'd already described his London one as rented only.

"A—" Fateh turns to Madame. "A-thens?"

At first he doesn't get it; she'd pronounced the *t*. Then he understands more than necessary. She's asking Madame's questions for her. She's the second wife.

"Athens, Georgia. I'm afraid it isn't my house."

"Not?" Fateh makes a pursy sound, chiding him. For not having it. Or not crediting him.

"My cousin's house."

"Ah—your cousin's." A quick glance at Madame and a rippling phrase. So Fateh, too, speaks French as well as she does English—and doesn't giggle in it. *O la la,* she'd said—we know about cousins.

So Madame owns Fereydoun's apartments here? He's not surprised. And on Bakh's money? A hunk of which she keeps in that pouch-bag of hers, ever-shifting on her lap? He glances up. All this may be Bakh's —and the day not ended yet. "We're always passing off our family junk on my cousin." He sees that they truly don't catch this. "I mean—the family's always asking her to store things. Because the house is so big. It was our great-grandfather's house. And some of us did go to be born in it."

They seem to understand this perfectly. As to a palace? He'll never be able to explain the difference.

"The beautiful ring is your cousin's—Fereydoun showed me," Madame says idly. Her first question.

"No—it was my wife's." No one's yet mentioned her. "My great-grandmother's, originally."

"Very pure stone. Rubies of that class are now more valuable than diamonds. In Switzerland, we know stones." She speaks to her pearl, her only ring, with a covert glance at Fateh's array. "Your cousin has daughters?"

"She's unmarried."

They cast up their eyes.

"Older than you?"

"Eighty."

"Ah. A pity she's not with you."

"She would certainly enjoy it."

"Fereydoun say—your cousin very angry." Fateh rolls her eyes at him. "Because the ring—you want to bury it. With your wife."

When he doesn't answer, Madame intervenes. "Fateh! And why not, Fateh? She was the first wife."

Fateh rises. If this is dismissal, she has no rancor.

A sense of the harem is wafted to him. Alliances between the women, in spite of themselves. Or because. With the big-screen husband, up there like Bakh, a still photograph always watching from the background of their collective submission. But he's heard they have their own insistences, powerful ones. "Madame . . . Manoucher's wife, Soraya. Where is she?"

Madame gets up. Inhaling, she addresses her body to rise, a royal chore. "My son's wife has her own *appartement*. Fereydoun!" He appears. "He will take you there."

On the way out, men waylay him, the younger deferring to the old. He's passed from one to the other, with cigars. Some are buying buildings here; others already have. He hears that shipping is for the Greek magnates; they do not poach. And thinks he hears, innuendo in Farsi, that they don't approve of these shippers' women. One of the younger men owns a bank. He's learned that a relative of Wert's is a banker in Baton Rouge. "A kissing cousin, actually." They have the same concept, the man says. A black sheep, sort of, Wert says. "Now pretty old. He keeps dogs. Whippets. Races them. Wants to leave me them. I've refused. Not my sport. And rather expensive." They look embarrassed, as the moneyed do at the mention of penury. Perhaps they worry he'll become a liability—not that they'd ignore that. His presence here's a guarantee of their solicitude for life—and of his. He sighs, answering absently from a kind of minor truth when asked what his sport is. "Horses." He's sometimes imagined that his pension will run to keeping a filly, on shares maybe, and boarding her out. But he sees that once again he's reassured them.

He and Fereydoun go up a staircase, Fereydoun plodding. Madame won't have an elevator. Because of the "Machine"? Soraya's household name. "You'll see why." They all have these nicknames, the women. Madame is Four Eyes.

"What's Fateh's?"

" 'Mouth.' "

Wert's guffaw echoes. Not a gentleman's. This place coarsens him. Well, it's needed. "Fereydoun . . . before we go in . . . what about Manoucher?"

The old man stops on the stair. "He stays with Bakh. Until."

Possibly a year, the boy'd said. But when we spoke, the regime was still hanging on. "Won't he be in danger now? Now that—"

Fereydoun waits. He's good at it.

"Now that—the Shah." Wert won't go further. How do these people say it among themselves? In time of revolution these people are the ones seldom asked. The New York papers hadn't, much. A revolution belongs to the poor.

The old man exhales, putting a finger across his lips—a signal Wert's been flipped in hotel rooms and embassies, seldom sure whether it comes from habit or romance. A world signal: the walls have ears. "You are with your government, Mr. Wert? Even in this house."

"Absolutely." The truth. But also the right answer.

"Manoucher—was already not with the UN."

"Oh? Since when."

"Since he marry Soraya."

"But Bakh—"

"Made the marriage, yes. From prison."

"Bakh?"

"Not *him.* The girl's grandfather was his friend. She is in prison a year."

"Did—Manoucher know that? Beforehand?"

"He is the *son.*" Fereydoun is a study, quizzical, sorrowful. "He is told. Later, he knows it for himself. Eh, eh."

"A university student, she was, he told me." One of those.

"Eh . . . But Manoucher is also the son of Madame." Fereydoun, fisting up, pulls on imaginary reins. "All his life, the mother and the father. A power—what you call it?"

"Struggle."

"Five years ago Bakh wants him out of the country—safe. He sees ahead. But she's a Pahlevi. So the bargain is—Manoucher can go, if he goes to *them,* at the UN. But he must not see his father. . . . So Bakh still gets his son out of the country. Eh?" Fereydoun twitters, looks pained, and stops himself, literally, by placing a hand on his Adam's apple, or against the lap of flesh that now covers it.

"At a sacrifice."

"Eh." The deepest yet. Perhaps the hand helps.

But as long as Manoucher stays—no grandson. "Will the wife go back now?" Now that the Shah . . .

"She cannot. How she is—you will see. For other women, enough revolution if they are—" He lapsed into Farsi.

"Out of the *chador*," Wert said, forgetting to pretend he knew none.

"Eh. Like Fateh—just give them a suit from Dior. Not Manoucher's Soraya. They would put her in prison again. This time—the mullahs."

"Was Bakh with the mullahs? All along?"

"Bakh?" Fereydoun spread his expressive hands. "They gossip suddenly that in Bakh's mother's family was the *muj'tabad* of Imam Reza in Meshed—you know what that is?"

"The Blue Mosque. Head priest."

"*I* never hear that rumor before." Fereydoun squints. "But in the case of wives, yes, Hossein is very religious there." That nervous laugh again. "So . . . now he marries again. It's late. The fox is at the throat. But an *imam* will be there. For all to see. And Manoucher, five years in America, is allowed to come home."

After a minute Fereydoun says, "Mr. Wert—you are not laughing? Eh no. What Bakh said is true then." He waits until Wert straightens his face. "You are the son from the West."

Ho, now. Ho, there. I had a father. Still, the breath holds for a healing moment.

Ferey's curiously modeled face—is he merely an old gay?—appears over his shoulder. "And still so young, so blond, so handsome," Fereydoun is cackling. "We are so surp—pleased. Still such a chance for happiness."

Bless them. For always saving you from themselves just in time. If you're the son from the West, Bill Wert, then act it. "Mr.—" He's never actually heard the man's last name. Fereydoun, he sees, isn't going to supply it. "Fereydoun—what's in store for me here?"

The old man grips the balustrade, very handsome in his black-and-white way. There's a decoration now in his buttonhole. His tongue moves under his lower lip, exploring it. "Eh, you don't know?"

"I know he must have his reasons for all this." What I want to know is—how am I one of them?

"Reasons? In the old days—there were reasons. Now it's one foot after the other for people like us—and don't look up at the third one, over your neck."

"I'm returning the *pishkesh,* by the way." Perhaps he's got the word wrong? "The gift pot they sent to me in London. Came from the museum in Teheran, I think, originally. It's in that box there. I've filled it with British biscuits, for Madame."

"Biscuits. You brought biscuits. Dear Mr. Beel, she is insane about them. Bloomingdale's has never enough. You must tell her at once."

"After you tell me."

But the old man's coy. It's none of his doing. He belongs to Madame. The pot—that amuses him.

"Manoucher arranged for it, no doubt."

"He does what his Soraya tells him, these days." A sly look. He glances at the door at the top of the stairs. "Of course, Bakh is a god to her—before. Like to everyone else. Eh? Even to me." A glance at his remarkable gold watch. He smooths it, turning his wrist for the caress. Downstairs Wert had noticed some of them still swinging the old-style worry-beads. "So tell me your instinct. I maybe have mine."

"Okay. I'm to be—the American connection—right?"

"Eh. Ah." He is overwhelmed. "That is smart. Yes. Like with the pot. Right." Thumbing his lip he looks long at Wert, eyes wide. "Ri-ight."

Wert's not sure of it. But he's tired of these colloquies in front of closed doors, instead of behind them. He knocks.

No immediate answer.

"Soraya has a guest," Fereydoun says over Wert's shoulder. "This week, from Teheran. Her aunt. And she will not keep a servant. Or not Madame's."

They hear steps, voices, women's. No giggles.

"I will tell you something." From his breath, the old man chews coriander. "You will not believe. Manoucher . . . Soraya, his wife, has not yet sleep with him."

The door opens inward to what he first mistakes for a flood of sunshine. Concealed lighting is shafting from all corners, spotted from niches and cornices, or bent in strips. Tinted glass, installed over what must be front windows, is lit from between. Because the ceiling is low, the effect is of a chapel cut in half with the top part missing, people below appearing stubbed. The girl of Manoucher's picture is before him. Awaits him. That's the stance. She's all in black—that loose "granny" dress almost to the ankles, with black stockings and sandals, too, which girls on the barricades of anything wear these days, or girls who follow that style; she could be at a "demo" in Boston, ready to demonstrate for the environment, or at an incendiary poetry reading in a Chelsea bar. No makeup, of course. That almost accusatory pallor the political ones seem to get. Some of those types wear handcraft decoration: she lacks even a wedding ring. The neck is goose-long, the brows meet over the nose—in the picture these must after all have been plucked, but she's still handsome, in an offended way. Doesn't she speak English? On the phone, hadn't she?

"Manoucher asked me to come."

She bows. Clearly she understands, but they're ushered further in, seated and offered the ritual bowl of nuts, without a speech. A bowl of pumpkin seeds as well. She's affecting the mode of the lower classes then? He realizes he's very angry—it must be for Manoucher. Taking a handful of seeds, he cracks one, spitting the husk into his palm. His tongue remembers its old agility. She's going over him top to toe, darting intelligences to herself. He cracks and splits.

"Will you have bourbon?" Fereydoun asks anxiously. "She has it."

He bows a stiff no. She's achieved a kind of personal *chador*, he's thinking. She'd doctrinairely unveiled. All over the world they do it, not just Iran, or South America, or here. His friend in Japan has a black-stocking wife like this one, tall too in the new-generation way, and by God with the same neck. The censorious way they all dress even has a kind of nineteenth-century force and battling charm. George Sand, Isadora Duncan, come to mind. Poor Manoucher. He spits a husk.

"Will you speak French? She knows American, but doesn't want to speak it." Fereydoun already has the harried air of a go-between trying to pour balm. "She wants me to tell you at once, though, that Bakh has allowed them to read your exchange of letters. She and her aunt. While they were in prison. Her aunt much admires them. And you."

Oh he did, did he? And didn't she admire them? But it's Bakh he's angry at. Friendship is to be used, he himself is no coolly off-hand Northerner. But these people never know where intensity should fall short. He's never been in prison, of course. "Why won't she speak it?" And who then was the rich-voiced girl on the telephone?

Ferey hesitates. Gets her nodded cue. "She has taken a vow. Until—" He gets a shake of her head. "A vow."

Insufferable. Wert gets up. "Full of vows, isn't she." She turns pink, a little. Now his choler's been released he can feel sorry. Poor things, they've always had to use their body-wiles. Even in the act of freeing themselves, they hang onto the method.

He wanders over to a row of black boxes and instrument panels which interest him, a whole row of ebony gadgetry set underneath the stained-glass windows. On the window seat, which runs the perimeter of the room as in old-fashioned rooms he's seen in Iran, there's a red catalogue, open face down. Hammacher Schlemmer's Instant Phone Order Gift Catalogue. Fascinated, he tracks what must be her purchases, none yet installed. Among them he notes a Spilhaus Space Clock "showing sun and moon positions, constellations, high tide and low, moonrise and set, Mean Solar Time and ordinary"; beyond it something called Marketline—"place your phone on terminal and get 7,000 stocks and options only 15 min. behind the tape"; a conference telephone amplifier; an automatic paper-shredder; and a cordless electric telephone index "accommodating one hundred and seventy names"—on which are inscribed two. He's aghast at what his country can provide a foreigner ardent for mechanization. But already mounted on the wall is something simpler, a Song Bird thermometer, a silly eighteen-inch disc with huge numbers and "birds in natural colors," which jolts his sympathies. It may be made in Western Germany and sold here, but those reds and blues and birds were once Persian taste.

"She didn't want to leave," Fereydoun is breathing behind him. "But it is only on this condition Bakh gets her out. And she is good girl—she makes modern home for Manoucher. Please come back to chair."

"Very modern." The doodled Farsi script on the telephone pad is familiar, but he hasn't time to place it. In his ear a whisper: "Manouch —she is really soft for him. Since before he is here. But she has pride, she wanted not to get out of prison like this. Also—there is Madame. Who wish them to live in Switzerland."

"Madame knows all this?"

"With us, what one woman does not know, the others tell her."

Never seeing when it's time to give up gossip and stand together? At times he fancies that women in search of autonomy need a male coordinator.

This is a big room, obviously made of several small ones. Can she hear them across it? She's sitting like Whistler's mother, in her younger black. Such a yackety sort her people are when together, yet he's often seen one of them apart like this, sitting in silence as if in extra air. She's watching them. Growing strong under their audience? A harem-habit, he thinks. Will it make for more tenacious female revolutionaries than we have in the West?

"She really won't speak English then?"

Ferey throws up his hands. "She has Ph.D. in it. In speech. And I must shop all over New York with her as interpreter. She say Fateh is not the right modern for her. Except at the drugstore."

Wert can't help laughing. "She's right."

Suddenly she whirls round at Fereydoun. *"Tell him."* In Farsi. A flood of it comes from her, too fast for Wert. Slowing, she addresses him lesson-style. Fereydoun, frowned over by those furry brows of hers, gives verse for verse: "She does it for the honor of the revolution."

"Oh—ff-augh." Wert can't help himself.

"At first, she swore not to speak it until you Americans left."

Wert shrugs.

"Now she finds she doesn't *want* to speak it here." Fereydoun shakes his head over her next sentence. But Wert has already heard it. She wishes she'd never learned American. She hates it here.

"But when she goes back—for the regime will change again, she says —they'll have to let her speak it if she wants to, teach the others even."

Same like coming out of *chador,* she hisses to Fereydoun, her lip trembling. I miss *chador,* even. But it is my right. . . . Don't tell him this.

Fereydoun looks from one to the other; bows his head.

"Oh my poor bitch—" Wert's already said under his breath. What a mix-up. He walks back to the chair in front of hers, sits, almost takes her hand in his, thinks better of it.

"Speak in French, you two," the old man says. "Go on."

Or break down into Farsi? Though probably he couldn't keep up with her. Besides, she's the kind of girl who on her own makes men feel hostile; it's not her ideas. *"Soyez bienvenue"*—he begins. But he can't hack it; he, too, has his pride. "Came here to say that, you know. To offer what I can. But this is my country. What it offers is in American."

She does have a glare. May even shine in the dark. Still, it's a wonder her Iranian husband hasn't got his rights from her.

It's the old man who explodes. *Get on with it, girl. We're not here to see you alone, remember?* To Wert he says, "I'm hungry. And it's almost time out there." He titters. "For the wedding." To her he adds, *It has to be done. In a hurry is better. Remember—what you and she both owe Bakh.*

She doesn't hurry. *Everybody always owes Bakh.*

The old guy stamps his foot.

This one will owe too, she adds, staring at Wert. *I did not admire those letters.* Shrugging, she stands up, clasping her arms in front of her. So be it. It's the gesture of the *chador.*

Standing in front of Wert, she's not as tall as the dark dress presents her. *Is this man worth it?* she flings over her shoulder. Then straight up into Wert's eyes—*I spend my life to watch.* Her eyes are the brilliant Kurdish blue which sometimes travels east into Azerbaijan. Suddenly she breaks her stare with a princess clap of hands, opening her mouth wide. Her yell splits just past him. For a minute he sees horse and cavalry in his head, and raised sabers, then a door to the next room opens and a skinny servant in *chador* runs toward them barefoot, though he sees no feet; this one is the floating kind the superior ones used to be. She's shaking her old head at Fereydoun. *She won't. I cannot force her. She won't wear the black.* The old man makes a sign. The woman wheels, catches sight of Wert, gives a shriek, spits a word at Soraya and turns her back, covering her face.

"Madame's *bodgi,* Mr. Beel," the old guy says. *"Pardon.* She did not know any man but me was here. *Now, Soraya, now. Tell the woman to bring her in now. Time's short.* Forgive me, Mr. Wert." He mutters to the servant. She doesn't move.

You old fool, Soraya says to Fereydoun, not turning her head. She's staring at Wert. Irish eyes, he used to pretend them, in the mountain-shadow of the Elburz. Sometimes a woman showed only one. *You old fool. Your Mr. Beel understands Farsi.*

She smiles slightly at him. How could he ever have thought this girl was—whatever he had thought her? "Vows are vows, Mr. Wert. But I also promised Bakhtiary." In English her voice is different, though it's not the voice heard on the phone. "I bring you a gift from him." She purses her mouth. Is she going to kiss—do they now? In Iran he was celibate. Flying occasionally to Thailand, where he had a girl, or when he could afford it, to Berlin. Most of the Iranian girl-students had had generals or other officials for fathers. He'd succeeded in thinking of even the westernized ones as shower-curtained from ear to floor. But the real anti-aphrodisiac had been their snaffled minds.

She whistles. *Peeoooooeuuuuuupewi.* No, a whistle can't be annotated. Call it the warning scratch a prince's cleats made, climbing up the glass mountain. When he should be hell-bent in the opposite direction.

There's a scuffle and a laugh from behind the door the servant skimmed back into; then a girl saunters from it—at first glance the kind of American girl he's just seen in Washington, or on the prinking streets of nearby Georgetown, airing along on white-stockinged legs which end in those fuzzy pink anklets and childish splat sandals, in just such a short skirt, too, and pink turtleneck, her head shining like a sheared button. A bag swings from her shoulder.

Seeing Wert she freezes, as if she hadn't expected to see him in the spot where he is. She's not a patch on Manoucher's wife for dramatic presence but informally prettier, in a candid way which might almost be American. She wears makeup, he sees, when she comes to stand in front of him. But she's certainly Iranian; the nose has the exact curve of Soraya's, though a freckle or two masks that. Now she's flushing, head bent. Perhaps she, too—like Bakh's bride-to-be—is only just out of *chador.*

"So you won't wear black," Wert says mischievously, as to a younger sister. *"Az molaqat e soma xeyli xosvaqt am*—I'm very glad to meet you."

Why does everybody look frightened but pleased?

"The *other* Soraya," Fereydoun says ceremoniously. "She was born the same year as Manoucher's Soraya here. And named the same. So that is what we call her."

Not a sister then. "Your half-sister?"

Manoucher's wife slips her arm around the girl's waist. They're of a height, but it's hard to believe them of an age. Though marriage hasn't fattened Manoucher's wife, it has filled in certain psychic outlines, as marriage does even if unconsummated. He sees now that though the other girl mustn't look her age, she's no teenager. Only unmistakably single. Manoucher's wife's smiling at him again. "No. My aunt."

Behind them all the door from the stairs opens, admitting Madame. She halts there, appearing to stare fixedly beyond them, as a sentry would, only toting a saddlebag instead of a gun. She bows to Manoucher's wife, who barely bows back. Slowly one woman after another files through the door, until Madame's surrounded by a thick circle of them; half the women from the other apartment must be here, at least thirty. In the stagey colored light they loom like a tribunal focused on him; what's he done? Their jewels flash red, green and blue with primary power, and with a holy white. Is this an auto-da-fé—for his being American?

It's as they trot forward on their high heels, herded in by grim Madame—but breaking up into their twos and threes because they're women and instinctively make any line a confab, that the truth comes on him, along with the shock that the name doodled twice on the telephone pad is his own. Just so, walking with a crony, one dusk in Tabriz, they'd met up with a clump of women, a perfumed cloud of them in *chadors* nothing like the servant-kind, being let into one of the blank, knockered doors in the long, continuous wall that concealed the houses, all with sizable courtyards, which made up that section of the city. The crony, a high-ranking clerk at his own Embassy, had excitedly pulled him back. "My sister Parvin—this is the third time those women have visited her—a very fine family. In our country the women pick the bride. This visit means yes. Better we not go in after all. She'll be making tea for them." As they'd walked on to an ordinary teahouse, where women were of course not admitted, a fact he knew as well had come upon him more forcibly. All along the wall, the brass knockers were women's hands.

The groom?—Wert had asked his companion. Oh, the women may bring him along, next time. Had the groom and the girl ever met? Oh yes, at the university. They like each other. We're not that old-fashioned. Mehrdad's teeth had been like Manoucher's Soraya's, almond-white, untouched by tobacco. "But when it's time for ritual, we revert. Don't you people do the same?"

Wert wished hard and sudden for his cousin, far away in a big old house now only a block from a gas station, yet in a town where certain people still did just that. Ordering the traditional magnolias from the florist if necessary—as had been done at his second-cousin-once-removed daughter's wedding—and tying them into the trees. He could telephone to ask her opinion, which she always gave overpoweringly. Cousin—under the circumstances, am I the bride, or the groom?

Better still, he could fly there. Away.

On second thought, he'd rather not let his cousin know. Women fester toward a wedding, their very skin irritated by the sight of the male in the single state.

His best gambit, the only decent one, is to be stupidly polite. Speak to the aunt.

"Do *you*—speak English?" Wert said. *Englisi harf mizanid?*

Everybody clapped.

Not the two girls, who look uncomfortable. Nor Fereydoun, who glances at his watch—and who may have an understandable lack of interest in weddings.

"Don't fuss, Ferey," Madame says in French. "That damnable program's been delayed another hour. Paris just telephoned." To Wert she says in English: "My husband's wedding will be broadcast from Isfahan, but on the—the—what is it, girls?"

Manoucher's wife doesn't answer her mother-in-law. Her neck grows an inch.

The aunt tucks in her chin, modestly. "Satellite."

The women purr admiration, passing the English word like a ball. He wants to clap.

"*Machines, tous les deux*, my nieces," Madame says. "This one"—she points to her daughter-in-law—" a speech machine. And the other Soraya—what are you, hmm?"

Wert waits, fascinated. That beautiful dove-voice, the voice of the phone, what'll float out on it? She's hanging her head, as one does in her country when young, subordinate, yet admitting a fact to one's credit. "Computer programmer."

"Are they not beautiful together!" bursts from one of the women.

His ears burn.

Fateh rescues him. "Brought up together, Mr. Wert, all their lives!"

A humming from the women. He recalls the cronies, their moist-eyed tales of masculine devotion. Are these girls the new-style heroines? "Did you say—nieces?"

Over there behind Madame, everyone giggles. Seems he can't make a wrong response.

Fereydoun intervenes. "It's very simple." But he's grinning. "The other Soraya's mother is Manoucher's Soraya's grandmother, married at twelve. The grandmother and her own daughter—Manoucher's Soraya's mother, had these two girls the same year, the grandmother first. The *father* of the other Soraya happens to be Madame's real brother. The father of Manoucher's Soraya is the half-brother of Madame by *her* father's second wife—although this half-brother was actually only adopted into that family, being the son of the second wife's dead sister. So Manoucher's wife is only an adopted niece; Madame made very sure of it."

"Otherwise my grandson might know all the parts of speech and still be an idiot," Madame murmurs rapidly. *"When* he arrives."

"Otherwise—" Fateh raises a ruby-nailed finger, pointing to the girl, "we would have send her first. As the aunt . . . and so talented, Mr. Wert."

"Bakh? He would have sent Manoucher both of them," Madame says gloomily. "Lucky, your country does not allow."

"Madame does not approve," Fereydoun says. "Of the old Islamic marriage. You may recall her family modernized it."

A silence. Everybody's recalling. *Shah.* No need to say it. Shah. "And Reza Shah," Wert says.

"You don't approve of more than one wife?" Fateh seems to be asking this question for herself. The shadow from her false lashes cross-hatches her pupils, reminding him of the x cartoonists used to put in the eyes of a character meant to be blotto. Under all her beige, yes, that other woman.

Only an Arabic answer is possible. "Madame Fateh—*qisma*—Kismet, gave me only one."

An abdominal groan from the ladies. He won't dare turn toward their starry expanse, agreeing now with what Bakh used gravely to tell him: *Chador* is a protection for the man. What's Ferey's allegiance, to men or women? To neither probably; that's his value. "Bakh's new wife, is she of the family, too?"

He's managed to say something wrong at last.

"She is of Ardebil. As one can see." Fereydoun confides, buttonhole to buttonhole.

A sudden keening from Manoucher's wife. "I did not want to leave prison first. *She* makes me." Palms outstretched toward the other Soraya, the Farsi trembling off her lips, she beats time to it. "We came into that prison nearly together; we should leave together." Her eyes are shut. Two drops squeeze from them, and a tiny voice from below. "Because she knows I am soft for Manoucher. Yes, it is true. 'Go,' she says. She is already getting too old for children she says. Already six months older than me, almost twenty-five." She opens her eyes. The other Soraya closes hers. They hang onto each other like a pair of just-revealed caryatids waiting for the archaeologist's pick. "So I say— 'I will wait. I will not have children. Until she, too, comes to America.' "

They remind him of his young cronies of yore. A touch of Damon and Pythias, the complications of the womb notwithstanding. Attacks of adolescent vowing—whose attitudinizings used to strike silvery shadows in his samovar.

He can't seem to remember that those two have been in prison. Prison, not jail; jail is apolitical. The fact keeps sliding away from him. As does his own possible role here. What's operating here is the clan, that engine always running during either the light or the dark of lives lived within its enclosure. He wants to get nearer it. Even if it burns.

At this moment, everyone's ignoring him for what's being revealed. Not that they didn't already know. But now the clan's obligatory scene is upon them.

For Madame is muttering to Fereydoun, in schoolgirl German. "To think. To think—that to ransom those two, Bakh let those *Schweine* have his last two opium fields."

"Shhh. *Hald dein Mund.*"

Wert gives no indication of having overheard. The special myopia of those who use a whispered other language as the last resort of intimacy always amuses him.

"I was just telling Madame," Fereydoun says, switching to English, "that her daughter-in-law really adores her. Adores you and admires you, Madame. What's she done but copy you—if I may say."

"You'll say it anyway. What hasn't he said to us, Mr. Wert. In the years he's managed us."

And how they smile at each other, the servility perfectly balancing the complicity.

"Then, I'll say it. Madame—what's Manoucher's Soraya done to him but copy what you did—to Bakh?"

"Das war persönlich! Nicht Radicalismus!"

Whether it was personal or radical, she likes being reminded of it. "But are those girls really—" Wert says. "Of course, country to country, radicalism changes."

"In my country, Mr. Wert, if you are in prison, then you are radical. How nice you speak German, too."

They watch her join the two girls, who are surrounded by the women. "Yes, how nice," Fereydoun whispers doubtfully. "For your information, Manoucher's wife was sent to prison for writing something. A lecture—about parts of speech. Very clever. Actually one more manifesto." He shrugs. "And one more university riot. But the other Soraya —she's been against the mullahs from the beginning. And that's serious. She can't go back."

"So—Bakh's really out of opium now?" Or again? He'll hear nothing good of the old man from now on. The clan being the clan.

"Ah—those fields were earmarked for Madame. Part of her—settlement. He'll compensate her. He now has interests in outer space." Fereydoun pets his watch, soothing it like a cat. "Not everyone can arrange a broadcast by satellite." He smiles at the word; his manner is loosening, his English, too. "The other Soraya—she's his favorite." He's scarcely moving his lips. "We think—he tried to marry her. To get her out of prison, of course. But he wanted to."

Wert stands rigid. The possibilities open like fans. "Who *sent* those girls to prison?"

But Madame's already at his elbow, shepherding the girl. "She is very like your American girls, *non, M'sieu* Wert? Like all our girls, she knows for the household—but like yours she is also modernly talented. The *spécialité* computer is very chic, *non?* But *of course* she can have children—if it is wanted. She is not like some." A glance at her daughter-in-law. And at Fereydoun. "It is understood—she would remain the only wife. But she is also so American she wish to choose her own husband." Madame's giggle rumbles in bronze. "She is very hard on us. We are supposed to arrange. *Méchante*, you went even to prison to avoid us. Hah! And then what happens, naughty girl?"

All the women sigh. Or a good many of them. He daren't look to see. *"Quand même, m'sieu,* a lovely thing happen." Madame's eye doesn't soften. *"Elle a de la chance,* this girl. She fall on her feet anywhere. We are *très embarrassé* but we are all agree, *non?"* A murmur from the others. "She is fallen in love, Mr. Wert. With your letters to Bakh."

The other Soraya is looking at him steadily. Her face is carved farther past youth than the prettiness he first saw: she can well be twenty-five. Why should that hearten him? When he can't bear those pink socks.

"They invited you early, Mr. Wert," she says. "Stop pretending to look at your watch, Fereydoun, you know it wasn't to be until four. And we all know who gave you the watch." All the while staring at Wert, her lashes unwavering. *Her* lip doesn't tremble. "Mr. Wert—I'll just give you what I have for you from Bakh." Even in the black that Manoucher's wife wanted to put her in, she wouldn't make a man hostile. Pity is, that won't help the revolution either. Though there are black circles under her eyes. So she was against the mullahs from the beginning—bright girl, if he can believe it. All that will have to be sorted out later. But if she herself's had a hand in this charade, it'll be doomsday before he'll know. What dignity, in either case.

An idea occurs to him, on how to save both their faces. What she'll have for him—in the ritual way they like to make wreaths of past friendship—will be the letters. Abide by the ritual then. Save her face, poor smart, muddled girl, prisoner of more than revolutions—and save his own skin. For in spite of all their effort, they know he's not the suitor here. His cousin has not applied for him.

"Then, if there's time—" Wert said. "I've come a long way. Perhaps—" he turns properly to Madame, "the other Soraya will make tea for me?"

How ridiculous—she's not a sixteen-year-old, to be made to show her jejune accomplishments. Head bent, she's swaying a little. Well, he won't ask her to sing. Or to dance. Immediately he's ashamed of himself. Manoucher's wife is hovering anxiously near the girl, who says palely, "I came far, too. From Isfahan, day before yesterday."

"And before that—" Manoucher's wife cries, but is hushed by the girl's hand.

"Hush—" the girl says in Farsi. *"You owe me nothing. Ah, Soraya, it's not each other we owe. Or even Bakhtiary."*

The Farsi cadence doesn't change her. Not like it does the others.

"And *he* owes us nothing," she says, looking at Wert. "In prison, any letter is precious. It's from the outside."

"When were you let out?" He speaks in Farsi.

"I—" She looks at Manoucher's wife. "A—month? I had no calendar."

"And three days. Manoucher flew her at once to the hospital in Shiraz. But she had bad dreams there. Then to Isfahan."

"I have no bad dreams in prison. I know what I am doing there." She's shaking, now. Wert puts out a hand. She fends him off. "It's nothing."

"Isfahan—" He can't help himself. "You saw Bakhtiary."

"I—saw him. Y-yes." Her teeth are chattering; is it ague? Malaria? "Ex-cuse me. I have pill for this." She slides the shoulder bag down, slowly, painfully opening it, moving constrictedly to take the glass of water the servant's already slipping her. So they know what the trouble is, then. The pill she extracts and swallows isn't big enough for quinine.

Fereydoun asks low: "You dreamed in Isfahan?"

"No, like in prison."

Watching her move slowly to open the bag again, it comes to him. They whip them there. She's been whipped. Out of the bag comes a letter—but only one, and not his handwriting. He recognizes the familiar stationery. An envelope like it is still on his mantel in London. What else can there be, to bring?

A box, a small, red morocco box. How small, to travel so far. Farther than either he or she. *Beautiful,* Bakhtiary said in Venice, the only time Wert ever saw him shy. *It came out so very beautiful, that mask, I had one made for myself.*

And better than a gravestone. Wert is reaching for it when the girl topples forward. Fereydoun catches her first, in his long, eighty-year-old arms. The box with Jenny's death mask in it, eluding all their fingers, has been dropped. No one will ever be able to say by whom.

They've laid the girl face-down on the cushioned seat which borders the room, Madame and Fateh waving all the other women back except the servant. The back of the pink turtleneck is stained wet and glaucous. "Not blood, what is it?" Fateh whispers. Manoucher's wife, bending over it, tosses back her head, agonized but proud. The sweater is slowly peeled off by the servant. Fateh, chafing the girl's wrists, moans like a cat. The girl's back rises and falls. The upper back is half scab, here and there oozing. Below, the healed small-of-the-back is like rose-colored leather.

"The hot plate," Manoucher's wife says loudly. "The *dastband e gapani* they put her in, first. Handcuffs from over the shoulder. The night they bring her in, the electricity is off in our part of the prison. And in the room where they use the grill. So they use coal-fire, and iron door. Shiraz Hospital say she's lucky. From the grill, you cannot have skin grafts."

Across that breathing body, Madame touches her daughter-in-law. "And you?"

"Only the lash, Madame. But twice."

"So that is why Manoucher. Why you refuse him."

"Oh no, Madame. I don't refuse him altogether. Not from the back." Swiftly the daughter-in-law turns her back to them all, kneels forward, and flips up her loose blouse. The lash marks, crossed vertically and horizontally, are perfectly healed.

"Madame! Watch out!" Fateh tries to pry Madame's nails from her own pearl string.

"*Jalel.* Moron. Let me be." Madame's hands tug at the heavy rope. She drops to her knees in a shower of beads. Beside her the two exposed girlish backs form a ruined folio, opened at the worst page.

Next to Wert, a nickering begins, a flute choking higher and higher. Fereydoun is tittering. He grasps his throat, squeezing the hysteria he can't stop. Mir-li-li-iiiiii-ton—ton. Gagging, he stops in front of Wert, the tears sprouting from his begging face. Before Wert can move, the servant does it, one long worn hand from behind the *chador*, crack, crack, on each smooth-powdered cheek. Fereydoun drops in a crouch, head down, arms hanging, heavy convulsive intakes . . . whooped breath . . . chip chip a-chip . . . and at last silence. "Madame usually does it for him," the servingwoman whispers. Above the veil her brows are grizzled, the lids papery. The blunt bazaar accent cackles. "He can't stand the sight of a chicken being cut into even; it's natural."

Madame kneels in her purple sweater behind the exposed wounds of the two girls, all three bowed as toward a prie-dieu. The other Soraya sits up, turning between the other two clasping women, her eyes still closed. The breasts that face Wert are unscarred, rose-swollen, milky-white. Fateh, swooping down upon her with a harem screech, covers the girl with a scarf. But unmistakably, he's been allowed a glimpse of her. The old servant, her veil between her teeth, is oblivious, picking up the pearls.

Fereydoun takes him by the arm. The aisle of women at the door, parting for him, gives off sparkles of gold tissue, black glitter, red-tinted black hair. Throwing off Fereydoun's arm, he retrieves the letter, which he stuffs in a side pocket—and the small box, which he cradles in both hands. They know it contains Jenny; he's sure of it. Blinking their mica eyelids they stand like sad eagles either side of a pyramid whose old marriage door he's expected to reenter. Making an apologetic cringe with his box, he passes them.

The bathroom Ferey leads him to is the women's. Two sunken tubs are separated by a broad ledge massed with tall vats of powder and bath salts, loofahs and towels, articles for the hair, all a replica of what one heard their finer bathhouses at home used to be. Fereydoun, at the toilet, is modestly slow at opening his pants. Wert turns his back. The note from Bakhtiary is a one-liner, not from his custom-made multilingual typewriter, but in hand. "Last letter. One sentiment. It's time." Scrawled beneath is an ankh.

Time for both of them. But he can't open the box, shrinking even from shaking it, to hear whether the old plaster-of-Paris has broken. The face inside already clings to his fingertips. Wish I felt nothing. Wish I felt something. Which is true?

"Shall I take care of that for you?" Ferey, washing his hands with a great yellow ball of heady-scented soap, regards him equivocally.

To guard it? Or to destroy? Smart equerry, he's not saying. Casually, Ferey seizes an atomizer and sprays his jowl. He's at home here. Leave it to him.

What better than to leave the past, seamless or smashed, to an old eunuch who knows what his trade is: certain peculiar services.

Wert passes him the box, and is freed to urinate, to use the soap—to share any of their domestic arrangements here, including a wife. And without compromise—which must always have been the value of eunuchs. A diplomat can't compete. He nods. "Probably you have closets galore."

Along the way back to the main apartment, the notes archways, tilings and cushionings subtly Middle East. Even the windows have been heightened and made mosquelike. But where they aren't draped the view is of dismally gimcrack low roofs, or that palely transitional modern brick which can't seem to make a firm imprint on space.

"But why are we here, you're asking—" Fereydoun says, "in this neighborhood? Everybody asks."

"Quite."

"Bakhtiary didn't want us to shine out. Now—it doesn't matter."

"Because he's dying?"

"Because we're all in this country now. Or—whoever can be."

"Bakhtiary would never come. I invited him."

"No. He would never come."

"Even to Manoucher?"

Perhaps he shouldn't have said that about dying, the old man is so pale.

"Will you excuse me, Beel. Only a moment." On their left there's a small room, door open, with a window on another vista—east. Ferey leaves the door ajar. There in the middle of the room, he's salaaming. No doubt about it; he's praying. Their movements make them supple beyond what Western devotions generally do for one. When he emerges he's noncommittal, but blowing his nose.

The main room's walls are a dazzle of rugs, making it one of their Arabian-nights enclosures. Now its deep burnishment sickens him. These rugs know too well the mahogany that blood turns to. Under their woolen astronomy of charming animal alembic and arboretums flattened for foot or eye, too often that spongy wound-color. Yet the inhabitants of this always migrant oasis can still thrall him. Crammed now on folding chairs, they're no longer his or a newspaper's invention. Their bank accounts have been streaming ahead of them for years against this possible moment; they'll be buying houses and schooling the children here, yet he can't imagine them on the world's chopping-board like other people; he can't see them as ever settling in. This tent of theirs floats with them, always perfectly aligned—and landing anywhere.

Up there on one side of the room Bakh presides on screen in his gnarled garden, armed for entry into the oldest eternity, with child-bride and at his feet a dish of sand, scrawled with religion. On the opposite wall there is now a hugely ready video installation—no doubt sent the way a five-pound box of candy "from your local merchant" used to be, by a conglomerate. Merely one of the contradictions daily exploding around the world, which any dutiful newscaster would report. Yet would such a reporter see what it is more than money which joins that beaky woman over there in her pared Paris black, that tail-coated patriarch who looks about to address the whole chattering fami-ly-wedding crowd yet is never seen to speak, Madame herself, just settling her own group on a separate dais, the boy teenagers stiffly Englished up in haircuts and jackets which ask for blond heads not black, and their awkwardly frothy girl counterparts—all the way down to the bright infant dots on a shoulder or a lap?

Except for their servants there's not a *chador* among them, or any remnant trace of the beads and saddles of the old donkey culture. Over the last seventy-five years most of these people wouldn't have slept toeing a brazier or even in the more formal quiltings but in beds imported from the West, and their Cartier jewelry may be thieved from them at the best hotels, yet they're joined to the old *bodgi* and her vast peasanthood by what they all share. A shallow *jube* of understanding runs through them all like that old water ditch of theirs, in the way that same dirty old life support used to frame their cities—and must still link their villages. The remarkableness of the *jube* was its shallowness, in which, stared into long enough, all their human commerce became clear. He must always have known what this people's enclosures contained. What unnerves him is that he may always have wanted it.

Up there on the grainy screen at his left, in that garden picture of erotic duties to self and who knows what obligations to truths greater than the self, his old friend's expression, that dignified alertness to advantage, hasn't changed. But did we in the Department ever consider what Bakh meant by advantage?

"Where'd you prefer to sit, Mr. Beel?"

Not with the men. Their poker-faced swapping dries up at his approach; he'll learn nothing. Where are his own letters to Bakh now? The daughter-in-law doesn't admire them; he'd be interested to know why; he admires her. A man would always know where he stood with her.

Madame and she are now on the dais, facing the crowd, where many of the women cling separate in the old style, leaving an admixture of couples of all ages, including several striking young pairs got up like internationally gilded statuary, and those few hormonally neuter old bodies who at their age were permitted anything. He doesn't see the girl. The aunt.

"Let's sit at the back."

Fereydoun hesitates. "You Americans. Such democrats."

Near the staircase to Manoucher's apartment is a short row of empties which must be reserved for the servants; two in *chador* are already at its farther end. He and Fereydoun seat themselves at the other.

"Who's that tall guy—he going to speak?"

"Our former chargé d'affaires. No—he's just—"

"Showing himself." Always a lot of that, anywhere in government. Power emeritus, among the displaced. "I suppose—Bakh won't speak?"

"The marriage ceremony does not require it."

Fereydoun's one hand, crumpling restlessly; opens to show a string of worry-beads, a fine one, small evenly worn globes of some cloudy quartz over which the thumb can move contentedly. At first sight of such beads, one might think them rosaries, but their use had been laic, subtly somewhere between the cigarette and the psychiatrist, a social admission that men must fiddle. In Iran, a colleague trying to use them to help break his cigarette habit had found them useless to someone lacking their intricate vocabulary of social reference. They were a habit always significantly of the background, and always masculine. He'd heard it was considered lower class to swing them. The cultivated could make them seem a sensuous pursuit, not a nervous one. They were old-fashioned now. Bakh had never used worry-beads. Or never in front of Westerners. But Fereydoun's watch must not be enough for him.

"And Manoucher . . . will it be dangerous for him to show himself?" Never *mind*, he thinks, watching the beads slide, jerk and slide. "Don't bother to explain, Fereydoun. There's no logic in revolution." Not even in history. We only lead ourselves to expect it. That is how we intellectually live—even the illiterate. Wert glanced at the two serving-maids. Maybe those most of all. Bakh, relinquishing his son only because he sensed the regime was falling, only to let the boy align himself with it —and now mending his own fences with the holy men, must have known this from the beginning. It's all a walking-on eggs, he'd written. Between versions of that greediest of all egalitarians, Bill—the natural ape.

There's no logic but compensation. That's what these people know best.

The old equerry's now looking at him in such open pain that he half wants to take him in his arms. "The bride, Mr. Beel—" he says in his high voice, "she doesn't need to speak either."

Wert sat. Terrible to see a man of that age pacify himself, a revolution, and God knows what all, with a canny string of amethysts. In Wert's own heavy daytime brogues his toes spread, seeking surface, and delicately retract. "I know. They're sent."

Fereydoun got up. "It's beginning." On the second screen, blank until now, an agitation of images has begun—a house, a garden torch-lighted, major-domos and waiters, food tables al fresco, and a trickle of guests in evening dress—from the embassies? Farther behind is a somber crowd, more solidly packed, from which the camera skitters back to tables stiff as cardboard, the food still unattacked. Whether the camera is badly maneuvered or psuedo-artistic is moot.

"Wait. What is that place?"

"The hospital. In Isfahan."

"And that?" Wert points to Bakh in his chair and the leaning girl.

"Their house in Teheran."

"When?"

"When? Why, I suppose when the girl first came. Some time ago. . . . But that up there. That's the hospital all right. The garden, yes." He leans forward judiciously. He must have been a palace man all his life. "I'll leave you now. My place is with Madame. But, Mr. Beel—that staircase behind you leads down also. We're very late. One of the maids can show you out." He flicked an eye toward them. "If you must fly."

THE COUNTRY BEHIND HIM

So they've tried—is he admitting? Starting all the way from London, or even earlier, from those palace reserves of obligation where they store people like Wert. Where ever since Venice, he must have been kept.

If he stays, what a confidant this Fereydoun could make. Mere colleagues like Nosy pale beside him—and his clan.

"I liked the boy," Wert said.

"Boy? Manoucher?" Is Fereydoun going to titter again? Instead, a surprisingly heavy fist comes down on Wert's shoulder. "He was there."

The lights dim as he leaves, a genie receding. Except for the two maids on the row, who don't count, Wert's left to himself for the first time. So abrupt is the plunge back into this familiar, slow-breathing, cud-in-the-mouth self of his when in crowds, that he examines it. Is this his favorite state of being? Or a cul-de-sac from which Bakhtiary, with ambush if necessary, hopes to rescue him?

Around him, conversation's not fading. Their sense of attention is different, requiring constant formal annotation aloud. Very out loud or very hush-hush; that's how they live, not much middle ground to them. He's all middle ground, Bakhtiary's told him. His country's taught him to be. Oh there's ashcan violence in your cities, Wert, stifled mass murder in your suburbs. And political murder, if you can call what's random or mad "political." Bakhtiary can't. All Wert's own aggression, he's pointed out, is now in his country's bombs, and all his once valuable personal secrecy. Your bombsights are now your people's chief organs of meditation. What barbarians you're teaching us to be.

There'd been a convention of Western philosophers at the Teheran-Hilton; Bakhtiary had wondered why. "Maybe to observe our code of violence, which is in our daily living, dear Bill? A head lopped off, here and there. A mild thumbscrew, to clear a man's head so that he may perhaps keep it. Or a skin-peeling, to correct a woman's. How civilized —to be able to suffer personally for one's views! There our women are even more equal than yours. They guard our secrets, you know, like the Pentagon does yours. So we must guard them."

On the video screen, Bakhtiary himself is now advancing. The short, sturdy feet plant themselves steadily as the camera travels forward. Wert can't see the backs of them. Bakh's wearing one of the deep black suits of thinnest silk which they used to affect in the worst heat for formal occasions. Here in Queens in snow weather, some of the men are wearing them. In that blazing garden of the still photograph at the left, Bakh's suit is white—for engagement time? The video garden on the right-hand screen is a nighttime one, but well illuminated, and as the saying goes—"live." Though even so, a viewer may be struck with certain cliché album conclusions on the passage of time.

The announcer comes on, to a low spate of "Ahs!" from the audience; he's a young Iranian whom many of them know from Paris. Speaking English with an Oxford accent interspersed with French, he ripples out a long list of Bakh's credits: —*industrial magnate, adviser to the new regime.* On that pause, the camera shifts. The ayatollah is coming forward. The audience sighs. "Ah, that one." We progress from comfort to comfort, Wert thinks. This mullah's name isn't yet known to Wert or his newspapers, but he is plainly an important one. His wrappings shine powerfully, properly subordinating the face, which appears to listen impassively. *This is Mr. Bakhtiary's third marriage. Though his holdings are in the most modern industries, and he is expected to help regularize the regime's management of these, he himself has always kept to the Islamic laws in his private life.*

And perhaps he has. With such scant outward change. Ninety years, what has he done with them; what's been done to him? Is that jaw slightly swollen, or merely thrust forward? The necktie loosened? People here are murmuring what people do; the tenderest audience can't help scavenging. "Those dark glasses, I wish he would take them off." Everybody wants him to look at him or her personally.

So does Wert.

The bride is from a family prominent in Ardebil. At last, a shot of the bride, in heavy white and a headdress, surrounded by women, somewhere inside the house. Silence. Then a cry from the dais: "Yes, her father has a string of sweet-shops, very prominent."

Fateh is made to shut up, not without laughter.

His eyes are getting used to the partial light; he can see Madame. She's shed her sweater set at last for a gown which should glitter when she moves. It doesn't. There's no code for translating her feelings. He tries to imagine his mother, separated for half a lifetime from his father, presiding in public acknowledgment of his father's remarriage. With these people, though, it's not remarrying—while we'll continue to say that even when a man is on his eighth wife. For them it's been onward-marrying, as much for clan as for the man. *Gallinaceous birds, we are* —Bakh had once informed him. *Look it up, pal.* He had to. Ordinary domestic fowl. But what Westerner, if reported this, would honor it?

Minutes ago he was hungry, now hunger's gone, down wherever other intensities send it. He can't name what these are, except that his chest seems to be surgically widening. There's always the staircase, if coming alive gets too much for him. Glancing along the row, he notes that the nearer *chador* is wearing dark glasses, a Western modesty. He's never seen those with a *chador*. Another reportable fact.

In front of the television screen here, someone's placing a tray of sand molded into hieroglyphs similar to those etched in the sand of the tray at the feet of Bakh and his girl in the still photo. Now the real Bakh—or the one moving on video, is seating himself. As the camera advances, a third tray can be seen on the screen, in front of Bakhtiary's chair. The trinity of them—in still, on video and one actually here on the floor before them all—is eerie past ritual, suggesting a fourth dimension behind all these submissive replicas. Bakh, the real Bakh, is now looking out at them here. Behind him is the real scene. Is he noting the differences?

There can't be many relatives up there in that sleuth-crowd pressing silently behind Bakhtiary's chair. For one thing, so many are here. On the other hand, there's no mullah here. No roses. Not a one; that's strange. Queens has florists, flowers. Maybe this crowd hasn't yet brought itself to believe in them. Though the row in front of him is rapt.

The mullah's now addressing the camera from beside Bakhtiary's chair, raising his right arm up down, up down. On the mullah's face, which Wert always thinks of as a single generic one, is the stare that such faces always had there, not inward or meditative but fanatically forward, past the flock itself, toward the letter of the law. Yet always full of secular gall. Wert had never seen one without it. They seem to him the most quick-tempered of man's priests. Is this one reading the Koran, each time scowling up from a scroll half in his sleeve? No, he's calling a roll—the names of people here. Each time he pronounces a name, Bakhtiary raises his own hand, in salute. Noises of assent come from the room here—an old woman's long, wan agreement, a boy's yell, quickly cut off, a man's sobbing. The mullah is doing it by families. Each is having a different response. There are silences.

Up there on the video, it's a duel between the two old men wielding their arms, one speaking, one mute. The mullah—a talon, a sleeve and a spitting voice protruding from the country those here have left—is he excommunicating? Standing right there, mouthing on, he's fading; he's upstaged. Hossein Bakhtiary, raising and lowering his right arm, on its wrist a watch like Fereydoun's, in its palm a long-stemmed rose, is winning. And why not? He's doing what these here have had to do. He's saying good-bye.

The last of the names, sputtered unintelligibly, almost passes Wert by. Just then, Bakh removes his sunglasses. The hand grasping the tea-colored flower moves forward, palm up. The eyes are the same. The mouth, closed until now, opens a swollen hole. Wert can hear its tongue-less gurgle. Buh-Beel.

They bring on the bride.

Wert wants not to watch. Ahead of him, an elder is rotating worry-beads in steady pinwheel. There's now no sound from this room, none of the woman-surf which hails a bride. Under the heavy headdress and costume which Ardebil has chosen for her, the slender body opens and closes obediently, a white fan manipulated from behind, twice refusing the gold bracelets offered her, a third time accepting, eyelashes fanned on her cheeks in the one close-up—while sugar is sprinkled by one of the two contending retinues, both sides in *chador*. *To sweeten the moth-er-in-law*, the announcer informs, his voice perfunctory. Even the cam-era is restive, disdaining this secondary creature with her trail of "old custom" dragging behind, and her not-to-be-dwelt-on life ahead—whose mother-in-law, dead in childbirth, as Wert happens to know, was a girl her own age, surely sweetened now by ninety years in the grave.

A camera is never embarrassed. One more flash for the bride's "beauty," whiter than the rest of her, then a close-up—of Bakh's. The lens moves on to the brilliantly lit food tables, pointing out epergnes. The smell from the Queens kitchen mingles with them.

All the wedding gifts go to the nation. They are on the longest table of all, in huge assortment, more ransacked than piled. The lens travels at table level, like a child's eye. "Look—Grandpa's silver samovar; did we give it?" a young girl two rows ahead hisses clearly. Finally, the camera traverses the crowd. There, tall as a trophy, between two mul-lahs, and behind him a third, is Manoucher.

Quiet now, not even a sound track humming. Over there in Iran, has noise been confiscated, too? Wert can hear the separate breathings around him—even at the end of his own row, from the nearer *chador*. The pinwheel up ahead has stopped.

A cry then from Manoucher's wife, from the dais. "Manoucher! How thin you are. It is only five weeks."

True. That same coat he was wearing in London now hangs on him. Taffy under the hot lights, it hangs from him in points, like his own flesh running from him. What are the seasons there now? Tabriz may be under snow, blue-glass afternoon ski slopes, with the brass samovar stuck in a drift. But Isfahan's warmer. Why's he wearing that coat?

The camera won't answer. It's scouring the façade of the hospital behind the crowd, running briefly over a plaque showing that Hossein

Bakhtiary was donor of it, returning frantically to rock past the tables of loot, saying without a word, "Palace to palace, to nation . . . loot eternally."

The smell from the kitchen here in Queens is imperative. In the deep iron skittles which they'll have brought over here whatever else they left, the long-kerneled rice is forming that bottom-crust which will be scooped out like brown lace, to be screamed for by the children, dropped on the plates of the favorite. Left too much longer, it will burn. But up there on the screen, the plates on the food tables are yet unserved, the heaped melons, green under the false rays, will warm and rot in memory, or be left forever celadon; the camera's done with them. Barging on, it's pushing Bakhtiary's chair, now seen to be on wheels, into the hospital façade; he's in a room of bright chintz—a suite, it is, and once more he's facing front. His hand no longer holds the rose. The dark glasses are on again. The bride is entering.

Where's her retinue of family women? Gone. Frantically as a gossip columnist, the camera hunts for them, finding only bowls of roses on tables, underscoring banks of these nodding on the deep windowsills— there are roses everywhere! It probes the dewy heart of one of them, and floating dreamily on, finds the bed. A hospital one. Quickly away —though not too quickly. Find the couple who'll lie on it. In a last roulade of the room, avoiding bric-a-brac now for final truth all in beautiful color, it finds them. Bakhtiary braces in his chair, his bride at his side. In the background, stage right, a *chador*'ed woman is briefly profiled, just entering. A proper royal touch. As the camera drains away, the married pair face it stolidly, like ancestors. It drains them away.

An announcer godspeeds them. *Ici Telefrance.*

This is no ordinary wedding babble. People are crowding in front of the dais, hiding it. Wert rises. He ought to leave here. He's going to learn too much. Six chairs away from him, the nearer *chador's* now alone. He's seeing it through the wrong end of the opera-glass, a minute ago big as life up on the video screen walking through that marriage-chamber door, then traveling thousands of miles to sit, infinitely reduced, on a folding chair. So that same pattern of dull gray flecked with orange is worn in Isfahan? How often with dark glasses as well?

Walking over he's off balance, stepping through arranged illusion. He stands over it. How many *chadors* wear such perfume, expensive stuff, no raw musk. Or is he bewitched by video roses? How right he is to fear machine shadow-play for not even spying, for being only the colorless agent of connection. How pleased to find it negligent. A camera's thought processes are as ingenuous as a child's. Its sins of omission have to be similarly forgiven. He stares down at the feet beside his. Pink socks.

The *chador* is silent. Once it was their women's desert mackintosh. Could they help it if their charms doubled inside it, or if they themselves doubled in another sense? What's it like inside that tent now, for a girl dressed like any girl from Georgetown? Blazing with new thoughts, yet still pressed with harem voices? Under which the muddy current of the dynasts is always creeping anyway, even in the smartly bared flesh of the women he knows.

That wasn't her doppelganger, up there just now in the honeymoon bedroom, yet somehow arrived here the day before yesterday—with those metallic words on her tongue: Programmer. Satellite. The apersonal procedures we give these people—they emotionalize even those to their own use.

Fereydoun said: Manoucher *was* there.

He bends over her. "What we saw and heard just now. It was a tape, wasn't it?"

The sunglasses lift. They're smoke-blue. He can just see her eyes behind them.

"Wasn't it?"

The *chador* turns its back.

"Why?"

"Bakhtiary—wanted it."

"Why?"

He can interrogate like this for hours. The *chador* hesitates; it can hear that. "The girl will have child." There's no dove-charm in this voice. "She is seven-months. The other picture was the real wedding."

Up ahead, people are finally oozing into the next room, where the baked meats must be. He can wait for the gossips he'll find there, unsure himself whether his revulsion is from cancer or death, or from such a child, ruthlessly inserted into life, between both. But that's what miracles are. Violences aimed toward impossible good. Tears smart his eyes. "When was this . . . second ceremony?"

The *chador* considers. "Three days past . . . four? I—"

"Hadn't a calendar, yes." Why's he so angry? "Why would Bakhtiary want it?"

"To help Manoucher. Everything—was for Manoucher."

From the dais, Fereydoun, seeing them talk, shrugs at them, nodding. He's supporting Madame on his arm.

"They all know then? That it was only tape?"

"Madame—Fereydoun was to tell her. Just before."

No one's helping Manoucher's Soraya, still on the dais, eyes fixed on the empty video screen, hands dragging against her black. The *chador*, taking off its glasses, has dropped its veil. Offering her its face, if she wants it near. Manoucher's wife's not looking, or not accepting.

"And Manoucher's wife?"

"Madame must just have told her."

Questions he doesn't want to ask crowd his head. Ask the least of them. "Why are you in *chador*?"

When she moves, closing herself up again, he can smell the perfume, waves of it. "It's—quiet, like this. And I am not—too much here yet."

Ask about her accent. Or run. "You were at school in Germany. Like Manouch?"

"Switzerland. Only Manoucher had to go to Germany. Like Madame. Then to England. Like Bakhtiary. It was the agreement."

And afterward to us. And now finally, back to Iran.

Manoucher's wife is standing up. In front of her, a train of women moves toward the next room, walking with the prinking body delays of the gauded-up. She walks starkly, but following. The girl from Ardebil's baby will precede Manoucher's and hers—if they ever have it—an infant aunt or uncle, to that putative nephew or niece. The father's child will precede the son's. No wonder their men love flowers, bending brotherly over them, their own body-gardens budding so inter-genera-tionally.

Where's Manoucher now? Who told Fereydoun? Why is Madame needing to be led away, that immobile dress of hers at last shaken to glitter? This ersatz Swiss miss—he'll bet it was Geneva where her tongue was trained to tick like a watch and her brain also—what was she doing in that bedroom, caught by the cameraman, not by accident, not that camera, at the aftermath door of a wedding already so after-the-fact? Who but Bakh could draw her there—this Soraya, this *other* one?

In the West, such a naming would be expected to have psychic effect, here it's merely a family position, where every member is doweled in from all directions, down to the half-brother, half-sister variations, not all of it remnant polygamy even now, and still so multiform that not to marry too near within the blood takes scrutiny. Within enclosures so close. Where for an old man to marry a young girl is more than respect-able, not necessarily to be frowned on because the girl happens to be the man's wife's blood-niece. If there are incestuous dreams attached to matching old with young—Wert can hear Bakhtiary say, indeed has a letter saying—then these are Western dreams. With us, Wert, such marriage is erotically just, and eugenically coveted. And—he didn't add —male. No business of the women.

The room's empty except for the two of them, and the blank video. It's Bakh's calendar, why confirm it? Leave with your own riches. A last letter, a box suitably disposed of. That's enough.

And he himself can answer all of this. "Bakh's dead, isn't he?"

Then he's shaking her, this wrapped woman who was sent to him like a rose-tree. Carrying a box to break for him. The *chador* falls from her, the glasses, too. His fingers inform how she's encased. White bandages rise out of the wide neck of her dress, expertly overlapping like a mummy's cerements. But they've persuaded her to something. The dress is black.

He kneels. "How can I—I'm sorry."

"It's only I heal. It draws together." Her teeth are chattering.

"You have fever."

"Not of the flesh." From the *chador*'s folds a long silver-mesh pouch emerges. Like a sword, he thinks, a bumpy female sword, and with some of the same medieval necessity. She dumps its contents into her lap. He's meant to study them. The pills are ordinary enough, the same compound the Embassy staff used to get at the PX pharmacy. Her hand brushes the bottle aside, the blunt, unpainted hand of any competent American girl, on it a signet ring. Under the bottle is an old iron key of the kind used to open their courtyard doors, a passport, a billfold, and a battered gold pen and pencil, on a chain. "My father's. They let me keep it."

"I have trouble remembering. Imagining, I mean. That you were in prison."

Her eyes are brown, not that fanatic blue. "Because, yes—of your wife. May I have a little water?"

In the bathroom, that sponge-strewn spa gilded with luxe from Paris and Venice, the toothbrush glass is an old etched tumbler in a cheap metal holder, the kind one used to get in any teahouse, but important to someone here. The money's been coming over here for years but now they're bringing whatever they can to remember with; even a Swiss bank account is not that restorative. His hand shakes, holding it. What she said was a shock, a shock, showing him not only what she knows but what she is. Bringing her the water, he can't help seeing it. He's brought two other women water in similar circumstance, Jenny during her menstrual cramps and his mother during her last illness. There's character in the way they take it. His mother was a dramatizer;

she drank her death in sips, and made him watch. Jenny drank with self-impatient shame. This girl's even shorter on self-pity. She wants the water. No upward thank-you glance as she drinks. He already knows her eyes are brown. He knows more about her than is fair—that back, those breasts. The mouse will be black.

With the pill, color and girlhood return to her. Aunthood—or is it clanhood?—fades. Would he always be able to tell the difference? He doubts it.

"Funny. When I need to be strong, I don't shiver. Only afterward. Over here. And on the plane."

He picked up the bottle, looked inside. Only the aspirin compound the bottle said it was.

"The customs inspector, he looks, too. I tell him—no, we don't hashish, we don't drink, even we don't smoke to like it. Only to be friendly with you. Our flesh is clean." Her teeth are indeed white.

"But you still tremble. And don't answer questions."

She's putting the articles in her lap back into the pouch, one by one. Under its silver mesh the shape of each is still decipherable, a support of a kind. "I did not admire Hossein Bakhtiary's letters to you. Yes, he is dead."

He turned his back. That video screen, what's it made of? Not linen. Nothing so mortal. "Of the disease?"

No answer from behind him. The screen too has no opinion.

"They kill him after the ceremony?" When she walked in there? Then why would they let her go, afterward?

A light, shuffled movement behind him, the kind kids make in games; you're guessing close, Wert, you're warm. Or she's gone, stolen away. She must want to. He wants her to.

He turns. She's at the head of the stairs, looking down them. On the way she's dropped the *chador*. That cha-cha black dress they've given her is much too big for her. Even so, a girl like her might accept it to mourn the revolution in—a girl more comfortable behind bars. Where there are matters to stand up for.

"You kill him?"

He's surprised her. People judge his exterior incapable of such conceptions.

"No? He wanted to marry you, though, Fereydoun said."

"Once, yes."

"But you refused."

"No one would believe it."

"Why?"

"My father was already dead. In prison. We are the stupid ones of the family." She's fumbling in that purse of hers again, holding out a palm. The iron key is in it. "I have nothing."

There's not a jewel on her except the signet ring; he should have noticed that. And they've given her none. According to his cousin, his great-grandmother's ring had been hidden in advance of the Northern army first in the craw of a stuffed owl, then in a sack of spoiled barley, and as houses and barns went for burning, was several times swallowed by a faithful slave. Some people progress through history via their objects. He had hoped not to, if only by default. Envying these others, who travel so light.

"Did Bakh—were you sent to prison because you refused?"

"I go to prison because of myself!" She picked up the *chador*, smoothing it. "Soraya follows me. I am to blame. So then I ask them, to let her go. To come here—they will do it." She tossed the *chador* on a chair. "So then—she ask for me." Her face is a study. Fatalism? Too modern a word for it. There's a rogue smile to it. "But yes, when I am first in trouble with the police, it is convenient for somebody. Fereydoun doesn't tell you that."

He sees it. "Madame."

"Oh—Fateh, too. Those two are used to each other. But I? For a third wife? Even that girl is better."

On the other screen the bride remains, high above them, in suppliant curve.

"So they found her—" the girl said. "Like you find a nurse."

Wert stared up at Bakh's thickened mouth. Relieving to conduct this inquiry in his presence, even a token one. Ritual: the uses of. He's learning. "He wouldn't have killed himself. Not for pain. Especially not."

"Not pain of the flesh," the girl said. "No. Or not of his own flesh."

From the other room, the dining quarters, there's silence now.

"He wanted to feel it there in the throat, he said. A knife. Nothing else would do, he said. He ask me to. I—could not give him that—satisfaction. But I agree—to watch."

So, the girl from Ardebil. Who will do for me, Wert, what I can no longer do for myself. She's still up there in the photograph, curving toward nothing. "So. That's when the camera caught you. When you came to watch. And—did she?"

"No. Because of the baby, she wouldn't. All these months what she does for him, you can imagine. She even lets him put the knife in her hand. But at the last minute, she wouldn't. Because of the son-to-be, she said. Hers. And she ran out."

"Leaving—you."

"He picked up the knife himself. He could still walk; he is only so weak. The chair was for television; they said the audience could see how much too weak. They are very criticizing. But to do what he wants he has to sit in chair."

Up there in the photograph the tray of hieroglyphed sand is still at Bakh's feet. Down here, the respondent tray has been cleared away. There's such silence behind those swinging doors to the dining room; somebody's telling them. The physical—everything in the universe is anticipated there. Dare a man say that? What then happens to him?

"And did you watch as he asked? Damn you—did you watch?"

I did. He heard it through a veil, a red thunder in his ears, the knife cold against his own throat, then warm. He found himself kneeling, collar choking him, the slide projector in front of him. He wrenched at the switch. The screen went blank. A white blackout, all the invisible girls gone, or kneeling. She isn't. Her perfume sickens him, or is it her strength!

His throat hurts but is whole. "Roses—all the way."

A death erotic to the end? A rosebed of mysteries, watched over by the unattainable girl, whose concept presides in all their heavens of the physical? Yet the pain which excused the old man to take himself off honorably wasn't of the flesh—or not of his flesh. Then it must be the clan's. Such an act, done in the stench of suicide blood but presided over by a white flutter of family honor, was what we called primitive. Two months from now, the babe would be born again, polymorphous as life itself. That is what we call perverse.

How the Koran resembled the Bible. Old testaments. Behold the fire and the wood, but where was the lamb, for a burnt offering? . . . And they came to a place God had told him of, and Abraham built an altar and laid the wood in order, and bound his son. . . . And the place is a hospital garden in Isfahan, where three mullahs guard the offering. With the father still thinking—I'll save him yet. . . . And the angel of the Lord called unto them Lay not thy hand upon the lad, for I know thou fearest God, seeing thou has not withheld thy son, thine only son, from me.

But the mullahs were not angels and hadn't withheld their hand. The stories were not the same; only the methods were. No ram appeared in the thicket, as substitute. And Bakh lost.

It could have happened right after the wedding just witnessed, and before the bedroom scene. The camera had simply omitted it. A camera has no obligation.

But I'm getting up from my knees with the answer in my mouth, as if I'm still Christian.

"By then, they'd killed the son, hadn't they?" he said. "Manoucher."

She's leaning forward and down the stairs, her black dress whipped against the banister, retching the name. One arm flails. "Manoucher. Manoucher."

How they mourn. He's envious. Such a fountain of grief, in Farsi of a range he'll never have. Careful of her back—he's remembering better —he stretches his arms to circle her.

Two men are coming up the stairs. One is Manoucher. Lumbering ox-eyed, he hunches past the girl to stand in front of Wert. It's the coat that's dead, torn at the breast, muddied with handprints, smeared with the orange turd dogs used to leave in the streets there, as if they ate turmeric. Even so it's kept its shape. The man inside hasn't. The coat's pockets clink as he shifts; there's metal weighting them. He's thin, but not enough to need such ballast. He has his arms and legs. Only the mustache is gone. Yet this body belongs to that coat.

Manoucher's cheek is laid against Wert's, once, twice and rests there. Wert's arms go round him as he heaves. This torn creature was never a boy.

"Easy now. Easy. Told you I'd get you here," the other man on the stairs is saying. A tall man with a face which could sit for Uncle Sam; he looks up. "Hello, Wert." Nosworthy has a tan, maybe from Jamaica, maybe from Ceylon. Sri Lanka. He leans on banisters round the world.

"What—"

Nosworthy holds up a warning hand. Manoucher's standing in front of the girl, his right arm moving in a plane between his face and hers; is he blind? Wert can't see whether or not his pupils are moving. Grunting, Manoucher finds her cheek. He stands back from her, his pockets clanking.

The slap makes her rock. A weighted dummy, returning upright the other cheek. Before the two men can act, he turns from her, breathing hard, a gone bull, the eyes red and small but seeing, and lumbers past them, threading the massed empty chairs with a nod here, there, as if to invisible occupants. At the door to the dining room he stops. "I bring them the keys." He speaks to the girl. "You already have yours." He bows to Nosworthy. "You will—you will be thanked." To Wert he says nothing. The door swings behind him.

Cheeks flaming, the girl's fingering a tooth. She wards off both men. "He had to—" she says to Wert in Farsi. "Ah, poor—he never hit a woman before."

When he's sure she's all right he turns to Nosworthy. "What are you doing here?" A departmental question. Who could ever really answer it?

"I was posted there," Nosworthy says, still leaning. "Ahead of our new, new ambassador. He never got there. Seems we're both *persona non*. On my way out, did a good deed on the way, that's all. Poor bugger." His long legs shift, tensing. Only symptom you could ever spot. "You don't believe that—fully? Try."

"He's not blind. What's wrong with him?"

"No. But he would rather be . . . *E*xcuse me. This lady—you're Soraya, young Bakhtiary's wife?"

"That's why Manoucher hit me," the girl says rapidly in Farsi. "Because he is head Bakhtiary now. And because I watched. . . . But this man, I won't speak with him."

"No, this is the other Soraya," Wert said.

It's not possible to tell whether or not Nosy has heard of her. He deserves his rise though—if one can call it that—even if he doesn't know Farsi. If one can be sure of anything about Wert's sometime mentor. He's a member of the Department. Leave it at that.

"They offered him a choice," Nosworthy said. "Blindness, or—it seems there are certain ritual—punishments. Though I've my doubts on the validity of this one. Young Bakhtiary chose blindness. They simply didn't keep their promise. He should have known. They're his people."

"What did they do to him?" He's afraid he already knows.

"She isn't the wife, then?"

"No."

Nosworthy's still uneasy. "We're not sure it was the mullahs, you know. Might have been—extremists."

"We don't have to know, you mean—" Wert said. "But I have—an interest."

"So I see," Nosworthy said. "She speak English?"

The girl flicked an eyelid.

"Maybe she's taken a vow not to."

Nosworthy gets it. But what's it to him if this girl in *chador* thinks he's dirt? Tax him with the one thing he can't take. "What they did to Manoucher," Wert said. "Something you can't tell Gail, is it?"

Target. Now he's lost a friend, if he ever had him. No cop-out that way, though. One's always responsible for what one's friends are.

All Nosworthy does is to stand a little straighter, away from the banister. One has to admire. "I just don't happen to, Bill. Tell her what I don't yet understand myself." His voice is gentle. Always was. Gentle hand, on Wert's shoulder. "Remember in Manila—Chip's time? That day we were in his office together?"

The ambassador who believed in real talk. Remanded to an insignificant post by a President who didn't.

"Yes, I remember." Nosworthy knew how we younger ones admired him. Uncle is pulling out all the stops. "And I recall the incident."

The ambassador had read out to the two of them a Manila newspaper account of a Filipino who'd cut off the testicles of a man who'd deflowered his sister, and had thrown them into a public refuse can. The paper had reported the victim as attempting to retrieve them, then exclaiming, "Oh, what's the use?" Shouldn't laugh—the ambassador had said—yet people do. Want to know why, boys? Just then an aide had come in, on the matter Wert and Nosworthy were there for. And the ambassador is dead now, and can't say.

"But that brand of punishment normally fits the crime, doesn't it, Uncle? Doesn't that bother you? Gail would never understand how Manoucher's helping out Uncle Sam could be a sexual offense."

"Watch yourself, Bill."

"Everybody's watching—everybody. I've a departmental interest in watching you and me face the violent facts."

"Don't you go cosmic on me, Wert."

The girl spoke from behind them.

"What's she saying, Bill?" Nosworthy waited. "You'd better say."

"Oh, I don't mind—interpreting. That was always my role, wasn't it? Even though I'm not coming back to it."

The girl is speaking softly, ice water on his back. "She says . . . that Manoucher will now occupy himself . . . with the business of the family . . . like their cousin . . . Fereydoun." Wert swallows. "That right now . . . Manoucher will be giving out the keys in there. . . . And that . . . I am welcome. To . . . join them." You only, the girl says.

"Oh, those keys—" Nosy said, with compatriot chumminess. "He wouldn't be parted from them, even in hospital. The Jews did that, you know, when they left Spain in the umpteenth century. Took their household keys with them. Very good hospital by the way. Old Bakhtiary saw to that. Saw to everything, didn't he, Bill? Saw to you."

"That makes two of you. How much did you already know—or plan —in Washington, that lunch we had?"

"Didn't take much to see it. That sending you a woman was what they had in mind. Gail—"

"Saw it at once, yes. And was it then you tried to recruit Manoucher?"

"Told you in Washington then I liked the sound of him. When I got to Teheran, I—simply got in touch with him."

"You and Gail never got to Ceylon?"

"Sri Lanka. No. Fell through. We're still *persona non* there."

As in Teheran, and other places. As even in Jamaica in your own garden, behind a steel hedge no orchids can hide.

"I only took soundings, Bill. Give me credit—he never even came to the Embassy."

To your hotel? Or a teahouse? What would that matter, in a bazaar-city teeming with as many small-boy runners as there are articles of merchandise? "And you used my name to put the screws on him."

Behind Wert, the girl says softly, "Manoucher would have gone anyway. On his own. As a Bakhtiary. You are not to blame."

Does Nosworthy really not know Farsi? He's staring at her. But what he mouths is for Wert. "I am extremely sorry for him, you know. But you saw him slap her. None of them acts like us, Bill. When are you going to face up to it?"

"I am facing it, Nosy." He sees him brighten at the old nickname.

From the diningroom he hears the mourning noises cognate anywhere, then above the rest a child's wail, loosed because the adults have given way. Does he also hear Fereydoun? He turns to the girl, who nods. "Fereydoun heard of it first." When she bows her head the bandage can be seen at her nape.

"Come away with me, Bill."

"That what you came for?" He knows it is. To the rescue. One of us is in danger of going cosmic.

"You can't just leave us, you know. There are—"

"Formalities." And you'll put the screws on me with them.

The noise inside there is trailing off now. There's a deeper hum. Prayer. Smelling as prayer always did in that country, stuffy with food.

"Bill." Nosworthy's too smart to come close. His long hands slide into his pockets, his pleasantly quizzical face, neatly bordered by its stateside collar, cocks wryly. "What's the use?"

The Farsi comes from behind Wert, iron in his back.

"What'd she say?"

So the man really doesn't know Farsi. Or not much. "She said—'Get rid of him.'"

How light on the stairs a man as tall as Nosy can be, going up or down. Halfway, he pauses. Framed in the stairwell window's harsh, poster glare, he looks more than ever like Uncle. "I feel responsible for you, Wert."

"Oh—I feel the same for you."

Wert didn't watch him go out. The years ahead would take care of it. He turned. "Soraya—?" First time he's said it.

She began to thread her own way through the empty chairs. He followed her. At the dining room door he took her hand. "Afterwards —you'll let me take you to my cousin's?" A formal proposal, which he thought she'd understand as such and indeed, she bowed. They led each other inside.

Once again these people themselves pull him back from sentiment.

Behind a long refectory table around which men and boys are ranged three-deep, the walls are a backdrop of silver, descending shelf by crammed shelf, from heraldic urns and huge ewers to samovars and lamps, to plaques and plates and goblets, to bud vases singly furled. A sheeny white shallowness came from the intricately matted surface of all Iranian silver, whether from content or the overiridescence of the engraving. The women are sitting directly underneath, clasping children, even teenagers, to their knees. Because he's never had children, he often looks at them as if they are people. Disaster's occurred somewhere above these small awed faces, even the youngest have a holy look of it; the oldest ones know their elders have horrors to keep. Keys lie all over the table.

Manoucher, at its head, is distributing them, each time to an answering murmur, imprecation or prayer. He has taken off the coat.

They seat Wert at the opposite end of the table, in the place saved. Ritual is in the room, good or bad; each time Manoucher hands out a key and hears the response, normality shudders closer to him. The keys are all of the same shape. When the last one's been dealt, Wert hears his own name. An object is passed down the table to him. "Hossein's—" the man next to him, no one he knows, mutters as he lays it in front of Wert. Flat, gradated segments of fine yellow ivory, incised in small double circles, form a fish of about four and a half inches long. He's seen those double circles before, on amulets against the evil eye. One segment toward the middle is out of place. Wert's eye is already mentally restringing it. Perhaps this is intended. The string itself is of the cheapest kind. One wouldn't twirl such an object, but in a pocket the abraded ivory might be subtle and comfortable to thumb. Carefully, he scooped up the white fish, feeling its blind scales, and stowed it away. He has caught it, and been caught. Nobody says anything.

Coffee, not tea, and powerfully sugared, is then whipped on the table by the women, with the same hushed but up-to-the-occasion air women anywhere assume in the sickroom, or after death. According to which women serve who he can begin to distinguish families, though there are enough of the tiny silver-framed cups for everyone.

They must have known all these five weeks that Manoucher was in danger, just as they had carried with them the more ordinary family portent of a patriarch's death. Bakh, gambling for his son, had even then entwined his gesture with his own roseate greed for life. A wedding—finally paid for? People repress their knowledge of violence as they repress their knowledge of death. Even these people? Or, scarcely knowing it, had they here made their first real entry into the new life? The new—ritual.

Only Manoucher perhaps had repressed nothing. The night he and Wert had dined at the Garrick he must have known what scrutiny might well be lying in wait for him in Iran, after the five years in New York. But he was the son.

Across the room, the two Sorayas are once more together. Manoucher's wife, recognizable only by her height and the way she clasps herself, is now in *chador*, a familiar one. They have exchanged. The other Soraya, in the borrowed black she has no temperament for, and bareheaded, is making no outer attempt to comfort her. There's no need. They are complements.

Manoucher's coming toward him, carrying his cup: Must anything more be said, commemorative? *Über allen Gipfeln—ist Ruh?* Wert's never been able to admire anything German separate from its nation —even Goethe. Probably these days many people feel the same about us. But death at least is always translatable.

Say nothing. Another kind of effort is being made. The petal-shaped cup shakes in Manoucher's palm. He drinks. "Some of these people have now no houses, Beel. In the past they have paid big house-deposit money here, which the agents will now not give back. But now these people get no more money from home. We have lawyers, but need perhaps a special one. You have names?" Manoucher's sweat-beaded upper lip, seen without its mustache, is as long as his father's. In boyhood he retrieved a motorcycle, kept all these years in a garden in Teheran. Whose wall now has no key. Or perhaps there's no longer a wall. But business will be done.

"I'll—see that you get one. In Washington."

"New York is better. We will all be here."

In a body. When people first come to a country, this is what they do.

"You'll be in London, Beel?"

"Not for long. Manoucher—I must speak to you personally." As if from the first we haven't. "I must tell you something." Which you already know or suspect. This being what ritual is. "You're the head of the family now." No harm mentioning it. "I want your permission to take the other Soraya to meet my cousin. She agrees."

Now that Manoucher is thin, pit his smooth face as if from smallpox and you would get old Bakhtiary's lineaments. No miracle. This is what happens between dead fathers and live sons. The minute Wert's father was dead people began to remark how he resembled him.

Manoucher set down his cup. "Rightfully, we should both speak to my mother. But she is—resting. She doesn't wish—to see me." His face is impassive. Gray is draining into it, but he persists. For him violence has logic. "She goes tomorrow to Switzerland. Soraya, my wife, goes with her." He's looking over at his wife, at the wrapped woman she has now become. "A lot of our money is there. They will . . . see to it." But money, the restorative, the bracer, isn't helping. He sways.

Wert rushed to the sideboard, to a silver decanter which indeed did hold whisky. "Here. None of us has et." In emergencies he became British now. As in sex, he became Southern again. The she-barrister had noted it. "Or perhaps you don't drink alcohol. I forgot." But Manoucher has already downed it. He sits with glass in hand. Over on the women's side, Fateh's two tarted-up daughters are kneeling in front of the two Sorayas chattering excitedly; news of the departure has spread. Of the two departures. Two and two; things are symmetrical here. Clans are. Ankhs.

Over there, tradition's inching again, this time by powder puff. The two gigglers, lips pursed, are lightly wielding long-handled ones over the other Soraya's still face. Now they're at the eyelashes with a brush, now intently at her lips, dipping each time into a tray between them piled bright with gilt jars, tiger-striped boxes and a suede roll of instruments. Life goes by tray here, and by whatever hieroglyph. The other Soraya sees he's watching her. Under a last brush of powder, she sneezes. Perfume wafts toward the two men.

"I had whisky first in London," Manoucher says, staring. Fateh's girls, deserting the finished Soraya, begin coaxing Manoucher's wife from her veil.

"At the Dorchester, I had it," Manoucher said, turning his back on them.

Children are drifting past, boys chasing girls, small toddling after big. "About London—" Wert says, "I'll be leaving now anyway."

Manoucher's head hangs. His profile gives the best of him, unaltered. Wert puts a hand on his shoulder. "Remember at the Garrick, eh? That cabby you hired? Soaking in oil you all were, he said." It gets a smile. Manouch puts a hand on Wert's hand. They stay so, clasped. After a bit, Manoucher takes a deep breath. "We were never in oil."

"I know."

"My father thought it always too—too—"

"Impermanent."

"A bubble," Manoucher says in Farsi. He releases Wert's hand. "But, Beel, must you resign?"

"Better so. I'll find something over here."

"Ah—New York. Perhaps the UN?"

"That haven for leftover diplomats? Sorry."

"Of which I am one." A pause. Manoucher's head comes up. "But yet with some—*clout.*" The usage is intended. It's Bakh's.

"No!" Wert said violently. "I can't. Go there. Not from *us.*"

He's forgotten the room of people. Their alerted faces are frightened, tender, vulnerable, proud, pleased. These two headmen have made a conspiratorial nest—and it's working.

"Ah, Beel—what a too young country you are." In Farsi, Manoucher sounds even fatherly. "Marvelous. In politics, how you still stop to blame." But the contempt seeps through. "It's a waste in anything. But most in politics."

Wert bursts out hysterically laughing. People smile. The West always cheers.

Manoucher nods back at them with dignity. "Besides"—he whispers in English—"that Uncle of yours. That baby papa? How could you think it? That it was him."

Wert's shaking. Not much, nothing heroic. *Just chicken-sick, that chile,* the old home kitchen help say in his head.

"Industry, yes— Much better to be there now, than in government." Suddenly Manoucher reaches out and collars a young boy just dribbling past them. The boy stands shyly, squirming in his jacket and tie, the skin like dark dew, the eyes pure, the lips full with hope. He's the hope of the world, Wert thinks—I never noticed it. Manouch cuffs the boy's cheek. "Get Mr. Ordoobadi." The kid rushes off, blushing like a page.

Ordoobadi turns out to be the man who knows about banks and

Wert's relative in Baton Rouge. He also knows the name of the lawyer Wert might best procure for them. He speaks a fast-blending patois of Farsi and English. The idiosyncracies of almost any major American city's country clubs are at his polished fingertips, and like the clubs, suffering from a certain industrial pollution. He's been everywhere in the service of the Bakhtiary interests, from Beverly Hills, where they don't scorn to be backers of a boutique which dresses the stars, "A whirlywind success!" to Huntsville, Alabama—"You know NASA?" and Florida—"You know Cape Canaveral?" Is Wert up on what Bakh these last years was into?

"Space, I believe. Outer space." The obverse of inner space? Wert's never thought of it that way before, but in this man's orbit it does obtrude.

"I like best Texas, though. Fine red people. Fine hearts. And in New York, of course, the Kinkerbocker Club. You belong?"

Hungry, light-headed, sick at heart—though that's curiously fading, or blending with what may be sexual hope; we won't call it love yet—he'll believe even Mr. Ordoobadi at the Knickerbocker Club. "No, I'm a Southerner. Georgia."

"Ahhh. They are more honey-butter there." Ordoobadi sparkles with what he knows well enough is his "line"—the more telling because he believes it. He's divided the people of this country by color, which is after all how it began. Florida girls tend to be fish-belly white. "The poor ones." He's noticed the poor—and hopes we're in control there. Thinks we are. "Also in Bridgeport. Very pale." Washington? "Ah—a girl rainbow. But not only from yours."

"You're a poet." And under the gloss, one of my old cronies, to the life.

Ordoobadi takes the compliment as due; all men of his race are. But at the moment real estate preoccupies him. Children are running everywhere with bowls of nuts and finger food; the intensive predinner nibbling has at last begun; the two old servants are circling. He waves a comprehensive hand, accepting a soft drink from one of them. Pity —but soon they must move from this neighborhood. "Too much brown." Not blacks, no, and not Puerto Ricans. He doesn't actually know what they are. He snaps a finger. A tall, good-looking boy appears. "My son. At Deerfield Academy. Mohammed, what are the people in this house? This neighborhood. Tell Mr. Wert."

"Doctors, nurses, orderlies, hospital staff mostly—from the nearby ones. Dentists." The boy shrugs. "Airline stewardesses, personnel. They team up."

"No, you know what I mean. What *are* they?" Ordoobadi turns to Wert. "Twenty years ago, they begin coming here, I am told. From when your people leave their country."

The boy's faintly smiling. "He means the Philippines." He's not being insolent. He's merely been born too late to know Bakh's generation and into circumstances which have made him wiser than his father. But two to one, he's no longer the hope of the world. "Couple of them were at our school."

His father dismisses him. "Not like these."

"No. I've been in the Philippines." Twenty years ago, that slow-moving squatter-crowd behind the Embassy—could some of those here —be some of them? This small, heartening seepage into Queens? "No, those boys would be the sons of the sugar land-holders, I fancy." In the Manila opera house, their wives wore spun-sugar dresses, Jenny had joked. "Or of diplomats."

A servant is at Wert's elbow, decanter in hand. They've noted him already. He pours himself one. "Whisky, Ordoobadi?"

"Eh—no thanks." He bows. "I have though many men in my busyi-ness, who drink it."

"I'm sure." Representative Americans. Who, like anyone who joins a clan, will never quite make it to the top—even if not brown.

From the grave, a voice he's incontinently glad to hear. *Now, Beel. Never think we're as stuck in our skins as you are. When among you, we're not observing our prejudices, but your statuses. Safest for us to be at the top.*

So the voice *will* go on. That's something.

"You ever think of busyness, Mr. Wert?"

"Often."

The card extended has Ordoobadi's name, four intercontinental offices and a cable line, but no company name.

"Sell space, eh? Just pure white space."

"Eh?"

Wert repeats it in Farsi.

"*What* good Farsi!"

"Honey-butter style."

But Ordoobadi is jubilant. "Listen to this, Manoucher! What do you think we sell? We sell—"

Manoucher is gone.

On the women's side, those two doll-babies, bending over from their four-inch heels with their round bottoms reared, have persuaded his wife from her veil. Her revealed face, rigid as a mask on a neck not its own, is untintable. Clearly even those two don't dare. All by herself she has a symmetry, of lap and knee, lax hands on them, of black brows dabbed. The blue eyes swim, blinking. There's a Bellini in the National Gallery looks like that, but it has an infant on its lap.

On impulse he walks over to her. Her eyes lower at once. She must know the effect they have on him. He's just identified it. When he kisses her hand, Fateh's girls breathe in as one. Or does the whole room already know what he's just found out? That he's been sent the wrong girl? Had she herself known at once? That they should have sent her to him?

Poor blue-eyed, bluestocking Machine, with a neck made to arch more under kisses than under doctrine, she does remind him of Jenny, but only because he recognizes that blend of the steadfast and the mercurial—and knows just how far it will go. Of all the people here, she'd have made it quickest to being an American.

He lets go her hand. In Switzerland, life under Madame's vengeance will assuage her guilt; it'll be like being in prison again. But after that, a girl like her must verge toward convicted action. Or toward a man, possibly a family one. Or will she become absorbed in their commerce, one of those muscular, charioteering Dianas in the new high-philosophical, female business style? Before that, he and the other Soraya must send for her. Hope is what she needs.

"Speak English," he says to her. "Oh, not to me. But generally. Break a vow, why don't you? Maybe it'll help." Cruel. He's learning. "And I'll write you, from America. Letters you might even like."

He sees that the other Soraya has vanished. A sharp-eyed chorus in duo at his elbow supplies the answer before he asks.

"She is waiting outside."

"*We* are ready to eat, *she* does not want to."

"She will help drive; she has international license."

"They have pack you a lunch."

"A very good lunch."

"Good-bye."

"Good-bye."

What practical girls they are, and she is. Prettier than Manoucher's wife, the other Soraya is also easier, with talents to more moderate scale. Tough and brave, she'll have his admiring tenderness forever. Plenty steadfast, too, she sees beyond ideals alone. She is the true heroine. Pink socks.

Manoucher's wife would have been—will be—neurotic enough to fight with him, sardonically knowing what is wrong with him. Living with him, or near, she'd wage war against the West in him—and so assuage his guilt.

Wert wants both of them—*in the house.* He understands that concept perfectly, wanting at once to talk over this marvel, and his devious progress to it, with the person who would understand each—perfectly. Who would agree that in both these solemnly breathtaking girls there are certain flecks of humor—discernible in each like the flakes in a glass of *Goldwasser,* which could flourish best in concert—which must be what harem humor is. Who would concede that for the time to come, or maybe for all time, the girl waiting outside for him is now Soraya, Manoucher's wife being now—the *other* one.

Extraordinary, what Bakh has done for him, considering the modern world. And Wert is going to accept. Knowing every nuance of the climb by which he's come to it—every horizontal traverse, crampon and pickax by which two mountaineers can climb from opposite sides to the top—new snow on old ice being specially dangerous.

Which top turns out to be a flat space just big enough for two pairs of boots, one of them worn down at the back.

Does such a space have any credit in the realms of higher conflict? —Probably not. Some human weaknesses are too small for international congresses.

. . . Oh don't be too sure about that, Wert. As I've hinted before—there's an underskin sexual thrill to the changeovers of nations, whether these come by codicil or a landing onshore. Take the spinster British— shrouding supple India in her own muslins and pongees. Or the French with their ferocious dictionaries, seducing Algiers from behind a coy fretwork of civil law. That latex-breasted sponginess of you and yours, Wert, we'll rape it yet. With our barbarian wedge.

But now they want him out of here, the whole crowd. Those men he's met are surrounding him, fiercely suave. He's theirs now. Those he hasn't met are smiling allegiances, crude or austere. But like any in-laws they have family secrets to mull over, feelings still to be kept from him. The wedding is over, of him to them.

"Good-bye."

"Good-bye."

This dark rug-room, spored with their moisture and light, is already growing them a world here, which can go anywhere. They'll penetrate the contradictory life over here—our bathrooms like hardened blanc-mange, our pavements dirtied with garbage gone beyond collection, the fat land gone nitrate-rich with wells our farmers themselves daren't drink from—yet all of it still gassed only with domestic stainings, for generations not browned with mass blood. Into it they'll insert themselves, arrowheads steelier than are known here, but bazaar people also, who understand merchandise, software, hardware, all the local words for what with them will end up in the clan machine, and in the gems wound like electric lace around the women. Where we bar them from our inns, they'll buy them. Their keys will grow here as these always grow, iron affecting the host soil.

It's nothing new. In London, all the stationers are Pakistani now; in New York, Korean all the fruiterers. Such a movement comes from below the money-mark as well, a lowly surf no United Nations dare legislate aloud, no bourse will bother with. The Bible and Koran are full of it. No diplomacy can hold out against it, it's the paranoia of what happens. Nations move.

How very tiring it has been, though, not to admit that ever-third world to consciousness.

"Good-bye."

"Oh, good-bye, Ordoobadi."

Ordoobadi's hand makes a feint at being firm, then lies limp in Wert's. But it's merely the bisexual handshake of half the polite men of Europe. "Outer space—it's the new opium, Misser Wert. You think about it."

Wert tiptoes from the room, closing its door behind him. Crossing the empty second room of chairs and screens, he closes that door as well, with caretaker heed. So, Smiley—my village. See you at the Kinkerbocker Club.

On the landing she's waiting patiently; a girl without a calendar. Otherwise, that girl has vanished. Or all versions of her yet seen. Brown coat now, brown cap, shoes to match—and stockings, soft plop of brown bag. The going-away clothes, who hasn't contributed them? Jewels in her ears. Collar up, one can't see the bandages. She'll do for him what he's never been able to do himself. She'll heal, but not too easily. She'll keep a sharp lookout.

But she's not alone.

Fereydoun's valise is at his feet. His hat is on his valise. "You can't think it, Mr. Beel. That they would let her go alone."

"Can't they. Or only to prison?"

She's already sneaking her glasses on, as if they're contraband.

"And your cousin. That charming lady. Would she approve?"

"My cousin has more than charm."

"I recall." Fereydoun squats to his hat. Smoothing it, he looks like a butler stirring a campfire. What bruised-blue bits of human offal, human history, he must grill there from time to time, some of it his own. There's a Tory glow about the old man, a stubbornness like the light seen through the stained-glass of badly reconstructed saints. What is it? "Madame—wishes me gone. It was never my house."

Why, he's honest, that's all. But with such a struggle to show it, under that equivocal voice, plumped countenance. Could one learn to divine it?

"And Manoucher—wishes not to look at me."

How easily Fereydoun might be arranged for, after all. Wert's cousin is already half in the room, consoling with all her native good: Oh, but, Mr. Fereydoun, your knees are still so good, for our age.

She, not Wert, could become Ferey's confidant, more hardened in the hands than Madame but as welcomely imperious. On her antebellum porch in old Athens—with their backs to the gas station—she and he can exchange old civil wars. She learning, for instance, how long before this Sunday in Queens Fereydoun had had to be the silent harborer of bad news. Hearing, too, what Wert only now surmises. Up to now he had visualized the old courtier ever behind a screenwork of telephone calls. Now, looking at the old man and the girl, he grasps the collusive innocence which has had to be meted out between them. She had carried the news. Wert looks over at the girl. "In that case—?"

A brown chirrup from her. "Okeh."

She's gone foreign on him again. Chill spreads in him like Luminal, half pleasurable. "Well then, Ferey—I expect my cousin'll be proud to have you. She liked you very much."

Fereydoun's already standing, fingertips together. His own story will remain inviolate, except for a tremor of it that Wert can guess at: And I, Fereydoun, will not have to bear the sight of Manoucher.

"Thank you," he says low. "Your car's a rented one, isn't it? Why don't we go in mine? It is mine." He blushes again. "Give me the registration. Fateh will take care of delivering it."

"She drives?"

"Like the wind." He goes off to take care of it.

"He'll have some money of his own," the girl says. "He doesn't know it yet. Bakhtiary saw to it. Your cousin will take him in?"

"For good? You'd want that?"

"Best for him." From behind the glasses, and the hat.

"Possibly she'll be glad to. They're about the same age. And tastes."

Crazy. How can he know what Ferey's tastes are, or even his own cousin's, during those intervals when all creatures are a lone unit of being? He's merely tired of clocking the differences between people; he wants likenesses. It's then we can make decisions for others. "And, that house of hers." With all its assembled family garniture. "He can organize it. Like a palace." Relieving me of that yoke. Wert finds he can smile. "Look—it won't take long to get to my hotel. They'll find rooms, for you and him. The manager's—a gentleman. Tomorrow you'll see a doctor." He's prepared to insist. No answer. "At my cousin's—we'll decide what next. That okay with you?" She has a right to know what to expect. So does he.

She's listening, but not to him. To a sound he can't identify, either what it is or where it's coming from, except that it's not coming from the dining room. Pillahil-ilah-allah-ilal. The voice of the wedding presents, wailing from the box-room downstairs? Or all the random birdcalls of his life come to plague him, as men are plagued when they find pleasures too strange for them? Peeah-ee-ahooo-eu-uu-pewi. Balooch.

No, it's the call to evening, from the mosque. Do they have an *imam*, here?

Together, they follow it.

In the small room off the hallway a slim figure, white-shirted, is touching its forehead to the floor over and over. It's a young man, a young man's voice, rasping and uncertain, new to heavenward allegation, testing it. Or greeting what presently exists. It's the Ordoobadi boy.

Finished, he passes their niche without seeing them. Wert has a view of his face. That face knows it is immigrant.

He checks an impulse to go after it. No more cronies for tea. This girl is bringing him dowry enough. The reasons for violence—he must always have wanted them.

Wert raises his head, sniffing. He knows that smell, long-grained in the nostril, Caspian, on the edge of char. They'll eat it anyway, as they always do. This meal is not on camera. Each child shall have a piece of its burnt lace. "The rice is burning."

That driver's cap she's wearing must be Fateh's. The long visor projects from her forehead like an antenna, over goggles that watch. He lifts the cap off, the glasses also, half wanting the guises never to end. She's to lead him to the wilderness.

Underneath, her eyelids are wrinkled shut in prune misery. Her mouth is moving, in his language. He bends his ear to it. "Make me be here. I am not here yet. Please—make me be here."

Ferey, passing them on his way out to the car, lowers his glance respectfully. They seem to be in a passage of love.

The small room Wert can see over her shoulder has nothing religious in it except an east window. It's reddening. Old Sol's going cosmic, once again. In the mean street down below, buildings hulk on their paws before him. South of Vancouver, on the last coast West, mountains slope to the sea, kitten in the starlight. Praise all the path between there and here—his country.

The game is always to enumerate, to praise, swallowing all ethical or aesthetic disappointment. To traipse across the steppes, the kraals, the wadis of whatever, the golf courses and the health stations of the new, new world, or the old, with heart-warming dinners everywhere. He can't. No more palaces, except for Fereydoun.

How give someone your country except by first in faith receiving it, taking it like communion on the tongue? In all its shames and glories.

He pressed a hard palm against her back, remembering exactly everything. "You'll dream here," he said.

We're the western approaches, limpid in the starlight. They haven't really seen us yet.

3

MYSTERIES OF MOTION

THE FREE ROOM

"OH MY HONIES—" Mulenberg writes to his daughters. The word processor has already corrected him—"honeys." After spending three of his daily Free Room hours in mute session with it, he isn't about to argue. Those are his first written words.

Behind him, Gilpin hunches in one of the silvery Easy Chairs, so labeled by its distant manufacturer. An easy chair shouldn't be luminous, he said the first day. He always has a book. Sometimes he annotates rapidly in what he says is a form of speed-writing but each day he politely refuses use of the processor. "Bravo," he says now. "Don't stop for me."

"I'm not. If you're sure you don't want it."

"Hath too lean and hungry a look for me. We won't have them at *The Sheet.*" At mention of his newspaper his face gives its usual gaunt twitch.

"Shakespeare—" the man now known to them as Cohen-Lievering says, making it out the airlock in one eel-hipped slide. His large head, bobbing on its rubber neck, recedes last.

"Some exit line," Mulenberg says.

"He once had to recite whole plays, for his stuttering." Gilpin nods toward the shelves of personal-history folders which line the forward wall. "Moves like an angel, though."

"Or like a bat. Extra-sensory vibrations in his nose. Where'd he go?" Mulenberg has no further reason to be envious of Lievering on Veronica's account, unless one is stupid enough to be envious of history. The man to be jealous of, for commanding love he hasn't sought, is sitting across from him.

"Second crew's cabin, next to the cockpit. He and Mole." Gilpin's face lights up. "That's where they've berthed the boy. The whistlers' cabin, Mole calls it."

"Kid's kind of their mascot, eh?"

"You might say—everybody's." Gilpin hunches further into the offending chair. He and Mulenberg are both in their more comfortable fatigue suits. He looks up from his usual brooding, the space pencil on its wrist-clip dangling idly. There's gravity here, but no loose objects are allowed. "According to Mole, Ship's Commander Captain Dove thinks Lievering looks like Jesus. A Jewish Jesus, the captain said." Gilpin grins until the joke takes.

"Mole—" Mulenberg says. "That the boy's name? Or his situation." He's not been too dazed by his own affairs to see that there is one.

"He was born to it." Gilpin shuts his lip.

The man can't lie; he even dislikes chairs for pretending to be Easy. But he can be sloppy about the facts. "Dove isn't the ship's commander," Mulenberg says gently. "Commander's an air-force cross-over none of us in Ordnance has met yet. Don't know if even Wert has. Keeping him under wraps."

Gilpin smiles at himself—the kind of man who would see his own drawbacks in perspective. "Should've known they'd never stand for a commander named Dove."

So even Gilpin isn't idealist enough to assume there are no military aspects to this mission? "The *Civilian Courier,*" Mulenberg says with a smile. Their brand of hype. So simple it works. For the great mass of the simple. For whom he has no contempt but no special feel, either. Except for his travels, he might have been one of them.

"Wert says that word acts on me like a glass of wine. Civilian."

"Wert doesn't get to go forward much, does he. For a man who's going to be administrative officer." Some show of equality was usually made by the military, when they wanted a man's services. There had been—for Mulenberg.

"Wert has—a lot of background. Old government man."

"Pretty dated, eh?"

The answer is just a headshake, but with more cussedness than maybe shows. Anyway, a man not to be lifted up by his own lapels. Yet accessible. Gilpin may make it his business to know about you, but this is why you can talk to him. Mulenberg sighs. "Wert had daughters, he'd know how dated he really is. Especially if they've got the idea you travel light." Veronica crosses his mind, like a wraith which can't get away this time. Where is she? Not far. "Promised to write them a full account. So as not to be just a—you know. Passenger freight. Maidie's the emotional one, though to see her you'd never know. Married to that town she lives in. Keeps their home on firehouse discipline." Though that broker husband of hers will never find the brass pole to slide down on for getaway. "I did something to shock her years ago, at her mother's funeral. Well, you might as well know. I tore the dress—from the body. She hadn't spoken to me since. Until the corridor."

Mulenberg stretched, staring up. Ceiling and walls here are some stuff the lay trade hasn't got the patents to yet. "So this trip must be of some use." Mulenberg's chuckle doesn't quite make it. He presses a wall slot, closes on the dropped lozenge and pops it in his mouth.

"Tessa's the *kind* one. The Californian. Lives in a Mendocino ravine, runs a commune." He grins. "No one person's supposed to run a commune. But Tessa does. With a lovely boy, now and then. Big girl, like her sister. Like me. Both of them with minds like their mother, sort I can talk business to. Miss that. Matter of fact, their college yearbook called them the two Kwan-Yins." Though Tessa isn't that neat a dresser, she's the one you can give presents of value which would horrify Maidie with price-guilt. But now, after years of drouth, he must find a present for Maidie, too. What can it be, from here?

"As for that lad—I like his spirit. Though that age, I never know what to say to them." He chuckles. The lozenge has helped. Everything here works as it's meant to. "Know what he said to Ver—Miss Oliphant? 'I feel at home with you because you're like me. By now you're just a little bit black.' "

"Smart boy."

"Where is she?" After that scene in the corridor he knows his offhandedness fools no one.

"She has to wander. Reporter habit." Gilpin smiles—since who can wander here? "My guess is she's in with Seat Six." In the Hygiene Unit, one side of which has become the two women's hangout. He smiles too for that female bonding.

"So does the Jew wander, eh? Habit." He's glad when Gilpin laughs. "Watch myself, eh. Lived too long in Islam."

"Ah. You meet Wert there?"

"I recommended him. But d'ya know, I can't remember. Whether I actually did meet him."

"He blends. It worries him."

Mulenberg shuffles his notes, gathered for him in Washington. "Well, better get on with it." He turned back to the machine. "You know—" he said dreamily, "I've been going on the idea, tell the emotional stuff to Maidie, the practical stuff to Tess. Divided like they always were, or trying to be. But maybe that's what's holding me up."

"Lucky—" comes from Gilpin behind him, "That you can tell the difference."

There speaks a man who's settled all that, Mulenberg thinks. Is it because I haven't yet, that I divide the girls? Gilpin would never humiliate a corpse. Or confuse love and the body. Or be in thrall to any of it? He's so safely in thrall to the multitude.

"I've read you," Mulenberg said.

Behind him, Gilpin writes: "How vulnerable they often are, the men with daughters only. Sometimes they have extra stature because of it, sensitivities they themselves don't identify. Their loves are often marked by being so much with women—surely this man's are. But the world can make them feel they're men without sons, so sometimes they hunt the male life? Bonding with the expense-account bars, the academic or commercial offices. And when they meet the 'lads'—other men's sons—are shy with them—"

"But, too easy for me to see what children are to people, since I have none. Like Wert here, up to now."

Otherwise, Wert's life is so outrun by the past decade that to men like Mulenberg it must read like history. Nothing so outmoded one political framework as the emergence of another. Wert, the foreign service officer, is getting to be the last of a certain kind of national, a man whose responses, geared to Earth politics, are of a kind which, along with the twentieth century, begins to disappear. Decades go faster toward the end of a century. The old politics is now as primitive-sounding as old land-grants. The new century is in the air.

So far according to what he's reading, Wert has no children. But unlike Gilpin, he's thought of it.

Quickly, Gilpin buries his head. Not before he sees Mulenberg's newest opener, transcribed on the lighted screen where the processor's user and any audience may follow his thoughts, reblinked: *Dear Kwan-Yins:*

Mulenberg's going to cheat. His file of space data, executed by research staff at his various offices, is merely a dictionary of heterogeneous fact designed to help him self-orient. He'll use it whether he understands it or not—as really the more honest reportage on his present condition. And in spite of that salutation, he'll alternate the two girls as it comes to him to do. As it comes to him! He trembles with communication, holding that abused word in his mouth like a lozenge. He's naked in this new limbo, with his two communicants. None of the three of them yet a corpse.

Girls:

—I'm in a kind of common room and library which we've taken to calling the Free Room, because we're on our own here—not otherwise programmed—and it has gravity. Pseudo of course, made by revolving the room, which is a cylinder, just as will be done in portions of the habitat. Or so I get it. You understand I hope that we're not en route to another planet. Excuse if I insult your intelligence. I find that notion still prevalent down below. We're of course en route to a man-made station, only one larger and farther than ever before.

And for longer inhabitance. No one's believed, you see, that we'd do it so soon. And perhaps we won't. When I look over the ordnance, one thing I do know down to the ground—ha, pun, Tessa—I have doubts. And no one's really said—permanent. But make it or not, the world'll be changed—already is. Doesn't take a philosopher to see that (though I've got one sitting next to me). For instance, not two weeks out, and we're already calling you Down Below. Not accurate. But we're calling you it.

Let me give you a rundown on our daily routine. So that—

He pauses to look behind him, as he'd done when he mentioned their philosopher. In sarcasm. Yet it's a comfort to have that man near. Turning back to the keyboard, Tessa's last blithe postcard comes to mind: *Daddy, I have something to share with you.* The dog, Gravy, named for gravitation and Mulenberg's voyage, had had bon voyage pups.

—So that I may better share with you two some of our delusions, which I must hope these are. For we begin to have them—

Yet perhaps it's Maidie, his worn coin of a girl, milled to the thinnest edge by the normal safeguards against madness, who'll understand him best. Who'd hung the week's schedule in her kitchen the morning after the honeymoon, and five years later, on a screen a safe thousand and more miles away from him, looked as if she still hung by it.

—We rise to a morning meal, sent by mechanical means from the galley, like all intake except dinner. Strictly, there are no mornings here. Our days and nights being of different lengths from each other as well as from yours, also get harder to distinguish—

As the blaze at a porthole of stars raining like snow will confuse his already shaky inner rhythms. But this he would rather not reveal. They will think it is him.

—Once at the landing station, we'll set our own day lengths—

What's he saying? On a mainly industrial station already manufacturing crystals to be used in electronic devices, the hours of the cycles must long since have been set.

Why should he be defensive about that or about any of it? For it now occurs to him that he is.

—But we maintain. Since we must wear our full life-support suits at all times in the cabin or at drill, the bath hour is welcome. Everything unisex, including a modified Jacuzzi. Privacy, though, can be calculated—

Scrounged, rather. The two women have more or less been allowed to be alone. Or so it's working out. Over and above the scheduled life —in this one-way mousehole, as his big body sometimes inveighs at him —there's always that other overlay. Of things working out.

—For circulation's sake, we're expected to use the massage aids, alone or mutually—

So far as he knows, nobody's been mutual, in Cabin Six.

—All our activities are closed-circuit monitored, the video-auditor being the computer only, of course—

Of course. But why think otherwise?

—We're then left to various drills which familiarize us with our sector of the ship, including the Sick Bay, the said Galley and Hygiene Units. As well as our sector's access to the Payload Bay—your daddy's special interest, heh, heh—and to the forward and aft Avionic Bays, which include—

Here he has to refer to his notes, which thank God and staff are as organized as a president's should be, for a minute returning him in delicious pain to what it had been to be one.

—radar altometers, general purpose computers, mass memories, rendezvous sensor electronics, microwave scan beam landing system, accelerometers and one-way Doppler extractor—all of those forward. Also rate gyros, aeroservice servo-amplifier units, all of these aft except the multiplexer-demultiplexer units, which are located in both. The names are by and large self-explanatory, except for that last one, whose function I confess I haven't yet learned. What a Doppler reaction is I haven't time for here, but any aerodynamics manual will explain—

Pure bluff, Mulenberg, as they'll know.

Somehow that cheers him. As a contact with the self which isn't up here yet.

That scares him.

—What we do not see are the passengers other than our own six, each cabin and service area being separate because of atmosphere maintenance. The Free Room has artificial sea-level atmosphere. We go in and out like at a bridge game. In fact, all our alternating arrangements are a damn beautiful cooperative game. Or ballet. Maidie, you'll know about that—

In which in the absence of any ballet master, the strangeness of what we do sometimes washes over us. Yet once, when by chance he was the one to dip out of a bay in order to allow Veronica entry—she lifting herself on the handrails with a face clearly ready for glory—he'd caught a sense of what they were here for.

He'll have to mention Veronica soon.

—Otherwise, except for no stewardesses—skyroom too precious— we're like guests at a dull resort managed by the aeroequivalent of the Cornell School of Hotel Administration. Haven't seen the other guests yet and haven't seen the sights. Though they promise us both.

That is—though we can't see each other all at once, or in sections, like in a jumbo jet, one hundred strong sipping from paper cups—an open-circuit viewing of all of us by all of us is on the prospectus. For the third week—no specified day. Most of our calendar is set. I understand there's already an events-calendar for two of your years ahead, on habitat—

The flow of ordnance requires it. But that three-week turnaround visit to and from earth of the *Courier,* in time will it come to seem like the visit of the cruise ship to the remote port—everybody down to the dock? Morale activities are to be planned—even Earth sells its opera tickets well ahead. But behind these happy exertions, all the equilibrations of an artificial sphere will have to be kept going. In his New York office, one entire wall-mapped room monitors company operations which span the globe. But no care had to be taken to keep the globe itself going. On the living-station, every inhabitant will spend some portion of time at that. Appointed time. As here.

Where then do the rumors come from?

—As for the sights, dear girls, we're promised EVA. Not any rival of yours. Extra-Vehicular Activity. *Planned EVA,* they call it, or *Unplanned EVA.* Until I see it I can't say for sure, but I think of it as crewmen dancing on the surface of the ship—

Maybe to pat and inspect that ceramic skin whose spotty resistance to the terrible heat of reentry is always being "confirmed." An uneasy word, industrially. Did that heat obtain not only at the moment of rendezvous between *Courier* and Earth as it reenters atmosphere from orbit, but also between *Courier* and habitat—as the *Courier* "docks"? He's never given it any thought. His notes don't say. But the diagrammed Orbiter, slate-blue on cloud and annotated like a psalm, made the blood surge.

Though if he's still talking more or less to Maidie, he won't point out the sexual naming that NASA goes in for, which he secretly finds jaunty. Planes are asexual, so far as a passenger is aware. But though an Orbiter, with maybe a nod to the plants, carries its propellants in "pods" and has all the old "wing" and "tail" analogies to the birds, it "mates" with its own booster rockets, has "umbilicals" on the fuselage and aspires at all times to the "rendezvous."

The bell rang, signaling the first third of the time here. Mulenberg turned around. Gilpin gives him a "hard at work, too?" smile.

Mulenberg smiles back. No—I can't separate Maidie. They've always complained we didn't separate them enough. Their mother used to call them "Messa-Taidie." Calling them in from play. He smells the leaf-smoke of long ago autumn dusks, sharper than any oxygenation within these NOLEX-felted portholes—and hears how he must sound to Gilpin. "I'm an obsessive. Not only on daughters. Most good businessmen are, you know. Dreamers. According to a psychological study done for our personnel department, the best of us don't even dream in money. Worse than artists, my doctor says. With even less to go on."

"You businessmen brought us here."

Polite man, if overcompassionate. Mulenberg wonders if Gilpin knows how literally that might be the case. Early on, the "international space effort" for the original long-term gravity-free environment had been mostly an affair of European prime and co-contractors, though he'd worked with them all in a way—Fokker Netherlands on the optical windows and scientific airlock, Alitalia and Micro for module and thermal control, SABCA Belgium for the film vault, INTA Spain and TERMA Denmark and FOKKER Germany for the management system integration and testing. Mulenberg's company had had paper in all of them. As well as actually collaborating with the United Kingdom on a large instrument pallet-structure which could be controlled from without in some configurations, and finally, on the tunnel-connect between crew-compartment and pressurized modules such as this very one— being the absolute main contractors with NASA itself. On the *Courier*, of course, all suppliers had had to be USA.

He's kept his long since diversified company out of application software, which he regards as pure flea-market and discount-store hell.

"Nowadays I only know the charts, Gilpin. And the bankers. Not even the engineers. Amazing, isn't it."

"Not to me."

"That's right. Heard you speak once."

"Oh? Oh, I'm only in the middle, far as dreaming goes," Gilpin says hastily. "Wobbly place."

"The lad doesn't think so."

In the silver-brown luminescence of the cabin, composed of many muted reflections of metal gone angle-soft under outer shadows which come and go, producing that rotogravure effect which once gave depth to faces in early-century Sunday supplements, they're all learning to translate facial expressions anew. Gilpin's face has clouded. But so has the porthole. "Mole? The boy's pure adventure. Don't know whether he knows it."

Mulenberg stares down at his page of daughters. So are they all— adventure. Sure they know, and hit you with it. But Gilpin, who's childless, romanticizes. Any confidences are wasted on him. "Guess I'm the only parent in Cabin Six."

"So far."

When Gilpin doesn't respond further, he's moved to personalize himself. Like when the staff used to hold back. "I say 'lad' maybe because the head nurseryman at my father's place used to. Used to call *me* that." And maybe because I haven't got one. " 'A lad is a boy with a nice streak of cussedness,' Dineen used to say."

"Mole's got that."

"Spends a lot of time up front. Forward."

"That berth he's been exchanging with Lievering now and then, yes. But they don't allow him in the cockpit."

"The—? I should think not. Though he gets around like sixty, he lacks a certain—"

"Training knowledge?" Gilpin seems now to want to swap glances with him.

"Being pals with Lievering should sure give him the hang of it. But the young ones all take everything once-over easy." Except Maidie. Who's like him. It's Maidie he could tell about following Veronica from that half-craved distance. "Tried to get him to talk about architecture; we've built factories around the world. But nix. Sure doesn't sound like what he is. Or act it. What the devil is a catabolist?"

Gilpin's laugh loosens up both of them. "It's a fancy school of Japanese architectural theory. More mystical than structural. Seems to work. It's not new. Started in the fifties."

These days it's the young who are the antiquarians of the decades. Falling in love with their grandfather's era, though not with its real properties. "He says he's lost interest, in favor of another profession. He tell you?"

"Afraid so."

" 'Reformer, student grade'?"

" 'Private, first-class.' "

When Gilpin throws up his hands the second book he's been reading sprawls—a small, dowdily old one, exotic on a floor which might be metal or grapholite. "We oughtn't to laugh," Gilpin says.

"None of our family has humor," Mulenberg says shyly. "I wish the girls."

They both bury themselves in their "work."

Gilpin takes up his pencil:

"I like Mulenberg, poor chap. What an extraordinary thing—one of Veronica's one-night stands to come so far. A man of considerable personal resource who is always deprecating that; he knows too well what the world usually thinks of tycoons. 'Here I'm a man suspended from my money,' he told me our first hour here, 'want to see how I do.' Yet he was clearly that, before. A space-dreamer all his life? Since he suffers from a poor sense of direction he's provided himself with a large NASA blueprint of the vehicle, which he's learned by rote. He's used to being coached by experts. Goddard sent him three to get him through the training, which he then crammed into half the time it took the rest of us, getting a deserved top score—a feat I heard nothing of from Mulenberg himself. Look at him, tending his data like a purist, hoping for the time—vainly I suspect—when he can dispense with it. It bothers him that I call the flight deck a cockpit. Up to now, his forays into self-knowledge have all been one-night stands also. Down beneath them is this other tenacious life of the emotions he's been taught to be ashamed of—which he'll peel to the bone to get to. Yes, I like him. He is my opposite.

"I say 'poor chap' because of Veronica. Who's known where she is since she was born, and wants only to go farther. Who maybe is the only true traveler here."

The pencil drops. Gilpin watches it sway on its chain. The claustrophobia of any space journey adheres not only to the vehicle but to the motion. One's walled up—in motion. A coffin of it, after a while static as a train at standstill in a station. Past which all eternity wheels.

The pencil crept toward him slightly. Not a delusion. Whatever degree of gravity is here, whatever air mix, Mulenberg will know, or know the place for it in his file. But the idea of the "delusions" Mulenberg alleges he's beginning to collect on his own is unnerving. "Baby idées fixes," he said yesterday, "can run through an office like wild rabbits." And journeys with a sense of mission breed abstractions of no more value than imaginary music; people think windily on Everest. What Gilpin wouldn't give for an old jet-liner crowd of ordinary travelers weaving their to-and-from-the-toilet rhythms. Florida-bound couples in identical vanilla checks and with the irritable lardiness of pensioners. Or one of those men who always sat over the wing, with profiles sharp as their portfolios.

If he and Mulenberg and the others come to share some idée-fixe which can pass for real, what then?

"The hazard here is eeriness," Gilpin says aloud. "It attracts. Like an emotion." Or it does me. But there'll be no opera in another town to fly me to. Maybe we can learn to wrap and unwrap one another in hot sheets. I like the design of the sick bay. Our cabin seems a tough community. Except for its persistent young guest—who thinks himself the toughest of all. Wonder how the other cabins have done? Hard to keep in mind that there are four such sick bays and four Free Rooms like this one, for a total of twelve passenger cabins, plus that cabin of whistlers, the relief crew. Plus all those on the flight deck—how many? We shall see. In little more than a week.

He sits up straighter. Even in the Free Room there's always a leaning. Mulenberg, who now has an array of newspaper clips spread before him, hasn't responded. The so-called silence here is cellular, capable of growth, composed of many small auricular coils of approach. The core of one's hearing is always being scratched. It's not unpleasant. But if Gilpin had a piano keyboard he would skitter it from bass to treble with the back of his hand. Or if he had a tuba—give one hippo snort. In his time he's played both, badly. He sees by the built-in ship's clock that the free hour, actually an hour and a half, will soon be half up.

"Stars don't twinkle here." Gilpin stares out through the thermal pane. "Rude of them." Far up ahead the wing rides steady as a coastline. Made of honeycomb aluminum.

Mulenberg pushes his half-lens reading-glasses up onto his Triton head of hair. He seems never to remember he can look over them. On his face is the blank smile of scholarship. "No atmosphere to." He sees that Gilpin knows this already. "Sorry."

His clips are disposed on the flip-out desk in front of him like a wreath of witnesses to what is still called "the space effort"—as if outer space is a still recalcitrant part of creation which refuses to recognize its own potential. It was in collecting this batch that Mulenberg, on one of the impulse errands by which he now and then removed himself from routine, had gone himself to the newly non-corporate floor in the Gulf & Western Building on which the clipping agency lodged, and there in that obscure cul-de-sac had caught sight of Veronica emerging from another elevator, so intent on a brace of shoulder bags marked Peene-münde-New York-Fragile This End Up that she hadn't seen him. A person had opened an adjacent door marked in dusty brown, THE SHEET, and had helped her in with them.

Inside the clipping agency, standing at the counter at which Any-thing in the World could be potentially furnished him, he hadn't been able to demand it, shattered by a glimpse at how his own life was mass-connected beyond what it supposed. A minute later he said, "Give me anything you have on *The Sheet*." His own Tessa subscribed to it. Later a secretary went back to get the file on the *Courier*. "Here— they've mixed the *Courier* clips with more stuff on that rag, *The Sheet* —aren't they something? I wouldn't use them again." To him that load in her arms seemed to issue out of some proper voodoo in which two lives were being wooed to their space-slot in destiny.

A "TRAFFIC-JAM" IN OUTER SPACE
OVERCROWDING: A PROBLEM FOR COMMUNICATIONS SATELLITES

An old clip from back in early 1980, with a diagram of the approximate location of the then existing satellites on the only geostationary orbit for these, 22,500 miles above the equator, and already showing that those orbital slots above the busiest markets, then U.S. and U.S.–Europe, were to be the most jammed.

He began to draw a similar diagram for the girls. "I suggest you girls make your own world map—for habitats and rival shuttle lanes."

Tessa, tracking world politics from her mountain longhouse in front of which the goats were milked, would see to that. It was Tessa (who'd posted above her personal hole in the outhouse: *All our Righteousnesses are as menstruous Rags*—BUNYAN, and followed her affinity with the moon, as she herself said, like a member of a rape committee) who'd long since alerted him to lunar politics.

TIME FOR EARTHLINGS TO SIGN A MOON TREATY

No, that was '79, and only from a letters column, though that loathsome word, Earthlings, had been the *Times*'s own.

PACT ON MOON'S RICHES APPROVED

Undated, which by now made no difference. Like the pact itself, finally emerged from an Outer Space Committee long-stalled by the Soviet's refusal to accept the concept that the moon's resources should be a common heritage—a touch he found hilariously like his maternal aunts' and uncles' refusal to share a belated U.S. Indian land-grant settlement with "any in-laws," some of whom they were married to.

He had wired Tessa a congratulatory message anyway. "Aren't you glad that now neither the moon's surface nor its subsurface can become the property of any country?" Refraining from unsportsmanlike crowing over the fact that her favorite "Third World" countries had wanted a moratorium on exploitation only until the establishment of a regulatory regime for getting down to it. How odd it was though, to have a child even now still back in the world of the "Third World."

Since then, she'd moved on. Returned once from Saudi, he'd sent her a pendant just presented him as deacquisitioned by an unidentified museum, a pure gold crescent with that faint, unreal finish the archaeological years bestowed. On his last visit to Mendocino she'd apologized for having had to hang his gift communally, above the kitchen sink—meanwhile shaking dun-clad breasts the plaque might have hung between, and hair of an ancient glow not unlike it. "Oh yeah, the moon," all there had said, admiring. The big news being that they were now into banning nuke explosions in outer space.

Tessa, shushing them, said: "I sent Maidie a pic of it." She knew he yearned to hear. Yes, Maidie'd sent pics in return—and knew he would clutch at them. Tessa's wide mouth, stained blue with the wine all in the commune drank *ritually*, a word they never explained, hung open, distressed. A lovely boy entering just in the nick squeezed her compassionately; they all knew each others' sagas. "Daddy—she sent pics of their new hedge."

Magnolia grandiflora seven foot high. In his head, as at Guilford, she stands behind it. There are facts in his file which seem to belong most to her.

—Did you know, Maidie, that the younger a woman is, the more sensitive to startle from sonic boom?—

He reread the aeromedical report on it, remembering how as an adolescent she had screamed at his overloud stereo.

—We find we're not as hungry in space. Less caloric outgo—

In the marvelously compensating balances of the body which he's learning to trust here, and maybe to fear, would passengers long in transit, or space-citizens of long duration, have to guard against gradual anorexia? He has always thought his straight, chiseled girl has a touch of it. Maybe her reaction to Tessa's curves, at fourteen self-confessedly open to "any man whose eyes take the you-darling position."

—We perambulate a little like your cakewalk—

Done at age eight to a section of the *Nutcracker Suite,* in a hat like a mushroom, and with Chinese'd brows and lips which half a dozen other sets of parents had told them made Maidie look like Myrna Loy.

—When one turns one's head here, for instance—

Here he has to refer to the notes, copying them painfully, though without quotes:

Space passengers experience surprises because of counter-rotational movement, and move only by action and reaction, which are always equal and opposite. When a person in non-gravity makes a movement with his right hand, left to right, his body moves a trifle to the left. The lighter the arm is, and the more heavily loaded the body, the less the body will move. Under weak gravity high jumps of thirty-five feet can be made, they say—after which you would float lightly down.

Your Dad hasn't done it—

Perhaps on habitat, and for manufacturing purposes, we'll make a practice of it. That wouldn't interest her. But her sister will want to know, though little will either surprise or disappoint Tessa, inured as she is to communes which start up in the most spiritual landscapes and upon the most stubbornly fixed absolutes, but more commonly end up admittedly like hers—"a soul boardinghouse, for lease by the week." Like Tessa.

Ah, she was a darling though, and likely he was wrong about the humor in her case.

He wrote on, busily.

"Which do you prefer?"

Mulenberg raises his head. How Gilpin could smile, asking that! But childless people—be gentle with their lack. One always smiles back. "Fathers can't. But I'll tell you a story." In hotels he sometimes has. He draws out two snapshots illegally in his breast pocket. "Had a fellow in our New York office, known the girls since they were two and three." Until they stopped coming there. And stopped taking my money. "He kind of uncled them. Asked me that question once. Gave him the answer I gave you. Fathers can't—prefer. But uncles can, I said. Which one do you?" Because it helped to know.

Mulenberg holds out the snapshots.

There they are, just about as Gilpin has imagined them. Maidie the classy lady whom everybody done wrong. Tessa all hound-dog soft, her boundaries oozing beyond the lens. And these are not girls. They're thirty now—thirty-five. "What did he say?"

"Said—'I prefer the bitch, of course.' " Mulenberg knocks his head, as narrators of an old story do. "And when I said, 'Yes, but which one of 'em is that?' you know what that damned old geezer said?" Mulenberg lets it out in his softest baritone. " 'Oh, Jack, I leave that to you.' "

All parental stories are the same—they don't hear their own overtones. What use to tell Mulenberg that Gilpin hadn't wanted to know which daughter he preferred but which atmosphere, the steady starry one or the red earthly twinkling? Gilpin has more pressing matters to bring up. "Well, of all your women, perhaps Miss Oliphant—looks most like a Kwan-Yin."

Is Mulenberg going to put up his dukes, as men still say in the fish house on Gilpin's island? No, Gilpin's statement seems to dazzle him. "Thanks. I'm just finding myself," he says hoarsely and sits down.

Watching, Gilpin sees him turn off the processor and shakily try the pencil chained like Gilpin's at his wrist. Twice he tries, straining red-faced, like a child at stool. Or a man in orgasm. No one should be watching this. Gilpin closes his eyes.

"I'm just finding myself," was said to the unmoving ring of faces in sales conference, or on the mat afterward—by those vice-presidents who weren't going to be given any more time at it. Remove their secretaries. Close the coffee-break door; cancel the lunch date. When their air conditioners break down, fumble the order for repair. Let even the office machines seem to ostracize. Better that way. One day such a man will finally get to Mulenberg on his own. Resign, you say? *Thought* you might be thinking of it. We don't want to stand in your way.

The door he's outside is his own. No lettering; everybody knows I'm the president. Here's my key.

He'd thought if he improved his "geographic" deficiencies, it would balance his other reason for being here. Not as a question of virtue. Not excusing himself but empowering himself, as well as occupying time as he always had. Space is travel, like any other. Just be more efficient at it. I vowed I would be. I promised the girls.

Suppose I tell them how when I leave here I'll spend the next thirty minutes on a bicycle ergometer? And that I've got the hang of it. Travel.

Or show them this little item—on how the data on hearing-threshold sensitivity in airline pilots had been used to profit by one of our own outfits?

Or here's his own speech—a long clipping from an industrial magazine, on how American business had no sense of history, how technology was often forgotten in the rush of events and already existent studies were reproposed. As a scrabble through the file shows him, several had been for the *Courier*.

His hand trembles over all the connections magnetizing toward this vehicle. I'm learning my place here, girls, that's all; I see it. That tight knot in the head which loosens when a problem in geometry dissolves into solution?—it's like that. The theorem was always there. And the proof for it. All of it counts. The girls are no pretext, only part of a search in which everything counts, and all his pile of notes. You have only to be in a closed world to see it. In a home even, like Maidie. How long since he's had one?

He swung his pencil toward him, using the left hand to snag it. The hand is abnormally hot—has he fever? The pencil doesn't work, not even an impress. The paper tears. He writes on, invisibly, sprawling it large. SPACE IS MORAL. SPACE IS LIFE. SPACE IS— He can't make that last perception come. But it will.

He turns around, exultant. "The Free Room. You know—it *is* that. Even if you're chained to it. Or because you are. Everything's together here. Climbing. And us with it."

Gilpin's eyes are shut. Mulenberg turns to the word processor. The girls are gone. They're women now. He types anyway. Let the machine edit if it can. TELL YOU THE TRUTH I FOLLOWED SOMEBODY HERE Yes, they're women. He doesn't have to spell it out for them. Only for the machine. He punches it savagely. Might as well punch a photo-electric cell. An answer lights up: *Wrong Direction*.

One tickle will erase his whole labors here. There, that lever. So cool to the touch. Response with no response. Businesslike. Rest a minute, Mulenberg. Then begin to learn your home. He feels as if he's eaten. He wants to sing.

Gilpin is in the fish house. Old Cap'n Treeve, the island's unofficial chieftain, is blading a cusk, farting as he goes. All the men are doing something. The cusk means it's not winter yet. Albert, who runs the dry goods store, is giving Cap'n a haircut. That he'll do the one means he'll do the other, neither of which any fisherman would. Treeve's wife is on the mainland, helping her ninety-five-year-old father with his fall canning. The haircut is to appease her when she comes back and finds the captain winding up his binge. No women come into it, except her when she returns. Sun is just leveling, so the poker deck and the whisky aren't out yet. No one there would eat the cusk, too close to an eel, but the Canuck hand on the *Winnie Mae*, which comes in tomorrow, will take it home to Rockland and leave Treeve a couple of pints. *Winnie Mae* comes in only twice a week now the tourists are gone. No lobstering for four months yet. The angle of the sun, gold on Albert's scissors, tells everything. These harmonies of information go unremarked.

But just at that time also, Gilpin's father was applying neat's-foot oil to a sharkskin, his boy watching. Gilpin has brought along the portfolio made from it. Deep in the hold with his other document, a bit of the shark, at first sophisticated to him, is once again mariner. The fish house would not be surprised.

Gilpin opens his eyes. The sun in their space path is on the left. The buzzer attached to the time clock here—which doesn't always work although Mulenberg says the system comes from the highest bidder— now beeps. He notes his place in the book clamped again to his lap desk. Sure, we're all climbing. He did hear what his cabinmate said. From a fish house where men hang out after catch, it hadn't seemed worth answering.

He sees that Mulenberg has set up a long accordion folder all across the panel in front of him and even over the screen of the word processor. A flattened dollhouse version of the *Courier* with three-dimensional fretworks which rise out of the pages, it must have been made for him. To help him find himself.

"Nobody's at home in the universe," Gilpin says. "But we're all busy at it." On his island the housewives curtained their windows, putting ruffles around the North Star. All the way back to the Ptolemies building their pyramids—give us any strong idea of future enclosure and we'll suffer up the stairs by the thousands.

Mulenberg sits back. "There. Look at this model . . . I can take off the rocket boosters. We've used them. But here're the external tanks. Look at how the slosh baffles are mounted in the oxidizer tank. Five interfaces, between the tank and the—the *Courier*. All of them insulated, except one. . . . Wonder why—well . . ." He shrugs. "And here're the main propulsion engines. Here's a diagram of the structure systems— and there's the thermal-protection one. . . . And I still haven't touched auxiliary power control, environmental control, communication. Tracking-data process, navigation, operational flight." His words come trippingly, with too rational a gleam of eye. "You seen how they deploy and retrieve payloads? Not just lights on booms and sidewalls. Remote-control television for *depth* perception." He closes the folder reverently, starts to put it back into its case and then into the storage bin but it won't go. He's refolded it wrong. Guiltily he slides it into the long stashpocket in his suit.

"I could fancy a slosh baffle," Gilpin says. "Is it to drink tea with? Only got as far as the azimuth on a mariner's compass, myself. Come on, Jack. We can't beat it, we can't join it, either. Not all the way. Not that way."

"Come on yourself. You were the smartest man your year, M.I.T. I never got beyond the Colorado School of Mines."

"You got to the mines."

"Ah, that's the rub, is it. The money."

"You know it isn't," Gilpin said. How quick his own hostility swells, after all the monkish years. Like love, that other tumor?

"Anyway—I'm staying, understand? At the station." This is the way Mulenberg's face must be when it's on the heights of negotiation— irradiated and chill. Or when at the edge of sex? "I just found out, writing to the girls. Thing to do is—leave them the business."

Gilpin widens his eyes. He has to force them. They feel sleepier than when closed. Mulenberg, sitting back, cracks the folder. They both sit up, straighter. At the window the stars rain.

"Stuffy in here." Mulenberg passes a palm over his face as if to wipe the violence from it.

"The absence of weather." With an effort Gilpin adds, "Should it worry us?" Funny—to consult one's opposite—or sensible? Impossible to think of Mulenberg as enemy. Though there ought to be one in every decent man's life. "People are colored by weather." Or were. "There'll be flowers up there, anyway. Hydroponic. And vegetables."

"No fauna."

"We'll—see ghosts of them."

"When I'm anxious," Mulenberg says, "I dream of deer. Don't know why. Except that we had them."

"I never dream of fish. When I dream. Haven't dreamed yet here. You?"

"No."

There's a pause. Real pauses are hard come by here. Fruitful ones. The journey is all one long pause, under which the itch of destination nags.

"I'm not a man of imagination," Mulenberg says.

That's what people say who think it shameful because they are, Gilpin thinks. Or who want to confess something. "What about those delusions you mentioned? In the galley, yesterday." If they hadn't been in that almost humdrum sector of bright ovens and lockers of trays attesting to a home-handling they were meant to visualize, Mulenberg, dipping a corpse of asparagus into a pink pouch of what appeared to be lava and swallowing it with a muttered prayer, might never have said: "Not gossip, you know." It was then he'd spoken of the little group-paranoias which could sweep an office. And the rabbits. They'd have had a lot of fauna on the Mulenberg ranch.

"Mirages, I've been thinking, Gilpin. More like mirages, that people share." Or could start to. Think of those streaked waterlines on American highways, which dried as one approached. Or out in the Saudi desert, what the driver has to tell you isn't a palm fringe with water plain as a jewel at its core. There were those who had seen whole architectures hanging from myth-rock. And all natural phenomena.

"Like what?"

"Well—like that boy, Mole. Acts like he has inside info. But like he can't help it. I could begin to think he was a spy. If I couldn't see he was just a lad."

Gilpin half-rises from the easy chair. His damn legs seemed to have ankylosed into one. "For who?"

"Say. Our space effort been that internationally cooperative lately?"

"Hasn't it?"

Mulenberg punches the side of his head—and misses. "Not since the first shuttle. Even my girls know that."

"The volume of what people don't know extends even to me." Gilpin coughs. "Where are those lozenges?" His hand is guided to them. "Thanks. But the boy knows more than he says, yes. More than he—is. I can't elaborate. But I vouch for him." He sucks gratefully. "God, my throat's dry. And my legs—"

"The air is—"

They both check the video, but it's blank. Perhaps it's only that now they're talking, air moves again in the old comfortable earthbound way.

"Particulars don't count with me enough, Gilpin. That's why I'm always checking them. I'm going to Telex the girls. And the office. Make it all shipshape."

"Telex?"

"Well, whatever. They'll have something."

"What confidence." But so they will, of course. And whatever it's called, Mulenberg will have access to it. "You ever—imagine—this crew has contempt for us?" Must have. At times Gilpin has felt it, seeping into Cabin Six from that flight deck. Or even from the vehicle itself, laughing at what it was carrying.

"Sure, they have it. For passengers. You gotta—" His thumb goes up, for all their asses.

"For that you have to see them. Why don't they show?"

"Beyond the call of duty. Keeping us safe is enough—and they are. Never saw a first-class in the tail before, where it belongs."

First? Well, why not? Hadn't he himself warned of it? "Shhh—" Gilpin says. "Hear anything?"

"You talking," Mulenberg spurts childishly. He sits up. Where's that sixth-grade giggle come from, him or his vis-à-vis? "Are we getting too *much* oxygen?" Turning, he blusters among his papers. "What's the mix here? I know they gave it to me. It's here somewhere."

He needs a subordinate, Gilpin hears his own thoughts voice thinly. I'm no good to him.

Mulenberg's found it. "Here. Environmental Control: Cabin temperature, pressure, humidity, carbon-dioxide level and odor . . . controlled by heat-exchanger and . . . associated equipment. Temp. between 61 and 90 Fahrenheit. Oxygen—*here!* Partial pressure of—" 22 065 $\pm$ 725 N/ m^2 (3. 20 $\pm$ 25 psi) is maintained and nitrogen added to achieve total pressure of 101 355 Nm^2 (14.7 psl). He couldn't read this correctly—and what if he could? " 'Cabin controlled by air ducted through cabin heat exch. ges.—' What's ges.?"

"Gauges? Are none for passengers anyway." Why would there be? "It's a classic situation." First-class. Because they can't open the door outward, which is computer-released. "Thirty minutes to the door," Gilpin said.

Or press an alarm? Warning plates, gamboge circled in black, are everywhere throughout.

Mulenberg sniffs upward, blond eyelashes batting like a cook tasting. "Little too much maybe. Oxygen. Not serious. Tough it out, eh?"

"Watch each other. In case we turn blue." Would it be blue?

They are both smiling wide.

"Gravity remains." Gilpin's feet are on the floor but another giggle isn't far. He swallows it. "You ever—fantasize—somebody might have it in for this whole ship?"

"I have had that delusion." Mulenberg hiccoughs. "Seeing the list of successful suppliers. But then I always want all the machines to stop. Always have. Especially any vehicle I'm on."

Funny stuff from a captain of industry. Where'd he get it?

"From a horse," Mulenberg answers, as if Gilpin has spoken aloud— perhaps he has. "Used to bolt whenever I had her out. And then lead me home, when I couldn't. That filly sent me East."

Now they're certainly laughing.

"And when it stops—in your head, I mean. When all the—prairie schooners, and the horses, and the—jets—all the tra*sh*portation—stops." Gilpin's hand leans out from him on its own. "Where d'you go? Where're you then, I mean? In your head."

Mulenberg has his eyes closed, breathing lightly. He opens them. One eyebrow goes up, but not at Gilpin. Mulenberg is in his head. "In the family room at the ranch. The home ranch."

But with the person one mustn't name. Or to the greenhouse, Mulenberg says to himself—to lie down there with the plants. But the person you mustn't name—the forbidden one—is always behind everything. For everyone. Until found. Watch the clerks in our office. The girls who still marry and give shower-parties for one another. Or those who loll in the "permanent relationship," now and then shifting it. Or even the jolly staff-golfers, who've done it out of the stud-book. All marrying certain masks, certain significances. The person you follow is always with you, whether or not. The one you can't name.

"Not for me, I guess. The family. I'm the one who stopped that rhythm, in ours." How old-fashioned of Mulenberg, though, to say "machine" for what we're in now, for this whole fusion of processes we've started and can't see the end of. "You know, I don't think we were the machine age," Gilpin said. Or thought he said. "We were just the over-symbolized one. Had a little rag myself, called *The Sheet*. Maybe you know it." Who really were the people he'd gathered there? The revolutionaries of what? Anti what? The people who *inhabit* revolution, Veronica said in awe when she first met them. A race he recognizes, yes, whenever he sees one of them—but which maybe dies in almost everyone by age forty. A race that only inhabits people for a while.

Soon he must mention Veronica. Again.

"Yes, I know *The Sheet*."

"Well—we did that. Oversymbolized. Oh, I wouldn't go back on it. See it better that's all. From here." Here? Looking down, Gilpin plants his foot on it, a shagless, fire-retarded something. "Maybe its never too safe to describe the machine, huh? Not the one you're on."

Mulenberg gets up, in sections. Leaning on the processor, he begins to ready his papers for tomorrow. "No? Then what am I going to tell the girls?"

Gilpin lies back, his eyes slitting and reopening. His chair seems easier now. More—receptive. Unless my buttocks are growing squarer. And the man does have humor. Or is growing it?

"That the bell? No." Mulenberg feels the gaucherie of looking for a kind ear. Of finding one. "You believe in the glory of this trip. Or don't you?"

"I was sure trained to. But then you have to believe in the delusions, too."

"Looked at any of those background folders yet?"

The wall of them looks ready, each dossier alphabetized large in white on black, each on magnetic hold. On a sidewall are the instructions for releasing one. At home in Gilpin's sold apartment, his beloved edition of the Encyclopaedia Britannica waits respectfully for its new owner, even at its great age so green of cover that chlorophyll might still be seeping from all the freshets of expectation enclosed there in 1911. "No." I believe in—something more.

"Lot of 'em are here because of *you*."

Shocked, Gilpin half sits up. "I suppose that is—my small autonomy. Never thought of it that way." So the ball falls on my side. If anything could fall, in this place I've immured myself. Is the man grinning?

"Maybe whoever brought you here will take it on. The responsibility."

"I brought myself," Gilpin shot out. "That I'll take on."

Immediately he hears all the great episcopals of time asserting how impossible that is, given our entanglement with one another. Plus the twang of the borrowed minister from the mainland who took the island chapel on once-a-month Sundays, his nose tweaked with drink.

Mulenberg gets up. His movements are often his answers. Standing in these close quarters, his bulk grows, suggesting how often he must have imposed it. He's worried at how lax the usually sharp Gilpin is. The oxygen mix may affect men according to size. By his own watch, they should be out of here by now. The watch, which has a chip that adjusts to their journey in a series of infinitesimal responses, was presented him by three grave men in a salon in Geneva, along with a little speech in which it was referred to as a Nuremberg egg. When he asked what that was, the head of the firm replied, The first watch. As yours will be. Out there.

He doesn't trust the time clock. "Who comes in here next?"

Gilpin is picking up his book, slowly. "Mulenberg—I can't raise my arm."

"Get down flat on the floor. Pronto." But that's for heat. Mulenberg had been a volunteer fireman once. His lips move soundlessly, missing his beard. *Oxygen is supplied from the cryo-genic tanks which also supply the fuel tanks. Nitrogen from pressure vessels mounted in mid-fuselage. For normal purposes,* his notes say. *Central-nervous system toxicity, from inhalation of hyperbaric oxygen, which at pressure over 5 ATA (atmospheres absolute) induces strychnine-like convulsions,*

*however has its tempered uses in cases of carbon-monoxide poisoning
and gas-gangrene tetanus.*

"One up for St. Paul," Gilpin murmurs, not moving.

Mulenberg has a blinding image of his two girls, united again, each flown from her coast to stand somewhere in the middle of his and their United States, maybe O'Hare Airport, looking up at him. Daddy will explain.

In the same minute he pulls Gilpin to the floor with him. Feeling along the wall of locked folders, he finds the warning plate above, and decides against warning *them*. Below, in a column of control boxes and stats, all talking to their computers, is one marked H. Ex. The inner gauge had three positions. He stretches to flick to the middle one: Norm., and slides to the floor again. What kind of floor is it has no smell, neither plastic nor dust? Breathe in, slowly. *Fac me cruce, custodieri—* his voice box sings silently. *Morte Christi, prae-mu-ni—*

"That isn't us laughing," Gilpin mumbles, his face close to Mulenberg's. "Is it the ship marvelous?"

Listen to its laughter, brewing between multifold wirings from which only satire can twang. In this ark carrying to the new world enough electronic chips of info to alert a small galaxy or regulate that gross watch of Mulenberg's, is a personality igniting—and are they hearing its first cry? In Italy once, he'd been present in a house where a baby was being born. He was in that *sala* now as the message-cry came from that odorous bedroom, twining the air with honeysuckle birth. A soul is ignited, the priest said.

The woman in Seat Six, Veronica told him yesterday, is making one. High in the heavens its *sala* waits.

And this complex we're in, trusting it to bear us on and on into the non-weather, along comprehensions known to no one telegrapher, is laughing. That is my *alluzinacione, illusione.*

"And that is *my* dee-lu-zhee-on," Gilpin says aloud, sleepily. But the Free Room doesn't smell of Tuscany. He opens his eyes. Mulenberg's already are. Gilpin's had no reclining face that near his for years, male or female. He sees the attraction of it, animal and kin. Pillow talk, while life-as-usual hangs by a thread. The collapsed closeness of those who've already extorted each others' private images. All that part of sex which isn't sexual per se but which people bring there, because—where else? Two men lying on the floor in forced eye-contact, breathing the oxygen which in a hospital would be called intensive care.

Mulenberg's remembering Ventura, those deathwatch eyes. Long-vanished eyeballs which had seen Veronica. Ventura's son has been given a trust fund to which Mulenberg adds annually, though he's never seen the boy; the shipment of Saudi crude never became possible. On account of that night he's here—and she is—and the man opposite.

"I'll eat with you—" she'd said, in the corridor. Hope seeped into him, simply because she remembered that last detail of their night. Though the nether side of obsession is that black hole down which all belief falls. In the corridor they of course couldn't eat, but while they perambulated—a word her mouth spat out in scorn—she fed him tidbit histories of herself and the other two men, in sketches so sharp they scratched on the air the outline of any person talked about. "Lievering?" she'd said, to his suggestion that the man might be aboard because of his connection with her. No, Lievering's pure chance. That's his way. We'd better be afraid of him.

He'd asked her about Gilpin point-blank. Not a brother to me, she'd said. No, I had a brother. I don't hear from him. I once thought my problem was to lose him. But we lose no one. Especially those. She'd seemed to Mulenberg to want to throw away every reticence, and to have him see why. He saw. Because she's so open with him, there's no hope for him. He doesn't loom with her as a lover must.

No, not my brother, she'd repeated. There were tonal changes to her repeats. He noted that like a husband. But Tom's more than a friend, even a heavy friend, she'd said. Put what I am with what he is—and together we might make a third sex. I've often thought of it. At the end of one of their turns on the parallelogram their path was tracing, she lifted a boxed foot. Out there—as sex gives me up—she shook the square boot—I'm fancying he'll come to it. Mulenberg planted his boot next to hers.

"He looms with you, doesn't he? I know why you're telling me all this. Because I don't." Pshaw, you're smart, she said. He'd stamped his own great boot, thinking of his first Indian-slender ones, in which he'd dreamed for hours before putting them in muck. "Not as I'd want to loom. But maybe—as an extra man?" He meant her to know any share would be acceptable. "Ah, I often thought of it," she said. "How with you, I could almost repeat a man." Her outline came clearer to him, a woman more often among her own thoughts. "What I did with women," he said, "you have done with me." "You're smart," she said, softer. "Know what, Mulenberg—" The office way she said his name smote him. "I've never met a man again—to talk with. That I slept with before."

When it came time to enter the vehicle he'd managed to be behind her. "You're in Cabin Six too?" she'd said. "Yes—I arranged it." If she'd slapped him, he'd have still hoped. She smiled. "Down below, Mulenberg. Maybe as extra man. But not—out there. It's not what I'm going for. What I'm going for—" The line in front of them was held up, as if waiting for her to declare. Her features were small for the strains and powers within. To one side of the hangar door where they waited there was a basket of roses. She touched one, shuddered back—and touched it again. "I'm going for the—the glass planet. Yes, that must be it. What I'm going for." She stared straight through him, seeing it.

He didn't know what that meant, didn't need to. He was back in Bahrein, Oman, Yemen, Baghdad, Teheran—countries which were like overheated mosques of such gestures. Honor. Virtue. Despair. Fate. Fortune. Peril. Redoubt. Eighteenth-century gestures, lingering on in the Western mind like swords brought home by travelers. *I'm falling through the air waiting for Allah to catch me*—the bazaar guide boy at the Hilton in Saudi said—and two days later was seen clinging to the rack of one of the Rolls-Royces which haunted government there, a Luger at his waist and his shrewd bargainer's eyes exalted past recognizing his own mother. In the hotel coffee shop in Oman, the Arab bank manager who every morning sat next to Mulenberg said: "You don't *despond* loudly enough in New York. I have been there. It is more like discomfort, yes? And vi-o-lence is for television." The fine shoes which hooked over the footrail were the same brand as Mulenberg's. He'd had one of their prouder faces, the nose jutting from the snowy headdress over the mustache which thickened the upper lip, the lower one curling outward over a jaw which declined straight into the throat without making the face chinless, as it would have an Anglo's. He wore a collar on that throat, and a Liberty tie. Yet not too long after he'd hung a rope around it—for the sake of one or the other of those words. Retribution. Shame.

About to board the *Courier,* Mulenberg had stretched to see the last of the sky. It flashed over him that if disaster came upon the *Courier,* it wouldn't become legend. His own company would merely repudiate the vehicle, its whole concept if need be—and try for another. His country would do the same. He put both clumsy canvas mitts around the woman beside him; the mitts were double ones, he'd forgotten why. Women weren't pushed toward the unknowns that were common enough to men. So that when one of those great unknowns came over them, they mightn't even know it. "You're going for glory—" he'd said.

Two gentlemen lying exhausted on the floor, as if after love. When that wasn't the case, or even the impulse, why should memory of love awaken in Gilpin after so long? The air had a lemony tang over a snuff underbase, like adolescent sweat. Even in his maturity he'd secretly felt that all sexuality belonged more rightfully to the young. His last involvement, with the woman photographer Purvis, had already had too much pity in it for health—though he'd never believed that her desire for a sex change was more than a forlorn grasp at a fashionable deliverance of the day, from one whose weakness of orientation hadn't been to sex but to the world. Those days, if one had to risk being publicly mad, to do so sexually was by far the easiest. Since to be publicly sexual in some sense was so much the norm.

As for him, not impotent, nor homosexual, though he'd had his experiences—he hadn't escaped the freakiness. Sexuality as it aged didn't lapse, only dispersed, gently polymorphous—though he wasn't that old. But he'd been drained, publicly too, by the open life. The Lord Newsworthy giveth and taketh away, a little of the psyche being smeared like printer's ink on the public thumb every morning—to the disadvantage of both parties. Men and women directly under the yellow news glare became publicly bedworthy. I went the other way—toward a public chastity—without even feeling it. Philanthropy can shrivel one. Mass love dissipates; the saints have that unfocused stare. One has to love singly—even daughters. I forgot to live privately.

Lying on his back, he sees that the Free Room's ceiling is stenciled with stars, as if there aren't enough of them around already. Centered in them is a photostat of the living-station. The private life—what a place to undertake it.

Gilpin bubbles laughter, and breathes free.

Mulenberg, stumbling to his feet, looks down at Gilpin in embarrassment. "It worked. Air's normalizing." He offers Gilpin a hand.

"Or what passes for it." Gilpin takes the hand and is raised to his feet. "Someone's always rescuing me. Thanks."

Mulenberg's reading his own palm. "First time I ever. Moved the machine. On my own. Well—always parlay."

"What?"

"Success."

That's a word Gilpin and his kind never use, on the grounds that only spiritual fools or knaves see such finish lines. But this man has an air of a maybe just as able half of the world which sees like that. He's already made Gilpin admit it exists, and made him yearn for Mulenberg's confidence. "Mulenberg, why don't you stay on out there with us?" To be that other half—of Wert. And maybe—of me? "Any real chance of it?"

Mulenberg is at the wall of dossiers, guardedly lifting a few to see if they unlock. They do.

"Looking for someone's? For Veronica's?"

"No, Tom. I've already found hers." Mulenberg's leaning toward him. Is it only from the gravity angle? "Tom—"

I hate this first-naming, Gilpin thinks, but it's the business way. His estimate of Mulenberg drops. "Yes, Jack?"

"She'll marry you in the end."

The hatch from the airlock opens. William Wert enters, helping in ahead of him the wife the rest of them call Seat Six. She bows, all she's done so far, even at mealtime. Never in here without Wert, and even with him unwillingly, preferring to stay in the Hygiene Unit, where she's under dispensation to take more than the limit of baths, according to Veronica lounging afterward in a non-NASA-issue smock, tacky yet female—the way they can be where she comes from, even when they're princesses.

"Gentlemen. My wife, Soraya."

This metal-plated room, giving off mini-illuminations which never come to much, isn't tooled for that style of address. Let it adjust then, Gilpin thinks. Wert would have said *Gentlemen* if he'd found the two of us men on the floor locked in mortal embrace. Isn't that the right temperament for the administrator of so many diverse souls? Whether Wert would have found the gauge as Mulenberg had, or known of it, is still to be demonstrated. The wife has her eyes lowered. Soraya, yes —but which of them, both so clear to him from Wert's memoir? Blue eyes—or brown? Gilpin has no time for it. "Mulenberg—"

Mulenberg's turned his back on the new occupants, taking folders from the shelf one after the other, opening each, slamming it closed and shoving it back in. When Gilpin nears he pays no attention. Behind them Wert reverentially seats his wife in an Easy Chair.

"Jack—" Gilpin says low, "you get that from Veronica herself?" Can he know what is known only to Gilpin's lawyer, and Rhoda of the old staff? "I can't imagine that she—"

Mulenberg's now strewing a bastion of the dossiers on the floor around him, his hand shaking. "She doesn't know it yet." He squats to the ring of folders. "Lots of roads to—glory. Why else would she come? If she isn't—following you?" He opens a dossier, peers in and smacks it shut. "Because she's free to? Because she's a citizen of the world?" Another folder smacks down—open and shut quickly; what can he have found there? Or not found. "No one's a citizen of the world. Not me. Maybe not even you."

"Maybe she already is. Married." He can't give the word Mulenberg's emphasis.

"Lievering? Puh. She told me that one. They never were. Nothing legal."

"No." So she hasn't told him. How Gilpin and she are married, if only legally. Six years ago, for the sake not of taxes, but of testimony. When they were about to clap him in jail. So he could transfer certain obligations. For the good of the paper. Rhoda Esher had suggested it.

But would businessman Mulenberg, even dreamer Mulenberg, have understood the three of us in that bar near City Hall afterward—the aura of the kind of people we are? Or were.

"It's Rhoda who's marrying," Gilpin had whispered, though Rhoda was right there at the table between the two of them. "She acts like she's the bride of the Lamb." And looked it, in a black hat whose wings hid the red pot-holder hair and came down to her wattles. "But which one of us is the Lamb?"

Veronica asks for Bejan rum and gets it. "Me. Now that I own *The Sheet.*"

Rhoda, staring at the two bartenders behind the long bar, two Humpty-Dumpty look-alikes, says: "And because she always answers my telephone calls, no matter how stewed I am. No matter how late." She leaned toward the bar. "There *are* two of you, aren't there?" The nearer of the two barkeeps laughed and said yes, they were twins, fraternal not identical. "That's the way to be," Gilpin said. Veronica lifted her glass. "To my brother, wherever he is." The barkeep, joining them in a drink, leaned over the bar. "Tell you a story." Once, when he and his brother worked a gay bar in Greenwich Village, his twin, trying to quell a noisy sailor who kept protesting he'd never seen twin barmen before, had snapped: "Well, there's nepotism everywhere!" The sailor had slammed his fist down, looking around him defiantly. "Well, and why not? This is the Village, ain't it?"

It had seemed just the right wedding anecdote, in their case. "We three just got married," Rhoda said. The barkeep stood them a round. "Three's a crowd—" he said, "though if you ever need four—?" Gilpin smiled at Veronica. "A crowd, yes. That's why we did it."

She'd nodded back, twirling her glass; it was the last of the Bejan.

She'd worn white, but then she often did. "Now I know what to do," she said. "Now I can lead a proper life." The aura at their table came of knowing one's own reasons and each other's. Rhoda had squinted at the barman for all of them. "But it's not the Village." Then they had each gone home, alone.

Here they're four, the room's tolerance, but by a convention fallen into the first week, privacy is always ceded the new occupants. Wert, if he wants this, would never say. Even in a fatigue suit he looks too fine-boned for authority, one who would exert it a mite too politely and maybe a little slowly—but in long sieges of any kind, still a man you'd like to have in the room. At the moment watching his wife, who's bent to the opposite wall, scanning it. "She checks every computer setup she can here. Of course, it's her field."

So she's that Soraya. Where's the one who went to Switzerland, by now? Surely not back in Iran. The minute Gilpin mentions countries to himself he experiences a strange dislocation. Since he's been aboard, no one's mentioned any. Once he'd spent nine weeks in Southern California without ever hearing the word Europe. But this is his first plane without travel talk. How could there be? "We had a little trouble with the air mix. Not enough to call for help." Had it been? "Seems all right now."

Soraya turns from the wall to focus on him. Yes, the eyes are brown. How she focuses. Now on Wert. What she murmurs must be Farsi. Are they very much married, or not?

"We'll be off now," Gilpin says, loud enough for Mulenberg to take the hint. "Time for the bicycle. I must have pumped halfway to Betelgeuse." All three men glance at the window. Such glances come like tics here. Then for hours they forget to. Whatever stars they see are nameless, any time they look. And that's distance for you.

Wert's been gazing out there the longest. "My wife wants me to tell you something. But first, I've news of my own. I'm not to be your civil administrator out there."

"Why not?"

"Protests from home."

"Home?" Gilpin horse-laughs, jerking a thumb at the window.

"We're still wired to it. With bands of steel, I'd say." Wert's tired smile, so attractive, is really a facial mold, years in the forming. It won't release him even in stress. "I'm not surprised. What surprised me was being appointed."

"Wrong politics?"

"Oh, I wouldn't mind that. Spent my life at it. And when I had to leave the Department a university gave me a chair for it. Seems it's my private life as well. I live with two women. Openly. Or did." Wert's smile does relax—when he regards his wife. Whose eyes are concealed again. "That's all right. You can't take them to state parties—but that's all right. Just don't have it occur that some scruffy, well-intended avant-gardists make a cause of you—which finally reaches Washington."

"Wash-ing-ton," Gilpin says, as if in some Hopi dialect. He's still eyeing the window.

"It's still there. As I've been informed." Wert's hand, held by his wife, twiddles itself from her grasp, opens and shuts, slaps his thigh. "My worry-beads. Had to leave them behind of course. But it's like cigarettes, breaking yourself. Even the voyaging is not enough." He says something under his breath.

"Eh?"

"I said, 'As I should know.' "

"Oh, there're things we should." It seems to Gilpin that everyone present aboard is linking these, pooling them, socializing each other down from the first peaks of the journey, when any remark had been as significant as a mountaineer's move. "We're going to bring down all the marvels to take tea with us. It's what the human animal does so well."

Seat Six is touching Wert's arm. "William." The rest is in a tongue soft and twirling as an awl.

"My wife thinks we should know the computer was programmed. For your air change. A rise in oxygen. Twenty minutes of it. Can you read computers?"

"No."

"Can Mulenberg?"

"I doubt it."

Mulenberg, still in his corner with his back to them, is coming out of his barrier of dossiers, slowly returning them one by one, like a man working himself out of an aberration.

And Wert and I? Why've we lowered our voices?

"She could be wrong. Not on the reading—she's tops. On the interpretation. She's been so upset all day."

How has this dignified man, who looks fifty but must be nearing sixty, got in the habit of speaking for his wife? What happened in that throwback household which must have come out of the events Gilpin's read of? What age would she be now—pushing forty? She still looks young, but not the way American women do. Nor like Veronica—delayed. He can't put his finger on it. "That the reason you won't speak English?" Gilpin says to her directly.

A half grave smile from her. A soft American "—No." But a shrug for the triviality of it.

"She reverted to Farsi the second we heard she was pregnant. I tell her she must be programming a son."

One sees how Wert's reverted, too. Handsome and straight-backed enough to impregnate a younger wife, maybe two, with mutual pleasure, he's newly, fussily rheumy at the eyes—a more than middle-aged first-time father, who'll become elderly the minute the child's born.

"What's upset her?"

"I can't—I scarcely know how to say—she's got this singular idea." Wert draws himself up. "I must tell you she's the least paranoid person I know. All her dangers have been real."

"I know of her background."

Mulenberg has glided up behind the three of them. "I don't know it." He turns to her. "Something about this—ve-hickle? Some naggy long-eared delusion buttin' you in the back? Like one of your burros in the back streets of Tabriz or Rezaiyeh, eh? I said 'Beg pardon' to one of those once." His drawl's suddenly Western American—and his bow to her. "Jack Mulenberg, Cabin Six. Your cabin. Like to tell us what's botherin' you?" Tell Daddy. He doesn't say that, but the womanizer magic is there. What a scare that may have been—for daughters.

"She—"

She hushes Wert. Speaking with her hand still in his of course, "Soraya here. Okeh, listen. I am often in the Hygiene Unit. I have to bathe for the back. Old troubles there." Her voice is low enough to please Shakespeare but matter-of-fact. "Yet for the baby I must not soak too much. So I must balance, I must think ahead. I am there often in the Jacuzzi, doing that." Her teeth are exceptionally white. What will the baby do to them, on the diet they all have here—does she supplement? Her polite smile doesn't compromise her, nor inform. Gilpin, having once held her very life story in his hand, is moved to see her.

The brown eyes aren't on him but on Mulenberg. "You know our Hygiene Unit—how it has the four doors? Three to our section—and also the door which would lead to the next cabin's Hygiene Unit?"

Each cabin has access to its unit from its galley, from the cabin proper and from the general corridor—and so on down the line, making each cabin an autonomous section, linked to the one ahead or behind only by their adjoining Hygiene Units. Bathrooms, for God's sake. Locked. As linking bathrooms often are in a house. Bordering all is the general corridor for access forward or aft and so to the general vehicle, enterable only on schedule, for it, too, has a set capacity.

"That's right." Gilpin enjoys going over it. Helps. "So we're the only cabin with a Hygiene Unit only on one side—the forward one. Since we're the last cabin in the tail. Excuse me—aft."

"So that door—" Soraya's saying. "That fourth door. To the next cabin's unit. Not used. Locked. Why? What a design. Multiple capability, but they don't allow." She flashes a competent look at her computer wall. Her very English gains ripple from it. "So I sit in my bath, or not in my bath, and I think of how we are not to see the other passengers until the last week. And how now and then the red light in the unit comes on over a door. Only never that door."

While the unit's video screen will warn you of someone's approach, though in vague outline. Whereupon, though the room's set up for two, you exit as soon as possible through one or another access doors. Doing this not for privacy really but because that was what one had once habitually done. And perhaps because there aren't that many such habits one may still exert?

Always remembering meanwhile—if you're returning cabinward, you'll change first from fatigue suit to the non-gravity one with its cumbersome life supports, taking yours from the hooked line of them. Or vice versa. Maybe cursing Congress for insisting on the heaviest model suit—which some say is like requiring every seat in a jet not only to have its personal oxygen mask but to wear it.

Always remembering also to rid yourself of other impedimenta. Such as the couple of Personal Wipes, so inscribed and luckily unsoiled, which had once come back to cabin with Gilpin, floating and sticking everywhere. The cabin being empty at the time, he'd never owned up to it.

"So I sit on that ledge. And because of the baby, in my head it bubbles like a fairy story, along with the Jacuzzi. I think—who is the person on the other side of the wall? A person from another cabin? I tell me maybe they do come into our Hygiene Unit, when we are not there. I tell me —maybe—I will stretch a hair across that door. Like in the old palaces, for the wife's lover. But really I do not feel that anyone will ever come." She breaks off, taking in the other two men, then homing back—to Mulenberg. "In prison one has eyes in the back of the head. Even on the skin. One can always tell if there is no one. Or someone. On the other side of the wall. What you call that?"

There's a hair stretched between her eyes and Mulenberg's.

"Subliminal," Gilpin says, breaking it.

She turns at once to Wert. Like in the traces, a matched pair? "So— tell them, Beel."

He hesitates. "Why—burden them?"

The buzzer rings. Time's up.

"Come on, Mulenberg—" Gilpin says uneasily. "I'll race you on the ergometer. Let's go."

"Allow us to." Wert's extended his hold on his wife to her arm. "Enclosures are difficult for her at best—but she would come along with me. She's easiest in the bath, because in prison they didn't have them. Or in the cabin, because we're all there." When he comes to speak plainly, he does it well. "Now of course, we could go home. On the turn-around flight."

She flashes him a long look, but is silent.

"So you've been in prison," Mulenberg bends to her. "I'm sure for good reason. Like with this one, eh, Gilpin? . . . Gilpin thinks this is a prison, and the living-station will be, but he's going anyway. Wouldn't miss it." Mulenberg smiles hard at him. I've read you, Tom. You didn't think me capable of it. "So tell us, little Seat Six. Your delusion. And I'll tell them mine."

"Seat Six?" Slipped from Wert's arm and leaning forward, she looks sturdier, stronger. Though not quite as young.

"What we call you. Because he keeps you to himself."

"Not him. I." She won't sparkle for Mulenberg. "Because I am not to myself." She means her belly. "So. You, too, have an impression. Tell me."

Under the video screen which is now jerkily rating their progress for them in coarse print, the intercom squawks. *Mmmrrrher-rher-guh. Fwah—deck.* They're all learning to interpret it.

"For Mulenberg, I fancy. They'll be wanting you on flight deck. They told me so."

"Why me, Wert?"

He already knows but it annoys him that Wert knew it first. He wants to make Wert say it. A hard man. When on business.

"I fancy they'll want you to take my place."

Always the gentleman. Misfortunately? Gilpin's not so sure. Wert seems to get what Wert wants. What he may want is to get that willful girl home.

"Will they now." Mulenberg is toneless. "Well, bully for them. But let them first explain this." The shelf he goes to has six of the black folders segregated. Some are as thick as books. "Here we all are. All with our names on the back, just like at the motel: J. Cohen-Lievering, T. Gilpin,

V. Oliphant, J. Mulenberg, W. Wert. And S. Wert." All lettered in gold-leaf. "All in order. I looked. And now—these others." With a back-hand sweep he riffled the two long shelves of folders below, bringing most of their contents to the floor again. "Look at them."

Books tumbled every which way are like women with their legs in the air. Gilpin peers. That one. That there. Over there. All of them.

"Blank—" Gilpin says, kneeling, scholar-horror in his voice. "They're all blank."

"All sixty-five of them. I counted. And yes—empty. All but ours. So I think—well, budget reasons. Four Free Rooms—they didn't Xerox for all. But then why have the folders? Or they didn't want us to spend the time here that way. Or even—they want us to work for it. The info. There's no crap like a psychologist's. Somebody's sold them a bill of it."

I say: blank, Gilpin thinks. He says: empty. He passed a hand over the folders, almost gently. "These don't have any names on them at all."

A cry from Soraya—a long Farsi moan.

"She's right to wonder. But Allah won't help." An almost libidinous satisfaction plays on Mulenberg's lips. "All right, then, girl. Tell me."

"No," her husband says. "Do not. It's destructive. We're all on a thin edge here. Until we arrive. But this is not prison. We're connected."

Gilpin stands up, tilting toward Wert. Does the vehicle help him there, though gravity's near normal? Maybe the *Courier* itself gets confused. "With, say—the military?"

Wert's long upper lip twitches—amusement at a child's plaint. "Let's say—" He bites the lip. "Let's say—I am not connected with it."

So was that the screw? But who's applied it to who? Who protested what? What would Wert not *do?* "You agree then—some factions might be very glad to see this mission disorganize?"

Wert shrugs, maybe back in his old world of honorably negotiated checks and balances. *Let's say—* that Wert would be a fine man to have at your side in a crisis, but can he ever be brought to it? "Gilpin, you and I might have our vanities of principle. I admire yours. But we'll never be the real enemy."

"Whose? Whose enemy aren't we—you and I—important enough to be? You've been out there. Tell us."

The warning light over the door is pulsing red. A person is about to enter. Gilpin hopes for Mole—his happy-nihilism-to-you grin. He sees Soraya arch her neck like a cat's, lift her nose, hunch her shoulders. She does know. She knows who it will be.

Veronica breezes in, the airlock seeming to deposit her astride a wind. But by now the movement is characteristic of all of them when moving in and out of gravity, a kind of brimming. In Mulenberg's heart a valve opens. The essence of to and fro—we'll have it always with us. We'll have her. He sees she's counting heads. "No, stay," he says. "Tom and I are just leaving."

"Yes, Jack and I."

Her eyebrows go up at both of them. In the fatigue suit, with her long bones boxed away, she's lost her model's leanness. Though she never wore makeup except at the eyes, she now looks as women do when washed pure of it—caught by age and youth at the same time. "Hey— what's that pile on the floor?"

"That's my delusion. Tom, want to tell her it?"

"Nobody here seems to want to tell his own."

"He thinks all those folders are blank," Mulenberg said.

"Yes, I think they're all blank."

"What are you two—?" She kneels, passing her hands over the white pages. She looks to Wert, away from the two men staring at her in concert, as if whatever she says might bind her to one of them. "They are blank, aren't they?"

Wert nods. Holding his woman tighter.

"Mulenberg's collecting delusions. How about you, Wert? Don't you have any?"

"Sure. Mine is—that I left mine all at home. And yours, Gilpin?"

"That he never had any," Mulenberg says, almost with affection.

"He's read me." And who says you don't have humor, Jack?

Soraya, tracking all this back and forth says softly to Wert: "Yes—they talk like the prison."

In truth, a jailhouse gaiety is rising here.

Or is it lack of air?

All four of them are standing closer, as in a street corner shell game. Veronica joins the circle. But in its center nobody's playing. The game's not here. Yet she seems to feel there is one.

"A penny for your thoughts." The porthole light aureoles Mulenberg's head. It's not clear which woman he's speaking to.

"No, Soraya. Come away." Wert edges her toward the hatch.

Mulenberg bars them. "Soraya. Say there's a hair across this door. Is there anyone outside it? . . . No? . . . Not Lievering? Not Mole?"

"N-not at the moment." Her accent turns Englishy, stiff, a schoolgirl's.

"Who might there be? Besides us?"

"No one." Her eyes are sleepwalker wide.

Veronica interrupts. "So she's told you that story, Mulenberg?"

"Not all of it."

"She won't. Bad for the baby."

Wert coughs. "That's my wife's delusion. That the womb protects the child." His restless hand seeks hers again. She's his worry-bead.

Veronica lays a tender hand on her. "Shall I tell them?"

Between the two women Mulenberg senses that sudden waxy flow which can join the most ill-assorted of them. Just so, Veronica stood over the blood-spattered black-gartered, foolish haunch of pimp's meat, the night of his and Ventura's exploit—only with a gilt dress on her arm, offering it.

Soraya gives her the nod.

"She thinks—that we in Cabin Six are the only passengers aboard the *Courier.*"

Someone's signaling to enter the hatch. No head turns.

To Mulenberg, the other four in the center of the Free Room look like a war monument, each figure stricken in its own attitude—with him the one off-side.

Wert's fingers, so restless by themselves, are locked firm across his wife's belly. No bulge there, but anyone would know what he guards. Veronica, the tallest, pivots slowly, half-left, half-right, a weather vane at the top.

"Listen—" Gilpin says, "hear it?" The silence has changed. Where in a jet plane the noise assures a sense of flight, here until now it has seemed rather the stars that moved, the sun, while they themselves hung fixed, dead-center of the universal change, their vessel a great loosed shark, plundering the same space waves over and over, often as if ahead of its passengers. Who haven't moved an inch since Canaveral.

This is what it means to be in orbit. The universe pulls past you.

But now—with that same slight dislocation which occurs between the moving train and the train at standstill in the station, they're pulling past the universe.

"We're moving—" Gilpin says. "Aren't we?" Because that's what we're here for. He's the man who always has to do what he's here for.

The others nod, abstracted.

"I felt it, didn't I?" Wert says. "The child, turning?"

"Too soon, too soon." But her eyes are shining ahead.

Veronica's stopped pivoting. "Does it strike you—all day I've been thinking so. We're shifting course."

They're letting go. Of time.

The video is blinking   RETURN TO CABIN   RETURN TO CABIN   RETURN TO CABIN

When Lievering enters—moving like the king of the tightrope walkers, for one can't burst through an airlock—his first thought is that he has at last joined the gas chamber of his longings.

They're all so still and clumped, in a sharper ozone than he's ever smelled here. The great hubcap of the sun is at the porthole. In its white vision they press together, their arms hung down and wavering. Death is not yet their dignity. They're mayflies, the wings of their past lives folded glossy, ephemera collected around the glass cage of space. Inside which is the gold icon-shoe of traveling.

In the minute it takes to count heads they're Cabin Six again, already filing past him. They must have forgot to count—that precaution which should by now be routine. His entrance has reminded them. They've surely dared too many for the Free Room's air, by the half-drugged way they pass by him, their eyes ark-dazed and liquid, like people just out of the theater.

He's counted. "Where's Mole?" And to the next one in line— "Where's Mole?" And to the next one, the echo following them. He trails after them.

Mulenberg's alone again with his two communicants, his daughters. The model of the *Courier* is warm against his hip. Over in that corner is the tumbled pile of folders—what the cook at the ranch, a believer in spiritualism, would call "the evidential." He'd never believed the cook's clairvoyant writings, brought to the kitchen table from a half-dozen assorted famous dead—and all in the same round penmanship. Or the tales of horses that spooked under a dead man's saddle, or mossy fingers brushing your face in the dark like your dead sister used to tease you with, and when there was no live-oak within two thousand miles. Or a prediction that broke someone's back last Saturday, within only three and a half weeks—and two rodeos—of the specified time. He hadn't believed any of it but he remembers. He's alone.

His flesh creeps—and he knows it for spiritual delight. I know where I am, and will from now on. In a minute I'll go forward to the flight deck and tell them anything they want to hear. That, yes, I'll stay up there, for the two-year contract—or who knows, forever? Though there's no more forever in space than there is anywhere and no competency they offer him can compare with his own. No evidential.

Oh my honies, I'm still the passenger. But I know where I am. I'm on EVA, in extra-vehicular activity. Let me describe my machine.

He's on the vehicle of himself. Where all the delusions may prove real.

THE SICK BAY

"FEAR OF HEIGHTS can be a fear of rising." Lievering stretches in his hammock in the Sick Bay, next to Mole's. "A metaphysical fear—in a foolish way."

The crewman who subs as aeronurse and medical aide has gone off for his mid-shift meal. During the hour Lievering subs for him he's dubbed Mole his assistant here—the sub's sub's sub, Mole said, accepting. He loves any category which will keep him a kind of student. Lievering, whom the flight deck has tabbed for several such fill-in tasks which might require his refined agility in case of emergency, has in his spare time been coaching Mole in the special pratfalls of non-gravity living. But here they rest, and exchange legends. It's Lievering's talent to be able to make a man of eighteen feel he has one.

"What the f—is—what's metaphysical?" With Lievering one doesn't swear. Too time-consuming. Mole has long since been escorted through the etymology of "fuck."

"The science of being. Of all your being that is not physical. Or is behind it."

"Oh yeah, *meta*." Mole has had Freshman Greek under The Chape, but is ashamed of it. He purses his nose in what he hopes is a high-powered sneer. Facial expressions go awry here. "What happened to plain old fear of falling?"

"That's for when you do fall. Most of the time you don't—which is when the other takes over." He believes that his attacks, which he feels no need of here, are a kind of falling and rising both.

"Tell me again about the camp." Mole has learned that his new friend half-wants to be drawn back.

"You know I was only a year old when we left. Germany." This is the nearest he comes to revealing that his parents had never been in a camp.

"Uh-huh. Tell me anyway." Mole habitually imagines himself as an ongoing cartoon. Any action of his that he doesn't want to examine goes quick-quick into the daily strip—the cartoon of Mole. He has reels of it. It's a way of getting through. Lievering's word obsessions, which stop all action like a sentry's "Halt!", or his word pictures of what he couldn't have seen are just Lievering's cartoon. Mole smiles, gently swinging. Dormitory convention, summer-sailor dusks at gnat-time, sleepy-time in shuttle-land; it's all the same. Men in adjacent hammocks swap.

"Well, then. You remember what an energumen is? Sometimes spelled with an added *e*. Energumene."

"A devil-possessed, yes," Mole quotes as taught. " *'If ever there was an energumene, the devil is speaking with that woman's* tongue'— Sir Walter Scott. Was it always just the women in the camp went like that?"

"No. But it's them, certain of them that I think of, that come to me." Certain little Jewish women, often very pretty when young, who when they age—the short grapple-hook nose, the swarthy skin, the hooded eyes—look like small, winning owls. Competent, with the smell of many milk puddings behind them. Or those like retired elementary-school teachers, their breasts molded into one gray bird-bodice spread with a few gold chains, their feet leather orthopedic stubs. "Tenacious women, who don't serve the devil easy, or go under with just a quack. So they become—" Lievering can still shudder at his old nightmares. "Black-tongued, from more than thirst. Harridans, but because of hunger." He pronounces it with the *g* soft, to rhyme with "lunger," then corrects himself. "Hunger. The eyes get a snot-glare. Like green glass."

Mole shivers pleasurably. "And the men?"

"I don't like to—remember."

"Yes you do. Come on."

"They become—mirrors. Torture-mirrors. Double ones. From the back they reflect the torturer. From the front—you. Or sometimes they are walking lopsided, with purple tongues. Or with the skin in tatters. They have been hanged, or boiled, but won't die. For which they apologize."

"Br-r-r."

"Don't make a game."

"Come on. You do."

"You—devil." But Lievering is pleased. No one's ever said that, even the doctors. Mole's truths go as deep—or are as gauche—as his own.

"Wolf, Vulf. Jay-queeze, Jacques—" Mole teases. When a man tutors your legs and arms, sending you on practice swoops down corridors, prying you off walls and showing you how to arch the small of the back to control the ballooning and haul in, even coaching you on how to drink in non-G without either dribbling or making yourself into a blooming fountain of Versailles—then, if you don't want to become his baby you become his junior intimate. "Cohen-Lievering. The only guy outside the flight deck to carry a gun."

"I've told you. It's just a—document. And I don't carry it."

"Got a bore, hasn't it. Got ammunition."

"Such ammunition. Like hundred-year-old bird droppings. I see when they dig it up."

Mole gets up on an elbow, steadying the hammock, which makes him motion-sick, a fact he conceals. "For your info—they polished it. Everything . . . to a sweet shine. Those boys are something."

Lievering rocks with his hammock. "Yes, they were."

"What you mean—were? They in the past or something?"

Lievering elbows up. For some reason this is harder today than it has been, as if there's resistance somewhere. "You looked at our private documents?"

"Gun's a breechloader. Never seen one. First I thought they got it assembled wrong. Uh-uh. Not those boys." Under Lievering's stare he says loftily, "That hope chest in the cabin? Somebody has to. Study it." That pose won't hold. "Gilpin peeks. Saw him." He shakes his head, though tenderly. "Wouldn't you know. Couple of peewee books."

"Those are his own."

" 'kay. Sorry."

"Seen anything else of mine?"

"You mean that gre' beeg hankie with the gre' beeg *Elise a Jacques* on it?" He bats his eyes vigorously. "No."

"Oh—Mole."

Mole subsides happily, that being an inflection he's used to. His bad character is maintained—in his own eyes, where it's most needed. As to his identity, he knows that this man of two names and episodic life has never questioned it. A Wolf-Jacques looks beyond such matters, into the *meta* behind a person. Though when Mole thinks of Tom Gilpin and Lievering together—the two men he likes best in the world or even loves, their innocence frightens him. Of course, to Fred and himself, older people had always seemed innocent to a degree, or else they couldn't have accepted life as they had. But back there, on a known planet, the collective incompetence hadn't been so frightening.

There'd been a kind of trust that the veteran planet itself, heavy with the secrets of the millennia, would somehow advise.

He knows only one older person he'd rate as not innocent.

"How do you know so much about guns, Mole?"

"My father hunted once." Fanatic for specimens, when he was still a poorly paid biologist. Yet not ignoring the social aspects of being the first black member of a Virginia hunt. Later dropping the hunt and biology both, for wider armaments.

"Wolf, why'd'ya suppose they've stowed all our documents in the cabin with us?" In that silly-marked wooden hold. He snorted. "LOOSE EQUIPMENT. PASSENGERS." It's the only amateurish object he's seen here. As an amateur, that outrages him. Handkerchiefs, white fur, books; even if germ-proofed, the silly medley keeps reminding him. That he will be on a kind of planet. But one bald and new. "Looks like my old toy box. Or my sisters' hope chests. Why'n't they stow that stuff in the Payload Bay?"

Lievering's making a cat's cradle with a piece of string, an exercise for finger sensitivity. His nails are grown long for that purpose. "You've answered yourself. Loose equipment—hope! In the Payload Bay? No room for it." Chuckling, he completes the cradle and with one pulled whirl destroys it, his middle nail rearing up, triumphant. "I tell you, Mole. Words. You have to watch them. Like string."

But you're watching your nail. No point in saying.

"First comes the meaning," Lievering says dreamily. "Then the use. So often different. Like—we are in the sick bay. But we are not si— Mole!"

Next minute he's cramming a vomit bag to Mole's mouth, holding his head. It's a dry retch. "Here. The hammock's no good for you. Sit on the cot." He hauls Mole onto one of the alcoved beds, each built over its own bin. Shelves of affixed supplies are at the foot of each. He whips a menthol impregnated wipe from one of these and laves Mole's face. How indented the snub face is, a child's face, not merry for the moment, tucked, in a man's long head. How oddly most move here though, even this man-child. All except that lightfooted Mulenberg. Who never knows where on the ship he is, or near what supplies. But direct him to execute a movement and he responds accurately, even rhythmically, like an overgrown danseur. Or like the men in that brothel in Paris, where, when Lievering came to protest the display of his picture, he'd been invited to stay a night for free. Hard as it was to refuse anything offered him, he had.

"Balance is compromise," Lievering says. "Of the muscles." Actually he's surprised. Mole had been getting good at it. "But also it is the muscles' brand of faith. To the center of things. Which is always change." Under the shaved-wool head whose rounded bone declines to the neck like a skinny pair of haunches, Mole's face is bent to the bag he still clutches. The young object to compromise and to faith both, as Lievering knows well. That's their trouble, their prime paradox. "You get sick because you are in the place for it, yes?"

"Lievering, know why I love you?" Mole gasps, reverting to school sarcasm. "Because you're so honking, rat-trap silly." He grabs a Wipe and blows his nose. "I barfed because I thought of my father." He chucks the Wipe into the bin for it, pauses over the mark on the next bin: WASTATS, and leans back, lordly. "So now you know. And know what? I feel fine."

"You have a problem with your father?"

Mole makes use of a second wipe and disposes of it. "My father—has a problem with me."

"Aha. So that's what Gilpin knows about you?"

Mole sits up. "He say?"

"Anybody can see. Gilpin worries like a priest. Who has no God to help him out with it."

"Yeah. Yeah! Like—he's such a great guy. But like—yet he gets things so *wrong*."

Each has turned red, Mole for the betrayal, Lievering shaken by that slangy I love you. Slang upsets him, as too intimate. He has no list for it.

"Funny you should say priest, Wolf. I been kicking an idea around. That what that Free Room needs is a confession box. Oh, not the kind you talk into. To complain to. Like—for complaints in a bank. Only more serious. Or for a joke."

"A serious joke."

"Yeah. *Yeah.*"

They are both smiling.

"You know what, Wolf? You remind me of The Chape. Mr. Chape."

"He is who?"

"Our headmaster. *He* put up a confession box. Boy. Did he take it down quick. I *miss* Chape . . . What's so funny?"

"You young, you are all *italics*. But no wonder you miss—many things. Real food, at your age. Girls. I see how you squint at Veronica." Mole's experienced leer had shocked him almost as much as Veronica's response to it—one rover appreciating another.

"I miss *missing* them. It's all so calm here. Fake calm." Picking idly at the hasp of the chest under the bed he's sitting on, Mole gives a smart shiver. *Anti-calm,* as Freddie would say. Who made use of that prefix for everything. All the hasps and drawer pulls are recessed here, but there's more purchase on this one than on most. When you drop it it should give a clunk, but it doesn't. Mole looks down at it. "Nothing *clunks* here. . . . So okay. So I *did* put up a— Not a box—where would I get a—?" He looks round him at the stacks of conforming providables. "Everything *meshes* here. So wadd'ya know—that gave me where. On that grillwork in the Free Room—I hung it. Not a box, a pouch. That little waterproof pouch from the shark kit; you can write on it. I used that." Marking it in indelible ink PUT YOUR BEEFS HERE. Just like the one at school. "No one's used it yet, up to yesterday. I checked." No one but him.

"On that grillwork next to the instrument panel? Mole! That's the exhaust." Lievering hesitates. "I didn't see it."

"Maybe it got sucked in. Or maybe—I didn't do it."

"Mole—" Lievering's recalling all the colleges he's taught in—Mexico City, Barbados, Valparaiso. Stupid or smart, all the student eyes are the same. Hangdog, yet judging. "Mole—maybe I was never in the camp." He waits. The boy waits too. Some won't. Some will. "Maybe I need the camp. Like you need the box."

"Sure, man," Mole says absently. "Like we all need the camp." But this is only an acquired wisdom. He's far away. He turns back, stubbornly. "The box is different. Like we have the life we're standing in, huh? And we have the loopholes. Like when I think of riding through Japan where I was this summer—Japan is now a loophole. Or sometimes a girl from before. Or one that's coming. Like anyplace or anything you aren't now or maybe never was yet—that's a loophole. That's the loophole life."

The boy means more than memories, or dreams—or he would say. He's said exactly what he means—the loophole life. The blend of past and future which is at every person's core.

"And the box?"

"Oh the box's only to let off steam. Like a go-between, the Chape said."

Under that glance Lievering isn't sure he isn't one. "I would like to meet that Chape."

"You almost could of. I went back to see him before I—right after graduation." To suggest he come along. To dare him to. "But he'd been axed. Oh, they all still stand behind him even so, the school said. But he'd been axed."

"But he sounded like an institution there. *The* institution."

"Watch those italics," Mole said. "Oh, he was."

"So?"

"He shot his girl friend. *Chape.* Oh, he's out on bail. Nobody at the school helped raise it. But he's out." Mole shrugged.

In the end they all shrug at us. All of them. "Mole—if there was a box. What would you put there?"

The boy reaches for the vomit bag, tosses it into the MISC. TRASH and stands, stretching. "I did put." He drops his arms hard, almost to the ground, head wagging. "I put—'I miss Freddie.'" He pulls up slowly, his chest out. The name on the breast pocket, Fred Kim, is fully visible.

"Now, Mole."

"No, I mean it."

"A real person?"

"A real other person."

"Aha. Freddie. A girl friend."

"No. And not a boyfriend either." Mole drops his hands to the floor, bearwalks the four steps across its width and pulls up with an abortive flying motion of his arms, flopping back heavily on the thinly padded chest-bed. "Ouch." He rubs his narrow buttocks. "I'm beginning to hate gravity." He rests his chin on his hands. "You could say Freddie is my anti-friend."

"You are not being fey?" Lievering asks softly.

"No more than usual," Mole said.

After a while Lievering says, "To add anything to this ship is to be against it. You have not yet learned the ways of this ship. That worries me. You have not yet learned how we are going to have to live out there."

"On the habitat. Nobody ever mentions it. It's cuckoo, how nobody does."

"Because we are all thinking of it. Maybe not so much of how it'll be, yet. Of why we came." He reaches over to nobble Mole's head. "But not you, eh?"

"Do you all—just worry?" Mole said.

Lievering flips up the Hydrostat and pees, keeping the arc within, then drinks from a nozzle, arching to it. When he turns it's no longer definitive, the way most people still turn here, but as if he peels one turn from a store of them. "I wouldn't teach again for a thousand pounds. You've been taught—we taught you—only what's wrong. Not what's dangerous. But that's how we're going to live, understand? Not what's wrong. What's dangerous." He waits, expecting nothing. "So now excuse me. I have to go."

"Yeah, I know. Training you for EVA, aren't they."

"Unplanned EVA only."

"Which means what? Emergency?"

"Contingency."

"What's that mean?"

"Shortage of crew."

"Yah. Whyn't they say what they mean? Whyn't you?" He got up and peed, inaccurately. Reaching for a Galley Wipe he mopped and then tossed the wipe in the trash-all, pausing again at the lid of the bin next to it. "WASTATS. Of course, I remember learning them. Waste stabilizer tablets. They can't bury in this sea." About to sit on the bed again, he jumped up as if burned, raised the mattress and flipped up the long board below, and peered in. Lowering it slowly, he let go of the hasp and sat down again. "Nothing in it. Can you imagine that? And in the sick bay, too. *Wasteful.*" He looked up. Lievering was still standing there. "Sorry, Vulfie. Just learning to worry."

"No you're not. At your age you despise death. That does not work here. That won't keep you safe."

"What will?" Search as Mole has among the antique heads which were reproduced in his old Latin books, he's never hit on one analagous to Lievering's.

"You must covet it."

No, Wolf's face is not what's familiar to Mole, nor its features, but a quality of its skin, of its voice, even of what it has just said. He remembers it, looming over the nightmare bedclothes until his mother came.

"Don't—don't look so *German* at me."

White—the face goes. And those black lines from the nostrils, framing the mouth. No one must ever have said that to it.

"Explain yourself."

He can't, though he could draw that look. His mother's *au pair* girls —always German rather than French because "they stay under your thumb better"—had all had it at times. Gleeful toward some inner authority that tortured yet exalted them, as if some goddess had lent them shoes which were killing them yet raised them up. The one girl had had it when he caught her praying, the other whenever she caught and punished him. He can see it on the face before him, limned by the day's beard. The German look. His own mother's phrase for it. Sweat, on stone.

"You're right—" it whispers. "I need the camp."

In silence, Mole passes him a Wipe, then another and another, carefully placing each in the proper bin, until the flinty gray space between Lievering's lip and nose relaxes into flesh again, the sweat now sprouting merely acrid and tan on the fairness.

No, you're sick, Mole wants to say—and not because you're in the place for it. But Lievering is plainly dealing with a process known to him.

When it was over Mole ventured: "Don't you have to go?" and Lievering mimed, "Not yet."

After a while Lievering mimes, "I'm okay," but lies back in his hammock. Mole remains on the bed. The air smells clean but pharmaceutical, like in a good hospital. But who is visiting whom?

After a while Lievering says, "I do think of it."

"Of what?"

"The new station. For the EVA practice they show NASA slides of it. A cylinder, but to such a scale that to anyone walking its outer surface it will seem like a globe."

Both their voices are hushed. Like convalescents, Mole thinks. "What'll you do that for?"

"To inspect. You think they put those things up there and just leave them?"

"They have." From the dinner table gab at home, the sky, or at least the nearer sky, was full of smaller installations, not all of them merely satellites. Durations unknown, on some of them. Locations lost.

"Not like this. Not to live in. Or monkeys maybe, dogs. But not when it's us. There will be constant maintenance. The outer skin of these constructions is always the most delicate to manage. Like on the *Courier.*" Lievering braces his arms against the ceiling, which was lower on one side of the bay. His hammock stops. "You know about that?"

"The house was full of it." Even his sisters when they visited: Dad, how's with the tile?

"The—house?"

"My father's with NASA."

"Aha. So that's how you— So young. You have—what do you call it here?" Lievering's face is ordinary again, for him. But he always grimaces for slang. "Pull."

"Mm-hmm," Mole says. "The whole force of gravitation. But go on."

"No, you. So you saw special pictures? Of the L-5. Of the interior, too?"

They've reached a new stage in their companionship. He's ahead. Not sure he wants to be. "Dunno, how special. Only, I maybe saw more."

Great green-studded maps spread out under the cigarette smoke and the pointing, always well-cared-for hands, some with the weighty signet rings of colleges, an American style his mother always made fun of as juvenile.

"So what did you think of it?"

What had he? "The stations are always going to be bigger next time. They always have to cut down. From what they want. NASA's always the underdog." He can hear the self-pitying voices. All but his father's, who never pities himself, even professionally. "But they're always very proud of the greenery. There are always the factories and yeah—a playing field. Even a made river. All very tiny. And then the rest—you know. Where they live and all."

"They. You don't see yourself there?"

"Oh—me? I'll board at the 'Y' or something." Mole grinned. "The Jewish one. If they have one. Oh yeah—they have a church." No graveyard. But there's a church. "A chapel, that is—with a triple-denominational sanctuary. Revolving." He'd been saving that to tell Chape, who'd had high-church leanings. He's surprised at how much he does know. "Of course, it was always just what they called 'artists' renderings.' I never saw the finish line."

And of course they never put in any people, not even dots. It was all architectural drawings and luscious photographic glossies. Strictly rearrangeable. Gilpin's lonesome tale of the lost civilians, which had so touched Mole and his friends—that had been a lovely cautionary tale —for children. The dinner table had never thought of people at all.

"Then there's the Tomb," Mole said. "That's always there."

"The—?"

"For the Unknown. Not a soldier necessarily. Just ready." Mole nods. "Kind of nice, huh?"

"Nice?"

"I mean, there's nobody in it yet. That's what's nice."

Aside from girls' breasts and men's peckers, Lievering has the most overt body-changes Mole has ever seen. He can't decide whether Lievering's cakewalks around space, each day more lucidly sinuous, are rarefying him or animalizing him. When he's excited as now, his eyes actually darken.

"Nobody?"

"Gives all of us a chance, eh, Vulfie?"

Swung down from the hammock and standing, Lievering's height, too short for the head, is still a pedestal. He'll never be as short as

Napoleon, but there's lodestone in him. People will follow him. If not with love.

Mole sat up, spreading his long thighs and waggling his bent head between them. It's like a boxer's corner here.

"You ever hear of the Messiah, Mole?"

This calls for a lift of the chin. "My mother was Jewish." You don't *say*-eee is what they usually come up with, and with a second look.

Lievering only smiles, "Was?" He bends to the water nozzle and drinks, like an orator. Wipes his mouth with the back of the hand, not at all his style. "My father wasn't very Jewish either. But he was a refugee. They had a weekly cabal, in a Bloomsbury pub. I could go along, if I could keep mum and not shame him. Since a stuttering Bar Mitzvah boy was not possible to him, this was the manhood offered me." He's being a Jew now, old Europe suddenly tailoring him. He takes another drink, swallowing hard. "That Messiah, how they needed him. All of them escaped the Holocaust early, and without trials. Either their relatives were already with them, or there were now none to rescue. So we never talked of the six million. We were its fat-cats, which could not be said. But we needed a future, like any refugee. Maybe even more than most. And being what we were to the London world around us, it had to be a Jewish one. So—the Messiah." He's still smiling. "They weren't all educated men like my father. But needy. So one day it would be Spinoza and another day questions like, 'Where is the Messiah right now? Is he waiting around from the beginning? Or would he be born a real boy-child and then chosen, like the Dalai Lama?' "

"Or like Christ."

The laugh explodes unexpected. Has anyone ever heard Wolf laugh before? "Or merely chosen," he says. "Like all of—us. Like you."

They're still laughing when the medical aide enters and goes to the fridge for the soft fizz he drinks by the gallon. "Jokes? I could use one." His voice is loud. Switching gravities often brings on a slight deafening. His name is Francis Tuohy. According to Gilpin, he's a paramedical whose trade has involved him in compassions he's had no training for. According to himself, he's signed up because at thirty-odd he already has five kids and the base pay here makes him hit the side of his head in wonder. He is the youngest and smartest of the second crew, and can whistle Schubert's "Ave Maria" with either double stops or a hot-lips riff —even though, as he says, he both hates priests and is white. "Sure— a nice joke. Not too close to the bone."

"Wolf's just telling about a club he belongs to." At once Mole's sorry. Three's never good. Never fair.

But Lievering's solemnity can't be betrayed. "We sometimes did talk about the Christ. We Jews are very sensitive to Jesus, even though we don't believe in Him."

"My mother—" Mole gulps. "She used to say—if we don't believe He's the son of God, it's only because each of us already thinks he is it. Jewish men."

"We—?" Francis stares. "I mean—excuse me. Mothers can be anything." He dives into the fridge, where he can be heard chirring.

"As didn't your God make clear?" Lievering calls out to his back.

The medic emerges, laughing. "Thank God for jokes, and soda pop. Go on, Professor."

Lievering's not been a teacher for nothing, Mole thinks. But is laughs all the medic is shaking with?

"I must go. But yes, Mole—our club. We often discussed whether Jesus was dead the three days before He arose, or only in a certain state of being, for which my father tells them the word."

Mole groans.

"Never mind then, about the word. But we study over and over about the tomb. You know that part in the Bible where—"

"Tomb?" the medic says. "Which tomb you talking?"

"Both," Mole says. "Go on, Wolf."

"So in our—club—we have a famous folklorist. He is from Romania, where even forty years after Hitler you could see the broken synagogues, village after village, still closed. Maybe even now. He tells us that after the war, certain villages want their own tombs for the unknown soldier. Who is not to be so unknown that he could turn out a gypsy, or something worse. So in his hometown they build one. But when they come to put in their own man, there is already a body there. So it happens in village after village, until all Romania is afraid of these monuments. Then of course appears a rabbi, out of one of the ruined synagogues. He will tell them how to prepare their tombs. 'Take down that sign that says in your language The Unknown. Put up a sign that says The Eternal Occupant. In Hebrew.' This of course they won't do. 'So don't,' says the *reb*. 'Saves us from building our own.'"

The medic with a wild laugh dives again into the fridge. His voice comes muffled. "Always something in the tomb." The open door shows so many medical bottles that Mole wonders whether the bottle brought out is pop. Tuohy closes the door with his hip. "Yea bo."

"So." Lievering is hoarse. His voice gives out fast. "S-so the folklorist says to my f-father. Who is always the last to laugh. If ever." His voice fades, his eyes bulge, his mouth opens and shuts like a bird's. "So the folklorist says, 'Why, Lievering, the Messiah's like us, he's a refugee. He's always looking for a new boardinghouse. But since he is the Messiah he always gets there first."

In the silence the medic's half-deaf grumble to himself can be heard: Somebuddy always does. He catches Mole's eye.

"You're like my father, Mole. You don't laugh."

"No," Mole says. "Like mine."

Lievering is suddenly shy. "I bore you, I beg your pardons. When the daze comes over me, I have to watch out."

"Daze of what, Mr. Lievering?" The medic leans forward, alert.

Lievering hesitates: "Of—brotherhood."

He's halfway out the bay in his graceful way when Mole calls out, "Hey—what's that word? Of your father's." He cocks an ear. "Oh boy. Spell it."

"P-s-y-c-h-o-p-a-n-n-y-c-h-y."

Mole fakes a retch. "What's it mean?"

Pedagogy is Lievering's only malice. "The state the Messiah would be in. If he's—already up ahead." He smiles. He's gone.

The medic and Mole look at one another.

"We have to watch him, you know. He has a history. Well, come on." Frank squats on the floor. They're about to play crap, which they often do.

Mole follows, pulling his legs into lotus position. "His features are sure —classical."

"Heh. Jews were all lady-killers once, weren't they? In the Bible. Except one." Frank's slow bringing out the dice. "What Jesus felt in the tomb. Sounds like my wife. She's very devout, you know."

Mole does. Frank reminds him of his brothers-in-law, once normal post-collegiates, now like stuck to the armpits in bowls of breakfast cereal, from which all their talk issues glutenized by family life. Though Frank has other backlogs of thought—at least when he shoots crap.

"Frank— On the station out there . . . that monument. *Is* it empty?"

The medic reaches out and slaps Mole's thigh. "Wish I could sit like that. Too much of this." He wedges the pop bottle in a wall slot.

"Frank—*is* that pop?"

"You go too far, kid. But yeah—it is. Surprised?"

"No. You're a good family man."

"Don't get too smart." But he hasn't brought out the dice. He's in one of those nostalgia pockets nobody's exempt from here. He's in a loop-hole.

"Frank. *I* know. Even my age, I get, you know. Like I spoke of my own mother like she's in the past."

"So you did." He's awarded a grin.

"So? Then bring out the dice."

They're pretty ones, gift of his oldest daughter, who's thirteen. They stay in Frank's palm. "Thanks. But you've got me all wrong."

Mole unfolds his legs, a dramatic effort. "So what singed your eyebrows off, Frank?"

He has good control. "So you noticed."

"Who wouldn't. All that grease."

"Your friend didn't."

"He's not geared to faces. Or not to ours. What happened to you?"

Frank shakes the dice gently, but doesn't roll. "Not supposed to say. Maybe I better. Since they tapped me to watch over you. You mischievous, interfering"—he stands up and bears down on Mole's shoulder—"absolutely first-class offspring." He reaches down, tugging at Mole's name tag. The dice scatter on the floor, blessedly staying there. In the sick bay, G-force is therapy. In silence Mole gathers them up.

"There was a fire in there. Still hot when they called me in with my stuff."

"In the Free Room?"

"The day salon? No. Why, anybody smoking?"

"Gee, no," Mole says righteously. "Would anybody?"

"Now and then—some of the guys think they smell—maybe the Iranian lady?"

"You been sniffing around our Hygiene Section, hah? No, that's for the baby, Veronica says. Some cream she's got."

"Veronica, huh."

"Look, Frank." Mole's hoarding the dice. "Tell me or not."

"Fire was on the flight deck. Big screen that maps deep space, which stars we're passing through. Behind there."

"Anybody hurt?"

"Not bad. Flash burns. When we went in, a smaller spot blew." Frank goes to a shaving mirror. The skin between his brows and his eyes is marked with a corona of red spokes, like when the oven exploded in Mole's mother's face. "Everything in this dreadnought comes out symmetrical," Frank murmurs at himself. "That's a World War I expression, dreadnought. But it didn't get my whistle." He trills a phrase that

Freddie, an oboeist when he could find a gig, would have cottoned to. "No, nobody hurt bad. The guy that would have been if he was in his seat, wasn't there."

Mole's trying to recall the manual, with that long diagram of the three-level flight deck, which came up from between the center pages like a pop-up. They wouldn't let you on the deck but they wanted to impress you with it. "Behind a screen. What could be there?"

Frank's daubing on more grease. "Ouch. Maybe I should use tannin. . . . Who knows? Anyway, we're now on Auxiliary Environment."

"Where was Dove?"

"Dove? Oh yes, Dove. Understudy Captain Dove? He was on break with the rest of us. When we bust in. Dove's beak is now a goodly pink." He turns. He has a glob of yellow on each red spoke. "Looka me. Sloppy Louie the Sun King, huh?" When Mole doesn't answer he drops to his haunches beside him. "Sorry. Five kids—you play games. But I see you're a man."

"I saw the deep-space map in the *Courier* model at the Goddard. Weird cobalt blue they'd painted it. You'd think they'd know better about the color of space. But they never got to installing the whole flight-deck panel."

"There is only one. Finished just in time. This one. Never saw it myself before." Hugging his knees, the medic inches across the floor on his haunches in one of the exercises mandated for the lower back.

Though Mole's buttocks are too scraggy for comfort, he sometimes joins in and they have a kind of butting cockfight, hands barred. Not today. "I saw a map once—for the habitat." At home, one of those evenings. "The Tomb was drawn on it." It was exactly the shape of those stone beehives still on some of the old thruways, usually near a thruway authority base. He'd always thought them kind of runic, a public shrine to the art of getting thru; the Japanese had such things. But asking a state trooper, he'd found they were only storage for road salt. "The map code was on it." Like for everything: Factory A. Factory B. Recreation Hall. Hospital. Factory C. "The Tomb was right on the main drag." With a big waste-space around it. Or so you would think, comparing other allotments. Marked Platform X, it was." Delivering or receiving? " 'What do you suppose that's for?' he'd said, pointing it out to his mother when they were clearing the table, no maids being allowed in at these sessions. 'Not for the Space Angel,' she'd said. She is still in the past tense.

"Frank, you're shivering."

"Burns do that. Body defense."

Even such a small burn? Mole eyes the labeled shelves here, where nothing rattles. No urns of ruby and blue, like the trick pharmacy in Georgetown. Everything here is space-serious. Add to it at your peril. Or subtract? "My mother's big on body defense. She says you have to be. And big on the mind. Or else the medicines will take over. The pharmacopoeia, she calls it." She has a wide range of such terms; she's not a tenth cousin of Freud's for nothing. Once, clearing up those maps and models to dump in his father's study, she'd snorted "Prosthetics!" He'd followed her into the study, which was lined with more models his father himself dusted, to ask what that meant. "Artificial limbs." She'd swept out a hand. Took him a minute to catch on she meant NASA— maybe all of it. It was she who taught her three to pit their bodies toward the world. Into it, she'd said—not against. And not always in a machine. Oh, come on, Elsa, you drive that Porsche breezy enough, his father said. Of course, Moleson. It's my *subordinate.*

It occurs to him that he gets his italics from her. And that he's here as much on her account as on his father's. Much in the same way, she'd sent his sisters, those Cathedral School types his father had insisted on, to the midwife instead of the hospital, where they did handily, almost too quick for their husbands to take flash-shots of the births. Whee, isn't he lovely, Elsa said, handing round to his father's colleagues the snapshot of her first grandchild pulping from between her elder daughter's engorged thighs. 'Scuse it, boys, his father said, red under his brown: Elsa thinks she did it. No I don't, Moleson. But I did wear out two fans.

Bitter and saucy behind him, she picks up the models of glory and mulls them. Because of her he is pitting his body into the universe. Without coveting death.

"Hurray, he's breathing," Francis says. "Our living Buddha. I was beginning to wonder. Or are you just having a BM?"

He's straining to drag her forward and over the miles set between him and her since a week ago Saturday. Hup, Mother, and over the stile. In a minute she'll be here, distant maybe but as alive as he—no loophole for me, sonny. No, Elsa. Wish I could hear her on Lievering. Probably she even knows his big word. Forward, Mother, out of the past.

"Seven, come eleven," Mole says, scooping the dice, throwing them and untangling his legs all in one graceful swoop which brings him back to the cot bed, where just as rhythmically he raises it, and holding it up, lowers himself into the box below.

"What the hell you—?"

The bed's resisting him, like a lid. He pushes against it, panting.

"Multiple Failure . . . Not Contemplated. Remember? On all those print-outs. Of the mission, they meant . . . Well, I'm—contemplating it." He's big for the box. But if he curves himself in, it fits.

"Get the fuck out of there." Tuohy, straining against the upraised cot, hauls him up and out. Red to their Adam's apples, they waver at each other like two cocks.

"I'm—gee, Frank, that lid was—weighs a ton."

"You fool, it's on a spring."

Mole stands up, weaving, vibration like an undercarriage beneath his feet. He misses his old sneakers. He tries to grin. "Tuohy, you're not shivering anymore." His own teeth are chattering.

"I should be. Suppose you'd done that while I wasn't here."

"I didn't . . . Hey, look." He's thrown a seven, and a four. Shakily, he throws again. A six. A five. "Hey—these dice loaded?"

He only meant it in fun. But the medic says gently, "Sure, Mole. That's the pair that are. Didn't you know? Thought you were just humoring the old guy. My kids do a lot of it." His voice is husky. "She just wanted me to have all the luck I could. Daddy's little baby girl." He whistles softly. *Mam-my's li-tle ba-bee loves short-nin bread,* the tune is. Mole stands at attention. Frank's bringing his baby girl over the stile.

Though when the elders are finished feeling, then better to make like you're sloping off; it's less embarrassing.

"Where you going, kid?"

"Galley. Time for—ah—that cold porpoise and purée of bog."

"Come on. It's not that bad."

Actually it isn't. Better than the airlines. Only the presentation is odd. Booger-shaped solids and virtuous essences. What he craves is a little home-style disorganization. What saddens him is he's getting used to the other. Not without a fight. "Sure. But I still have my standards."

"You sure do. That's what we cherish you for."

"You what?"

"That's what I said."

They are both embarrassed.

"Then level with me."

The corona framing Frank's eyes goes up. "Ouch." He claps a hand to it. "About what?"

Once, playing tic-tac-toe in an office anteroom, he'd overheard his father interrogate. He reached out a finger, lightly spreading the grease on those red marks. "What else on the flight deck scared you shitless, Frank?"

In a similar silence, had his father offered the guy a cig? No—asked for one. Mole stretched. "Think I'll have some of your pop."

When Frank comes back with the bottle, he says: "The deck did. The deck itself. I can only tell you what I saw."

"Please." His father had said—"Do."

"I never been in Outer before. But I been a rocket buff since I was in jeans. Seen every model they ever had at Canaveral. Never seen a panel like that one. Yards of it. The controls alone are like jewelery. Some of the screens longer than a man. Than a big man. And like three-dimensional. Like you could almost live in them. Who knows, maybe four dimensions, once you get the hang of it. They've even got that radio-communications setup broadcasts signals —you know—for pickup. In case of other peer groups hacking around the universe."

"Like at Goldstone. That desert one? But those discs are huge."

"They've brought it all down to size. Things when I was your age were spread out a whole hangar. Or like—remember the old comput- ers? No, you wouldn't. That's the first rule, kid. Bring it all down to size." He crouched forward. "That's what we do best. And it's marvelous. Want to know the truth? I'd pay to come."

"And the men in there? On the flight deck. What size are they?"

"And the men are there—" the medic says in a dramatic whisper. "In their shirt-sleeves. They have perfect G-force there, perfect environ- ment. Royalty. And don't begrudge them it. You barge in like we had to; there they are. Like those cookie-cutter men in toy cars or like in a drag race. All profile. No full face. Because all five are glued to the panel. The three who're on inside break can ease more, or take turns leaving deck. Or help put out a fire. They did that."

"Dove was on outside break?"

"Yeah. He hauled me in. And my kit."

Throughout this narration the medic's excitement has grown on him as if it comes from an outside agent, pounding his fist in his palm for him, rolling his eyes. Now he walks on tiptoe, his arms stretched graph- ically, watching the story issue from between his own fingertips.

"Frank. Five and three makes eight."

The medic stops in his tracks.

"And one makes nine."

"So it does."

"But the manual calls for—" A flight-deck crew of ten.

Foolish Mole. Never interrogate in a straight line. Frank's strong fingers are at his elbow, the coronaed eyes too close. "Kid. Go eat."

In his grasp Mole goes cunningly limp. "Frank—you like being scared?"

He's released. "Told you I'm a buff. Maybe I do. When there's—good reason for it." He can't resist a slight smile. "Sends my wife up the wall."

"When there's Quaker duty, huh?"

"Somebody told you about that. Yeah."

"And I'm part of that duty, huh? You were never tapped. To watch over me. Frank? Thanks."

Now wait. Say nothing. Let him come down on it.

"To let you come aboard like that," Frank says slowly. "Cold. Men with boys of their own. For a joke. And when—"

"When what?"

"Nothing."

Repeat their name, his father said once, in a rare briefing on how Mole should deal with a touchy housemaster. Names never tire. "Frank—"

"Space is curved, they say," the medic says angrily. "That mean we people using it have to be crooked to match?" He bangs a fist against his head. "Ouch. Look, leave me be, will you? I have to write a letter home. Every week, I promised them. Hey. Hey, Mole. Don't go all dreamy on me." The medic's voice softens, but like they all do when they've had enough of you, and hard tit to you. Like they have your interests at heart, but now scram. He can't know of the three syllables which have entered Mole like a silver corkscrew. *Using space.*

When Mole draws to his full height he's almost six-five. Girls saw. Men noted only the shamble, and bone sockets wrong for basketball. Or if they knew his father—the flecked eyes. He'll say "Frank" one more time, he thinks. You, Frank—answer, hear? Or else I'll—I'll swallow your dice. Though there's no porthole, the sick bay has a reflector to the corridor. Out there he can see the medic's life-support suit hanging on its hook. When Lievering goes for simulation practice on how to maneuver on the surface of the *Courier,* he wears a heavier version called an EVA Mobility Unit. It's all the same thing. Maybe if I had my life-support on, this would be easier. Because I have this problem. I'm a joke, yes. But I'm also the Joker. "Frank—"

The medic raises his head.

"Does my father—does Canaveral know it yet. That I'm here?" Using space?

"Come here, kid. I won't bite. But if you weren't such a lummox I'd take you on my lap. *And* your sidekick." He snorts. "Some of us are psycho, yeah. Some of us are only panicky."

The dice lie on the floor. Mole kicks at them. "You're going to tell me —I know what you're going to say." At what passes for night here he's awakened and gone into the Hygiene Unit to squat and think of it. Or gone to the document box for Fred's gift book, which dealt with all space as if it was only an architecture meant to soothe, whereby inconvenient people could be prayed away. He's not sure what his prayer is. "Maybe—that my father's aboard?"

The medic gets up, goes to the fridge. Instead of opening it, he leans his face to cool there. "Your age, I worked Amnesty International awhile. We talk to a guy in jail, or a woman, we always do like this, for good-bye." He turns up his hands at the wrists, "See? Put your hands against mine. They always do like this, for good-bye. They always did it, no matter what language. Paddy-cake. Through the bars."

Mole puts his palms against the medic's, which are horny and greasy both.

"We don't fly like the canaries here, kid. Everybody knows they work us from outside. Like the wardens did. That's what shook me up. That one gray screen that's responsible—to them. Then one little hot spot and it goes blank. Like my old Murray switch-box at home, when a fuse blows. But *they're* the ones at home."

Mole can see their own box in a closet under the cellar stairs.

"For a minute you're in the dark, that's all," the medic is saying.

"Then what?"

"Then you repair. Or they do. And that's the glory of it." Tuohy removes his hands from Mole's. At the mirror again he pats his face all over delicately, with a Kleenex, like a man using aftershave before a date. "Us—against the universe." He drums his feet on the floor as if the universe stops there. "Glory, hear? All those wars've made us ashamed to say it. Teaching kids like you only bad men have it. Or want it." He reaches behind him. "Here. Have some of my fizz."

Mole drinks. It tastes like—fizz. "Thanks, Frank. Now I am a man."

The medic chuckles. "Everybody needs a little . . . paddy-cake. You all right now?"

You're the one needed it. "Thanks. You must be a very good father."

"Right." The medic brings out a pencil, free of its string. Here and there the rules break down. Here and there. "So—"

"I'll scram."

"Enjoy your meal. Hah—porpoise. I'll write the kids that."

"We had it in the Bahamas, on a rented schooner. The captain insisted." Mole lingers.

"Honest? What's it taste like?"

"Like the inside of a girl."

Frank's head comes up, slowly.

That's right, Frank, revise me. Still think I need a lap? "Silly idea aren't they, Frank. Captains." Mole ha-ha's giddily. "On a bridge, with a spyglass. Passenger idea."

The red coronas are hard and shiny now. They still can wrinkle.

"Tuohy?"

The medic sits up.

"Which side you on?"

"Side?"

"The men or the kids?"

"Heh. Close to the bone. Very close to the bone." He doesn't smile.

"Maybe I should ask Dove a few things."

"That stooge? You ask Dove anything, Dove is what you get. Kid—" He shakes his head, flicking Mole's breast pocket. "Okay, *Mr.* Kim. Whyn't you just hold tight and wait till you're called?" He mutters under his breath.

"I heard that. And pray you won't be, you said. Then why won't you level with me?"

"You walked into it." He's moving his letter page in a circle under the pencil, as if he can't figure out how to intersect with it. "And so did I."

"Walk—" Mole says. "When we can *fly.* Who wants to *walk* anymore?"

"You mean that?"

"Almost." He's dizzy with it. High—on fizz.

"I keep wondering what my kids will think about that when they're old enough. So now I know." He flaps his arms like wings. "Like father, like kids. So you're a buff, too? Like the rest of us? Then settle down to it."

"What is this fizz?" Mole said.

"Potassium juice. For the athaletic muscles. People win Olympics on it. I just take my cut. Expect to do a lot of running, out there. Be in a factory, they said. In a medical capacity. What the factory makes, I dunno."

"Well, you have the run of the ship here. You're crew."

"Second crew. The others on it understudy the deck. Which means they don't get away from it. My bailiwick's here. I run the supernourishment supply." He shook the bottle. "With other supplements."

"We don't get this in the cabin. Cabin Six, I mean."

"No-o. You're administrative bigwigs. You're not going to be athaletes."

"Frank—who are—the rest of us?"

But the medic, taking up his pencil, is lettering a large HOW ARE THE   HOW IS   In the first space he draws two rabbits with their ears intertwined, in the second a plump cat holding up its name. He's quite good at it. The finished letter will be processed to wait for the return voyage and then at last go local to the Canadian border where his family lives as Americanly close as possible to his wife's Quebec. Months may pass, more.

"You're a talented guy. Drawing, whistling."

"The wife takes care of their mortal souls." Tuohy now limns in a houseboat marked WE, with a brace of giraffes nodding from behind its smokestack toward toward two horses, one bonneted, the other dropping a turd. Then come a number of auditing birds and finally a far shore with a crowd of minute button-faces, labeled YOU. Presiding over the deck is his own face recognizably hung in the air and rayed like a sun. Below it is a woolly-haired figure with its hind end in a tub. YOUR DAD AND A CUSTOMER.

"Stand me up *straight*," Mole said.

"Me, too." Gilpin enters. He and Mole smile shyly. Since Mole's apprenticeship to Wolf they haven't more than greeted during the routines, often taking their places silent throughout, well-drilled pupils with nothing more to exchange. Since that time in the Free Room, everybody's doing it.

"Bad knee again, Frank," Gilpin says. "What I need's a space walking-stick. I dream of what it could be. An electric grip, like a baseball glove for buttocks only, that follows after you like a nanny does a toddler. Or a crystal cane, really an elongated ray, that springs from your palm. Both palms. Or a floating walker, with ball-bearings that react weightfully." He groans. "Dear, dear weight, remember how steady it was? I would like to eat some—like chocolate."

"I'm your nanny," Frank said. "Strip."

In order to have his knee examined, Gilpin has to. "Jump suits. Rightly named. Always jumping from them to get in touch with yourself all at once." He hangs his canvas fatigue suit on a hook where it slowly reshapes itself. Ditto his thermal underwear. His anatomy is solid and much younger than his face, whose skin, even in their short time aloft crinkled further by the dryness, has begun to distance itself from its own features, a much used atlas showing these valleys and peaks.

"You have a Maine skeleton."

"So I do. How'd you know that, Mole?"

"We used to classify ourselves, at school."

"What were you?"

"Ibo aristocrat from the Niger. Mixed with Silesian cattle-dealer, from the mountains of Glatz." His and Gilpin's laugh chime together. It's a relief to talk on his own level. He suddenly feels great.

Frank removes a clear plastic bracket from Gilpin's left knee. He holds it dangling. "NASA aeromedical brace." Shrugging, he opened a drawer full of other lustrous shapes—my moonbeam drawer, he calls it —and tosses the brace in. He pokes a greenish area just below Gilpin's kneecap. "Old synavitis, looks like."

"Had that since I was sixteen. Wave smashed me on the dory once, lobstering."

"Oh? Catholics love lobster," Frank says glumly. "My wife."

"So do Silesians," Mole grins. "But aren't stinkpots used for lobster runs now?"

"Outboards, sure. But there are still the waves." Gilpin sighs. "The January sea."

"Golly, I could use a real swim."

Both older men look at him silently.

Gilpin breaks it. "Where'd you get that sunburn, Frank?"

Frank, poking in other drawers, ignores them.

"Bartendering," Mole says. "On the flight deck. Tom—you know a word—psychopannychy?"

"You've been talking to Lievering," Gilpin says sharply. "Mole— you'd better understand about him. Everybody's head is—plagued with symbols. Look at me. Look at Frank here. Look at you. But Wolf lives by them. He's like a man brought up on wine instead of water—or in his glass everything turns to it."

"He's some man to put on EVA then."

"Maybe that extra coordination comes of it. Of being all of a piece." Tom is bent to the striations left by the brace on his knee, smoothing them.

"They have a little cart travels along the surface of the ship, to examine it."

"Oh?"

"He doesn't like carts."

"Why not?"

"Hitler took away the Jews in them."

Tom's hand stops. "There you are."

"So—it's not just—brave of him?"

"What's brave? Sure, admire him. Pushing his little diagnostic hut along, like that old Geiger counter he brought with him. Testing what we've put into the universe. Meanwhile, the universe is streaming past him. The others, they'll be intent on the job. But Lievering, he can't admit that this trip's in the end like any other—just travel. He's looking ahead."

"To death?"

"Farther than that. To legend. He'll tell you it."

"He did."

"The unknown in the tomb? Waiting for us? No matter how far we go? And when we get there already there?"

"You take any stock in it?"

"Sure I do."

Frank has lifted his head out of the drawer.

"The one who goes before?" Gilpin says it lightly but like Scripture.

"Sure. But I'm a popularist. Look in any grave."

Frank's ready to impart information. He always does it with pomp. "In the erect position, Mr. Gilpin, a vertical line from the center of gravity passes in front of the knee."

"Hear that. And me with my center now so—moot." He looks down himself, shaking his head.

Mole looks shyly away from the distinguished pubis.

"Not Mole's. His runs straight down the middle, eh, Mole?" Frank's brought out a small packet he's tossing from hand to hand. "Why'ncha try the Jacuzzi, Mole, maybe it'll run cold for you. Or maybe one of the girls'll let you in. Watch out though for that feisty Iranian."

"Lay off him, Frank. Remember your youth."

"I prefer to remember my middle age. My early middle age. On a Sunday afternoon, a nap with the wife. With the kids at the rink. You know—I believe this is Sunday afternoon."

"Where?" Gilpin says.

"Here," Mole says passionately. It has welled in his throat. "Here, too. Anyplace, you can always feel the Sunday molecules gathering." Around Washington, about 1 A.M. Saturday night. "According to a friend." His live-in girl, that was.

"So this is already a place to you, then," Gilpin said.

"I have a present for you, Mr. Gilpin. Rare, very rare. Only one within a million miles far's I know. I brought two."

"Why, Frank, that's very kind of you. What is it?"

Frank unrolls it slowly. "An Ace bandage."

"An Ace bandage. My dear Frank."

Slowly, firmly, the homely stretch of pinkish cloth is bound in overlapping circles around the swollen joint. Mole, kneeling to watch, can smell the menthols of the locker room after track.

The bandaging is done with art. Gilpin's knee is scarcely thicker. "God it feels good." He extends the leg. "Hermann Oberth couldn't have designed it better."

"Those little metal Ace fasteners shaped like dog pads—what about them?" Mole says huskily. He's been waiting for them.

"Can't risk those in heat; this cloth self-locks," the medic says absently. He's staring joyously at Gilpin. "Never knew you were a rocket-buff. Oberth—wasn't he a fast man though? And how about Wernher von Braun?"

"Still have a spot of resistance to those other Teutons. Okay, Von Braun—even though he wanted metal space suits, like armor." They all laugh. "But the ghouls like Krafft-Ehricke—ever hear his Extra-Terrestrial Imperative? No? Heard him give it in Alabama, once." Gilpin half-closes his eyes. He is lecturing. "Confi-*denz* in a soaring future is the ess*enz* uff our techno-scientific civilization. Und Vestern Mann's greatest message to *Mann*kind." He opens an eye to wink at Mole. "Erosion uff ziss confi-*denz*, threatens—zee Vahlue Sys-tem." He opens both.

Mole's clocking their two faces, his and Tuohy's, like a boy in a bar, waiting to be asked to drink.

Gilpin's arm is quickly around his shoulder. "Well, here we are. Three —buffs." He unhooks his suit and eases in the game leg. "Good old ACE."

"Brought 'em along for my own varicose." Frank gives him a hand with the suit. They all do it for each other without a thought, the women, too. "In non-G, liquid pools in the lower extremities. Then I go and spend most of my time in artificial G. Does the job, good enough."

Gilpin is dressed. "Cheap candy. Not the real stuff. But we'll get used to it."

"R-r—right. Trouble is, too many people round here have too much imagination." Frank has a prop cigarette he sticks in his lip now and then. He reaches for it. "Extra-Terrestrial Imperative. My God, I never heard it better said."

"Nor worse."

"Ah, come on, Mr. Gilpin. Your bark's worse'n your bite."

"So it is, alas." Gilpin prepares to leave.

"Well, ta-ta. Any trouble, come by and I'll rewind that for you. Or we'll shoot a little crap." The medic winks at Mole, or tries to, reaches for the grease, slaps some on, stows the tube in its drawer and takes up his pencil again, all in one go.

"Your hands are your imagination, Frank, but they won't let you know. What was it on the flight deck? What's going on?"

The pause now hasn't the comfort of a bar's or a Sunday's. Mole steps in. "The other bandage, Frank, where's that one?"

"Why? Want me to save it for you? Ah, come on, both of you. Off me." He twiddles his pencil. "I'll tell you where. It's on that gutsy Iranian gal's back. The posture changes here are rotten for it. Some nights she can't sleep, I bind it for her. I couldn't see how they qualified her, till she told me. She really comes in here to talk to me. Midwife stuff."

"Seat Six?"

"Seat Six to you, boy. A princess born—and she is one. You know they're gonna do half the parturition out there in non-G, to see if there's pain or isn't there—a test case? Why'd she agree to it? It's not the pain is it, I said; it's not the limelight." He chuckles. "She answers, 'Mr. Tuohy—did your babies breast-feed?' " Over his saw-toothed red eyelid the forehead itself is now a faint pink. "So. Time for my sleep-shift. You guys never gonna eat?" He makes for the cot, tapping a pill-dispenser, tearing open the packet, popping the pill in his mouth and flinging the empty in the bin all the way, a soda-jerk ballet.

"Frank—whistle something first. I get hungry for live music." Mole knows he really is hungry for the friends whose secret image of themselves comes out in the music they cluster to. It's the kind of key to yourself you can safely hand around, a form of comradeship.

But Frank's whistling is a form of speech. An ironic commentary on his thoughts.

This time it's a medley, bits of anthems thrown together. There's the "Marseillaise." Then something German. Then the "Volga Boat Song." Through them the "Star-Spangled Banner" rides triumphant, giving in to a marine-band drill style catch for some bars, rising in a virtuoso trilling toward the awful high note of "Fre-ee" and flattening just as the voice always does, to the not quite lame "ah-ah of—the brave."

"I always like that sour ending," Mole says. "After that impossible high." Bringing back those shrieking school periods in postures of Attention warm with body-smell, and the imminent release onto the grass of recess—always with the same large sense of belonging to a great if bumbling nation. Not one too neat, like the French.

"Doesn't do to save from war to war," Gilpin says. "The glory never quite fits."

Frank's already snoozing, braced against his moonbeam drawer whose contents he sometimes toys with, shifting the prosthetics there like instructive playthings, cannily estimating their non-performance. The dummy cigarette is lax between his fingers. Though his eyes are shut the flashburns make them seem open in a secondary mask of fright.

Gilpin, bending to slip the cigarette into the sleeper's breastpocket, nicks in his head at the sight. "Or the rocket's red glare."

It has grown cold in the Sick Bay. The Auxiliary Environment maybe takes a while to come up to scratch. Mole unsnaps the thermal coverlet from the base of the cot and draws it over the sleeper to protect his body defenses.

"People when they sleep—they look so—Unknown."

Outside in the general corridor he and Gilpin part. Gilpin eats in the cabin's galley. Mole eats with the second crew, where he also sleeps. Though now and then—he suspects, when something hush-hush is going on there, they let him sleep in Cabin Six, for which they've given him a super hang-style sleeping bag. They've been nice to him.

During liftoff this corridor was in total non-G. as it will be again during docking. Meanwhile, a kind of limbo gravity is maintained here, not as forceful as in the main rooms of their section of the ship but sufficient to allow for "ground" walking, and freeing them to wear their fatigues. If it weren't for the gymnastics in the drill room, where he and Lievering nose-dive and float like giddy Wordsworths in daffodil light —"Which poem are we walking to, today?" Lievering will shout in the gaiety that overtakes him only in non-G—Mole might altogether forget the altered world they're going to.

This corridor's also the least demanding part of the vehicle, having none of the labelings which define and instruct everywhere else. There are even no handrails, though the manual showed them. Perhaps an economy. No one will be here anyway in the crucial times of ascent or descent—or entry and reentry, as he must learn to think of it. Now its long bare limbo is soothing. He's standing in a cylinder slightly more than man-high, flattened enough at its base to accommodate his in-flight passenger-sandal, or even—he can imagine it—the soles of men soon to be walking into a new century. Or riding.

It's a kind of log cabin of the mind, here. A small, unadorned place, of the sort minds have gone to since the beginning of mind, hoping for clarity.

What's the medic so afraid of? What frightened him on the flight deck, that he almost certainly knew of, well before? That he saw in extension, in the weird shine of the star-screen? Or in the unexpected flame from behind it? Against which he'd carried in his kit.

"I-Ching, a-ching, ching," Mole says, tapping the no-color almost soft wall with the nails he's let grow long here, imitating Lievering. That is what he and his live-in girl—the one no one knew about, not even Fred —used to say, tossing the omen-sticks onto the counterpane or his drawing table, or flinging sticks of kindling onto the open fire of the apartment he'd moved to because of her, refusing to occupy hers. She, transferred back now by the consular office she worked for, had sometimes chanted in Finnish along with the sticks. She wasn't too old for him, her sticks had always foretold. But whenever he tossed them, he was too young. I-Ching. A-ching, ching.

She'd been the most diagnostic of his girls. In glimpses, he still likes to talk to her.

This is a glimpse. Loopholes are fine and necessary, like the bedtime-past one scrutinizes, but they don't move you on. A glimpse is wet with the future, like the foal Chape once sent all the senior form to watch get born, saying: Should have done it when you first came.

In it he can see what scared Frank. The robot vehicle itself, moving on. Not a true robot, the *Courier*. Nothing like the goofy single-task satellites that seeded earth's almost suburban belt of them, one or more at this moment reporting the *Courier* into the homes of civilians who may or may not look at it. Seeable in Finland, too, she'd said. No, the *Courier*, half-rocket, half-plane, is also a hybrid in brain. Humans cached somewhere on Canaveral or elsewhere are breathing over it as they can. To those cached here. On the not quite robotomized, yet less than autonomous *Courier*. That's what Frank saw.

It's on the edge of glory, too, that combination. A glory suitable for a man Mole's own age. Mole raises an arm.

"No captains here yet, Freddie—" Mole shouts. "Nobody in the main seat."

IN THE GALLEY

GILPIN, ON HIS WAY to the cabin to consult the dictionary in his documents box, checks in at the galley first for what his stomach now recognizes as dinner and even looks forward to. He's always late. Mulenberg and Wert are already there. They always wait for him in that blend of mutual anxiety, irritation and necessary affection which has come over all of them as a result of their locked-in propinquity. The minute he arrives the punching of buttons begins. Some are on the wall, some at tableside. In a minute their menu is assembled. Touching to see how first this man then that will give a nudge to a packet so that the table will have a semblance of place-setting—men who in most of their lives never set a table before.

They've long since developed a joke routine. "Noisette of lamb—" Wert will say, fingering the stew packet. "With mint jelly? Odd. And I'm afraid the champagne's only Spanish." The nozzle for soft drink pulls up from the table, like those for water, milky coffee and a juice which tastes heavily of ascorbic acid. In a pinch—if the mechanical spinning which produces the galley's modicum of G-force should fail that is—a nozzle can be sprayed directly into a mouth clamped tightly over it, but they've almost forgotten this. Like ordinary air travelers they repress all thoughts of any pinch. At least at table.

The first day all were outraged at the thought that the coffee could have as easily been black, allowing one of the options which meant so much here. For three days running Mulenberg, proud of his winesmanship, pretended to offer them Pouilly Fuissé of different years, to no avail; nobody will touch the soft drink. "No tea?" Wert said early. "That'll be hard on my wife." What joy, when powdered tea was discovered. Gilpin yearned for mineral water, Italian preferred. Salads were wistfully spoken of, with some talk as to whether hydroponic vegetables were already in production on habitat. Now all that's over; they merely eat, even the ever-present ice cream, a welcome solvent for dry throat. Almost by convention now, Gilpin's thinking, we're all optimists.

"There'll be beer," Mulenberg says today, sitting down. "Saw to it myself before leaving Washington. Some in the Payload Bay too. Forgot all about it until yesterday. When I talked to them. Man, that's a setup in there. Makes our company's communications room look a toy. One whole end of the flight deck."

"You talk about the beer?" Gilpin said.

Mulenberg laughs. On matters of power he's not to be embarrassed.

Wert, who eats unconcernedly of anything and with broadly functional manners, now has a dark mustache of bean sludge. On him it looks grandee. He's the only one who doesn't miss cutlery.

Mulenberg continues stoking in his usual double ration. "No, I bargained. Said I wouldn't serve except jointly, along with you, Wert. You surprised?"

"Nothing surprises me about bargaining. Only if there weren't any."

"But you don't mind I asked?"

"Not at all."

"Don't you want to hear their answer?"

"They agreed to it. For say—five and a half months."

Gilpin realizes what he's watching. One negotiator who thinks he's a master and doesn't care who sees it. One who is, but would rather not let it show.

"How'd you know?"

"My wife has an—aeromedical agreement with them. For about that time."

"That when her baby's due?"

"She'll have it in their lab. On habitat. Less birth trauma, they allege, for the child. My wife's on her way to forty—a first child. And she has certain—muscular rigidities—extending from the fascia of the lower back."

So that's how he bargained to get her here—both with her and with Washington?

"They said—" Jack hesitates. "That for the look of the thing, I'll have to appear to make the decisions. You mind that?"

"I'm used to it."

"So they said. Well. That gets everybody out of the hole." Mulenberg gets up. "Excuse me." On the way to the Hygiene Unit he reaches back to pat Wert's shoulder. They hear him try one unit door, then enter the other side.

Wert looks after him quizzically. He wipes the mustache from his face.

"What a bargainer you are," Gilpin says. "They'll use your experience —which is what they need—and big business will be satisfied."

Wert's looking amused. "Big business, as you call it, always goes to the toilet after a deal's closed. It's second only to the cigar."

"But you and your wife would have stayed on in any case?"

"As she wishes."

"Then why bother? To consent to it."

"I was brought up to serve. Not always being sure of the intention." Wert's response is quick, his voice hard. "The bargaining you learn. Then you learn—that it never stops." He got up, walked tensely round the table and sat down, again the lazy, tentative Wert they know. "At the end of the time period they'll let Mulenberg go, too, of course. Care to guess why? No? Don't blame you. So simple it took me a lifetime to learn." Wert looked over his shoulder. "They'll do exactly as the Russians would. Or the Chinese. They'll let him go for having displayed personal allegiances."

"You have none of those? Except to the lady, of course."

"Not at all. Have them. Just don't let them show." Wert's smile appears, the tired one. "And always bargain short-term. Never let yourself see the end of it."

"Ah?" The food's depressed Gilpin. Or blame the food. "I'm a— long-term man, myself. See though why you'd hesitate—constitutionally."

When Wert laughs aloud he can look quite young. "That's such a Southernism. We have everything like we have the rheumatiz—constitutionally. How'd you come by it?"

"Boston, my mother. Southerners of the North. Anyway, it was good of you, not to embarrass him."

"He cuts his losses. He and I'll do very well. Though I suspect my household might embarrass him."

"Lordy, of course. That Southerner?" Gilpin said. "First the double wedding everybody read about, years back? Rome, Georgia?"

"Athens, Georgia. My Christian wedding, yes. They tied magnolias to the trees. My old cousin likes to make the South exist again."

"She married the butler, both of them in their eighties."

"In their nineties now. She and Fereydoun preceded us down the aisle. She said she wanted to go to bed with a man at least once, now that it was safe. Though I doubt they did. But Fereydoun was never exactly a butler. And had inherited a great deal of Iranian money. Which he was unexpectedly allowed to keep."

"But you didn't take *your* inheritance, by all accounts."

"Er, no, I didn't. That went to my other wife, Soraya, in Switzerland, where it had been banked. She wasn't yet my wife, at the time. She invested it to considerable advantage for her family's sake, then returned the original sum to Iran. In exchange for certain—promises. To all of them. In our case so that she and I—so that there could be a wedding. And so that nobody would be assassinated at the reception. Even in Paris, they have a very long arm—my two Sorayas' enemies." He waited politely for possible comment. Many people must want to. When Gilpin made none, Wert ducked in acknowledgment, and went on. "That's where Mulenberg and I did meet. At the wedding reception. My Muslim one."

"The second one?" Gilpin said. "Oh well yes. The Christian one would've had to be first."

They both look up at Mulenberg reentering.

"Wert says you were at his Paris wedding."

"Only been to one in Paris. The Elysée. Packed. Man from Ottoman Grindlay's Bank in Oman took me. Never did see the groom. Thought he must be some kin to all those Iranian beauties from Switzerland." His eyes narrow at Wert. "You mean—"

"I was from there. At the time. So was my boss, Ordoobadi—remember him? Friend of your friend from Grindlay's Bank. You came there by appointment. To meet him."

"The Elysée?" Gilpin said. "Who gave the party, the President of France?"

"Oh nothing like that," Wert said. "Just one of the smaller rooms. That's why it was packed."

"No, not the President." Mulenberg's rocking on his heels, as much as sandals allow. "But tell him who."

"Matter of fact, um—the Sultan. The former Sultan of Muscat."

"A mutual friend," Mulenberg said. "Of my friend and Wert's."

"Friends of friends of friends. It's confusing."

"Not when they're in armaments, Tom. Or looking for them." Mulenberg's laughter rolls. "Your head nipped in at that like a falcon's, Tom. Had a pet one, once. No, the Sultan on that occasion was a general customer. I'm only in industrial aerospace. Poor Ordoobadi, Wert's friend—he's only in software. Yes, he introduced you and me, Wert. Just didn't catch on you were the groom."

"The Sultan was just then presenting Mulenberg with a handsome gold artifact," Wert said. "What a piece. A breast ornament presumed to date from the Portuguese occupation. Or even earlier. But first he modeled it on the nearest woman. Who wore no jewelry. He remarked on it. A bride."

Mulenberg inclines his big head. "A beauty. I remember her very—Bride?"

"The other Soraya?" Gilpin can't help himself.

"At the moment," Wert says.

"I beg your pardon," Gilpin says low. "From your memoir, I see them so plain."

"Oh, that's their family characteristic. One does. That's why people like me take up with them."

"And what of—Manoucher?"

"Doing very well. In Rio, with a horde of relatives." Wert turns back to Mulenberg. "Both my wives are named Soraya."

"I gave the Sultan's gift to my *daughter*," Mulenberg says stiffly.

"Ah?" Gilpin can't help saying it. "Which one?"

Wert stands up between them, quickly.

"An Amazon of Ephesus, it was," Mulenberg adds, sullen. "But Tessa's commune isn't fussy. So it's hanging in Mendocino. Safe as anything is above a sink."

"Good God." Gilpin walks his long gallery in the apartment now sold. Did deserted objects somewhere in their molecules scream for us? "Once saw a vase of your description in Isfahan, Wert. I recall you sent yours to Madame—Manoucher's mother?—in a biscuit box. Still keep her in supply?"

"Madame died two years ago. But happily. Bought herself two hotels in Vevey, grew thin with the help of the spas and expired in the arms of a gigolo who turned out to be richer than she. He'd simply had the temperament."

"Biscuits. Bath Olivers?"

"Romary's Tunbridge Wells."

"Ah God—the absolute pearls. With cheese."

The table, littered with silvery transparencies emptied of their liquids and solids, reminds Gilpin of Tuohy's moonbeam drawer.

"Tessa won't have anything to do with the business. I spoke with both of them," Mulenberg says.

"And Maidie?"

"The one present I could have given her years ago. She jumped at it."

"From—so far."

Mulenberg slaps the table. "For men like you, Tom, all miracles have to come by faith. Any from our own efforts, you despise. Like"—he makes a grand, enveloping gesture—"this."

"I apologize." Gilpin stamps his foot at himself. "Ow. Had my shooting-stick, wouldn't happen."

"Someone has to be historian," Wert says. "If—I could make a—ah, suggestion, Gilpin?"

"So early in my career?"

"Keep this trip—keep seeing us—in the particular. Don't be too—"

"Say it."

"Universalist."

"You must have read *The Sheet*," Gilpin says sadly.

"The Department always did. I even heard you once."

"Did you now." He claps his hands. "Okay, lads. Why don't I start now. Take Mr. William Wert—in particular. Now let's see. Ah, Mr. Wert's—hesitancy? A form of administration. He's administering you and me, Jack, right now."

Wert bows.

"And now—Mr. John Mulenberg. John T. Mulenberg, in the dossier. I make a guess: Theocritus. Your father being a famous nurseryman."

"Tehachapi," Mulenberg said. "Mountains where my mother was born."

"Ha. At odd moments Mr. Mulenberg swings thumb and forefinger under chin. As if fingering a tie? Left to right. That's it. One of those Western metal-tipped string ties."

Caught in the very act, Mulenberg bows too.

"And now me, boys," Gilpin cries. "What about me?"

It takes him a minute to catch on that those two are brimming with a silent belly-laugh which at his look splutters over. Jack's the first to wheeze to a final Haw. Wert waves a weak hand, wiping his eyes. "Okay. I'll do it." He clears his throat. "Ahem. Mr. Gilpin is always—himself. A ver-ee consistent personali-tee. How can a man possibly be himself, and so faithfully like himself—at the same time? Tom Gilpin will give us a little lecture on how." Wert's a fine mimic. "But we listen." He has returned to his own voice. "And it helps."

Jack chimes in musically: "He—can't hel-lup it, pip, pip. But—it helps. *And*—we lis-ten, *yes*, we listen—"

Wert joins in, baritone. "To this man so ma-ha-hah-velously like himself."

Both men beam. They share a joke he's not onto. Jack lunges for the table, grabbing the soft-drink nozzle. Holding it high he squirts a stream into his mouth, then at Wert lightly, at Gilpin harder, on himself hardest, and at last high over the table, drenching it until the nozzle hangs limp on its stem. "Piña colada, boys. Let's all have some."

They know him, they've read him. Maybe not the full dossier, only the selected Gilpin, but they know that long-ago young man making up his recipe, which will last him for life.

Wert says low, "I liked your island." The big fellow studies his own wet legs.

Gilpin says shakily, "Drove for a hayload-ride concession that next summer, out of Newburyport. Kept the wagonful in giggles, every moonlit night. Finally the concession fired me. 'The front seat has to be quiet,' they said."

This time his friends' joint laughter laps him, old friends sherry-voiced at dusk. There almost could be dusk here.

"Ah—rr—haven't had a laugh like that—since," the big one says. "Almost takes the place of sex."

"I haven't laughed yet," Gilpin says. "But I will."

They're three stubbled men who've lost the passenger's gloss. Not dirty yet—no dirt can appear here, but each day their human smell is stronger, maybe working to preserve its particular. In spite of all drills, they have the lounger's smell, and though not prisoners, they have some of the prisoner's undependability, hoarding certain secrets as if these are privately designated work.

Mulenberg won't yet tell about yesterday's chat with Dove, who'd explained the blank dossiers in the Free Room as belonging to listed passengers at the last minute motel-detained. For whom "substitute personnel"—not further described, has been arranged. The corner of perforated wall off the flight deck, where Mulenberg had been allowed to send and receive his own messages, had reminded him of the complimentary long-lines telephone his own company offered visitors. "That telex booth—" he says. "Or whatever it is. Not too private. But it seems to get there."

Gilpin's been wondering when to tell them of the facsimile *Sheet* he's received here, headlined: Architect's Son Injured Tokyo; subheaded, Eminent Architect Questioned on Identity Fred Kim on *Courier*. He says, "The computer sends me *The Sheet* once a week. Yes, it's a miracle." On-Island, when he was ten, the teacher, preachy but heeded because she was their first, used the same wintry, shining word, drawing on the wet blackboard, pale with January sun, the structure of a snow-flake.

Wert smiles tiredly. In every camaraderie there's a point where one becomes solo again. Too often, he achieves it first. The enormity of this voyage will disappear like a shipboard romance the minute they touch down on habitat. And the enormity of the living-station will begin.

He sees the cool gray barracks he hasn't told them of, entered matter-of-factly at the top by maintenance crews in from non-G, and the startling lawns, which seem to be acting out green, in front of land-rises like false bosoms; both saying: This was Scenery, once. In one factory great weights hung like parallelograms done on paper, the craftsmen appearing to manipulate shadows. In another, crystals worked to form themselves in intense cold, behind doors tiger-striped for danger. The white labs are the shrines, hissing small table-size blessings. It's all small scale, a nursery for what comes next in the universe. In one of those labs his wife will have her labor. He won't be there—no room. The child is known to be a boy. To think of him is like testing the beautiful ache of a new tooth. He plunges into that deep, saline comfort, then opens his eyes, "Beer—" Wert grunts, "that'll be welcome."

Mole enters the galley in one bravura sweep.

"Perfect landing," Mulenberg says acidly.

"Just practicing." He stands there weaving a little in the way they do at that age, as if their muscles are eating them—and they have to battle everybody else because of it.

"Thought you et."

"Did, Tom. With the whistlers. Wonderful rendition they have, when they're high."

Mulenberg juts at him. "Smoking *stuff?*"

Mole gives him a cool look. "Not after today. This time they nibbled it."

"You too?"

"Not my bag."

"What is?"

"Sir?"

Mulenberg's never been to boarding school. It shows. "Your bag."

Mole has a mooching elegance, but he's not lounging, he's patroniz-ing. A young blood gazing past the sports car salesman's paunch at the future only he can afford. "Space user, sir. Runs in my family."

"Oh yes, your father. The architect."

Gilpin and Wert stare like abbots at their own thumbs.

"The Kim who turned us down on subcontracting for the *Courier?* Any idea why?"

"Yes, sir. But maybe Mr. Gilpin'll want to tell you something first. About my father. About me."

"That can wait," Mulenberg says. "What's happening to the discipline on this ship?"

Mole grins at him.

"Stop wanting to be a hero, Mole," Gilpin says.

"Why shouldn't the boy want to be one? Since he's found out none of us are," Wert says lightly. "How elated you look at the news you bring, Mole. Like a—son." He reaches out to tap Mole's shoulder. "Like the first time we met."

"Yes, sir," Mole said. "How did you tell?"

"I was on *my* way. To being a father."

"So you did recognize me. When we came aboard. Dumb of me. Like I underestimate people. So whyn't you come out with it?"

"Thought maybe you had a bargain going. With your father."

"On my way to it," Mole said.

"Who the devil is he?" Mulenberg hates to ask.

Mole gives Wert a nod.

"Met him at his father's house. He's not the architect Kim's son. He's —Admiral Perdue's."

Mole heaves forgetfully high, smacking his fists against aluminum. Crouching bright-eyed, he nurses them happily.

"And I fancy he has news for us," Wert says under his breath.

Mulenberg's roar interrupts. "Perdue? Wait'll I see that son-of-a." It's half a laugh. "So he shipped on after all . . . After letting the entire industry beg."

Mole's caught short. What have been his hopes?

"Afraid not. Not till the second trip out, he told me. The admiral." Under Mole's stare Gilpin shrinks as if caught name-dropping. "I was in his office to check the civilian list."

"Sure, Tom. Sure. So here you are. All three of you. Plus Wolf. Plus the girls." Mole stretches again, in that curious well-being. Is he even relieved?

Gilpin sits up sharp. Do the others know what they're watching— youth the stowaway, about to come into its own?

"Plus me," Mole says.

Jack rears up. "Been meaning to tell you two. They've explained about the blank dossiers. Seems certain people, ah, were held back, at the motel. So they've had to fill the slots with new people. From the waiting list." He veers around to Mole. "But you mean—we're the only civilians aboard? That Seat Six was right?" He veers to Wert. "What your wife said. That we're the only—passengers."

"Not that, Jack. But I was wrong to try and keep it from her. That we have a—military presence here. Dear God, we always have." Wert has the clearest hazel irises. Their clarity will attract some women like the murk in the irises of men who drink. The wife now in Switzerland, or in South America, would she flee from it, feeling it most? "I can't say how many. But I felt I had been—misrepresented too." He has spent a lifetime at that. "So I—bowed out."

"You should have—stayed on?" Instead of me, Jack means.

"They—put it to me." Wert must be unaware of how straight he's standing. For the many times his peculiar honor must have had to be maintained.

Gilpin is watching the death of heroes, on Mole's face. First that of Gilpin himself, begun long since. Now the flick of interest that for a moment had been for Wert. Not enough. Maybe the son in Soraya's womb, of whose existence Wert's confided, already feels the same.

"More's the bloody fool you," Mulenberg says, mimicking Wert's occasional Pall Mall overlay. "Now then. What about Perdue? You there. Kid. You're not here because of your father?"

Mole's very still—for him.

"I mean—you're not with him?"

"No!"

Gilpin closes his eyes. Oh, Mole, I begin to see your bargain. I don't want to.

"Then—who's in real command here, that asshole with the signet ring? That born-again subordinate?"

"How well you describe us all, Jack." Wert's voice is acid. "But Dove's an astronaut, not a captain of industry. He'll do well enough."

Gilpin's eyes remain shut. The better to hear Mole say it.

"Nobody is. In command."

It should be said all at once, for dignity. Or sung to get used to, like in church. No-bo-dee-ee is in space-command.

"What do you mean, you—"

"Kid—?" Mole says. Gilpin can hear the smile on him. "But out here, I'm learning. Lot of heavy fathers in the world. But maybe no captains."

Oh, Mole. You could have learned that at home.

Wert has. "That all your news?"

"No. Take a look at that diagram Mr. Mulenberg's always toting. Let him open it."

There's a rustling.

"There. The flight deck—see? The tenth seat."

"What about it, kid?"

"Nobody in it."

At the yell from Mulenberg, Gilpin opens his eyes.

"That's the *dummy* seat, boy. Has no controls. Never has had. They cut the specifications, cost-estimate went to sky-high. Perdue's own command okayed every cut. You have to decide between the human element and the—" By now Mulenberg's braying. "Every spacecraft they tested *unmanned* they could have cut the test and flown *manned* the first time. And been okay. Or most of them. But people remember what's in a budget proposal. So you cut the human equivalent. When it helps make a five-hundred-million-dollar difference. After all—you people are on computer here." He stops short, his jaw hanging. It's an awesome sight. The president, catching up with the passenger.

"Yeah." Mole coughs. "Dad always said the human component wore out first, anyway. So, maybe that's why discipline's a little hard to maintain. Now they know the equipment specifications they're flying. And that's why Kim—my friend Kim's father, Mr. Mulenberg—wouldn't subcontract. Any more questions?"

"No," Gilpin groans.

"Yes, Moleson," Wert says. "What have you really come to tell us?"

He's choosing. He's being as specific as he can. He's going to be better at it than they are. "Lievering's on EVA. With four others from the flight deck. . . . We keep veering."

The word bounces off the galley's shining surfaces, coming to rest on the table. Is the frail waste there moving, very slightly or not?"

"Who says, kid?"

"The whistlers."

"Who the hell are they to—"

"Second crew, Jack. But no drop in quality." Gilpin hopes he's right. "But I thought a rocket couldn't veer." Too late he remembers they no longer are one.

"Hell no. Woman got the patent on it some years back. Or applied." Mulenberg winks. "Nowadays a rocket can change orbit, mid-flight. But we're on Orbiter. Canaveral must know what they're doing." He bends suddenly toward his left boot. It's sliding almost imperceptibly toward his right one, which is creeping also. Away from it. All their boots are moving similarly. All of them stand up, vainly pressing their boots to the floor.

Gilpin is reminded of his briefcase, gallantly upright in the draining sea.

"Simpler to lean the other way." Mole, with a queasy expression, is doing so.

"We may be imagining this, you know." Mulenberg is making for the door, touching walls deftly. "I'll get on to Canaveral."

"Dove already has." Mole has turned his back to them. "Or to wherever Joint Command now is."

"And?" Wert's worry-hand is already in action, seeking its mate.

"They're having trouble keeping in touch with us."

Wert, too, makes for the hatch. Not doing quite so well as Jack.

The slanting is more pronounced now. A ship would be almost on its side. Gilpin, a good sailor, steadies Mole from behind. "If you have to toss up, go on."

"No." Mole lifts his head, turning. "I don't barf at it anymore. Any of it."

Suddenly they're righted. Feet solid on the floor again, or as solid as here can be. All three men expel their breath, testing. It lasts, it hangs firm—this particular vertical.

There was a time, Gilpin thinks, when I was under the impression there was only one vertical to a man. Later on, I settled for a few, wreathing around the once-and-former true like Saturday afternoon hang-gliders.

It's Mole who shakes his clasped hands at what used to be heaven— or up. "Little EVA. Wuddya know."

From the hatch Mulenberg snarls, "That kid know the answer to everything?"

Mole slowly lowers his hands. "Not hard to."

"You don't say."

Wert says, "Shut up, Mulenberg. Yes, Mole?"

If Mole doesn't hide his face again, it'll break up. He doesn't. His lip quivers for that hero within who might die on him. "Ship's a bummer."

THE DOCUMENTS BOX

AND THAT WAS NO NEWS to him, Gilpin thinks. Gilpin is back in the cabin, poring over his section of the documents locker. If the ship is a bummer, it's no news to Mole. But the glory is. Some kind of glory—I can't yet figure it. Maybe the horrendous bargain he made by coming here—he's facing up to it. But what a time for the glory to hit him. Maybe that's when it does. I wouldn't know.

He's alone in the cabin. All in the galley had dispersed, Mulenberg and Wert to go to Dove, the one to demand he be put in touch with Canaveral "direct," the other to suggest that before docking they all be informed of the real terms of the flight, that is, who and how many others are here with them?—or are absent. And by whose leave?—Gilpin reminded him. Ah, that's maybe harder, Wert said. Mole's gone off in awed expectancy of his gym period with a Lievering down from the heights. Though Gilpin has guessed Mole's quixotic reason for being here and feels a responsible pain when he thinks of it, he's as grateful as the others at getting rid of him, a valued dog, but ever at heel.

All along the way here the video screens said ON COURSE. Behind him now the cabin's screen says the same, though reassurance is unnecessary. Restored balance is in his limbs like a convalescence. He can't even find ominous the item now seeping along the bottom of the screen in reduced letters. *Jettisoning schedule,* the craft will be *trying for a docking* tomorrow. Or whenever tomorrow is. For psychological reasons alone this would be well advised. They are beginning to confuse space with time.

The locker, communal yet ingeniously private for each, has an oriental capacity beyond its size, suggesting it may have been one of the small preliminaries Kim did design. Its smell is heartening; there's wood

in it. At the top of his own pile of goods is the Moore drawing of the
sleepers. He's glad it's a reproduction, which at home it mightn't have
been. It must stand for all the world scenery he's left behind. Air travel
must have been the first to be without scenery either human or animal
or vegetable—until then that tender or cruel cottage industry always
set before the traveler on train or horse or car, or even under or over
the sea.

In the air age, the long preamble to his kneeling here, men and
women in flight had become their own scenery and any airliner a kind
of mass play-action between passenger and crew, ritualized with music
and warnings, entr'acte strolling—and conversation passed along like a
rope.

Here men and women are the only originals. And in a new world
ought to be? Excitement tremors him. In middle age one has so few
reversals of thought. On habitat—a word he's finally given in to—he
expects the scenery not to be much advanced. Conversation has these
past days been their drama, the talk that on any voyage is a song hiding
the shuddering of the wheel. Now that's over. Exchange has stopped.
In the last hour a familiar self-hoarding mood has overtaken all of them.
God knows it's premature, but they're all passing each other with that
hurried reticence which means destination is near.

Down at the bottom of his pile is his *Decameron* with its inflamed old
red cover, gnawed from island days when he'd first scavenged it for
what he thought was porn—and had found a human narrative he's still
in. Next to it is an older volume, small like so many from the early
eighteen hundreds, a Voyage also. Discovered in his Boston library
days, bought for himself only recently, it is fairly rare, but there are
copies, one for sure he knows of, in the New York Society Library. He's
only spot reread it. It's here for that ultimate emergency, nothing new
to read.

The dictionary makes him smile. All of them do; they have the ampli-
tude of religions open to change. He can hear the variorum voices
which have made this one, the committeemen chattering like senior
apes, the dullards hired by the yard, their mouths as full of syllables as
a carpenter's with nails. Here and there a holier scholar is made to
intervene, in a quote. Milton is his favorite. What fun it could be to
catalogue all the quotes cited in one or other of the standard editions
—has anyone ever? He has an idea the Oxford feels safest with Sir
Walter Scott.

Here it is. Psychopannychy: 1642. [From the medieval Latin *psy-*

chopannychia and the Greek ψυχο —plus παννχιος lasting all night.]
All-night sleep of the soul; a state in which (according to some) the soul
sleeps between death and the day of judgment.

A tic goes over him. He feels the glory that streams from the far
reaches of the yet undefined.

There is no quote.

THE HYGIENE UNIT

"SCARS—THAT'S WHAT LIEVERING WANTS." Veronica is lightly cream-ing the welted purple grid on Soraya's lower back. That rectangle so opposed to the curved lines of any body no longer makes her gasp. "From some holocaust the world could honor. War's not good enough. Nor death either. Death would kill him."

Soraya giggles. "Holy wounds. He can have them."

"He won't get them out there."

Both women glance up and away from the video screen on which the boxily white-suited and masked figures alternately float toward and recede from the looming curve, thrust from left-screen like a shoulder, of the vehicle which is bearing them all on. Lievering's own position is constantly televised for him out there; he juggles that equation as he goes. At the moment his other companions are not visible, nor any reflection from the creeping plastic sheath in which they are at times enclosed.

Soraya's wing-bone quivers. "Who knows?"

"Space-martyrs aren't publicized."

Another shrug. Sometimes Soraya's back seems more expressive than her face. "Many kinds are not." She rolls over and lies face up on the Jacuzzi's broad rim, which ingeniously houses both the waste system and exercise gear. Veronica lies on the opposite rim. Both are naked—the ultimate luxury aboard. Though they have only the tube of unper-fumed cream, have nothing to boudoir-litter with and Soraya's hair is razored as close to the skull as Veronica's corn-rows, the pliant walls and air have acceded to their flesh and conversation; for the hour this is a feminine retreat. More likely, they'll find a way to stretch the hour to two.

The martyr Soraya must be thinking of is Manoucher. Each always knows who the other means, as if she herself had lived the life opposite; each has by now heard the other's story so exhaustively. For Veronica, who has never had a confidante, even whose beloved stepmother never knew her inner life, these hours are like afternoons in a Platonic cave she never knew existed. For Soraya, whose whole early life and confidence had been wedded to women, this allegiance is expected—and never emotionalized. Though they're sufficiently fond and Veronica has the single woman's awe of the pregnant one, this hothouse closeness hasn't necessarily made them love one another and will likely grow feeble when they part. There's even an extra ease to it in that their minds are so unlike, as if their temperaments will moderate what their tongues can't.

Meanwhile, this part of their day is felinely cozy. The motion of the *Courier* is reduced to a kind of hibernation. Its designers made no provision for the harem gene, which may be why the harem gene persists. Veronica sometimes thinks of saying such things, but never does.

Soraya, taking all this for granted, clearly never thinks of it. Her motto is: For Now. She admires German cars, Swiss hotels, but says it is better not to like any one country too much—a true internationalist. Skis, but doesn't like ski people. Is anti-cinema. A world without children is dust. Torturers believe in the world still, she says; murderers have given up—death is their answer. While she was being tortured she gave them just enough of her life for them to go on with her. They gave her one bad fingernail, to match the brand on her back. That same week her cousin, the still-reigning Queen, sent home to the palace an entire plane full of pink marble; it was the death-wish monument. But Soraya still loves pink.

When she met Wert in their first bedroom, every naked inch of him was scrutinized. She showed him the nail. "My scar he had already seen." On the way south, he solicitously wouldn't let her drive because of it: she correctly took this as token of their married life-to-be. But certain dowries had had to be settled first.

Driving along, he wondered what she read—if she read? Islam, and Francis Macomber from an American short-story anthology at the university? Or the writer Reza Baraheni, who'd been in prison also, and maybe Che? She had answered only that she was not a virgin, which had been a lie. She had insisted Wert come to the bedroom she'd been allotted at his cousin's, after the doctor, come to examine her back, had gone. There he might see the book left for him to see, on top of the open suitcase filled with the lingerie all the women behind her had contributed. Ah yes, he says, taking it up, expecting as he said later one of those soft French-oriental novels which household women seem to grab for and find anywhere—half Beardsley, half Lalique. She has since looked those up. He doesn't ask who gave her this one tattered book she carries about, a cheap copy of the *Gulshan-i-Raz;* perhaps he guessed. If he had asked, she would not have lied. He says: "So you do read." She is standing patiently, not naked yet, though she approves of his body. "Can you have children?" she says. He knew what she meant—would a son of hers be his first?—and had answered appropriately. I'm like you, Soraya; I don't yet know. Then, with that smile, he began to show her that he knew everything else.

In the wedding picture her legs are slenderer. Pink silk socks in Paris-version little-girl sandals—and a Folies Bergère maribou jacket soft against the lashes. She is not perverse, not at all, but her emotions, never on the surface, are blocks of marble down below. He can expect the grand from her, never knowing what. Americans are by nature a sad, depressed people, she thinks, lacking real jollity; that's why they are the itchy leaders in transportation. She doesn't care a hoot about the physical style of such things, gravity or not. Absorb the method, the style—like a ski suit—and go on from there. If you are detached enough you can do that. "If you have nothing."

But now she has. She has a calendar.

She believes that she and Wert took so long to conceive a child because she once lied.

There is of course no picture of her in *chador.*

"In Brazil?" Veronica says now. "In Rio? Well, at least you all know where he is. Even if he never gets in touch." It's understood that she is still referring to Manoucher.

"The other Soraya may not wish it. Nobody may wish it."

"I know."

"You do not wish it either, maybe." It's understood that Soraya refers to Veronica's brother, Ollie. "For you, too, not knowing may be better. Even whether he's dead or alive."

"A brother means the past, the family one. But maybe you're right. Listen, was Manoucher ever more than a brother to the other Soraya? In her mind, I mean. Even though she married him?"

"She was sent—" Soraya said. "Yes, she was soft for him. But she was sent."

"I used to think people who didn't keep track of all family members or for any reason didn't know where some were—that the only people who would let that happen were scum."

"Ah-hah. And now we are the elite." When Soraya feels broody she doesn't say so but will perform a little something from body-lore, like pinching her nose-tip to keep it from age's broadening, or flexing toes upward to keep the metatarsal pads, those pedestals of the spine, open for energy, or in extremity plucking all her leg hairs. Now, of course, she has her belly to feel, for the fourth-month sign of life.

"Stop looking," Veronica says. "A watched pot never boils."

They chuckle.

"That poor girl from Ardebil," Soraya says. "She lost hers." She is, of course, referring to old Bakhtiary's child-wife.

"What happened to her?"

"Who knows? We have no one left over there. Not for years. But you know what?" Her voice lowers. Some new tidbit, as yet untalked of, is about to be dropped. "The other Soraya, when she is—not with Beel and me, you know?" She waits for Veronica's acknowledgment. "She is supposed to be in Switzerland, at our house there. But I dream she is not." Soraya appears to use the words "dream" and "think" almost interchangeably. But one is never sure.

"She goes back, you mean? To Iran?"

Soraya seizes the cocoa butter, which is what the tube contains, and begins circling her nipples with it, to make them supple for the nursing. "And maybe—to him?" She's asking, not telling. What they do for each other is to unravel.

"I don't know about revolutionaries any more. Maybe I never did." Veronica picks up the greasy tube, weighing it uncertainly. "Gilpin says —we inhabit revolution—like a house. Then, one day, we move on. Or the house is gone. But I suppose—you could keep going back for it."

"Like to a poem?" Soraya always hits below the belt. And then acts. Horrified at Veronica's tale of abandoning the poem at the motel— confessed only after Soraya had revealed who she herself had been and would be in love with eternally, and oh what a release for both women —she had made Veronica grudgingly reconstruct it, line by line, she herself taking it down, since Veronica couldn't bear to, and proving so good at her nagging sorties and pressing, hypnotic silences that the poem now existed again, if in the feathery Arab script its own author couldn't hope to read. Soraya doesn't understand the poem but she vows to set a computer to retranslating as soon as they arrive. She understands completely what the poem means to Veronica, diagnosing

this in one shaft—"Oh yaas, it is why you could have so many mens."
She always pluralizes it that way. Though she owns many inherited
adages beginning: "Mens—" they emerge sparingly out of the slim
darkish face and steady brown eyes. It may be she's beginning not to
believe in them—or never has.

"Manoucher was never a revolutionary," she says now. "What they
did to his body—it happens more than you think, in our history. Afterwards, such mens, to still feel—you know"—she raises a fisted arm,
flexing a tiny bicep—"they have to have money, power. Money he has.
But people also tell such men their secrets. So he would go back. To
show Soraya." She smooths the cream over her breasts so that they
shine like armor. Her smile is rare, Wert normally smiling for both of
them. "So—they show each other. But different."

"How?"

"Because *she* is the revolutionary. They were the real ones. She and
Bakh." This is the name she's been leading up to. To mention it a dozen
times, probing for the opportunity.

"And you," Veronica says, proud for her.

"Not me. I have the baby." She shrugs, mock-deprecating. But triumph glistens on her. "For—all of us."

Veronica knows the story. In that still fairly recent ménage-à-trois,
which she fancies the women have been as much parties to as Wert if
not more, the race to be pregnant had been constant between the two
wives, though kept from Wert, the women being united on that score,
as on so much. Veronica has learned not to assume anything about that
relationship. The one time Soraya had been infuriated was when
Veronica idly assumed they must all three sometimes bed together. No,
she had hissed, beet-red—"We are not whores."

"Do you dream—that the other Soraya will stay over there? And
Manoucher?"

"No! They quarrel. He will leave. Or maybe I dream wrong that he
would come back to Iran at all. Maybe only she is there. To find out once
again the revolution there is not for us. In South Africa, Latin America,
we are, all over. Fateh in Washington, where her girls have married so
well. She wants to marry, too, but she is so enthusiastic. And those rings
she wears go off in a men's eyes like bombs. Yet she has no money. She
spent it all bringing Bakh's library here. Thousands of crates, you cannot
imagine. And thousands' worth of bribes. Through the Greek port of
Piraeus she did it. Such a giddy woman, to do such a holy job. But the
mens, that library puts them off, too. So she is giving half the library to

other libraries. And half to Wert." Often she calls him that, rather than Bill. "For the boy."

"He's probably reading Latin in there already. Let me listen." Veronica applies her ear to the belly.

"Silly. We won't hear. We will feel." She flutters a hand.

"So we will." That "we" touches Veronica. So generous, so maternally blind. If she herself were pregnant would she still be able to make these fine distinctions? Or, as in the other kind of love is there a blunting of the finest mind—and no turning back?

"Why Latin? No, he is studying the *Gulshan-i-Raz*. So he can be trusted with his father's precious copy."

The one Bakh gave Wert so many years ago, yes. This time the name doesn't come, only the wise look over the kind of pawky detail even a devoted wife will share, or a devout—rememberer. Seems that Wert's copy, though authentic, isn't as precious as he thinks. Bakh, like many collectors, could be overweeningly generous with objects whose flaws only he knew. There was even a secret pleasure in that. But Bakh always denied suffering from the worst grossnesses of ownership. For his best objects he was only trustee, only waiting for a recipient as worthy as he. How did Soraya know all this? When her father went to prison Bakh bought her family's collection, one by one. She herself used to bring each object to Bakh's house, at which time the great appreciator would instruct her on it. In fairness, he often bought things of little value—though he would always point this out. Wert's copy, which was one of them, is presently on loan to a university which luckily thinks quite well of it. In exchange, Bakh had given her the cheap English translation which went to prison with her later, where being in English it was suspect. She was tortured extra for refusing to say where she got it.

"All these objects, always having to be rerouted, or left behind," Veronica said, the day Tom moved from his flat, having disposed of everything to where everything should properly go. He can be a good donor because he's not a collector; none of that stickiness adheres to him. He goes straight to an object's interest; only now and then an interest clutches at him. Earth's moving day, she said. Going to be that way from now on. Nothing new, he said. Always has been. It's just that you and I—we're not Pharaohs. Though you have maybe the look of one.

Nothing new?—she said back to him. Tom, you always say that. That'll be the day—when you find something new.

Soraya's waiting. "Or no—you know what he is reading inside there?"
She pats her belly. "Yo-yo. He is reading yo-yo."

"Whatever's that?"

"Little magazines. Thick paper, big print. Thin paper, little print.
Fancy language always. Bakh's desk was always covered with them. His
second desk." The first desk, as Veronica knows, was swept clean of all
but the roses, the onionskin paper and the pen. "Bulletins from the
University of Double Meaning, he called them—when I myself was at
university he was always showing me. Over a hundred prescriptions to
them he had—quarterly, they would arrive, or sixterly. Come, have a
little laugh, he would say—Summer or Winter Issue?"

"*Sub*scriptions." Veronica is under strict promise to correct. "And
sixterly," she laughs. "A good word. But we don't have it."

"And always he hummed the same over them." Soraya bends over
her belly. The cicatrice on her back bends with her, an embracing
purple spider. She vibrates softly, a nighttime woman with carved eyelids and loosening mouth-curves. "*Yo-yo. Yo-yo.*"

She was sent. To Wert by Bakh. Who'd first had her sent to prison for
her views, because she wouldn't marry him. Who before sending her
to Wert dispatched Fereydoun to inquire of the prison matrons the
color of her pubic hair. The color of my *place*, she'd said, soaping it.
When I watched him die, she said, it was like watching an Alp die, that
you have always lived under. That I had to be against.

Does she know that she was always in love with him? Of course. So
must Wert. And so they are joined, all three of them. To all the lost ones,
as well.

She wants not to dream. But she won't get her wish.

"Look—" Veronica says, "Lievering's disappeared." The screen is
blank. "Sometimes do you wish they all would? Mens?"

"They are not here by accident," Soraya says sharply, but smirking.
"And we are not."

Bakh hasn't taught her double meanings for nothing. Nor Wert, who
has explained to her how the recruitment of Cabin Six has centered
around Mulenberg—"and around you, Veronica." How Wert had been
recommended merely because Mulenberg vaguely recalled meeting
him in important company. "Businessmen of his class like to keep a
handle on their world. Or what they assume to be theirs." For Wert the
possibility of easing what Soraya would undergo has clinched it.

You learn too much from your men, Veronica told her, though she
knows this to be an idea Soraya has no room for. To find that Gilpin
himself had had his path smoothed because Mulenberg wanted to as-

sure himself of her own presence—which Soraya had guessed at, was a blow, but believed at once.

Shivering, she flips the tube from hand to hand. The gravity stipulated here is almost normal. Today it's not quite that.

Soraya's watching her. "Wert says you can have any one of them. The big man. Or your friend. Or even—them, there."

The screen is still empty. "Lievering? He shows no sign of it." She shudders. "I hope not."

"Or all, of course; you could have all," Soraya says calmly. What other people might do doesn't shock her, only what she might; she's admitted it. In the old days yes, that was how the harem was made to work. "I say—you'll have none."

"Or all and none." As she's always done. Though she hasn't felt like it since coming aboard, owing to the same medication provided women astronauts, which has stopped her menses as well. What the men have been administered she doesn't know, though Tom has complained the coffee tastes like his old boarding-school slosh, in those days rumored to be doctored with saltpeter obtained at the nearby naval base. She can imagine him as a partner, though she has never let her mind run that way—toward what might turn out to be incestuous heat. But could she give up, even if he would, his company as it always has been, the quirky, cocky, asexual life-monitor ever at her elbow? Who knows everything about the world and himself—except that he's not a reformer but an adventurer?

As for Mulenberg, he's diagnosed his position with her correctly. He counts just little enough so that she might begin to be tender with him. Lievering moves her most. Of him she is sincerely afraid. He has the Indian sign on her, of her own youth. While over his own once crippled attraction there hangs now the shadowy *in hoc signo* of some spiritual chase whose stigmata might suddenly boil in his palm.

This leaves Mole, whom Soraya hasn't mentioned. Plainly no victim of saltpeter, his open, bee-stung admiration makes her bridle—and smile. He already has a solemnity which the journalist in her recognizes, encountered in both the civilized and uncivilized corners of the world, and as often in broken men and women as in great ones. His virtue is not going to be separable from his intelligence.

All and none, that's my trouble. Once, in Paraguay, she'd been taken by a French ornithologist to see a rare and celebrated bird-courting. The great males, naively lifting and lowering their seven-league wings for permission, picking up feet red-hot from inner burning, danced closer until rebuffed. The females, tall, angular specimens with faces as black as her own—even she saw the resemblance surmising that the laughing Frenchman had brought her for this purpose—stood averted, each in the hereditary sullenness. Then each had pounced. There had been more than enough males. There was no doubt which of the genders was the more prurient. She hadn't spent the night with the ornithologist. Grinning mightily to herself the next morning, she'd sent him a bouquet.

She got up now and walked the Jacuzzi tub's rim, her bare feet cuddling metal lukewarm as a rug. To her, one of the pleasures of this vehicle is its varied surfaces, and above all the gradations of motion provided her animal restlessness, those shiftings, in her since puberty, which Vivie had counseled were her "natural sex-nerves." She is savoring her diet of gravities and atmospheres the way a recruit to radicalism might relish the new dogmas. The very suit-changes they must make seem to her bracing, like what one might do for sport. What she had known of flying now seems to her naïve and all ego—the monocycle thrill of piloting her small plane, or the soaring of the glider which hung over the earth like a soliloquy. The ordinary travel she did so much of down below now seems to her indiscriminate. Movement here is in phalanx, and within the thrill of fixed boundaries. She won't describe this to Tom, who would see fascism in it. For what the vehicle offers them all is that wholeness of sensation which is geared not only to motion but to containment. So will the habitat.

Soraya's still watching the screen. "It can't be over yet."

"What?"

"That repair. It shouldn't be."

EVA—you've flown, why don't you train for it, Tom said, needling her, and like most of his sort equating any "air" activity with another. As well as mistaking this for why she had come.

For glory, Mulenberg, entering the *Courier* at her side, had said, flushed with the humility which made her cruel to him. You're going for glory. At once she had stripped off one of the artificial roses flickering in the wind at the hangar's doorside and had thrust it from her gloved hand to his.

Lievering has followed no one. He's here as usual via the pure accident of himself. Seated next to him in the galley their first week out, she trembled, though the palm of the hand he ate with was unmarked. The curl of his lip, no longer so godly, still has no scorn in it. But now that he no longer stammers one sees that the defect had rendered pitiable a man who is really to be feared. He is one of those in whose presence people remember their own inner scourges. Women have to stop somewhere, he'd said—and here she is. I don't ever want to stop, she'd cried, and had run from him straight toward the great arched categories she hoped to evade. We make nets of language but the blood always comes through, he'd warned. But he never really needed language. Wherever he is, the blood of the world comes through to him. For sure, one will never know which is character in him, and which experience. He is one of those rare ones in whom these are the same. When he rose from the table, Mole got up and followed him.

She's here to leave her experience behind, to break through into ordinary life and maybe stay. By will a member of Mole's aerospace generation, she sees no oddity in the extreme setting she's chosen. As what her world sleazily calls a celebrity, she has no hope of being an ordinary person, or not until old age, when all have that possibility. Yet all ordinary lives need not be the same. She's so muscularly happy here; mayn't she be acting from instinct—though this, too, Tom would deny. Nowadays, as he often sighs, we act bodily for such intellectual reasons; it's the late-century's neo-primitive curse. Even the dopes are doing it. He'd like to have lived in one of those Restoration comedies where as a matter of course everyone had his or her shark-teeth out for satisfaction. If you and I can't do that, Veronica, it's because we share the classically poor judgment of those who look ahead.

So for years they've immobilized each other. As in their statutory marriage.

Yet she's had two of those fake-legal affairs. Careful, Veronica. Don't blame the mens.

She's tired of her own secrets. As with the manuscript, she's trying to dispose of them. For a long while after Mulenberg she'd found herself chaste, the fever stopped, along with the excitement which used to come from repetitive sexual action secretly pursued. Knocking about Paris she had often observed certain women, beauties or *jolies laides*, not all of them with many lovers but all with some, suddenly pull up short into a kind of false middle age. Since they were also types who could do nothing without style, they externalized their new state, clipping their skulls close in what was more than chic, strutting the effigy bone structure as less vulgar for them now than any further striving toward the proud-flesh of youth. Though not homosexual themselves, they often gravitated to the company of the gay, inviting gently appreciative male souls to tea at the blue hour formerly devoted to love, and later joining those mixed crowds of any sex who knew how to waste the white, sleepless hours by turning them into scarecrow night. Widows of the hormone, such women are. She's still too young for it.

Before she embarked, her most notable public admirer came to wish her well and regret her leaving. He knows the secret which includes all of the others, that she suffers from a lack of recognition by herself, over the work done. She still does those articles in which she invades an environment, or a matter of principle, abused or eccentric ones preferable, with her hypertensive eye—and still has her claque for it, thanks to which she's known in her nation and even beyond, if in the shallows of the name and the photograph.

What she'd wanted was to be a good enough artist so that when she chose she could afford to confuse the power of the adoration with the power of the work—a disease deadly when chronic, but if not, often supportive to the sufferer, and in the case of a supreme gift now and then producing, like a self-inoculation, further good work. "Ah, but you're going off," he says shrewdly. "People of that sort do not." They do not adventure but imagine, and record from the star-strewn casement only. Yet he doesn't want her to be ordinary—for he's written about her; it would reflect on him. It was he who years ago said of her: "The language of nihilism—and full of hope." He is sure she will admire herself again. Nuh, she answered. "That's what they say to children." He laid his gouty, puffed hand against her cheek. "Yes." She took him to her door, now an anonymity in a tower always royal with sun and overlooking no small buildings, and said good-bye without further talk. He knows what's happened to her; she's not the first. The nihilism is what has gone, over the far hills, to wait for the next contender. She has been left with the hope.

"Allah—" Soraya says, still watching the screen, "bismillah. There is Mole."

Extraordinary that they can tell it is he. Thanks to living so close they have triumphed over uniforms; in spite of all, they can differentiate. Mulenberg is Size, Lievering Grace, Tom alas Clumsy, without reflexes he will trust. And here is Mole, floating diagonally across the screen, at the end of two thick, corrugated tubings which attach to his shoulder and must connect to the vehicle somewhere off-screen. He is no longer awkward, now daring, now tentative. Now he stops peering toward the vehicular surface and floats straight at them, goggles wide. Soraya draws in her breath. "S-fffff. They should not let him." Mole is modern, insolent. He's the tester, not yet nameable. He is judging space.

Now he, too, is gone.

The Hygiene Unit is itself again. Curtainless, without a porthole to the crammed stars; it's once again part of a mechanism skimming these bright wastes. The rocket probe with phallic nose has long since been dropped behind. A universe's curve may or may not be construed as uterine. But they are in the belly of the *Courier*, as Soraya's fetus is in hers; there's nothing further of the erotic here. To look for it would be —unproductive. Would mean that we are dragging our old home with us toward an absolute, in whose focus no dream can apply. No voyage other than that of the measurer, measuring.

"Lost." Soraya's dove-voice cracks on it.

"Him? Mole? No, he's just—"

"We all."

"What do you mean?"

"Wert thinks it."

"Did he say?"

"Not with the tongue." Soraya's trying to hide her grimace. She bends toward her belly, an arm sliding forward alongside, on the rim of the Jacuzzi. She wants the impossible, to lay her face on where the child is. "I mind for him."

Veronica runs round the side of the tub to kneel in front of her. "Soraya. Look up. Don't worry; they'll find us. Mission Control. The computers will. *You* know that." It doesn't hit her as strange that she should be reassuring a person trained to them. Confidence flows where it can. "Come on, duck." She lays her long palm on the belly, almost covering it. "The universe is too small, nuh, for him to be lost." She's talking like Vivie did to her when, waking in the dark hole of the midnight cot, the coifed head appeared over her, its earrings shaking, medicine rattles against all giants. Come, duck, what you need's some hot milk.

"Soraya, honey." She smooths the outstretched arms, so much shorter than her own. "Tell me again, nuh? How that baby going to be born, that lab we're taking him to. Like how they going to manage it? How you?"

Soraya half raises up. Not that the two of them aren't grown women severe on the ways of the world, but now they tap a complicity risen up in them. "Come on, hon duck. You compute it for me. Compute, poot. You know what a pootie is, that li'l sound a baby makes in his didie?" Gibberish such as the island women talked, severe women, too, in other circumstances—which popped out of Vivie to disprove her daytime counsel: No woman a baby-style woman just from she born to it.

"Raise up, Soraya."

Where's that stern voice coming from? Veronica stands as if she, too, doesn't know, her neck stiff and high. Soraya raises up as if she's already on that birth table.

"It will be like—I am to be in restraint. Those straps. Like in any hospital. But inside them—I will float. I will push, but not against. Nothing will drag at me. It will be all my push. And he will push, too, but so light—" Her arms lift, undulating. "Even they say the *pain* will float. They care for the research, not for me. But the doctors say I myself have not much push; some of the muscles are cut. And the abdominals, too." The words issue odd and strict from between those dancing arms. "The pain, psssh—those men with their pencils. But this way the baby they say will cry only for the air. When he cries." Her face is all delight. Then she sighs. "I will tell you something. I am three years older than I say." She gives a little shrug. "Only the other Soraya knows. And Fateh." She rolls her eyes. "No mens."

Veronica scratches her head, her finger delicate down its center. "I'll tell *you*. I'm two and a half years younger. Than my supposed legal. I wasn't ten when I started menstruating, and just about to start a fancy school. My stepmother was ashamed for me, especially with the whites. We were in Ottawa by then. She said those wishy-washy English didn't start till they were fourteen. And I was grades ahead in my classwork anyway—so she just switched me. Daddy never knew."

They face each other, shoulders hunched. The giggles come by fits and starts, then louder and louder, one spell after another until they're exhausted, when Soraya gives a shout. "And then—they will catch him. The boy. Maybe for a minute he will float, too, out, out, but quick they will catch him, in a net. Like a mosquito."

"Little mens." Veronica whispers it.

Turning as one, they check the screen. Empty. Then a boot comes on, in close-up. Another boot joins it. They hang there, their stubby bulldog fronts forward. Impossible to say whether they're a pair or belong to space-walkers halted side by side. Both women hug their breasts, feeling their nudity. Then the boots are snatched up and away.

"Must be no small repair." Veronica cocks her head. "Hey, listen." A siren. Once. Twice. And again. "Is that the all-clear?"

"Or the emergency?"

Can you believe it? They've both forgotten which is which. "Told us so many times, too," Veronica says between her teeth. "Beginning with that motel."

The humdrum word hits like a pebble slung at a barred window. They're silent.

"This laughing we make together—" Soraya says. "The name for it?"

"Giggling."

"You think—we do it too much?"

"No," Veronica says. "All considered."

When the screen springs to radiant life the shiny walls dapple with it.

ON COURSE

The video wouldn't lie. It's not used to it. Or not in such short syllables.

All clear, Soraya whispers to her belly. *La la. Yo-yo.* You and I know it has to be. All clear for you and me. There—didn't he move? Or is it the digestion only? When it happens you won't have to ask, Frank the medic said—he'll give a kick that'll send you to kingdom come.

She sees that Veronica, halfway across the Hygiene Unit, is no longer squatting in her usual style—head lax between her piston knees, or lying full length along the pool's rim. She's standing up, her eyes like one of the pair of onyx statuettes originally plundered from the site of the Great Oasis at Gharga, which Bakh had hidden in his walled Teheran garden. The museum, Bakh had chortled, was begging the pair back on a promise to return them ceremonially to Khartoum, where until A.D. 400 or so, they had stood in a temple marking the confluence of the Blue Nile and the White. Which promise neither party had expected to be kept.

Both women are dreaming.

"Veronica—what are you looking at."

"I'm watching birds."

"Birds? Here—you are watching birds?" But they are both tolerant.

"Three of them. Maybe four. All dancing."

"There's a bird in my belly. Come feel." She's not a video; she's lying. She wants her fetus constantly monitored during its long dream to become a child. Shifting head and arm to massage her nape, she is transfixed. "Look! Look what you are *doing.*"

Veronica looks down at herself. All this time her right hand has been holding the open tube of cocoa butter. Her left hand, more knowing, and somewhere along the path of reflection holding out its palm, is now circling one of her nipples then the other one, round and round, creaming them.

Wert, come to the corridor side of the unit to reassure his wife, smiles to himself. The door here reminds him of the smart but jerry-built door of their apartment at home, a nasty modern flat and more than he can

afford, but the layout convenient for a double establishment. Through
such doors the lowest conversation carries. The bathhouse cackle reas-
sures him now as always, giving him a double dose late in life of what
he'd learned so tardily to respect—that life's smaller details are often
its holiest. At home, too, the voices often change timbres, the wife now
in Switzerland softening hers to a dove's. The Soraya here, since her
fertility, has now and then taken to a cawing which amuses and heart-
ens him. He lingers to hear it before he knocks. The *Courier* at times
reminds him of his entire apartment house.

Look, what you are doing!

Veronica, with her crow's croak, can usually be heard keeping her
end up. Today she answers so softly the words are inaudible.

He's always tried to keep up with what he thinks of as the particulars.
His whole career has been formally drummed by those small gestures,
less than deed but more than manners, and local to no country. No need
to be nostalgic about them. The little details called human, which
merely means they take place well short of the emotions, are the likeli-
est to go on happening. Catastrophe doesn't dislodge them. Sometimes
they're part of the horror; sometimes they appear to assuage it. NASA
has no manual concerning them.

He has in his hand a blunt plastic container not intended for aerated
stuff but adaptable. Tuohy stores his "pop" in them. By further adapta-
tion one may drink from them. They are for vomit. Carrying an empty,
he has broken into certain stores in the Payload Bay and made a sweating, dangerous and illegal transfer of federal property.

In that country farthest behind him, his childhood, those who were
confronting death, or often only life, were often persuaded to partake
of a little liquid refreshment beforehand. Women awaiting their time
were especially urged to it. He is bringing his wife a beer.

Veronica studies her breasts. They're small cone shapes with large
nipples, puffed now, which purse at her like the sly lips of neighbors.
So that's it, huh—she's tired of the ethical life. As led alongside of friend
Tom. While saving their lives for their memoirs.

But who'll she choose? All—and/or none?

She reaches over to pat Hossein Bakhtiary Wert to be, child of many
mothers, still in his seed-pouch tum. Soraya herself seems asleep, her
mouth wide though not gullible. According to her, they are brought up
to begin anointing their bellies and sides the minute they've slept with
a man—pardon, *the* man. The nipples can wait until conception.

All right, then. She gives each of her own nipples a tap for its trouble and begins buttering her belly. By rights she should have begun at fourteen. Her child will have many fathers.

Soraya's not asleep. Her eyelids are quivering.

"Go on, look," Veronica says. "The past makes all of us whores."

4

THE VIEWING

PASSENGERS KNOW A LOT already, but never trust their own expertise. Even any old mother who's never flown has had a pursuit in heart from the beginning, or a flight. Even Wert's son has already begun his brilliantly designed impulsion toward the light. Wert, a tense sleeper, inches vainly in his restraint bag, worn during the shift that is night. One can't toss in it. But if he lies yoga-still he can woo to him the arch of the Foget couch. Semi-awake, he rides the balance line between the expertise floating him on, and his own. Ahead of him, Seats One to Four —Mulenberg, Oliphant, Cohen-Lievering, Gilpin and, behind him, Soraya, do the same. He wakes.

In the other civilian cabins of the *Courier,* what are they doing? How little they've merged with this cabin's consciousness. No wonder Soraya doubts the existence of those other small, six-sided worlds. If that they are. He sits up, yearning for tea.

ON COURSE

Each hour of that colophon, once so reassuring, is more impatiently unacceptable. The end of a journey as it nears always downgrades the journey itself. But that won't account for why their long-promised intramural viewing of the spacecraft has been shunted into the scant prayer time before breakfast, or why their whole schedule has been telescoped. Two civilian administrators-to-be here, and neither of them told what-all—a divide and conquer habit of government which his old boss Nosworthy, a one-time Rhodes scholar, used to call *bye-fellowing*—a bye-fellow being one belonging to the college but not a member of its foundation. Wert's been arguing in his head with Nosworthy for several days, asleep and awake. After a lifetime of reports to that silent interlocutor he still hopes that the actual Nosworthy, long vanished into retirement, is alive somewhere. Arguing with the dead is unprofitable.

Wert pulls a nozzle from his armrest and drinks. In his and Soraya's documents box is the brigadier general's collapsible traveling cup he'd sent to Madame in Switzerland, found in her effects after her decease. Soraya, intent on her son's American heritage, had insisted on bringing it. He stares at the nozzle, as it retracts. Unlike most objects he's been used to, it doesn't stare back. It has no historical past, to help make it real. An air of exaggeration always attaches to the real—only look close enough at people with noses, gas stations and foreshortened dogs. The norm is seldom very natural.

On the *Courier* the case is the opposite. Such an exaggeration lies at the core of the life possible here that every execution of it has had to be routine. Surfaces repeat themselves so steadily that it becomes useless to observe them as distinct. Even people are lessened. The pull of space is the main feature of every face. On his arrival at the living-station, his first trip out, he'd been disturbed to see that same muzzle on all faces waiting at the dock. He'd assumed that the larger rotor movement inside of which they lived would have relaxed them. Instead, each face is prognathous with intent, as with those aborigines for whom each moment is a gamble with the gods.

Indeed, Nosworthy, you'd have recognized us—as well as an old process. As Wert toured a wheel station twice as far from the sun as the Earth, yet made of ferronickel or asteroid, and currented by thermal prime movers, with refrigeration rooms for ice and oxygen cannily deep in the shadows of the rear walls, while other competences beyond his ken swarmed toward him in the Aztec light, he still thought: colonial?

Recalling certain specifications from his days with Ordoobadi's company, he'd primed himself to watch for bombs hung on what had been called "Ross-Smith arms," or rather to ask for them, since as defense ordnance they might be on the outer surface only. "Ross-Smith?" the commander leading him around said. "Not for years." Remembering that bland face, Wert understands the quality Dove and his crew have been picked for. The best colonials were like the sturdiest equipment, not rare but satisfactorily routine. That's why he, Wert, won't do.

Indeed, Uncle, they've done their best here to remove all drama from us, so that, as deliverably tailored packets of consciousness we may better enter and exit what NASA calls the "man-machine relationship in space." Any irruption, if it comes, will be that much more exaggerated. When it comes. Life having no obligation to teach us anything useful about life. Not in time to use it, like say—an old cup.

"Sleepers, awake!" Wert calls out. He's taken to doing this each "morning."

Everybody is except Soraya, who lives in sleep these days as in an old surplice. Gently, having to get up and step behind his own couch, he lays a hand on her cheek.

Up ahead, Gilpin bursts out laughing. The screen, which he's always watching, now says THE VIEW. After a pause it corrects itself, adding the ING.

Mulenberg yawns. "Wish to God I had some cologne." His head looms over his seat-back. "Whatsit you have on, Oliphant?" Lately he calls her that. "Smell it all the way from here."

"Cocoa butter. Soraya lent me it." Her voice is lazy, deep in her chair. Soraya laughs.

Yes, there's a new intimacy here. Office party at Christmas. End of summer, the yacht club. Leaving Soon. Is he mad to think this, considering where they are? Not at all. It's our way.

For Lievering is saying, *"Unser Gott im Himmel. Kaffee."*

They can smell it above their own odor, which isn't a rank stench but a blanketed one of vinyl linings, bagged urine and sweat nullified.

Tuohy the medic, a Galley Wipe adhered round his crown pirate-style, is bearing in one of his plastic unmentionables, on it a row of the covered cups they collect their own test-specimen in. Gravity's waiter himself, he lays the other hand's forefinger against his nose. What's wafting from his tray is no school-smelling emulsion. There's one of him at every Embassy, and at least one of these celebrations. Wert's reminded of a picnic at the base of Mt. Ararat, trundled over the Azer-baijani border with a load of *nun* bread, Jamison whisky and Kraft cheese from their post, and met by their compatriots from the Turkish side with Coca-Cola, a box of French almond-dragées from Ankara and a roast kid. Plus a tent, borne all the way by the beaming newest young guy from home, who when complimented, for the sun was fearsome and their side had only hats, said modestly: It's our way. "And sugar—" Tuohy says. "And—well—cream." He indicates the packets.

They all take it black. The old statement floats out like a caroling. The brew is strong, wineberry of their own earth.

Lievering, standing, has drunk up. Is there more? He whispers it. There is, though not enough for all. The ladies are served again. Wert watches the long Oliphant arm reach out, hand its portion to Lievering. Blinking back tears, he accepts.

Wert's own cheek is damp. Whatever, they're not going to down us. We'll live in the little particulars, no matter from what source. So softened, or weakened, he awaits the viewing. A rumor that home will see it at the same instant has circulated from somewhere forward. The medic has gone. "I wonder—"

"What?" comes from Soraya behind him. But hers is only a murmur, marital.

What the social tenderness is, where it stands among the emotions? Between charity, and what else?—that brush with another which the gruffest of us must have. Which behind all the avowed reasons, even to a reform bill for humanity and to giving birth without pain, he believes has brought all of them here. The emotion under all the rest, though he would never say that to this wife. Such reflections are for his other one. "I—was wondering whether there was a medic like Tuohy sent to every room."

"Room? No one's ever called this cabin that before." Veronica makes her laugh intentionally crude. Why does she do that, and as if she herself doesn't know?

It occurs to Wert that he now knows the people here like a member of a congregation. From which, like any found wanting in loyalty, he may be about to be dispossessed. For who knows better than he that in even the smallest of statehoods the wise neither criticize the facts nor predict them? Diplomacy is what is practiced after-the-fact. Never be too right too soon—as any smart Uncle will tell you. The man who guesses what will happen will be blamed for it. No one will believe he has merely guessed.

Why should he have shouldered so early the burden of statehood, and of his country's virtue, as the true burden and virtue of his own life? Was it the Pledge of Allegiance, said solemn and breast-crossed in the sunlit classroom, with spring flickering outside on the Civil War monument? Or the stunted primer, with its echoes of Edmund Burke. Or the old canvas of a family member obscurely at the Treaty of Paris, whose vast white-weskited abdomen hung in the dining room at the level of young William's eye? It had had a hole in it.

"Hey, Mole—" Veronica says, "come on in."

Mole, swanning in his long neck, follows with the gosling rest of him. "I—just wanted to check. Seen anything yet?"

"Have you?"

"No, sir." He still calls Wert sir. "Hear they're going to show us the official film of our own liftoff. Before they show us the whole ship."

"So we're in touch again."

"I believe so, sir." Mole's no longer debonair. "Cabin Two's not talking."

"Or whistling?" Though Gilpin gets messages, he's not been forward since the first day, nor invited.

"Take my seat, Mole." Lievering gets up. "I'm going forward." There are no spare seats in Cabin Six.

"Or—mine?" Gilpin says, hesitant. He knows he's a liability. "You've both been on EVA." He admires them for it. He's not a man who despises the prowess he doesn't have. "Must be tired."

"Not Lievering—" Mole says. "He thrives on it."

"Find anything?" Wert asked.

Lievering turns. His eyes glitter like the eyes of racing drivers when lifted from their cars at Le Mans. They already have a view in them. "Nothing to repair."

"The tile—" Mole said. "I *saw* it. Nothing wrong with it." Like most of the young, he loiters well. He's come to be with them for the viewing. It's touching, how at any crisis he prefers to be in Cabin Six. But Wert can't offer. His place is with his wife. This wife, a distant blue-eyed voice reminds him.

"You can have half my seat," Veronica drawls.

They all hoot, except Mole. A Foget couch can't be divided.

Soraya stands up. "I am going to the bath. No, Mole, my pleasure. Sit here."

"Go on, Mole. She doesn't want to see." Wert stands up, putting an arm around her. Up to now he's been careful not to emphasize their coupledom. He stares down at his brown-eyed wife, admiring both his wives for the rhythmic instinct with which they use self-sacrifice.

"You will tell me." She starts forward. "And, Veronica, you change seats with Wert. Mole won't mind the smell." Her merry look has the iron mirth of ranks of matchmakers behind it.

They both do as told, just in time. The video, unfolding to wide lens, no longer looks bumbling. Used to its single-line clichés, they are awed, ready to meet themselves.

The camera begins like any travelogue, lyrically scudding coastlines, bridging alps. Its intention is at once plain—to dismiss the Earth. But on that they aren't amateurs. *Isn't* that Italy's San Marco Platform? . . . *That's* off east of Kenya, only for satellites. . . . *Ah*—Thumba Equatorial Rocket-Launching Station, India. . . . Mar del Plata, Argentina, *or used to be*. Where the joint Apollo-Soyuz with the U.S.S.R. was launched, *back then*. . . . The U.S.S.R. does not appear. Australia does. And now again they are at sea. No ships. Cloud.

"Europe has disappeared," Wert says, with wry intention. Not even Gilpin bothers to echo him—for here they are: NASA's Johnson Space Center, Houston. A President picked it. They circle it, long enough for Oliphant to whisper, They lost a piece of our action, Mole; they're no longer set to bring us in.

And now—why it's Greenbelt, Maryland, where we first started sending hopeful signals to other worlds. One of the symbols they send, Wert remembers, resembles an ankh. "Much bigger installations now in Arizona," he hears Oliphant mutter. "But other worlds have not yet come forward."

Cabin Six falls still. Back and forth we go, along our own dear country's edge, the rest of the world annulled, as in any love affair.

"There it is, from the sea," Gilpin breathes. "Gantry Row."

It is a beautiful coastline. Flocks of birds. They approach at dusk.

"What are those shapes?" Lievering says. "I never saw anything like."

"Lost EVAS," Gilpin answers. "Look."

The camera is slow and grand now, hovering in a magnificent sunset. Below they spot a kind of ladder, with ungainly squares at its sides. They near it. They pass it. "Crawler Transport to move the old *Saturn V* rocket," Oliphant says. "Only about forty feet high. They called it 'The Train Wreck.' And there, that tiny job, the old Lunar Model Mission-Simulator, I think."

Mole says softly, "I been in it. You can move the moon's landscape past you by the controls."

The thing is full of birds. So is another ancient sculpture, pretty with vines. Gilpin and Oliphant exclaim at it.

"What the—" Mulenberg rouses himself. "Can't they find anything better?"

"Model of the old *Vanguard* dud," Gilpin said. "Blew the men up on launch pad. Don't think the camera realizes what it's looking at."

Mole says softly: "They're photoing the birds."

"Twenty miles of Teflon-coated wire were in it," Oliphant whispers clear. "Water-glycol system to protect on reentry, from the intense heat. Glycol's corrosive, and its dry residues are combustible. They also used non-certified paints, epoxy and tape."

"How do you know all this, *Ronchen!*"

The two back couches are silent. It must be the endearment makes her hesitate. "I wrote an article on it."

The camera is now taking them into fog. "Maintenance crew of the *Vanguard* were overworked," Oliphant continues in a drone. "And said to have been drinking cleaning alcohol, ninety proof. Afterwards, a leftover wrench was found in the spacecraft. According to the House Investigation Committee."

"They are very proud of still having the birds," Mole said.

"I find you two—uncalled for," Mulenberg said. "Your attitude."

"The report was called *NASA Oversight*," Veronica said.

On camera, the lights of a great, sweeping peninsula are now below. Wert says: "Now, now, folks. Here we are. Canaveral."

Once again Gilpin notes the dish-antennae on their triangular turrets. "We go much deeper in space, they'll have to radio-impulse symbol language to *us*."

Mulenberg snaps, "Now then. Merritt Island. Four miles from the sea. And there's the new VAB."

"Par*don?*" Lievering.

"Vehicle Assembly Building. The *Courier* was put together in it. You could fit a pyramid in it. Or a whole thunderstorm. Or that new piece of ordnance called 'The Blind Boy.'"

"Whatever *for*," Mole says.

"To blow up troubled rockets, for one thing." Her voice comes low and rich.

"Troubled?" Mole says.

Can't stop the two of them, Wert thinks. It's a wooing. Do civil administrators do the marrying? Not that those two would bother, but on habitat there'll be chapbooks for conduct. All the rulebooks of the world, to be done again. He should groan, yet it dazzles him. A clean slate. He should know better—he does. Yet it shimmers before him. That white hero-hall of the human mechanism, with all the old inscriptions coming on again, slow.

"Here *we* are," Mulenberg says. *"That's* whatever for."

On the screen, the launch pad is still empty, the *Courier* not yet arrived. The pad is a concrete base which has been compared to a Mayan temple. Any craft on it will stand slightly above terrain. Underneath is the flame deflector, brilliant yellow. Nearby is the gangling service tower and its companion gantry, red and clumsy, though with a white room inside. Those huge tanks in the distance store fuel. Those asbestos ones are for viewers. And rescuers.

Here it comes: The Roll-out. Theirs.

Looking out from Mission Control, there would be no human scale by which to measure it. The way soldier ants look, huge, crawling a white asphalt day in summer Georgia, with the street cleared by the sun's cannon. Inch by inch now, slow as lava, the towering mass. In its blind

self-knowledge it is not unlike a waterspout. When did it stop? For it
has stopped.

How it and we loom. Universe, accept us into your quantity.

The dawn is behind us. The view is from the east.

WE HAVE LIFTOFF

Someone in the Firing Room back there must have said that. It
sounded like surf.

They watch themselves soar.

The screen goes blank. Cabin Six won't see how its rocket dropped
away into the ocean to join or not join the recoverable. The cabin waits,
like hide-and-seekers closeted. It knows it is here, to be found.

"Those onion-domes back there," Lievering said hoarsely, "those
were the tracking-ships."

Have they slept again? Wert, missing Soraya, checks the watch he's
allowed to wear here, constructed on habitat. Since the fire on the flight
deck destroyed some circuits, the *Courier* has used the backup system,
which sounds like ship's bells. Only fifteen minutes have passed. Should
he recall Soraya from the Hygiene Unit? Better not. The baby has made
her boss of herself. Also, like many men from his region, the women,
black and white both, have trained him to believe that women apprehend everything. If after Jenny he hadn't let women into his serious life
sooner, that must be why. Like those Irishmen who marry late out of
their respect for the church, but not too late to have a large family—
out of respect for it.

"Do you suppose—that coffee? I feel unwontedly calm," Gilpin says.

"Oh no," Wert answers at once, out of Embassy habit. Allay panic
where you can. "End of journey stress maybe. The brain takes care of
it. I dropped off, too, actually. Did anyone else?"

Oliphant thinks she has not.

"Indeed not—" Mulenberg says.

"Are we all awake now?"

Lievering has to be roused.

Two cups. No one likes to say it. Maybe only one of the natural herbal
restoratives their contracts specified. "I like to be forewarned," Gilpin
said.

"Mole?"

"I have been awake," Mole said.

"I still would drink that *Kaffee*," Lievering murmurs. *"Entschuldigen Sie, bitte!* The screen!"

STAND BY STAND BY STAND BY

"I confess I am eager to see them," Gilpin said. "Our constituency."

But it's Dove. Full-face, a patch of plaster on his cheek, he speaks slowly, at some length. They can't hear a word he says. He continues, unaware. A final phrase they catch in mime.

Veronica says it dreamily, " 'Is that clear?' "

"Not yet," Mole says. But not smart-alecky. What makes the boy this sad? It's plain that Veronica will take him on. Already has? Wert thinks not; where could they? But Mole's not one to wait to be asked. What a marvelous, complicated kid—would he want one like him?

Wert's shaken by the answering physical rush, swelling his chest, opening his hands. How the empathy rises, tumid as sex. When you have a son.

"Get . . . on . . . with . . . it," Mulenberg says to the blank screen. That gray voice must have a separate pipeline through his easy, floppy bulk.

The screen, a vapid, uneasy mauve, activates in white script, agitated but obedient.

WE HAVE PARTIAL VIDEO FAILURE
PICTURE AND SOUND DO NOT
SYNCH WE HAVE JUST RECEIVED
JOINT COMMAND'S REPORT WHICH
FOLLOWS THEY ARE TRACKING US
LIVE

When the screen blanks again, Mulenberg's fist rears up and comes down with a crack. His knuckles? Or the couch.

With the new seating, Wert is right behind him. In his head he reviews the two arrangements, not sure why. What had been Mulenberg, Oliphant, Lievering, Gilpin, himself, and Soraya, is now: Mulenberg, himself, Lievering, Gilpin, Oliphant—and Mole. In emergency, their deployment can make only accidental difference. But he can hear Mulenberg's heavy breathing, feel the balked energy, always so evasively sexual. They all have some of that now, though nothing like Jack. Gilpin shows it least, but one too-sharp twit from him, or one more twinned whisper from the two end-seats, and that raw intake in front of Wert could blow. Wert's in the right place, if anyone has to take charge.

In front of him, he sees a descending moisture, falling slowly, in accordance with G-force. From Mulenberg's couch.

Dove here. The screen is blank. *Can you hear me?* The voice clears its throat. *All cabins attend.* The voice has already shrunk. *Cabins Three and Four in particular stand by for command report. Followed by film if we can pick it up. They have us on world satellite.* The voice fades, replaced by a flash of the flight deck. Dove is reading from a panel, in clogged static, blurred with squeals. They hear a blurted *One eighty-five* and what may be a *Please God.* The flight deck vanishes.

"What are the wild waves saying, Dove?" Mole's voice from the rear. "Give us the script."

Mulenberg, with a growl, leaps from his seat.

"Hold it, Jack. He's using the intercom on my seat." Wert's just realized it.

"Give us the screen alone, please. The audio has a glitch in it." Mole has the pebble-smooth space-command voice down to perfection. But shouldn't he identify them, Cabin Six to Flight Deck? Maybe they know.

They do. The cabin is irradiated by a large white message, in caps moving left to right: NASA JOINT COMMAND TO COURIER: ACCORDING TO ATTITUDE INFORMATION COURSE DEFLECTION DUE TO UNIDENTIFIED RESISTANCE NOW MODERATING . . . INERTIAL MEASURING UNITS NOW PROVIDING CORRECT NAVIGATIONAL REFERENCE . . . VECTOR UPDATE INITIALIZATION AND EXTRAPOLATION NOW PROCEEDING . . . TACAN INTERROGATOR ON FORWARD AVIONIC BAY WAS KNOCKED OUT NOW FUNCTIONING . . . PAYLOAD S-BAND INTERROGATOR WAS OFF . . . NOW IN ORDER . . . YOU ARE NOW OPERATIONAL . . . BUT KEEP CHECKING MSBLS

YOU ARE NOW TOO FAR OFF POSITION FOR DOCKING PLAN ALPHA BUT WILL ATTAIN CAPABILITY FOR CONTINGENCY TERMINAL RENDEZVOUS IN 185 MINUTES . . . WE HAD EXPECTED TO INITIATE A POINTING VECTOR TOWARD TARGET WITHIN AN ACCURACY OF PLUS-MINUS ZERO POINT 5 DEGREES HOWEVER YOU SHOWING PAYLOAD MISALIGNMENT ERROR AS REPORTED PREVIOUSLY . . . CHECK PRIORITY PAYLOAD VIA PLANNED EVA . . . REPEAT . . . CHECK PRIORITY PAYLOAD VIA PLANNED EVA . . . ALL CABINS STAND BY FOR ACTIVE RENDEZVOUS DRILL . . . REPEAT . . . YOU ARE TOO FAR . . .

They watch it through twice. There is no PLEASE GOD. The cabin is dark.

"Software—" Mulenberg says then. "The muddy software. I told them."

"What's MSBLS?" Gilpin says. "Look in your pocket, Jack." For the diagram he carries everywhere.

"Don't have to. Microwave Scan Beam Landing System. Know the company who makes it. I told Quality Control, might as well depend on extra-sensory perception."

"But you still—came aboard."

"Yes, Oliphant. I'm aboard."

"But, Mr. Mulenberg—Jack." Lievering has never before called him that. "Are we not depending on that all the time? When I am on EVA I feel it especially." He waits, a man used to hostility. "Not just for me, please. A force."

"You never said. When we were out there."

"But you felt it, yes, Mole? You felt it."

"For you, Vulfie," Mole said.

After a pause, Veronica says, "That force, Lievering. Are you for it? Or against."

No answer is expected. None comes.

"Soraya—" Wert says. "I must go to her. If it's going to be this dark."

"Hush—" Gilpin says. "All of you. They're tracking us. They'll be showing us. Live. Us *now.*"

He's so humbled here, by the physical. They've forgotten who he is —the most public man here. And the passenger with the longest expertise—in comradeship.

It grows hot in the cabin. Or seems so, as closets do. Are all their temples pounding as Wert's are? Pleading to be found?

"Jesus God—" the seat in front of him mutters, "pick us up, will you!"

To estimate time in the dark is an acquired faculty. In prison, Soraya did it. You travel on your breath, she said once—like in sex. And whom do you copulate with, then—God? Wert hadn't asked. Her first month pregnant she lost the power anyway. I cannot even estimate my child, she'll say, laughing. That's so my son will have all the time he wants, in his dark. She has the sudden humor of the submissive. His other wife, who bends in his arms like a rod which understands everything and denies it, has none. She is like Lievering.

All these indemnifying and subtracting powers, how they swirl around him. In the computing dark.

Dove's voice comes, through the keyhole. *They have us.*

On the screen a white dot, growing larger. Is it nearing, or are we nearing it? Child-in-the-dark, how absurd. We are it.

The voice comes again, shakily. *This is us, folks.*

There we are. That white fly, long since shed of its hard sheath. In shape exactly like the deerfly which haunts a scroungy stable, or will settle for a man's scalp.

They stare, deep in their own marvelous continuity.

"Soar on!" Somebody says it aloud. The civil administrator.

Soar. Soar. Soar. Soar. It comes in a Gregorian rumble, from all.

Oh we float, the administrator says, deep within himself. Freed of nations or not—we float.

"Keep seeing us as we are, Down Below," Gilpin says shakily.

"Oh, Tom—" Oliphant cries, "there we go."

The fly's becoming a dot again. They watch it recede. Dying is like this, some Tractarians say. The soul hangs over the body, watching it.

"We are still here, *Ronchen.* In our chariot." Lately, Lievering has a way of returning her to seriousness he plainly thinks she has missed. Lately, she tolerates it.

Wert no longer sees the frivolous or stark as that divisible. In the constant assemblage of light and dark which is the mind here, even a shoelace he has to bend to becomes part of all capability. Space invades the being from any crack. Words are merely Lievering's crack. And he's always hunting words for brotherhood. But the ancient Britons had a chariot whose wheels, mounted with sickle-blades, cut to pieces whatever came its way. Lievering's words—like those of a woman too deep in emotion, are often over-apposite.

Like Wert's other wife, for instance, who is forever leaving, and puts all her life on her tongue tip when she says good-bye.

"Yes, Veronica." Gilpin always gives her her full name. "Gone."

How many of the 185 minutes have passed? Wert can't recall what a rendezvous drill is. All instruction has oozed from him, like the trickle from the couch in front. He wishes he could see the face of his watch. Though strictly it has no face. Like so much made on Island Five.

COURIER YOU ARE NOW GOING OUT OF RANGE

Of whose? Canaveral's? And is that good or bad? Where are we now?

Passengers who attempt the other expertise create their own suspense. In the eddying vacuum Wert feels for what his black nurse used to call his mind-truths. Two weeks ago, knowing very well where he was, he'd turned his back on the gawpers scanning his mare before the handicap, off-track bettors who came one day a year, armed with tip sheets just as Cabin Six had been, and in the same state of demi-ignorance. To whom he could have said: at the sale the mare looked to me for all the world like that old engraving of Blink Bonny, the great runner and a good dam—one of whose foals was brought to this very county a century and a half ago, and lost sight of. Got her cheap, because of the native curl in her tail.

He yearns unbearably—for that dot.

U.S. NASA JOINT SPACE COMMAND

WE HAVE COURIER

The screen-shine of this Mission Control, wherever it is, is bright. The sectored room looks much as any space command. High above its winking panels one may glimpse though not quite read that blazon now on every NASA facility, the living-station as well: MAN IS BOTH THE WEAKEST AND THE MOST IMPORTANT LINK IN THE CHAIN

The men working at the many panels have their backs to the viewers. Those on a short uniformed line of five men in front do not. One officer in the center is capless. Like the legend, he is too far for details, but not for outline. A tall, frizzed head on its long Mole-neck. Surely that's Perdue. All the officers have their right arms raised in the familiar space gesture. They are in salute.

Mulenberg bursts into song. *"Morte-e—"* His voice cracks on it. Standing to face the screen, he bawls on anyway. He has the old Italianate pronunciation, the vowels long. High syllables, linking Wert to old Sundays. He finishes head bowed.

"That a prayer?" Gilpin says, not harshly.

"Only one I know."

"What's it say?"

He turns, red-faced. "I never knew."

"I used to know Latin," Wert said. "But no prayers."

"Sorry. If I blocked the screen for anyone." Mulenberg sank into his seat.

"You didn't," Mole said.

If we could—Wert feels—we should swivel to look at Mole, show some kind of faith in him. To swear to his worth. But the whole cabin's now bathed in the video's alternate flashes, brown to white.

EARTH TO COURIER   COURIER TO EARTH
L-5 VIA ALL SATELLITES
STAND BY

"Veronica—" Gilpin says, "your tidy pals at Peenemünde must have briefed you on this. Do us the honor."

"They briefed me, nuh. But not on what you think. Sure we'll watch you, Peenemünde said. *Und auch Der L-Fünf. Will we watch them to*

the Ode of Joy? . . . Our cargo shuttles lift off and dock to it, you know
. . . Beethoven belongs to the world, I told them. Ah, but you people
—they said—*Sie wunschen die Ganze Welt haüslich machen*. You wish
to domesticate the whole world."

"Germans," Lievering said.

"No—everywhere. That's what they brief you. That they won't disappear."

"We lack tact," Wert said. It was always said to him.

"The English, too, *Ronchen*. Before I leave I get letter from a poet
friend. They are shocked the *Courier* is not international."

"Space is any man's glory. We'll do it for them." But suddenly Mulenberg makes the squeezed sound which comes from that other plexus in
him, involuntary.

There it is on the screen, the Earth. Colorless but charged with silver,
like all video. Moving at the pace of the tears of things, that impercepti-
ble motion. It is as they think; it is everything they think. Have they
escaped it? More than half of its population will be looking at them.
Wert feels—not homesickness. The malaise of the linked.

"Superfly," Mole whispers. "Here comes Superfly."

The *Courier* is now flying on full camera, so close that they might be
looking at it from an escort plane. They can see that queer, proud
embossment on the wings—NΛSΛ—as other worlds might see it. Two
plane points. Or missiles. Or pyramids.

And as it vanishes, in replacement the *Courier*'s passengers see its
own interior for the first time in entirety, spread out cockpit to tail, aft
to forward as seen from above, like some diagram an even huger Mulenberg might have in his pocket. Is it a model? Or what interpenetrated
slide-magic has imaged all those tiny figures slumped forward in their
couches?

"One hundred of us? By God, there are." Behind Wert, Tom Gilpin
must have risen to his feet. In the long, opened-up belly of the *Courier*
—like an alligator slit from snout to toe, the top half laid back and all
its organs plain, do they almost see a tiny figure rise?

"Look, Veronica," Mulenberg babbles, "here we are again. On television. That's how we met. But on the street. You had a gun in my back.
Or nearly." He speaks in a lover's voice.

The diagram regards them steadily. Will it never leave? Perhaps
they're to see themselves so until docking—a page from a magic manual. Wert puts his head in his hands. To rest his eyes? His hands tremble;
they know he's kidding. His body feels Soraya's absence like a guilt; he's
let her stay away; he admits it. And the other in Switzerland, he's let

her stay away, too—or go. You are maybe a man who should only be in public life she'd said, shrewdly unfair. For this was their kinship, yet she would be leaving him to the more private one. He has come away, or been led, rather than decided.

But it's public service that rests him, in the profound relief which adherence to early precept always brings. As if his right hand had early been sewn to his breast in a certain posture. So armed, he can sleep at night in face of the bloodiest event. He has his village, which he cannot get away from—sometimes behind him, sometimes before.

"That fifth cabin—" Mole says. "Why's it dark?"

The screen switches now, coolly normal, filled as it is in the whitish living-room style, with three cleanly seen talking heads. This is the home studio, commenting on their flight. Behind is the controllable, backdrop sky which each tired citizen yearns toward at evening. The two men on the ends are those same interlocutors who performed in the corridor before liftoff. The stage-left one is the more famous. Between them, cinched like a plainer animal in a fancy trap, will be the usual "expert." A table borders them. But with that sky and the twinkle of mike on each, it might be an arête they are gazing from, or a battlefield. Yet they chat.

So familiar is the scene, Wert almost fails to realize that the screen is again in synch. So fluent and easy now the voices of the commentators, swallowing all events. Briefed to the ears with destiny, taking responsibility for none, it's their alternation which is so brilliantly shoddy. The man in the middle, hugging his expertise, looks uncomfortable.

Neatly the other two bounce out the *Courier*'s situation, by turns tickling danger, reassurance and history:

We proceed to the docking, which will be at Eastern Standard Time Central   Western   To rendezvous with Island 5 the Courier will have to pass through   For those who don't know what is meant by EVA   Contingency EVA   A fire in the avionic bays   temporarily   but now   The Courier has been flying during the anniversary week of the first orbital flight of the pioneer space-shuttle Columbia, which initiated   Since then the number of technical and military missions   exceeds   Island 5 is the first built in space itself, and will launch an industrial effort whose working population is expected to reach   If the eight-year plan on Island 5 is successful our coun-

*try will be the first to   Though other nations are assumed to
have long-range laser capacity for missile and spacecraft intercep-
tion, none is known to function beyond a range of   Island 5,
whose concept has for the present superseded NASA's interplanetary
exploration, lies at a range deemed beyond   It is estimated
that the number of Islands, of which other prototypes are under
NASA study for similar locations, could by the middle of the coming
century reach*

Such facts become raindrops. One doesn't listen. But now the two
interlocutors stumble—like over a pram left at the bottom of the stairs.
"It has just been reported—"
How glossily they recover. Yet this joint voice—though doubling between them: "Yes, Dick" and "No—Harry"—is real:

*"We've just been informed that prior to liftoff an undisclosed num-
ber of passengers and ground personnel were overcome by what may
have been hydrochloric gas or other fumes leaking into the embarkation corridor while it was undergoing sterilization precautions. There
were no casualties. Those more seriously affected are recovering in Walter Reed Hospital. Others are being held for medical check before being
returned to their families. All passengers unable to embark have been
replaced with stand-by personnel trained for such contingency. Since
not all these had undergone complete pre-liftoff biologicals, they have
been kept isolated. All these and other passengers aboard are reported
in excellent health and spirits, including the mother of the first child
likely to be born in space. The substitute personnel are expected to take
on living-station duty without hitch and indeed may add to its talent
pool, since among last-minute additions is a ballistic expert whose
proposals, five years ago put into escrow because of budget, can now be
tested under cheaper space-cost, and an astronomer"*—a fumble here,
Commander *who?*—*"first to study X rays in extra-galactic space . . ."*
Whew.
    "*Finally, one sad note—the dog which apparently slipped through
security patrol at liftoff and was consumed in the retro-blast from the
launch pad—some of you may have seen that shot—has been identified
as escaped from a nearby kennel, probably in search of his owner, a
correspondent inside Mission Control at the time.*
    "*We now are about to see the interior of the* Courier—*live from its
own cameras. We remind you that during docking, the* Courier *will be
under manual control and not visible. Docking will be seen from the*

*living-station itself, and relayed. The screening you now see begins
forward, or in the nose of the spacecraft, and ends aft, or in the tail.
Here goes:*
"The flight deck—and technically Cabin One:—"

Is just as it should be, as every boy and girl in the sunny classroom
will see it. They may even see the empty seat, not filled even by a
substitute.

"The second crew—Cabin Two—"

Though unlike the flight deck they're in short sleeves, they look less
casual. They are not in profile but full-face. If their mouths have gone
too sour for whistling, this can't be seen. Shoulders squared, they are
now as hup hup as any town band being West Point on Decoration Day
morning.

*"Cabins Three and Four, quartering the replacement personnel, iso-
lated for respiratory and other checks during the mission, have had the
partitions between removed, to allow freedom of movement during
special exercises for circulation, and other drill. You see them together."*
"Do we have them, Harry? Not yet, Dick. Stand by, folks—"

And now an exchange of some of that rubbery filler always kept to
hand. The man in the middle is being consulted.

To Wert, who thinks he knows what's coming—whose professional
sense of intrigue has quickened through years of opéra-bouffe coups,
attacks on embassies and all the more submerged violences back to a
custard apple mistaken for a grenade—the facts when they finally
emerge will protrude like extra bones from a skeleton truth already
assembled. The true corpus of the story lies in what has been going on
in all their imaginations, and will so survive—if it survives. He strains
to see what he can of his cabin mates. The facts should be anti-climax
to the united vision of these six. Though what's coming will be the facts.

Until the last moment he looks everywhere but at the screen.

There they are, the substitutes. Later on, as we settle into habitat, will
we be able to sort out precisely who was left behind? That paraplegic,
whose limb loss was to be so valuable? The two mentals, reclaimed for
sanity and sent forth to it with a ceremony Wert had attended in the
ward at St. Elizabeth's? And divers others, to a certain selection. Or

even that fell choice of beauty and promise which so often adheres to a true accident? For one may not rule that out.

They are—the forty or so whose folders he guesses were Mulenberg's empties—in the same fatigue suits from which Cabin Six will shortly be changing. As in the cabin here, they are unhelmeted. They recline similarly, and in every respect except its double size their cabin is identical. Perhaps their hairstyle is more conforming; which of them is male or female is moot. What they share is a quality. As they stand up in a body, this unity, which maybe the authorities didn't anticipate as so photographically clear, rises with them. They are white, black or other, yet a certain lack of variation supersedes even that. *Are* they— say it flat out—civilians? What matters, doesn't it, was that they were ready? And such fine specimens. Bridegrooms of the physical. For he now doubts that any are women. What a sight row by row it is though —the whittled modeling of handsome young men's mouths!

They are in salute.

"Cabin Five will not be seen. It contains priority payload not storable in the bay."
"Cabin Six—the last."

All of whom are surely feeling what Wert does, the admiration one can't begrudge any event however brutal or mean which has had the nerve to effect itself. And the corresponding tympani in the blood.

"Cabin Six, composed of a prestigious group who are well known to you—"

The camera traverses them one by one, the voices giving each inmate a character, like an offside kick. They have no time to bend their heads, if they think to, in shame. He hears that France is awarding Gilpin, the "controversial environmentalist," a post-liminary—"not posthumous, Harry"—Legion of Honor. Gilpin's eyes are lowered. The "beauteous Barbadian journalist" has averted her face. Soraya's absence is noted, and tenderly explained. Wert does not look at himself, the "diplomat." Lievering is passed over. Mulenberg smiles to the camera, but does not wave.

And Mole, after a fumble identified as "possibly a translator"—stares straight ahead.

It's good of time to move on.

"And now, people, Island Five, relayed from the Courier's *own cameras, now sighting it, the world's first public view:"*

—There it is, tilted hexagonal, the side toward them shining, in no cloud. Unlike his old brown ball, it has no hoary striations, can never be allowed them. Yet he feels a pity for it. He is its fauna-to-be, and like any good fox, he knows what those forty men are. They are the unknown, without which no world is a world. He breathes deeper, as he always does, over a map—

Wert waits. The video is now blank again except for its stand-by dream, but the air in Cabin Six is fetid, as if forty more persons than should be are breathing near. Alien lungs, pumping from afar the way propaganda does in wartime, exhausting all the country lanes and city bedchambers of civilian air. He waits hoping for Gilpin's usual oath, his Elizabethan "S'death, s'death, *s'death,"* swearing triply agnostic by the death of God. Oaths are like birthmarks; now and then you must show them. Or surely Lievering will evince a holocaust interest in the hydrochloric gas. A monomania can be like an earned oath.

Nothing? He is ashamed before Nosworthy.

"We are in the world's blood," the administrator said.

After some thirty minutes Wert begins to feel he has heard all the responses of his congregation. The grudging light is filled with their silences. Gilpin has admitted to having been forewarned. Mulenberg, ever double-voiced, after confiding to his business-heir daughter: *Priority Payload, that's military ordnance; there's always some,* is apologizing to his California one. *Honey, I did know Strategic Command had dibs on shuttle-space for forty trips this year; I just didn't know this was one of them.* Lievering is laughing to himself: An unidentified force resisting us—did they think they were going to be able to give it a name? Veronica will have no trouble believing all forces in outer space have national names on them. Wert has solved the riddle of her laugh. She has the cynicism of all those who believe themselves to be corrupt. And Soraya, plashing ruefully in her bath with her eye on his son's habitat, is already counseling the boy that we are all in public prisons, of which the *Courier* is only the latest version, but that she will use her influence. She considers it to be all in the hands of the authorities. Among whom, with loving worldliness, she has always included Wert.

"Well, folks—I'm off. Bye-bye all. And thanks."

He's forgotten Mole. That stowaway from youth-time, whom one ought never forget, what's he been saying?— Sure, we're the bummers: Us—? That young man who's having such trouble joining his country, such trouble leaving it; Wert understands him well. But there's no room for him.

"Mole—" Gilpin says "Godspeed. Be careful."

"Careful?" Is the boy thinking it's always unsettling when an agnostic invokes God? He's answering so gently. "Yes, Tom."

The hatch opens, admitting the medic. He has Soraya half in his arms.

Wert, rushing toward them, recalling too late one can't rush here even in partial G-force, slams against the wall. "Soraya, are you all right?"

"Is she ever. Came into the sick bay, to watch the movie with me." Tuohy's burns have faded. Another kind of flush is on him. "My wife first felt Mary Agnes in a movie. And Denis slipped her his first poke on the way to one. All fetuses are movie buffs." He gives her a pat. "Go put your feet up. Later on you can give 'em all a feel." His face sobers. "Later on."

"Let me feel." Mole is debonair again. "For luck."

"You again, kid? What you up to now?"

"Just a—rendezvous."

"Zat so. Well, here's your pill for it." The medic's yellow pouch is well known to them. "Here's everybody's." He hands them out.

"Don't take them!" Gilpin says sharply.

"If it isn't Mr. Gee. Say, how's your knee? Listen, I just handed out damn near my whole round." He flicks the pouch's dispenser with a smoker's thumbnail. "Sixty-four of them. What you think I am, a mass-murderer?" He pops a pill into his mouth. "Plus one makes sixty-five. Capacity." The pouch is empty. "Where's your WASTAT bin." He tosses the pouch in.

"Nothing personal. Just think we ought to go in—natural."

"Go in—?" Tuohy says. "How about that." His face is abstracted. "Everything we do here is natural. I know what's eating you, Mr. Gee. You seen those guys." He feels in a pocket. "Hey, Mole. 'Fore you go, wanna shoot a little crap? There's time for it."

"No." His eyes glow. "Let's butt."

They're on the floor, crouching, thighs spread. The medic, digging into a pocket, ties one of his extra-large Wipes around his head and tosses one to Mole. Both clasp their hands behind their backs. They begin to hop in clumsy footwork.

Wert watches, his hand on Soraya's belly. So far, he hasn't felt movement there. Suddenly the medic's head darts forward. Forehead hits forehead. Mole's knocked back but recovers. His leg length gives him an edge but Tuohy's bullet head could be dangerous. The strain on the loins must be terrific. Wert's own loins clench—and the hand. He uncurls the hand, abashed. Soraya, on her Foget, eyes shut, whispers smiling, "I wish *she* could know it—that funnybone push." Brown-eyed and blue, his two wives' union, chaste and solemn as it is, means as much to them as any they've had with him—yet they never mistake the difference.

The two down on the floor are now panting rawly, circling. There's just enough room for it. "Oh-oh—" Soraya murmurs, "if it would only come again, Wert. It is like having a friend inside me." A new friend, Wert says. His hand on her is electric, waiting. All's quiet there. Maybe his son doesn't like fights.

Yet born of a double marriage, according to his mother he will have a reinforcement, to her entirely literal; he will be "a double boy." Maybe so, but Wert, listening again to his other wife leave him—for Switzerland, for revolution, for Manoucher?—hears how, with the delicacy of the childless, she has left him to this Soraya. And to the likelihood that from now on he will be monogamous. His hand on the belly, he hears her: If you want to know the future, Wert, pick a life.

Crack! Mole, with a grunting surge of his loins, claps his legs together, catapulting forward. The medic goes over backward. His legs hang in the air. Mole's head-aim was true.

They both stand up, shakily. "Don't tell my wife," Tuohy says, with a leer he can't hold onto. He pulls up Mole's right arm. Mole hugs him with his left, on the shoulder of each a head.

"Take it easy." The medic, removing Mole's bandanna, pushes him toward the hatch. Darting out of his clutch, Mole leans over Soraya with a sheepish grin at Wert, touching first her cheek, then her belly, and goes.

The medic, taking off his own bandanna, folds both with finicky neatness and stows them away. "You all know he's had a message? Yeah. He's on the carpet. They want him up front." On his way out he pats Gilpin's knee. "Hang onto that bandage. I'll rewrap it for you on the Island."

"I will."

"And those guys in Three and Four—don't worry yourself. Maybe they have a fix on Oberth, too, not on the other rocket-man. You never know."

When he's gone, Lievering says, "Oberth? Do I know that name?"

"He believed in lie detectors," Gilpin said.

Mulenberg is contemplating the pill ration in his palm. "Nine for the flight deck, ditto for the second crew, six for us. Plus one makes twenty-five. From sixty-five, leaves forty. Yop. There's your evidential, Tom."

"For what?"

"You were never meant to have it. Your constituency of one hundred —civilians. Or any, turns out."

"Oh, I dunno, Jack."

"Eh?"

"I'll settle for six." Gilpin clears his throat. "Plus one."

Veronica is staring at some inked markings on her sleeve.

"What are those, Ronchen?"

"Mole was explaining to me. About burnup. How he and his friend Fred maybe got that wrong. Friction heat on orbit reentry? That's for Earth. Island Five has no surrounding atmosphere. But—we miss the docking, we could still—? On her sleeve, a small, overlapping circle, drawn in the water-soluble pale-blue tracery of all their pencils, goes round and round. "Overshoot?"

Nobody answers, though they are all standing now, ringed around that sleeve. Nobody knows enough.

Mulenberg has moved in close to her. He hasn't done that since the *Courier* lofted. "Balls. We'd have backup. If the computers fail."

"How? What? Do they build it?"

He is uneasy. "I don't know of any—existing contracts."

Bent, their heads almost touch. To Wert, watching them straighten, they appear to climb the ladder of one another, eye to eye. "Fool that I am—" Mulenberg breathes. "Another shuttle, of course. They'd send that." He lifts a huge fist to touch her earlobe, incredulous. It is a remarkably beautiful ear; Wert, too, has noticed them. "Or else—" His hands shakily bracelet her neck, move on to flatten the breasts under the fatigue suit. "Or they'd pull us in. By Island computers. They'd have to. With the payload we've got."

Lievering is watching, too. "Or we could . . . detonate."

Is Mulenberg going to tear her suit? She breaks from him.

Wert, roused from his family cocoon, says: "What you've been doing on EVA, Lievering. Tell them."

"We are shifting payload. Trying to."

Gilpin, all this time nursing his knee, looks up.

"Oliphant—"

"Yes, Mulenberg?"

His head hangs, defeated, the voice small. "What's that kid pervert up to? He is one, isn't he?"

"I don't know that yet." When she stretches, she's the taller. "I don't yet know him well enough." She steps past him, which in these quarters takes deliberation. "Soraya? May I feel?"

His wife, long since listening with vibrating eyelids, opens them. "He is quiet now. But try."

Wert lifts his hand away.

Veronica puts hers in its place. There is really as yet no arc there. "No, nothing. But he's had a shock. Soraya—you saw them? The new passengers?"

"*He* did. He does the seeing for me now. In the dark." She giggles, displacing Veronica's hand from that hardening belly. "All mens, they were."

"All men, nuh. Not a woman in the lot."

"Funny you should mind."

Veronica is trembling. "I do mind."

Ah, the harem can insult, Wert reminds himself. She didn't know.

His wife sits up. His only wife. If she has a bosom friend now, it's no longer Veronica, and he has a hunch it isn't going to be him.

Soraya yawns. "Have a son."

In the drill before docking, a cabin is lit up the way the great liners used to be when crossing the equator. In the same way the passengers in Cabin Six are dressing up for it. A life-support suit is like a small spacecraft—or sailboat. It has to be threaded and rethreaded. The overhead lights, bracing as any ballroom's, show every shoelace. As each passenger helps another, sentimentalists might think they clumsily embrace. The ceiling camera, when and if got to, will show otherwise. They have been through their group delusions, like any passenger list. It was merely that in preparation for docking the G-force was lowering, causing changes of balance. The mood in Cabin Six, and the attention paid to detail, was as stable as you might ask for, of any on that craft.

5

DOCKING

LIEVERING ON EVA

LIEVERING'S ALONE ON EVA. Consider how. Not literally alone, he has a power beyond most people's to step outside the vehicle of himself. In those rare seizures, with the eyes of his mind rolled upward, he has savored super-cool moments at that vehicle's edge. Moving along out here, goggled and visored in the center of a filmy octopus of other lenses, at times he has to quell an impulse to shed all this gear and float out in his nakedness for one moment's purity against all the hedgings which keep a person alive from the minute born. He sees his body snapped up by the cosmos, can feel the crumpling. But he has his second-rate sanity; he never will.

Downstairs he savors the danger of the work to come, hopes for it. In grammar school he had once immediately eaten a couple of stinging liqueur-chocolates which a malicious boy with a father in Intelligence had told him were "spy-savers," for use when cornered. He had wanted that cornering; it was not to be. He still craves it. But the rhythm of fearlessness, which one can neither fake nor avoid, takes care of him—and does his work.

Tonight three other payload specialists are strung out along the mid-fuselage structure of the bay, which stretches for 120 feet. One man is at the payload-handling station, facing aft. This man can open and close the Payload Bay's door, deploy the manipulator arms and control the lights and cameras mounted inside the bay. Four closed-circuit television monitors are displaying video from those cameras, to check all maneuvers. The second of the three other men stands there. The whole system is known as a "remote" one. It reminds Lievering of his own. Remote, but demanding men in chariotry.

Long ago, when the space push was still quasi-international, the first such manipulator system had been designed by Canadians. They did well. In those days one manipulator arm used to be standard, a second one optional. Now he doesn't know how many there are. What he and the others are about to do—135 minutes before docking—is not standard. They are going to retrieve a package unfortunately misaligned—in order to deploy it for more stringent pointing and stability accuracy.

He thinks of this process as akin to what was done to him in the British hospital, so long ago. For, this payload item, like him requiring such special handling, has too its own controls for what is termed in technical space language, "its particular experiment." Like a man's life. But "since structural deformation error sources always exist between the sensors"—one can never point a payload as exactly as a vehicle. For vehicle, translate: the world.

To be able to get outside one's world even if only when contingency calls—how marvelous. He's been out here twice before. The first time he actively assisted in the inspection of photographs, against a possible manual override of certain components. Next time, he merely watched repairs and calibrations of antennae and other instrumentation, to whose vibrations he tremored as to an opened brain. That time, he'd been stationed at an airlock outside the cabin on the aft bulkhead. This time he's nearer the docking module itself. During docking, this module, should they still be on EVA, must serve as their EVA airlock. If they are no longer on EVA it will mean they have performed their mission well. Or as well as can be.

What he hopes one day to see is the launching of a satellite into orbit —the Island's orbit, he assumes that to be, no longer the Earth's. A *Courier,* they say, can deliver as many as ten on a single mission. First, the satellite would be serviced, checked out and loaded—they would have done all that in the ship. On reaching the orbit desired—and after further predeployment checks—the satellite will lift from the cargo-bay retention structures, then extend away from whatever Orbiter—and release!

Its final activation would of course be by radio command.

To recover a satellite, one would rendezvous with it, maneuver close and grab it with one of those "remote" arms. After that—simply deactivate, stow in the bay and lock it up for further use.

He laughs when he thinks of this process, both in theory and execution so resembling the ingenious laundry pullies, much envied by the English, which his mother had had installed between house and tool shed at their London residence, after a design carried in her head all the way from Berlin.

The item they are handling now would be launched in much the same way. Retrieval, he suspects, might be moot. Though it is obviously a deep-space item, and requires a propulsion stage of its own, he doesn't know its precise function. What he does know is that the *Courier*'s retention structure is not quite what it should be—yet they're carrying two of what the head crewman calls "the little beauties." Lievering has heard no other name for them. But feeling his way with words, as always, he has put together enough syllables dropped like crumbs during the last two repair jobs, and one fringe ejaculation—"If I knew the activation phrase for this thing I wouldn't even think it"—to surmise the blinker word going on and off in all heads during tonight's operation. Detonate.

They like to fool about, and then deny. Unless a vehicle itself goes all to blazes—they've declared to him—a little beauty is utterly safe. And maybe even then. It cannot self-detonate. "Unlike a man—" he said to them. They hadn't replied. He had expected none. But he expects to see the item shortly.

The fourth man, the head crewman himself, is inside the bay, next to it.

The airlock hatch to the bay is D-shaped. In shuttles to date, the flat side of the *D* had a minimum clearance of thirty-six inches, the inside diameter of the airlock being sixty-three and its length eighty-three. For the *Courier*—triple it. Men haven't magnified since the old days. But loads in order to pay off may have to. The same thing used to happen to his father's library in Berlin—ever being outmoded, and ever more books. Though there, "the old days" had meant more than a decade or so. Still to Lievering rejoicing here, his whole life seems to have deployed and prepared him toward this securely threatened edge.

He's not anything like a real specialist. Yet *Pass me the Nijinsky*, they'll say of him—and down or up or sideways he'll go for them. Just so the Paris brothel would have gambled on his face to make do for the ordinary rest of him. That wouldn't happen to his face now, and he is glad. Only a woman may offer to the fate she craves a mere face.

What he's so far done on EVA is minor compared with what he may be used for now—depending on word from the bay. Last time, while he never touched the radiator panels being installed for increased heat rejection—for what reason they hadn't said—he was there in time when one of the others, in spite of foot restraints, slipped in the matter of space judgment, and might have soared wide. At present he's keeping watch at the handrails which extend along the aft bulkhead, down the hinge line of the hatch door and into the bay—and though he has nothing to do with the transfer of the equipment itself, if he has a suggestion for body-handling, the men will follow it. Down in the bay itself are what are called "translation-aids," for moving about. He is their translation-aid out here.

Tonight he also has charge of the mission kit of life-support expendables. Since their two previous six-hour stints out here have depleted these, the kit now contains only a supply for the remaining emergency EVA allowed them—so in one way his load is light.

The other half of his responsibility is an informal one, like him, not in any manual. As they are aligning the beauties down there in the bay, should there come a spot too tight for normal agility, he'll fill in for them. While—hopefully or foolishly, they post themselves well away. He is their life-expendable. They may think he isn't aware of it. They can't know he relishes it. Or perhaps they may. He doesn't crave absolutes the way Gilpin does—to help nourish the world. He wants to be one. This is hard to conceal. It would never occur to him to try.

Or to wonder why all his life the idea of rank for himself has horrified him, and the menial task has calmed him best. Down at the bottom of the rich London households—once even a royal one—to which refugee children of his class had now and then been bid, there might still be encountered a man-of-all-work and no one trade, Victorian in job and name, who performed any task the other help had no time or will for, from running to the post to scrubbing out a grate. This man, serving the servants themselves but outdoing them all in randomness, had a shuffling, kitchen-grub freedom they never caught onto. His title was "the useful man," and the young Wolf, when once teased at his father's club to tell his ambition, had elected to be one—to veiled smiles from the merchandisers who disliked his father's airs, and a chorus of praise from the Fabians. A day after, the agonized years of word-memorizing and list-reading had begun, done in their skylighted attic at home, with his father shouting *Recite to the Gods.*

Yes, I am in place, Lievering now mimes to the first crewman to enter the hatch. They both have intercoms, but they all mime when they can; it seems to go better with space. Now the two men still out here must be kept in the tail of his concertmeister eye. Finally both have passed him, descending. Down there the lights on booms and side walls illumine all four now in the bay. Two are moving along the sides, which accept the longitudinal and vertical loads. Two are along the keel, which accepts the lateral ones. Now the four conjoin, maybe in conference on just where the two beauties are. He would like to turn off his intercom, but dares not. In compromise, he impels himself along the vehicle to a point from which, though he can spring to duty on command, those four are out of sight.

He is alone. He can dare to look up. He never before has. The secret of his rhythm is that unlike even a pirouetting dancer, it never fixes the eye except on an inner recess. Those possessors of a body rhythm which moves from the loins are accepted readily enough by their fellows. Those in whom it moves from the brain via the restless funnel of the mouth are often scarcely acceptable to themselves. Until he came to the *Courier* he was ashamed of his gift except when he taught.

He grasps a handrail, for dizziness. Even if he could, he wouldn't wish to float off clothed. Stealthily, from eyes lowered but observing through what *Der Vater* had called their *Seitenflügeln*—their "side-aisles"—a practice forbidden him in the attic, he can see the universe streaming past him. In a second, he is going to cede it his innerness. Unlike in the wranglings of sex, during which some men illusion the same—the movement will not be mutual. He isn't fool enough, like some, to expect that even of a universe.

What he fears is that when he at last stares fully at this gold-black Eden in which the *Courier* rides frictionless, once again he will see only a setting—for him. Shutting his eyes tight, riding his wedged feet like a skier, Lievering lifts his arms, his chin—and stares wide.

It is an attic. But through its chinks one may address the gods. Here in this place, there will be almost no gap between the live and the dead, or between a proposal and its destiny. Fact will fulfill itself like dream, and beyond any smirch of the logic which is also gravitational. How else could he have begun to feel—against all the weight of reason—that there must be a buried Savior already on Island, ready to rise with their coming? Because they themselves, the multiple saviors floating out on all the *Couriers*, will have brought Him there, along with them?

His audience of stars, those fixed points which he can stare at now, tell him it makes no difference why.

Was it Christian or Jewish, or even anti-Jewish, to have proposed such a thing?

Answer: Out here is the sacristy, and the rabbinate.

Now the final heresy: Is it I also who am buried there?

The answer comes as it still must to morning scholars everywhere bent over their cabalas in all the ghettos—or out free: This place sees no difference in the quality of thought as to where it is bred.

And any answer is only his own, like the one given to Mole yesterday, when that imp of a scholar—for that's what he will be, no matter what headmasters say—asked, shivering, "Wolf—are you, are we really in that all-night sleep of the soul? Am I?" And he'd answered diffidently: "Sure. Sure, all of us," unable to add as he should have: But you surround me, all of you.

Is that a star falling? If so, not in reply. If the word *colleague* brings tears to some eyes, those gold auras tell him, that is not our lookout.

What's happening to his life-supports? He's so cold now that a tomb might not be a chilly place. He sees the need for jokes. Could he make one? *Come in, Wolf,* Dr. Larry said one day. *We are going to have a little practice session. We are going to act as if you exist.* He hadn't replied. Across the years, Lievering, another refugee, now answers him.

"Ah, Doctor—" Lievering says to the state of things, "always arguing."

Ah, ah—the deep throb of the craft's silent progress endorses him. Sure   Sure   Sure   Sure   Sure   Sure.

His mouth is stiffening. Speech is what you perpetrate upon the world. "Though   it   is of no importance—" he manages to eke out, "I am trying to understand myself. And. You. Attack me."

Out of the fund of situations offered him through life and refused, his own mouth chooses, chanting. He can see the words it speaks just as these were written down for it, some capitalized, some lowercase. At first he'd been required to know the meaning of all words on his father's lists, but sometimes failed to. Those were the words he articulated best. Once his father caught on, the definitions were let go, though sometimes the voice at his side couldn't forbear murmuring them, in that threatening library undertone which yet had brought the family so far. Of all the lists, loathed for being forced on him but still compelling, this one, a parable of all journeys out, had been his favorite.

> Whip-tom-kelly
> Beebread
> hemule
> Venery
> Nichil
> nighness
> hellward
> Flotant

He is going to push off. Calling out whip-whip the name of a bird, chosen for its aspirate. With traces of honeycomb on his lips. And having for company on the way one roebuck in its third year, he will surge out into the sea of venery—*mind the two meanings, son: sexual pleasure and the hunting of game.*

But he is already past that, and navigating deep into the old spelling of nothingness, on two next words chosen surely for their directional help. At last, he is Flotant—*a term applied to anything flying in the air, or so displayed.*

All those *h*'s, and *ch*'s, and *gh*'s, chosen so cunningly for a Teuton in England, and the *v* in *venery* the hardest; he has done it faultlessly, as never before. All the while on the journey he must have had always in mind.

He floats. On the L-5 they will have—just as is done at an Olympics —Flotant Sports. He will aim instead for those gold points which now cram toward him and recede. Come by elephant, Wolf, or by chariot, or crashing through sonnets or shopping for speech on *Der Vater*'s grocery lists; it is all the same to them.

In this attic the vision seizes one because it is already here. Even memory is returned to those who have escaped it. Ahead of him, the faces he passed by in life are filling the haunted picture frames he kept bare for martyrs he had never seen.

This is a real attack. His tongue, falling back, fills his mouth with its tremendous joke. He is the boy who kept crying "Wolf!"

The voice calling back to him is not his own. A voice! Of Brotherhood! He catapults toward it and is pulled up short, all the time attached to the craft by those wavering deep-sea divers' coils which plumb his back. His tongue's his own again. His fists, clawed in his mitts, relax. Upright, he jounces toward the hatch. In its metal wall he peers at himself, mirrored there. Behind that visor, is there a face he hasn't seen recently, purer at the cheeks and mouth and temples than a man's ought to be? It has suffered an attack of space, but it will be a useful man's yet.

"Lievering—" the voice of the intercom says again, "come down into the bay."

MOLE'S RENDEZVOUS

MOLE WANTS NOTHING FROM GUNS. He's annexed this one because it has twice belonged to a boy his age. He has left its ammunition behind. He's taking it along to the flight deck because it is a document. Dead and buried in a war, revived with the help of Geiger counters and slung over his fatigue suit's shoulder by its slim new leather, it blends quite well with his other strappings and might be some newfangled implement against shark. *It's a British Enfield,* the note accompanying it had said. *We wish it was one of ours, a Winchester. But my father says the war in these parts didn't get those in time, not till 1865. I think he's wrong. But anyway, it isn't one.*

That boy, too, believes his father is wrong.

On his way, he stops in at the Free Room. He has an itch to see whether anyone ever did use that little confession-pouch. If it's still there.

He's managed not to be in the Free Room since he hung it there. Now of course the room is empty. Empty rooms used to bug his girl, when she came into their flat alone. They know they can dispense with you, she said. But that was because she was leaving. The Free Room knows he is, too. The pouch is there. Someone has detached it from the grillwork and laid it neatly on a shelf. He half hopes. But it is empty, too.

"We missed you. At the suiting-up."

In his sandals still, he could easily whirl and grab her, as in old courtships. His flesh creeps toward that. He answers as he is, bent to the shelf, back turned. "That why you followed me?"

"To leave a note for you."

"Saying what?"

"Hadn't decided yet. Just knew I wanted to."

He turns. Suited up as she is except for bare head and hands, there still remain visible the nostrils that so please him, cut like the eyelets in his mother's table-linen, also her height, matched against his, and most of all her skin—but why choose? There wouldn't be time for it. There hasn't been.

She agrees without a word. Much has been saved here, by their being in the same slot, much bypassed. He thinks of it.

"Where will you? Suit up?"

"Cabin Two."

"And to dock? Where will you hole in?"

Nobody's said. He's been so much a part of the drills—and so adept at finding a place, at times he's forgotten his own status. "Probably there. If Lievering's on EVA though—I could come to your place."

She laughs like a riff. He likes that best.

He flicked the empty pouch, addressing it: "Wish me luck, hear?"

Two Cabin is so silent, so ready. Entering from aft, he finds no one lounging. No more locker-room sprawl, or lilting chitchat. Though the second crew's chaff is kindergarten stuff to the brain-scanning in Cabin Six, he's liked it here. He sees that his usual seat—up in front of Arthur Shefflin, the next best whistler after the medic—is occupied. No sweat, now and then he's found it so, the guy in it either telling him to buzz off to drill or galley, or in with Tuohy, or getting up himself to go back to the Pit. Which is what the flight deck is called here, manual or not.

Nobody's moving. Though faced away from him, they have an odd symmetry. Not strapped in yet, but their visors are down. Soldier ants are said to give off odor when in swarm. He can't smell anything new. But nobody's turning round to him. Cabin Two is full up.

Aw, come *on.* He doesn't say it. That's his pituitary taking over—that on-the-mark rush. The antennae tightness of his scalp is fear—a protective mechanism. Name it, Wolf says; then stand pat. He forces himself to. The man in the rear seat nearest him stands up. That should be Ervin. He was on EVA when Mole was. He mimes for Mole to approach the flight deck. Mole mimes back, an easy acknowledgment, staring into the other's visor as he goes forward. It isn't Ervin.

Passing the next two seats he manages to lean friendly on each shoulder. Neither face is known to him. He passes up a couple. Seat Four is Arthur. *Ringers?* Mole says without lips as he bends over. Old Arthur blinks. "That was some cockfight, kid," Arthur says, falsely loud. "Saw you on the monitor." Mole passes his own usual seat without bending to its occupant.

He stands at the flight deck hatch. On the closed-circuit monitor they'll have a view of him standing here. They've got used to him toting the gun. But reminded of what was cautioned him when he was led on the ship he resumes his old earth-slouch. The hatch is opening.

"Don't shoot," Mole said.

The flight deck is blinding bright. Icy stalagmites of chairs encrust upward from the removable floor panels. Display-and-control panels are drip-winking down. The line of crewmen is pinched between. They're too busy to look up. Too steadfast. They wear the face-exposing chin-strapped helmets which make all men look-alikes. There is no empty seat, though there is a tenth one. He has time to count. Left of it in a fire-blackened frame is the giant star-screen which had awed the medic. Big enough for a man to walk into. Or from. Nearest it, a head turns. "Your father's expecting you," Dove said.

"Where?" he says humbly.

"Telephone Booth."

The simplest directions weigh heavy here. Everything in spacecraft has a nickname. Dove, at the weekly home-dinners, had been full of them, Crawler Transports turning into Train Wrecks and one vast apparatus, whose function they were quiet about, into The Four Horsemen. It was one more way of joking. His father never joined in.

"Back there, kid."

Offset from the rest of the avionics array, but surrounded by the ever-present computer panels and yellow alarms, is the communications center Mulenberg had half described—a whole inner box of trapped light. Well, they have to woo it far. Pride seeps to him, for workmanship in spite of all muddle. "Looks like a fortune-teller's booth." Going in he hangs back; in close quarters he doesn't fancy a person behind him. No great ape does. Dove's paw is at his elbow. He isn't wearing his college signet ring; can't here. His hand looks less plump without it. "Yeah, kid, that was a fight. Worried us. You're valuable cargo. To one and all."

They're now concealed by the niche's high-molded angle.

"You have visitors, Charlie. You still in command?"

Dove's leftover burns go redder. "Never was, and you know it. Even a little kid, you were never fooled. Or about him." Dove put his lips to Mole's ear. "They came in the carts, at launch-time. Put in their own passengers. Your dear father had us traveling so light. That'll teach him. Anti-civilians—he's got 'em now." Dove pressed a button, or what stood for buttons here. A timer dial lit up. "Seven minutes, then you're on with him."

"He asked for me?"

"Burnt up the wires, when he heard."

"From where?"

"Joint Command—where else? Wanted to *see* you." Dove smiled at his own ring finger. "We sure let him."

It gets to him. On EVA. They showed him to his father on EVA. That's why he was allowed.

"I was terrible."

"Boy, you were. Lucky your sidekick."

"Lievering still out there?"

Dove stares afar. "Yeah, I guess. Until we dock. If."

They both let a half-minute go by.

"Then it is a bummer? The *Courier.*"

He's watching a curious act—Dove smoothing his chin, rubbing his singed nose, knuckling his palms in a washing motion, finally stretching his arms to the physical riches glittering close, all in what must be a loyalty to the thing itself. He moves like a snake unable to rid itself of its sheath. "Look at it—how can it be? Sure, they all have glitches. But we could make it. What we've had is a weak link. Oh, not you, Mole. But it's in the family.

"The timer's gone to four. Why else would you have come—" Dove says, "why else would we have been crazy enough to let you." His lips are swollen. "Dumb enough."

"Why did you?" Mole's voice cracks. He's ashamed.

Behind Dove, the man who isn't Ervin appears, his lean face jutting. So revealed, Mole has seen it somewhere. In a group of men, the only one with shaven head. "Told him yet? What's expected of him?"

"Just on." Dove edges Mole farther in. "Precious—you're our backup. Don't tell me you didn't know."

"They couldn't shift the load," the other man said. By that arm-embroidery, he's no NASA commander. "We'll ditch it. Then come in for terminal-rendezvous. I've warned Joint. They won't agree to it." He shifts what weight he has. The movement of a spacesuit can be hilarious, or sinister. "That's where you come in, Junior Perdue. Get that across to him. To yon Admiral. Maybe passengers can wait around. Maybe indefinitely. We can't. We won't. We want to land. Alpha rendezvous as planned. We'll do it by manual control if necessary. We have—that option. We'll come in nice and tidy, speed less than Mach 5."

He poked Mole's chest. "Say the normal ninety-five miles per." He lifts a boot and watches it descend. He has a lot of G-force on his own. "So explain to him. How it isn't fair—for a passenger like you to be expendable." He straightens; he's one of those who has to move. "Bawl, if you have to."

Maybe it was that bawl. Maybe it was the Junior. Maybe it was the Perdue. "I won't explain anything," Mole said, "except what you explain to me."

"What did I tell you?" Dove said. "A chip of *him.* Better let me." He took Mole by the hand, gazing with distaste at the botched purple wrist. The dial in the niche has gone to five. "*One*—that extra payload. We didn't know about it until after. NASA's nose is clean. Or my mission crew's is. *Two:* Our visitors—they did know." He is counting on Mole's fingers. "*Three:* Maybe that payload's why we had a bump back there *nobody* knows from what. No matter what else they know. *Four:* We daren't dock with that load positioned as it now is; we can't seem to shift it. *Five:*" his voice lowers, "We can ditch it." He grabbed Mole's other hand, first missing it. "*Six* and *Seven:* Command doesn't want us to; *we* can do it anyway." He drew breath. "*Eight:* If we do, Command will not cooperate. And that we can't do alone. A rendezvous takes two." Dove sighs. "*Nine?* Or we could do as they say. Not drop the payload. Which would avoid international complications. And wait like good boys. In orbit. Until they come for us." His grip is crushing. "Mister here, is not willing."

Over that other face comes a flick of contempt. Among the Washington parents there are one or two fathers like him. Machines don't satisfy this kind, not down at the bottom of their competence. At a point when, because there are so many machines, ordinary men in service to them give in to them and go home to tree-culture or ritual massage or swing-sex, this man will simply trample the balky machines themselves, in order to get on with it. Only animal confrontation will satisfy—all the more because it can't be had.

"You're Army, aren't you?" Mole said. "Used to see you at the general's. You're one of the ones who swat Linda for listening."

The man has a watch like Wert's. He glances at it.

"*Ten.*" Dove drops Mole's hand. "Mole? That's you."

The dial is counting, too. Six minutes have gone.

"What's that hanging on him?" the man said. "A gun?"

"An ancient document," Mole says. "It has no ammo."

"That's how the young shoot these days," Dove said. "Aw, let him keep it. He's not a bad kid. Used to see him at his father's. When we came to dinner, Mole—so your father could spread himself, and his pure intentions. Over the week's contracts. And those maps."

"There were never any people on them," Mole says.

"We're the people," Dove said. "The guys who run this mission. Dummysville, Grade A."

The other man lifts an eyebrow. The insignia on his breast rise. "Want to know why we can't shift, Dove? The bay is like stacked with consumables. Unbelievable amounts of them. Any idea why?"

"Wuddya know." Dove is pushing at panels in the niche. Filmy screens begin to close around Mole.

"Hey, what are those?" He's afraid his voice is panicky.

"For shadow," the man says. "Optics." There is still the contempt.

Dove watches him go. "Hope they've noticed the star-sensor is off," he murmurs. "But you do like they say. Save all our necks." He pokes his head back in, pointing to a yellow button. "Push that when you're through. No time to monitor you. You have ten minutes; then we need this place." His eyes gleam like signet rings. "Shoot him for *me*," Dove said.

He's alone. The screen in front of him begins working like a soup before it boils. He himself is standing in the deep pollution of the facts. Fred, brought up to a business, will do better at that; he won't expect his houses to be all dream; he has said so. As he deals with his Osaka contractors, he'll plunge for the builders' dream in them, mixing up only his *r*'s and his *l*'s. An honorable business. Which in time will make him an eminent Kim.

There's another tradition. Good or bad, he, Mole, comes from it. Dummysville, itemizing his fingers for him, tossed that in for finders— how with a man like his father the dream itself can pollute the facts, as well as the anti-dreams which follow after. Gilpin must all along have been watching him, Mole, pilot himself through the optics of that.

The screen, graining toward image, is filling in the grubby, graphed outline of a head. His father bears forward at him, in black and white. But he can fill in the colors himself, if he cares to.

He doesn't. He doesn't even have to keep away. He already is. In another century. From which he can stare.

"Son?"

That's what the face would say, though it doesn't move. Half mist, half dot, a glassy refraction of codes; that's only a kind of still shot they're showing. Like when a correspondent broadcasts from darkest nowhere, and having only the sound-tape, they shine his photo steady above his by-line.

"Pa." And only a by-line.

"We have to be short."

You taught me. "Yop."

"Why'd you go?"

Why had he—to be a good boy? A hero? A Gilpin, a Chape? For my values? For my mother's?

To learn how to tell cloud from monument. To be identifiable, in space.

"For you."

A groan. He hadn't counted on that. "How—is my mother?"

He wishes that face could move.

"We'll come to that."

"We have."

"You've grown hard," Perdue said. With pride?

"Short." Because though I've got over you, I cannot bear, I cannot bear to go into it.

"She's left me."

Hup mother, and over the stile.

"You don't ask me why? You don't express any—"

"She has my consent."

The face doesn't show anything. But then it never had.

"Father—" He's begun to shiver. He grips the gun. "To come so far. To talk." Like two shadows. And only of a domestic relationship. "It gives me the creeps. I mean—is that all? I mean—is that all right?"

"You didn't have to go," his father said. What's happening to his voice? "But yes, Mole. It's all right."

"But I did have to." The gun grips him. "I'm *their* backup. The passengers." He waits. "But I didn't mean it to be—for those."

No answer.

"I've a message—" Mole said into the miles between them—how many trillion? "Let me get it right. I'm bad on the flight facts." He concentrates on his hands. "First—they're going to ditch, orders or not. They do not intend to be expendable. I'm to say that. They said it the other way round, but that's what they mean. Then—they're keeping to Alpha plan rendezvous. We're going to dock."

Is the booth swaying, or is it just the optics? He wishes he hadn't had his kind of education. With those groans coming at him like Banquo's ghost. But he's doing fine. They're not his groans.

"What's that?" his father said. "On your shoulder."

He flattened backward. "You can see me?"

"They didn't tell you? That's the way it works, yes." Any detail and the admiral is himself again. "*Joint* can't be on live, because of the security. We may even have had a little—interference. All the more reason—not to be provocative. Mole . . . *what's that gun for?*"

He looked down at it. "It's a—go-between." Between the mystery and the facts.

"Oh, Mole, Mole."

"We get fancy out here. Fred warned me." If he mentions Fred he won't bawl. And her. "Anything you don't understand, ask my mother. Where'd she go?"

"Down in Virginia. To the old house. You remember it?"

He suddenly craves a stick of chewing gum. All his girls knew what that meant. The world was too much for him.

They had given that name to the old house high in the Blue Ridge, the one they used to rent when he was little. When his father was still a biologist.

"I didn't know it was still around," his father said.

It isn't. Not really. That's the trouble. She's gone back to summer. Those. Thinking maybe you'll come for her? No. She knows you won't. We were the ones who knew you best. But will she come back? Wolf is right; hatred is hard to keep. He droops, then remembers he can be seen. "I've made so many friends here, Pa. Friends for life."

No answer. The *I-Ching* doesn't like you to mention life directly. Nor love nor hate, any of those.

One more of their minutes has gone by. "Give my mother my love. And tell her I'm doing what she taught me."

His father doesn't ask what. He must know. "How did those bastards ever let you on?"

Because they are stupid. Like you taught them to be. Like you taught me not to bawl. Everybody's always teaching everybody.

The dial's moving in on you, Mole. Pit your body against the universe. Even in a machine.

"Go on, Pa. Give me the message."

Though it seems to him he hears only groans, he gets it. Jettison is not contemplated.

"Didn't think it would be." In a glass case at the Goddard there was a note pad from a famous old mission's checklist, on it printed Multiple Failures Will Not Be Considered. It lay above a display of "Freedom survival equipment," including a police whistle, a radio beacon and a self-inflating raft. Wow, the boy who'd tagged after Fred and him had said: That's kind of beautiful.

"Command won't order it. And I have to tell you." His father's voice breaks. "Neither can I."

No, you don't have to tell me. But one detail you do. "Pa? You did anyway, didn't you? Play the *Courier* to lose?"

No answer. He doesn't expect any, except from himself. "So. And you would have let Fred come."

"So your mother was right," his father said. "You came in his stead."

"Jeez—" Mole said, "we never thought of it that way." Did I? Bending to the gun, he fondles it.

"Sometime back"—his father is saying from a great distance—"Mr. Kim sent me a letter, offering a design. For retrieval, in case of just such an—orbital situation. I've just gotten in touch with him. We'd ignored them. But Kimco began it anyway. He counsels us—to hang on."

Hang on. It echoes.

His father's head has disappeared. "I—" his voice says, "—there's also a cable. For you. I'll put it on." His father is bawling.

The screen is as calm as an inland sea. The cable comes on in slow-traveling letters. Its by-line is Osaka. The letters fall into place like autumn leaves do in Japan.

Fred Kim to his friend Moreson Peldue aboard the U.S. *Courier* WISH YOU WERE HERE AM BUILDING YOU A HOUSE

Gad ap the floor, Mole.

Is this the floor of the Goddard? Was that the guard?

He can't move his neck to see. He can open only one eye.

The eye is almost flat against a no-color wall. He knows this wall, which has no angle where most floors meet a wall. He knows that curving. He must be in that little cylindrical cabin-in-the-sky, the *Courier*'s general corridor. Which must still have its limbo gravity. For he is on the floor. Have they docked?

Not yet. It's not entirely known, even aeromedically, how the plish-plash of even the steadiest vehicle is intuited by the passenger. Those on his own planet took long enough to do so. Centuries.

He closes his eye. Everything's moving along as always. Except him. Other than his . . . eyes. He can now open both of them. The left one must be swollen from where he banged it. When he fell. He cannot turn his neck. He opens both eyes wide.

Dove and the other man never came back for him. Maybe the Army man thought Mole could have tried harder, maybe Dove knew better, but the facts are that when he came out of that booth with a message somebody would already have monitored—there was no place for him. To ride out the docking in. There is a hierarchy even for stowaways. Two of the strangers edged him out of the Cabin Two hatch. He had the feeling that from now on where he was concerned the *Courier* would be all brinks. Though it may have been Dove who threw after him his life-support, a great limp Teddy bear. He recalls starting to put it on, alone. Wondering where he's meant to hole in. He knows better. He's not meant to.

In Cabin Six, his restraint bag is still hanging; it might have to do. He wishes it could. But in the Sick Bay there's a better deal, a couch to which he can be strapped. The one on top of that box whose lock has no clunk. He recalls struggling with the suit, having no purchase in this cylinder for his feet or his haunches, intent meanwhile on whether it should be the cabin or the bay—all along aware it will be what he can get to. When—what was it met his eyes, right there, where wall meets floor? Though he knows it amazed him, he's blank on what it was. He remembers hunkering over it, gratified. When—caught in a lurching of the *Courier* in which his own bowels joined—he slipped. There are no handrails here. And now his neck won't move. Foolish economies, both of them.

Or is he immobilized in one of those loopholes which come just before dawn, from which, while boarding train after train, arms and speech powerless—all are gathered; only he will not be on time—he is unable to awake?

Or is it the delirium to which no mother comes, while the bed turns to rock?

No, that one's long outgrown, together with that drama, always staged in a dull afternoon's pewter-gray, with him upstairs at his nap time, while downstairs his mother, who during their poor years cooked when she was upset, is silent in the kitchen against the cry from the dining room—"I'm drowning in food." Whereafter, a chair being shunted, a door slammed, he feels them float up the stairwell hand-in-hand to the bedroom next to his, to clench there as he once caught them. Wherefore the next time he lay as now, mummy-still in his toys.

No, he's much older now. He's hungry, morning-hungry. His girl-in-bed—who?—is murmuring to his blanket-twisted figure, All the covers are on your side. And for a split second, a frenzied second, he is locked in them, bound with hairs so fine he cannot feel them, or with cord so strong it must have paralyzed all sensation, wanting to scratch his nose with a forefinger that won't—move.

He's grown up by these loopholes and dreams, and grown out of them. He's here. Lying so he can't see his toes or even the curve of his chest. He can see his faithful nose now, slightly akimbo to the left, and an arm flung upward, atop of the fallen gun. That must be uncomfortable. He can't feel it. Butt, Mole, *butt.* How lucky. He is so lucky. He has very slightly moved his head. He can open and shut his eyes.

This is not a loophole. This is a glimpse. Wet with the future. Has he pissed? He can't say. Or shat? Does one, in such a—contingency? Or get that same awkward protrusion which happens to men hanged? He can't see. Or feel. Go higher, Mole, above the waist. Higher. Don't swarrow, Mole. You can't.

He will not close his eyes. He is about to know the flight facts.

I am the vehicle. Always was. Nobody else can horn in on it. Quick, bearers, I'm arriving. On Platform X. Quick, medic, toward me. Can't move my fingers. Somebody counted on them. I press yours anyway. Paddy-cake.

Time is in his limbs. He's heard talk of this since he was born. Who do they always want for it? Angels. Grotty little space-angels, calling you over the edge. He's grown out of that, too.

He stares straight up. He sees the speck he saw. On the low ceiling above him, a traveling dot. Just before he slipped, he bent down to it, yelled to it. Not a vision of the retina. A live mote, of the kind one sees in winter libraries, on the white page, traveling.

Let it be that mote please, crawled up that far. It is. A stowaway. He stretches to see.

One neck-click. Dock.

A giant hand has pushed his shoulders square. Nothing shows on his face.

HOLDINGS

THE SILENCE IN Cabin Six is now the quiet of some ordinary plane in a holding pattern over a city—holding up, holding on, holding out—too long. In its whine they feel to the quick what they are. Passengers. Ear-stopped, they hear themselves. In all their voices.

Bad luck, to think of a destination while landing. But the idea of Island 5, held back all these weeks, fills the cabin with floundering cloud. Spinning into a glittering city, on whose sharp roof-points only a holy *saddhu* can walk. Declining into burrows half sheepfold and open to every rapine, half bank vaults to which they have no key. Now that finally it's no use to think of the small holdings they left back home, they do—the flight bag which held everything, the old pair of shoes crocked and bunioned like the very soul of transportation, the tea-bag life-supports of a house. A hand going cosmic finds itself searching for carfare. They are losing altitude to the small, draining images of the ordinary. The grand manner of space is abandoning them. And they aren't yet safe.

Tom Gilpin is holding his breath. He's going through all the stages of his flighthood from his first time. Called back then from the mainland because of his father, he and the pilot of the tiny Coast Guard plane bobbing through a nor'easter like a tandem bike, he had been convinced that he, too, was flying it. Out of the hundreds of flights logged since, certain are bound to flash on during any new landing.

Coming in on the most insignificant hop, he will follow his first transcontinental one over the ranches of Montana and Idaho, black Morse code in the snow. Tokyo non-stop from New York approaches in sultry autumn, its oriental wind machines already babble-bowing him to a Maple Leaf Viewing, while with a first class shrimp in him for every air pocket and his cells floozy with champagne he himself is negotiating the touchdown. Over the green death-cones of Cebu where the air currents draw you in like the answer to a theorem, he sucks his breath in harder, in reverse. He likes best those flimsy carriers of Southeast Asia and Africa; in them he has more influence.

Over Bonn, Belgrade, Budapest, Prague and other secondary European cities—a qualification to be avoided when angling in on them— he invariably clutches his briefcase for political guidance on their ancient Reichstags—but works his lungs nevertheless. The capitals of the world overween him; coming in on Orly his eyes bulge like a gargoyle's from the provinces; hover-hovering on the ever-ever London fog his breath dissipates in bell-chime; about to fall on New York's scalpels, he closes his mind entirely—but never fails to keep going the good faith, the abiding breath.

Up ahead, Veronica will be hang-gliding among the narrow ecstasies of her own choice. Mulenberg is no doubt back again in what the airlines call the V.(ery) I.(mportant) P.(erson) Lounge, leaving it all to his importance, and to them. The Werts, in the parentdom which now obsesses them, are made physically fearless by the proper world-hopes —and by a lack of the shakier concerns beyond. Though they will never fly higher than internationally.

Lievering is to be envied. A religious by default and surely doomed to the separate life, he is out there putting both conditions to work. Mole's case is still too young to settle. Also, in realms other than the physical he shows signs of a flighthood not unlike Gilpin's own. He can only be loved.

He, Gilpin, is the ultimate passenger. Ignorant and broken-lanced as he is out here, his consciousness insists on its role. He is breathing for all of them. Just as he does on the ground. Always ready to explain, to Christ Jesus if need be, why people should be saved.

He's wiser now though, on why even the common people will be drafted, and will want to come on these missions from an earth ever more trapped in its history. Only a Boston philosopher, and one who'd ended his life with the nuns as Santayana had, would expect history to be understandable. Gilpin would not now write in emulation what he once had: "We can be pioneers again—but will there be time for it? Oh yes. Vandalism is the architecture of the future. For people who want to burn the past, there is always time."

From here, what a perspective he has, far chillier than the moon's. In whose atmosphere, since Leonardo's perspective, yes the best we have, does not pertain, a distant mountain is as sharp as a pebble six inches away. Why shouldn't our new lives be like that—not from history but from present intent? As it seems to him his life on the *Courier* has been. History has never been logical enough to help. Any art it has is post-mortem, and heavy with that odd vanity which comes of posthumously rapping the knuckles of emperors. Island 5 may not be claustrophobe, at least not at first. Possibly for long enough to make heroes which time will not despise?

"Ha."

They're used to his ejaculations here, those laughs and expletives which he has explained make him feel concrete "after a lifetime of the vapors." Their acquiescence has become one of the many courtesies he'll be sorry to leave. But this time it's no use. He's begun again to hyperventilate. Call it that. The aeromedics will.

They'd prefer him to be busy noting changes in his "cardiac silhouette." All here have noted some in their own, except for Soraya whose heart, doubly anchored, does not fibrillate. Walkers on the moon maintained their C.S. at preflight value. Maybe lack of perspective contributed. But he hasn't much walked. After these days of even partial weightlessness, the brutally headward acceleration of any reentry can't help but warp that dim profile he carries within him. Who will be the "recovery doctors" waiting for them? He imagines himself confounding them. This one has a complaint, Doc, about his silhouette. Used to feel pretty butch there. Doesn't like *l'art nouveau*.

No jokes will cover over what he's found out the world he deplores and incontinently loves is in for. Nobody really expected the extraterrestrial imperative to soar by spiritual affirmation wholly—if only because it was so glib about it. Yet he'd still assumed it must somewhere continue to acknowledge what we humbly are. It does—oh how it does —but only as a basis for altering that. The whole external process of this greatest of pioneer splurges is to move toward and by—a denial of what we are.

"Oh Lord—" Tom Gilpin said. "Lord—in the hour of our descent shall not the heart skip?"

In the *Courier*'s Cabin Six, courtesy prevailed.

The light is now that phenomenon which comes rarely, a trick of the dust specks they don't have. Old afternoon tawniness, with the slub of fake silk. When it comes, the cabin's heads go up as if listening. The old sense-confusions which on Earth used to come so reliably—there's so little chance for them.

The last person to speak out in this silence—perhaps twenty minutes ago?—had been Mulenberg, pathetically eager. "That film of us—they will see it? In all cities?" The vast blondness which has kept him youthful now has heavier facial lines. Though he'll have a giant lightness of foot until he dies, he's the only one who hasn't lost weight; he is flatulent with lost hope. Sexual abstinence has aged his self-confidence. Gilpin has had fantasies of reviving him under the group ministrations of some space-brothel to come, where he will bloom if he can be made to enter it. Not even Veronica now teases him. They had all reassured him at once that his daughters would see the film, all of them overcome at the scope of how tender they are going to have to be with him. To read of such a business-type being pierced by his own enigmas might once have filled them with glee; now his conundrums are theirs, and maybe soon his same lineaments. "Of course, of course," they all said. Cabin Six had never before spoken in chorus.

"I—want to share something with you—" he'd then blurted. That phrase from his California darling must have cost him something. "Has it occurred to you—that our hearts might be being monitored?"

What delusion is he asking them to share this time—as always in that flat, office-voice guise of informing them? For of course they have all worn heart-monitors from the outset. In dismay, they hadn't answered. He'd sat back in his seat without comment. The curve of his visor-bubble rears just visible above it, as it has always done. The trickle from his couch has stopped.

The cabin's radiance is now oppressing, a Fort Knox of solar gold. Are they flying directly toward the sun, that hole with its *tutu* of flame? Or would that put them in shadow. Deep enough into the magnetic field so as not to worry about solar fires. Though of course there are water hoses, foam bottles and U.V. sensors in all areas. U.V.—ultraviolet. It now occurs to Gilpin that Jack may have meant—not monitored by their own crowd. He can't deal with that. He won't.

He sees that their counsel these last hours: STAND BY—is now turned off. Probably all such circuits are. Time's up. They are going to dock. "The sweetest sound in space—" an early astronaut called it, "the click when two spacecrafts have completed docking." For old passenger cargo like himself, it's when the undercarriage bump-bumps the runway, grinding on without flare. Newer commercial planes now have rubbery, bendable wings, with subtler leanings. Stewardesses on landing remain the same, vestal in their corners, navels calm. He wishes with all that had been his uncontrolled heart—to see the faces of his companions.

As the headlong rush begins, he thinks he sees them. Not so much faces as crimps of light, as if he stares through the branches of a mountain laurel bearing toward him its own gravitation, demonstrating its force. His heart? A focus, too. His heart is being monitored, toward those. But he does not have to breathe for them.

Thank God. Thank whatever is about to be conceived as God, whose ovens must be drawing near. He is tired of the world he was born to. So was the world. There was only so much of the illimitable a man, a world, could take. Only so much, yet more and yet more, for this is what illimitability is. Until at last the mind stopped. At the new intergalactic pub, if need be. And got off.

He wept with the relief of it. Tears coursed warmly through his stubble of beard, blinding him to any sight of his neighbors, who might be undergoing the same. Each tear stood in his eye, golden. Each was crosshatched with that massing of light—which thus entered him. He began to sob deep in the larynx, or laugh deep in the abdomen. His sphincter let go, only slightly, so that a warm bit of his inner self must be staining his quasi-uniform; at the same time his penis rose excitedly, like a man hanged, or ready as it hadn't been in years. Probably he was not at all suited to non-gravity living or at best was not going to be one of its aristocrats. What did it matter? His pupils were all gold now, all idolatrous. Continents chased briefly over his cornea and were gone. A trace of war cloud hemorrhaged near the tear gland of one eyelid; there was the smallest tic in the other, as if a vestige image of an inferno Earth or of its innocently starved skeletons had lodged there; then all were gone in the rage of relief that spent from him. Agh. Ugh. Agh. Dazed, he entered Paradise. There was going to be somebody else to take the responsibility.

6

ORBITING
SOME ETERNITY

O   B   A   F   G   K   M   R   N   S

O Bring A Full Grown Kangaroo My Recipe Needs Some
O Brutal And Fearless Gorilla Kill My Roommate Next Sunday

THOSE CAPITAL LETTERS refer to star categories in that great work of
nineteenth-century spectrum analysis, the old Henry Draper catalogue.

Those two lines beneath are how a couple of Harvard students of the
era, reeling from the telescope, tried to remember them.

Idling at the porthole here, I compose my own jargons. In continuous
star-weather it takes stamina not to be Olympian. The *Courier* might
be some cracked palace in which a small royal clan is under house
arrest, at standstill in an omnipresent golden cave of carbuncles whose
fires burn well back or are extinct. While the populace, though at
enormous distance, may stroll by to view. Prison used to be more private. Prisons open to view are the last refinement of my century.

But no one can prevent us from leaving our century. No one. My
heart, which after strange infarction seems once more coiled red in its
original factory tubings, leaps at that. The nature of nature is always to
begin again.

As I, Gilpin, begin this log:

We cannot tell you where we are except by intuition. We speak often
of how we came. There was a moment—we decided after many sittings
on the question—which must have been the one when a try for jettison
was made. This moment we reverted to again and again, describing the
sensation in the flesh as we dropped, yet our cells held fast, as bottom-

less loss sucked us downward, to a point where in our former lives we would have smashed, fallen from a skyscraper's pinnacle to the Lilliputian pavement below. Then, at the nadir, came that stony reply—we all felt it—from space itself: *No. Gather them.* There has been some discussion about the No.

At the moment we speak of, Lievering was in the Payload Bay, alone. The special cargo he'd been left to shift—by means of a set of computer commands he can still repeat like the stations of a rosary—had not budged. Later, as each of us in turn became his apprentice to carry back to the cabin the day's ration of consumables, he would point out how the rest of the payload around it had. So, our consensus is that the *Courier* still has in its belly a terrible beauty which may be born—Wolf's own phrase for it—but not by any push from him. It's the least he can do, he'll say, with that stiffish grin of his; he doesn't say for or against whom. Considering the work he has done on the flight deck since, we can only bow to it.

For we did not dock, did we. During those first hours—or days?— after that fierce pull-up, it seemed to us, in our numbed, almost pleasant state, that we had, and were merely being held for embarkation in some customs process under which all clocks were stopped. I remember hunting for my scrip. For, during the next days—or hours?—we were still in communication with you—it can only have been you, just as we had been during those two apogee weeks of what we now think of as the *Courier*'s youth.

Certain never before activated remote-call boxes—our ignorant term for them, located in the public rooms, which installations Mulenberg has since explained are on unique radio-telephonic circuits decoding to ordinary ones—did bring you in, in one of your ordinary broadcasts. We heard nothing from Joint Command itself and of course had no way of talking back—though if we could have got to the flight deck, whose circuits to us were out, we would have tried. But like all watches and dials in the cabin, which had stopped, the door to the corridor had self-sealed, as it would at docking, according to its own dial, and like our watches, at half-past two. This has since become our calendar.

(Since then the call-boxes have subsided. Though not operable in reverse, or not by us, we think of them as ever on the ready, a solace from waning corridor to corridor. The cabin keeps bright. The video never revived.)

Can you imagine us then, having to construct our position via your brilliantly wigged juries of the newsbreaks (we recognized the anchormen & women's voices), of the self-perfected faces in which a jaw by

Daumier, a wrinkle by Breughel, never appears? Perhaps you no longer find it a peculiar way to learn one's destiny, since so many of you do, but by now we have had a perspective. We thank you for it, and for the news as well.

Gradually it became clear to us from those dutifully opaque releases and guarded voices that it might be a while before the world was revealed our whereabouts—that intransitive phrase being theirs. We were a security matter. Joint Command was quoted only, their location also being under risk. What was happening on the platforms of the world? On the subject of civilian missions, Congress performed loudly, and on us in particular very affectingly. The laiety stormed predictably, falling back like a well-divided apple, in equal parts. The broadcasters kept the best faith with us after all, mentioning us hourly, especially when signing off.

Then you left us. One fact seemed to have been spared us. We did not know where we were. Yet an impression persisted that everybody else did.

So we have taken what we could from you, putting together what Wert suspected, Mulenberg had not yet told us and Mole had let drop. To which we have since added that intuited sense of its own motion which even the babe in arms, fearful of falling yet trusting some arms subliminally, is said to have.

We are in orbit, quite apparently. We assume ourselves to be in orbit around Island Five. Perhaps—indefinitely? Or perhaps you are pursuing the matter. We await your call. Giving you news of us meanwhile, which you may never receive. We have had our conferences on whether you may or may not wish to.

We, on the other hand, wish to reveal all.

Log of the U.S. Civilian Shuttle *Courier*, on what we have decreed to be the thirty-first of May.

Orbiter Characteristics

(Values are approximate)

LENGTH: 74 m (244 ft.)
HEIGHT: 34 m (144 ft.)
WINGSPAN: 48 m (156 ft.)
WEIGHT: Gross lift of 4 000 000 kg (9 000 000 lb.)
THRUST:

Main Engines (6)
4 200 000 N (940 000 lb. each)

CARGO BAY: Said to be at least four times that of
                      commercial shuttle dimensions, which last
                      were 18 m (60 ft.) long; 5 m (15 ft.) in
                      diameter

ACCOMMODATIONS: Unmanned spacecraft to fully equipped
                               scientific laboratories

(My apologies for any error. We study as we can.)

When Lievering emerged from the cargo or Payload Bay, saved by
those very protections which had overzealously guarded the two beauties in there, he was not surprised to find himself alone. On the other
side of the bay, massive shiftings had effected little breakage, but a
creative disorder. Consumables were in siege supply. One nearby box
had already been raided—beer. He took a bottle along with him to the
flight deck, to which he had been instructed, if equivocally, to report
back, but found it sealed, as all forward hatches appeared to be, perhaps
for secret operations. The vehicle must already have been engaged in
that wide sweep of the heavens which has continued. (You will excuse
the word heavens; a log engenders such usages—and perhaps our present life.) When he had twice tried the signal-plate on the flight deck
entry and the alarm as well, he sat down on a housing and had his beer.
Finding himself alive had made him meditative. He may have slept.

On his way aft to us through the length of the ship, he tried every
hatch along the path. Cabin Two was as silent as the flight deck—not
a whistle. On Cabins Three and Four, which quartered the replacement
personnel, he admits to having fudged or delayed his report to us,
wanting to spare us immediate decisions which might be hard to make.
Though he was never to admit that there had been any reply.

It had by now occurred to him that all sectors of the vehicle might
be sealed. He knew from the viewing that Cabin Five contained further
Priority Payload (inventory since found shows it to harbor a complete
lab for the manufacture of viral insecticides). He tried that door too, as
he says—For luck. His humor grows increasingly Germanic. I mean to
say—his humor grows. No doubt concomitant with those duties which
(for some months, we think?) he soon set himself, shanghaiing Jack
Mulenberg to help.

After Cabin Five, he says, he stood at the entrance to our own sector
for some time, unable to make himself go on. When he found by the
signal-plate that it was unsealed, though apparently immovable, at first
he told himself that this was all a friend could ask for, then stood

narcotized by how much it was not—all. When he tells us this, as he often does now, we are embarrassed, for he tends to spell out to each of us our value to him, one by one. And we must all be wary here. Emotion takes energy. The median is best.

He must then have been emerging from one of those attacks, now familiar to us, which lend him temporary powers beyond any of ours. The entry, like all throughout the ship perhaps, was sealed only to those inside; from his side it was merely stuck fast to any except extraordinary strength. Perhaps this was true of Cabins Three and Four also. I would not care to say.

He decided to urge his way in—one doesn't slam-bang an airlock. If successful, he would find himself in our general corridor. At last he did so. There he found Mole.

Death does not need to be intuited. Much else about Mole did, on which we have all since collaborated, though I have had the main hand. By a second effort at our own cabin's hatch, Lievering was able to satisfy his need to see all of us summoned at once—which is interesting in the light of what our conduct was to be. I shall give a name to that, but not yet—to the way we act in concert more and more.

I have myself seen early shots done with box cameras of a group of people standing over one of their own tumuli, hands hanging. The presence of burial mounds may even affect an otherwise primitive drawing. Druid groups around their dolmens or cromlechs may well have been in similar attitude. Longboats come to mind. I saw such a group once around a dory which had no man in it. There need not be a body, but there has to have been a ritual death. The group is always consanguineous, or as with us now, has the look of it. They are assigning the death its role.

Mole's body lay in a triangle no living body could make, its head doll-sideways on the neck, though looking straight up. The left forearm, lying on the gun, looked most natural. Mulenberg was the first to bend down to him. There was no connection other than his posture to remind me that this was the same man who had once torn open the dress of a corpse dear to him, but I was so reminded, as perhaps the others were. When many in a group know bits of each others' history, these tend to unite. Delicacy has so grown upon Mulenberg here. We were watching its growth in us.

He turned upward Mole's left wrist. I could report aeromedically on the progress of rigor mortis in partial G-force, but will not trouble you here. What we saw was that the purple identification mark was gone.

Lievering at once jerked his own wrist upward. We followed suit. We were all still clearly marked. Later we would recall that since these brands have a time limit—two years—we may at least once be able to know accurately the duration of our stay here—but as yet we had no apprehension it might be that long.

Veronica was the next to kneel. I felt our collective presence nudge her to it. She made no attempt to close Mole's eyes, but then she was not his next-of-kin. I thought at first she might not have heard of this kindly custom of shielding the eyes of the living from the dead ones. For of course—as Jack has said since—it is done for us. Instead, in one whip-tip motion she laid her head alongside Mole's. Her body's angle, though fearfully contorted, was alive; that is, comparing the two bodies, one saw what life was. Then though still lying there, she moved, her face traversing the 180-degree arc from the base of one wall, up and across the ceiling, down the other. "He saw something. I know Mole." We thought both of those allegations unlikely. Increasingly though, it is our habit not to contradict. The data will in time shape itself to our needs.

She stood up then, tossing her head with the defiance I saw in her at seventeen, and thought then would keep her limber. "I didn't close Vivie's eyes either. My stepmother's. They have to know what they know." The word *know* is the key to Veronica, isn't it.

When she stepped back into our group Soraya shrank from her, shuddering against Wert, and I saw who would comply most in the burning of widows. Soraya pointed at the body with a long Muslim nail. In Persian art there is often one such fluid extension, snaked from the phalanx of faces behind. "He was the mascot, yes? The mascot is always the youngest, yes?" From behind her waist Wert clasped hands over his child. "Not if you don't name it. A mascot has to be named." Their relationship has changed. His face was almost sly. Though he will not win that battle, we can understand why he resists having a child called Hossein. And once you name them, the gods do notice them.

"He was the messenger." Lievering said no more.

It was my turn. I could assent to that. From my own classical education. But I am always a little out of the ritual. Or that is my hope. I knelt down. All heard my knee snap. It has never recovered. I prefer that. Little enough. A man must have a mark of what he has been and seen. Though the knee worsens, it serves as a spur to my own duty, this log, and we need constant reminders here. Orbiting ultimately penetrates the inhabitants of any heavenly body, man-made or not—just as the cyclic patterns of your own earth—one or more of which has caused us to be where we are, attest. So far, we experience only those brief hazes of forgetfulness which occur in people of middle age. Perhaps we age quicker here; certainly the skin does. My own face is riddled as if from bittern, which is what my island called the salt lye crystallized from seawater. All six of us are what the elders there used to call cabin-thin, a phrase descended to them from the days of sail. Otherwise it seems to us that our mental faculties per se have been quickened, the way a body in a centrifuge might have all its blood fly to its brain. In an orbit like ours we seem to ourselves constantly flung toward the a priori principles—and to brood on them.

Nevertheless, it is my opinion that with one sad exception we continue to be what is called sane. During this first period, perhaps what one might call hyper-sane. Stress takes its toll, and we are human still. I trust you will be glad to hear that. Though reassurance would be welcome.

To return to Mole. I knelt to him. In that other corridor, the germ-proofing one, through which we had been passed like show animals being defleaed in the anteroom of a good veterinary, he had approached me to inquire my identity, or award me it. I could only do the same for him. "You Mole?"

The eyes answered as I had known they would. I was just getting to my feet awkwardly when Soraya screamed.

Left of the body where the wall curved into the floor, we saw two— how shall I describe them to you? Not gnats, for they did not fly. Perhaps midges, if any of the Chironomidae move that infinitesimally. We could not see their motion by any stare. But Mulenberg interrupting to check what we saw, when we bent again, they had shifted position in tandem. Toward the body.

None of us moved. I suppose we might have. I doubt I need to explain, though. The motives from which one does or does not kill a midge.

"We must bury him," Wert said.

We shifted our stare. One does not bury in that sea.

But Wert never suggests what can't be done. In the face of constant rebuff he keeps the practicality of his lost statesmanship, plus a store of handy items observed. He led us to the Sick Bay.

Lievering was too spent to help us there. Mulenberg pushed the hardest, cursing loudly. He thinks the sealing can only have been intentional. I would prefer to blame the vehicle. Wert won't say. But we got into the Bay, carrying Mole in cortege.

The medic is our live casualty. You may think it pitiable that a man who hates priests, if not the fecundity of Catholic wives, should expend his madness in crossing himself. We think it the way he stays in touch with his family. Otherwise he keeps to his corner, considering us his jailers. He saw too many prisons perhaps. But as you and we know, it's no use becoming a space-buff because of that.

He still has his uses. Sometimes we can get a sharp medical hint from him, especially if we petition as a group. And if we have a task which falls outside the assigned, he likes to have us throw his dice for it. But as yet, while we lifted the hasp of the box-bed Wert indicated, the two women holding up the lid, and lowered Mole into it, what the medic was doing seemed as yet only appropriate. He never makes a sound at it.

Then they all looked to me. For the rites of emphasis, I suppose, and continuity. A role ridiculed behind one's back, though my cabinmates are kinder than you below ever were. All groups must have someone like me. And I am used to it.

I did not kneel again, though perhaps I could have. Nor did I look into the box. While I hunted for words, Wert, waving Soraya off, took her corner of the lid. No one dared relieve Veronica. Though the lid, as you no doubt know, is on a spring which takes strength to resist. I knew without question that he and she would uphold the lid until words were found. We had already begun to be a group, but were only halfway along, and if we had docked, would have been dispersible. Your command sealed us; that is what gods do. The rites evolve.

I spoke first for all of us. Perhaps pompously, though I saw no one wince. I can't say as to any of you, if you had been monitoring. Including Perdue. Though I spoke for him, too. "It's possible to remember in one's own cells the morality of the young—" I said, "and to do nothing."

Then I spoke for Mole. Telling why I did not need to see his face again. I could hear his voice: People when they sleep, they look so Unknown. "You are not Unknown," I said.

These boxes you have provided us with make fine platforms. Better even than the ones marked X. Anyone may make use of them.

U.S. *Courier,* on what we have decreed to be the fourteenth of July.

Bastille Day? Seems the day for it. To set forth for you what are the major divisions of lives anywhere, but are more starkly evident for groups like ours. I won't say—primitive ones. Though we exhibit certain —reversions, your anthropologists might call them, or retreats. We think of these, or begin to, as advances.

After Mole, we were hungry, and since our respects had been paid, not ashamed of it. One eats to live, and to be able to remember among whom. The Galley's consumables, weighed in for the voyage, were almost gone. Did we still think we were only in delay? People in any kind of craft which keeps them one or more steps away from the elements—even a sinking boat in sight of those drowning or blown away from it—are until the last optimistic. We are so yet.

"I felt—"

Each of us said it, still trying to phrase that moment of non-impact. Suddenly the table was pounded. The debris there jumped like a second meal offered.

Lievering has never made loud gestures, or anti-social ones, or those of personal enmity. Yet he can never be private enough for our comfort; his is a channel which can neither close nor be stanched. Now he seemed to us at last outside himself. In his effort to get closer to us? Or away from you?

"When the Moment came—" he said, Germanizing it, "ah you knew it at once. That stone in the heel, the brace in the back. That wooing in the hands—ah you knew." This was the gentle chiding of the pulpit, drawing out the better or worse side of a constituent but always the unconscious one. I was never that good at it. Pure reason can never take its place. As soon as he spoke even I recognized the identity of that once-simple reaction: the tendency of every particle of matter toward every other.

"Gravity. *Gravity*. We felt gravity." Not all of us shouted. But it was a chorus. "Yes, perhaps that's what it was. The Moment."

Afterward, we each confessed to doubts. His is the shaman-face in which our century professes not to believe. But we were agreeing with the essence of this man—which we seem now to do in turn for each of us—and it is true that gravitation, the full-force variant, no longer haunts our dreams. Even I, who craved it most, am ascetic now. What I remember instead is—that moment. Which in our folklore—yes, call it that—is now the birth one, the big or little bang which initiated our present small voyage—and universe. With your same gods holding our fate in the balance—your Joint Command. As they hold yours.

Do I mock? Yes. When I can.

When it came to us we were not in dockage?
When it came to us that we were in orbit?

When it came to us that the flight deck was no longer with us
When it came to us that we might be alone in our universe

We were passing through these shocks in that timeless state in which peoples form religions to help explain where they are, and in what condition. We were to go over those statements again and again, as I have printed them. They had become our psalter.

As you will know from similar sessions on us, we were preparing our excuses. After which we set about paying our tithe.

How much time elapsed before we gave thought to whether others were alive behind those sealed hatches, I hesitate to say. Once we got to it, we debated agreeably long. If they were alive, were they in willful non-communication? If so, then were we the ones being left to wither as we might, on what they assumed were our scant remaining rations. "To twist in the wind?" Wert said. He still smiles.

That old government phrase for the expendable was the first tonic one. Crisping us in mind. For as I strive to show here, though except for the medic we are not in any sense mad, we go in and out of psychic states ranging from the depressed to the exalted—just as you. And in somewhat tighter quarters. With information at best restricted and now entirely withheld. We do have one advantage over you. I'll come to it.

Finally it was decided we must make every effort—but only as we could—toward the flight deck. It was not so brave of us. By now, no one seemed to be holding us back.

We went as a body, the women, too. We had never traversed the whole length of the *Courier* in a body. It is the kind of travel people do in their own houses, huts or condominiums, circling beyond habit, approval or repulsion, testing their place. When we passed Cabins Three and Four we checked our speech, took stock of each others' faces and stole by as past an ambush. Though we keep them in conscience, we have since come to believe this the best way of dealing with Cabins Three and Four.

Yet when we came to the flight deck, behind which were men of the same order, we halted in awe. Stupid men though these officers inside might be in other contexts, here we had been hostages to their expertise. Also we felt some pleasure, for we had been trained to defer to them as invulnerable. Finally, though, we felt generous. They had the computers. For this we would free them, if they needed it.

So we stood before the hatch. Who was it prewarned us to don our oxygen masks? As so often happens between close inmates, most likely a common impulse arose in all of us.

First off we pressed the signal-plate, then the hidden spare. Then, the four men abreast, the women leaning their weight behind, we pushed. The door gave. Then we tried to hold the women back. Those two would have none of that. It was a necessary rite, to file in one by one —to see what could happen here—and file out again.

They had died at their posts. Steadfast. In their Auxiliary Environment. Which we civilians had not been allowed. Though an inhalation of hyperbaric oxygen over 5 ATA (atmospheres absolute), and possibly beyond, does indeed induce convulsion, the harness they died in gave them no leeway. As each scarab-dyed face with its *risus sardonicus* testified. Identification could not be routine, but we managed some. Flight Commander Charles Dove (or Mission Captain or Head Pilot, since we are not sure of these distinctions, but most certainly alumnus of a college whose class ring, found in his breast pocket, is an amethyst in sterling) died in the extra or jumpseat. The head seat, or head astronaut's, was occupied by a male, probably white, in Army uniform, rank major general, identity unknown.

Though the atmosphere had returned to normal, our masks were needed. For your aeromedicals: either death from central-nervous toxicity has a special morbidity or in spite of the dryness here other factors make decomposition quick. Or else we were deceived, as we so often are now, on how much duration had passed.

But flesh—one cannot simply close the door on it. Or not immediately. In our next log I hope to record what has been done. Though promises congeal here. Action proposed retrogrades into performance already accomplished. Motion is catatonic, and sometimes occurs only in the head. On occasion we have even used mirrors—the walls serve as they can—to confirm our acts. But of this I am sure. Jettison—of those bodies—will be contemplated.

LOG FOUR: Timeless

From the need to clear the flight deck of those bodies have come all our assigned tasks. Indeed, is it not the same with you and your work? What is one of your decades at bottom, other than a process by which bodies are got rid of, to provide space for those to come? And that is its motion.

Lievering refused volunteers. So, though Jack each time helps him remove and transfer a body to the designated point outside the vehicle, he stops there; it is Wolf who jettisons. The satisfaction he gets from this is clearly a form of justice the rest of us couldn't attain to but can respect. (We grow ever more tolerant here. In certain reprises of clarity, the kind you might have at the end of a hard day's work, or gazing suddenly at a friend immersed in his, this worries me.)

Our other great task has been to classify the supplies in the bay and arrange a system of provendering the Galley. Solids are in impressive supply, and as the Galley nozzles run dry—the soft drink one, lately more popular, already has—we shall broach the cases of distilled water which were for manufacturing use but appear drinkable. What we have not fathomed is how to restock the Galley mechanically, so we must in a sense shop in the Bay and carry home each day. Day? Without ways to sector our duration would we not grow abstracted, even anarchic? The weather at the portholes is no help diurnally. To our relief, our circadian rhythms have taken over, not only privately, as with the bowels, but collectively. Certain rhythms were to come naturally, from living close.

For sleep, we return to the cabin, and it is remarkable how we begin to converge upon it from whatever point in our small terrain, at an hour we tend to think coincides with your dusk, Wolf and Jack in from the hunt as it were, stopping by at the Hygiene Unit for the necessary ablutions afterward, followed by each of us, in from one of the domestic chores we have so handily divided. A toy satisfaction can come of that alone. The danger, as you know, is its comfort, in which one can sink larger concerns. So we have our discipline, which is each "night" to don our support-suits, for excusable display to you—and in the hope that the call will come.

When, however, you do not, all our problems recoil on us. Well supplied as the Bay is, we cannot replenish. Though the WASTAT bins and Dry Johns appear stable, chemicals have their limits. Our situation cannot go on as is forever. Of course, neither can yours, and you too are veterans of unanswered prayer. Under this analogy, a kind of blessing, we are able to fall asleep. It is almost a religious experience. So, by the careful manipulation of this and other analogies, we survive, to arrive at the next stage of what it may please you to dub our culture. If you do monitor us, you may be expecting it, cast in your image as we are. For there has always to be an enemy, doesn't there? Your Joint Command, who indeed presented themselves, were too remote. Carefully we repressed any thought of engaging you down there in toto, even psychologically. As I warned, an island may never entirely reject the mainland. Interdependent, and permanently land-locked as we were, only an ideological quarrel was open to us. So ours was, yet like any of yours still based on supply and demand.

One day Wolf came to us. You must understand that the disposal of each of the dead was a project in itself, involving what may have been weeks of logistical planning, even at the outset some mechanical drawing, followed by the construction of slings, preparation of cerements for each poor scarab—whose weight loss did help—all the way to the final execution, to which the rest of us, trouping forward, contributed a few simple choirings. *Basta, you know the process!* But now our supply had run out. Wolf had long since sent the tenth body into space. Moreover, not wishing to disturb us with questions of sentiment, and knowing how badly we kept track, he had proceeded on. The whistlers were also already in space.

With your resources, you may have no notion how that disquieted us. A rite was gone with them. It was then we allowed ourselves to think consciously of Cabins Three and Four. We had long suspected that the substitute passengers there might have life in them. Or—we had not fully convinced ourselves they were dead. Allowing ourselves this suspension we had never tried those hatches and never spoke of it. As yet we had had no need of them. Now we did.

I'll spare you our arguments—radical and conservative, voluble, lyrical, profound. Prisons were now mentioned in stifled accents—and passed over. Youth—those handsome mouths—was eulogized. Honor, Decency, Shame—or the beginnings of them, for we were by now at the opposite end of the road from you, you see—were somewhat explored. Vengeance—was finally mentioned. Jack was for it. Wert advised a prudent wait. Soraya agreed passionately, for two. Lievering, wanting his bodies, stood mute. I myself, of course, locked in my lifelong role, perhaps sustained by being safely the weakest, went and pounded on the doors. Veronica, though hardened by the death of Mole, and reminding us there were no women there, came and listened behind me. We were never able to agree on what we had heard.

Was there a response from those cabins? I still think so. But then my philoprogenitive love of my fellow humans, which lies so heavy on this narrative and on me, has never been trustworthy. I always overhear. We could have bored a hole, I thought later. And perhaps I would have done so, if I had had my shooting-stick.

We were in the end the kind of jury you know well—able to demur privately and concur publicly. It was suddenly recalled that in their doubled quarters they must have double provisions. The suggestion which carried came spontaneously, as it often does. Even vivaciously. "Why don't we wait until rescue?" several said.

Until then, no one had dared mention the word. But in this context, not to draw spiritual help from all the reserves of science, as well as your own good will would be remiss. No one could object to hope. Or to equality in it for all.

So we generously gave up our routine, but did not abandon them. We left them to you.

So, for some cycles, and still in a state of primitive shock, we led a life similar to yours as we ourselves had once known it—a regulated existence, beneath which lurked certain secrets, dirty or arcane.

But in the end, is there any spur to change quite like unanswered prayer? Wolf had served us in his way, so had Jack. The women in a way were already serving, as was I. Even Mole had had his turn. Now it was Wert's.

One day at dusk we were again converging on our cabin. In our restlessness we have become what the American Indians of yore called "walkers," those who must wander their hours instead of fixate them, very like those urban ones who parse your city streets. Within the *Courier's* limits we were becoming nomad, after any task always compulsively on the wander again, often taking up some little bundle for company. Even among close tribes the persona can become sick of its kind. Performance was already affected. Though we helped each other suit up, we did so without the usual solicitude. There might even come a dusk when we would not bother to suit up for the possible reentry which would pull us out and back to you. We might simply present ourselves to you bare, in our aboriginal state. I see I have at last named our condition to you. One comes to it.

But we are after all like you—or like those of you I address. Men and women of responsibility—even of a chosen one, if half by circumstance. All of us are now agreed that in the recesses of our awakening intellects we were: *noting.* Or walking, we had arrived. But it was Wert's turn to speak. Or he felt our collective pressure, and bowed to it. Not to you. Even though we had all settled in our couches for the daily prayer. Plea.

Wert leaped up, facing us as accommodations allow. Indeed we have those to thank in that once cabined we seldom have orations of length. "This has got to stop—" he shouted. "We are worshiping them."

We were stunned. Wert never shouts. We knew he spoke the truth.

Wert pointed downward. As you in your devotions look upward. Saying in the deepest voice he could manage, penetrating indeed to the depths restirring in us, "They are no different from us."

Only more powerful. Only at the—moment. No one had to say it. We were passengers once again.

And perhaps there's no sharper spur to meditation than answered prayer.

Two dusks ago, just as most of us were settling in, the call-boxes all over the ship began emitting a white sound. The poor medic came running into the cabin; he does that at anything untoward. The others sat him in my seat.

I was in the Hygiene Unit. For fear of weight loss, and the gradual anorexia which can come of it, we take appetite pills. When I first saw the stodged walls and spilled crates in the Payload Bay, supplies enough to last us for years, I was encouraged; at least cannibalism will not be a problem, or not soon. Passing by there now I see that whole *étape* as a mound we shall have to excrete—the bombs too, if that's what they are. Waste will be our problem in the midst of plenty. So I must eat, but I constipate. I am public-spirited even in the bowel.

As I sat, a video high on the wall opposite began to activate. In the cabin, the others told me later, our old home-video, spider-gray in its corner, did not; instead, the ceiling camera, long since forgotten, opened wide. Leaning back, they opened their mouths to you, and let your news fall in. As for me, I said at once: Kidney failure. I hallucinate.

I do it well. There they seem to me to be again, your newscasters, bringing us our destiny exactly as they bring it to the rest of you, though I see them not pink and lemony in their happy-skins but dotted in black and gray high frequency on the white gist of space. Age has not got to them, nor art either, but otherwise the picture has such painful verisimilitude I have to watch—and listen.

They are speaking of the *Courier* as they do of all the luckless, in the third person only, in their evenly festival voices. (Confirming—that we have intuited well. And may have to go on doing it.) They don't yet know that they have got through to us. Or else my subconscious will not allow them to know what it overhears the world say, being always a little shamed.

Still, when I get back to the cabin, I may hint that it seems we are a security risk—though I'll spare them the details. Why should the medic have to hear it suggested that we are to be in orbit indefinitely? Would Soraya be happier to hear that though neither Earth nor an expensive installation like the Island is yet prepared to receive us in our present state, ultimately a rendezvous with us is planned—if we can hold out?

Nevertheless I sit there spellbound at how a masterly subconscious can secrete detail utterly foreign to it. You newsmen are by now describing the radio-emissions designed to attract our call-boxes, as being not too dissimilar from the coded picture once sent by the Arecibo Observatory in Puerto Rico, designed to alert advanced beings to our existence. That message included numerical representations of hydrogen, carbon, nitrogen, oxygen and phosphorus atoms, a graphic illustration of a twisted DNA molecule in binary numerical symbols and a human figure of a height in terms of the transmitted wavelength (12.6 centimeters), all of this to indicate that on the third planet out from the sun there exists a civilization whose beings depend on molecules of DNA deoxyribonucleic acid for the continuity of their species. It is not the message I would send. To the target star-cluster Messier 13. Even at the speed of light. But then, look how well I am receiving, even in a Hygiene Unit. Whereas Messier cannot possibly reply until the year 49,975.

I'm afraid my attention wandered from you some. I'm always sore when my symbols are chosen for me—even by myself.

Then—I sat up hard, on my pot. You are telling each other how concerned you have been for the state of our minds. In your most lulling tones, you decree what is in store for us: to hold out.

I stand up. The Dry John, grown so familiar, now looks like a dream. Yet I had shat in it.

Going back to the cabin, I want only to look into companion eyes. There they are. My seat blessedly waits. I'm in a bad way, I'm about to say, no longer fit to be their historian; I hallucinate. Just then they point upward, just a flicker of the eye and finger, as children do when nursey is back. I look where they're pointing. My comrades' hallucination and mine are the same.

And we have pulled ourselves up. For re-entry. Into the modern world? Or the old? Though it appeared we were going to be looked after, we do not yet know the terms of it. Or whether you do. Whether the *Courier* can be returned to Earth direct from here, or will be drawn onto Island, or as seems more likely we ourselves might be transferred in some midspace operation, we have not been apprised. Or whether anything can be done without crew. The word rescue, implying a past disaster, is never spoken. On grounds of security we are in Limited Access I believe the communications term is. The limits being ours, the access yours. Having monitored us all through a period of what I prefer to call a variant sanity, you found us purportedly in a state of disorientation which your medics pronounced either a Jungian reversion to the primitive, or a fetal progression from barbarian to man. For psychological steadying, your calendar was beamed us, but now that has stopped.

Shortly, we feel, you will stop monitoring us. We feel so very cleverly, more and more. Perhaps you have come up against your own limitations. Or you will be on the way to forgetting us. Are we now to you what Cabins Three and Four are to us. Now and then a haunting? A non-noise from another apartment, heard by the last tenant of the deserted housing project, in the East Bronx.

Disorientation, my beloved dictionary says, is only a turning from the east. Who can say whether, as we turn and turn, ours is not an adaption new to the world? Well worth monitoring. More and more in our own minds we are passengers of one century, our destination another. And we are almost there.

In return, we want to give you something. Should that surprise you? It comes of the dusk—of circumstance. It comes of our location.

So, say that one dusk, we hear that sweetest click, and all the hatches opening—and you coming through to greet us, or your chosen representatives. Say—six of them.

This is how you will find us:

The cabin dapples now, an old loved place. It is real. Real as the light that each night comes through the portholes with you, as you leap through to us in your jumpsuits, your life-supports. We lie on our couches, suited-up also, but in reality we are bare, all our crammed cells revolving. As are yours, though your stories are still ahead of you.

Nowadays, I use the word processor. I must rush on. While all around me the stillness becomes so lovable.

I say at once—don't think of us as an image of life squeezed—as a hospital is a paranoia of the sick. We remind ourselves more of birds at a continual nesting-time, domestic with chirps. Though glory, which I see now should only be dwelt on in duration, creeps in.

Soraya's belly is our true calendar. Laughably vain of it as she is, we find ourselves worshiping it. There we are aborigines still. By its persuasion we are getting many things done. Among these—a net for the birth. The medic, now partially recovered to the point of resuming drawings for his children, is making it. He does not draw us.

I recount our activities in no special order. What order could there be? As part of our regimen, we often change seats. In orbit, order is too much what you have. Consequently, when piecing together Mulenberg's Latin song—Pergolesi's "Stabat Mater," as it one night came to him—while Wolf-Jacques obligingly Englishes it we may break off to help Soraya pry out from the Farsi Veronica's poem. Lievering refuses to be consulted there, alleging it is not his style of poetry. He suspects all wordage of being minor. The poet herself is reluctant to help, even though it is suspected that she now has another stanza in her head. In their hearts those two have always doubted the motion of words. Perhaps only an amateur like myself can revel in them—and with my eye on something else.

The word processor is no serious help. I should be sunk if it was. The

Courier's laboring mathematics of the wilderness, ever creakier, is enough to contend with. A machine doesn't have failings one can love —or not eternally. While as I watch our ring-around-rosy of bent heads, inclined over their grand mals and other epilepsies or rising to the constant rhythm of their delusions, I observe that we are more tolerable for being somewhat fallible. Look at Soraya there, whose maternal fatuity we accept like a widow's, who would stretch backward to any orbit if the boy in her could be Bakhtiary's; look at Wert tending her, while the beads in his hand twirl toward the other wife. They are not his amethysts but a string of lucky-beans given Mole by some girl and found in his documents box, which we rifled almost at once; we are untrustworthy, too. Like you. Mole's beans, light as aspic, float.

The military has written us off. That's what "for security reasons" means. Wert, our interpreter there, is sure of it. Civilians are now our hope. That as you may suspect is my contribution—with the addendum that we always come in late. If food does get to siege scarcity then will we be like any hamlet with all the tribal growlings of home? For doubting our own nobility, forgive us. We prefer it perhaps to trusting you.

But that's my last bitterness. I now come to the drills we have perfected on our own.

You must all along have been expecting me to speak of despair. We do not all experience eternity in the same way. For those of us most used to the mobility and interests of the world, there would be the silent, claustrophobic terror, the strain of hearing the unremitting tuning fork of the status quo. We all know that the note being sounded is death. But with us there is a complication. Death is an eternity of being shut away from one's kin, and one descends to it alone. That is not our case. When we see the dark imprint on another's cheekbone, or in the eye above our bony image, one or the other of us will talk to it.

Veronica's game is to travel us. How many places we have been with her, all the time on our cots! She will not tour a country. She doesn't want the cities. She is like a travel agent who will deal only in the specific place but understands our needs with singular empathy. There her art expands. We shall not forget Minot, North Dakota at dawn from a train, how after the Wisconsin flats the sour green swells which will become the badlands begin. How until then one doesn't know that the Wisconsin dells, those quirky castellations of limestone, were a warning. At Minot, the train crawls over a viaduct. We left it there, for a plane hovering low in the bauxite stench of clouds furled around a condominium straddling the traffic of a major bridge—was it Brasilia?—where behind ranks of windows sealed like the *Courier*'s, the tenants strangle slowly among the cocktails, on divans laid out for the only intercourse left. And once she took us back to the motel, that grotesque Eden—though all Edens may be grotesque. We left quickly. But she doesn't deal in warnings only; none of us does, not even I. Winding up, she always brings us to the same villages, hot and baking on a Saturday night, the beery wind from the Bejan pothouses reeking the streets, the windows broad with maternal light.

And that is the Cabin Drill.

But there's an end to pretending places where you are. We are the outside people to you now, less than that unknown passing on the pavement beside you, hard-smelling in the armpits even though his other life is an aquarium apart. We're like the finger-giraffes projected on the walls of childhood, for your kids when you get home to them.

When that wans our faces, Wert rises to explain. He likes us to be in the Free Room for it. It's here, freed of our visor-bubbles and in the light gloss which part-gravity lends the flesh, that we can see, fortunately or not, how we've changed. Corn-rows, no matter how neat, or how beautiful the head, grow fuzzy in duration, and mouth lines hold fast (once you know what you know) like the riffle that detains the current in the riverbed and produces the gold. Jack, between shavings or between beards, has the indecisive air this gives, but his thinned frame casting its long lantern-shadow, is making its racked decision clear. Soraya no longer blooms pink as her dreams; the late-month mask of pregnancy monkeys her. Below, the new life juts. One sees that Lievering's head, a marble bust almost freed of its *putti* angelhood, is a Jew's. I am at the word processor, where Wert likes me to be. I perambulated least during our mission; duration has compensated by crippling me most. That's fair, but I can't much hand-notate now.

How many times I have been in such a hall! Where the speaker will lambast us, then give us hope. While the audience, come to have its own say, bears with him—the speaker being beyond their informing him. Wert will inform us of what we already know. That is what we want to hear.

He looks the best of any of us, thin, but only fined-down. Nature often allows late parents a longer span. Though he has parenthood always in mind, he will talk to us about nations. From where we are in this regard, even yawns are ingenuous. But Wert's oratory is not the usual.

Wert's the bellwether a country doesn't make much of. Where you see him in government, he won't be on top. His type used to be much seen in the law, though not anymore. It still lingers in your classrooms, that untamable refuge. He's the one whose ideas and heart one knows by the cut of his weskit, which may have more than one hole in it. My guess is that down the ages he has always been the man whose ideas are going out.

Wert's are nothing new. He'd learned when a stripling, he says, that we'll think we're the authority wherever we are. When he says "we" he means "the nation." By the time he came here he'd been acting for years on the principle that "we" meant any nation—yet his own remains like a sinkhole in his breast. *Our minds are so good,* the cabin once heard him groan—in his sleep, and when Jack later asked if that excluded the military, he said, with his gray shyness at the explicit: "Those are whom I meant." Though Wert has been born an American for close to two hundred years, it's sometimes hard for him to be sure he is one. When he brought me for process his letter to his unborn son, I saw that this might be why he had written it.

For though there was still the Thoreau in us, he wrote, and alas Emerson, by now there were all the other waves of inspired emigrants from the stale or cruel known—that ever-hopeful diaspora. He wrote to his son as to a member of it. I saw how he approved of the Asiatics washed to us from the late wars, for bringing to the slippery hodge-podge of the way our lives were lived the industriously slim, pearly ethic of Eastern existence. Thoreau he did love, for his particularity—a man who knew what a stringbean was. Emerson he saw as a third-rate transcendentalist on the world scale, and far too responsible for our self-satisfaction, though sterling of intent in his sage's pallid style. Of his own prospects Wert spoke guardedly. They thought him outmoded, he said. But if he lived, he was certain that new dying statehoods would be provided him.

Soldier-scholars once wrote such letters, at predawn. Though it contained much else more intimate, these remarks seemed to me the most personal. I was sad to see what he thought of Emerson, that mentor of my own youth, especially as I now agreed with him. I saw that he felt guilty; he needn't have. He speaks only to the best in us.

When we had settled the disposition of the letter—it's to go with this log—I dared to say I thought any son would be glad of it. On the desk-shelf the fragile papers trembled with our movement, and our destiny. Neither of us is a praying man. "I believe in correspondence," Wert said.

I had a mentor once who resembled him. Our teacher on my own island. Because of her job she had to speak routinely and did. When pressed for her own opinion she would give it. But only of the snow-flake.

What Wert has us do here in the Free Room—is to count. Whenever you lose your bearings, the briefers at the motel told us, *count*. Today we did so as usual. Silently. To do this in company can be very healing. One may be counting up anything, blessings included, and there is a sense that much more is being taken care of. When the interjections come, I record. For when you come. We already know most of them.

Today Wolf's was the first. When we lose grandeur he returns us to it. Which some at home think an illness we should evade. Careful under its weight he speaks with head in his hands, voice muffled. "—The martyrs cannot be deserted," the processor repeats after him. "But they can be joined."

After that usually no one speaks.

Jack keeps waiting for these meetings to be "executive." Deafening slightly, he doesn't know we hear him mumble: "Space is moral. Space is life. Space is—" He never finishes. We do it for him. Space is Earth.

When our counting is over, at a quiet Quaker signal which may come from anyone, we will sometimes fancy we see—not our planet, but its surrogate. How can it possibly be there at the porthole, that cheese-face floating silvery in our own atmosphere of an evening, in summer huge and lavender, while a child is falling asleep? But one day Soraya said, "Look, Hossein. The moon."

Apol-lo. A-aa-pollo.

And that is the Free Room Drill.

The third drill we have not named. One day, we were filing into the Sick Bay, for the medic to give us our potassium. It had helped him considerably to perform these small duties and we were always creating them for him; indeed, that is how the stumbling train of our mutual kindnesses began. It is always pleasant to crowd into the Sick Bay even if briefly, a little closer than our wont. And as we each have our swig, we might be at a soda fountain. Or as Jack reminds us, with a crosshatched grin caused by the loss of two of his excellent tooth-caps to what was not food after all, or not edible, we might be modern farm animals. Whereupon we are likely to reply that if we could, we would be fauna for him. Our understanding of each other is frighteningly deep.

Just then the medic, his head in the refrigerator, begins to howl. It leaps to all minds that the midges have arrived there, but no; inside all is sparkling. The medic, hauled out in our circling arms, is counting his family, his face yellow with grief. Over and over he does it until, anthem-high, the theme of it breaks for home. It seems they depend on him to count them. But he cannot get their number right.

In these padded walls the noise penetrates us. Shelves hold injections; we have no lore. We can't let go of him. It's I who remember a remedy. Those sheets we wrapped Mole in before putting him in the box there? Winding sheets. We wrapped the medic as tight as we could, passing the long, serviceable cloth from shoulder to shoulder, for first we had circled him with the warmth of ourselves. So quietly do we breathe, that so far in this drill, which we practice only in extremis, the atmosphere in the Sick Bay has never yet been exhausted.

Wrapped so, we can feel the *Courier* lumbering on. What a ship you have after all given us. What experience. Grateful, without other means of expressing it, we feel like apostles on a vaulted ceiling, unable to inform or bless the masses come to light a candle to see us from the cathedral below.

Perhaps it is in this attitude you will find us, when you come.

What an elite we are.

That entry was to have been my last. Graceful enough. My forefinger lay rigid on its key. Just so it had stopped me in the Forty-second Street Library when, tracing down the UN's list of objects in space, it had come to the lost ones.

But Soraya, claiming to be now in her seventh month and restless, begged to be allowed to work at a computer which apparently interprets other computers, on the now no longer noxious flight deck. Or as she says—to play with it. So far, she has found no messages from you except superannuated ones, but she continues to try to beam out. If she goes on, I must. Since then we have all begun leaving notes for her to send when she can. There is no reason why I should be our sole representative. Or this log.

Sometimes, on my way aft for the dusk's discipline, I contrive to be the last, and nip into the flight deck. Once it had the best atmosphere of all. Now it has a faint musk of—what shall I call it?—the after-life. One wouldn't want to be here in one's shirt sleeves. Though it has the widest view in all the craft. I stand here in the brilliant orbit—how many times have we traveled it by now, Henry Draper? Should we be beginning to know that large star which flashes by like a Stop—and those milky ones? Send Us A Kangaroo.

Will there come a time when all except your catalogues let go of us?

When will we fall? No use asking where. I have intervals, even, of finding us luckier than you. Whom can you look forward to, on your vehicle, for rescue? Some dusks I see a resemblance in our plight.

For support I look over at our graffiti, which we scrawl on a computer panel now covered with them. Veronica has affixed a pad and one of her special pens, but we are not often so neat. Those remarks inscribed earliest begin to fade. I see one which looks familiar: *Disperse like a field of stars, yet cohere.* Is that from Alfred Whitehead, whose parties for favored students still echoed in the Cambridge of my own day? Or from that old crock, me?

Here's one says merely, *How do we ever get to you?* A wide audience once cherished Veronica for her bewilderment. Now at least she knows who you are. Here's another one, below: *On the flotation rafts of return, we shall come to you—* Alas, my own scratchings here are as fatally recognizable as bell-buoys. I come from an era when alliteration was respectable. The cows of my island spoke Beowulf.

I detach a few of the more embarrassing and crumple them in my breast pocket, though disposal here grows ever more difficult. The WASTAT bins are almost full. When young, I too was of the school which my own age has brought to apogee—according to which it is their garbage which most reminds people they are real. Now our problem grows as fast as your Malthusian one. Down at the bottom of the panel is a note to you in drawing pencil from our medic, whose madness grows dearer: *Your prosthetics are N.G.*

Our mottoes, unsigned as raindrops, will puzzle you. Should they ever fall.

On the way deck to aft we have to pass Cabins Three and Four. The more Christian of you will grade that as our scourge. But as an old if retired revolutionary I have to tell you that such guilt lived with over a period becomes reverence—half for the punishment, half for the crime.

In the corridor, I pause. Orbiting, like any routine, causes the mind's voice to repeat itself, yet accumulate. Suddenly a bit that is new may arrive. Like those motes we saw here. Each time I dawdle here I expect to see them, perhaps multiplied. Soraya says she would like to cage a pair, for Hossein. The future is now our joke.

I bestir myself. Forward!—to the present. I make these divisions consciously, worried that the others do so less. Reformer that I am, I am critical even of eternity. Yet compelled to describe it.

The hatch to our own cabin opens easily now but I am reluctant to enter. Once, in an antique shop in Amsterdam, a group I was with for an afternoon came upon a body-box. The owner had placed it high on a shelf where it would directly meet the eye, yet when out of a common urge, and already suspecting, we asked him what it was, he told us slyly, as if he knew it wouldn't sell. Made in one of those tropics which handle death comfortably it was no cheap wicker or rattan but woven of sisal and modestly oval at the ends, after a satisfactory length. We each had an urge to try it, it was so deliciously to human size, yet all of us shrank back, and of course we did not buy.

That is the way I feel about the hatch, yet I enter it.

Once in the cabin, I still delay, even hunting out my briefcase and neglected note pad. There is still so much to tell you, or that you may wonder at missing; I may not have selected what you most want to be told. Quick—what about our copulations here? Two women and four men—surely there's been a corner for it? Soraya and the medic at their midwife consultations, he a family man at lickerish ease with a protruding navel and the safe hole beneath, she trusting him to be careful, wanting for once to try a man brutally young? Veronica and Lievering, Mulenberg and Veronica—what an aphrodisiac memory is, or what a triumph for each in turn to lay the other low? And what a rhomboid, if I myself joined in, not yet so leached or sophisticate, as I had thought —and more than affectionate. Be coarse enough to imagine as people do.

I have. So must the others—and we are great hopers, all of us. Though already practiced at other solutions, or overpracticed at that one. From the beginning we were also on expedition, which fact inflected everything. We were also an enormous experiment in physical adjustment, which we are yet. My guess is that whatever would or would not have happened earlier in our journey does now, wilder in purpose then, less submerged now, but in the same pattern. As for the Werts, with a married pair one is never sure what goes on. We try to leave them opportunity but have never smelled it exercised. As the hour for possible rendezvous looms for the ship, we are busily chaste to all but that. As doubt creeps in, the other interest creeps with it; a hand may fumble for a breast, a crotch—and nowadays of any gender, duration having less of it. My guess is that the hand usually subsides. We move polymorphously here but toward the supremer emotion, whose kindness kills. Though that's as I observe us, and by now you know my character. I copulate best with Paradise.

However Wolf's yearnings for us don't quite yet apply. We're not always in chariotry here, which we should hate. Nor in the all-night sleep of the soul awaiting judgment, from which we most certainly wake. To work. To eat. Not too differently from some of you—and like you, in orbit. The movement toward each other's mystery is the only life we know. How is it with you these days?

In one way, we are no longer representative of our planet. Down below, once you get safely past youth's morbid death-interest, which is for most of them a quackery, your invidiously lively rivalries are often what keep you from brooding on your most certain end. But we here have only this everlasting kindness, almost a vice. In which there grows on us the conscious privilege—don't flinch; we no longer do—of having been preselected for a companion death. Changes can come even in eternity, when it goes on so long. We have not discussed this, but I think of it. I think of how we will observe endless courtesies to each others' wanings, to the child in us, to the skeleton.

Time for the last drill. Mine.

I am the man in the fourth seat. I have a book clamped in the reading vise. It is not the *Decameron* of Boccaccio. Time may not move on here, but we do. We are our own decameron now, having fewer people than in Boccaccio, but more days. Due to atmospheric decline beyond our control the book buckles slightly, making me fear for it, since it is also quite old. It is the one I brought with me for that unimaginable hour when I would tire of the dictionary. Dated 1827, it is entitled *A Voyage to the Moon (People of Morosofia)*—by Joseph Atterley, pseud., George Tucker. A familiar by now, we call him either, one day reading from Joseph, one day from George. I would not wish to say which day this is. I read from him:

The machine in which we propose to embark was a copper vessel that would have been an exact cube of 6 ft. if the corners and edges had not been rounded off. It had an opening large enough to receive our bodies, which was closed by double sliding panels with quilted cloth between them. When these were properly adjusted, the machine was perfectly airtight and strong, enclosed by means of iron bars running inside and out to resist the pressure of the atmosphere when the machine should be exhausted of its air by means of its air pump. On top of the copper chest and on the outside we had as much of the metal (which I shall call lunarium) as we find by calculation and experiment would overcome the weight of the machine and take us to the moon on the seventh Day.

At times I have to close the book and clear my eyes. Optically. We six are people who have been swung head over heels and drained of our simple objects. Though we have done well, those objects which have been left to us do confuse—the real ones, the memory ones—into a state resembling old age, or a senility not quite divine, but not without divinity either. Or perhaps it is the food. We have it, but we are harder put to get to it, now.

I read on, to how they "condensed" air, for every six hours of respiration, and of how on each of the six sides they had a small circular window made of thick, clear glass. So many sympathetic sixes they had —though I can never remember from day to day how many passengers. (Our own sun, standard at the portholes, no longer disturbs.) As to their "lunarium": they fastened pieces of it to screws which passed directly through the top of the machine, so that by turning them in one direction those metallic pieces would fly into the air "with the velocity of a rocket."

Robert—I say. Robert Hutchings—who? On a good day, I can recall in toto. Goddard. This is a good day.

At some point the medic will come in and then we have to find a place for him. There are always corners. He likes to hear the part about the ladies of that region, how they wear fireflies in silver tissue cages on their heads, or live butterflies in stiff open gauze. So does Veronica, who one day opened the documents box for him to see her white fur. When I come to the section—"At first as we partook of the diurnal motion of the earth our course was consequently oblique"—laughter always spurts. But the people of Morosofia were classified by their shadows, which we consider exceptionally intelligent. And no matter what section I read of this piece of curiosa, I always end with the one of its author's sentiments which always brings a silence. "Human pity is always the same."

Then, drill being over, we suit up for our daily performance. The medic leaves. Up in the nose of our vessel, all the instruments are still chattering and screening; the dial hands swing like a coquette's eyelashes. Someone else is taking the responsibility. The feeble circuits of our cabin strain to glow. We are freed—each to his or her own kaleidoscope. In mine, a woman walking the street of her own exploit is suddenly treading the streets of Iran, along with a harem intimate. The cab which held a dead man in front of the plaza, is found in London, brass-polished to a fare-thee-well and in front of the Garrick Club. Yards away from a dog lying on the runway at Canaveral there is a glint in the bushes like a turned soup spoon: the birds are back. In many places.

In the mountains of Tehachapi the geography is now clear. My father Giovanni the Portygee, lost from his dory, is riding the waterspout, over what was once the sea. Soraya swings in her net.

My pockets are full of crumpled paper. Ideas come on here like the silk of motion, with no air between them and the carriage of meaning. There's a thinness here, a purging. A convalescence from worldliness. We watch the indolent sidle of light into shade. Maybe we no longer expect to see our heirs. Maybe even Hossein no longer expects it. Our eyes glaze, exuding time, that mere by-product. We are time; we make it by enduring space until we are done for. How is it with you?

It occurs to me that you may get to us, but never quite reach us, where we are now. Though I hear—I hear the sweetest click. Or on this, perhaps the thousandth-and-one night—hear you hearing it. We are not as we were. On our foreheads may be the sweated drop of dew which contains all biologies. It comes of our location. Where we are now we can just glimpse—the balance between the voyage and the voyager. It seems to us we are brimming over with the mysteries of motion; our hands are cupped with them. We wear the great mask of transportation and know it for a mask. Are we the country behind you, or the one before?

We are the dark behind the migration. Bend over us as the Romans bent over the guts of cocks to see their own lunes. In our sunken entrails you may see the difference between the way things work and the way things are. I hear your cry—They felt gravity! Cover us, with your glory and rage.

Then I will rise up, from the all-night sleep. I know what I have been compiling here—a civilization. The *Courier* was only one of its missions. We were what the military calls a civilizade. A nonce word, i.e., created for a special occasion. Blessed are the dictionaries, for they shall see God.

We never knew for sure the drill for rendezvous. We were only non-footprints in space. But there have to be passengers. There have to be. What can we offer you—broken time, broken language, broken lives always fusing again—breaking the mold? It will happen. The broken best represents you. But the tragedy must be enough. Islands will happen. If we can bring our suffering with us, I'm thinking; if they can—

Foolish. It comes.

What a wind your entry makes. My papers are blown up. Handwritten, they swarm the cabin, soiled but afloat. They circle lazily, like snowflakes. The miracle is that they will never fall.

We wish you might have trusted us

Goddard

. like a field of stars yet there

We think often of that dog

Comprehendo

In the new time

Prs. of return we will come to you

according to the manual

Know what I know

torch

We wish we could have trusted you

Nations indivisible

. . . martyrs . . .

Count when

Enduring space

Pick a Life

Ride with us

We

From my Foget couch, I watch them. I feel the extra-territorial imperative. Dangling from its hook, Mole's empty restraint bag, veering right when we veer left, left when we veer right, says to me what it has from the beginning: Comprehendo.

Reader, I was Gilpin. Who are you? Bend over and I will tell you. An infinite number of people could have been brought into this account; in fact it was my guilt not to have you all here. Then I looked up, and saw that you were.